FORTEAN TIMES 68-72
MEMORIES OF HELL

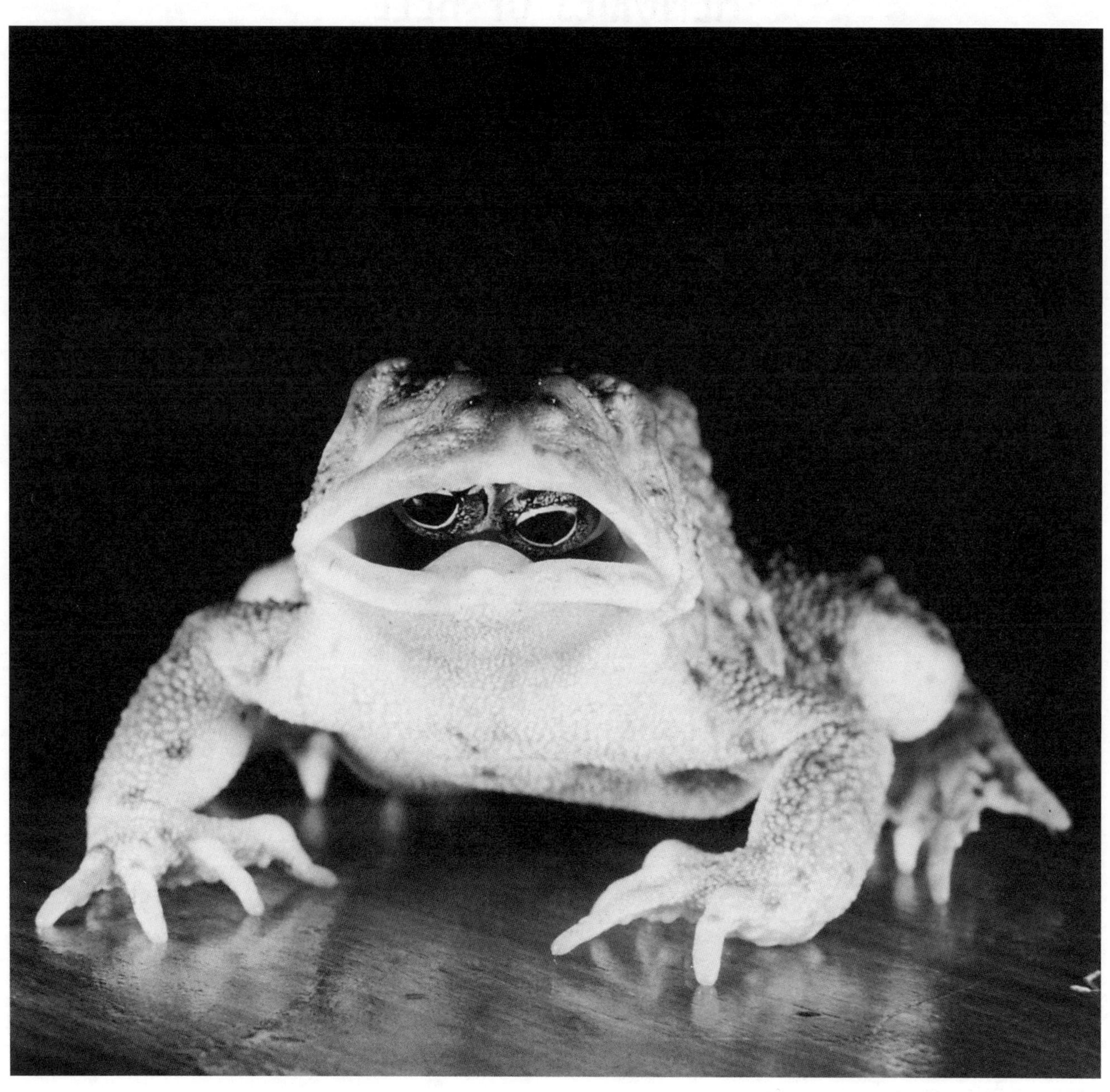

'Gollum', a toad found in Ontario with eyes inside its mouth. See ***FT68:5***.

FORTEAN TIMES 68-72
MEMORIES OF HELL

This edition was prepared by *Fortean Times* (PO Box 2409, London NW5 4NP) and was published in March 1997 by John Brown Publishing Ltd.

Fortean Times is now published every month by John Brown Publishing Ltd.
It is also available on subscription — inquiries to:
***Fortean Times*, FREEPOST (SW6096), Bristol BS12 0BR, UK.**
Tel: 01454 202515. Fax: 01454 620080. E-mail: ft@johnbrown.co.uk

British Library Cataloguing-in-Publication data available.
Fortean Times 68-72: Memories of Hell

ISBN 1-870870-905

Printed in Great Britain by
Redwood Books, Trowbridge, Wilts.

PREFACE

The five magazines in this book are reproduced facsimile, although not with the original spot colours. Our thanks again go to Steve Moore for compiling the contents lists, which are as detailed as possible to compensate for the lack of a full index. The consolidated index for *Fortean Times* 1–66 is nearing completion and we hope to see it in print quite soon.

With issues 68 to 72, the circulation gradually increased from 17,000 to 20,000. Contributors include Gerald Baker, Janet Bord, Peter Brookesmith, Peter Carr, Tony Clark, Loren Coleman, Tim Coleman, Jonathan Downes, Karma Tendzin Dorje, CP Drapkin, Glenn Fleming, Michael Goss, Yvonne Green, Richard Halstead, Tom Hodgkinson, Brian Inglis, Martyn Kollins, David Lazell, Kevin McClure, Anthony McLuskey, John Michell, Alan Mitchell, Ralph Noyes, Rolf Olsson, Mike O'Neill, Lynn Picknett, Guy Lyon Playfair, Jim Schnabel, Paul Sharville, Pat Shipman, Karl Shuker, Dennis Stacy, Dennis Stillings, Chris Tinsley, Stephen Volk, Simon Whittaker, Robert Anton Wilson, Colin Wood – and the regular Gang of Fort (Mike Dash, Steve Moore, Bob Rickard and Paul Sieveking).

Our title comes from the feature on "false memories" by Jim Schnabel (***FT71:23***).

Paul Sieveking February 1997

FORTEAN TIMES 68–72 (1993–1994)
CONTENTS

FORTEAN TIMES 68 – April/May 1993

4 EDITORIAL – Ghosts in the machine

5 STRANGE DAYS – 5 – looking down in the mouth – 6 – Fortean almanac – starling cook–out – 7 – fax be to God – boom time for melons – return to sender – Barbie news – simulacra corner – sidelines – 8 – man bites alien (headlines) – troglodyte expelled – gone to pieces – hook, line and sinker – a load of squalls – wrong numbers – 9 – Filipino fervour (kneecap raiders – footprints stir religious fervour – 'devil' spotted – Mary cries bloody tears – incorruption) – 10 – fluttering by – woolly comforters – goat news – 11 – Rasputin lives! – girl with X–ray eyes – 12 – vampire news – mystery of the orienteer – The Far Side [***Gary Larson***] – 13 – primate strippers – house–napper – the mother of all slime–moulds – not their day – 14 – Danielle & the Lyons den – rivers of blood – gone with the wind – singing outbreak – 15 – a sting in its tail – mass–murdering plants – 16 – obituary: Brian Inglis [*Ruth West*] – 17 – the 'aye–up' ghost – foulmouth doll – 18 – medical bag (young mother – DIY tonsillectomy – sneezing cured – plague death) – identified flying disks – 19 – momentous marrow – tiny spider eats woman – gas guzzlers – Brezhnev lives! – strange deaths – 20 – crooked cross – is it a cloud?

21 COMIC STRIP: PHENOMENOMIX by ***Hunt Emerson***.

23 POOR COW – an overview of American cattle–mutilations – Part One: tales of madness and mutilation – ***Paul Sieveking*** with a history of cut–up cows – Part Two: killing the golden calf – ***Dennis Stillings*** offers a mythical analogy – Listing: American animal mutilations 1990–1993.

30 THE FT INTERVIEW: MARY SEAL. THEM AND US. The conspiracy researcher and conference organiser talks to ***Simon Whittaker***.

34 ANGELS TO THE RESCUE. ***Kevin McClure*** re-investigates contradictory rumours of divine intervention at the World War I battle of Mons.

39 HOAX! THE VAMPIRE OF CROGLIN GRANGE. An alleged tale of a 19th century Cumbrian vampire, exposed by ***CM Drapkin***.

42 UNEARTHED. Fresco fiasco. Cave art finds and frauds in southern Europe. [***Steve Moore***]

43 THE CROP THICKENS. 1992 crop circles, rounded up by ***John Michell***.

44 THE OTHER HALF. ***Bob Rickard*** on separated Siamese twins. Katie & Eilish Holton – Yvonne & Yvette McCarther – Hussein & Hassan Saleh – Page & Sara Johnson.

46 HORSEWATCH. Madness in the Home Counties. ***Paul Sieveking*** chronicles the development of the English horseripping epidemic.

48 ARCHIVE GEMS 2: THE BLACK MADONNA OF MONTSERRAT. A photo showing the statue crowned with an apparent halo, examined by ***Janet Bord***.

49 DIARY OF A MAD PLANET. December 1992–January 1993. Geophysical highlights.

50 THE LOVECATS. ***Karl Shuker*** on the hybrids turning up among Britain's Alien Big Cats – strange–coloured hybrids – a feline fox.

52 SECRET COUNTRY 8: Eildon Hills, Roxburghshire. The folklore of the region, summarised by ***Janet & Colin Bord***.

53–56 FORUM

53 PSYCHIC RESEARCH: AN HALLUCINATION TO SIT ON. ***Brian Inglis*** on tangible apparitions.

54 CRYPTOZOOLOGY: THE ART OF JUMPING TO CONCLUSIONS. Zoological mysteries under our noses, by ***Jonathan Downes***.

55 SCIENCE WATCH: ALIEN BASTARDS! ***Dennis Stacy*** on the abduction scenario and its hybrid baby lore.

56 METAPHYSICS: ATHEISTIC RELIGIONS. The 'religious' dogmatism of CSICOP, by ***Robert Anton Wilson***.

56 COMIC STRIP: GURU by ***Pierre Hollins***.

59 REVIEWS – *The Sign and the Seal* (Hancock) – *Tibetan Medical Paintings* (Parfionovitch, Dorje & Meyer) – *Finders Keepers* (Purcell & Gould) – *UFO Encounters* (Clark) – *Millennium Prophecies* (Mann) – *Caspar Hauser* (Wassermann) – *The Gemstone File* (Keith) – *The Enchantment of the Trossachs* (Stott) – *The Columbus Myth* (Wilson) – *Méliès: Father of Film Fantasy* (exhibition) – *Vampyres* (Frayling) – Magwatch.

63 LETTERS – vegetable lambs and the drunkard's fate – dream ticket – Grimsby portents – weird – Sheerwater fish fall – a matter of meteors – respect for alien abductions – silent cities in the sky – radiometric dating – reds in the pond – letter–box amputations – rigor tortoise – herald angel.

66 NOTICEBOARD

FORTEAN TIMES 69 – June/July 1993

4 **EDITORIAL** – getting to know you.
5 **STRANGE DAYS** – 5 – I bring you mad tidings – 6 – Fortean almanac – the tale of Yagamo – 7 – stonehenge on the sun – bull about a bear – black widow – quick drink and flood – sidelines – 8 – extra! extra! (headlines) – demon scratcher – trans–sexual trout – polar puppy – gold caps – 9 – Indian incidents (Brahmin ghostbuster – breathless feat – Ganesh reincarnation) – simulacra corner – 10 – a new primate – 'triangle' swallows again – fast lane to heaven – 11 – pig vicious (pig mugs digger – 1992 boar wars) – 12 – nowt so queer – seeing is believing – 13 – nest foils plane – tight ass – hot foot – telecom terror – 14 – electric farming – 15 – officer not a gentleman – seeds of time – with this ring – Ireland's first oil? – eye eye – 16 – Coutts haunted – spring fever – 17 – silence of the lambs – the Andronov cure – ear trouble foreseen – crying boy returns – 'Edouard', the secret wine drinker – 18 – it's a crime – buried alive – The Far Side [***Gary Larson***] – 19 – Geller gets Randi – damned mummy – strange deaths – 20 – bloody Mary.
21 **COMIC STRIP: PHENOMENOMIX** by ***Hunt Emerson***.
23 **HOT STUFF.** The Pons & Fleischmann Cold Fusion debate, and its aftermath, by ***Chris Tinsley***. The new power age – Mills cells – sound + light = heat!
27 **THE FT INTERVIEW: DAVID JACOBS. SECRET INVASION.** The UFO abduction researcher talks to ***Tim Coleman***.
30 **GOLDEN CHILD.** ***Karma Tendzin Dorje*** on the intrigues, disputes and hi–jinks surrounding the enthronement of the Karmapa in Tibet.
34 **LUNCHTIME AT THE PHANTOM DINER**. Iran, 1956, and a tale of a restaurant that may or may not have been. By ***Tony Clark***.
37 **HOAX! PICK OF THE CROPS**. A field guide to English crop circle makers, compiled by ***Jim Schnabel***. Doug & Dave – the Bill Bailey gang – Merlin & Co. – the Wessex Skeptics – the Snake – United Bureau of Investigation – Spiderman & Catwoman.
42 **THE CASE OF THE MISSING MOA.** ***Karl Shuker*** evaluates recent sightings of big birds in New Zealand.
44 **DEADLY ALCHEMY**. Rumours of red mercury, apparently used in nuclear weapons, medicine and voodoo, rounded up by ***Paul Sieveking***.
47 **UNEARTHED** – mini mammoths linger longer – footprints in the sands of time [***Steve Moore***].
48 **HARD TO SWALLOW**. Modern cannibalism tales from China and Japan, chewed over by ***Bob Rickard***.
49 **DIARY OF A MAD PLANET**. February–March 1993. Geophysical highlights.
50 **THE MIA PHOTO MYSTERY**. ***Richard Halstead*** casts his eye over some alleged photos of missing US servicemen. Fat, happy campers – poorly manipulated fake – World War Two prisoners – the myth of survival.
52 **SECRET COUNTRY 9**: Cerne Abbas, Dorset. The giant hill–figure and his associations, by ***Janet & Colin Bord***.
53–56 **FORUM**
53 **ASTROLOGY: THE IMPORTANCE OF TIMING.** ***Mike O'Neill*** on astrological research using the study of twins.
54 **EVOLUTION: MISSING LINKS**. Darwinist Richard Dawkins gets a going over from ***Colin Wood***.
55 **PSYCHICAL RESEARCH: THE ID, THE EGO AND THE SUPERNATURAL**. ***Ralph Noyes*** looks at the parallels between sexuality and the paranormal.
56 **CRYPTOZOOLOGY: REALLY OUT–OF–PLACE.** Real and imaginary animals in out–of–place reports, by ***Loren Coleman***.
56 **COMIC STRIP: GURU** by ***Pierre Hollins***.
59 **REVIEWS** – *The Matter Myth* (Davies & Gribbin) – *Demons, Doctors and Aliens* (Pontolillo) – *Robin Hood* (Wilson) – *Arktos* (Godwin) – *Fractals* (Briggs) – *The Goddess Hekate* (Ronan) – *The Year of the Sorrats* (Richards) – *America's First Crop Circle* (Cyr) – *The Afterlife* (Randles & Hough) – *Missing Pieces* (Baker & Nickell) – Magwatch – *Fire in the Sky* (film).
63 **LETTERS** – largest fish clarification – prudes from space – bollock! – trolley travel – another face on Mars – age of the earth – Sai Baba's miracles – music to our ears – given the bird – parrot chicken minder – bird death mystery – the face(s) in the window – von Däniken got there first.
66 **NOTICEBOARD**

FORTEAN TIMES 70 – August/September 1993

4 EDITORIAL – will the real impostor please stand up!
5 STRANGE DAYS – 5 – nice to see you – 6 – extra! extra! (headlines) – The Far Side [***Gary Larson***] – bloody ants – naff's the word – electronic demons – 7 – simulacra corner – fax from limbo – crossed wires – 8 – wakey! wakey! – dramatic reunion – the blue flash – 9 Chinese whispers (chicken and egg – robots, worms and spies – Shanghai skylarks – eat this...) – 10 – sidelines – Swedish stunners – 11 – who killed Bambi? – sidelines – 12 – bar code madness – love's labour locked – water too clean – fish falls – 13 – meteor news – 14 – sex, libels and audio tape (James Randi lawsuit) – 15 – a captive audience – lost in Romania – shoes that pass in the night – blind faith – death to cannibals – 16 – elephant news (rum do in jungle – the elephant's revenge – tusker road blocks) – funny money – snake removal – 17 – the curse of Uluru – attack of the eight foot birds – 18 – medical bag (triplet trek – lizard eggs – babies in baby – self–replicating (almost)) – best feet forward – professional waif – lunch on the wing – 19 – quake gods – dialling the dead – gun ho! – 20 – Fortean almanac.
21 COMIC STRIP: PHENOMENOMIX by ***Hunt Emerson***.
22 THE MÜNCH BUNCH. ***Jim Schnabel*** on Münchausen's syndrome and its relation to paranormal experiences. Beverley Allitt, a case history – conversion neuroses – alter egos – Münchausen's syndrome – pious fraud – the shamanic reflex – Venus unhinged – tricks as rituals – sexual ambiguity.
30 THE FT INTERVIEW: JOHN BLASHFORD SNELL. THE EXPEDITIONIST. The noted explorer interviewed by ***Bob Rickard***. Mammoth footsteps – meeting the giants – murderous bull – monstrous projects – wildmen and Nessie – bizarre banquets.
SPECIAL INSERT. THE BUTTERFLY ALPHABET. Kjell B Sandved and his photographs of the alphabetical and numerical simulacra appearing on butterfly wings. Snap happy – riddle of the skull. [***Bob Rickard***]
35 I–CON MAN. Artist Jeffrey Valance and his exhibition of faked religious relics, reviewed by ***Edward Young***. The spear of destiny – the clowns of Turin.
38 ROVERS RETURN. Dogs that make epic journeys to return to their original homes or human companions, put on a lead by ***Paul Sieveking***. Fortean Times league table of canine trekking.
42 HOAX! BONEHEADS. The Indonesian industry of skull faking, exposed by ***Pat Shipman***.
44 EGG VOYAGERS. Monstrous eggs washing up on Australian beaches, unscrambled by ***Dr Karl P.N. Shuker***.
46 THE DRAGONS OF VANCOUVER. ***Mike Dash*** on the west Canadian sea serpent, Cadborosaurus.
49 DIARY OF A MAD PLANET. April–May 1993. Geophysical highlights.
51 UNEARTHED. Mystery of the pharaohs. The hidden chamber in the Great Pyramid [***Steve Moore***].
52 SECRET COUNTRY 10: Trellech, Gwent. Standing stones, sacred wells and fairy lore, by ***Janet & Colin Bord***.
53–56 FORUM.
53 BIOLOGY: EVOLUTIONARY FAST FOOD. Debates about evolution, discussed by ***Martyn Kollins***.
54 RELICS: THE ANSWER'S IN THE NEGATIVE. ***Lynn Picknett*** on rows among Turin Shroud researchers.
55 DENDROLOGY: TRICKS OF THE TREES. Appearing and disappearing trees, tracked by ***Alan Mitchell***.
56 THEATRE: 'FOXING THE PUBLIC'. ***Stephen Volk*** discusses the relationship between actors and mediums.
56 COMIC STRIP: GURU by ***Pierre Hollins.***
59 REVIEWS – *Round in Circles* (Schnabel) – *Superstitions* (Lorie) – *Spaceship Conspiracy* (Knap) – *The Plains of San Agustin Controversy* (Eberhart) – *Blast Your Way to Megabuck$ with my Secret Sex–Power Formula* (Dukes) – *Unusual Personal Experiences* (Anon) – *Healey and Glanvill's Urban Myths* (Healey & Glanvill) – *An Introduction to the Magical Elements of the Bible* (Stutley) – *The Science Gap* (Rothman) – *The Character of Physical Law* (Feynman) – *The Struggle to Understand* (Corben) – Magwatch – *The Silbury Treasure* (Dames) – *The Devil's Notebook* (LaVey) – *Columbus was Last* (Huyghe) – *On Jung* (Stevens) – *In Search of the Dead* (Iverson) – *Jung for Beginners* (Hyde & McGuinness) – *The Whole Person Catalogue* (Considine) – *The Universe and I* (Ferris & Pinn) – *Passport to Magonia* (Vallée) – *Dao De King* (Lao Tzu).
63 LETTERS – lenticular cloud – Black Lagoon revisited – of cats and shopping trolleys – cabin fever – albino lobsters – the end was not nigh – fractal freaks – icy mist – hijacked? – elephant sits on mini—again – dead funny – a brush with a black dog – we stand corrected – devil's footprints.
66 NOTICEBOARD

FORTEAN TIMES 71 – October/November 1993

4 EDITORIAL – are memories made of this?

5 STRANGE DAYS – 5 – mental floss – 6 – extra! extra! (headlines) – The Far Side [***Gary Larson***] – murderous water goddess – missed! – bear–faced cheek – eagle snatches dog – 7 – micky finn – don't mention sex! – bottles tops with islanders – heretic dinosaurs – ancient gum – 8 – simulacra corner – secret blindness – look who's talking – animals serve time – 9 – talking Turkey (ancient space module? – venerable olive tree – monster mice – world's oldest cloth – catnip – doom of the dentist) – 10 – sidelines – the lady is a vamp – 11 – Jesus in the dishwasher – sidelines – 12 – the Taos hum – Bechstein's bat – baffling beads – 13 – necrolog (obituaries – Aimé Michel – Sun Ra – David Bohm – Gordon Higginson – Jan Oort – Ishiro Honda – Margaret, Duchess of Argyll) – 14 – not their day – providence strikes – if you park here, you're dead – the madness of sevens – 15 – ghosts on tv – 16 – loose lions – 17 – Floydada outing – organ kidnapping – yo! Boris! – 18 – underneath the arches – 19 – taking the ashes – many happy returns – Toyota twins – strange deaths – 20 – Fortean almanac.

21 COMIC STRIP: PHENOMENOMIX by ***Hunt Emerson***.

23 MEMORIES OF HELL. True or false, the 'repressed' memories of childhood trauma uncovered by hypnotherapy and other means have lessons for all witness–testimony cases. *Jim Schnabel* probes the depths. Hoaxed crimes: lying for help – truth, justice and the Salem way – Michelle re–remembers – it happens in the UK too – abuse excuse – the showbiz shaman.

34 THE WEBS OF WAR. Cobweb falls and rumours of secret weapons in former Yugoslavia, by ***Paul Sieveking***.

SPECIAL INSERT. IT CAME FROM OUTER SPACE! A chronological, illustrated guide to the changing shape of 20th century aliens, both in the media and in UFO reports, by ***Mike Dash***.

35 THE FT INTERVIEW: TERENCE McKENNA. RADICAL MUSHROOM REALITY. The psychedelics advocate and reality–theorist interviewed by ***Tom Hodgkinson***. Telepathic world – mushroom reality – alien abduction – psychedelic epiphany.

39 MODERN FAIRY TALES. ***David Lazell*** collects tales of fairy encounters from the 1930s. The hearth creature – roadside glimpse – silvery sounds – midnight protest – picking berries – goblin shapes – pretty in pink.

42 FAIRY TREE IN PERIL. ***Bob Rickard*** laments the state of the Elfin Oak in Kensington Gardens.

43 HOAX! THE GREAT MIRABELLI. Brazil's most prodigious medium of the early 1900s, brought down to earth by ***Guy Lyon Playfair***.

46 ARCHIVE GEMS 3: THE BOWHEAD INCIDENT. A great goat escape from 1938.

47 DIARY OF A MAD PLANET. June–July 1993. Geophysical highlights.

48 FEELING CROSS. ***Bob Rickard*** discusses stigmatic Heather Woods, who displays the wounds of Christ.

52 SECRET COUNTRY 11: Callanish, Isle of Lewis. The famous standing stones and their lore. ***Janet & Colin Bord***

53–56 FORUM

53 UFOLOGY: FOETAL MEMORY METAPHORS. Abductions and Birth Trauma, discussed by ***Yvonne Greene***.

54 ASTROLOGY: UNEXPECTED BIRTH CYCLES. ***Gerald Baker*** on the birth dates of chess champions and Roman emperors.

55 BRAIN RESEARCH: FRANKENSTEIN VIBRATIONS. Brain cycles and consciousness, by ***Peter Carr***.

56 SPECULATION: COMMUTING AT 186,000 MILES PER HOUR. ***Paul Sharville*** looks at the perils of matter transmission.

56 COMIC STRIP: GURU by ***Pierre Hollins***.

59 REVIEWS – *Sasquatch/Bigfoot* (Hunter & Dahinden) – *Haunted Nottinghamshire, Vol. 2* (Moakes) – *Encyclopedia of Strange and Unexplained Physical Phenomena* (Clark) – *Unexplained! 347 Strange Sightings, Incredible Occurrences and Puzzling Phenomena* (Clark) – *A Confusion of Prophets* (Curry) – *The Beast of Exmoor* (Francis) – *The Terrestrial Connection* (video) – *The Warp* (video) – *Messengers of Destiny* (video) – *Biological Anomalies: Humans 2* (Corliss) – *Materialisations* (Boddington) – *The Holy Place* (Lincoln) – Magwatch – *In Search of the Neanderthals* (Stringer & Gamble) – *The SLI Effect* (Evans) – *Crop Circles: A Mystery Solved* (Randles & Hough) – *Where Science and Magic Meet* (Roney–Dougall) – *The Temple* (Lundquist) – *Atlantis* (Ashe) – *Ultima Thule* (King) – *Fearful Symmetry: Is God a Geometer?* (Stuart & Golubitsky) – *Hecate's Fountain* (Grant) – *Dowsing: New Light on an Ancient Art* (Williamson).

63 LETTERS – fainting goats – fax not from limbo – crop correction – rational debate – Che in the clouds? – birds, sheep and cremation accidents – bibliomania – it was crap – the haunted billabong – bird rains – Randi replies – shrouded retort – levitation – odd rings – Jung's dream.

66 NOTICEBOARD

FORTEAN TIMES 72 – December 1993/January 1994

4 EDITORIAL – sleeping beauties.

5 STRANGE DAYS – 5 – Santa stuck – 6 – extra! extra! (headlines) – The Far Side [***Gary Larson***] – termination claws – Mekong monster – balloon wonder – 7 – simulacra corner – crapsicle misses cop – Indian tragedy – not you again! – postbox perils – 8 – mountain man misses the mark – nailed – 9 – Siamese sundries (meteorite returned – spirit snatchers – Bangkok sting – spirits blamed for fire – science in action) – 10 – sidelines – final curtain: 24 November – horse lover – 11 – a contentious new skull – sidelines – 12 – forget me knot – 13 – slam bam – it's a miracle? – wild humans savage dog warden – old cobblers – environment–friendly jewellery – 14 – egg scramble – new mammal – a grizzly sight – alien sting – hold tight – 15 – it's raining men – 16 – snack attacks – now you're talking – 17 – river surprises – assault on the battery – fish counter–attack – a modern caveman – 18 – tales of divine ingratitude – 19 – Russian enterprise – Fijian spectre – strange deaths – 20 – Fortean almanac.

21 COMIC STRIP: PHENOMENOMIX by ***Hunt Emerson***.

23 THE BIG SLEEP. Long sleeps, multiple personalities and sleeping prophets. Nodding off [***Bob Rickard***] – the sleeping preachers – the Brooklyn enigma – Carolina dreaming [***Rolf J.K. Olsson***] – sleepyheads (sleeper's league table).

30 SHOOTING DOWN THE MYTH. The Kennedy assassination reassessed, by ***Glen B. Fleming***. The Lincoln–Kennedy coincidences – two interpretations of the Zapruder film – the assassination of Lee Harvey Oswald.

36 THE FT INTERVIEW: JENNY COCKELL. MARY'S CHILDREN. The woman who claims to have reincarnated, and now to have been reunited with the children of her former life, interviewed by ***Bob Rickard***.

42 HOAX! DRILLER CHILLER. The story that Hell had been discovered by a drilling team in Siberia, laid to rest by ***Paul Sieveking***.

44 MISSING TIME. The 1993 Sheffield UFO conference: a report by ***Peter Brookesmith***.

46 LOVECATS: THE NEXT GENERATION. Possible jungle cat hybrids, examined by ***Dr Karl P.N. Shuker***.

47 BEDEVILLED. The continuing saga of 'Satanic Child Abuse', updated by ***Mike Dash***. New Zealand – shark sentence – peanut bitter – Orkney saga – Northolt news.

50 UNEARTHED. Subterranean submarine. Rediscovered submarines, dug up by ***Steve Moore***.

52 SECRET COUNTRY 11: Silbury Hill and West Kennet long barrow. History and legend, by ***Janet & Colin Bord***.

53–56 FORUM

53 GENETICS: CLONING RECIPES. ***Anthony McLuskey*** demystifies DNA research.

54 PHENOMENOLOGY: PREPOSTEROUS PERCEPTION. Memory, hypnosis and perception, by ***Robert Anton Wilson***.

55 SCIENCE WATCH: ROSWELL THE TERRIBLE. ***Dennis Stacy*** on the alleged 1947 saucer crash.

56 FOLKLORE: DOWN IN THE JUNGLE. The folklore of the Candyman, discussed by ***Michael Goss***.

56 COMICSTRIP: GURU by ***Pierre Hollins.***

59 REVIEWS – *Forbidden Archeology* (Cremo & Thompson) – *The Paranormal Year* (Randles) – *Prime Chaos* (Hine) – *The Only Planet of Choice* (Schlemma & Jenkins) – *Shamanism and the Mystery Lines* (Devereux) – *Symbolic Landscapes* (Devereux) – *A Theory of Almost Everything* (Barry) – *The Damned Universe of Charles Fort* (Kaplan) – Magwatch – *Other Meridians: Another Greenwich* (Gale) – *Fandemonium!* (Vermorel) – *Gmicalzoma* (Vinci) – *The Beast Within* – (Douglas) – *Sell Yourself to Science* (Hogshire) – *Schwa* (Barker) – *The Avalonians* (Benham) – *Ghosts and Legends of Yorkshire* (Roberts) – *The Best of British Men/Women* (Anon) – *The Coldrum Line* (Clampitt & Peters – *Extra Sensory Perception* (MacLellan) – *The Little Dutch Boy* (Hearn).

63 LETTERS – an 'impossible' solid? – fractal challenge – who's in charge here? – elusive pig – rip–off – marketing blunder – meeting Pan – solar phenomenon – Münchausen's syndrome – flashes in the dark – localised combustions – quake miracle.

66 NOTICEBOARD

NUMBER 68

UK £2
USA $4.95

FORTEAN TIMES

THE JOURNAL OF STRANGE PHENOMENA

CATTLE MUTILATION IN AMERICA

STRANGER THAN FICTION

FREE PHOTO SUPPLEMENT

Angels of War • Horse Ripping • ESP Orgasms • Siamese Twins
Mary Seal Interview • The Vampire of Croglin Grange

Contents

Issue 68 April/May 1993

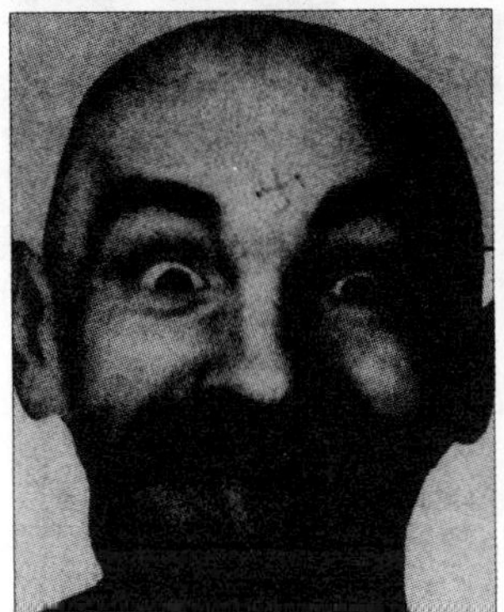

P25 RIPPING YARNS

P30 CONSPIRACY QUEEN

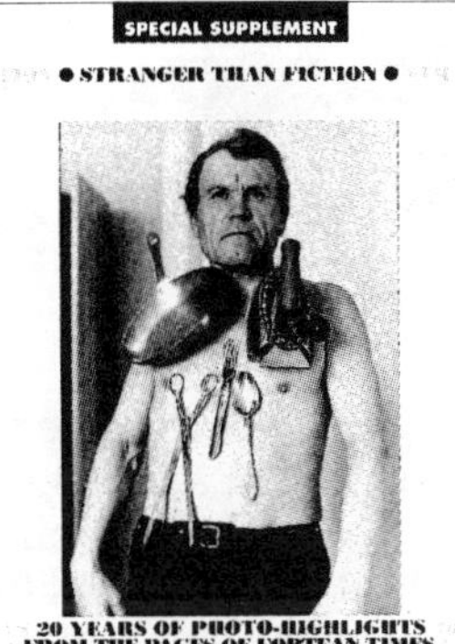
SPECIAL SUPPLEMENT
● STRANGER THAN FICTION ●
20 YEARS OF PHOTO-HIGHLIGHTS FROM THE PAGES OF FORTEAN TIMES

FREE WITH THIS ISSUE

4 EDITORIAL

The Waco siege ● Paranormal software ● No Moa!

5 STRANGE DAYS

● Frog with eyes in mouth ● Unexplained bird deaths ● Faxing heaven ● Filipino fervour ● Rasputin lives! ● Vampire news ● Poison bird ● The 'Danielle' mystery ● Swearing dolls ● Landscape swastikas

21 PHENOMENOMIX

HUNT EMERSON's humorous look at the world

23 POOR COW: U.S. CATTLE MUTILATIONS

PAUL SIEVEKING reviews the 1970s wave of mutilations and the range of explanatory theories. DENNIS STILLINGS offers a mythical analogy in the story of the golden calf

30 THE FT INTERVIEW: MARY SEAL

SIMON WHITTAKER talks to the conspiracy theorist about her ideas and the Wembley conference she organised last January

34 ANGELS TO THE RESCUE

KEVIN MCCLURE investigates the various rumours of supernatural intervention in WWI

38 FROM OUR FILES

- *HOAX: The Vampire of Croglin Grange*
- *UNEARTHED: Recently discovered cave paintings in France and Spain*
- *THE CROP THICKENS: The 1992 harvest of crop circles*
- *THE OTHER HALF: Cases of Siamese twin separation*
- *HORSEWATCH: Equine attacks across England*
- *ARCHIVE GEMS: The Black Madonna of Montserrat*
- *DIARY OF A MAD PLANET: Weather watch December 92 to January 93*
- *THE LOVECATS: Hybrid solution to the big cat mystery*
- *SECRET COUNTRY : Eildon Hills, Roxburghshire*

53 FORUM

● Brian Inglis ● Jonathan Downes ● Dennis Stacy ● Robert Anton Wilson

59 REVIEWS

● The lost Ark of the Covenant ● Tibetan medical paintings ● Vampyres ● UFO Encounters ● The Gemstone File

63 LETTERS

● Vegetable lambs ● Spontaneous combustion by Jules Verne ● Fishfall in Surrey ● Meteor news ● Herald angel

66 NOTICEBOARD

Fortean meetings, lectures, events, products and offers

Cover by Hunt Emerson

WHY 'FORTEAN'?

CHARLES FORT (1874-1932)

Fortean Times is a bi-monthly magazine of news, reviews and research on all manner of strange phenomena and experiences, curiosities, prodigies and portents, formed in 1973 to continue the work of the iconoclastic philosopher CHARLES FORT. Fort was sceptical about scientific explanations, observing how scientists argued for and against various theories and phenomena according to their own beliefs, rather than the rules of evidence. He was appalled that data not fitting the collective paradigm was ignored, suppressed, discredited or explained away (which is quite different from explaining a thing).

Fort was perhaps the first to speculate that mysterious lights seen in the sky might be craft from outer space. He coined the term 'teleportation' which has passed into general usage through science fiction. His dictum "One measures a circle beginning anywhere" expresses his philosophy of Continuity and the 'doctrine of the hyphen', in which everything is in an intermediate state between extremes. He had notions of the universe-as-organism and the transient nature of all apparent phenomena. Far from being an over-credulous man, Fort cut at the very roots of credulity: "I cannot accept that the products of minds are subject matter for beliefs ... I conceive of nothing, in religion, science, or philosophy, that is more than the proper thing to wear, for a while."

Fort was born in Albany, New York, in 1874 into a family of Dutch immigrants. Beatings by a tyrannical father helped set him against authority and dogma, and on leaving home at the age of 18 he hitch-hiked around the world to put some "capital into the bank of experience." At 22 he contracted malaria, married his nurse and settled down to 20 years of impoverished journalism in the Bronx. During this time he read extensively in the literature of science, taking notes on small squares of paper in a cramped shorthand of his own invention, which he filed in shoe boxes.

In 1916, when he was 42, Fort came into a modest inheritance, just enough to relieve him of the necessity of having to earn a living. He started writing *The Book of the Damned*, which his friend, the novelist Theodore Dreiser, bullied his own publisher into printing in 1919. Fort fell into a depression, burnt all his notes (which numbered some 40,000) as he had done a few years earlier, and in 1921 set sail for London, where he spent eight years living near the British Museum (39 Marchmont Street) and wrote *New Lands* (1923). Returning to New York, he published *Lo!* in 1931 and *Wild Talents* in 1932, shortly before he died. He left 60,000 notes, now in the New York Public Library.

THE GANG OF FORT:
Editors:
Bob Rickard
& Paul Sieveking

Contributing Editors:
Steve Moore
& Mike Dash

ISSN 0308 5899

Bob Rickard

EDITORIAL
Ghosts in the Machine

Paul Sieveking

● On page seven we note that Jews can now fax their prayers to the Wailing Wall in Jerusalem and also the debate amongst Catholic theologians about whether to permit the faxing of confessions to priests. Whatever next? We are familiar with the new folklore of 'demon possessed' computers so it was with wry amusement that we noticed the forthcoming release of *Word For Windows 3.0* includes a feature called 'automatic writing' which not only checks your spelling and grammar while you are lost in an electronic seance, but pops up to suggest any rewrites it thinks necessary. Of course computer commands 'invoke' programs which 'initialise entities' in 'hex'code, but can chips really channel? Booting up your 'ghost writer' may need 'hands on' after all!

● As we go to press, the maverick messiah David Koresh – aka Vernon Howell, a renegade Seventh Day Adventist – continues to hold out against the FBI in Waco, Texas. Stymied, the FBA are rattling the fortress cage of the Branch Davidians (as they call themselves) by blasting non-stop recordings of Buddhist chants. An earlier Koresh was Dr Cyrus Teed (1839-1908). Howell – who once penned a song called 'There's A Madman In Waco' – has a charismatic hold over a flock largely composed of women, as did Teed. Teed, however, is more interesting: he experimented with electro-magnetic alchemy, planned to build a New Jerusalem in Florida, and believed in a hollow earth. 'Korenshanity', designed as a scientific replacement for Christianity, flourished for a while before WW1 (for more information see John Michell's *Eccentric Lives*). Millennial flutters – like those at Waco, and in Korea (see ***FT66***) – are bound to increase as we approach 2000 AD, and we promise to keep a spare eye on developments.

● The English horse-ripping continues, and we give a bulletin on page 46. The chief mystery is how the uncatchable assailant(s) are able to do their dirty work without being kicked to bits. By contrast, the questions raised by the cattle mutilations in the USA over the last 20 years are much more various and intractable, and have led to a host of whacky theories, outlined in our feature 'Poor Cow' on page 23.

● We were to have a report in this issue on the claim that a moa, long presumed extinct, had been photographed on New Zealand's South Island. Although discounted by local authorities, our preliminary enquiries reveal that there is more to this case – indeed, a new search is underway, led by Paddy Freaney, who made the original sighting. Information is accumulating and we hope to include a more substantial report next issue.

● CHRISTMAS COMPETITION: The correct answers were: 1B (Hoy); 2B (*The Book of the Damned*); 3C (Mary – changed to Marie by Conan Doyle when he fictionised the story); 4A (crocodile); 5C (Angelsey). The winner of the sun dial was Ms Dionne Jones of Truro. Runners-up: Angela Arnell, Mr Jay Arnold, Miss Deisrée Atkinson, Dave Baldock, Wayne Bee, Claire Blamey, Miss R Cody, Miss H B Duncan, Mr A Foxton, Mr M K Griffiths, Mr B Hughes, Mr A B Kent, C P Lazenby, Mr A McBeath, Mrs A Mirfin, Sarah Morcom, Steve Slaughter, Graham Whiberley.

THE EDITORS

EDITORIAL ADDRESS
Fortean Times: Box 2409, London NW5 4NP, UK.
Tel & Fax: 071 485 5002 or 081 552 5466.

SUBMISSIONS
Submissions are invited of suitable articles, news, art, cartoons, reviews, and especially clippings. Preliminary discussion with the editors is advisable. Text can be submitted on floppy disks, but check with the editors first. Submissions may be edited. FT assumes no responsibility for submissions, but all reasonable care will be taken while they are in FT's possession. Requests for return of material should be accompanied by stamped addressed envelope.

CLIPPINGS
All clippings, references, etc, should be identified by source, date and clipster's name. Mail or fax them to the editorial address (above).

SUBSCRIPTIONS
RATES – One year (6 issues). UK: £12. Overseas inc. USA: £15.00 or US$30. For two years (12 issues) UK: £20, overseas inc USA £26 or US$50.
PAYMENT – US cheques acceptable; payments from all other countries should be in sterling drawn upon a London bank. Major credit cards accepted – just phone details on 0800 581409. Make cheque/money orders payable to:
JOHN BROWN PUBLISHING
Freepost SW6096, Frome, Somerset BA11 1YA, UK.

ADVERTISING ENQUIRIES
DISPLAY or CLASSIFIED: contact Ronnie Hackston or Dan Squirrell at John Brown Publishing Ltd: The Boathouse, Crabtree Lane, Fulham, London SW6 8NJ, UK. ☎ 071 381 6007 or Fax: 071 381 3930.
BOOKSELLERS' LISTING items – contact the editorial address (above).

PUBLISHER
John Brown Publishing Ltd, The Boathouse, Crabtree Lane, Fulham, London SW6 8NJ, UK. ☎ 071 381 6007 or Fax: 071 381 3930.
Managing Editor: Fiona Jerome.
Publisher: Vic Lime.

DISTRIBUTION
UK trade distribution by UMD, 1 Benwell Road, Holloway, London N7 7AX. ☎ 071 700 4600 or Fax: 071 607 3352.
USA newsstand distribution by Eastern News Distributors Inc, 2020 Superior St, Sandusky, OH 44870, USA.

STRANGE DAYS

16 pages of worldwide weirdness

LOOKING DOWN IN THE MOUTH

Yes, we did a double-take, too, when we first saw this portrait of a toad whose eyes have developed upside-down from the roof of its mouth. 'Gollum' was found by Deirdre Warren, 20, in the garden pond of her home in Burlington, Ontario, when she noticed it hopping, apparently with its 'eyes' closed.

Deidre took Gollum to Jim Bogart, professor of herpetology at the University of Guelph, who identified it as an otherwise normal male American toad, quite common in Ontario. There are no openings or rudimentary eyes where its eyes should normally be. Prof. Bogart had never heard of such a deformity and was surprised it had survived so long.

Christine Bishop, a toxicologist with the Canadian Wildlife Service, planned to make a special study of the pond's environs and other residents. Ms Bishop and other officials stressed that they had no reason to believe this mutation is pollution-related without further investigation. *Hamilton (Ont) Spectator, 4 Sept 1992.*

So far, Gollum seems to be unique – a sport of nature. Perhaps an ingenious reader can suggest what the evolutionary advantage might be of seeing your food at such close quarters, just before it vanishes down your gullet.

FORTEAN ALMANAC 13 April – 14 June 1993

Notable feasts and anniversaries in the coming weeks

WEDNESDAY 14 APRIL: Birthday of Erich von Däniken (1935), the uncritical but immensely popular proponent of ancient alien intervention.
FRIDAY 16 APRIL: Dr Albert Hofmann had the first LSD trip today in 1943 and fell off his bicycle.
SATURDAY 17 APRIL: On this day in 1976, June Melling, 12, saw a menacing 'owl man' near Mawnan church in Cornwall.
TUESDAY 20 APRIL: According to English folklore, the cuckoo sings today for the first time.
FRIDAY 23 APRIL: St George's Day. The dragon killer, England's patron saint, is a combination of the Nordic hero Siegfried, the Green Man or wodewose, and a bishop of Alexandria.
SATURDAY 24 APRIL: In 1964 police officer Lonnie Zamora witnessed a metallic 'flying saucer' take off near Socorro, New Mexico.
FRIDAY 30 APRIL: Walpurgisnacht. Feast Day of St Sophia, the spirit of female wisdom symbolised by the dove of Aphrodite, later transformed into the dove of the Holy Ghost.
SATURDAY 1 MAY: Beltane, one of the eight great pagan festivals of the year, from the Gaelic *Bealltainn* (fire). The beginning of summer.
THURSDAY 6 MAY: Two explorers were born today in 1856: Sigmund Freud and Robert Peary.
SATURDAY 8 MAY: The Apparition of St Michael. Climbing one of the hills dedicated to Mercury/Hermes/Michael is guaranteed to cure madness.
SATURDAY 15 MAY: Feast Day of St Dymphna, patron saint of the insane.
FRIDAY 21 MAY: New moon, with partial solar eclipse, 14:06 GMT. Prodigious frog fall in Gibraltar (1921).
WEDNESDAY 26 MAY: Shavuot (Jewish Pentecost). In 1907 hailstones containing the image of a robed woman, "like the Virgin of the Hermits", fell at Remirement in France.
FRIDAY 28 MAY: Feast Day of St Theodolous the Stylite. Fall of periwinkles and crabs in Worcester (1881).
MONDAY 31 MAY: The apparent teleportation of Dr Geraldo and his wife in their car from Bahia Blanca, Argentina, to Mexico (1968).
WEDNESDAY 2 JUNE: Feast day of St Elmo. 'St Elmo's Fire', the electrical discharge sometimes seen around the masthead of ships, was taken as a sign of the saint's protection.
MONDAY 7 JUNE: A train arrived in Chicago with a dead trout inside its shattered headlight (1937).
FRIDAY 11 JUNE: Feast Day of St Barnabas. A white-robed man, identified by the crowd as Jesus Christ, appeared in a Nairobi slum (1988).

STARLING COOK OUT

Mystery surrounds the hundreds of starlings found dead or dying in a remote lane in Anglesey. About 300 birds were found along a 20-yard stretch of the lane near Bodedern, some heaped on top of each other, some in hedgerows.

Alistair Moralee, senior RSPB warden on the island, said he'd never known anything like it in his 10 years with the Society. He has sent specimens to various agencies for investigation. Theories range from poison to being zapped by lightning as they perched on overhead cables.

An unofficial post mortem seems to suggest the birds' livers had been cooked. How did Mr Moralee deduce this? "I was told the livers appeared bronze coloured, which is how they would look if cooked." Whatever happened - poison, lightning or perhaps even microwave radiation - it did not affect any other internal organ. "It is strange that only the liver was affected," he said.

A battle of starlings over Cork in 1621 – from an old account – which left thousands dead. Did something similar happen in Angelsey?

Mr Moralee remains puzzled by another detail: "There were no dead birds in the fields on either side of the track." And why only starlings?

Later, Gareth Jones – of the Welsh Office Agricultural Development Advisory Service (ADAS) at Trawsgoed, near Aberystwyth – said their tests showed the birds had not been poisoned by any kind of pesticide. He did reveal, though, that someone phoned ADAS saying that they recalled a similar incident occurring on the Llyn Peninsula "many years ago". *D.Post, 7 & 8 Dec 1992.*

Perhaps the birds fell from the sky, as happened near Campeche, on the coast of Mexico last October. This mystery – baffling experts – has involved many hundreds of members of 16 different species. They fall with head injuries, it is said – but how this can be distinguished from impact injuries is *not* said. *[PA] 22 Oct 1992.*

FAX BE TO GOD

People who want to plant notes to God in Jerusalem's Wailing Wall can now do so by fax. Every day, hundreds of notes seeking divine intervention are stuffed into cracks in the wall, once part of the Second Temple (destroyed in 70 AD), and now Judaism's holiest shrine. The fax line was set up by Bezeq, the Israeli telephone company, on 20 January. A member of staff collects the messages, folds them and takes them to the wall. The number is Jerusalem (0109722) 612 222.

The Catholics are not far behind: a new confession fax machine is to be unveiled at Italy's annual church fair in Vincenza in May. The idea of 'confaxion' has stirred fierce theological controversy. Traditional teaching holds that the sacrament requires the presence of the priest and the person confessing. *[AP] 19 Jan, Int. Herald Tribune, 22 Jan, Observer, 24 Jan 1993.*

BOOM TIME FOR MELONS

The American Deep South has been hit by an outbreak of exploding melons – in fields, stores, fridges and kitchens. Tom McElroy, of Dadeville, Alabama, took a ten-pounder home and left it in his kitchen. "Ten minutes later", he said, "I was dripping in juice and my place looked like a war zone." Experts speculated about a bacterial disease causing gas build-ups. *The People, 21 Feb 1993.*

RETURN TO SENDER

Tom Field, 42, from Turnditch, Derbyshire, was baffled when the postman brought him two £20 fixed penalty tickets for illegally parking a steamroller in Edinburgh last December. He had never been to Edinburgh in his life, and he doesn't own a steamroller. *Sunday Mail, 7 Feb 1993.*

BARBIE NEWS

Someone in Sandusky, Illinois, is preying on Barbie dolls. He rips off their clothes and slashes them across the breasts and crotch with a knife. So far 24 dolls have been attacked. *Daily Record, 15 Jan 1993.*

Our correspondent Karma Tenzin Dorje spotted the following in the American paper *Common Ground* (Winter 1992): "I channel Barbie, archetypal feminine plastic essence who embodies the stereotypical wisdom of the 60s and 70s. Since childhood I have been gifted with an intensely personal, growth-oriented relationship with Barbie, the polyethylene essence who is 700 million teaching entities. [..] I'm happy to answer your questions, and my enlightening newsletter shares my experiences as also guided by Skipper, Ken, Poindexter, and my own Higher Inner Child. Send questions with $3 to Barbara, 23 Ross Avenue, San Anselmo, CA 94960."

Sidelines

Helen Sanger underwent surgery to alter her palm prints after a fortune teller in Duluth, Minnesota, predicted her life lines spelled an early grave. *Sunday Mail (Scotland) 29 Nov 1992.*

• • • • • • • • • • • • •

The mummified body of a 200-year-old mouse was found squashed flat inside an 18th century hymnbook by a librarian at Salisbury Cathedral, Wiltshire. *D.Star, 29 Jan 1993.*

• • • • • • • • • • • • •

Silent Ernst Hort spoke an average of 3.5 words a day over a two month period, a divorce court, in Bielefeld, Germany, heard. His wife Suzanne told the judge: "We never have any rows because he never says anything." She kept a notebook, in which his longest recorded utterance was: "This coffee tastes like dish-water," and when asked for a divorce, he simply scribbled, "I agree." *D.Express, 10 Sept 1992.*

• • • • • • • • • • • • •

Angry cowboy Ross Howard of Denver, protesting about men being allowed to marry men, was refused a licence to marry his horse. The hitch was a technicality; the law says three-year-olds need parental consent. *D.Record, 28 Sept 1992.*

• • • • • • • • • • • • •

Harriet Lasky put a piece of bubble gum in her mouth when she was seven and she is still chewing it, 33 years later. She keeps it in a glass of water overnight at her home in Denver, Colorado – and says "it gets better with age." *Sunday Mail, 21 Feb 1993.*

SIMULACRA CORNER

An old woman went to sleep under this tree near Fountain's Abbey, North Yorkshire, in Studley Royal Park, and was turned to wood. The photograph was taken by John Billingsley early in 1992.

We forgot to say that the giant sunbathing stone woman last issue was on the island of La Digue in the Seychelles.

We are always glad to receive pictures of spontaneous forms and figures, or any curious images. Send your snaps to the editorial address – with SAE – and we'll pay a fiver for any we use.

MAN BITES ALIEN!

An occasional selection of Fortean headlines from newspapers around the world.

ICE FROM HEAVENS STARTLES NUNS
Cincinnati Enquirer, 20 Nov 1989.

GLUE VICTIM DIALS 999 WITH HIS NOSE
D.Star, 4 June 1991.

OWLS WITH SPECS EXPLAIN VENTRILOQUISM D.Telegraph, 9 July 1991.

COUPLE LIVE IN FEAR OF DANGER HEDGE
Evening Leader (Clwyd & Chester), 30 July 1991.

JAPAN'S MAJOR TRAFFIC PROBLEM: DEAD RACCOONS
Nairobi Sunday Times, 18 Aug 1991.

2M ALLIGATORS BESIEGE TOWN
D.Express, 19 Aug 1991.

FAECES-TOSSING INARTISTIC, JURY RULES
Victoria (BC) Times-Colonist, 24 Aug 1991.

RELIEF FROM SMELL SOON Manchester Metro News, 30 Aug 1991.

TROGLODYTE EXPELLED

A 39-year-old Norwegian student was expelled from the University of Oslo because he smelled too bad. He then sued the university for £120,000, because they wouldn't let him sit his exams. He came from northern Norway to Oslo in 1978, and appeared to be normal; but in the early 1980s he started to live in a small cavern in the ground at Nordmarka, Ulleval, which led to the neglect of personal hygiene; as early as 1983, he was asked to study in a separate room from his fellow students.

The man makes his own clothes by sewing scraps of textiles together. Recently he was seen wearing boots made of birch bark and carrying a rucksack of plaited branches and leaves. Although he stinks and is infested with lice, the man is, according to many at the university, very intelligent, good at his subject (astrophysics) and a nice person.

On 11 January, he lost his court case and was ordered to pay costs and take a shower. He is appealing (but not very, as one journalist added). *Idag, 14 Dec; Guardian, 29 Dec 1992 + 12 Jan 1993.*

GONE TO PIECES

On 19 August 1992, the Prest family were getting ready for supper when one of them noticed a skull on the balcony 12 miles south of Prince George, Canada. It had been brought there by the family dog, Animal, an eight-month-old huskie-lab cross. In the following days, Animal brought home more human bones, which were collected by the Mounties.

Police dogs were unable to find the rest of the corpse, but Bert Prest thought it must be their neighbour, Toivo Haaparanta, 44, who had lived in a trailer up the road and had last been seen walking into the bush in 1990. By 10 September, the identity of the bones had been confirmed, but Animal had only retrieved the skull, pelvis, a portion of limb, boot and several vertebrae. *Victoria (BC) Times-Colonist, 24 Aug + 10 Sept 1992.*

HOOK, LINE AND SINKER

In China's Shaanxi province, an angler thought he'd hooked a giant fish. He reeled it in, saw a human head and promptly fainted. His 'catch' was a farmer, trying to drown himself because of personal problems. Passers-by pulled the drowning man out of the river, which presumably left two deeply unsatisfied participants in the drama. *South China Morning Post (etc), 28 July 1992.*

A LOAD OF SQUALLS

Kenji Ozawa – a Japanese meteorologist and inventor – told a conference that he has perfected a method of making miniature rain clouds that would be useful for watering lawns. The 4ft-wide clouds, which hover close to the ground, can deliver 15 gallons of water in an hour, and even have 2ft lightning bolts. "I simply extract humidity from the air with a special machine, and release small clouds of charged particles, which are zapped by an electric impulse to begin raining." We suspect that humidity isn't the only thing Mr Ozawa is extracting... *D.Telegraph, 24 Oct 1992.*

WRONG NUMBERS

● As Jason Pegler, a salesman with the AA in Dover, left his house in Folkestone, he heard the phone ringing in one of the phone boxes outside. On impulse, he picked it up. It was a colleague at work. "Hello Jason, it's Sue, the fax machine isn't working". At first she didn't believe she had rung a public telephone; then she realised what had happened. She knew Jason lived in Folkestone, so dialled 0303, and then by mistake dialled his staff number instead of his telephone number. The first five digits happened to be the number of the phone box. *Kent Messenger, 24 Oct 1992.*

● On 2 October 1992, Jan Morris answered the telephone at home in Llanystumdwy, Gwynedd. A man and a woman, without announcing themselves, sang in pleasant unison a verse of 'Happy Birthday to You'. They addressed the greeting to someone called Denis. They had got the wrong number. However, it was Jan Morris's birthday as well. *Independent, 3 Oct 1992.*

FILIPINO FERVOUR

Fortean phenomena from the Philippines

KNEE CAP RAIDERS

On the morning of 13 January 1993, it was found that 29 graves in the public cemetery in Barangay Sagasa, Bago City, had been broken into, and the bodies, some quite fresh, strewn around with their knee caps missing. It was believed that the patellæ or knee caps, known locally as *tuway-tuway*, were used by cultists as *anting-anting* (talismans) or to produce healing concoctions.

The cemetery caretaker said a tricycle with about eight men stopped in front of the graveyard at 9:00am on 12 January, and hammering sounds were heard until 2:00am the next morning. Police suspected a group of cultists, three of whom had been arrested and charged with the same offence in May 1991 in Pulupandan, Negros Occidental. They were set free after paying relatives of the 85 dead people they had disturbed. *The Philippine Star, 23 Feb 1993.*

FOOTPRINTS STIR RELIGIOUS FERVOUR

Human footprints in concrete and asphalt, ranging from five to seven inches in length and half an inch in depth, appeared overnight in several streets of Lucena City two days before Christmas. Traffic jams were caused by curious bystanders, and Roman Catholics lit candles near the footprints, which they believed might have divine origins. *Bangkok Post, 24 Dec 1992.*

'DEVIL' SPOTTED

On 22 January, Joy Bolante, 12, saw "a black man with a tail and horns" after she and some of her classmates burned some wood at the foot of a narra [tamarind] tree at the Camp Crame Elementary School in Quezon City. Another witness, Marilyn Umpat, described the horned figure as 'gigantic'. The next day, Joy collapsed and was sent home by her teachers. Then she regained consciousness and with a man's voice shouted "There is no God!".

On the morning of 27 January, five other pupils started acting strangely and soon 15 others collapsed. Priests and relatives said they were talking in various voices and showed 'extraordinary strength'. The children were rushed to a nearby Roman Catholic chapel where a priest dabbed them with holy water and said prayers. *People's Journal Tonight (Philippines), 28 Jan; [Reuters] 29 Jan 1993.*

MARY CRIES BLOODY TEARS

On 11 February, on the Feast Day of Our Lady of Lourdes, hundreds of devotees saw a wooden statue of the Blessed Virgin Mary shed tears of blood at an altar in Baringay San Antonio, Agoo, La Union. The sun allegedly 'danced' ('a universal sign of Mary's presence') and a luminous white cloud hung over the head of the young visionary Judiel Nieva during a bright, cloudless day. Hours later at the Agoo Basilica, many saw at close range the dried blood on the statue's eyes, cheeks, lips, neck and chest. Her white, flowing robes had bloodstains. According to Father Roger Cortez, appointed spiritual director for the young visionary, the statue had wept blood six times. *People's Journal Tonight, 11 Feb; Manila Bulletin, 13 Feb 1993.*

INCORRUPTION

Jose Ilagan, 86, of San Luis, Batangas, suddenly succumbed to an unknown illness on 16 November 1972, and was embalmed and buried in the family crypt three days later. The crypt was opened in 1978 to bury one of his sons-in-law, and it was discovered that his body had not decomposed. They dressed the body in new clothes and placed it in a new coffin. When Ilagan's widow died in 1985, the old man's tomb was reopened and the body found to be still fresh. He was again dressed in new clothes and placed in a new casket. This time a new tomb was built on top of the old one.

On 10 January 1993, the tomb was opened again after Ilagan's daughter, now a resident of Rizal province, complained of having strange dreams.

The body appeared to be intact, including the hair, nails and penis. However, some deterioration was noticed in the eyeballs, and the body weight had been reduced to about three kilos.

The body was moved to the church and large crowds came to see and touch the 'miracle'. Sceptics maintained that the preservation was due to an unusually large amount of formalin in the body. The family intended to take the remains back to the old house in the barrio and build a glass crypt for it. *People's Journal Tonight, 13 Jan 1993.*

AND HIS CLOTHES HAVE HARDLY GONE OUT OF DATE EITHER.
Hunt Emerson

FLUTTERING BY

According to the Biological Records Centre – a vast archive of data on British wildlife at the Institute of Terrestrial Ecology, at Monks Wood, near Huntingdon – many species of moths and butterflies are hatching earlier and extending their range northwards further and faster than some plants. Something similar, it seems, happened whenever this part of the world warmed up after various ice ages, and is taken as an indication of climatic change.

May 1992 saw an 'unprecedented' migration of large numbers of butterflies of many species recorded in Northern Ireland, including Clouded Yellows, and the earliest ever sighting of a Speckled Wood. About the same time (mid-May), naturalist Tristan ap Rheinallt saw Clouded Yellows on the Isle of Arran; these visitors, usually blown over from the Mediterranean, are rarely seen so far north.

A massive invasion of East Anglia by the Cabbage White occurred in July 1992. Stephen Piotrowski, the official butterfly recorder for Suffolk, reckoned their numbers could be 50 times higher than usual. They were blown on winds from France and the Low Countries, and appeared to be dispersing inland.

A swarm of white butterflies, heading for England, encountered off Normandy in July 1903.

That last report prompted a letter from A.W. Kimberley, of Colchester, pointing out that such invasions are not always one-way. "On July 16, during a three-hour passage in a yacht between Dungeness and Dover, some three to five miles offshore, I observed a continuous flow of Cabbage Whites moving out to sea towards France. They were flying 6-10 feet above the waves in good weather conditions with a light cross-wind from the SW, so their movement towards France was a deliberate one. They were not blown across."

Times, 13 Aug, Butterfly Conservation News 51, Arran Banner, 30 May, D.Telegraph, 29+31 July 1992.

WOOLLY COMFORTERS

Teams of women and brownies in Washford, Somerset, spent weeks knitting gaily-coloured 'birdigans', with 'arm'-holes for oily wings, after an appeal went out to make coats for the puffins and guillemots recovering in Inverkeithing bird sanctuary, Fife, after the *Braer* Shetland oil spill. It is not stated who made the appeal.

Officials at the sanctuary, run by the Scottish RSPCA, threw away the 100 miniature body-warmers. "They overheat the birds and they start preening them and ingesting the material", explained Sandra Hogben, the sanctuary manager. "They also unbalance the birds because they're not used to wearing coats and they fall over."

The RSPCA's attitude annoyed the birdigan's inventor, Jim Ward, a veteran seagull rescuer in Scarborough, North Yorkshire. Only last year, after an oil spill off the South African coast, wildlife experts asked Mr Ward for a knitting pattern and put hundreds of Zulus to work making dwarf jumpers for their own oil-slicked birds. *D.Mail, 20 Feb; Independent, 23 Feb 1993.*

GOAT NEWS

● Three months after Uganda's talking goat [see ***FT66:9***], another one appeared in Jamaica. It spoke to Miss Adele Brown of St Anne's Bay and her mother as they collected pa fruit near Albany. The goat prophesied that unless the Green Party of Jamaica came to power very soon the destruction of the planet would accelerate. They asked the goat what they should do and it said: "There are no limits to creativity and no limits to subversion. Vote for any candidate opposed to the Year 2000 Party." Then it wandered off into the trees. *Brisbane Telegraph, 16 Sept, via Private Eye 6 Nov 1992.*

● Dennis the beer-swilling goat, one of the more innocent victims of South Africa's political violence, was offered a dignified farewell to the Great Pasture in the Sky by a white animal-lovers group. Dennis, inseparable companion of self-styled Zulu warrior Xolani Sabelo, was a regular on the pub circuit of Umlazi, a picturesque but dishevelled settlement in Zululand, until he was strangled by marauding killers last August. *[AFP] 1 Sept 1992.*

● Ringo, an 18-month-old billy goat, had sired 45 kids by September last and also produced a fresh glass of milk every night. Farmer François Ruiz of Port-Vendres in south-western France said that the rare hermaphrodite goat had two small nipples near its male genital organs. *[AFP] 5 Sept 1992.*

RASPUTIN LIVES!

Faith healer Boris Zolotov claims the power to induce orgasms by thought alone. Women from all over Russia attend the sexual healing seminars in provincial cities. The press brands Zolotov a 'sex maniac' and the Russian orthodox church accuses him of breaking up marriages and associating with the devil.

Four hundred followers warm up for a session at a 'pioneer' camp outside Zelenograd, near Moscow. A huge communal bed is covered with mattresses and blankets. A sea of tracksuited bodies writhes in unison to American soul music and the air is dense with the smell of sweat. Zolotov, a tall, chunky man with blond hair, dressed in jeans and shirt, believes that man's role is to make women happy. He bellows "Who wants an orgasm?" Dozens of women scream back, "I do!" He strides about waving his hand like a conductor and grimacing with concentration. As the music pulsates, everyone gathers in a large circle. One by one, women and men jump into the ring, flinging themselves about to the throbbing beat in a feverish ecstasy. The

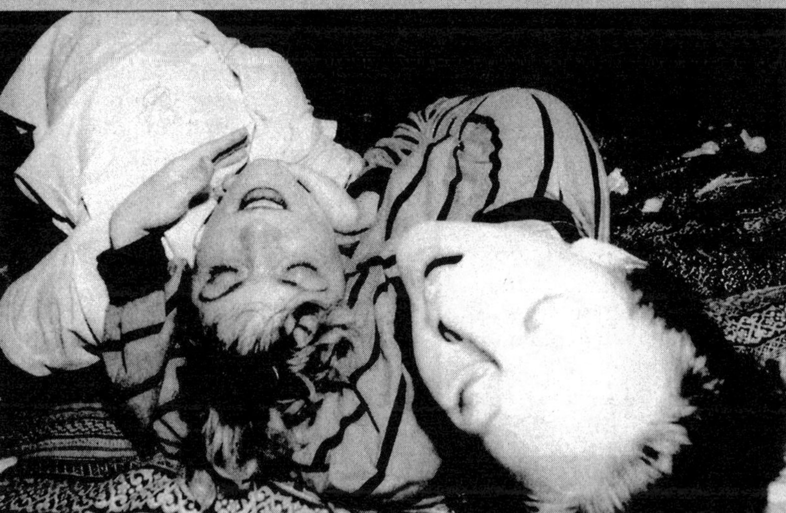

music stops abruptly, leaving about 50 devotees lying in a heap, moaning. About 30 appear to have had a sexual climax. (We are not told about the remaining 350.)

Then Zolotov makes them 'speak in tongues' – supposedly French and Chinese. They scream and mutter gibberish. Some followers say that after intensive work with Zolotov, they can communicate and induce orgasms with one another by telepathy. They say it beats ordinary sex with a partner. Zolotov means 'gold' and he calls his method 'The Golden Way'. Most of his followers are women between 20 and 30. Graduates receive qualification certificates, which they say are accepted in Russian hospitals.

"Some women have massive orgasms, they fall in love with him and project their fantasies on to him", said one participant, Australian psychiatrist Adam Rosenblatt. "He releases their creative energy and some start to write poetry and draw." Zolotov, a married man with a family, hugs and kisses the women. He analyses their poems and pictures, which are eventually displayed in an exhibition. Seminars cost £20, an average monthly wage; but in Zelenograd nearly half slip through without paying. *South China Morning Post, 29 Nov 1992.*

GIRL WITH X-RAY EYES

In the summer of 1991, Georgian schoolgirl Maiko Ramishvili, 14, complained of headaches and started describing to her mother, a professor of biology, the internal organs of the human body in graphic detail. By the autumn, with just a slight effort, she could 'see' all the internal organs in a person and even a network of acupuncture dots. By massaging these 'black spots', Maiko improved the health of everybody she worked on.

A more graphic, if rather less useful, talent was her ability to magnetise books as well as plastic and metal objects. In her palm, a pen could be made to dance to a tune 'independently'. 'Experts' blustered obscurely about her "ability to sense high-frequency fluctuations". *Soviet Weekly, 24 Oct 1991.*

For other women with X-ray eyes, see ***FT49:8*** + ***FT57:27***; and for 'magnetic' Russians, see ***FT59:11***.

VAMPIRE NEWS

■ The Vampire Anti-Defamation League (VADL), launched by the Ghost Story Society, is concerned to correct pejorative horror-fiction terminology to help eliminate 'prejudice against otherly-abled individuals in our society'. It proposes that 'vampire' be replaced by 'nutritionally-hæmatologically challenged person' and 'zombie' by 'otherly-animate individual of Haitian origin'. *Sunday Times, 18 Oct 1992.*

■ On 16 June 1992, Mark Heggie, 23, of Kentish Town in London, was sent to a secure mental hospital for an unlimited term by a judge at the Old Bailey. On 27 July 1991, the day after making bail from a burglary charge, he stole drink, got plastered and met fellow Scot Alison da Costa, 63, in the Royal Free Hospital in Hampstead.

She took him to her house in Golders Green, where he attacked her with a pipe and length of metal tube, with which he tried to garotte her. Thinking she was dead, he drank the blood from her head wounds before running into the street covered with blood, where he was arrested. He told police he had always tried to find work in abattoirs so that he could drink blood. *Independent, 1 Feb + 17 June; Camden New Journal, 6 Feb 1992.*

■ A 'vampire' was caught in the act in the Hungarian town of Debrecen in July. The 22-year-old unemployed man had bitten a goat's neck open and had sucked out its blood almost to the last drop. When caught in the act by the goat's owner, he was so drunk he couldn't even say his name. After sobering up, he was unable to explain his behaviour. *Die Tageszeitung (Germany) 14 July 1992.* [For other recent vampire cases, see *FT58:6*.]

■ Mohammad Ali, 26, of Barking, Essex, was jailed for six years last year for biting a lump of flesh out of a policeman's neck while resisting arrest after he had been speeding on the M11. *D.Telegraph, 1 April 1992.*

■ According to an opinion poll published in *Russky Sever*, the local paper in the northern Russian city of Vologda, what the local people feared most were vampires – specifically the 'energy vampire', a supernatural beast whose greatest delight is to suck people's 'life energy'. Running a close second were witches and black magic, followed by 'silly bosses and their stupid orders'. Three of the 40 questioned said that they feared an earthquake, a flood or the arrival of aliens from outer space; while four told the poll they were afraid of nothing. *[AP] 14 Nov 1992.*

MYSTERY OF THE ORIENTEER

Orienteering, the tough cross-country sport that crosses fell-running with map-reading, breeds some of the world's fittest athletes. In the last three years, however, a mystery illness has killed seven of Sweden's top competitors, forcing the national teams of Sweden and Denmark to stop training while doctors investigate the problem.

The latest death, in the first week of November, was that of Swedish international orienteer Melker Karlsson. Karlsson, 23, collapsed in a post-training sauna, and after hurried consultations, doctors ordered 200 other top athletes to suspend their training programmes.

The precaution seems to have been taken because Karlsson's death did not fit the pattern medics thought was appearing. Suspicions had fallen on a respiratory condition known as Taiwan Acute Respiratory Infection, which can kill if the infection spreads to inflame the heart muscle. But Stig Carlsson of the Swedish Orienteering Association admitted: "The doctors said one thing is clear: this sudden death can't be explained merely by TARI. There must be another reason."

The Swedes report that all of the dead athletes had previously exercised while feeling ill, but further research is to be done on animal-borne infection and to test links between the deaths and the taking of baths after exercise (a theory that somehow smacks of the 19th century). In the meantime, doctors will also have to establish whether the mystery illness is unique to orienteers or whether the problem was noticed among the athletes simply because they were under closer medical supervision. *Independent on Sunday, 15 Nov 1992.*

THE FAR SIDE By GARY LARSON

"Well, Donald — forgot your sun block, I see."

PRIMATE STRIPPERS

An anonymous French tourist was strolling with his wife in the orangutan sanctuary in Sandakan, Borneo, on 16 October 1992, when Raja, a 14-year-old male orangutan grabbed him and stripped him naked. The ape didn't disturb his wife. The Frenchman, in his 30s, kept still for fear of being attacked. Raja fled into the forest with trousers, shirt and underwear, while the tourist rushed to the park office where someone lent him a pair of trousers.

A park official said that Raja was not violent, but could be 'inquisitive' at times. It was the first time such an incident had happened at the sanctuary. He advised visitors not to wear clothes which could be removed easily. *[AFP] 21 Oct 1992.*

Two months later, a pack of wild monkeys apparently desperate for food raided a Japanese village northwest of Tokyo and made off with men's and women's underwear from a washing line. *Edinburgh Eve. News, 15 Dec 1992.*

HOUSE-NAPPER

Someone – or something – has been stealing houses – one from northern Russia and the other from New Zealand. In the first case, a man arriving at his country retreat near Arkhangelsk, on the White Sea, found the entire building stolen, complete with outhouses and fences, leaving just a vegetable patch. Two months later, an entire house disappeared from its site on forestry land at Pipawi, New Zealand. Police were holding a suspect. *Leicester Mercury, 31 Aug; Sunday Mail (Scotland) 4 Oct 1992.*

A few years ago, we noted the disappearance of two bridges, both complete, one from Wales and the other from Uruguay. Perhaps, on some alien planet, a museum curator has just added to his collection of artifacts from our solar system.

THE MOTHER OF ALL SLIME MOULDS

Slime moulds, those strange carnivorous fungi neither wholly plant nor wholly animal, usually weigh an ounce or two. Some which can move several centimetres a day have been found on rotting wood, while one soared into space in January 1992 on the shuttle Discovery so its daily rhythms could be measured. Now Xinhua, the Chinese official news agency, have announced the discovery of one weighing 77lb. Spotted in a river in Shaanxi province in August 1992, it put on 22lb in three days.

"It is usually found in cool, moist and dark places such as grassland, rotted logs and withered leaves" said the agency report, "and it can move across the ground slowly on its own. Its flesh is pure white with explicit layers, and it feels soft." The news caused ripples of delight and disbelief among slime mould specialists. A 77lb mould would be the size of a small donkey or a large dog, trailing spaghetti-like tendrils. Professor John Bonner of Princeton said that he could not image one of that size. Slime moulds surge backwards and forwards like waves at the shoreline. In lab tests, they surge towards food. "They are the physiological equivalent of the wolf pack", said Professor Bonner. *[Reuters], Guardian, 14 Oct 1992.*

NOT THEIR DAY

■ Doctors in California hit a snag with a prototype electronic implant which helps impotent men rise to the occasion by remote control. A 52-year-old patient complained that he got a lift every time his neighbours used their electronic car doors. *D.Record, 23 Oct 1992.*

■ A 36-year-old man who had lost his memory asked police in Hamburg to find out who he was. He wished he hadn't bothered when they discovered he was wanted for fraud and arrested him. *D.Star, 21 Jan 1993.*

■ Note from a recent *Lloyd's List*: "The average seal rehabilitated after the Exxon Valdez oil spill had $80,000 spent on it. Two of the most expensive were put back into the bay at a special ceremony. Within two minutes they were both eaten by a killer whale." *Observer, 4 Oct 1992.*

■ During the body count of the *Braer* oil disaster off the Shetlands, the corpses of four sea otters were brought in, but only one was found to have died as a result of the oil. 'Natural causes' did for two more, and the fourth was run over by a Norwegian film crew reporting the disaster. *Independent, 19 Jan 1993.*

■ According to *Police* magazine, a suspicious-looking cardboard box was recently found outside a Territorial Army centre in Bristol. The TA called the police, who called an Army bomb disposal unit, which blew the box up – to find it full of leaflets on how to deal with suspicious-looking packages. *Independent, 20 Jan 1993.*

■ A telegram firm were obliged to pay £1,000 damages by a Filipino court for sending a death condolence message in a birthday card... in a Christmas envelope. *D.Record, 3 April 1991.*

■ Village policeman Marc Fagny, 48, from Arlon in Belgium, was sent to shoot a rabid Alsatian – and killed the woman who owned it instead. At his trial for manslaughter, he said that everybody in the village knew he couldn't shoot straight. *D.Record, 12 Oct 1991.*

■ A man was so annoyed when a fortune teller forecast he would go to jail that he shot him, for which he was jailed in Naples. *Sun, 13 Jan 1992.*

■ A Dutchman who went into hospital to be circumcised awoke to be told by doctors that he had been given a vasectomy because of a mix-up in patient cards. "He was getting married and went to the hospital to get his circumcision done by professionals", said a spokeswoman for the Dutch patients' rights group. The man's reaction is unrecorded. *[Reuters] 4 Sept 1992.*

DANIELLE & THE LYON DEN

French police and the local media spent more than three months chasing their tails last summer in an attempt to solve the mystery of an apparently deaf-and-dumb teenage girl who turned up in Paris and whom they believed might have been the victim of a sect of witches. All they knew about the girl, who wrote her name as Danielle Sanchez, came from a series of drawings she executed for them. In one, she showed herself weeping as her mother kills her pet cat and collects its blood in a container. In another, her mother and a group of hooded 'witches' gather to sacrifice animals.

'Danielle' also drew herself being forced to take part in a ceremony while bound to a bed, lying on a floor while her mother stands holding a syringe and a key, and in a hospital undergoing a brain scan while her father watches her.

All police could say for sure was that not all the information in the girl's pictures checked out. One of the most elaborate showed her in a chateau complete with vineyards, tennis court, stables and a swimming pool; it was captioned "Danielle Sanchez, the big manor in Lyon". But a thorough check of the area failed to turn up a similar building, or anyone who knew the girl.

'Danielle' first turned up in Paris one night in August. She was wearing designer clothes with the labels cut out, and carried two cuddly toys in a rucksack and about 70 francs in cash. A brief spell in a psychiatric hospital showed that while the girl appeared to be deaf-and-dumb, she had no knowledge of sign language or hearing aids.

Police suspected the girl might actually be able to hear, but that she had been struck dumb with shock. The authorities seemed unsure whether 'Danielle' was really the victim of a cult or simply had an active imagination, but they treated her as a possible kidnap victim.

There was a parallel case in 1988. A young mute boy turned up in Mexico, unable to give even a name; he drew pictures that suggested he might have been the survivor of an air crash. After a nine-month investigation, the boy was identified as a runaway from Tampico with an active imagination [*FT54:5*].

Sure enough, further investigation revealed that 'Danielle' was Karen Ponsford, a weighbridge manager's daughter from Crediton, Devon. She was seeing a consultant psychiatrist near her home but was not, apparently, in institutional care. Informed by her French doctors that they now knew who she was, she still declined to talk, but indicated in writing she would like to go home. How Karen got to France and why she went there remain a mystery. *Today, 10 + 26 Nov 1992.*

One drawing shows a vast chateau with cars and servants. 'Danielle' (pictured top) is at a fourth-floor window

RIVERS OF BLOOD

Villagers in Three Crosses, West Glamorgan, awoke to find their gardens swamped in blood. Lawns and pavements were red and an awful stench filled the air. Blood from an abattoir seeped from drains, "officials believe". *D.Star, 6 Oct 1992.* We are not told whether there *was* an abattoir in the vicinity… Perhaps clippers of the local press could provide us with more data.

GONE WITH THE WIND

A girl of nine was playing at Songjiang, near Shanghai, when a whirlwind lifted her into the air and set her down unhurt in a treetop almost two miles away, according to an official Chinese newspaper, the *Xinmin Evening News. D.Mail, 22 July 1992.* We were reminded of a Reuters report of 30 May 1986: a freak wind lifted 13 children into the air in the oasis of Hami in western China, depositing them unharmed in sand dunes and scrub 12 miles away.

SINGING OUTBREAK

Last summer, psychologists were sent to a village in northeast India to investigate strange behaviour by residents. Tripura State Health Services Director K.L. Roy said some people in Garo Para village had been behaving abnormally for several days. They would sing, dance and cry until exhausted as though affected by mass hysteria. Others had fled the village in panic. *Edinburgh Evening News, 31 Aug 1992.*

A STING IN ITS TAIL

A remarkable new species of bird, unlike any other, was discovered accidentally by American biologists working in New Guinea. The feathers, skin and flesh of the starling-sized hooded pitohui, *Pitohui dichrous* are saturated with a powerful natural poison. They were found, over a period of two years, trapped in nets intended to catch birds of paradise.

John Dumbacher, of the University of Chicago, said: "We were trying to release them as quickly as possible, but they were able to cut our hands with their sharp beaks and claws. They are pretty feisty." When he licked his wound his mouth began to tingle and go numb. The other scientists reported similar effects. The immediate reaction was numbness, burning and sneezing.

The poison was identified as a neurotoxin containing *homobatrachotoxin*, 10mg of which is enough to kill a mouse or frog. The only other creature known to produce it is the poisonous frog whose secretions are used by hunters in South America on their arrows and blow-darts. Local people, of course, already knew the bird; they called it a "rubbish bird" because it was not worth catching to eat.

Two other types of pitohui were found – the rusty and the variable pitohuis – but neither were as poisonous as the hooded variety. The toxin is thought to have evolved as a defence, because snakes and hawks tend to leave them alone; there are even birds which mimic the pitohui's distinctive black and orange markings to share this defence. It seems to demonstrate the mystery of convergent evolution. But how did the pitohuis acquired the ability to synthesize the toxin in the first place, and at the same time develop immunity to their own weapon?

Sources: *Science 28 Oct; Times, D. Telegraph, Int. Herald Tribune, New Scientist (and many others), 31 Oct 1992.*

MASS-MURDERING PLANTS

Meat-eating vegetables – like Venus fly-traps – have always provided Forteans with a giggle. They fascinate by inverting the usual predatory arrangements, which is what makes a report in last August's *Nature* rather interesting. It sheds new light on how dinoflagellates (single-celled algae, a major constituent of plankton) are responsible for the 'red tide' phenomenon which can kill fish in their millions.

A 'red tide' occurs mostly in the spring when the algae bloom in abundance; occasionally they produce massive clouds of toxins which poison all the fish in the vicinity, and sometimes also the humans who eat shellfish contaminated with those toxins. Until now, it was thought that the toxin cloud was a defence against huge shoals of fish, but the work of JoAnne Burkholder and colleagues at the North Carolina State University, in Raleigh, shows that if these tiny single-celled plants had a mind, collectively, it would have the mass-murder of another lifeform in it.

The algae lurk dormant in the mud of tidal rivers until they detect (it is not said how) large schools of fish in their vicinity. They are not fooled, it seems, by crabs or shellfish, but are only excited by their herbivorous finny enemies. They drift up out of the mud, floating to the surface, exuding a powerful nerve-poison as they go. As the fish succumb, the toxin causes their skin to disintegrate. What happens next has been described as an orgy of gluttony and sex on a scale that beggars the imagination. The dinoflagellates gorge themselves on skin particles, then mate in countless millions, and their progeny sink back into the ooze awaiting their turn.

Observers have noted that 'red tides', and their characteristic billowing acres of rotting fish, have become more frequent in American estuaries in the last 20 years. Some marine biologists have suggested that this might be because the voracious piscivors are actually thriving on the phosphates polluting the rivers.

OBITUARY:

BRIAN INGLIS

21 July 1916 — 11 February 1993

I had put in a phone call from Brian out there in the 'beyond' – but after discussions with his sceptic friends (there were many of them at his 'wake', most going back to his days as Editor of *The Spectator*), it was decided that nothing less than a fax from Brian would do to convince them that he was right after all.

That, however, would not be Brian's style. In all my 15 years of knowing him, nothing paranormal ever happened to him. The closest he ever came to experiencing phenomena was secondhand, through his association with the psychics Uri Geller and Matthew Manning, to whom he gave an arm of friendship, staunchly standing up for them in the press whenever their detractors had a go at them. He used to greatly enjoy describing the David Dimbleby TV show with Geller that launched his career in the UK. At the press meeting afterwards he was standing with the other journalists while Geller demonstrated his metal-bending. He watched a colleague suddenly slap his hand to his trouser pocket and with horror bring out his door keys. One had bent.

An historian by training, Brian's main contribution to psychic research was to provide an in-depth history of the paranormal. He completed two volumes, taking readers from early civilisation to the present day. He was well aware of the difficulties of the task. As he put it in his introduction to volume one: "The supernatural presents a problem, because one man's facts are another man's superstitions."

And that was exactly the reception given to the book. Bernard Levin saw it coming. In his review of *Natural and Supernatural* in *The Times* (1978) he described his old friend and ex-colleague's technique as 'ruthless overkill'. "He has piled up a mountain of evidence, searchingly examined and scrupulously evaluated, so gigantic, multifarious, honestly attested and unshaken, that [..] it is simply not possible [..] for any sane person to deny that there have been a vast, an unaccountable, number of supernatural happenings [..] Yet it will be done [..] [because of] the terror that seems to seize many intelligent and large-minded people at the suggestion that the universe may contain, may even run on, principles either beyond their control or their understanding."

Brian's response was to begin classifying the 'sceptocæmia' as he called it. There was, for example, retrocognitive dissonance. This described how someone could first witness a paranormal event (such as a poltergeist phenomenon or metal-bending) and declare it for real, but subsequently deny that it took place. It happens a lot. Professor John Taylor is an example. He appeared on the original Geller-Dimbleby show and was totally overwhelmed by what he saw. He set himself to research the child metal-benders who had watched Geller on TV and started to copy him. Several years later, retrocognitive dissonance set in. He could not prove that electromagnetic phenomena had 'caused' the metal-bending; as there was no other explanation that he could find in science, the phenomenon did not exist.

Brian admitted his own mild version of the disease. He would on occasion come up against his 'boggle threshold', a term coined by the late Rene Tickell describing that point – different for each of us – at which we say: "No, that defies my commonsense; it cannot be."

He never, though, saw himself as a fighter for causes; and was embarrassed when *The Daily Telegraph*, in the headline to an article on alternative medicine he wrote in January this year, described him as 'an enthusiast'. Another label he shied from was that of 'believer'. "I don't know", was his reply to anyone who – over a jar or two at his flat in Belsize Park – tried pushing him for a statement about the existence of God, or purpose, or other grand themes. It was, rather, his integrity – together of course with his Irishness, that drove him on. He would never let go of an issue, no matter how unpopular that might make him. But he also relished academic argument; no scientist would be allowed to get away with a sloppy argument or mechanistic assumption.

His third volume on the history of the paranormal was to be different. He had, he wrote last July in the introduction, at last seen the very changes happening to science that he had worked so hard for. The new statistical methods of meta-analysis meant scientific (though grudging) admission of evidence of paranormal phenomena. Rigorously conducted trials could be individually dismissed – for all sorts of reasons (statistical error and fraud being the most popular); but taken as a whole they were now acceptable. More importantly, Brian believed, the assault on scientific materialism was now happening from within. In particular, developments in physics had meant that the old way of viewing paranormal phenomena as somehow taking place at the interface of mind and matter was no longer relevant. The stuff of the world is all 'mind stuff'. He was now to 'explore psi as if the new paradigm were in place'.

... Fax me, Inglis.

Ruth West *February 1993*

THE 'AYE-UP' GHOST

Susan Griggs, 42, rented a terraced house in Agincourt Road, Buckland, Portsmouth, from the Portsmouth Housing Association in August 1991 and moved in with her daughters Nicola, 23, and Sarah, eight, and Nicola's daughter Jasmin, who is now two. Poltergeist activity started a month later, when they began to decorate. A year later, Nicola told the local press that Jasmin had befriended a ghost and she asked for the family to be rehoused.

Medium Ron Pomroy and his colleague Margaret have told Nicola that the ghost is "a miserable old sod" called Percy and comes from the North. He once lived in the house and promised to look after it after his wife died. "No-one round her says 'aye-up' to Jasmin" said Nicola, "but that's how she answers me."

Ghostly activities are said to include cups of tea snatched from people's hands and thrown into a gas fire; clock hands suddenly moving on several hours; neatly-piled clothes strew over bedrooms; a kitchen chair thrown at Nicola, who was also pushed down the stairs, breaking her wrist; the oven door opening and shutting on its own; strong cooking smells when no food was being prepared; cutlery flying around and taps being turned on. The Rev Len Fox, vicar of All Saints, Portsea, blessed the house, which only made things worse. *Streetlife (Portsmouth), 27 Aug; The News (Portsmouth), 27 Aug + 31 Oct; Guardian, 28 Aug; The Big Issue, 16-29 Oct 1992.*

Jasmin Griggs with her mother Nicola in the kitchen at Agincourt Road, where she talked with the ghost

FOULMOUTH DOLL

The Willis family gathered round the tree on Christmas Day to open the presents. Gemma, 10, took the wrapping off 'Tummy Talks', a round-faced, big-eyed talking doll, which was supposed to make happy gurgling noises. Instead, when she pressed its stomach, the doll shouted "Mama, mama, eff-off... ha! ha! ha!" Gemma's father John, who bought the doll at Tesco in Redditch, thought his ears were playing tricks on him, but he played it again and heard it again. "It put a bit of a dampener on Christmas", he said. "We want compensation."

In Peterlee, Co Durham, a shocked Shirley Adamson heard the same thing a week before Christmas when she checked whether the £13.99 doll she had bought from Asda for her granddaughter worked.

After Christmas, Tesco investigated the Chinese-made doll, while managers and toy buyers at Asda were forced to listen to dozens of Tummy Talks talking: their conclusion was that what sounded like 'eff-off' was really just a giggle with a Chinese accent. "We sell tens of thousands of these dolls" said an Asda spokesman, "and this is our first complaint." It sounds to us like an aural simulacrum. *Independent, 3 Jan 1993.*

John Willis with his daughter Gemma and the allegedly foul-mouthed 'Tummy Talks' doll.

MEDICAL BAG

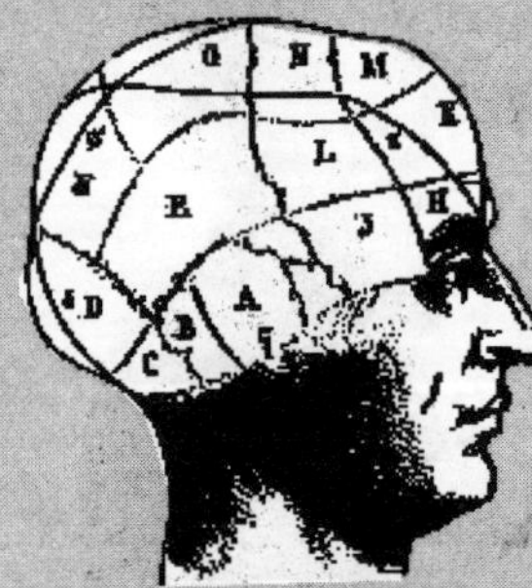

YOUNG MOTHER

An eight-year-old girl became what is believed to be Mexico's youngest mother when she gave birth to a healthy boy. Mother and baby were said to be in 'perfect condition' after the Cæsarean delivery in a Guadalajara hospital on 12 January. *Edinburgh Eve. News, 15 Jan 1993.*

DIY TONSILLECTOMY

Poppy Faldmo, 21, of Salt Lake City, took out her own tonsils because she didn't have medical insurance to cover the £700 hospital bills. She spent hours every day in front of a mirror, removing the inflamed tonsils a bit at a time with nail scissors, a modelling knife and a toothache gel as an anæsthetic. Doctors say she did a perfect job. *D.Mirror, 9 Feb 1993.*

SNEEZING CURED

Nicole Kane, 9, from Greenford, could not stop sneezing for nearly two months despite visits to doctors, a hospital and a hypnotist. Then she had a tooth extracted to allow a new one to grow properly and the sneezing stopped. A doctor speculated that the new tooth might have been affecting a nerve connected to the girl's nose. *Eve. Standard, 21 April 1993.*

PLAGUE DEATH

A 31-year-old man from Tucson, Arizona, died after contracting pneumonic plague in rural Chaffee County, Colorado. The man's friends had several cats, one of which was sick. On 19 August, he crawled under the house in an attempt to drag the sick animal out. It was coughing, wheezing and sneezing, and died later that day. The man returned to Tucson where, four days later, he developed stomach ache, high fever, diarrhoea and vomiting. He died on 26 August, the first plague death in the United States since 1987. The disease has been confirmed last year in 21 of Colorado's 63 counties, a rate said to be unprecedented.

Usually, plague is spread by infected rodents, such as rock squirrels, mice, chipmunks and prairie dogs. Infected rodents are widespread in parts of Arizona, California, Colorado, Nevada, New Mexico, Oregon and Utah. Pneumonic plague attacks the lungs, bubonic the lymph nodes, and septicæmic the bloodstream. All three types are contracted from rodents' fleas, although pneumonic may also be spread by coughing, as in the latest fatality. Colorado usually averages two plague cases a year during plague season, which ends in October. It fluctuates in cycles of five years. There were a lot of cases in 1984-86, none in 1988-90, and then three cases late in 1991. *Denver (CO) Post, 16 Sept; Hackensack (NJ) Record, 9 Oct 1992.*

IDENTIFIED FLYING DISKS

The flying saucers in question are manhole covers which suddenly become airborne. This particular phenomenon was first identified by Mike Dash in 1990 *[**FT54:6** & **FT57:29**.]*

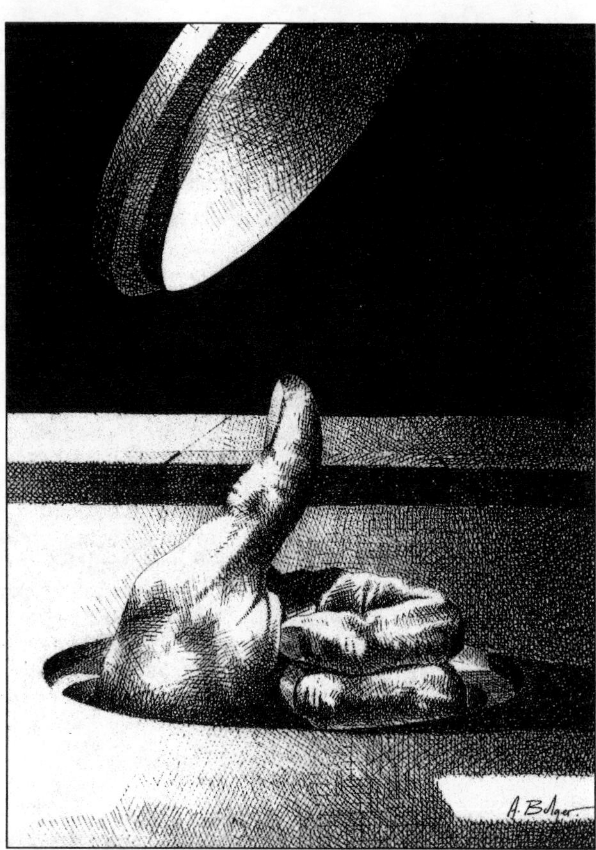

■ A manhole cover blew into the air in Pittsburgh after a power failure on 1 August 1991 and crashed through the windshield of a car, killing the driver, Mary Vehec, 23.

■ Minutes before a carnival procession was due to pass by on 20 June 1992, a manhole cover blew out of King's Heath High Street, Birmingham. The police quickly sealed off 150 yards of the road and diverted the procession.

■ Another one blew out of Milton Road West in Edinburgh some time in August, possibly by pressure of storm water. At least two cars were damaged after failing to spot the hole and driving into it.

■ Another one flew six feet across a pavement in Guildford Road, South Lambeth, London, on 2 September when an electrical link box under the pavement blew up. The hot lid gave severe burns to Corrine Cordner, 11.

■ At 3:00pm on 5 February, a manhole cover blasted into the air from the Greenfield Caravan Park, Lincoln, and crashed down on the roof of a bungalow 30 feet away, smashing eight tiles. Caravan park owner John Conyers had the tiles mended and the sewer tested. "It was completely clear of any gas", he said. "We just don't know what happened."

[AP] 2 Aug 1991; Birmingham Eve. Mail, 20 June; Edinburgh Eve. News, 13 Aug; South London Press, 4 Sept; 1992; Lincolnshire Standard, 12 Feb 1993.

MOMENTOUS MARROW

In September 1992, hundreds of visitors admired a strange marrow brought into the editorial office of *Calauze*, a newspaper in Deva, Romania, by a peasant who grew it in Certeja, a village in central Romania. On the marrow could be seen the letters L,I,T,D,N,R,S,I,C,D,S,U and the numbers 6,9,5,4,4. Agronomists confirmed that these were natural and not man-made. Clairvoyant Natasa Serban declared that she had decoded the letters and numbers: the letters symbolised "the struggle between good and evil" and the numbers were a code for the country which will unleash the Third World War. Ms Serban would not name the country. *Tineretul Liber, 21 Oct 1992.*

TINY SPIDER EATS WOMAN

Valerie Slimp, 39, was bitten by a Brown Recluse Spider at her home in San Bernardino, California. By the time doctors discovered what was wrong, the tissue in her legs and arms had already been eaten away and she had to fight for her life. She faced losing all her limbs.

Expert Dr Rick Vetter said: "The Brown Recluse – also known as the Violin Spider because of its shape – is more dangerous than the notorious Black Widow. A native of America's Midwest, it is so tiny that humans do not feel the bite. It can take a month before you know you are bitten." *D.Mirror, 21 Aug 1992.*

GAS GUZZLERS

Strange tube worms up to six feet long have been discovered off the Spanish coast, dining on the hydrogen sulphide from rotting beans in the hold of a ship that sank 13 years ago. Lacking mouth, gut and anus, they rely on bacteria to process the nutrients in minerals dissolved in sea water. They had been found previously in the Pacific and the Gulf of Mexico. It was thought they liked to live in huge colonies around cracks in the ocean floor where hot, mineral-rich lava pours out and areas where oil and gas leak from the seabed. *D.Telegraph, 22 June 1992.*

BREZHNEV LIVES!

After those tales of how Leonid Brezhnev was actually dead for years before he ceased to rule, it made a change to read in the Estonian paper *Esmaspaev* that there was a rumour going round Estonia that he never died at all. It seems that a body very like the Soviet leader was requisitioned from Morgue 36 in Moscow; B. Alexandrov, senior doctor at the morgue, says he was given no explanation, but was sworn to silence. Watching Brezhnev's funeral on the box later, he was amazed to recognise his former client.

The rumour goes that the old boy (then nearly 76) had fallen in love with an 18-year-old nymphet, but knew the politburo wouldn't let him ditch his wife to remarry. So, with the help of his successor, then KGB chief Yuri Andropov, he staged his own demise, and soon afterwards an elderly cove with large eyebrows, and a beautiful maiden, were sighted taking up residence in a heavily-guarded villa on Samoa. *Soviet Weekly, 15 Aug 1991.*

STRANGE DEATHS

† David Wayne Godin, 22, drowned near Dartmouth, Nova Scotia, last September as he was returning from his bachelor stag party, when his vehicle plunged into a lake. Attached to Godin's leg, courtesy of his friends at the party, was an authentic ball and chain. *Hartford (CT) Advocate, 3 Dec 1992.*

† An elderly woman in Donetsk, Ukraine, probably a vagrant, was blown to pieces near the city's railway station when she pulled the pin out of a hand grenade she had mistaken for a can of beer. Seventeen other people were injured. *Police Review, 16 Oct 1992.*

† Psychiatrist Oscar Dominguez, 45, shot dead a woman patient in his Sao Paulo office as she told him about her sex life. "I couldn't take those nutcases any more", he told a court, where he faced a 25-year sentence. *D.Star, 27 Nov 1992.*

† Hardial Singh, 41, a married hosiery knitter from Leicester, slipped and impaled himself on a broom handle as he rested on it while trying to open a window after taking a bath. The handle perforated his rectal wall, he had a colostomy the next day, but died two weeks later, probably from blood clots in his legs which had entered his lungs. *Leicester Mercury, D. Mirror, Sun, 20 Nov 1992.*

† Shy married couple Sachi and Tomio Hidaka, both 34, waited 14 years to make love – and died of heart attacks the first time they tried it. They had no history of heart trouble, according to their doctor in Chiba, Japan. *D.Mirror, 11 Oct 1992.*

† Mrs Evelyn Houser, 70, driving near Waynesburg, Pennsylvania, struck an embankment and overturned. She escaped unhurt. As she stood near a guard-rail while police investigated, she was fatally injured by a 16-year-old firefighter who lost control of his car on his way to the accident. *Belfast Telegraph, 19 Mar 1992.*

† Charles Millbank, 25, crashed into an electricity pole on the A127 near Brentwood on 22 January and plunged over an embankment. He escaped unhurt, scrambled up the embankment, touched the 11,000 volt cable trailing across the grass and was killed instantly. *Independent, Today, 23 Jan 1993.*

† Born-again Christian Herbert Pickney committed suicide in Charleston Jail, South Carolina, by eating eight bars of soap and five cans of shaving cream. "The Lord told me to do it" he confided to warders. *Weekly News, 25 July 1992.*

CROOKED CROSS

Both these giant swastikas went unnoticed until spotted in 1992 from ærial photographs. ABOVE: a 100 metre-square of larch trees planted by a forest ranger in 1930 near Dedelow in eastern Germany. BELOW: Wesley Place, a housing complex in Decatur, Alabama, comprising 100 apartments for retired church folk. Allegedly, it achieved its final shape by accident, because funds ran out during construction in 1980-81, before the full square was completed. *[Reuters] 3 May; [AP] 22 Sept 1992.*

IS IT A CLOUD?

Mrs Mariah Brown photographed a strange cloud - see photo - over the Cumbrian town of Sedgwick, and sent it to the *Westmorland Gazette* which published it mid-August 1992. Other sightings came forward from all over the Lake District, and the same paper (for 28 August) reconstructs its route from Hincaster to Sedgwick, then to Kendal, Selside, Stavely, Windermere and Kentmere.

It was not, as many claimed and feared, a UFO, but an unusual 'lenticular' cloud, formed by a wave action in different temperature layers of air.

More curious is the mass observation of pictographic clouds over Klang, in the Malaysian state of Selangor, on 26 July 1992. Among 26 distinct images

reported, were the word Allah (in Jawi script), a foetus in a womb, two corpses, and "women with their *aurat* (parts of their body) exposed".

The event was interpreted by devout Muslims as depicting the ascension of the Prophet Muhammad, and it will be studied by the National Islamic Centre, headed by a bigwig from the Islamic Affairs section of the Prime Minister's Department. *Straits Times (date unknown, but late July/early August 1992 likely).*

PHENOMENOMIX – HUNT EMERSON ©93

IN TODAY'S COMPLEX SOCIETY IT BECOMES MORE AND MORE DIFFICULT FOR A VAMPIRE TO FIND A DECENT MEAL...

FORTEAN FANCIES

T-SHIRTS

100% WHITE COTTON T-SHIRTS, ONE SIZE XL.
£7.99 EACH
Charles Fort's portrait and the slogan "One Measures A Circle Beginning Anywhere"

BOOKS

FORTEAN TOMES is a series of facsimile reprints of early issues of The Fortean Times (formerly simply titled The News). Each book covers a wide range of fascinating subjects from feral children to spontaneous human combustion to UFO abduction.

FORTEAN TIMES 1 - 15
Yesterday's News Tomorrow **£19.99**
ISBN: 1 870870 263 400 page paperback, colour cover, illustrated throughout.

FORTEAN TIMES 16-25
Diary of a mad planet **£19.50**
ISBN: 1 870021 258 416 page paperback, colour cover, illustrated throughout.

FORTEAN TIMES 26 - 30
Seeing out the seventies **£14.99**
ISBN: 1 870021 207 320 page paperback, colour cover, illustrated throughout.

FORTEAN TIMES 1993 DIARY

NOW HALF PRICE - ONLY £5.00!!
HURRY WHILE STOCKS LAST!
ISBN: 1 870870 247 128 page hardback (250mm x 156mm)

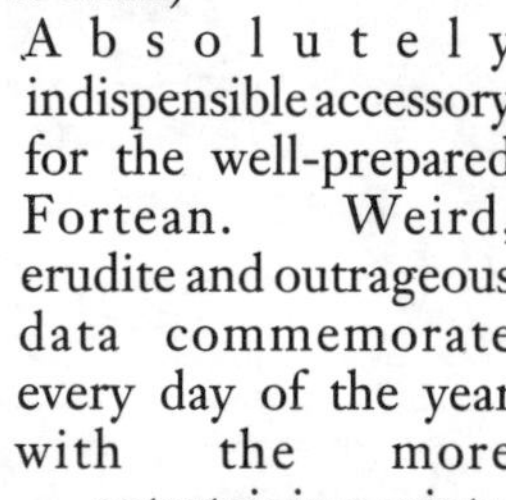

Absolutely indispensible accessory for the well-prepared Fortean. Weird, erudite and outrageous data commemorate every day of the year with the more entertaining saints, religious feasts and over 1,000 birthdays of the famous and the notorious. There is ample space for your own entries.

SUBSCRIPTIONS

If you have enjoyed this issue, why not make sure that you receive a copy on a regular basis? Order a year's supply of Fortean Times for yourself or a friend and get it delivered direct to your doorstep. And that's not all: every new subscriber receives a FREE copy of Doc Shiels' Monstrum book (DIY monster hunting - worth £8.95). Fortean Times back issues also available (see below).

BACK ISSUES

FT51 - South Carolina's Lizard Man, albino frog fall and Yorkshire's water wolf.
FT53 - Crop circles, invasion of the slime creatures and Islamic simulacra.
FT58 - Lesbian vampires, trepanning today and alien abduction.
FT60 - Alpine ice man, Father Christmas as Odin and the Lake Erie monster.
FT61 - Homing treks by cats, everlasting light bulbs and social panics.
FT62 - The Piltdown Hoax, World's Heaviest Man dies and puddle - creating poltergeists.
FT63 - Crop Circle colour pull-out, acid tattoo panic and British alien big cats.
FT64 - Spielberg, Satanic witch hunts and the pregnant male hoax.
FT65 - Colour pull-out on Martian monuments, kidney kidnapping rumours and blood miracles.
FT66 - Florida's penguin panic, bogus social workers and horse-ripping.
FT67 - BBC's Ghostwatch hoax unravelled, 20th Century Dinosaurs and Italian Martians.

Please send me the following items:

Item	UK Price	US Price	Overseas	Qty	Value
Yesterday's News Tomorrow	£19.99	$44.00	£22.00		
Diary of a Mad Planet	£19.50	$44.00	£22.00		
Seeing Out the Seventies	£14.99	$34.00	£17.00		
Fortean Times 1993 Diary	£5.00	$14.00	£7.00		
Charles Fort T-shirt	£7.99	$18.00	£9.50		

Postage and packing free. **Total £** ______

I would like to subscribe to Fortean Times from issue ______
***Please tick for free Monstrum book** ☐

For one year (6 issues) £12 ☐
Overseas inc USA £15 US$30 ☐

For two years (12 issues) £20 ☐
Overseas inc USA £26 US$50 ☐

Back issues £2 each (£2.50 overseas or US$5.00) Please circle your selection:

35	**36**	**37**	**38**	**39**	**42**	**43**	**44**	**46**
50	**51**	**52**	**53**	**54**	**55**	**56**	**57**	**58**
59	**60**	**61**	**62**	**63**	**64**	**65**	**66**	**67**

Name: Mrs/Miss/Ms/Mr ______

Address ______

______

______ Postcode ______

I enclose a total payment of £ ______ made payable to: John Brown Publishing Ltd, or debit the above amount from my Access/Visa/ Mastercard/Eurocard (delete where applicable) account.

Account No ☐☐☐☐

Expiry Date ☐☐

Signature ______

Date ______

Please return this order form to:
Fortean Times, Freepost SW6096, Frome, Somerset BA11 1YA, U.K. or Freephone credit card details on (44) 0800 581409

FT68

POOR COW

Throughout most of the 1970s, large areas of the American Great Plains witnessed thousands of enigmatic cattle deaths which led to much excitement, fear and speculation. Panics over waves of animal deaths date back many centuries. In 16th century France, for instance, unexplained attacks on sheepfolds led to hunts for *loup-garoux* or werewolves. Several accused persons confessed to changing into animal form and, urged on by the devil, mangling as many sheep as possible. Charles Fort chronicled several outbreaks of livestock ripping (mostly sheep) in the 19th and early 20th century, including the horse-ripping outbreak in Wyrley, Staffordshire, in 1903, for which George Edalji was the scapegoat (see Fort's *Books* p878ff & *FT21:8*). Sometimes, 'mystery animals' such as wolves or escaped big cats are blamed. The draining of blood, a distinctive feature of the 'classic mutilations' of the 1970s wave, was prefigured in many of the sheep deaths chronicled by Fort, and in 1966 when an Ohio dairy farmer found a number of her cows "expertly butchered in part and the bodies [..] bloodless". Similar deaths were reported in Pennsylvania. In September 1967, the mutilated body of a three-year-old horse called Snippy was found at Alamosa, Colorado. The brain was missing, the flesh on the head and neck down to the withers was totally gone, and the demarcation between the missing and the remaining flesh was described as surgically precise. The carcass was bloodless.

The mutilated remains of Snippy the horse, 1967.

PART ONE: TALES OF MADNESS AND MUTILATION

Paul Sieveking reviews a puzzling and unsavoury phenomenon that has sparked many bizarre explanations

In the summer of 1973, panic gripped north-central Kansas after a large number of mutilations of cows, most of which had black hides. Sex organs and ears had been removed. In one case, the intestines had been drawn out through a hole in the cow's side and piled neatly by its head (recalling a similar gesture by Jack the Ripper). A lengthy article in the *Kansas City Times* (22 Dec 1973) implied that 'hippies', sex fiends or satanic cults were to blame. The scare spread to Nebraska the following April and was given national prominence by *Newsweek* on 30 September 1974.

At the crest of the wave in 1976, 23 states were affected, and by the end of the decade statewide investigations had been carried out in Iowa, Oklahoma, Texas, Colorado and New Mexico; and in Canada in Alberta and Saskatchewan. In 1980, a major study by former FBI agent Kenneth Rommel concluded that nothing extraordinary was going on beyond mass hysteria. He put the deaths down to natural causes and the mutilation to natural predators. After further sceptical assessments, mass media attention tailed off, although both the mutilations and the discussion among groups of enthusiasts, exchanging photocopied documents, has continued. Most notably, no-one has ever been caught in over 20 years of American cattle ripping.

> "The 'classic' American mutilation includes the removal of sexual organs, one or both eyes or ears, the tongue or flesh of the lower jaw."

The 'classic' American cattle mutilation includes the removal of sexual organs, one or both eyes or ears, the tongue or flesh of the lower jaw. The bodies appeared to have been drained of blood and the incisions described as 'surgically precise'. Some cuts suggested a scalpel while others showed an odd 'pinking shears' effect. Some mutilations appeared to have been made without a knife, either by separating cell from cell or burning the flesh apart with a laser beam. In the more elaborate cases, the head might be stripped of flesh, the anus 'cored out' and organs such as the heart removed. There would be no tracks or footprints visible around the carcases, even on muddy or snow-covered ground, and predators gave them a wide berth. The body parts usually devoured by predators would be left intact.

The final component of the 'classic mutilation' was an associated anomalous activity such as reports of mystery animals, unmarked aircraft or strangers in robes. Chemicals like nicotine sulphate or PCP ('angel dust') were detected in some livestock corpses; in others, puncture marks were found in the jugular vein. There were also unsubstantiated rumours of radiation and burned vegetation at mutilation sites.

The first explanatory framework for the 1970s mutilations was the satanic cult mythology. In 1970, while researching *The Family*, his book on Charles Manson, Ed Sanders had already encountered rumours of Californian occultists who performed blood sacrifices and made 'snuff' movies. The death of a teenager in Vineland, New Jersey, in 1971, allegedly during a ritual, was linked by police to 'sacrificed' animals as part of Satanists' ordinary *modus operandi*. In 1972 the evangelist Morris Cerullo was touring the country in a 'witchmobile' warning against the dangers of Satanism and blood-drinking orgies. Sinister notes were found on some of the dead cattle, such as: "This time it's a cow, next time it will be your daughter" (Minneapolis *Tribune*, 20 April 1975). This is a strange echo of one of the anonymous letters in the 1903 Edalji case: "There will be merry times at Wyrley in November when they start on little girls, for they will do twenty wenches like the horses before next March".

The satanic scenario took its most elaborate form in the 1973 ravings of Kenneth Bankston, an inmate of Leavenworth Federal Penitentiary, accepted at face value by several police forces and even the Federal authorities, who wasted much time and money on investigations. According to Bankston, a group called 'The Occult' patrolled the Great Plains in a fleet of black, unmarked, helicopters. They would land, place large sheets of cardboard to avoid leaving footprints, stun cattle with angel dust, pump their blood out and cut off their sex organs to use in black mass sex orgies.

'The Occult' also featured in Beatrice Sparks's popular novel, *Jay's Journal* (1979), the story of a teenager enticed into New Age meditation by a satanic recruiter. After mutilating cattle and bathing in their drug-laced blood, he is possessed by a demon named Raoul and commits suicide. Details from the plot soon began turning up in stories offered to the police by self-styled 'survivors' of cults.

GOVERNMENT EXPERIMENTS

When the police found no evidence for the satanic cult scenario, investigators such as Ed Sanders and others from the prevalent counter-culture began to suspect the military-industrial complex. It is curious that the main mutilation wave started as the Vietnam war came to an

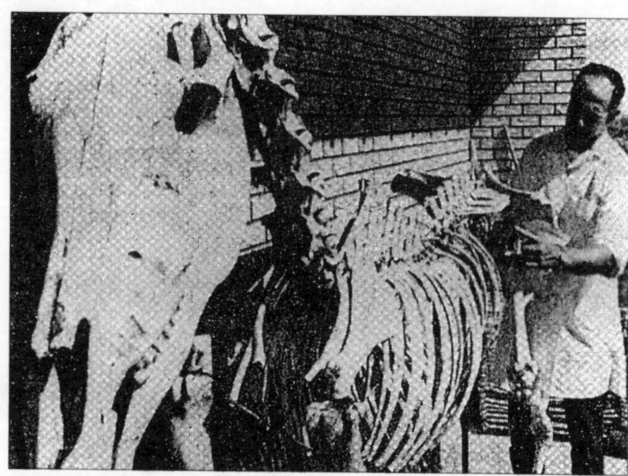

The skeleton of Snippy the horse, killed at Alamosa, Colorado. No explanation was ever found for the bizarre wounds, the missing brain and vital organs, and the skin stripped cleanly from head and neck

end. During that conflict, there were many stories circulating of body parts stripped from dead Vietnamese as grim souvenirs. (Similar rumours circulate during most wars, and surfaced again during the 1991 Gulf War). The clearest military link was the oft-reported unmarked helicopters in the vicinity of mutilations. It was thought that the blood lust of some of the war veterans, deprived of a human target, was redirected towards American cattle. However, Sanders thought the mutilations were too sophisticated to be simply the product of joyriding veterans.

After the extensive use of 'dirty tricks' was exposed in Watergate (1973), it seemed quite feasible that the government was conducting some secret programme while deflecting blame on the satanists. Active military research into poison gas and germ warfare was outlawed in 1970, as was the testing of chemical weapons on most animals in 1974, and investigators inferred that the mutilations were part of a secret government weapons testing programme. This hypothesis died on its feet when no evidence of a cover-up emerged and, in any case, it was nonsensical that the government would attract attention by randomly killing ranchers' cattle when they could have bought animals and experimented on them in secret.

ALIEN RIPPERS

There remained the UFO scenario, one which avoided any awkward lack of terrestrial evidence. The UFO link to mutilated or kidnapped animals can be traced back to the rustlers from the land of Magonia in the clouds alluded to in the ninth century by Archbishop Agobard. The *Miami Herald* of 16 October 1973 reported that police in Dayton, Ohio, had received about 80 reports of flashing UFOs in the area, one of them from a woman who claimed 'hysterically' that a UFO had landed, killing a couple of cows.

By 1974, reports of strange lights and unmarked helicopters had become inextricably tied up with cattle mutilation reports right across the USA. In December of that year, Minnesota investigator Terence Mitchell noted a series of circles in fields near mutilated cattle. Such circles had already been interpreted as 'saucer nests' or UFO landing sites. Mitchell's circles were eventually found to be snow-covered silage, but by then the UFO link was well established in the national consciousness. UFOs could move silently at will and advanced alien laser beams could mutilate with 'surgical precision'; the *why* of mutilation, however, remained unanswered.

A partial resolution emerged after the hypnotic regression of UFO abductees by Leo Sprinkle and others in 1980: aliens were excising body parts from cattle and conducting medical examination of humans as part of some inscrutable biological research. This was the basic thesis of Linda Moulton Howe's award-winning documentary, *A Strange Harvest* (1980). It was assumed that the US Government had covert contact and even agreement with the EBEs (extra-biological entities). The aliens were like the witches of old, who harmed cattle and stole children; the government's collusion with these 'satanic' forces was a kind of Faustian bargain. The 'secret treaty' scenario still inspires many mutilation investigators today.

All the mythologies elaborated to explain the mutilations are part of what Veronique Campion-Vincent has called the 'immemorial fable' of the blood sacrifice: victims (usually young children) are "drained of their blood, symbol and essence of life [and] cannibalised by evil outsiders who need our vital force." Besides the literal castrations, unexplained cattle ripping gives form to inchoate fears of social impotence. Thomas E. Bearden, for instance, sensed the use of Soviet psychotronic weaponry behind the mutilation of cows, "the Western female symbol par excellence", which would culminate, he predicted, in the sexual mutilation of a human female as the prelude to Armageddon (see his 1977 article, *Species Metapsychology, UFOs and Cattle Mutilation*, ***FT26:14-20***.)

Mutilated steer, Caldwell, Kansas, photographed by Chuck Pine on Feb 3 1992.

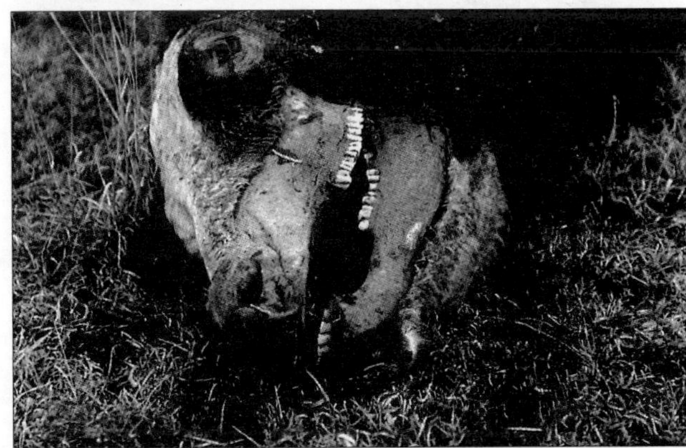

Steer's head showing excision of jaw tissue, bone and teeth.

Oval cut in belly of Brahma steer, genitals removed. Calumet, Oklahoma.

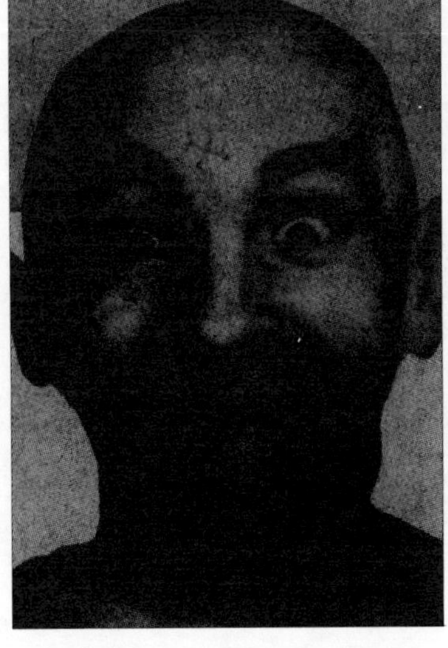

Charles Manson, whose hippy following committed some famous murders, including that of Sharon Tate in 1969 Hollywood. There were unsubstantiated rumours, current at the time, that such 'Satanic' groupings as the Manson 'Family' were performing blood sacrifices of animals and making 'snuff' movies.

RIGHT: Rancher Steve Somsen next to mutilated female cow, July 23 1989.

BELOW: The most popular theory of cattle mutilation involved aliens and flying saucers attacking the animals with bizarre weaponry.

NOTE:
Much of the material for this summary is abstracted from Bill Ellis: "Cattle Mutilation: contemporary legends and contemporary mythologies" in *Contemporary Legend* vol 1 1991, the Journal of the International Society for Contemporary Legend Research, published by Hisarlik Press, 4 Catisfield Rd, Enfield Lock, Middlesex EN3 6BD. This new publication is warmly recommended.

PART TWO: KILLING THE GOLDEN CALF

Dennis Stillings, editor of *Artifex*, offers a mythical analogy

Robert Oppenheimer, chief scientist on the Manhattan Project, which produced the atom bomb in 1945.

Whether or not certain phenomena are considered anomalous or 'paranormal' depends largely on their relationship to an unconscious background matrix of folklore and mythological imagery. Certain putative anomalies, such as mysterious cattle mutilations and phantom helicopters, can be demonstrated to evoke specific images of a highly numinous quality. These collective images then provide the basis for emotional reactions to the supposed anomalies, reactions that are typical, persistent, and widespread. 'Explanations' of the phenomena will also tend to be based on these unconscious collective associations with the object or event.

In the spirit of mythopoeia, or mythmaking, I would like to tell a 'story' to illustrate how cattle mutilations and phantom helicopters have to do with the viscera-suckers of the Philippines, the North American Indian Trickster stories, the development of nuclear weaponry, and Moses and the Golden Calf.

There are few events of significance in history that do not eventually become embedded in a matrix of folkloric and mythological material. It makes little difference whether or not the event 'really' happened. To the extent that the occurrence remains unexplained, a psychological vacuum is created which is readily filled by the mythic imaginings of the human psyche.

WAR IN HEAVEN

This mythogenesis is not confined to such elusive things as Bigfoot or flying saucers; it can just as well accompany completely real and concrete manifestations. The SDI ('Star Wars') scenario, for example, is exactly analogous to the ancient notion of a War in Heaven at the end of time. The development of nuclear weapons, in their overwhelming fearfulness, in their relentless and all-pervasive influence on our economics, politics and religious thinking, can be – and has often been – compared to a return of Jahweh, a god who also appeared as a cloud and a pillar of fire. Scientific theorising is itself not free of mythological projections. Speculations upon the 'ghost planet' Nemesis [1] and 'dark matter' [2] provide some of the best examples of this.

There is a very odd relationship between helicopters and UFOs and connections can be made between helicopter 'folklore' and the Trickster stories of certain North American Indian tribes. There are also some mythic and folkloric linkages between the cattle mutilation phenomenon of the 1970s and the imagery of nuclear power, also between cattle mutilations, UFOs, and phantom helicopters [3].

Mythopoeia or mythopoesis means simply 'mythmaking'. What I am going to discuss here is an instance of my own spontaneous creation of a myth and what that might imply with regard to the nature of reports of anomalies of certain kinds, which are modern pieces of folklore. The stories about anomalous cattle mutilations, which reached a peak during the middle and late 1970s, are one example; however, I believe that the relevance of what I have to say extends to other types of anomalies.

The 'classic' anomalous mutilation usually involves cattle, although there are reports of mutilated horses, pets, and even people. These mutilations involve removal of various body parts, usually the genitals or anus – which is 'cored out'. Ears, eyelids, and other regions of tissue have been removed with what is often reported to be 'surgical precision'. Skin patches may be excised in geometrical shapes. Claims are made that the animals were completely drained of blood; bones and horns have been broken as though the animal had been dropped from a height; 'clamp' marks have been reported from time to time, indicating that the beast was lifted and then dropped.

"Now, if Oppenheimer was Moses on the mountain, the Golden Calf would be in the valley. When Moses came down from the mountain after his momentous visit with Jahweh, he had the Golden Calf torn to pieces."

There have been a number of studies of the phenomenon (which still goes on sporadically), perhaps the most comprehensive and sceptical of which is *Mute Evidence* by Kagan and Summers [4]. There was even a small periodical on the subject called, interestingly enough, *Stigmata*.[5]

A myth can operate in the collective consciousness without any awareness of the dynamic mythological configuration that has taken root. This has been amply demonstrated by depth psychology and other disciplines. Occasionally, one or more people formulate a partial or even complete mythology based on the real or imagined facts surrounding the anomaly. This happened to me in the following way:

For several years I have studied the symbolism behind nuclear weapons and have paid several visits to such places as Three Mile Island, Lawrence-Livermore, and Los Alamos. While driving back to Minneapolis from Santa Fe, I went to Los Alamos to get the flavour of the place. As I arrived, the sun was coming up, giving an orange glow to the high desert mountains. In the draws, the ground fog was still quite heavy. My impression of all this was of a biblical landscape.

OPPENHEIMER AS MOSES

Los Alamos lies high up on a mesa that I am told has a significant religious history among the Indians. My tour of the town was brief. Nothing was open, and I didn't know anyone there. As I left to go back down the mountain, I went around a sweeping curve, giving me a panoramic view of northeastern New Mexico and (at least in my imagination) southeastern Colorado. It struck me that I was looking out at some of the really prime cattle mutilation country.

At that moment, it came to me that I had just left an area high on the mountain where a group of 'high priests' of science, almost all of Jewish extraction (J. Robert Oppenheimer, Leo Szilard, Jeremy Bernstein, Erich von Neumann, and many others), had invoked the presence of Jahweh as the cloud and pillar of fire of the Old Testament. There is a passage in a history of the development of the Manhattan Project where the author says, straight-faced and with no reference to the Old Testament sources: "Army searchlights were laid on to follow by simple triangulation the ball of fire by night and the mushroom cloud by day."[6]

Now, if Oppenheimer was Moses on the mountain, the Golden Calf would be in the valley. When Moses came down from the mountain after his momentous visit with Jahweh, he

had the Golden Calf torn to pieces. Here the cattle mutilations become part of the myth. The focus of cattle mutilations around Los Alamos has been noted by those who study these phenomena. They have also noticed the frequency of mysterious mutilations near nuclear sites in other parts of the country.[7]

It makes no difference to my argument whether these assertions about nuclear installations and the reports of mutilations are true or not in the ordinary sense. What is of interest is the psychic fact that such assertions are made.

Let me emphasise that these Old Testament-based fantasies were not constructions of my conscious mind. They simply came to me, like movies in the mind. I thought it all very funny and decided to write it up as one of the little joking articles I often do for Artifex.[8] But the 'joke' turned somewhat more serious upon my return to Minneapolis.

While browsing through a local bookstore, I came upon an issue of the Jungian journal *Spring* containing an article by the well-known German scholar and theologian Wolfgang Giegerich entitled, 'The Nuclear Bomb and the Fate of God: On the First Nuclear Fission.' [9] The author traces the development of nuclear weaponry and its attendant imagery and symbols from the story of Moses and the Golden Calf. The argument is well documented in the best European scholarly tradition. I was quite shocked to find this, as it echoed my bizarre fantasies.

I remained unsatisfied with the comparison between Moses and the Golden Calf, the development of the bomb and the cattle mutilations, because the Golden Calf had been made out of the jewellry of the Israelites. Where was the 'jewellry' in this parallel? Three days later, I found the answer in the *Wall Street Journal*, which contained a short article about a peculiar individual who made jewellry out of animal parts. [10] I then remembered the simple fact that we often associate jewellry with parts of the body; ruby lips, emerald eyes, the 'family jewels', pearly teeth, skin like alabaster or ivory, shell-like ears, golden hair, etc. I then thought about the mythology of the American West in general, much of which is tied up with Old Testament imagery, especially by way of Mormonism.

That an Old Testament myth might actually be operating behind the scenes to organise and energise the mass hysteria over cattle mutilations began to seem probable, especially since this mythologem had sprung up spontaneously in my own mind and had formed the theme of a scholarly essay by a German theologian. Another theologian, the ex-Jesuit Salvador Freixedo, connects UFOs and the cattle mutilations directly with Jahweh, thereby generating a myth of his own. According to Freixedo, Jahweh, no longer able to make people sacrifice animals to him, appears in the form of UFO manifestations in order to mutilate animals and obtain the blood and entrails for himself. [11]

TRICKSTER-RIPPER

These unconscious factors that organise perceptions around typical themes were termed 'archetypes' by Jung, and his theories about synchronicity are based on the conception of the archetype. According to Jungian thinking, a powerful, emotion-laden myth might be capable of generating paranormal events, such as real psychokinetic cattle mutilations. I just mention this in passing, since I am concerned here with psychodynamic processes associated with reported anomalies – not with whether they are, in fact, paranormal in nature.

I have lately extended my researches into American Indian folklore about the Trickster. Trickster is a formless entity – usually called Coyote, or Raven, or Hare – that plays all sorts of tricks on other animals and human beings. There are hundreds of Indian stories about the adventures and misadventures of Trickster. This figure is also nearly universal. One variety of Trickster is the viscera-sucker of the Philippines. [12] This disgusting creature flies about at night, extracting the organs, body fluids and foetuses of its victims by means of its long, thin, razor-sharp tongue. (Foetus extraction has also been reported in cases of cattle mutilation.)

In the Trickster lore of the North American Indian, Trickster is almost continually involved in animal and human mutilations – decapitating, skinning, and eviscerating his victims. Remarkably enough, Trickster is even described as coring out the anus of animals [13], a staple feature of the reports of cattle mutilations. The Trickster is related by Jung to the unformed, pre-adolescent ego, which occasionally constellates the Trickster archetype to such an extent that poltergeist phenomena occur.[14]

Trickster thus manifests in at least two aspects: first, he appears to be a sort of folk personification of the normal events that might lead to erroneous reports of anomalous animal mutilations. (He is, after all, called Raven and Coyote, the animals that pick at the carcasses of animals that died of natural causes.) Secondly, he is a supernatural, 'formless' entity that personifies certain reported phenomena of psychokinesis. Unfortunately, the cattle mutilation phenomenon – like that of the UFO – has not yet learned how to conform to our particular categories of behaviour.

Whatever the true meaning of the mutilations, it appears to me that certain prevalent notions deriving from both the Judeo-Christian and North American Indian traditions may well be operating on an unconscious level to organise our perceptions and ideas along certain lines consistent with the myth. The energetic quality of the anomaly emerges out of a subterranean interplay of archetypal imagery. This interplay gives rise to a whole fabric of connections with ideas of 'messages from the beyond' [15] and other apparently unrelated phenomena such as UFOs.

It is my feeling that a thorough study of such things as the Bigfoot legends and the 'abductee' cases from the standpoint of myth, folklore and current sociological and religious issues may reveal the underlying structure of these webs of relationships that touch and affect the real living psychology of the times. We may then find it easier to address the question of what sorts of reality we are dealing with and what methods are appropriate for their study.

NOTES

1 – A summary of evidence, theories, and speculations is to be found in David M. Raup, *The Nemesis Affair: A Story of Dinosaurs and the Ways of Science* (New York: W.W. Norton, 1986).

2 – Dennis Stillings: 'Images of High Numinosity in Current Popular Culture,' *Artifex* 6, 2 (April 1987), esp. 'Addendum: The Mythology of Dark Matter.'

3 – Tom Adams: *The Choppers...and the Choppers: Mystery Helicopters and Animal Mutilations*, (Paris, Texas: Project Stigma, 1980).

4 – Daniel Kagan and Ian Summers, *Mute Evidence* (New York: Bantam, 1984), pp.312, 403.

5 – *Stigmata: The Project Stigma Report on the Continuing Investigation into the Occurrence of Animal Mutilations.* Published sporadically between 1978 and 1989. Available from Tom Adams, Ed., Project Stigma, P.O. Box 1094, Paris, TX 75460.

6 – Leona Marshall Libby, *The Uranium People* (New York: Charles Scribner's Sons, 1979), p.220. Compare with Exodus 13:21: "And all the time the Lord went before them, by day a pillar of cloud to guide them on their journey, by night a pillar of fire to give them light, so they could travel night and day."

7 – Dave Perkins, *Altered Steaks: A Colloquium on the Cattle Mutilation Question* (Santa Barbara, Calif.: am here books, 1982), p.17.

8 – *Artifex* is a quarterly publication of Archaeus Project, 2402 University Ave., St.Paul, MN 55114.

9 – *Spring: An Annual of Archetypal Psychology and Jungian Thought* (1985): 1-27.

10 – *Wall Street Journal*, March 29, 1986. 'Give her Roses, but Remember That Only a Fish Head Is Forever.' Jung, in the *Visions Seminars* (Zurich, Spring Publications, 1976), p.87, analyses a dream in which the entrails are torn out of a sheep by Indians. The intestines are then draped around their necks where they change into 'great red jewels.'

11 – For a brief summary of Salvador Freixedo's ideas, see *Crux 1* (Summer 1985). Available from Tom Adams.

12 – Maximo D. Ramos, *Creatures of Philippine Lower Mythology* (Manila: University of the Philippines Press, 1971).

13 – Paul Radin, *The Trickster: A Study in American Indian Mythology* (New York: Bell Publishing Co., 1956), p.36.

14 - Radin, op cit, p. 195.

15 – The 'message' aspect of the cattle mutilation myth is put forward in different forms by Leo Sprinkle and by Thomas E. Bearden. The former sees the mutilations as a coded message from extraterrestrials (Kagan and Summers, *Mute Evidence*, pp.312, 403), while Bearden (in *Excalibur Briefing* [San Francisco: Strawberry Hill Press, 1980], p.97) sees the phenomenon as arising from exteriorised psychokinetic manifestations of the collective unconscious, the symbolism of which, in Bearden's view, refers to the threat of a Russian attack on the heartland of the United States.

AMERICAN ANIMAL MUTILATIONS 1990-1993

ARIZONA

Nov 1990 – June 1991 – eight cattle and one horse mutilated in southeastern Arizona. Udders, genitalia and anuses cut out, blood drained. Local police claimed to have found evidence of satanic cults, such as rock altars and numbered trees (!)

ARKANSAS

20 Aug 1990 – cow found in Griffin Valley with right ear, parts of the udder, anus and genitalia cut off. A lot of blood near the left ear.

2 Feb 1991 – cow found dead on James H. Thorne's farm in Berryville, Carroll County, with eyes, sex organs and tongue removed and blood drained. Ground completely undisturbed 'as if the body had just floated down to it'. Other animals refused to go near the carcass. Thorne had found a dead heifer in the same area on 4 Nov 1990, with one eye and ear missing as well as the sexual organs, anus, tongue and blood. He had lost heifers mutilated in the same way in 1978, 1985 and 1986.

A local vet maintained that the latest death was caused by blackleg, and the organs had been removed by buzzards. However, the tongue was cut off from the back of the mouth and the jaw clenched shut.

19 Oct 1991 – newborn female calf found in Wooster, with tongue, one eye and reproductive organs missing.

MISSISSIPPI

8 April 1990 – 200-pound calf found dead in Lee County, with the cornea of one eyeball and half the tongue cut out. No blood. A heifer was found in July with the left ear and 18 inches of skin from its left rib cage cleanly severed. A hole had been bored through to the heart, which had not been removed.

NORTH CAROLINA

17 Jan 1990 – cow and deer found in Cabarrus County with tongues and left eyes removed. Eight mutilations investigated in the preceding year.

2 Nov 1990 – remains of young Black Angus calf found in Gaston County with two cuts, three inches apart, from the scrotum to the neck; intestines, lungs, heart, legs and hooves removed. The hide strip was left dangling from a branch over the animal's liver and severed head.

OKLAHOMA

Jan 1992 – Kingfisher County, mid-month: three yearling heifers found drained of blood, with eyes, ears, tongues, lips, sexual organs missing. The liver was removed from one animal. Okfuskee County, 25 Jan: cow found with heart and udder removed, bloodlessly. Other mutilations in Blaine, Garfield, Grant and Kingfisher Counties. Sheriff Archie Yearick of Grant County puzzled "because there aren't any tracks around any of these carcasses".

16 June 1992 – cow found in Comanche County, with eyeballs, heart and anus removed. A calf had been pulled from the cow's stomach and cut up.

29 August 1992 – cow found north of Tipton, with heart, tongue and udder removed, apparently with a scalpel.

TEXAS

Sept 1991 – six cats found dissected with a sharp instrument in Plano, in one instance the internal organs removed. In addition, 30-35 cats were reported missing since July.

Nov 1991 – remains of at least 800 animals – mostly young goats and sheep, but including chickens and turkeys – discovered at three sites between Weatherford and Azle, Parker County. A deer was missing heart and sexual organs; its stomach had been removed and "set up on a hill with several deer legs around it". Also found were several beer cans and a paint bucket containing less than a pint of blood. Some carcasses were fresh, others over a year old.

WASHINGTON STATE

26 June 1990 – body of a year-old steer found in Clark County with genitals removed. At least seven cattle mutilations reported in Clark County between May and December 1990. Skin samples were studied by Denver pathologist John Altshauler, who concluded that the skin was cut using high temperatures, suggesting lasers, because of the way the cells were intact.

OTHER STATES

There were also mutilations reported in Idaho (four in Mar-July 1990), Kentucky (unspecified number in April 1991) and Missouri (11 in Spring 1992).

Avoid unwanted and tragic Cattle Mutilations in your family!
WATCH FOR THESE WARNING SIGNS: 1) NO FOOTPRINTS, 2) U.F.O. SIGHTINGS, 3) SURGICAL INCISIONS, 4) NO BLOOD, 5) MISSING ORGANS, 6) RADIATION...
BEWARE! THIS MYSTERIOUS MENACE CAN STRIKE AT ANY TIME!

Illustration: Jay Kinney

CANADA

Feb 1991 – six-year-old pregnant cow found north-east of Edmonton, with tongue and foetus cut out, one eye pulled from socket and cheek peeled back.

1 July 1991 – Charolais-cross cow found in a pasture south of Saskatoon, with udder and anus removed. A patch of worn-down grass suggested that the animal had lived for some time after the mutilation. A vet suggested the animal had died of a metabolic condition called hypomagnisemia brought on by the wet weather, and the organ theft performed by magpies and crows.

July 1992 – seven heifers killed south of Edmonton since the previous September, six had sexual organs removed, and 'often' their blood had been drained. Frightened beef farmer Doris Verchomin blamed 'dumb Druids'.

MEXICO

May – August 1990 – 50 to 100 horses found hanging from trees around San Luis San Pedro, north of Acapulco. Many showed signs of ritualist mutilation, with puncture marks and deep incisions along the throat through which the animals' blood was drained. Town commissioner Gaston Estrada said that a note had been found at one mutilation site, signed by the 'Green Scorpions', proclaiming a pact with the devil to kill 150 horses.

Others suspected 'drug addicts from the mountains'. The town lies in the shadow of the Sierra Madre de Guerrero, for 20 years Mexico's most fertile marijuana-growing region. When the army and federal police arrived in July to curb the drug harvest, the horse killings declined, but kidnappings started.

HEAD TO HEAD

THEM & US

"I may be paranoid, but am I paranoid enough?"

SIMON WHITTAKER talks to MARY SEAL, conspiracy researcher

Mary Seal, a former public relations officer aged 48, shot to media prominence by organising the First International Conference That Exposes A Global Deception, held at Wembley over the weekend of 9-10 January. The hall was paid for by Mary and her partner Keith Mears and guest speakers were flown in from America and Europe.

Although there are many researchers delving into the mad, the bad and the dangerous to know, Mary Seal is a rarity in attempting to weave the many different strands together into a consistent and apocalyptic worldview, one too rich for English publishers to stomach, judging by the reception of the manuscript outlining her theories. FT spoke to Mary in her suburban home on the outskirts of Birmingham.

FT Who are you and where are you from?
MS: I'm just a normal person who started researching a long time ago. What set me off was a UFO sighting when I was about 18 or 19. It was so clear during daytime and there was no doubt that it was a physical object – nothing hazy or paranormal about it.

FT: Was it in this country?
MS: Yes, in Aldridge, near Walsall. I was sitting in a car, not thinking about anything and I looked up to see this huge Mothership type affair; and I thought: "My God, I'm going to get someone else to look at this with me." I was about to get out of the car and I realised I'd been *made* to look up. Out of it came three discs, much darker than the coppery-coloured Mothership. They got up to a certain height then shot off. I'd never considered UFOs before, but after that I started thinking things weren't as they appeared and began reading into a variety of fields.

FT: Just to get a grasp on your worldview, what do you think UFOs are?
MS: Well, they're man-made machines, undoubtedly. Advanced technology kept secret by Government. They pretend free energy is a Utopian dream because it wouldn't do for people to stop using petrol. I would have thought that was obvious to anyone. Go to America and talk to top scientists and they'll tell you quite openly what can be done. Getting them to come over and say it on a stage is a different matter. It can be proved the Nazis had this technology. In the Public Records Office there's quite a few documents that have been sealed for years, newspaper clippings and scientific reports. Nazi anti-gravity is one of the best-kept secrets of the last war.

FT: How did this lead to your conference?
MS: I had so much information and stuff on UFOs, but most of it came

from America. I put a book together, but couldn't get it published. Finally I thought the only way to get this information out – and I had to do it – was to put on this conference in London. The public must be able to hear this information.

FT: Were your speakers chosen to fit in with your world view?
MS: I was trying to get a global picture – there are people who know the political conspiracies, they know officially-sanctioned drug trafficking goes on – they may not understand why. They know the United Nations is moving in a particular manner – they think they're separate issues. People in this country haven't got a clue, but in America there *is* discussion. Here, people think of UFOs as little lights in the sky. They're not aware of the technology certain governments have got. They're not aware of what is going on, it's quite incredible. Of course, trying to get my speakers to present the whole picture was difficult... each one goes off at pet tangents and we did have some problems.

FT: Did you have personality clashes?
MS: No, but two failed to turn up – they'd been threatened and one had 'personal problems'. Another speaker, Vladimir Terziski, I'd engaged purely as a physicist to explain anti-gravity; instead of which he started talking of different races. He ruined it for me. I personally don't subscribe to that stuff. I'm sure there's no ET element doing all the cattle mutilations and abduction. Neither do I think there are grey beings from out of this world. I think they're clones. One of the things that Terziski said was that Nazi UFOs were at the South Pole. I'm sure that's disinformation. I think the Allies came across all this incredible technology and promptly absorbed it. I'm sure the Vatican, who were very much 'in' with the Nazis, were involved in the scientific work. But I think *now* there is something going on at the South Pole – a study to train people to work in extreme conditions, but no legacy of the Nazis.

FT:You said two of your would-be speakers were threatened?
MS: Yeah, one of them [Norio Hayakawa] working for Nippon TV at the Nevada desert test site had hours and hours of footage clearly showing anti-gravity 'UFO' manoeuvres – there's no doubt what they are. I've seen them. A week before the conference, we had a fax from him saying he'd been advised by some of the intelligence community he'd been in touch with, that the Ministry of Defence had sent a notice over saying he'd be arrested for espionage if he entered this country with this information and it'd be sequestered. I asked the MOD to see this official document and they said we couldn't until two months after the conference. The other speaker [Jordan Maxwell] had some mysterious men in a BMW draw up and they threatened him...

FT: Not 'Men In Black'?
MS: [laughs] No, I don't think so – these were real ones... and that was that.

FT: Who were the speakers you did get?
MS: Well, the first was Dr Robert Strecker – a Los Angeles doctor who's been looking into the AIDS question for years and has arrived at the theory that it's a genetically-engineered disease straight out of Fort Detrick and deliberately introduced into the African countries through the smallpox vaccinations. Eustace Mullins – he's written about 35 books on the Federal Reserve systems, the banking cover-up, the legal cover-up. He's been branded anti-semitic, but he's not. People haven't understood what he's been talking about – it's true that he's affiliated to some extreme right-wing Christian groups, but he himself remains objective.

Then there was Vladimir Terziski. There was an Australian journalist, David Summers, who's written a lot about the Trilateral Commission, the Bilderburgs [two of the supposed one-world-government think-tank groups touting hidden agendas] and, of course, William Cooper [a former US Naval Intelligence operative and UFO investigator].

FT: There's said to be a lot of intelligence disinformation passed out through UFO groups and indeed Bill Cooper has owned up to that. Aren't you afraid your conference could be a mouthpiece for this?
Ms: Oh, I'm well aware of this. What I

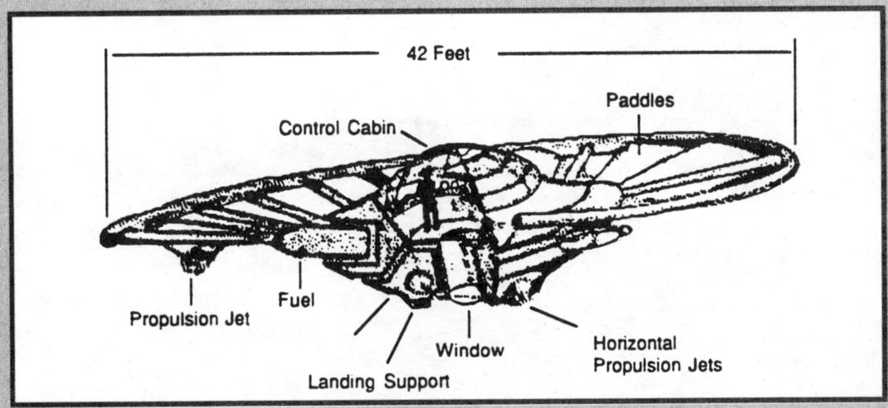

ABOVE: Many hollow-earth believers have long suspected that after World War II the Nazis withdrew to underground bases in Antarctica where they started a flying saucer assembley line. This advertisement is by Christof Friedrich (pseudonym of Ernst Zündel), author of *UFOs: Nazi Secret Weapon?*

LEFT: One of the German flying saucer designs published in the English language version of *Der Spiegel* in 1950.

admire about Bill Cooper is that where he's been fed disinformation he's owned up to it while a lot of UFO groups carry on spouting the same things they said in 1989 and it's all coming out of the government. People suspect us of being agents of the government or Nazis. They couldn't see why we did this conference. When we went to the States to vet people for the conference we met an awful lot of them who said things they weren't prepared to repeat on stage so there's no doubt in my mind of the genuine information – you can sift it out if you're careful. I had to pursue Cooper very hard to make him come to Britain, but that just makes me think he's not got anything to sell. The amount of disinformation They're putting on him is incredible. I think he must be one of the most targeted individuals in the world.

Financially, the conference was a disaster, but in terms of awareness it's gone all over the world. We'd like to do another, but we'd need funding. It's something we're actively pursuing. We've had offers, but as soon as you accept someone's financial offer you have to do their bidding. It's obvious to me who *They* are and what *They* want. Certain groups that say they're working for the betterment of mankind or on certain questions, you later find are being manipulated by those running the show...

FT: It's said that if you sign a petition in this country against the government, someone in intelligence will enter your name in their records. Do you worry you're targeted?

MS: I already am. I'm absolutely sure of it. I've been told I am by more than one party – but if you get out in the open, *They're* hardly likely to do anything to you. I don't know why people get so worried. The more exposed you are, the safer you are. I know my phone's tapped because I've had certain conversations repeated by a third party. He's working for certain people in UK intelligence who're not *for* what's gone down. He didn't approach me – in fact I'm very sceptical of people who come looking for me. There are also certain UK politicians who're very worried and would like to put a stop to it.

FT: Who is this *Them*, the Secret Government?

MS: It's just made up of people who've been machinating

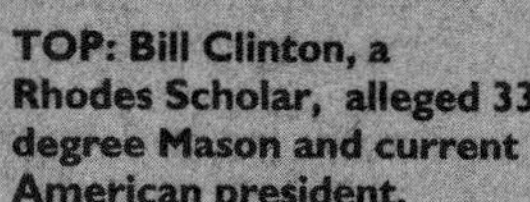

TOP: Bill Clinton, a Rhodes Scholar, alleged 33 degree Mason and current American president.

ABOVE: Bobby Fischer, the paranoid chess Grand Master, who had all his dental fillings removed to stop Russian radio transmissions into his head.

RIGHT: Conference organiser Mary Seal receiving a proof of her Wembley brochure.

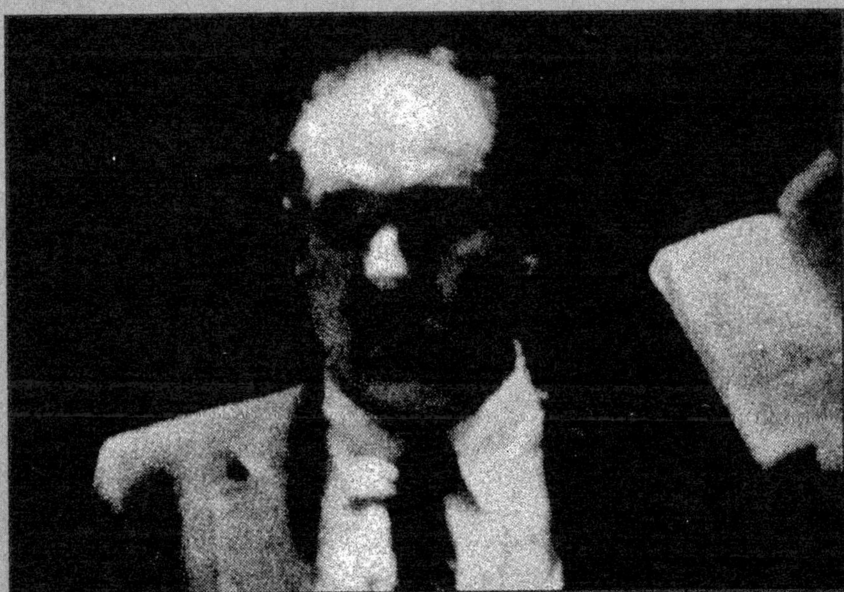

A rare photograph of William Cooper, a UFO buff formerly with US Naval Intelligence, who spoke at the Wembley conference.

for years to control the world through resources and manpower and of course they have infiltrated key positions – government, media, intelligence communities – and are pulling the strings. I don't think governments themselves are guilty. *They're* being manipulated through aid money – it's the only way to manipulate governments. They have to go to war, are lent money and then told what to do.

FT: To conspiracy theorists there's always a *They*. You've said 'How'. But who is it – the Trilateral Commission? The CFR? The Illuminati? Who's at the top of the pyramid?

MS: The Illuminati, definitely. I think this is a plot going back thousands of years. I believe they've known about free energy for ever, but only now can they put it into place – since the development of quantum physics this century. I believe there's much more to Tesla's inventions than *They* say and maybe he was actually working for *Them*. I think Einstein was a stooge. Of course, we're all made to think it's ridiculous. I think *They*'re aware the Earth has an energy grid system, antigravity. The same people who control the oil companies are behind government, behind what's taking place. *They*'re all in key positions now. Clinton was a 33 degree Mason, a Cecil Rhodes scholar linked to Carol Quigley, a Trilateral Commissioner. People say there's no proof, but it's easy to follow the trail – it's provable. Ultimately what you're talking about through the Masons, the Illuminati, is the continuation of the Holy Roman Empire against someone else with a power struggle going on at the very top. Who knows?

FT: So what of Bush's New World Order, the invasions of Somalia, Bosnia, etc?

MS: The world's being policed by the UN. I think it may have started as well-intentioned, but look at the League of Nations and who was behind that... Civil aviation pilots say UN tanks are all over America, positioned, thousands and thousands in desert places. I think the LA riots were an experiment. I think that's how *They*'ll create a state of emergency with a long-range goal of taking over the world. But, and this is just personal speculation, I think *They* know *something's* going to take place – geological or whatever. From the information I've been able to gather, I think we're coming to another Ice Age. *They* know and are making plans for evacuation off this planet. *They've* colonised the moon, *They* have bases up there and on Mars. NASA has a secret space programme...

FT: Since you're reaching a *Fortean Times* audience who may be more aware of the issues you're talking of, what other areas of concern have you?

MS: I think we should be aware of the incredible mind-control and brainwashing the security agencies have been developing. Everyone thinks of MKULTRA as being the last major exercise – it's not.

FT: Yeah, even the paranoid chess-player Bobby Fischer had all his fillings removed for his comeback to stop Russian radio transmissions into his head.

MS: He's not so paranoid because all the work that's gone into microwave technology, ELF technology, is provable. It's proven that certain low-frequency waves can affect your immune system. I don't think AIDS is just a virus. I think certain areas of the world are being 'zapped'. *They've* got hold of all the mineral resources through debt payments and don't want a 'useless population' – *Their* words.

Brain implants are provable – doctors in Sweden have proved it. *They* can completely manipulate the human mind now – implant pictures, cause behaviour. That's the most atrocious thing – that, and the cloning.

FT: What have you unearthed about cloning?

MS: Rumours about ET labs under the desert in Dulce, New Mexico, are disinformation. Those labs are certainly for genetic engineering carried on from the Nazi period. *They* can, without a shadow of a doubt, make a being. *They've* made about 40,000 and utilised these abduction scenarios. I believe they're used for two purposes: one, to plant the idea of extraterrestrials and two, as a future labour force to work under extreme conditions. This is one thing I am going to pursue until I can get some proof. The Nazi experiments have been taken onto the Illuminati agenda. It's like playing God, isn't it? Trying to create a super-race – the Nazi dream.

FT: So does this scenario explain Men In Black reports?

MS: Well, I think... actually, I don't think, I've been told that the whole of the contactee scenario is mind-control. The subjects are genuine. The abductions, some may be hallucinations, some physical events with a genetic angle and some may be just hoaxes to reinforce the ET belief. But you try and tell a contactee it's a hoax...

They obviously have an extremely urgent need for the creation of a New World Order. *They* can't just put it into place. One means could be a declared threat from outer space – you know, "We must unite". I think the SETI programme [Search for Extra Terrestrial Intelligence, using radio telescopes] will be manipulated to come up with threatening signals. Another could be an environmental threat – the ozone layer hole is a complete hoax... **FT**

The interviewer, Simon Whittaker, is writing a book on Conspiracy Theory, historic and current, and welcomes any comments, clippings or source material on the subject. He can be contacted c/o 2 Hillside, Station Road, Purton, Swindon, SN5 9AL A 2-video set of selected conference highlights plus other information is available from 60 Fallowfield, Orchard Hills, Walsall, W Midlands, WS5 3DH for £25 (incl p&p). Cheques payable to Nightlink Communications.

At the outset of World War One, the British Expeditionary Force was pinned down near the French/Belgian border town of Mons, whereupon something quite inexplicable is reported to have taken place. Kevin McClure re-investigates contradictory rumours of divine intervention...

ANGELS TO THE RESCUE

Debunking is a pretty merciless process. It is seldom that, once debunked, an account of a supposedly paranormal event will ever again achieve credibility.

In the vast majority of cases, this is no loss. I have helped dispatch a number of claims of the extraordinary, and I'm happy to have done so. Much of what is claimed and reported has no substance at all, and we can well do without it.

Occasionally though, something of value and significance risks being trampled in the rush to purge what seems unacceptable. This can occur where a rational explanation easily deals with a number of the elements of a complex investigation, but not necessarily with *all* the elements. The reports arising from alleged events during the retreat of the British Expeditionary Force from Mons in 1914 constitute just such a complex and confusing case. Resoundingly debunked since the summer of 1915 onwards, it is time to reconsider these reports. I think that an injustice has been done, though the details of that injustice remain difficult to define.

The Mons legends have always fascinated me. They bring together several of my own areas of interest: the Great War, religious visions, divine intervention, folklore, the writer Arthur Machen and the role the paranormal plays in the lives of people – and nations – under great stress. I've been gathering material on the subject for more than 10 years, but have only recently had the opportunity to bring it all together.

Many will be aware of reports that Saint George and the Agincourt bowmen – or maybe some angels, or possibly both – came between the British and German forces, halting the German advance long enough for an organised withdrawal and regrouping to take place. Many, too, will have read that the reports were all a myth, arising entirely from the retelling – Chinese Whispers style – of a short story by Arthur Machen entitled 'The Bowmen', first published in the *London Evening Standard* on 29 September 1914. It's an explanation Machen himself originated in the summer of 1915. It was probably misleading then, and has been ever since.

If anything wonderful happened, then it happened in the last days of August 1914, as superior German forces pushed a tired, but heroic, BEF back through France from the Belgian border. I must stress that no contemporary history of the war mentions any visionary event of any kind, the earliest account from a *named* military source being published in 1931, though apparently taken from letters written at the time. Certainly, when Machen's exquisite little story of a beleaguered British soldier invoking Saint George, and the saint arriving with a host of bowmen to drive back the Germans, first appeared in print, the public had read nothing of any claim of divine intervention. Few, though, doubted that we had 'God on our Side'.

When 'The Bowmen' was first published, the two leading paranormal journals of the time, *Light* and *The Occult Review*, both reported on its content and both enquired of Machen whether there was any truth in the tale. He replied that there was not, and both reported back to their readership accordingly. By the end of October 1914, it seemed that the matter had been forgotten.

One of the intriguing mysteries of the Mons legends is what happened next. After a full six months without tales of bowmen, or anything else, an account appeared in *Light* for 24 April 1915 under the title 'The Invisible Allies: Strange Story from the Front'. This refers back to Machen's story and continues in part:

"A few days ago, we received a visit from a military officer, who asked to see the issue of *Light* containing the article in question. He explained that, whether Mr Machen's story was pure invention or not, it was certainly stated in some quarters that a curious phenomenon had been witnessed by several officers and men in connection with the retreat from Mons. It took the form of a strange cloud interposed between the Germans and the British. Other wonders were heard or seen in connection with this cloud which, it seems, had the effect of protecting the British against the overwhelming hordes of the enemy."

Early in May, a fuller version of a similar account turned up in the All Saints, Clifton, *Parish Magazine*. This was quoted in papers and magazines all over the country,

LEFT: St George and the spectral bowmen defending WW1 British soldiers as depicted by Alfred Pearse. The belief in apparitions of celestial armies is ancient and widespread. Sometimes they are echoes of past battles, but during a war, they are taken as a sign of divine protection, as in Edouard Detaille's painting, ABOVE, of troops sleeping safely at the Front.

"They therefore turned round and faced the enemy, expecting nothing but instant death, when to their wonder they saw, between them and the enemy a whole troop of angels."

attracting attention from the national press and also from senior churchmen wanting to present patriotic material in their sermons. It seems that the editor of the *Parish Magazine* had met the daughter of one Canon Marrable, who relayed to him what she had been told by "...two officers, both of whom had themselves seen the angels who saved our left wing from the Germans when they came right upon them during the retreat from Mons.

They expected annihilation, as they were almost helpless, when to their amazement they stood like dazed men, never so much as touched their guns: nor stirred till we had turned round and escaped by some crossroads. One of Miss Marrable's friends, who was not a religious man, told her that he saw a troop of angels between us and the enemy. He has been a changed man ever since. The other man she met in London. She asked him if he had heard the wonderful stories of angels. He said he had seen them himself, and under the following circumstances:-

"While he and his company were retreating, they heard the German cavalry tearing after them. They saw a place where they thought a stand might be made, with sure hope of safety; but before they could reach it, the German cavalry were upon them. They therefore turned round and faced the enemy, expecting nothing but instant death, when to their wonder they saw, between them and the enemy, a whole troop of angels. The German horses turned round terrified and regularly stampeded. The men tugged at their bridles, while the poor beasts tore away in every direction from our men."

In the meantime, stories featuring bowmen were also appearing, the first in, of all places, the Roman Catholic paper *The Universe* for 30 April 1915:

"The story is told by a Catholic officer in a letter from the front, and is told with a simplicity which shows the narrator's own conviction of its genuineness . . .

"A party of about thirty men was cut off in a trench, when the officer said to his men, 'Look here, we must either stay here and be caught like rats in a trap, or make a sortie against the enemy. We haven't much of a chance, but personally I don't want to be caught here.' The men all agreed with him, and with a yell of 'St George for England!' they dashed out into the open. The officer tells how, as they ran on, he became aware of a large company of men with bows and arrows going along with them, and even leading them on against the enemy's trenches, and afterwards when he was talking to a German prisoner, the man asked him who was the officer on a great white horse who led them, for although he was such a conspicuous figure, they had none of them been able to hit him. I must also add that the German dead appeared to have no wounds on them. The officer who told the story (adds the writer of the letter) was a friend of ours. He did not see St George on the white horse, but he saw the archers with his own eyes."

"It was stated in some quarters that a curious phenomenon had been witnessed by several officers and men in connection with the retreat from Mons. It took the form of a strange cloud interposed between the Germans and the British."

And so it went on through the summer and autumn on 1915. Many accounts were published, though some were deliberately fraudulent, and at no time was an account by any named individual proved true. Arthur Machen wrote some more delightful stories along the lines of 'The Bowmen', with a long introduction explaining that all the accounts derived from his own story, and the resulting book sold remarkable well. Other writers backed the reali-

After the famous 'Mons' incident passed into legend, similar experiences were openly reported. This painting by A.C. Michael, c.1916, illustrates the white crucifix seen by British troops around midnight, described by a sergeant in a letter home.

The legend quickly passed into popular belief. ABOVE: The cover of Arthur Machen's collection of short stories in which the 'The Bowmen' first appeared c.1915. BELOW: A music sheet cover c.1915

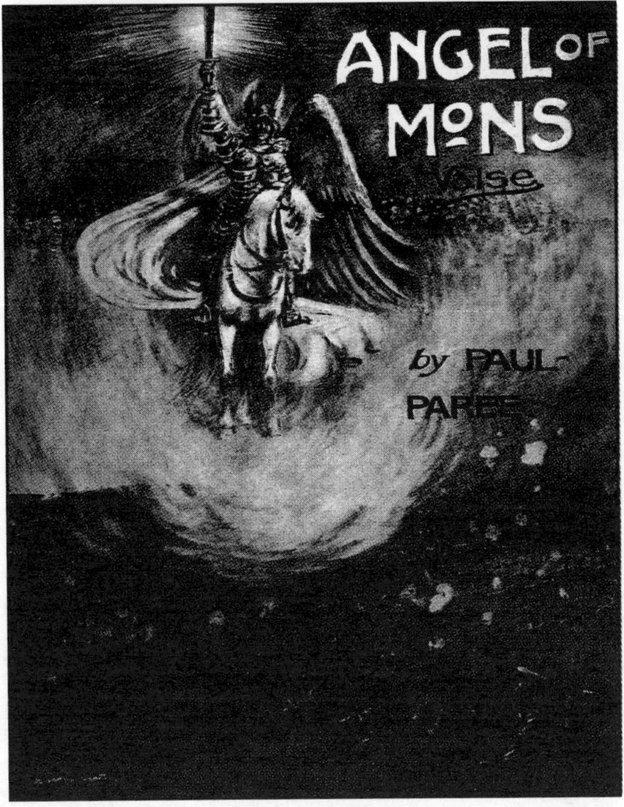

ty of some or all of the legends and one, 'The Showmen', even parodies the whole affair. Phyllis Campbell, apparently a front-line nurse, mixed some of the legends in with the 'atrocity mythos' that prevailed at the time, recounting the acts of the ghastly Hun in gut-wrenching detail, but providing no evidence for either the paranormal or the psychopathic. The Mons Legends achieved wide publicity and great popularity.

It has not been easy to unravel the huge amount of material published on this subject. There are all sorts of additions and variations in the accounts from 1915, and some intriguing detail in those reported years later. Many sensible comments were made at the time about the effects of extreme fatigue on perception, and the Inquiry conducted by the Society for Psychical Research – a model of its kind – found great difficulty in locating alleged witnesses and in verifying what they were reported to have said. Yet in spite of all these problems, I have come to one firm conclusion, one put tentatively at the time by both the SPR and by the editor of the All Saint's, Clifton, *Parish Magazine*, who received a great many letters giving various versions of the legends.

There were two *separate* stories of divine intervention during the retreat from Mons, one of which – the 'angels' vision – I think probably originated before the publication of 'The Bowmen', and almost certainly within the BEF itself. Such evidence as there is suggests that it was current during, or days after, the retreat.

One certainly derives from 'The Bowmen', with archers and St George featuring consistently. In the 'bowmen' version, the soldiers, under extreme pressure, decide to 'take a chance'. There is someone present who remembers a form of invocation (in the original story, the words 'Adsit Anglis Sanctus Georgius' had been printed on the plates in a vegetarian restaurant). The invocation works, the warriors and their leader appear, a battle cry is heard and the German troops are actually killed, albeit in some mysterious way.

The 'angels' version is substantially different, and I think it significant that the earliest published account – and some later – speak of a 'strange cloud' rather than of defined figures. Though the British soldiers are in a similarly difficult situation, the 'angels' come unbidden, without invocation, and they interpose themselves between the British and German forces. They have no leader and no weapons. There is no battle cry. If the Germans are harmed, it is incidentally, not directly – by their horses bolting or their haste to retreat. The 'angels' kill no one: their role is entirely passive. Neither the events nor their effects bear any resemblance to Machen's work of fiction.

In my booklet *Visions of Bowmen and Angels*, I have gathered together further key contemporary sources for both the Mons Legends and for other reports of extraordinary events during the war; particularly of the remarkable healing figure, the 'Comrade in White'. I hope that I will receive further reports and accounts of which I am unaware, and I will compile a revised version in due course if sufficient new material emerges. For now, I am happy to have rescued a genuine mystery from a premature burial. It makes a refreshing change from debunking! FT

ADVERTISEMENT

Hoax!

The Vampire of Croglin Grange

C M DRAPKIN SINKS HIS TEETH INTO A FAMOUS CASE OF BLOOD-SUCKING IN CUMBRIA THAT PRE-DATES DRACULA BY MORE THAN 20 YEARS

'How graves give up their dead, And how the night air hideous grows with shrieks!' Illustration for chapter I of Varney the Vampire, the forgotten vampire story that pre-dates Dracula, showing the protagonist assaulting an innocent maiden.

We all know that vampires do not exist. They are just an old folk-myth, exploited by Bram Stoker and others for the future benefit of film-stars, producers and special-effects men. Or are they? The Vampire Research Center (VRC) of New York does not think so. It claims to have documentary evidence of 810 vampires around the world. Their most favoured area is not Transylvania, but California. In Britain, they say, there are between 20 and 30.

There is no suggestion, either by the VRC or by *Fortean Times*, which has featured a number of contemporary reports of vampirism worldwide, that these cases are in any way supernatural. Dr Stephen Kaplan, director of VRC and "the world's leading authority on vampires", says they are "mainly nice people" who drink only a few ounces of blood at a time, presumably not directly from source, avoid strong sunlight, and occasionally sleep in coffins. [1] There's no accounting for taste.

"But do Dracula-types exist, with insatiable blood-lust, propagating by turning the corpses of their victims into vampires, immortal unless killed by one of the prescribed methods?"

But, do Dracula-types exist, with insatiable blood-lust, propagating by turning the corpses of their victims into vampires, immortal unless killed by one of the prescribed methods? Captain Edward Rowe Fisher of Thorncombe, near Guildford, evidently thought so. A retired army officer, active throughout the Crimean War as a cornet, later a lieutenant, in the 4th Dragoons, he sounds like an impeccable witness. [2] One of those to whom he told his story was Augustus Hare, in June 1874, 23 years before Stoker's *Dracula* was published. Hare recorded it in his diary and later published it in his autobiography. [3]

Thomas Fisher – Edward's father – migrated from Cumberland in about the middle of the last century. Their home – Croglin Grange – was some centuries old. By a curious tradition it had never been more than one storey high. The village of Croglin still exists; you can find it on the B6413, about 20 miles southeast of Carlisle. The Grange was let to a family of two brothers and a sister, who settled down happily in their new home.

One night, after they had all retired to bed, the sister lay, enjoying, through her window, the view of the moonlit countryside and the little church nearby. Presently, she noticed

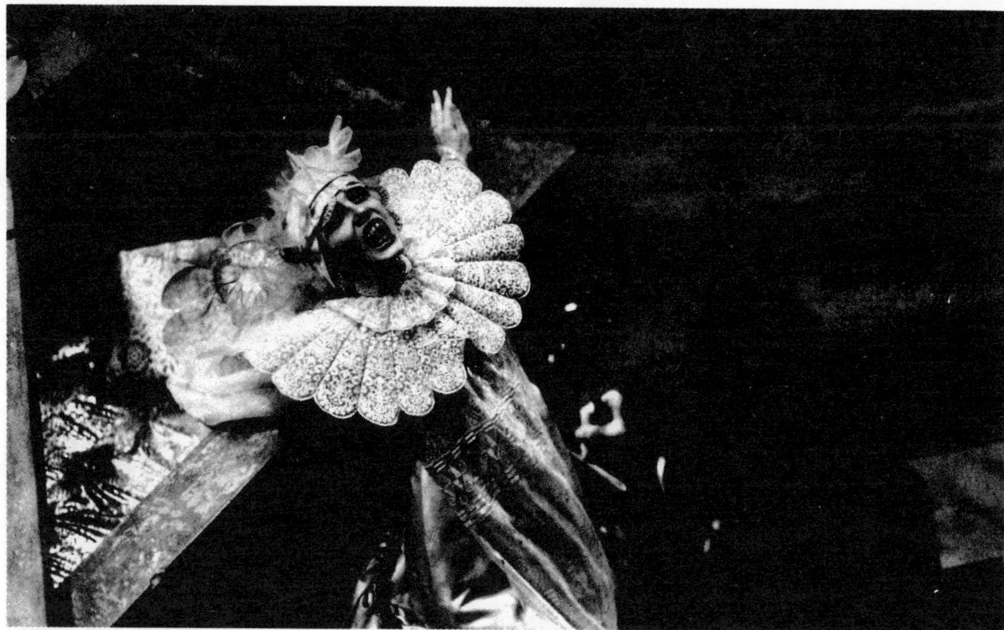

A scene from the new cinematic celebration of the mythology of the undead, *Dracula* (Columbia TriStar, 1993) by Francis Ford Coppola. Below: Augustus J C Hare (1834-1903). Gullible enough to fall for Fisher's tall story?

two lights flickering in the trees between the house and the churchyard. To her horror, she realised that they were the eyes of a monstrous figure, gliding inexorably closer, stopping outside her window.

Her bedroom door was next to the window; to escape she would have to go towards *the thing*. She cowered in her bed, too terrified even to scream, as the red eyes glared from a brown, withered face. The creature scratched on the glass, and she heard a pecking noise as it picked at the lead holding a diamond-shaped pane of glass. As the section fell out, a bony hand reached in and turned the catch; it entered the room, seized her by the hair and bit her throat. Finally finding her voice, she screamed. Her brothers rushed in to find her bleeding and unconscious. The intruder fled from the room, climbed over the garden wall and disappeared into the churchyard.

"To her horror, she realised that they were the eyes of a monstrous figure, gliding inexorably closer, stopping outside her window."

The young lady evidently did not have a morbid imagination; when she recovered, she suggested that her attacker was probably an escaped lunatic rather than a supernatural creature. However, her doctor insisted that her brothers take her abroad to get over the shock.

The following year, they returned to the Grange. This time, the brothers slept in the room next to hers, with loaded pistols by their beds. One night in March, she was awakened by the familiar scratching at her window, to see the same wizened face peering in at her. At her scream, the brothers rushed out into the garden to confront the creature. One fired his pistol and hit *the thing* in the leg. It limped away, scrambled over the wall and slipped into the vault of a long-extinct family.

The next morning, the brothers, with their servants and neighbours, broke open the vault. Inside, they found the coffins burst open, their contents hideously mangled and strewn over the floor. Only one remained intact. When they opened it, inside lay the brown, shrivelled creature that had twice attacked their sister, with a fresh bullet-wound in its leg. They burned the body, and nothing more was ever heard of the ghoulish assailant of Croglin Grange.

This story has fascinated students of the occult. Anthony Masters simply repeats Fisher's account, as set down by Hare, without comment. [4] Peter Haining credits the story on the grounds that it was told some time before the publication of *Dracula*. [5]

The principal champion of the Croglin Grange vampire was the learned occultist Montague Summers [6], who overcame several important objections to the story. There is no record of a Croglin Grange in the vicinity of Croglin, so Summers suggested that a house, known as Croglin Low Hall, sufficiently answered the description. It is possible that Hare might have recorded the name wrongly. Furthermore, the local churchyard does not contain a family vault, nor is there a record of one. No doubt, Summers argues, the local people destroyed it along with the vampire, having no wish to publicise the story.

So, what are we to make of this rather ineffective vampire? Not a lot. The identification of Croglin Grange with Croglin Low Hall is a triumph of faith over reason. The Grange was evidently a gentleman's residence, located near the church. Croglin Low Hall was a farmhouse, situated a mile from the churchyard. A sketch of it by Charles G. Harper clearly shows it as being two storeys high. Harper himself discounted the vampire story. [7]

The Fisher family did indeed come from Cumberland. The first mention of them is of a "Joseph Fisher of Scarrowhill, parish of Cumwhitton, later of Ruckcroft, parish of Ainstable". [8] Both places are within a few miles of Croglin. (Captain Fisher never actually said that Croglin

Grange was in Croglin, but it is a reasonable assumption to make.) Early directories of Cumberland mention Fishers at Coathill and Moorthwaite, Cumwhitton and at Dale, Ainstable. None are mentioned at Croglin, whose name is perfect for anyone inventing a creepy story; it means 'rock (by the) water'.

But why should a manifestly honest man like Fisher invent such a story? Presumably, the answer lies in the character of Augustus Hare. This distinguished writer was also a rather comic figure, a humourless snob with an insatiable appetite for scandal and tall stories. (I am bound to say that he sounds rather likeable, nevertheless.) He tells of several supernatural events, including the famous story of Lord Dufferin's escape from a fatal lift-accident thanks to a premonitory dream, which has since been discredited.

Another of his tales is about a supernatural visitation before the death of "Mr (or Colonel) McPherson of Glen Truim". Colonel Lachlan McPherson, who was the first member of the McPherson family to live at Glentruim House, Inverness-shire, outlived Hare by a year. [10] He served in the Crimea as a lieutenant in the 30th Cambridgeshire Regiment, where Lieutenant Fisher may have met or heard of him; for it was Fisher who told Hare this palpably false story. The Captain wasn't a liar; he merely had a sense of humour. Unfortunately, Hare took him seriously.

The fact that his vampire story was told years before *Dracula* is a blood-red herring. There were several fictional vampires before 1874, such as J.S. LeFanu's *Carmilla*, published in 1874; and T.P Prest's lengthy *Varney the Vampire*, in 1847, whose first chapter has the vampire entering his victim's bedroom by unpicking the lead from a diamond-shaped window-pane. Fancy! FT

The vampire at his awful feast. From *Varney the Vampire* (1847)

Croglin Low Hall, drawn by C G Harper. Captain Fisher was quite specific that the Grange (in his story) never had an upper storey. Montague Summers said this, and the absence of any record of a Croglin Grange, "does not affect the story in the slightest". For him the Low Hall was "exactly Croglin Grange". (*The Vampire in Europe*, p130.)

NOTES

1 - *Sunday Telegraph* 19 August 1992.
2 - *Burke's Landed Gentry*, 'Army List' (1855).
3 - Augustus Hare, *The Story of My Life* (1900); reprinted as *In My Solitary Life* (G. Allen & Unwin, Lonson, 1953).
4 - Anthony Masters, *The Natural History of the Vampire* (Hart-Davis, London, 1972).
5 - Peter Haining, *Vampire* (WH Allen, London, 1985).
6 - Montague Summers, *The Vampire in Europe* (Kegan Paul, London, 1929; reprinted by Aquarian Press, Wellingborough, 1980).
7 - Charles G. Harper, *Haunted Houses* (1907; reprinted by EP Publishing, Whitehaven, 1974).
8 - *Burke's Landed Gentry* (1871).
9 - *Parson & White's Directory of Cumberland, 1829* (Michael Moon, Whitehaven, 1984). *Mannix & Whellan's Directory of Cumberland, 1847* (Michael Moon, 1974).
10 - *Burke's Landed Gentry* (1906).

FOOTNOTE

The prevalence of military men, as both witnesses and victims, in the 18th and 19th century studies of eastern European vampire lore, may be significant. Besides travelling to faraway places, they lent both heroism and authority to the tales. Vampire adventures were, most likely, a familiar form of tall-story among the troops in the Crimea, where the spinner of the Croglin yarn, Captain Edward Fisher, had himself served, surrounded by the very lands - from Greece to Russia (see Summers, note 6, above) - that nurtured the original vampiric folklore. In one of the classic accounts, the teller, like Fisher, is a *cornet* in the cavalry. Fisher might also have been influenced by tales of the mystery beast that terrorized Ennerdale, in his native Cumbria, in 1810, which, according to Fort killed sheep by "biting into the jugular vein and sucking the blood" *(Books* p643). **RJMR**

This article first appeared in *The Skeptic* (Sept 1992) and is reproduced with kind permission. [The Skeptic: PO Box 475, Manchester M60 2TH, UK.] C M Drapkin is a writer with an interest in the occult and criminology.

UNEARTHED
Fresco Fiasco

Steve Moore investigates ancient cave art near the Spanish town of Alava

It's been a strange few months in the field of prehistoric cave-art. October 1991 brought the announcement that a new grotto had been discovered at Sormiou near Marseilles, with paintings of bison, horses, hand-prints and so-on. The entrance to the cave was 100 feet under water, and had been discovered a few months earlier by diver Henri Cosquer; the cave itself was 600 feet inland, just above sea-level.

The tunnel-approach was dangerous – on a previous occasion, Cosquer had discovered the bodies of three young skin divers trapped in it – but he later led a party of archæologists under Jean Courtin to the cave, for investigation and photography. After that, the tunnel mouth was sealed with rocks to prevent further deaths; originally it was above sea-level.

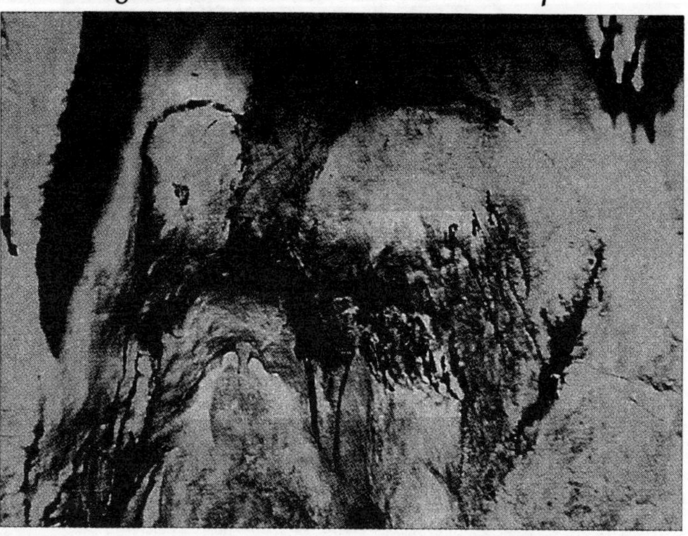

The drawing of a mammoth in a Zubialde cave near Alava. The drawings, found some two years ago and according to experts the best saved of its kind, were now uncovered as a forgery. It is supposed that an archæology student, who discovered the drawings, faked them himself.

The animal paintings were judged to be contemporary with those of Lascaux, about 12-14,000 years old; the hand-prints were thought to be 8,000 years older. Samples of charcoal from an ancient hearth in the cave gave a radiocarbon date of about 18,000 BC. So far, so good. By January 1992, though, the possibility was being raised that the paintings might be fakes. The problem is basically style: the Sormiou paintings are very like the Lascaux ones, in a style which has previously only been found in southwestern France and northwestern Spain. Other cave-paintings from the same area as Sormiou tend to be in the more schematic 'Mediterranean' style.

"There are other rare features: a bison shown in three-quarter face, the sex of bison and horse shown, and a strange flippered bird-like creature that looks like a cross between a seal and a penguin."

There are other rare features: a bison shown in three-quarter face, the sex of bison and horses shown, and a strange flippered bird-like creature that looks like a cross between a seal and a penguin. With the cave sealed and no further investigation likely until later this year, we have to leave this one in the pending file.

After the Sormiou news, things went downhill fast. The Tarn-et-Garonne cave, in southwestern France, was discovered in 1952. Over the years, a number of visitors made their way along 200 feet of tunnel to see the 15,000-year-old bison paintings the cave contained and, as visitors will, some of them left graffiti behind. So the local cavers, the Albigeois Speleo-Club, decided to have the place cleaned up and brought in 70 members of a Protestant youth group, the Eclaireurs de France. Unfortunately, they didn't tell the authorities; nor, it seems, did they tell the Eclaireurs exactly what to do with their steel brushes. Hey presto...two bison disappeared! Oops. The French Culture Ministry is now suing both groups.

In 1990, Serafin Ruiz Selva, a history student and amateur potholer, discovered paintings in a cave at Zigoitia in the Basque region of northern Spain. There were 20 paintings of animals (rhinoceroses, mammoths, horses and bison), 49 symbols and splashes of colour. 'Experts' from Spanish universities pronounced the paintings to be 13,000 years old and in superb condition.

Moreover, the paintings provided evidence that animals like the rhinoceros were present in Europe much earlier than usually thought, and so European prehistory was going to have to be revised. Ruiz was presented with ten million pesetas (£55,000) and hailed as a hero. The cave became a tourist attraction.

Alas, further examination has shown the paintings to be 'near-perfect' forgeries. Although painted in natural pigments containing iron and manganese, it seems that the drawings were made with a modern sponge. The horns have been put in the wrong place on some animals, and the legs of spiders and insects were found embedded in the paint; these would not have been preserved over so many centuries. Also, chemical analysis has shown the paint itself to be no more than 30 months old. As for Serafin Ruiz, reports vary. Some say he's not suspected of the hoax; others that he's being questioned by the authorities; others that he's mysteriously disappeared. In the meantime, paint on walls seems to equal egg on face.

[AP+UPI] 18 Oct 1991; Independent on Sunday, 12 Jan 1992; Newark (NJ) Star-Ledger, 22 Mar 1992; D.Telegraph, D.Mail, Guardian, Independent, 14 Aug 1992.

THE CROP THICKENS

John Mitchell, editor of *The Cerealogist*, looks back on the 1992 harvests of crop circles

The crop circles phenomenon is something Forteans have always wanted; a highly visible, totally mysterious excitement, which affects people widely in many different ways, and can be studied in all its aspects over a period of years. To take this opportunity of recording a new Fortean phenomenon, as it develops, is the main purpose of *The Cerealogist* magazine.

Issue 8 of *The Cerealogist* provides a round-up of the 1992 season, including reports of circle formations in Surrey, Sussex, Gloucester, Devon and other counties – including outbreaks in Belgium and Hungary. But the main action, as usual, was in Wiltshire, particularly around Avebury and the famous nearby centre of circle infestation at Alton Barnes.

Alton Barnes is in one of the most beautiful districts of England, and ideal for circle spotting. Its open, rolling fields of wheat and barley are overlooked by green, chalk hills, studded with barrows and antiquities from which watchers can, in theory at least, see everything going on below them. Sadly though, it did not turn out like that. Enthusiasts patrolled the fields or camped out on the hills, peering and pointing cameras through the gloom of Wiltshire nights. There were plenty of reports of strange lights and assorted UFO effects, and many dawns revealed newly-made crop formations, but these appeared as mysteriously as ever, and nothing significant was seen by the watchers.

Frustration was followed by an epidemic of paranoia. The watchers fell to accusing each other of faking circles under each others' noses. Certain individuals were fingered as closet circle-haters; suspected of knowing everyone's movements and, by posing as genuine researchers, secretly making circles to discredit the whole phenomenon.

It went further. Leading researcher George Wingfield, of the Centre for Crop Circle Studies, saw an international, government plot against the crop circles. He stormed off to the United States and spread the news across the lecture circuit and TV networks.

1992 highlight: the 'Charm Bracelet' near Silbury Hill. It appears in a record of the 1992 season by 'The Phenomenon Collective', available in sets of prints or a 40min video. Contact Grant Wakefield, 0273 747746, for details

Meanwhile, at Alton Barnes, Mike Chorost's Anglo-American team of scientists and near-scientists laboured diligently, collecting soil and plant samples from dozens of circle sites and sending them off for analysis. From preliminary reports, it seems that the sensational results claimed after the previous year's analysis (ie. 1991) have not been repeated.

A highlight of the year was *The Cerealogist*'s crop circle making contest, held on the night of 11-12 July in a Buckinghamshire wheatfield. Twelve teams, including some known, skilled circle-fakers, competed for a first prize of £3,000 to reproduce a given pictogram pattern. The results were as you care to see them. Many people said the reproductions were about as good as the real thing. The experts, on the other hand, thought they lacked something. [See **FT64:7**]

The most impressive, beautifully designed and detailed crop circle of the year appeared late in the season, only a few yards from the 'Waggon and Horses' inn at Beckhampton, a traditional resort where crop watchers take their ale on summer evenings. Known as the 'Charm Bracelet', the design was a ring with eight symbols on its circumference, and these symbols included types which had appeared in formations earlier that year. It was like the menu following the dinner.

It is thought that there were not quite so many circles in 1992 as in the year before, and none of the main researchers is prepared to say which, or how many, of them were fakes. Clearly some were, but in other cases the circumstances were so puzzling that neither the hoax theorists nor others could find a good explanation. So the plot thickens, the mystery deepens, and everyone is looking forward to further surprises next season.

The latest and back issues of *The Cerealogist* can be had for £2.50 / $6 each – or £7.50 / $18 for a 3-issue sub – from SKS, 20 Paul St, Frome, Somerset BA11 1DX. (Tel: 0373 451777)

THE OTHER HALF

Bob Rickard discovers that surgically parted Siamese twins feel their separation as a tangible grief

KATIE & EILISH HOLTON

The plight of Catherine and Eilish Holton received considerable exposure through many newspaper articles and a number of documentaries on ITV. The twins were born in Dublin's Coombe Hospital in August 1988, weighing 10lb. Their parents – Liam and Mary, from Donadea in Co.Kildare – introduced their other children – Claire, Therese and Mairead – to their new sisters, and the twins were quickly absorbed into their loving and active family.

The Holton twins were joined from shoulder to hip, with rudimentary arms behind their fused shoulders and a single pair of legs from an enlarged single pelvis. Although they had separate spines and sets of internal organs, these were progressively fused downwards through the body. Their rib cages were fused at their tips, and their hearts shared a protective sac.

They grew up as normally as possible (fighting as well as playing) and shared difficult tasks; to open a bottle, for example, one would hold it while the other unscrewed the cap. Physically Katie and Eilish appeared to be thriving, but doctors advised Liam and Mary that there was an increasing possibility that they could die if not separated. The operation was explained to Eilish and Katie by using specially adapted Cabbage Patch dolls joined with Velcro. "We had to give them the chance, " said Liam. "We felt that when we explained it to them, they wanted to take that chance."

We can only imagine what the family went through at this time. The Holtons agreed, but insisted that the girls should have an equal chance and organs would be shared equally. They obtained expert help from Dr Lewis Spitz, Nuffield Professor of Pædiatric Surgery, who had performed ten separations of Siamese twins, and who, in turn, consulted other similarly-experienced surgeons in the USA and Canada.

When the twins were aged three and a half, Prof Spitz began to gather a 25-strong team at Great Ormond Street Hospital for Sick Children, London. The operation – not a "first" as some reporters called it – began on 1st April 1992, lasting 15 hours and involving seven surgeons and five anæsthetists. "It was a major undertaking," said Prof Spitz. "We started at the top and worked down. Half the hospital was on stand-by."

Sadly, Katie died four days later; her heart failed. It seems that Eilish's body was the stronger, and her organs did about two-thirds of the work of keeping them alive. This weakness would have become more apparent as they got older, jeopardising both their lives.

In the days that followed Katie's death, Eilish showed strong signs of a grief that was tangible as well as emotional. She was still withdrawn long after the sedation had worn off. Liam said: "She would wake up from deep sleep and look towards the side where Katie had been and give a jerk before starting to cry." Eilish is still severely handicapped, and will have to undergo long-term therapy for her curved spine and undeveloped arm. At London's Roehampton Rehabilitation Centre, when she is strong enough, she will be fitted with an artificial leg.

Recovery has been swift and sound because of the family's deep love, openness and

YVONNE & YVETTE McCARTHER

Yvonne and Yvette were both found dead, on 2 Jan 1993, by a visitor who called at their home in Long Beach, California. Aged 43, they were the world's oldest surviving craniopagus twins – joined at the top of their heads and having separate bodies except for a shared circulatory system. Curiously, one could have a cold while the other didn't.

Born on 14 May 1949 (a breach delivery), they survived the prognosis of early death, participating actively in school and church life. Their divorced mother Willia already had five children, so part of their childhood was spent in an institution. Another time, poverty forced them to spend some time travelling with the Clyde Beatty Circus, a freak show.

Fed up with life passing them by, at the age of 38 the twins moved out of the family home in Los Angeles, to Long Beach and studied nursing at Compton College. They were inveterate smokers (protesting vociferously about the campus no-smoking zones) and (if the *Sunday Sport* is to be believed) shared cruel hangovers from occasional boozing excesses. (Sources on file.)

commonsense. In a follow-up documentary – made for Carlton TV's *3D*, shown on 25 Feb 1993 – Eilish is shown crawling around the house, on and off the sofa, happy and smiling. There are pre-separation photographs of the twins all around the house, and whenever Katy is mentioned, Eilish looks up at them. Although no one can take Katie's place, the family say, Eilish has formed a strong friendship with her 5yr-old sister Mairead. Mark Galloway, producer of two earlier documentaries for Yorkshire TV, said: "They are always playing hide and seek together."

"Since she's been home, Eilish has been the life of this house," says Mary. "On a bad day you have a lump in your throat when you see Katie's picture. On a good day, you can be like Eilish and you can talk freely about her." A curious thing has happened; the family are becoming convinced that Eilish has inherited some of Katie's characteristics. "Before the operation," said Liam, "Katie was the bossy, outgoing one and Eilish was the quieter of the two. It's hard to pinpoint exactly what has taken place in Eilish's mind, but she has matured enormously and is more playful."

Pictured together in June 1992, Hussein and Hassan Saleh look like any pair of 5yr-old lads. They share more than their good looks. They were born joined from shoulder to hip in 1986, genetically identical but with different personalities.

Liam and Mary Holton say they do not regret the operation; they realise that without it they could have lost *both* their daughters. "When we see the quality of Eilish's life today," says Mary, "I know in my heart Katie would have wanted that too. Now she has a lot of the gigging and playfulness that would have been Katie. We look at Eilish and see them both." (Sources on file.)

HUSSEIN & HASSAN SALEH

Prof Spitz's previous success was with the Saleh twins, whom he separated in April 1987 – when they were eight months old – in an operation also lasting 15 hours and involving 25 staff. Hussein and Hassan were joined in a similar way to Katy and Eilish, but unlike them shared a lower colon and bowel. "We used to be like this," Hussein told Lois Rogers (London *Evening Standard* 16 June 1992), squashing himself up against his brother. "They just cut us in half," interrupts Hassan, making a slicing gesture down the right of his body.

Hussein and Hassan were born in southern Sudan in 1986. When their father's brother, who was working as a pædiatrician in Riyadh, was sent a photo of them, he petitioned King Fahd of Saudi Arabia, who agreed to pay for their operation at Great Ormond Street, and for their 10-year period of post-operative therapy, including their regularly-replaced artificial legs.

As part of Prof Spitz' preparation for the separation of the Holton Twins, he introduced Hassan and Hussein to the Holton family at a time when they were all at GOSH together. It was the sight of these happy, healthy and handsome boys that helped the Holtons make up their minds about separation.

The boys have found it hard to adjust to life apart, and for some time after their separation they were obviously feeling the same kind of grief as Eilish Holton. Prof Spitz said: "They are very, very close. It was only when they were put together in the same bed that their recovery progressed." For years after, they needed to sleep entwined, and even now minutes do not pass without small gestures of affection towards each other. If one is sick, the other can hardly bear to go to school alone. And when one speaks, the other butts in, endorsing his brothers statement as his own. (Other sources on file.)

PAGE & SARA JOHNSON

The Johnson twins were born by Cæsarian section on 12 June 1991. Where the Holton twins were almost side by side, Page and Sara were born directly facing each other like Hassan and Hussein. The area of the join was smaller, from mid-chest to just below the belly button, and several organs were fused together through the opening. Apart from that, their bodies were robust and normal.

Their six-hour separation was carried out on 29 August 1992 at the Mayo Clinic in Rochester, Minnesota, under the direction of Dr John Wesley aided by a team of 29 people. They utilised a complex 3D computer imaging system to minimise scarring. Dr Wesley said "We could rotate the images of their bodies and even separate them to work out how much extra skin would be needed to cover the gap."

"The toughest decision was choosing who got the belly button," joked Dr Wesley. "We gave it to Sara because she was smaller and didn't cry so much." Life, for the Johnsons, is now proceeding normally, which, as far as they are concerned, is the miracle they hardly dared hope for.

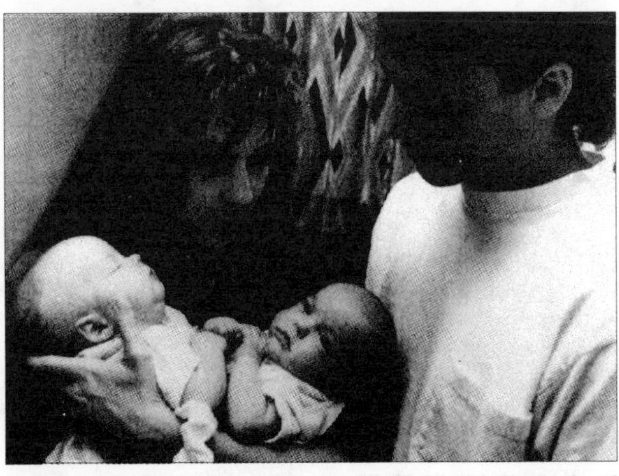

Page and Sara Johnson with parents Tom and Kimberly of Fargo, North Dakota, just before their separation in 1992.

HORSEWATCH

Madness in the Home Counties

PAUL SIEVEKING CHRONICLES THE DEVELOPMENT OF THE ENGLISH HORSERIPPING EPIDEMIC

Since our bulletins on the English and Swedish horse-ripping epidemics at the end of last year [***FT64:18 & 66:12***], there has been a considerable increase in these baffling atrocities in Humberside, Buckinghamshire and Hampshire.

In late November 1992, horse owners in the area round Scunthorpe, Humberside, set up a horsewatch scheme after several attacks in the county resulted in the death of one 18-year-old mare. Three mares had been attacked at Welton near Hull in October, one of which almost died from internal injuries.

"Of the 40 or so horse-rippings in southern England in the last two years which are known to the police, most have occurred in Hampshire."

The 1993 horse rippings began in heavy fog during the small hours of Saturday, 2 January – probably between 3:00 and 5:00 am. Chiltern Hills (nicknamed Nell), a 23-year-old mare and former hunter, suffered a foot-long wound, 4-6 inches deep, to her genitals; it was curiously jagged for a knife wound. She was in a stable with another mare on the 53-acre estate of Barclay's Bank director Sir Nigel Mobbs in Lacey Green, near Princes Risborough, Bucks. She would probably have bled to death if the groom had not found her at 7:00am. The wound required 30 stitches and the clitoris had to be completely excised during the 90-minute operation. Nell will no longer be able to breed.

There were two further attacks later that month. On 17 January, Little Jay, a chestnut brood mare, 11, suffered anal bruising and a deep gash across the left hind leg, at Widmer Farm, Lacey Green. Then, on 21 January at Moses Platt Farm, Speen, about a mile away, Ragtime Blues ('Bluey'), a piebald mare, eight, was stabbed in the genitals, leaving a wound six inches deep. Unusually, this was in broad daylight – between 10:30am and 3:30pm – in a field overlooked on all sides by houses and footpaths.

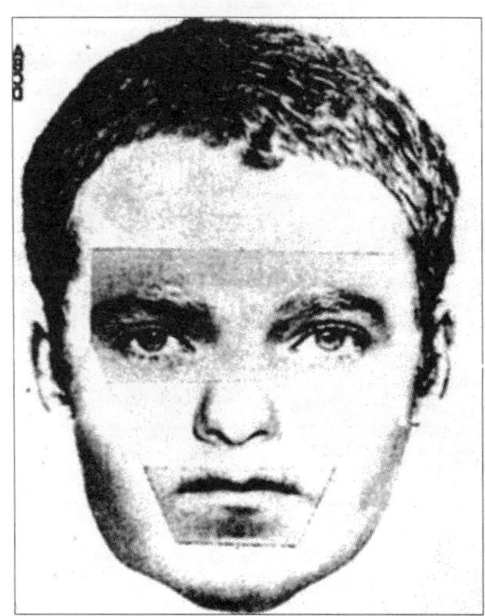

Horse ripping made banner headlines with the death of Mountbatten on 22 January. This 11-year-old, 16-hands-high, Irish hunter mare was attacked in her stable at Cobbs Farm, Four Marks, near Alton in Hampshire. There was deep cuts in her neck and hindquarters. Owner Robert Broderick shut her up for the night after her last feed at 8:00pm and discovered her dead with her head against the door at 9:30 the next morning.

Veterinary surgeon Colin Baxter concluded Mountbatten died between 9:00pm and midnight, of shock or from drugs such as detomidine or ketamine. She had been sexually assaulted and hit across the shoulder with a sharp instrument that could have been a knife.

Mr Broderick's daughter, Fiona, 24, was watching television until midnight, but didn't hear a thing. Her bedroom overlooks the stable and she could normally hear Mountbatten snorting and neighing. (The stable is variously described as 200 yards away or under 100 yards.) But this time she heard nothing, not even the 'lively and very strong' mare lashing out with her feet: a metal bucket was twisted and buckled and the stable showed signs of a struggle.

Of the 40 or so horse-rippings in southern England in the last two years which are known to the police, most have occurred in Hampshire – particularly in the New Forest and Meon Valley. About 25% of assaults involved genital mutilation. Stallions and geldings are stabbed or battered, often around the head, while mares, many of them pregnant, are sexually assaulted with broomstick handles and posts.

There are many variations, however: in the New Forest on 14 September, for instance, battery acid was poured on a mare. Two incidents near Winchester (13 June 1991 and 13 August 1992) involved rope burns. Other incidents have included wire attached to a stallion's penis, claw hammer marks on a horse's back and an airgun wound. As many of the attacks have occurred at the full moon – 14 out of 20 in 1992, for instance – some believe they are connected with Satanism, although substantive evidence is zilch: after all, bright moonlight merely makes it easier to get around at night.

Others suspect rivalry within the Hampshire horse community as the knifings have reduced the value of the animals. The assailant has – or the assailants have – detailed anatomical knowledge, as well as remarkable empathy with the horses to avoid being kicked to bits. The majority view is that the motive is sexual, psychotic, or both.

Speculation is rife among psychologists and journalists about stable hands or vets with grudges or obeying inner

ABOVE: Photofit of the ripper suspect issued by the Hampshire police.
RIGHT: Photograph of the knife found in the fiield.

Owner Katie Buckett comforts her injured mare, Georgie Girl (see 3 Feb opposite).

voices, hunt saboteurs and networking gangs of sado-masochistic zoophiles. There is no perceivable pattern of method, weapon, timing, target, or location and each time the attacker disappears without trace. A horsewatch scheme has been set up in Hampshire, but the task is enormous with 50,000 horses in the county, many kept in huts or fields miles from their owners.

White witches Kevin and Ingrid Carlyon of St Leonards were asked by a Hampshire horse owner last December to investigate possible occult ramifications of the horse attacks. Though they are careful to say there is no ostensible link between these rippings and the occult, they have performed some full moon rituals to track down the attackers, so far without success. They told *FT* that "animal fluids were once used to enhance sexual prowess and stamina, and we think that the people responsible may be trying to aid someone with a sexual problem, possibly a female who cannot bear children." Witchcraft as a motive was also suggested by the British Horse Society. Livestock ripping is often blamed upon pagan rituals.

Many news reports recalled Peter Shaffer's 1973 play *Equus* in which Alan, a stable boy, gouges out the eyes of six horses with an iron spike after a horse witnessed his first and unsuccessful sexual encounter with a girl. It was based on a true story set near Winchester between the wars in which a boy blinded 26 horses.

Some time around 23 January, a man of about 35, with a green jacket and black wellies with a yellow C on them, was seen staring without expression for half an hour at horses in a field near Corehampton, Hampshire. Around the same time, two military policemen from High Wycombe noticed a man lurking near a field where horses were grazing at Speen in Buckinghamshire, scene of an attack on 21 January. He ran away when challenged. A footprint was found and photographed.

On 28 January, police issued the descriptions of two suspects. A young man, about 5ft 7in with mousy hair **[see photofit]**, attacked a cow near Alton, Hampshire, on 3 October 1990, which had to be put down; while another man in his 60s, 5ft 3in, with a ruddy complexion and grey hair, was seen interfering with a mare near Alton on 16 March 1991. He was accompanied by two black and white border collies. Police also issued a picture of an eight-inch French kitchen knife found at Park Gate, Hants, near a field in which a Shetland gelding was wounded on 12 July 1992. It had a wooden handle and the letters 'INOX – NUGENT***' engraved on the blade **[see photo]**. By 29 January, reward money for information totalled £18,000. An 18-year-old man from Winchester was questioned on 23 February, but released on police bail.

As a crime, livestock maiming appears to have peaked in the first half of the 19th century, mainly as a way of attacking wealthy farmers and landowners. Methods included poisoning, hamstringing, shooting, strangulation, ear-cutting, stabbing, throat-slitting, stick-thrusting and straightforward ripping. Horses were by far the most common target. In 1840 a Norfolk labourer was transported for 15 years for three attacks on the sexual organs of horses and one of the worst documented cases involved another labourer who tore out the entrails of a live sheep with his bare hands.

Under the Waltham Black Act (1723-1832), anyone caught maiming farm animals was hanged. After 1832, the punishment was transportation and later penal servitude. Anyone caught today would face up to 10 years for criminal damage, or 'sectioned' under the 1983 Mental Health Act, in which case they would probably be released within two years. However, equine vigilantes are out for revenge, and rippers could face lynching.

TABLE OF INCIDENTS

There were horse rippings in Hampshire in 1983 (1 case), 1984 (2), 1985 (1), 1988 (5), 1989 (4), 1990 (4), 1991 (5) and 1992 (20). All the following incidents were in Hampshire unless otherwise stated.

1993: 2 Jan – Lacey Green, Bucks; Chiltern Hills, mare (23), had genitals cut. **4 Jan** – Owslebury: mare (20) had genitals cut and suffered internal bruising from blunt instrument in communal stables. Door had been forced off its hinges and mare found wandering in field. Pages ripped from pornographic magazines had been found on roadsides and in nearby woods. **6 Jan** – Kilmeston: Snow Simball, mare (23) in foal, attacked internally in field. **6 Jan** – Alton: mare found bleeding from her hindquarters in field. **17 Jan** – Lacey Green, Bucks: Little Jay, brood mare (11), suffered cuts to genitals and rear leg. Part of hoof cut off with axe. **21 Jan** – Speen, Bucks: Ragtime Blues, mare (8), stabbed in genitals. **22 Jan** – Four Marks: Mountbatten, Irish hunter mare (11), fatally attacked. **23 Jan** – Newton Abbot, Devon: 3 horses burned to death in probable arson attack. **27 Jan** – Wroughton, Wilts: Chester Barnes, gelding (17), had tail, forelock and mane docked in his stable. **28 Jan** – Peterchurch, Herefordshire: litter of piglets tortured and mutilated. **30 Jan** – Burford, Oxfordshire: stable boy Tim West had green hair dye sprayed in his face when he disturbed two (or three) men who had docked the tales and manes of four horses with sheep shears. One had been sprayed with dye and 'H SCUM' painted on the wall. **1 Feb** – Farnham, Surrey: chestnut mare (23) found with bruising to genitalia and left eye shut due to swelling. Human blood on the floor suggested the attacker had been injured. **2 Feb** – Landford, Wilts: Fax and Leo, two ponies aged seven, had manes and tails clipped. **3 Feb** – Upham: Georgie Girl, pregnant mare (16), mutilated and sexually assaulted with a large object in a field overlooked by several houses. The foal, due in April, was apparently unharmed. A man and a blonde woman in her 30s were seen parked nearby in an F-registered black BMW saloon car. **12 Feb** – Botley: gelding had part of its tail cut off. **15 Feb** – Reddich, Worcs: Arab chestnut mare stabbed to the bone through a thick blanket. Telford, Shropshire: chestnut mare had legs tightly bound with tape. **18 Feb** – Harby, Leics: mare (16) had genitals slashed with sharp instrument. **19 Feb** – Halwill, near Okehampton, Devon: Ralph, grey gelding (9), suffered 4in wound to right shoulder. Whitehill: Lorna, mare (14) sexually assaulted with broom handle, ran into barbed wire, ripping chest. Near Grantham, Lincs: mare (16) slashed with sharp instrument. **21 Feb** – Near Epping, Essex: attack 'of a sexual nature' on mare in field. **26 Feb** – Blythwood Farm, Gypsy Lane, near Bishop's Stortford, Herts: mare in a field had genitals slashed with a knife. **1 Mar** – Botley: two geldings, aged 4 and 12, had tails cut off. **2 Mar** – Langton Herring, Dorset: tails and manes hacked off 17 colts. **5 Mar** – Par, Cornwall: Gypsy, black and white cob (9) in foal, found dead in field with ear cut off, eye gouged out and genitals sliced open. Tara, another mare, had tail and mane hacked off. Trethowel, Cornwall: Natasha, light brown mare (12), stabbed in shoulder and knee.

SOURCES: About 200 national and local newspaper clippings, available in the Archives for Fortean Research.

ARCHIVE GEMS
2: The Black Madonna of Montserrat

JANET BORD, OF THE FORTEAN PICTURE LIBRARY, EXAMINES A STRANGE PHOTO FROM 1984

The reason why some images of the Virgin Mary are black, together with a gazetteer of places where they can be seen, is given in Ean Begg's book *The Cult of the Black Virgin*, published by Arkana in 1985. A fine example of such a black madonna can be found at Montserrat in north-east Spain. According to legend, she was carved in Palestine by St Luke and brought to Montserrat by St Peter. She was hidden in the rocks to save her from the Moors and then rediscovered in the eighth or ninth century. The bishop tried to move the statue to his cathedral, but couldn't shift it, so a shrine was built in the cave. Documentary evidence for devotion to Our Lady of Montserrat dates back as far as 932. Today, a replica stands in the holy cave, while the original is in the hilltop basilica, visited by many pilgrims who come to venerate the Madonna.

In February 1984, P.W. Wheeler, on holiday in Spain from his home in southern England, visited Montserrat and took a photograph of the Madonna on colour print film. When his prints came back, he was surprised to find that the Madonna had a halo around her head, something that was definitely not to be seen when he took the photograph. The halo is especially clear on the right-hand side, and it will be seen that the circle of light does not pass across the face of the statue, but stops at the edge of the head, as though it is passing behind it, and appears as would a real halo, were it suspended over the figure's head.

One's natural reaction is to assume that a light has caused a reflection which coincidentally resembles a halo, and this may be the prosaic explanation for this image; but, even if this is the case, it is a happy and indeed Fortean accident that the reflection gives Our Lady such an appropriate decoration.

DIARY OF A MAD PLANET

DECEMBER 1992–JANUARY 1993

This diary aims to record, in two-month segments, the geophysical highlights of our planet: the tempests and tantrums, the oddities and extremities. Compiled by the editors and various correspondents.

MUDSLIDE **8 December BOLIVIA**:
Following torrential rains, mud avalanche buried gold-mining camp at Llipi in about 700,000 cubic feet of mud. Side of mountain collapsed. Hundreds reported dead [at least 210, possible as many as 500]; precise numbers will never be known. Rescue work hindered by continuing rainstorms.

STORM **11December NEW YORK CITY:**
Worst storm in decades; fierce winds, heavy rain. Flooding and power problems virtually shut down the subway system for part of the day; considerable disruption to other rail services; bridges closed due to wind-blown debris, major roadways closed due to high water, six feet above normal. "We literally had scuba divers taking people out of their cars on FDR Drive" according to a transportation department spokesperson. Winds gusting to 77 mph caused La Guardia Airport to be closed. The same storm system removed seven feet of beach from several points on the New Jersey coast; a church steeple was blown on to the Franklin bridge. The storms raged from Georgia to New England, killing at least 5 in Pennsylvania.

EARTHQUAKE

12 December INDONESIA: Flores (8.482S 121.930E) Depth: 36km. Magnitude: 7.5R. At least 2,200 killed or missing, 500 injured and 40,000 left homeless. A further 19 killed and 130 houses destroyed on Kalaotoa island. Coastal town of Maumere, 20 miles from the offshore epicentre, almost completely wiped out. Tsunami run-ups of 1000ft with wave hieights of 85ft, along with many landslides, were responsible for most of the deaths. The quake was felt throughout the Sunda Islands, on Sumba and Timor and in southern parts of Sulawesi. Rescue operations hindered by continuing aftershocks, tropical storms and power failures.

WIND **11 January SCOTLAND:**
Low pressure of 916 millibars recorded near the Faroe Islands, equalling the British record and causing hurricane-force winds. 100mph winds and 50-foot waves caused further damage to stranded oil-tanker *Braer* in Shetlands. During January, Scotland had some of the windiest weather ever recorded. Glasgow: 57mph gales, gusting to 88mph, highest since 98mph in 1968. Edinburgh: gusting to 81mph. Cairngorm: winds of 106mph, gusting to 169mph.

Road on Hokkaido Island, Japan, ripped apart by the earthquake on 16 January.

ERUPTION **14 January COLOMBIA:**
Sudden eruption of the Galeras volcano, killing nine scientists, including Professor Geoffrey Brown, who had entered the crater to monitor gas emissions in an attempt to predict eruptions. They were trying to replace equipment rendered useless by a strong eruption on 22 July 1992. Professor Brown, head of earth sciences at the OPen University, was an expert on measing the minute drop of gravity prior to eruptions; his team had successfully predicted an eruption recently in Costa Rica, but Galeras stole a march on them. The 13,996ft Galeras, declared 'volcano of the decade', has erupted 21 times since 1580. This time, rocks and gases were blasted out in a thick column of smoke that rose 10,000ft.

EARTHQUAKE **16 January JAPAN:**
Hokkaido (43.403N 143.259E) Depth: 100km. Magnitude: 7.1R. Strongest to hit Japan in 11 years; 2 killed, 614 injured. Landslide, fires, damage to buildings and roads in Kushiro, Hokkaido and Hachinohe on Honshu. The quake was felt in Tokyo and Yokohama.

FLOOD **18 January TURKEY:**
Ozengeli, near Bayburt. A "sheet of white" buried 50 houses, killing 16 people trapped under tons of snow, 50 people believed still buried, and voices were still heard under the rubble a day later.

Special thanks to the Global Seismology Group of the British Geological Survey for the earthquake data.

THE LOVECATS

Leading cryptozoologist KARL SHUKER proposes a new solution to the diversity of Big Cat sightings

Dr Karl Shuker with the stuffed Asian jungle cat killed by a car near Ludlow in February 1989.

I recently purchased an authentic alien big cat (ABC). It was responsible for many reports of a strange lynx-like creature seen in the Ludlow area of Shropshire – reports dismissed by officialdom as misidentifications of domestic cats, dogs or foxes, before it was killed by a car. On 3 February 1989, farmer Norman Evans found its body near his home; it was tall, with tawny pelage, tufted ears, a fairly short black-ringed tail, striking one-inch-long fangs, and stripes on its upper limbs. It was an adult male specimen of the Asian jungle (swamp) cat, *Felis chaus*, which is not native to Britain or anywhere else in Europe. Investigations revealed that it was a captive-bred escapee that had been living around Ludlow for many months. **[1,2]**

This was not the first jungle cat found in Britain; another adult specimen was killed by a car in Hampshire's Hayling Island on 26 July 1988; as in the Ludlow case, its procurement followed months of discounted sightings. **[3]** In autumn 1992, I succeeded in locating the Ludlow jungle cat, which had been preserved, magnificently, by a taxidermist. After confirming that the relevant ministries had no objection, I purchased it – because it not only provides unequivocal proof that non-native cats are indeed escaping and surviving in our countryside, but, together with the Hayling Island cat, it adds a hitherto-unrecognised yet potentially dramatic dimension to Britain's mystery cat situation.

There are much larger non-native cats roaming Britain, including pumas, lynxes and black panthers. **[4]** These animals could even breed in the wild here, but only if a male and female of the same species met up. Interbreeding between the larger cat species occurs rarely, and the offspring tend to be sterile. The jungle cat is a significant exception to this because it is so closely related genetically to the domestic cat – despite being three times larger. Not only can it mate and reproduce with cats of other species, particularly the

Recent sightings of jungle cats or their hybrids in the West Midlands. 1 - Ludlow (Feb 1989, dead jungle cat found). 2 - Penn (summer 1991). 3 - Weston (summer 1991). 4 - Shrewsbury (Aug 1991). 5 - Telford (Jan 1992). 6 - Great Witley (May 1992). 7 - Tipton (May/June 1992). 8 - Great Bridge (June 1992). 9 - Bridgnorth (June 1992, and spasmodically afterwards). 10 - Wednesbury (Nov-Dec 1992). 11 - West Bromwich (Dec 1992). 12 - Welshpool (Jan 1992). 13 - Llanfyllin (Jan-Feb 1993). 14 - Lake Vyrnwy environs (Feb 1993). I wish to express my especial thanks to Jan Williams for kindly contributing sightings from her files to this map.

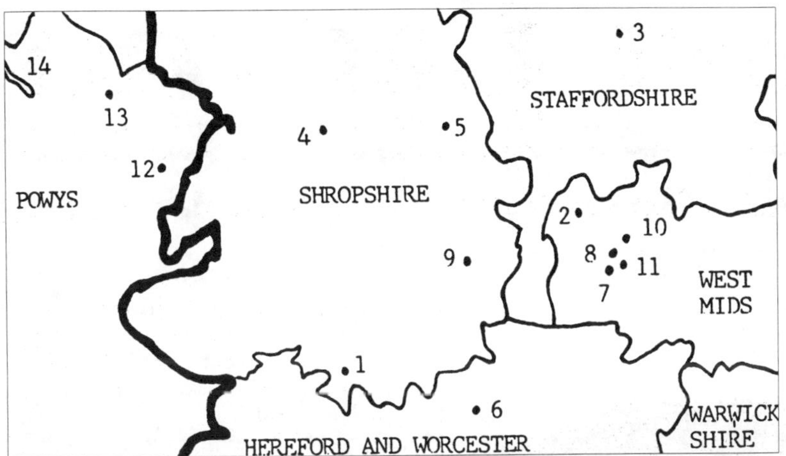

domestic cat, but successful matings with domestic cats in captivity have yielded *fertile* offspring. Furthermore, these offspring – after mating with other such hybrids or with either of their parental species – have themselves yielded offspring, and so on. **[5]** Interbreeding may also have occurred in the jungle cat's native Indian habitat. **[6]**

STRANGE-COLOURED HYBRIDS

What has particularly intrigued me about the Hayling Island and Ludlow incidents is the continuation of sightings in both areas long *after* the two specimens were killed – **[7,8]** – suggesting the presence of further jungle cats: for instance, in the Hill Top district of West Bromwich, West Midlands **[9]**; in the Bridgnorth area, not far from Ludlow **[10]**; and near Lake Vyrnwy, just inside Wales' border with Shropshire **[11]**. In other cases, although the cats described seem like jungle cats in general size and shape, their coat colours are different: jet black (near Hayling Island **[8]**); almost white (Penn district of Wolverhampton **[12]**); and pale brown with swirl-like blotches (Tipton, West Midlands **[13]**). Jungle cat *cubs* have spots, but these vanish as they mature.

As I have recently revealed to the media **[14,15]**, from my investigation of cat hybridisation and field research in the West Midlands, I consider it plausible that these strange-coloured cats are hybrids of jungle cats and feral domestic cats. First-generation hybrids tend to resemble their jungle cat parent in general size and shape – including their distinctive tufted ears and relatively short tail – but possess the coat colouration of their domestic cat parent. **[5]** This could explain the odd variations in ABC descriptions from localities known to be the haunts of adult jungle cats.

A FELINE FOX

To obtain an independent authoritative opinion, I discussed these ideas with the internationally-renowned felid geneticist Roy Robinson; he agreed that jungle-domestic cat hybrids were certainly possible, given the close genetic relationship between the two species and the docility (despite its large size) of the jungle cat. **[16]**

Another noteworthy aspect is the apparent presence of one or more jungle cats and hybrids in the West Midlands, a highly industrialised region where one would not expect such cats to survive. Yet, the jungle cat associates closely with man in its native India, living in deserted buildings and prowling close to villages. **[17]** Indeed, it is almost the feline equivalent of our own urban foxes, and may well be invading the same ecological niche here in the West Midlands. I have on file a report of a possible jungle-domestic cat hybrid that was startled by car headlights as it scavenged around dustbins on a Tipton housing estate before dawn in 1992 **[13]**; and reports of a likely pure-bred jungle cat seen at twilight, wandering through a caravan park near Bridgnorth, apparently looking for scraps of food, from June 1992 **[10]**.

Lastly, but no less compelling, is the fact that breeding between the Asian leopard cat, *Felis bengalensis*, and the domestic cat can also yield, sometimes, fertile offspring. **[18]** Indeed, a new breed of 'domestic cat' – the Bengal – is actually a hybrid of these two species, but one whose development, following the initial stage of interspecific hybridisation, has largely involved successive backcrossing between hybrids and domestic cats, reducing the aggressive behaviour inherited from its leopard cat ancestor while retaining that species' highly attractive spotted pelage. **[19]** With this in mind, I note that in 1988, an escapee leopard cat was shot dead on Dartmoor **[20]** and another in Scotland **[21]**; and in 1990 one was killed in Scotland by a car **[22]**. All three seem to have been on the loose for some time, offering the possibility that they mated with feral domestic cats during their freedom, and that hybrids now exist in the wild in those regions.

There is a realistic chance that interbreeding between escapee jungle cats, leopard cats and feral domestic cats has begun in Britain's countryside. If this continues, eventually a self-perpetuating strain of notably large hybrids could become established here – hybrids, moreover, that possess genes from a wild, *non-native* species (unlike the hybrids produced by interbreeding between feral domestic cats and the native Scottish wildcat). The result would be a startling feline parallel to the cross-breeding between native red deer and naturalised Asian sika deer – and an unpredictable addition to the British ecosystem.

NOTES

1 – "Killer found dead', *South Shropshire Journal* 10 Feb 1989. **2** – 'Wild cat sightings', *South Shropshire Journal* 17 Feb 1989. **3** – 'Hit and run driver kills mystery wildcat', *The News*, Portsmouth, 28 July 1988. **4** – Karl P.N. Shuker, *Mystery Cats of the World* (Robert Hale, 1989) pp33-69. **5** – J.M. Jackson & J. Jackson, 'The hybrid jungle cat', *Newsletter of the Long Island Ocelot Club*, 1970, v11, p45. **6** – Reginald I. Pocock, 'On English domestic cats', *Proceedings of the Zoological Society of London*, 1907, pp143-168. **7** – Jan Williams, 'A confusion of cats', *SCAN News*, Jan 1993, n1, pp5-8. **8** – Nick Maloret, 'Swamp cat fever', *Fortean Times*, autumn 1990, n55, pp44-46. **9** – Fred Rackham, personal communication, 2 Feb 1993. **10** – Robert Baker, personal communication, 27 Feb 1993. **11** – Harry Wilson, personal communications, 29 Jan & 14 Feb 1993. **12** – Jan Williams, personal communication, 27 Jan 1993. **13** – Ron Mills, personal communication, 27 Jan 1993. **14** – Alison Jones, 'The missing lynx', *Birmingham Eve. Mail* 29 Jan 1993. **15** – 'Danger cats roaming region', *Wolverhampton Express & Star* 30 Jan 1993. **16** – Roy Robinson, personal communication, 1 Feb 1993. **17** – C.A.W. Guggisberg, *Wild Cats of the World* (David & Charles, 1975) p45. **18** – Ralph Luce, 'Hybrid cats', *Cats Magazine*, Jan 1974, pp8-9. **19** – 'Gentle whimsey proves a leopard *can* change its spots', *Daily Mail* 24 June 1991. **20** – Karl P.N. Shuker, 'Feline clues on the Moors', ***Fortean Times***, summer 1989, n52, pp26-27. **21** – Mark Porter, 'Scots leopard shot', *Sunday Telegraph* 6 March 1988. **22** – 'Leopard type cat found dead on moor', *Berwickshire News* 23 Aug 1990.

SECRET COUNTRY

Mysterious places to visit in Great Britain compiled by Janet & Colin Bord

8: Eildon Hills, Roxburghshire, Borders Region

Eildon Hills dominate the gentle countryside around them

In legend, the hills got their prominent shape when an evil spirit, at the command of the magician Michael Scot, split one large hill into three. In the Iron Age, a great hillfort was built on top of the northernmost hill, the still visible ramparts forming the largest hillfort in Scotland.

A Roman fort was also built in this area, at Newstead, east of Melrose, and it was somewhere near here that Thomas the Rhymer (Thomas of Erceldoune) met the Fairy Queen. She took him into her kingdom under Eildon and he lived in fairyland for three years, though it seemed like three days to him.

In another tale, Canonbie Dick, a horse trader who was riding over the hills at night, saw an old man who bought the horses Dick had been unable to sell. Dick made several sales to the old man on subsequent occasions, and one night was taken by him into the hill called Lucken Hare. Inside Dick saw a large cavern where lay horses and knights all sleeping - and the old man revealed himself to be Thomas of Erceldoune. He gave Dick the choice of drawing a sword or blowing a horn, saying he would die if he chose wrongly. Dick chose the horn and blew a blast on it, whereupon all the knights and horses awoke. He grabbed the sword and heard a voice crying:

Woe to the coward that ever he was born;
Who did not draw the sword before he blew the horn.

Then he found himself whisked out of the hill in a whirlwind and was discovered lying on a bank by some shepherds, to whom he told his strange tale before he died.

Though steep in places, the four-mile Eildon Walk leading off the B6359 in Melrose will take you through the hills and past the place where Dick entered them; the hills can also be clearly seen from the surrounding roads.

In one version of the tale, the knights inside the hill were King Arthur's men; and there are many other hills in Britain where they are believed to lie sleeping, awaiting the call to come to the country's aid. It is also said that there is so much gold in the Eildon Hills that sheep grazing there develop yellow teeth!

In Melrose Abbey to the north, Michael Scot is said to lie buried: his alleged grave is next to the double piscina in the south transept chapel nearest to the presbytery, set into the floor and with a cross on it. He was a real person who lived in the 13th century, but there is no proof that he practised magic. Jennifer Westwood in *Albion* calls him 'perhaps the leading scholar of Western Europe in the early thirteenth century'. In his writings he condemned magic, but he was interested in science and astrology, and somehow an assortment of tales of magical feats, mostly located in Cumbria, Northumberland and southern Scotland, have become attached to his name. He was said to have powers like those of the giants and, with the Devil's help, it was he who built Hadrian's Wall; in one night the two also made Watling Street.'Michael the Warlock' was said to have controlled the witches in Glenluce in Wigtown. To keep them out of mischief, he made them perform tasks like spinning ropes from sea-sand and threshing barley chaff. Scot was believed to be buried with his magic books - including such works as *The Fire Spangs of Faustus* and *Black Clud's Wyme Laid Open* - in the abbey at Glenluce. Scot was also said to be buried at the Abbey of Holm Cultram in Cumberland.

Whether or not Scot is buried at Melrose Abbey, the substantial ruins are worth visiting, as too are the fairy-haunted hills of Eildon. **FT**

The now ruined Glenluce Abbey where Scot once cast his magic spells

PSYCHIC RESEARCH: Brian Inglis was a past editor of The Spectator and veteran of over 20 books on parapsychology and fringe medicine. See obituary on page 16.

CRYPTOZOOLOGY: Jonathan Downes is a writer and researcher in zoology and co-founder of the Centre for Fortean Zoology in Exeter, Devon.

SCIENCE WATCH: Dennis Stacy, a freelance journalist living in Texas, edits the monthly *Journal* of MUFON, the largest UFO research organisation in the USA.

METAPHYSICS: Robert Anton Wilson, best known for his *Illuminatus* novels, has published 26 books and lectures at Futurist conferences.

Psychic Research

An Hallucination To Sit On

Brian Inglis sees no reason why apparitions should not be tangible

Of the teachers who tried to instil some discipline into my passion for history, one whom I remember with particular affection was 'Thompy' – J.M. Thompson. In retrospect this is surprising, as he was a sceptic; a species which, though there have been other exceptions, I have not found to be congenial.

Thompson's 1911 *Miracles in the New Testament*, in which he explained them away along rationalist lines, had led to his being thrown out of the Church of England – 'de-frocked', as the term was then: maybe still is? Though if so, the Bishop of Durham ought surely to have had the same treatment. Having myself just shed the Protestantism of my upbringing, I had no inclination to argue with Thompy at the time. I would now.

The other day, for example, I heard or read of somebody – perhaps it *was* the Bishop of Durham? – dismissing the Resurrection. Wary though I am of the New Testament as history, I can see no problem in accepting that the disciples may have hallucinated Jesus after his crucifixion, in a form real enough for doubting Thomas to carry out the celebrated test, and to be convinced that it really was Jesus, risen from the dead.

This brought back to my mind a story I had come across earlier, and which had set me wondering about the power of hallucinations to create what to all appearances is 'matter' – a much less implausible notion than it used to be, thanks to the quantum physicists.

In 1954, Mr and Mrs Allan (not their real names), out for a walk in the country, were taking a rest on a bench in a clearing when Mrs Allan was suddenly overcome by a feeling of intense fear. Without looking round, she 'saw' behind her three men in clerical garb, whose appearance suggested they belonged to a time past; two of them radiating hostility. Her husband, touching her, said she felt like a corpse; they got up and walked away.

> "Sitters at D D Home's gatherings were able to shake disembodied hands"

A fairly commonplace ghost story, certainly, except for the mystery of the way Mrs Allan 'saw' behind her back (she was too paralysed with fear to turn round). But there was a sequel. She felt she must, at some point, return and exorcise the experience. Two years later she did, only to find that there was no clearing of the kind where they had sat on the bench; nor, she was assured, were there ever benches on that part of the estate.

Recounting the tale in *The Seen and the Unseen*, published in 1977, Andrew MacKenzie suggested there was a link between Mrs Allan's experience and the Versailles 'adventure' of the Misses Moberly and Jordain in 1901 (which sceptics are still trying, unavailingly, to explain away). Perhaps Mrs Allan had been in the grip of a retrocognitive hallucination. But, if so, how do we account for the fact that they sat down? "It is not possible to sit on a spectral bench", MacKenzie asserted. "Anybody who tries to do so will land on the earth with a bump."

This raises a curious issue. There are many well-attested accounts of séances at which the sitters have been allowed to test for themselves that the materialisations are 'real'. In light good enough to see what was happening, sitters at D.D. Home's gatherings reported, they were able not merely to observe disembodied hands, but also to shake them. Charles Richet, a Nobel prizewinner in physiology, found that forms he watched materialising were anatomically correct.

In the Allan story, the case for materialisation is admittedly weakened by the fact that only Mrs Allan hallucinated. But in general, "I fail to see" (as I wrote in a review of MacKenzie's book), "why one should not be able to sit on a materialised bench".

The Art of Jumping To Conclusions

Jonathan Downes shows that there are zoological mysteries right under our noses

In 1955, Belgian zoologist and jazz musician Bernard Heuvelmans published his *Sur la Piste des Betes Ignorées* (later translated as *On the Track of Unknown Animals*), an extraordinary book bristling with ideas which convincingly revealed the whereabouts of 30 or 40 hitherto unknown large animal species around the world. He also invented the science of cryptozoology, the study of unknown animals.

Unfortunately, none of the animals he described have been formally identified. Every major investigation into relict hominids, serpentiform lake monsters or surviving dinosaurs has been a remarkable failure; the Nessie photographs of Frank Searle and Lachlan Stuart along with Florida's giant penguin footprints have been exposed as fakes; severe doubt has been cast on the yeti footprint photographs of Eric Shipton; and the Minnesota Iceman and Patterson Bigfoot movie are decidedly iffy.

Russian yeti investigator Boris Porshnev has been accused of manipulating his data to suit his own ends. The so-called 'gargoyle head' photographed in Loch Ness by the Rhines/Edgerton team is very similar to a tree stump dredged from the loch bottom at the same location. Even the famous 'surgeon's photograph' of Nessie, described as having "the unmistakable mark of a living object", has had serious doubts raised about it.

While the sceptics claim that these animals do not exist, I would merely suggest that many cannot be accounted for within a purely zoological framework; they are unlikely to be put behind bars or stuffed for a South Kensington glass case.

In common with many amateur naturalists, as a schoolboy I bemoaned the fact that British natural history seemed dull and staid when compared with exotic foreign lands. I no longer share this sentiment. Over the past three years, I have been doing research for a book on the cryptofauna of southwestern England, and my findings bear out Heuvelmans' maxim that there are lost worlds everywhere.

There is evidence that a wide range of native British species such as red squirrels, pine martens, polecats, wild cats and possibly even the magnificent white-tailed sea eagle were not, as is usually believed, wiped out in the region by the Victorian gamekeeper, but that relict populations survive. They coexist with hitherto overlooked feral populations of introduced pumas, lynxes, wolves and so on which stalk the high moorlands. If such a diversity of unsuspected fauna can exist in a heavily populated and traversed region, then what mysteries remain to be discovered within the depths of Brazil and Borneo?

> "It is now thought, for instance, that there are wider genetic gaps between left-handed and right-handed people than between members of different races."

Today, we face the greatest upheaval in the taxonomic zoology of our biosphere since the last Ice Age, and cryptozoological disciplines will certainly be needed in coming to terms with it. Firstly, as the average mean temperature of the world increases, either through pollution or natural mechanisms unknown to us, western Europe becomes habitable to species traditionally confined to warmer areas further south.

Secondly, over the last 30 years, the gun laws across Europe have been tightened up dramatically in response to terrorism and peasant farmers no longer have high-powered rifles to pick off rare animals. Thirdly, the physical barriers of the Iron Curtain have been removed, allowing the freer passage of animals moving west. Wolves have been seen in France, Switzerland and Austria for the first time in decades and there are also rumours that bears are making a comeback. The Channel Tunnel will also facilitate the movement of species from the mainland to the British Isles.

One of the great fallacies of cryptozoology is that it is concerned with relict populations of ancient species when it is the emergent species which are of far greater interest. The discovery of three apparently new cat species (the onza, the Kellas cat and the king cheetah) apparently emerging from known species throws interesting new light on the mechanics of feline genetics, especially as all three, though apparently unrelated, have emerged at approximately the same time and share a startling number of characteristics.

Taxonomy governed by purely Linnæan rules has been overtaken by recent advances in genetic fingerprinting, which suggest that differences between species may be far more subtle than we realised. It is now thought, for instance, that there are wider genetic gaps between left-handed and right-handed people than between members of different races. The omniverse is governed by a multitude of laws, only a fraction of which are known to us. Traditional zoology has had its day; it is time for a transformation analogous to the changes in mathematics wrought by chaos theory.

During my research, I repeatedly met scepticism and even hostility from established scientists whom I thought would be only too willing to help me. More disturbingly, I had similar reactions from what has become the hidebound and reactionary cryptozoological establishment. Cryptozoologists should lead the way with a new methodology for the new millennium.

FORUM is a column in which anyone with something to say about a particular field, theory or incident can share their thoughts with our readership. If you'd like to join in with an opinion on any area of Forteana, send it in to the editorial address. Ideal length: 500-1000 words. Please enclose a head and shoulders photo of yourself with all Forum submissions.

Alien Bastards!

Dennis Stacy charts new developments in the standard Abduction Scenario

For years, the UFO abduction phenomenon seemed fairly static. The Standard Abduction Scenario, first outlined in detail by American folklorist Eddie Bullard in his massive two-volume 1987 study *UFO Abductions: The Measure of a Mystery*, delineated eight discrete steps or stages of the experience. In order, these were capture, examination, conference, tour, otherworldly journey, theophany, return and aftermath.

Bullard based his analysis on a review of some 300 abduction cases then extant in the world literature. While the underlying structure wasn't absolutely rigid – some 'abductees' might not undergo all eight stages; in other cases the sequence wasn't exactly the same – it did seem to be there in general, just underneath the surface, in ways that would mitigate against random dreams, individual daytime fantasising and so on. In other words, it seemed to reflect a *physical* procedure – with a beginning, middle and end – in the same way that, say, a terrestrial appendectomy or other surgical process would. The minor details might vary from time to time, but the basic whole remained largely and essentially intact. [See the FT interview with Bullard, ***FT60:46-49***.]

But a funny thing happened on the way to the hospital. In the same year that Bullard published his monumental survey of the subject (under the auspices of the Fund for UFO Research), New York artist and author Budd Hopkins came out with his second commercially popular study of the abduction phenomenon, *Intruders: The Incredible Visitations at Copley Woods*. The first had been *Missing Time* (1981). Shifts subtle and not so subtle were suddenly introduced into the original 'staid' abduction scenario, so much so that I believe we can now begin to think in terms of a New Revised Abduction Scenario (NRAS). This feeling was reinforced recently by the appearance of Dr David Jacobs' *Secret Life: Firsthand Accounts of UFO Abductions* (1992). Jacobs, a professor of history at Temple University, Philadelphia, draws many, if not most, of his own abduction cases straight from Hopkins' own databank, primarily as personal referrals.

In a word, this major new wrinkle in the evolution of the Standard Abduction Scenario has to do with the abrupt appearance of *hybrid babies*, presumably the genetically engineered byproduct of close encounters between unwitting (and unwilling) humans and extraterrestrial beings. When Bullard did his research, such 'star children' simply weren't there. The closest hint that any extraterrestrial visitor might be up to terrestrial hanky-panky was a single 1957 case involving a Brazilian farmer, Antonio Villas Boas, who claimed he was frogmarched aboard a UFO late one night and forced to submit to sex with a fair, reddish-haired (both above and below) beauty from outer space. She reportedly pointed to her belly and then to the sky above to signify that the sex act had been successful. But beginning with *Intruders* and culminating in *Secret Life*, reports of alien bastards are now almost as commonplace as crop circles and shopping mall sightings of Elvis Presley.

> "...reports of alien bastards are now almost as commonplace as crop circles and shopping mall sightings of Elvis Presley."

In the interval, Bullard's otherworldly journey seems to have dropped off the abduction map altogether. Perhaps the aliens were simply cutting back on their travel expenses like everyone else, or perhaps Hopkins and Jacobs were somehow – consciously or otherwise – selecting their cases to fit the new scenario. Two other of Bullard's original stages also appear to be suffering from recession – or inflation. What was once a general medical examination, for instance, now involves sex-specific procedures. Men report having their sperm extracted, women their ova, both under externally constrained conditions equivalent to cosmic rape.

Reports of nasal and cranial 'implants' are also bruited about, along with cases of 'missing' fœtuses, none of which have currently been substantiated by objective medical evidence. In addition, the onboard tour of the UFO is now confined in the main to a visit to the ship's nursery or incubatorium, where female abductees in particular are frequently asked to hold and nurse their supposedly hybrid offspring. Hundreds of other wan, seemingly premature, babies may be glimpsed – or at least remembered – under such circumstances. For the most part, these 'memories' are obtained in the course of regressive hypnosis; that is, while the percipient is in an altered state of consciousness.

The abducting 'Greys' – so-called because of their skin colour – are routinely described as less than four feet tall, often much less. They appear to consist of little more than oversized heads and eyes, the latter commonly characterised as a deep pool of liquid black. Their other physical features seem indistinct at best; if they have any obvious external genitalia, for example, they are rarely if ever reported. Ditto for nipples, navels, ears, body hair, tattoos, or any other readily identifiable physical 'defects' which would lend them a significant semblance of individual personality. Noses and mouths are said to be vestigial. If they communicate at all, it is by telepathy, words heard in the head. Conspicuous by its absence is anything remotely resembling a sense of humour. Displays of curiosity are cursory, if that.

So, what *is* going on? I wish I knew. What I do doubt is that the abduction phenomenon, as such, is taking place in real space and time. Some abductionists have recently suggested – based on a poll of 6,000 adults conducted by the prestigious Roper Organization – that as many as four million people in the US alone may have had the abduction experience. For some reason, abductions – like Madonna and Big Macs – remain a peculiarly American export. Still, when such numbers are extrapolated worldwide, and when we take into consideration the fact that many abductees report experiences dating back to early childhood, we are forced to consider two choices: either humanity is the collective victim of several hundred *million* forced abductions by humanoid beings from another planet in just the last 30 years or so; or else the fault, and origin, dear Brutus, lies not among the stars, but within ourselves.

More thoughts about the latter possibility next time. Assuming, of course, that you haven't been abducted in the meantime.

Atheistic Religions

Robert Anton Wilson exposes the dogmatic circular reasoning of the self-styled 'skeptics'

A year ago, I met three members of the Committee for Scientific Investigation for Claims of the Paranormal at a UFO convention. They all confronted me with undisguised hostility.

Of course, as a professional satirist, I have gotten accustomed to encountering displeasure from people with emotionally deep opinions, but the CSICOPeans really shocked me. Other dogmatic people these days at least put up a 'front' of courtesy and adult behaviour. The CSICOP faction had no 'front' at all. To say it in a positive rather than a negative way, they showed a refreshing lack of adult hypocrisy, and seemed "as open and honest as children at play".

It took me a while to realise that the attitude I had encountered deserves the title of 'devout religiosity' as much as anything one reads about in histories of the Dark Ages. CSICOP's use of the word 'scientific' in their organisational title had confused me. Actually CSICOP *hasn't even attempted scientific investigation since 1982*, after their first effort in that direction ended in fiasco. (Their principal investigator, Dr Dennis Rawlins, saying they had altered his data, cried 'Foul!' and resigned.)

CSICOP keeps the word 'science' for the sake of swank, like the Creation Scientists and Christian Scientists. It makes them seem 'modern'. (For similar reasons, Marx offered his Millennialist Utopia as a kind of 'science'.)

Regarding some atheistic movements as religions may perplex those who think religiosity requires a God or Goddess of some sort. However, several writers - including Carl Jung, Arnold Toynbee and Eric Hoffer – suggest that we should consider communism and fascism as 'atheistic religions' or 'religions without god'.

In 1960 I met Ayn Rand, the creator of Objectivism, another religion without God, which claimed to have the final solution to *all* problems in epistemology, ontology, economics and politics. If anybody disagreed with Objectivist dogma, Rand said (in several books and in my meeting with her) that they just hadn't learned to reason correctly: all *objective people* did agree with Objectivism. Since in her system 'objective people' meant those who agreed with Objectivism, this logic remained as impenetrable as any closed circle.

> "God has nothing to do with religiosity. One becomes part of a religion by group-sharing of certain enthusiastic opinions."

'God', you see, has nothing to do with religiosity. One becomes part of a religion by group-sharing of certain enthusiastic opinions (eg. Christian and Islamic fundamentalism, fascism, communism, Objectivism, the CSICOP catechism). The idea of 'God' may attach to these group-bonds, or may remain totally absent. 'Religion' essentially means the group-bonding itself, as the etymology should have told us. (*Religare*, to bind together; cf. *fascis*, to bind rods and sticks in a bundle, origin of 'fascism'.)

I think this explains why CSICOP has naively blundered into a succession of libel suits. The two latest suits, by Uri Geller and Dr Elton Byrd, seem likely to bankrupt CSICOP, some say. (A CSICOP spokesman had accused Geller of driving a man to suicide, and it appears that the man died of diabetes; and the same spokesman accused Dr Byrd of serving time for child molestation, and Byrd never served time for that or any crime.)

CSICOPeans commit libels and slanders with a wayward and childish innocence, because they genuinely believe that anyone who disagrees with their Final Answers must belong to the criminal class. Similarly, in the Dr Rawlins case, they simply changed his data with no bad conscience at all, because they had a Higher Morality. Historians calls this 'pious fraud' when theists do it; I think it remains equally pious when done by atheists.

Dr Marcello Truzzi resigned from CSICOP because they would not print dissident views in their journal, *Skeptical Enquirer*. But no religious journal prints Satan's side of an argument, does it? Well, anyone who dissents from CSICOP dogma appears to them as Satanic.

Once one recognises fascism, communism, Objectivism and the CSICOP belief system as modern religions, none of the behaviour of these groups appears surprising anymore. Religious people simply exist in a different symbolic universe from lawyers, philosophers or scientists, who all recognise that we can never find any final 'truth' – that all seeming truth can still provoke honest debate and may still need revision.

The religious have, or think they have, Eternal Truths that can never change – and CSICOP, like Scientology, remains firmly entrenched in the camp of the True Believers even when invoking the name of science.

New Age Sourcebook

Your Guide to Enlightenment

1993 edition 536 pages
£20 (US$28.95) inc p&p

- *What organizations specialize in Astrology?*
- *Where can I find a museum dedicated to UFO's?*
- *Who are the leading experts in the field of hypnotism?*
- *What centers promote the practice of holistic health?*
- *Which magazines offer information for Psychics?*
- *What stores sell the best crystals?*
- *Which schools teach meditation?*
- *Where can I purchase a tape on dreams?*

Now you can get answers to all these questions and thousands more just by turning the pages of,

Parapsychology New Age And The Occult - A Source Encyclopedia

It contains more than 10,000 hard-to-find sources and covers 62 topics from Astrology to Yoga. It's also loaded with information on Holistic Health. Search out your sources by category (such as schools, products, centers, music, etc.) or in the easy-to-use topic index. Find even more sources in the extensive bibliography or periodical sections and in the Publishers Index. Have a New Age product or service to sell? Market it using this remarkable New Age sourcebook.

Its Your Complete Guide to the New Age

Order It Today From: Fortean Times, Dept RP1•The Boathouse• Crabtree Lane• Fulham•London SW6 6LU• (cheques payable to "Reference Press")

SMART DRUGS

SAFE & LEGAL MEDICINES FROM THE WORLDS LEADING PHARMACEUTICAL COMPANIES THAT CAN -

INCREASE INTELLIGENCE
IMPROVE MEMORY & RECALL
ENHANCE CONCENTRATION

WIDELY USED IN USA & EUROPE
FOR INFORMATION TELEPHONE
071 483 3963 24 HRS

Mc.BIG JAYS

PROUDLY PRESENTS THE
"GRIM REEFER"
IMPRESS YOUR FRIENDS AND
AARDVARK WITH YOUR
8"s YES 8"s OF
ROLLING MACHINE PERFECTION
YOU'LL NEVER SKIN UP BY
HAND AGAIN! NO BULLSHIT!!
JUST SEND £3.50 & 75P P&P
CHEQUES & POSTAL ORDERS ONLY
TO Mc BIG JAYS. P.O. BOX 93
WIDNES, CHESHIRE, ENGLAND.
ALLOWING 32 DAYS FOR DELIVERY

COUNTER PRODUCTIONS

PO Box 556 London SE5 0RL

Astounding publications
including

John Keel, *Mothman Prophecies*, £12.50. The classic account of unpleasant goings-on in Point Pleasant, West Virginia: a fortean masterpiece.
Simon McKeown (ed), *Monstrous Births*, £5.00. The indispensable primer of teratology, with classic examples, 1562-1652.
Salvador Freixedo, *Visionaries, Mystics & Contactees*, £8.50. Superb study of the paranormal and ufology, introduced by John Keel.
Jim Keith (ed), *The Gemstone File*, £11.50. The conspiracy theorist's bedside book, with commentaries by RA Wilson, Kerry Thornley, Ben Price, Jonathan Vankin and others.
All prices include postage and packing. Payment in sterling only.

Send sae/irc for extensive descriptive mail-order catalogue of extraordinary, unusual and hard-to-find publications from the marginals milieu and beyond.

REVIEWS

THE SIGN AND THE SEAL

A QUEST FOR THE LOST ARK OF THE COVENANT by Graham Hancock.

Heinemann, London. 1992, hb £16.99, pp588, illus, notes, refs, index.

Warning! I am about to reveal a great and sacred mystery. Those who don't want the surprise spoilt should cover the next paragraph.

The lost Ark of the Covenant currently resides in the Holy of Holies of the Church of St Mary of Zion, in the town of Axum in Tigrayan-occupied Ethiopia. It is guarded by a single monk, though there are a few armed Tigrayan rebels in the town itself. A small assault team, a couple of helicopters, some smoke bombs and it's yours.

That's right! The Big Box of Goodies made by Belazeel for Moses' two tablets – which brought the house down at Jericho and smote the Philistines without the Israelites lifting a finger – is sitting quietly in a small town in war-torn Africa. This is Hancock's thesis, though it must be said that he didn't actually *see* the Ark itself – that is a privilege reserved for the reluctant monk guarding it with his life.

The Sign and the Seal, which is structured as a quest for the Ark, starts badly with a rounding-up of suspects familiar to anyone who has skimmed the *Holy Blood, Holy Grail* genre: Chartres cathedral, the Knights Templar, and Wolfram von Eschenbach's *Parsifal*. The *Kebra Nagast* and a number of other ancient texts are given the once-over for clues, and Hancock finds it easy to unearth hidden agendas in his source material. The Scottish adventurer James Bruce – he authored the classic *Travels to Discover the Source of the Nile in the Years 1768-1773* – comes across as scheming and duplicitous in his desire to avoid telling the truth about the secrets of North Africa. And, of course, he was a Mason, which ties him in neatly with the Knights Templar.

Chartres cathedral, on the other hand, is a positive mine of coincidence and meaning; the notion of secret knowledge being one of the author's powerful obsessions. Hancock happens to go there on holiday and engages in a thorough analysis of the Old Testament secrets encrypted into the sculptures and official guidebook. They lead him to the saga of Parsifal, and one gigantic leap follows another until Hancock has reconstructed the Greatest Secret of All Time.

Once his obsessions have been taken aboard, the book speeds up as Hancock jets around Europe and the Middle East in his quest to prove that God's Box was carted off to Ethiopia by a group of Jewish priests who fled the bad King Manasseh during the latter part of the seventh century BC.

Though the author's style is that of an interested amateur, he has astonishing access to the major academics in the relevant disciplines and an equal willingness to rubbish any orthodoxy he happens to disagree with. Following Hancock's own line of enquiry, however, requires the reader to make regular leaps of faith.

I remain unconvinced that the Knights Templar were necessarily the white strangers wandering around Ethiopia in the late 12th century, though Hancock sees their 'Croix Pattes' everywhere. One has to wonder how, if the Ark was so important to the relationship between God and his Old Testament Israelites, Ethopia's Nestorian Christian upstarts were able to swipe it. The argument of the *Kebra Nagast*, a 13th century Ethiopian text, that "the Kingdom of the Jews shall be made an end of and the Kingdom of Christ shall be constituted" really doesn't wash. The Ark had spent much of the previous two millennia effortlessly zapping anyone who tried to snaffle it.

The Sign and the Seal has clearly not been written for religious reasons; Hancock supports the theory that although miracles can be associated with the Ark, they were worked by the ancient hi-tech used in its construction. This is the launch-pad for a voyage into the mysteries of the ancients – particularly the Egyptians – whose stock of secret knowledge (see von Däniken) was passed to a select bunch of Pharaoh's closest advisors. They included Moses, who, after the bullrushes and Pharaoh's daughter incidents, went on to acquire the technical wizardry need to build the 'Ark as Gizmo'.

The book's chief weakness is that Hancock sets out determined to prove his thesis. To make matters worse, he depends on so many "accidental strokes of luck" that one is tempted to ask whether he himself is not of the Masonic persuasion. With disbelief firmly suspended, and critical safety-valve tightly screwed down, *The Sign and the Seal* is a thoroughly engaging read, written in an easy-to-follow, breathless style by someone who is absorbed by his task. Highly recommended for conspiracy fans; unsuitable for historians and archæologists.

Richard Furlong

TIBETAN MEDICAL PAINTINGS

edited by Yuri Parfionovitch, Gyurme Dorje and Fernand Meyer.

Serinda (10 Parkfields, London SW15 6NH); & Abrams, New York. Two vols, hb silkbound, slipcased £130 / $195. Vol 1 has 76 colour plates, vol 2 has 77 b&w plates, notes, bib, index.

The drawing open of the Iron Curtain has revealed vast eastern panoramas. Amongst the many religious artifacts stored in the 'Museum of Atheism' in Ulan-Ude, near Lake Baikal in Buryiat, was discovered a magnificent collection of 76 paintings illustrating the *Blue Beryl*, a famous 17th century Tibetan treatise on medicine. The *Blue Beryl* (or *Vaidurya Nyonpo*) was compiled by Desi Sangye Gyamtso (1653-1705), regent to the fifth Dalai Lama, during whose reign both the

Potala and the adjacent medical college of Chakpori were constructed. The Buryiat paintings, produced around 1920, are exact replicas of the original 17th century illustrations commissioned by Sangye Gyamtso. Their prime purpose was to visually impress the entire medical teachings into the memories of generations of Tibetan doctors.

Many of the vivid paintings can be read in cartoon-like strips, from top to bottom, with more than 10,000 individual illustrations conveying the whole spectrum of Tibetan medicine. The subjects illustrated include many intricate anatomical charts showing the structures of the skeleton, muscles, vital organs, blood system, nerves, and the systems of psychic nerve channels and points used in acupuncture, moxibustion, cauterization and blood-letting. There are chapters on embryology; sexuality; diet and conduct; omens and dream interpretation; demon possession; surgical instruments; diagnosis by pulse, tongue and urine analysis.

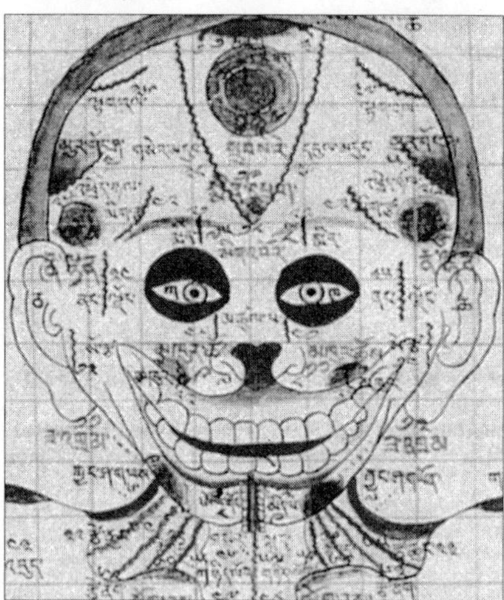

The *materia medica* is extremely fascinating, with hundreds of botanical, mineral and animal extracts, meticulously painted and identified. Who would conceive that the leather sole, heel and instep of an old shoe could have different medical properties? Or that a widow's underpants guard against epilepsy? Or that earth from a mousehole that faces east can be applied as a compress for cold wind disorders? The three sisters of *Macbeth*'s blasted heath would surely have given an arm and a leg for this knowledge.

Volume One comprises the colour plates with facing summary chapters, translated from the *Blue Beryl*. Volume Two consists of numbered monochrome plates, with individual captions translated on the facing page. The work is simply magnificent and unique, exquisitely produced and certainly one of the most important publications of this century. There are no fences bounding this field of alternative medicine, because it represents a synthesis of Ayurvedic, Central Asian, Chinese and indigenous Tibetan medicine – the wisdom of more than two millennia distilled into beautiful holistic imagery, which fills the viewer with awe, wonder and humility.

Robert Beer

FINDERS KEEPERS by Rosamund Wolff Purcell and Stephen Jay Gould.

Peter the Great – the larger than life (6ft 7ins and with appetites to match) czar of Russia – was catholic in his kleptomania. As well as locks of his own hair and keepsakes from his interest in dentistry (including a tooth from an unfortunate "fast-walking messenger"), he bought complete collections from all over Europe, among them Frederick Ruysch's stock of around 2,000 anatomical preparations. A child's severed arm rises gracefully from a lace sleeve, gently holding an eye socket. A fœtal skeleton holding a string of pearls asks: "Why should I long for the things of the world?" Skulls bemoan their fate by weeping into handkerchiefs made of brain meninges.

The eight collectors featured in this book seem, in many ways, as strange as their collections. Van Heurn went for symmetry; perfectly arranged rows of flattened moles with pale little paws; or a tableau of domestic dogs with identikit snarls. With perfect economy, a flat rat pokes out of a recycled envelope, its Latin name replacing the original recipient's. Eugen Dubois collected casts of brains – bats, tigers, squirrels, monkeys – all neatly labelled and prettily boxed. Walter Rothschild found banking distasteful and instead drove his zebras down Piccadilly and collected Birds of Paradise (nearly all the known species and 17 that he described for the first time).

Purcell's photographs are haunting; all taken in natural light and eschewing all trickery. Gould's writing illuminates them. It is beautifully produced and well-edited, though there is no index. *Hutchinson Radius (Random Century), London. 1992, hb £19.99, pp158.*

Val Stevenson

UFO ENCOUNTERS by Jerome Clark.

It would be too easy to dismiss this richly-illustrated and glossily-presented large-format book as yet another of those high-volume compilation works that pre-digest a subject for the thousands of subscribers who are more interested in a good-looking row of book spines. The large type and larger leading suggests that a slim work was padded out, and that no amount of nicely printed colour illustrations can disguise the fact that this is a comparatively thin book.

Don't let that deter you. *UFO Encounters* is, in fact, a very concise overview of the UFO phenomenon in all its facets, written by a skilled and knowledgable historian of the subject (Clark), aided by Marcello Truzzi, an equally respected scholar of the anomalous. The subject is divided into bite-sized chunks dealing with key people, places, incidents, objects and ideas. It is ideal for young people or a first encounter with a complex subject, and does not baffle the newcomer with too many details, references or footnotes. A serious ufologist might consider this shallow and worthless, but it doesn't pretend to be anything other than a well-presented, well-written introduction. That is something we could do with more of – and it is good to see that Jerome Clark can find time away from his absorbing encyclopædic work to write for the 'common man'. *Publications International, 7373 N. Cicero Ave, Lincolnwood, IL 60646, USA. 1992, hb price unknown, pp128, illus, index.*

Bob Rickard

MILLENNIUM PROPHECIES by A.T. Mann.

Dramatic events, such as the Second Coming and the End of the World, have been forecast many times, but don't appear to have happened yet. As the year 2000 looms, both modern prophets and those of earlier times seem to be in agreement about the momentous changes that will mark this period. I remain unconvinced because I can't see why the date should be significant, as the chronology is manmade and quite arbitrary.

This book covers a wide range of prophets (eg. Nostradamus, Cayce, the Great Pyramid, Mother Shipton, etc) and prophecies (eg. Age of Aquarius, cataclysms, End of World, Antichrist, etc), and will be of interest to everyone who wants to know what is supposed to happen. A good read for those of an apprehensive disposition – and now that millennarianism figures so strongly in the news, a relevant one. *Element Books, Shaftesbury & Rockport, MA, USA. 1992, pb £5.99, pp143, notes, bib, index, illus.*

Janet Bord

CASPAR HAUSER by Jakob Wassermann.

The true story of this mysterious youth who appeared in Nuremberg in 1828 knowing only his name and apparently possessing supernatural powers has inspired many artists, including Verlaine, Rilke and Werner Herzog. Wassermann was one of the world's most popular novelists of the 1920s and 30s. His book about Hauser is a luxuriant allegory of man's inhumanity to man, a Gothic study of crime and innocence betrayed. *Penguin, London. 1992, pb £6.99, pp407.*

Paul Sieveking

THE GEMSTONE FILE edited by Jim Keith.

This is a symposium on that much-copied and circulated paranoid samizdat of 1975 that suggested the late Greek shipping magnate, Aristotle Onassis, was one of the chief figures in the secret government of the USA, having started out as an opium smuggler in the 1930s and subsequently made deals with the Rockefellers and Roosevelts. He kidnapped Howard Hughes in 1957 and arranged the assassination of Kennedy in 1963. The 'Skeleton Key to the Gemstone File', reproduced here, is a summary by Stephanie Caruana of an alleged 1,000-page dossier by Bruce Roberts, a manufacturer of artificial gemstones who died in 1976. The 'Key' has a large cast, including most of the Watergate gang, assorted mafiosi, and features the 'sodium morphate', apple-pie-smelling, poisoning technique, supposedly favoured by the Mob.

A second-generation Xerox of the Key was initially shown to me in Wales by a worried George Andrews, and I passed it to Heathcote Williams for publication in an English underground magazine called *The Fanatic* (1977). Jim Keith's book has interesting background narratives from Stephanie Caruana and Mae Brussell, the west coast queen of conspiracy theorists. There are also musings and analyses from a number of people including Robert Anton Wilson and Jonathan Vankin. A stimulating read, isolating the obviously daft from the feasible. Overall, a nice balance between crackpottery and common sense. *IllumiNet Press, PO Box 746, Avondales Estates, GA 30002 USA. 1992, pb $14.95, pp222.*

Paul Sieveking

THE ENCHANTMENT OF THE TROSSACHS by Louis Stott.

1992 marked the 300th anniversary of the Reverend Robert Kirk's famous disappearance, allegedly into fairyland. To commemorate this event, Louis Stott has written and published a useful booklet containing some fairy traditions from the surrounding region, the Trossachs. Apart from being a very beautiful part of Scotland, this area is the location of Kirk's fateful encounter with the Little People which took place on a hill near his home at Aberfoyle [see **FT61:29**]. Stott points out the places in Kirk's story which can still be seen; and, delving deeper into Kirk's life and death, lists other local fairylore and an account of Kirk's literary influence.

It's a nicely produced publication, illustrated with some old photographs, and well worth having in one's collection of fairy books. It might even inspire you to visit Doon Hill and walk in Kirk's footsteps. *Creag Darach Publications, Milton-of-Aberfoyle, Stirling FK8 3TD, Scotland. 1992, pb £2.40 (payable to Louis Stott), pp32, illus.*

Janet Bord

THE COLUMBUS MYTH by Ian Wilson.

An excellent summary of recent research on the murky background to Columbus' voyage of "discovery", and the compiling of early information about the New World. Wilson quickly disposes of the idea of Columbus being the 'first' to reach America, and deals succinctly with the well-proven Norse settlement in Newfoundland. His main interest is in the possibility of Bristol seamen finding and fishing the rich cod grounds of Newfoundland in the 1480s.

The evidence is circumstantial but cogent; there's also much fascinating material on the competition between Columbus and Cabot to be the first to set foot on the American mainland. It is well argued and thoroughly researched; my only quibble is that, although well annotated, there is nothing in the body of the text to locate the notes. I found this infuriating – but the book is highly recommended nevertheless. *Simon & Schuster, London. 1992, pb £8.99, pp256, illus, chronology, refs, bib, index.*

Steve Moore

EXHIBITION:
The Surrealchemist of Light

Charles Chaplin called Georges Méliès "the alchemist of light"; and the Paris Surrealists acknowledged him as a "wizard of dreams". Currently, London's Museum of the Moving Image is presenting a celebratory exhibition and the NFT is screening a 'major season' of his marvellous films.

Towards the end of the 18th century, a Belgian showman, called Robertson, manipulated *lanterna* 'phantasmgorias'; and Katterfelto, with his 'solar microscope' and 'caprimantic art', projected scary images of gigantic insects. These 'scientific' sorcerers may have inspired M.R. James when he described Karswell's magic lantern show in *Casting the Runes:*

"And then, if you please, he switched on another slide, which showed a great mass of snakes, centipedes, and disgusting creatures with wings, and somehow or other he made it seem as if they were climbing out of the picture and getting in amongst the audience."

Méliès (1861-1938) was a stage magician who, in 1888, took over the celebrated *Théatre Robert Hardin*, in Paris. Like other illusionists of the period, he was fascinated by an invention of the Lumière brothers, the Cinematograph. In 1895, Méliès purchased his first cine-camera/projector (not from the Lumières) and soon surreal 'objective chance' played its preordained role in the history of the cinema. One day, Méliès was filming the passing traffic in a Paris street, when his camera jammed. It only took a couple of seconds to fix the fault, then our hero continued to shoot the scene. When the resulting film was projected, Méliès was surprised and delighted to see an omnibus magically transform into a hearse.

The Parisian prestidigitator quickly became the world's first film director, and built the world's first (glass-walled, glass-roofed) film studio. Georges Méliès invented a new language of 'special effects' and – between 1896 and 1913 – produced an amazing series of magical movies featuring Faust, Gulliver, Cagliostro, Mesmer, Cinderella, Bluebeard, pantomime demons and dancing skeletons. His theatrical painted (monochrome) sets had a Rousseau-like quality, against which buxom chorus girls cavorted with acrobatic goblins.

He shot a Jules Verne rocket, full of top-hatted astronauts, into the eye of the man-in-the-moon (in *Voyage dans la Lune*, 1909). He inflated and exploded his own head. He made a hydra writhe. He *conjured* in a bizarre picturesque-postcard style. Forteans should take note of such thaumatatropic marvels, or their umbrellas will mushroom and their hats will be hare-filled.

Echoes of Méliès can be seen in the work of several Surrealist artists such as Magritte, Trouille, Ernst, Delvaux and others. He certainly had an influence upon me, as a fledgling film-maker, magician and painter. At the age of 14, I even made a crude 16mm movie about a trip to the moon, which I exhibited as part of my (equally crude) magic show, advertised with (let's call them crude) pictorial posters. Méliès's art was, and still is, invocatory.

Georges Méliès was a wizard. His 'Abominable Snowman' devoured a person and winked at King Kong, while leggy lasses capered with Méliès-as-Mephisto. Without doubt, he had a surreal sympathy for the devil, and enjoyed playing the part. No harm was ever meant; he was concerned only with entertainment, fantasy and fun. George (another George) Lucas is, today, involved with the same old stuff: 'Industrial Light and Magic'.

Tony 'Doc' Shiels

Méliès: Father of Film Fantasy – special exhibition at the Museum of the Moving Image (MOMI), South Bank, London SE1 8XT (Tel: 071 928 3232); open daily 10am-6pm – until 12 June 1993. An accompanying programme of Méliès's films will be shown at the National Film Theatre throughout April and May. Special all-in tickets available £10.

VAMPYRES
by Christopher Frayling.

Vampires, as we all know, keep on coming back from the dead, and the merest glance at the media shows that the graves are opening once again. The lore of the vampire, too, is a curious beast, compounded of 'fact' and 'fantasy' which often cannot, or should not, be disentangled. It may seem that the development is quite straightforward: from ancient myths to the reported-as-fact vampire panics of eastern Europe in the 18th century, to the pure fiction of the literary vampire and its modern media offshoots. But the reported-as-fact tales still remain, as in the notorious case of the 'Highgate vampire' of the early 1970s. And these tales, of course, have to be seen and evaluated in their context... a context largely moulded by the fictions of the last two centuries, and by *Dracula* in particular.

Christopher Frayling's fat book concentrates mainly on the literature of the 19th century, and thus provides valuable background material to vampire studies in all their forms. A lengthy introduction traces the developments in the genre – from the panics to Dracula – and defines the major elements (the Byronic lord, the femme fatale, the folklore material, etc). Even so, at 85 pages, it still seems rather compressed – especially when discussing the famous Byron/Shelley/Godwin/Polidori 'ghost story' session, where Frayling assumes too much prior knowledge on the reader's part.

The anthology section naturally includes such classics as Polidori's *The Vampyre*, and the obligatory extracts from *Varney the Vampyre* and *Dracula*, but there are a number of rarely-seen tales besides. Perhaps the most interesting are the extracts from Stoker's notes and researches for *Dracula* and, as usual, the extracts from Calmet's *Treatise on the Vampires of Hungary, etc.* The book concludes with extracts from psychiatric works on *hæmosexuality*, which, being no fan of Freud, I found tedious. Still, they are undoubtedly part of the larger picture and so not to be ignored. All in all, *Vampyres* is a worthy addition to the literature of blood-sucking... Slurp it while you can. *Faber & Faber, London. 1992, pb £9.99, pp429, illus, bib.*

Steve Moore

MAG WATCH

THE CEREALOGIST

Most periodicals dealing with crop circles are becoming increasingly partisan and directionless; so it is a pleasure to see the heroically independent *Cerealogist* (under John Michell's educated editorship) as strong and informative as ever. Issue 8 (Winter 1993) contains much excellent material, including coverage of 1992 circles abroad as well as southern England; George Wakefield blasting the hoaxers and tricksters; Christine Rhone on how Wakefield was ousted as editor of *The Circular*; Andy Collins interpreting circles as manifestations of Reichian 'orgone'; and assessment of the famous circle-making competition. *TC: SKS, 20 Paul St, Frome, Somerset BA11 1DX, UK.*

THE LEY HUNTER

Under the aegis of TLH editor Paul Devereux, the followers of the 'old straight track' are in the throes of a philosophical and spiritual convulsion, throwing off the labcoat of technology-based notions of energies and dowsing and donning shamanic horns and hides, the better to interpret leys as 'spirit paths' etc. Issue 118 (Winter 1993) contains a richly varied symposium of articles on the new approach. *TLH: Box 92, Penzance, Cornwall TR18 2XL, UK.*

SKEPTICAL INQUIRER

Despite their proclaimed intention of disabusing us of all our misconceptions, most of the contents of this quarterly journal of the CSICOPs is well-written and well worth the consideration. Among subjects dealt with in the Winter 1993 issue are... the anthropologist Margaret Mead's invention of myths about Samoan culture; the police use of psychics; a recent survey of Americans showing increasing belief in UFOs, supernatural, etc; and ongoing debates about miracles, abductions and Creationist 'facts'. *SK: PO Box 703, Buffalo, NY 14226-0703, USA.*

INFO JOURNAL

The journal of the International Fortean Organization (founded 1965) is still publishing good Fortean material. Issue 67 (Oct 1992) reexamines Fort's case of meteoric stones in India; the relevance of Forteana to science; an alignment of churches in Germany. *INFO: PO Box 367, Arlington, VA 22210-0367, USA.*

ARTIFEX

The Winter 1993 issue of this journal of the Archaeus Project – researching consciousness and self-regulation – features articles by Martin Kottmeyer and Richard Leigh exploring the undying belief in a Flat Earth, as it is today and as it was for Columbus and Magellan. *AP: 2402 University Ave, St Paul, MN 55114, USA.*

NEXUS

This lively information-exchange-based magazine from Australia covers New Age, paranormal, ufology, conspiracy and Fortean related topics. The Feb-Mar 1993 issue examines microwave effects on health; the Mexican UFO waves of 1991-92; and the relationship between energy sources and political power. *Nexus: PO Box 30, Mapleton, Queensland 4560, Australia.*

INT. UFO REPORTER

The Jan-Feb 1993 issue of this journal of the J. Allen Hynek Centre for UFO Studies has an interesting memoir of astronomer Hynek's early encounters with the USAF and the UFO problem; more disputes over the Corona and San Agustin 'UFO crashes'; Budd Hopkins reproaches Carl Sagan over SETI. *CUFOS: 2457 West Peterson, Chicago, IL 60659, USA.*

DEAR FT...

VEGETABLE LAMBS AND THE DRUNKARD'S FATE

■ Besides the Vegetable Lamb in the Tradescant collection [**FT66:34**], there are other examples in the British Museum of Natural History and the College of Surgeons (or there were). However, these toys made in South China (where they are called *Kew-tsie*) provide only a partial explanation of the legend.

In all the early accounts, the Vegetable Lamb is located around the Caspian Sea – the region from which Astrakhan fur, made from the pelts of unborn lambs, comes. In his classic study of the matter in 1877, Henry Lee established that the root origin of the Vegetable Lamb was the Cotton Plant, which does indeed produce 'wool' from a plant. There is a full account of the legend, quoting all the early reports and later explanations, in my book *The Magic Zoo* (London, 1979).

A hitherto overlooked account of spontaneous human combustion is to be found in Jules Verne's novel *Captain at Fifteen (Un Capitaine de Quinze Ans)* (Paris: Hetzel, 1878, part II, ch.11), which is set in Angola in the early part of 1873. The alcoholic king of Kazonnde [Kasange] becomes the victim of his craving for white traders' spirits when a basin of spiced punch is brewed up one night.

Moini Loungga came forward. He seized the ladle from the hands of the trader, plunged it into the basin, then withdrawing it filled with flaming punch, put it to his lips.

What a cry came from the king of Kazonnde!

A spontaneous combustion had resulted. The king flamed up like a demijohn of paraffin. The fire developed little heat, but devoured him nevertheless.

At this sight, the natives' dance came to a sudden halt.

A minister of Moini Loungga threw himself upon his ruler to put him out; but, no less alcoholised than his master, he in turn burst into flames.

At this rate the entire court of Moini Loungga was in danger of being burnt alive!

Alvez and Negoro made no attempt to help the king. The terrified women took flight. As for Coimbra, he took to his heels, well knowing his own inflammable nature.

Striking a light in darkest Africa

The king and his minister, who had fallen to the ground, writhed in terrible agonies.

In bodies so completely alcoholised, the combustion produced a light bluish flame that water could not put out. Even if extinguished on the surface, it would continue to burn internally. When the alcohol had penetrated through all the tissues, there is no way of stopping the combustion.

Moments later the king and his minister were dead, but their bodies continued to burn. Soon, in the spot where they had fallen, there was nothing to be seen but some fragile cinders, one or two fragments of vertebræ fingers and nails which in cases of spontaneous combustion, the fire does not consume, but which it covers with a stinking, revolting soot.

It was all that remained of the king of Kazonnde and his minister.

[pp412-414, Livre de Poche ed.]

This grim scene of the king going up in flames was illustrated by Henri Meyer and engraved on wood by Charles Barbant, a vignette worth adding to the slim corpus of SHC pictures (**see illustration**).

Verne was a great admirer of Dickens and would have known of the celebrated scene in *Bleak House*. Here he accepts the theory that alcoholism plays a significant part in SHC. But he was also an avid reader of science magazines, geographical journals and other documentary sources. It would be interesting to know if this fictional incident is based on the death of an actual Angolan chief in the 1870s, rather than on an adaptation of a contemporary account in a French magazine of the phenomenon in a European setting.

Peter Costello
Dublin

DREAM TICKET

■ A workmate of mine came in one morning and said that he had a dream the previous night that he was having a drink in a pub at a place called Stoke Bardolf, near Nottingham, when a friend came up and said that he had won on the horses and handed over £35. He looked in the paper for that day's racing and found that a horse was running at Goodwood at 2:30 called Bardolf. So one or two of us, me included, backed it on a straight win and it came in at 7 to 1. Total winnings came to £35. Coincidence?

D. Johnson
Sherwood, Nottingham

GRIMSBY PORTENTS

■ The unexplained object described as a 'cup-like pram' witnessed by Art Wetherell in Grimsby in 1975 [**FT63:64**] bears a marked similarity to descriptions of an apparition witnessed on at least three occasions by Grimsby fishermen in the Humber estuary off Spurn Point in 1952/53. See the booklet *Humber Lights: Tall Tales of the Grimsby Trawlermen* by G. Farrell (Dock Tower Press 1991). It's an amusing notion that, with the decline of the Humberside fishing industry in the 1970s, this unidentified floating object came inland to weave its strange enchantment among the Grimbarians.

Ainslie Parker
Grimsby

WEIRD

■ Ian Simmons's review of *The Circlemakers* [**FT66:61**] incorrectly quoted Hunter S. Thompson. The correct version is: "When the going gets weird, the weird turn pro". Obviously not a trifling matter.

Steven Preston
Ealing, London

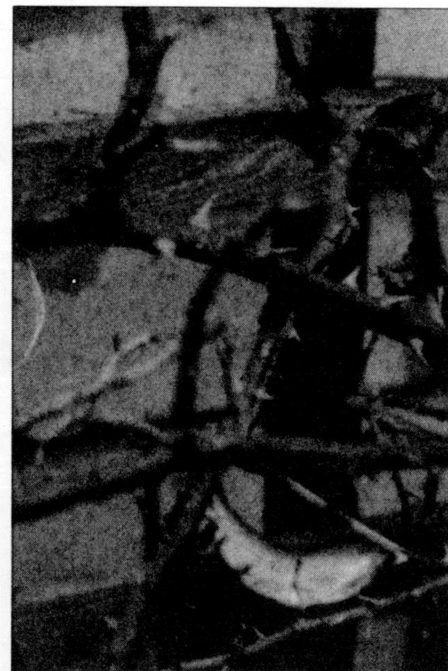

SHEERWATER FISH FALL

■ On the morning of Friday 15 January at around 7:30am I walked to the bottom of my garden in St Michael's Road, Sheerwater, and saw a fish on the path. There were others on the lawn, in the rose bush and on the shed roof, all within a 15ft radius – see photos. I counted 12 in all, ranging from four to five inches and looking like sprats. I couldn't see any in adjacent gardens.

The previous night had been very windy and stormy, with winds from the south-west. I contacted the *Woking Review* who carried a short report on 23 January. Later I heard that John Field, who lives next door but one, had found 11 fish within a small area in his garden. He is a keen fisherman and also thought they looked like sprats, which are of course seawater fish. The sea is almost 40 miles away, and the Thames over six miles. The fish smelled, so they could have been out of the water a long time.

Derek Gosling
Sheerwater, Surrey

A MATTER OF METEORS

■ I feel I should correct your note on the 'meteor shower' over the eastern United States on 9 October 1992 [*FT67:49*]. Press reports of this event were inaccurate. The Draconid shower, also sometimes referred to as the Giacobinids after its parent comet P/Giacobini-Zinner, is not an annual event. Indeed, meteors from the shower have so far only been definitely detected in some of the years when the comet returns to the solar vicinity (roughly every six years).

The last detected shower was in 1986, and although the comet returned to perihelion in 1992, I have heard of no reports of any unusual meteor activity produced as a result. This is much as expected since the material which seems to produce the shower is concentrated very close to the comet itself. We hope for better things at the 1998 return. Furthermore, there is still no recorded meteorite fall associated with a meteor shower, despite reasonably systematic observations for about 150 years. It would be most interesting if this situation were to change.

As for the actual fall in question, which took place at around 23:50 UTC, the meteorite track started over West Virginia and ended over the Pennsylvania/New York border. This track, SSW to NNE, is incompatible with a Draconid origin, since any genuine shower meteor would be moving north to south. The visible flight lasted for about 30 seconds. The meteorite was later classified as an L6 chondrite weighing 13kg, and was sold some weeks later for a reported $69,000.

At least 24 video recordings were made of the brilliant meteor, which was probably in excess of magnitude -14 (as bright as full moon). These show that very heavy fragmentation occurred towards the end of the visible flight – at least 20 fragments can be made out on the better recordings. Other possible meteorite falls cannot therefore be ruled out, although it is unlikely that they will be found since chondrites look much like terrestrial rocks.

I also noted your short note on Comet P/Swift-Tuttle [*FT66:7*], which reported another misleading media event. This comet is the apparent parent of the major northern hemisphere meteor shower the Perseids, visible from the end of July to mid-August every year. In 1991 and 1992, short-lived bursts much brighter than usual were detected. We now think that these were precursors of the approaching comet, and we are hopeful that another outburst will occur this August – specifically on the night of 11/12 August between 23-02 hours UTC, which will mean European observers should catch the best from the shower, with luck and clear skies.

Unfortunately, rather than take up this exciting prospect for the immediate future, the press chose the more distant though spectacular 'end of the world' story. With an orbital period of about 130 years at present, Swift-Tuttle should indeed return to perihelion in about 2126AD. It will probably be a bright, naked-eye object in our skies. If it passes through the Earth's orbit during a critical three-minute period, we could be in trouble, but even then the chances of a collision are far, far smaller than the quoted 400:1. The Perseids should be well worth seeing that year at least!

Alastair McBeath
(Vice-President of the International Meteor Organization)
Morpeth, Northumberland

RESPECT FOR ALIEN ABDUCTIONS

■ One can only marvel at Andy Roberts' declaration, whose sole inspiration seems to be wishful thinking, that the controversial – and suspiciously atypical – Linda Napolitano abduction story "is going to be *the* case on which abductions as alien events stand or fall" [*FT67:53*]. Roberts further tips his hand when he informs us that when "it all falls down, the nonsense that aliens are abducting human beings can be laid to rest". In your dreams, Andy.

Here on this side of the pond, abduction research has benefited from the active investigations, not only of serious ufologists, but of scientists and mental health professionals, some of them (e.g. John Mack of the Harvard Medical School) leading figures in their disciplines. I have yet to meet one – I here exclude, of course, armchair 'experts' – who deems the alien hypothesis mere 'nonsense'. Even those who have not specifically embraced it acknowledge that such an hypothesis merits a respectful hearing. After all, none of the others have proven notably successful.

It is disheartening to encounter, in FT of all places, the sort of empty rhetorical posturing exemplified by Roberts' remarks. Save that sort of rubbish for the rubes who read *Skeptical Enquirer*.

Jerome Clark
Canby, Minnesota

SILENT CITIES IN THE SKY

■ I recall thinking that the mystery of the Alaskan sky cities [*FT66:36*] had been resolved some time ago. One of the big American science glossies – most probably *Scientific American*, but just possibly *American Scientist* – carried a long photo-feature demonstrating that optical effects in certain atmospheric conditions can result in massive magnified images of ice crystals being displayed in the sky. These could easily be mistaken for images of built structures, given their regularities and angularity. I would guess that this article appeared in the early 1980s. Perhaps some other reader will recall this article, or have access to an index of the magazines.

Ian Miles
Manchester

RADIOMETRIC DATING

■ I was quite disappointed to see Richard Milton's highly misleading article on radiometric dating [*FT66:24*]. Milton relies, uncritically, on the work of Mormon creationist Melvin Cook and on Henry Morris, President of the Institute for Creation Research. It appears that he has not consulted the original sources he cites. For instance, he claims that Hans Petterson estimated the rate of meteoric dust fall on the earth's surface to be 14 million tons per year, but Petterson himself considered this to be an overestimate and suggested a figure of five million to be more accurate. His measurement, done in 1960, was performed with smog measurement devices at the summit of Hawaii's Mauna Loa volcano. In the 33 years since those measurements, accumulated satellite data show the actual rate of meteoric dust fall to be 11,000 to 18,000 tons per annum. Milton's information is not only out of date, but inflated more than 700 times.

Milton brings up discordant potassium-argon dates on Hawaiian lava flows, but fails to note that the very sources he cites explain that the inaccurate dates are caused by the presence of olivine xenoliths, which carry less argon. This is the sort of thing that is allowed for in radiometric dating. To cite Funkhouser and Naughton's 1968 study of xenoliths as evidence against the general accuracy of potassium-argon dating is simply dishonest.

Finally, Milton wrongly claims that "the sole method [..] of arriving at this immense age [of the Earth] is radiometric dating". He not only overlooks the fact that there are independent and self-checking radiometric techniques (isochron dating), but he ignores non-radiometric techniques such as ice-core dating, palæometric reversal data, geologic data (such as varves) and dendrochronology (tree-ring dating). Dates from all of these techniques converge, confirming the general accuracy of radiometric dating.

For a history of different methods of dating the Earth and discussion of the misguided objections Milton raises, I recommend G. Brent Dalrymple's recent book, *The Age of the Earth* and Arthur N. Strahler's *Science and Earth History*.

Jim Lippard
Tucson, Arizona

■ If you take a rate of radioactive decay that has been measured for a few decades and then claim that it has been going on at the same rate for four billion years, you are making an unsupported assumption. The æons generated by radiometric clocks, going back long before the corroboration of other dating methods, are just assumptions. Nothing compels us to accept that a radioactive decay constant has been invariant. Personally, I'm rather sceptical about any talk of millions of years of past time, let alone billions.

Nick Kollerstrom
Guildford, Surrey

REDS IN THE POND

■ As a footnote to the feature on the Hampstead Seal [*FT65:47*], I enclose a cartoon from the *Evening News* (3 Nov 1926). It seems that the whole thing was a Red Plot. John Citizen explains to the bewildered authorities that the *real* cause of industrial unrest is the influence of Moscow.

Jeremy Harte
Ewell, Surrey

LETTER-BOX AMPUTATIONS

■ You recently reported the story of a girl who suffered the loss of a finger due to an accident involving a letter-box [*FT65:9*]. The same event happened to one of my patients last year – she lost the tip of one finger after posting a letter through a door. I wonder if this is more common than we realise. I would be grateful to hear of any more such incidents.

Dr John Leigh
43 Larchwood,
Harraton, Washington,
NE38 9BT, UK

RIGOR TORTOISE

■ Your 'Pet's Corner' column [*FT64:19*] demonstrated one of the hazards of keeping hamsters. If the temperature of their surroundings falls sufficiently, they go into hibernation. To avoid burial alive, any hamster suddenly found 'dead' should be put in a warm spot for a few hours. Tortoises are equally worrying: it is often very difficult to determine if they are dead until they start to hum, I mean smell!

Ian T. Peters, BVMS, MRCVS
Lamberhurst

HERALD ANGEL

■ I'd like to submit the story of a strange experience I had in 1905 when I was seven years old.

Each Saturday morning I used to visit my friend's house where we'd spend hours playing. However, on this particular Saturday, my mother told me to go up and see my grandfather who lived in the next village along the road, Pensarn, which was about a mile away. He hadn't been too well and, although I loved him dearly, I decided to ignore my mother's request and sneak off to see my friend instead.

Leaving our house, I didn't feel guilty at all and continued along the streets to my friend's house, but just as I was about to turn the corner, an angel appeared in front of me and blocked my path by stretching out both his arms – he didn't say anything, but I got the impression that he wanted to prevent me from going on my way. I didn't feel any shock or surprise. He had golden or fair hair and small white wings which seemed to come out the middle of his back rather than his shoulders. He didn't seem to tower above me, but hovered slightly off the ground and yet remained still. Apart from his white gown I didn't take in any other details and whilst he didn't speak I seemed to get the 'message' that I should return home.

When I got in I didn't tell my mother what I had seen, I just seemed to accept it, although I can't think why! Later that night, we received news of my grandfather's death. I don't know if the two events were connected. I've never told anyone about this, not even my mother.

Mrs M. Treharne
Maesteg, Mid-Glamorganshire

[This letter is one of many accounts of supernatural experiences collected by Sharon Campbell, via appeals in local papers. Would any publisher interested in making a book from her collection please contact her through the FT editorial address?]

noticeboard

EXCHANGE & MART

■ **SURPLUS BOOKS FOR SALE** – from the library of Janet & Colin Bord (archæology, folklore, Britain, gardening, ecology, crafts, psychology, UFOs, religion, supernatural, New Age, etc), including signed copies of some of their out-of-print books. Send 18p stamp for list to: Janet Bord, Melysfan, Llangwm, Corwen, Clwyd Ll21 0RD, Wales.

■ **THE ENIGMA** – Articles on horror, politics, psychology, the occult and religion, plus subjects enigmatic for we are the ENIGMA. But not a puzzle. £1.50 UK, £2.00 overseas. Payment to: The Enigma, 1 Austin Close, Ircester, Northhants NN9 7AX.

■ **COUNTER PRODUCTIONS**, PO Box 556, London SE5 0RL: SAE for free descriptive catalogue of unusual titles – false prophets, virtual reality, conspiracies, anarchy, weirdness.

■ **ENIGMAS** – Scotland's leading journal on UFOs and the paranormal. £10.00 five issues. Single issue £2.00 (US$4.00) From Malcolm Robinson, 41 The Braes, Tullibooy, Clackmanannshire, Scotland FK10 2TT.

■ **MK1V CARR-SCHMIDT DREAM MACHINE:** Bio-feedback linked strobe shades. Illuminatory my dear Watson. SAE to Highland Psionics, Scoraig, Scotland IV23 2RE.

■ **THE MYSTERIOUS AND BEAUTIFUL** crop circle symbols silk-screen printed on top quality t-shirts and sweatshirts. For coloured leaflet write to Judy Young, Lazy Moon Farm, Upper Brailes, Banbury, Oxon OX15 5BA.

■ **SCAN** – New forum for open-minded appraisal of mysteries of nature. Alien animals, crop circles, earth energies, frog falls, ley lines, peculiar plants, sea serpents – and much more! Open membership, quarterly newsletter. Subscription £5.00 pa (£7.50 overseas) payable to Scan. Contact Jan Williams, 72 Leek Rd, Congleton, Cheshire CW12 3HU.

■ **WANTED** – "Yesterdays shopping – The Army and Navy Stores Catalogue 1907", 1972 reprint published by David and Charles Reprints, any condition, reasonable price paid, please contact Simon Queen, 23 Cyprus Road, Cambridge CB1 3QA. Tel 0223 240393 evenings.

■ **UFO BOOKS, MAGAZINES, VIDEOS** Lists SAE SR Stebbing, 41 Terminus Drive, Herne Bay, Kent CT6 6PR.

■ **PORTRAITS OF ALIEN ENCOUNTERS** UFO case histories and much more! Hardback £12.00, Valis Books, 52a Lascotts Road, London N22 4JN.

■ **WANTED** any information/ books/refs on aphrodisiacs. Contact: M Richardson, Pelham Land, Chapel Hill, LN4 4PX.

■ **A TRUE MYSTERY** written by F Russell Clampitt, geocryptologist. "The Coldrum Line" may be the strangest ley line in Britain, stretching from an ancient burial mound in Kent to the far depths of the North Sea. Maps, diagrams and photographs. Price £3.95 inc p&p. Cheques/POs payable to Akhelarre, PO Box 3, Llandeilo, Dyfed, SA19 6YJ. USA dollar bills only. $10 surface mail, $13 air.

■ **CRAZY CRITTERS ARE HERE!** Create life from a packet! A miracle? No, amazing! Each kit includes aquarium, food, solutions, magnifier etc. Watch your creations grow, swim, play. Fun for all ages! Kits available at £10.95 inc postage. Cheques/POs to Thermabond, 1 Sandy Close, Hertford, SE14 2BB.

■ **LEGAL HIGHS** – a detailed study of over 70 plants with hallucinogenic, stimulant and tranquillising properties. Don't buy expensive, pre-mixed preparations of anonymous herbs, send for this book and explore the botanicals for yourself. £7.50 or SAE for more details: Sirius, PO Box 524, Reading, Berks RG1 3YZ.

■ **YOUR LAST CHANCE** to discover matchless magic of the caring kind. Unique brochure £3 (profits to wildlife sanctuary). Margaret Bruce, High Rigg House, St John's Chapel, Bishop Auckland, Co Durham DL13 3QT.

■ **NEW DIMENSIONS** – the monthly magazine of esoteric information. The best for occult articles, qabalah, metaphysicas, psychology, book & music reviews. Dynamic in origin. The best all-rounder. Magic at its best £1.25 UD, £175 overseas. Dept MS, 1 Austin Close, Irchester, Northans NN9 7AX.

■ **UFO NEWSCLIPPING SERVICE** – keeps you up with the real 'close encounters'. Many fascinating UFO reports from the world's press are reproduced facsimile, along with news-wire items from the major agencies. UFONS is 20 foolscap pages monthly, with a Fortean section strong on cryptozoology. Foreign language reports are provided in translation. For information and sample pages, write today to: UFONS – Lucius Farrish, Route 1 – Box 220, Plumerville, AR 72127, USA.

■ **VOICES FROM HEAVEN?** – Investigating contact with non-human intelligences. A new magazine from Kevin McClure: 42 Victoria Road, Mount St Charles, St Austell,Cornwall PL25 4QD, UK. £2 or US$5 for one issue (cash or sterling cheques only). Inquire for sub rates.

■ **THE SKEPTIC** – takes an entertaining, rational and humourous look at pseudoscience and claims of the paranormal. Articles, reviews, columns, cartoons and much more. If you like FT you'll like The Skeptic. Sample issue £1.85; annual sub (6 issues) £12. The Skeptic, PO Box 475, Manchester M60 2TH.

■ **FREE LEY HUNTERS** – but would like postage repayed. Old series 33-35, 37, 45, 51, 58, 60, 61, 64-71; new series 73-84. Contact Phil Ledger, The Old Manse, 57 The Causeway, Carlton, Beds MK43 7LU. 2

RESEARCH

■ **ASTRONET** – is a computer bulletin board network operating in Australia with links to the MUFON BBS in the USA. Free access to discussions on UFOs, alternative science, Tesla, the paranormal and Fortean-related subjects. AstroNet would like to make a connection with the UK. Contact Bob Fletcher, 2/35 Cash St, Kingsbury, Victoria, Australia. BBS: +61-3-467-8090. Voice: +61-3-467-8065. 2

■ **`GORILLA WOMAN'** info needed - I am researching Julia Pastrana, the famous freak (d.1860). Any details/life-story/source recommendations etc gratefully received. Contact Stephen Volk, 9 Coppice Hill, Bradford-on-Avon, Wilts BA15 1ST. Fax: 0225 862281

EVENTS

■ **LONDON UNVEILED.** ASAP (Association for the Scientific Study of Anomalous Phenomena) presents a weekend symposium on the mystical and mysterious aspects of London. Speakers: Nigel Pennick, Chesca Potter, Andrew Collins, Steve Wilson, Rob Stephenson, Caroline Wise. Lectures 15 May, 10-15 Conway Halls, Red Lion Square, London WC1. Walking tour 16 May. Tickets (ASSAP members £7.50) from London Unveiled, PO Box 196, London WC1A 2LY.

■ **GLASGOW** - I'm thinking of starting a local Fortean society. All those interested with ideas for dates, venues, agendas for meetings please contact Desi Atkinson, 21 Kent Road, Glasgow, G3 7EH or phone 041 204 4207.

■ ***PUBLICISE YOUR EVENT HERE*** – Fax us details on 081 552 5466.

■ **UFOs – FACT, FRAUD OR FANTASY?** – Independent UFO Network international conference. Speakers include: Bud Hopkins, Jenny Randles, Cynthis Hind, Paul Devereux, Hilary Evans, Dr Sue Blackmore and others. 14-15 August 1993 at Sheffield Polytechnic. For full details send SAE to: Stu Smith, 15 Rydal St, Burnley, Lancs BB10 1HS – or Phone: 0282 24837.

■ **ORGONE93** – conference on how the works of Wilhelm Reich relate to UFOs, crop circles and earth mysteries. 4 Sept at Conway Hall, Red Lion Sq, London. Lectures, evening social + Sunday tour. Tickets £10 (inc. donation to charity). For details contact Andy Collins: Box 189, Leigh-on-Sea, Essex SS9 1NF.

■ **FOLKLORE SOCIETY EVENTS** – Informal evenings at the Jeremy Bentham pub in University St, London WC1, 6:30pm for 7: 21 April, 'Contemporary legends'. 15 May, Annual Children's Folklore Conference (Conway Hall, London); 4-6 June, British Folklore Studies weekend (University of Glamorgan). For details on these and other events, phone Steve Roud at the Folklore Society: 071 380 7095 (messages 071 387 5894).

■ **SOCIETY FOR PSYCHICAL RESEARCH** – Lectures: 20 May, 'Alien contact, the inner space dimension of the UFO mystery' (Jenny Randles). 17 June, 'A psychophysics approach to PSI research' (Peter Maddock). Venue: the Lecture Hall of Kensington Central Library, Campden Hill Road, London W8, at 6:30pm. Non-members £3, student cards £1. Further information from the SPR at 49 Marloes Rd, Kensington, London W8 6LA. Tel: 071 937 8984.

■ **LONDON EARTH MYSTERIES CIRCLE** – Evening meetings in St Andrew's Seminar Room, Maria Assumpta Centre, 23 Kensington Square, London W8, at 7pm on the 2nd and 4th Tuesdays in each month. Members £1.00, non-members £2.00, unwaged £1.50. 23 Feb, social evening, all welcome. There are also field trips and outings. Contact: Rob Stephenson, 136 Bravington Rd, London W9 3AL.

■ **TEMS** – social and study group for paranormal phenomena and earth mysteries. Lectures: 25 April, 'The best ley in Surrey (Eileen Roche); 22 May, field trip to Hampshire ; 30 May, 'Big cat sightings' (Steve Ashcroft). For details of venue etc, ring Lionel Beer on 081 979 3148, or Eileen Grimshaw on 0483 69583.

■ **BUFORA** – Lectures: 1 May, 'Contactees ungagged' (Ken Phillips); 5 June, 'The ET origin of consciousness' (Caroline Thomas). For details of venue etc, ring 0582-763218.

■ **ASSAP** – 15'16 May, London Unveiled symposium at Conway Hall, Red Lion Sq, London. SAE for details to: London Unveiled, Box 196, London WC1A 2LY. Monthly talk and social evenings, first Thursday of every month, 6:30pm, at the Tattershall Castle (it's a moored paddle steamer on the Thames), close to Embankment underground station, London.

MISCELANEOUS

■ **HOUSE FOR SALE** – Large stone house in North Wales, spacious but cosy, with outbuildings, in 2.5 acres: trees, shrubs, organic veg garden; quiet location near village in south-west Clwyd – £120,000. For more details phone 049 082 472 or fax 049 082 321.

■ **LOVER OF THE MACABRE** needs serious correspondent: Tony, 15 Circuit Close, Willenhall, West Midlands, UK.

■ **CONTACT WANTED WITH GENUINE MAGICIANS** or practitioners of black magic. Discretion assured. Any distance. Po Box 321, Prestatyn, Clwyd, LL19 9YA.

■ **DRUIDS!** – Discover what they really do and how Druidry answers our need for a spirituality that is connected to the land and our ancient heritage. For info send SAE to: ODOB (FT), 260 Kew Road, Richmond, Surrey TW9 3EG.

TO ADVERTISE ON THE NOTICEBOARD OR BOOKMART simply fill in the form below and send, together with payment of 25p per word (VAT inc), to: FT Classifieds, John Brown Publishing Ltd. The Boathouse, Crabtree Lane, Fulham SW6 8NJ.

I enclose my message of __________ words plus payment of £__________

Message reads: ____

Preferred section: ❑ Exchange & Mart ❑ Research ❑ Bookmart ❑ Miscellaneous ❑ Events

Please make cheques payable to John Brown Publishing.

CREDITS FOR THIS ISSUE

CLIPPINGS & TRANSLATION

Jayne Amat, Dr Gail-Nina Anderson, Sherry Baker, Aonghus de Barra, K.A.Beer, Lionel Beer, Claire Blamey, Janet & Colin Bord, Iosif Boszov, David Bourgoin, David J.Burns, Kevin Busby, ByRon, Cain, Kevin & Ingrid Carlyon, Brian Chapman, Arthur Chrenkoff, Peter Christie, Terry Colvin, COUD-I, Mat Coward, Tim Cridland, Paul Cropper, Joy Crutchley, Jim Darroch, Mike Dash, Nick Devonport, Karma Tenzin Dorje, Jill Doubleday, Peter Hope-Evans, George Featherston, Larry Fiander, Eric Fitch, Neil Frary, Rob Gandy, Alan Gardiner, Paul Garner, Robert Gifford, Mark Gillings, Ian Glasby, Andrew Green, D.A. Haines, Slim Haines, Chris Hall, P.G. Harfield, Jim Haslam, Peter Hassall, Tony Healy, Stuart A.Herkes, Steve Hexter, Richard Holland, M.A.Howard, Ronnie Hoyle, R.Hudspith, Alan H. Hyde Jaimovich, Peter James, Ros Jay, Dionne Jones, Dan Kahn, Walter J.Langbein, Jenny Lawes, Alexis Lykiard, John Macmillan, Dave Malin, Nick Maloret, G. Markle, Valerie Martin, Dave McKinnon, Barbara Millspaw, Andy Milner, Ian Morgan, N.J. Morgan, Jan Mura, L. Naylor, Ray Nelke, C.W. Nicholas, Roger O'Donnell, T.J.P., Robin Pascoe, Naomi Reed, David Rider, Jim Riecken, Sven Rosén, John Rowe, Tom Ruffles, Mel Saunders, Ronnie Scott, Paul Screeton, Keith Seddon, Chuck Shepherd, Ian Sherred, Doc Shiels, Caryl Sibbett, Karl Shuker, Ian Simmons, Alan Smith, Andy Smith, Richard Smith, Keith Snell, Peter Stallard, Alan M. Stracy, G.M. Stocker, Paul R.Thomas, Fred Thomsett, Mike Travers, Mike Truelove, Richard Turner, UFONS, Kevin Venters, John Viney, Sarah Walsh, P. Warren, Dwight Whalin, John Whiskin, Owen Whiteoak, Anette Will, Ion Will, Jan Williams, Jason Winter, Steve Wrathall.

ILLUSTRATION COPYRIGHTS

5 Hamilton (Ontario) Observer. 6 Fortean Picture Library. 7 John Billingsley. 9 Merrily Harpur. 10t FPL. 11t Associated Press (AP). 11b Novosti. 12 Intercontinental Features. 15 AP. 16 Topham. 17t Zac Austin. 17b NewsTeam. 18 Alan Bolger. 20 (both left) AP. 20r Mariah Brown. 21 Hunt Emerson. 24 FPL. 25 (top three) Linda Moulton Howe. 26tl Hal Crawford. 26tr Ellen Cartney/Idaho State Journal. 26b Paul Popper. 27 Mary Evans Picture Library (MEPL). 30 Mary Seal. 32m Topham 32b Daily Telegraph. 33 Don Ecker. 34-37 MEPL. 40t Columbia Pictures. 40b MEPL. 42 Popperfoto. 43 Grant Wakefield. 44 Scope Features. 45t Alison McDonald/Mail Newspapers. 45b AP. 47 Solent News & Pictures. 48 FPL. 49 Popperfoto. 50 Wolverhampton Express & Star. 52 FPL. 56 Pierre Hollins. 60 Serindia. 64 Derek Gosling.

NUMBER 69

UK £2
USA $4.95

FORTEAN TIMES

THE JOURNAL OF STRANGE PHENOMENA

PICK OF THE CROPS

1 STALK STOMPER • DOUG & DAVE
2 BISHOP CANNINGS • UNITED BUREAU OF INVESTIGATION
3 WOODFORD RINGS • THE BILL BAILEY GANG
4 OPERATION BLACKBIRD • MERLIN & CO
5 GARDEN ROLLER • THE WESSEX SKEPTICS
6 WILTSHIRE PICTOGRAMS • SPIDERMAN & CATWOMAN
7 DHARMIC WHEEL • THE SNAKE
STRAWBERRY FIELD • DOUG & DAVE
CRANFORD ST. ANDREW • THE BILL BAILEY GANG
10 CHARM BRACELET • THE SNAKE

IT'S CROPTASTIC, MATES!

WHO ARE THE CIRCLEMAKERS?

HOW STRANGE ARE YOU?

Take part in our unique survey and have a chance to win the revolutionary new AMSTRAD PEN PAD computer!

Cold Fusion Cover-up • Red Mercury • Moa Mystery
Lama Drama • Chinese Cannibalism • Pig Attacks

Contents

ISSUE 72 : DECEMBER/JANUARY 1994

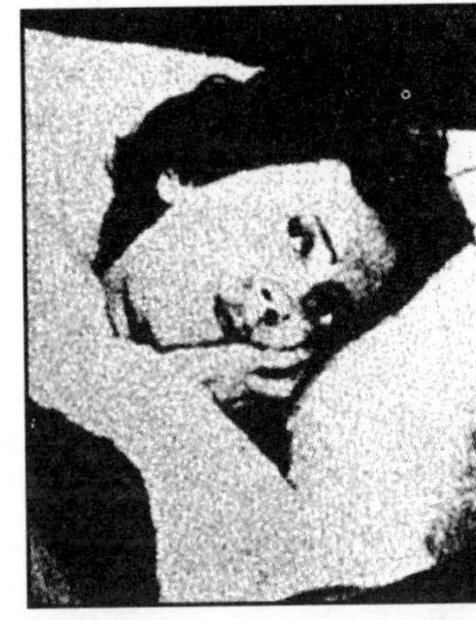

CAROLINA OLSSON - **PAGE 27**

EDITORIAL 4

The Fortean Convention • Improved service for US subscribers • Christmas competition

STRANGE DAYS 5

Bullseye projectile survivals • Siamese sundries • New Java skull • Absent-minded drivers • Amazing bridge hands • It's raining men • Snack attacks • Talking cats • Divine ingratitude

PHENOMENOMIX 21

HUNT EMERSON'S humorous look at the world

THE BIG SLEEP 23

BOB RICKARD reviews some of the more extreme examples of the 'Sleeping Beauty' syndrome. The prodigious 32-year sleep of Carolina Olsson is described by ROLF J.K. OLSSON

SHOOTING DOWN THE MYTH 30

Thirty years after the Kennedy assassination, GLENN B. FLEMING outlines the range of conspiracy theories about this ever-intriguing puzzle

THE FT INTERVIEW: MARY'S CHILDREN 36

BOB RICKARD talks to JENNY COCKELL, who claims to recall a former life as Mary Sutton

FROM OUR FILES 42

- HOAX: Rumours of drilling down to Hell analysed by *Paul Sieveking*
- MISSING TIME: *Peter Brookesmith* goes to the Sheffield UFO Conference
- LOVECATS - THE NEXT GENERATION: Possible jungle cat hybrids examined by *Dr Karl P. N. Shuker*
- BEDEVILLED: *Mike Dash* on the latest Satanic ritual abuse cases
- UNEARTHED: Four recent submarine discoveries reported by *Steve Moore*
- DIARY OF A MAD PLANET: Weather watch August/September 1993
- SECRET COUNTRY: Silbury Hill and West Kennet long barrow *Janet and Colin Bord*

FORUM 53

Anthony McLuskey • Robert Anton Wilson • Dennis Stacy • Michael Goss

REVIEWS 59

Forbidden Archælogy • The Only Planet of Choice • A Theory of Almost Everything • Dreamtime, Dreamspace • The Damned Universe of Charles Fort • Magwatch

LETTERS 63

An 'impossible' solid? • Flashes in the dark • Localised combustions • Solar phenomenon • Meeting Pan

NOTICEBOARD 66

Fortean meetings, lectures, events, research, products and offers

JENNY COCKELL **PAGE 36**

COVER: MAIN PICTURE MARY EVANS PICTURE LIBRARY
INSET: THE HULTON-DEUTSCH COLLECTION

WHY 'FORTEAN'?

CHARLES FORT (1874-1932)

Fortean Times is a bi-monthly magazine of news, reviews and research on all manner of strange phenomena and experiences, curiosities, prodigies and portents, formed in 1973 to continue the work of the iconoclastic philosopher CHARLES FORT. Fort was sceptical about scientific explanations, observing how scientists argued for and against various theories and phenomena according to their own beliefs, rather than the rules of evidence. He was appalled that data not fitting the collective paradigm was ignored, suppressed, discredited or explained away (which is quite different from explaining a thing).

Fort was perhaps the first to speculate that mysterious lights seen in the sky might be craft from outer space. He coined the term 'teleportation' which has passed into general usage through science fiction. His dictum "One measures a circle beginning anywhere" expresses his philosophy of Continuity and the 'doctrine of the hyphen', in which everything is in an intermediate state between extremes. He had notions of the universe-as-organism and the transient nature of all apparent phenomena. Far from being an over-credulous man, Fort cut at the very roots of credulity: "I cannot accept that the products of minds are subject matter for beliefs ... I conceive of nothing, in religion, science, or philosophy, that is more than the proper thing to wear, for a while."

Fort was born in Albany, New York, in 1874 into a family of Dutch immigrants. Beatings by a tyrannical father helped set him against authority and dogma, and on leaving home at the age of 18 he hitch-hiked around the world to put some "capital into the bank of experience." At 22 he contracted malaria, married his nurse and settled down to 20 years of impoverished journalism in the Bronx. During this time he read extensively in the literature of science, taking notes on small squares of paper in a cramped shorthand of his own invention, which he filed in shoe boxes.

In 1916, when he was 42, Fort came into a modest inheritance, just enough to relieve him of the necessity of having to earn a living. He started writing *The Book of the Damned*, which his friend, the novelist Theodore Dreiser, bullied his own publisher into printing in 1919. Fort fell into a depression, burnt all his notes (which numbered some 40,000) as he had done a few years earlier, and in 1921 set sail for London, where he spent eight years living near the British Museum (39 Marchmont Street) and wrote *New Lands* (1923). Returning to New York, he published *Lo!* in 1931 and *Wild Talents* in 1932, shortly before he died. He left 60,000 notes, now in the New York Public Library.

THE GANG OF FORT:
Editors:
Bob Rickard
& Paul Sieveking

Contributing Editors:
Steve Moore
& Mike Dash

ISSN 0308 5899

Bob Rickard

EDITORIAL

Getting to know you

Paul Sieveking

EDITORIAL ADDRESS
Fortean Times: Box 2409, London NW5 4NP, UK.
Tel & Fax: 071 485 5002 or 081 552 5466.

SUBMISSIONS
Submissions are invited of suitable articles, news, art, cartoons, reviews, and especially clippings. Preliminary discussion with the editors is advisable. Text can be submitted on floppy disks, but check with the editors first. Submissions may be edited. FT assumes no responsibility for submissions, but all reasonable care will be taken while they are in FT's possession. Requests for return of material should be accompanied by stamped addressed envelope.

CLIPPINGS
All clippings, references, etc, should be identified by source, date and clipster's name. Mail or fax them to the editorial address (above).

SUBSCRIPTIONS
RATES – One year (6 issues). UK: £12. Overseas inc. USA: £15.00 or US$30. For two years (12 issues) UK: £20, overseas inc USA £26 or US$50.
PAYMENT – US cheques acceptable; payments from all other countries should be in sterling drawn upon a London bank. Major credit cards accepted – just phone details on 0800 581409*. Make cheque/money orders payable to:
JOHN BROWN PUBLISHING Freepost* SW6096, Frome, Somerset BA11 1YA, UK.* For UK only

PUBLISHER
John Brown Publishing Ltd, The Boathouse, Crabtree Lane, Fulham, London SW6 8NJ, UK. ☎ 071 381 6007 or Fax: 071 381 3930.
Managing Editor: Fiona Jerome.
Publisher: Vic Lime.

DISTRIBUTION
UK trade distribution by UMD, 1 Benwell Road, Holloway, London N7 7AX. ☎ 071 700 4600 or Fax: 071 607 3352.
USA newsstand distribution by Eastern News Distributors Inc, 2020 Superior St, Sandusky, OH 44870, USA.

● To celebrate our 20th year – an anniversary we share with the Hynek Center for UFO Studies in Chicago – we are making plans. It's time we knew more about you, your attitudes towards the paranormal and perhaps your experiences of it. Consequently, this issue includes our first extensive reader survey. The results will be published in due course and will allow us, we hope, to make a direct comparison with a recent survey of paranormal experiences in the USA.

You may have caught sight or sound of us recently launching our quest for strange objects and photographs from private and museum collections for an exhibition of curiosities. We also have in mind an annual convention beginning next year. As you might imagine, these will take quite a bit of organising and lacking a mammoth staff (see 'Unearthed' on p47) the full details may take a few months to materialise.

● Our lead article this issue concerns the dramatic progress of Cold Fusion research. Cold Fusion is a demonstrable low-tech and pollution-free way to generate cheap power – by contrast, expensive nuclear 'Hot Fusion' plants won't be with us until after the millennium, and carry the risk of pollution, melt-down, and immortal waste-products. Cold Fusion is still scorned in the scientific press and anathematised in the club-rooms of orthodoxy and academe. Read Chris Tinsley's report on p23.

● On 13 May, a madman took children hostage in a Paris nursery school. Even though we are used to the way reality mimics fiction, we shivered. Two issues ago we told of a rumour that gripped a Calais slum, that a madman had taken children prisoner in a school and slit their throats – *see **FT67:48***. Fortunately, in the real case, the kids were delivered safely when RAID officers stormed the building two days later and shot Algerian Eric Schmitt in the head.

The other notable siege - irreverently called the 'Wacopalypse' – has also played out, but in a ghastly bonfire on 19 April in which over 70 people perished, 17 of them children who had no choice in their martyrdom. David Koresh – the roasted 'Lamb' – has been identified from X-ray and dental records – however, this has not prevented the expected rumour arising (*Sun* 22 April 1993) that Koresh escaped through tunnels. Doubtless he is, this very minute, sharing a burger with Elvis, Jim Morrison, and Robert Maxwell.

● Media attention has focussed on cannibalism lately. We have seen features on the making of *Alive!* and the original Andean plane crash which inspired it; the story of the Dodder wagon-train, stranded in the Sierra Nevada in 1847; the incident behind Gericault's painting *The Raft of the Medusa*; and now *Alferd Packer, The Musical* a bio-pic about Colorado's most famous (alleged) cannibal. And yes, it's Alferd, not Alfred. This makes our report on recent revelations of cannibalism in the East – see 'Hard to Swallow' on p48 – quite topical.

● Signs of arrival? A fragment of our interview with Julian Cope starred in *Private Eye*'s 'Pseud's Corner' (15 Jan 1993). Extracts from ***FT*** have featured in at least three publications used for teaching English as a foreign language. Vindication of Paul's attention to linguistic detail came when Lynn Barber called ***FT*** "a model of elegant English" whose "style cannot be faulted."
(*Independent on Sunday* 25 April 1993).

Paul Sieveking

THE EDITORS

MA' COLOURED SNOWS & RAINS WEATHER SUPERLATIV
OUS HUMAN COMBUSTION STIGMATA LEVITATION MIRA
ULT CRIMES FISH FALLS ICE FROM THE SKY DEMONIC
GE DAYS STRANGE DAYS STRANGE DAYS STRANGE DAY
SSESSIONS VANISHING PEOPLE RAT KINGS SIMULACRA

STRANGE DAYS

16 pages of worldwide weirdness

I BRING YOU MAD TIDINGS

Kevin 'Mad Dog" Mudford, former leader of the Devil's Disciples biker gang and charged with murder at 15, is seen here in Melbourne as he travels around Australia preaching Christianity. However, police told him he needed a trailer licence for his cross. [AP] 15 Feb 1992.

NDS URBAN FOLKLORE ENCOUNTERS WITH ANGELS MI
OT SAVANTS STRANGE PLANTS ALIEN ENCOUNTERS PS

FORTEAN ALMANAC 15 June – 15 Aug 1993

Notable feasts and anniversaries in the coming weeks

TUESDAY 15 JUNE: St Vitus' Day. His bones were supposed to be able to cure St Vitus' Dance, a sort of violent chorea.

WEDNESDAY 16 JUNE: In 1882, two hailstones which fell in Dubuque, Iowa, melted to reveal 'small living frogs'.

MONDAY 21 JUNE: Litha, the Summer Solstice. Sun enters cancer 09:00 GMT. In the old days, bonfires were lit on the highest points in the district.

THURSDAY 24 JUNE: Feast Day of St John the Baptist. In 1947, Kenneth Arnold saw silvery discs while flying over Mount Rainier, Washington. He told the press that they looked like saucers skipped across water (hence 'Flying Saucers').

WEDNESDAY 30 JUNE: In 1908, something fell and exploded in the Tunguska valley, Siberia, with a force more violent than the Hiroshima bomb of 1945. The argument over its identity – meteor, comet, black hole, spacecraft – continues.

WEDNESDAY 7 JULY: Feast Day of Saint Cronaparva, the patron saint of dwarves. Also Consualia, the pagan festival of Consus, god of harvests.

SUNDAY 11 JULY: In 1881, George, Prince of Wales (later George V), as a 16-year-old naval cadet on *HMS Inconstant* off the Australian coast, saw the *Flying Dutchman*, "a strange red light as of a phantom ship all aglow".

THURSDAY 15 JULY: St Swithin's Day. An unreliable tradition has it that the weather today – fair or foul – reflects that of the following 40 days.

THURSDAY 22 JULY: Feast Day of St Mary Magdalene, patron saint of harlots. Various churches, including Notre Dame, are actually dedicated to her and not the Virgin Mary.

MONDAY 26 JULY: Birthday of the psychologist Carl Gustav Jung (1875), whose theories of archetypes and synchronicity are much employed by students of anomalistics.

SUNDAY 1 AUGUST: Lughnassadh (named after Lugh, the Celtic god of wisdom and illumination) or Lammas (the Saxon 'Loaf-mass') is one of the great pagan festivals of the year. It marks the first harvest and the beginning of Autumn.

WEDNESDAY 4 AUGUST: In 1642, "a fearful and terrible noise" was heard above Aldeburgh, Suffolk, for over an hour, during which time "a stone of great weight" fell from the sky.

FRIDAY 6 AUGUST: Birthday both of Charles Hoy Fort (1874) and the first 'nosy parker', Matthew Parker, Archbishop of Canterbury (1504).

SATURDAY 14 AUGUST: Anniversary of the Hampstead Deluge (1975), when three million tons of water fell in three hours – the equivalent of almost four months' summer rain.

THE TALE OF YAGAMO

A pintail duck flew around Tokyo for almost three weeks impaled with an arrow. First spotted on a park pond in late January, the duck inspired public sympathy and anger, and the sort of media frenzy usually reserved for TV starlets and sumo wrestlers. Newspapers and networks quickly dubbed it Yagamo (the arrowed duck) and assigned hordes of reporters to cover the drama around the clock.

Although the 30-centimetre pink carbon-fibre arrow, apparently fired from a crossbow, had completely transfixed the duck's body, it did not seem to feel pain, and could walk or fly with apparent ease. Scared and deeply suspicious of the crowds, however, the bird ignored trails of food laid down to trap it and took to commuting from pond to pond in central Tokyo to find some peace. Eventually, zoo officials appealed to the media pack to back off, and Yagamo walked into a net at 11:08am on 12 February and was captured by officer Terumoto Komiya.

The pintailed duck, transfixed by an arrow, flies over Shinobazu Pond in Tokyo on 5 February 1993.

The arrow was removed at Ueno Zoo; although X-rays showed the famous bird had also been hit by two shot gun pellets, surgeons decided not to remove them for fear another operation would prove fatal. None of the projectiles pierced a vital organ. Yagamo was released on 23 February watched by 100 cheering kindergarten children, and joined several hundred other ducks in a pond nearby. Zoo officials hoped he would be strong enough to go with the other ducks when they migrated to Siberia in March or April. Commentators wondered how long he would live to enjoy his fame, since duck shooting is perfectly legal in Japan – although not with bows and arrows.
[Reuters] 13+24 Feb; Guardian, 13 Feb 1993.

STONEHENGE ON THE SUN

Retired draughtsman Edward Barnes, 70, from Ringwood near Southampton, has built this three-foot-long, four-lens telescope, which produces a glare-free image of the sun. "As far as I know, nobody else in the world has this invention", he said. "It would be very useful in the astronomy world. When astronomers look at the sun they project the image onto a piece of paper. The image is extremely poor. I can see things on the sun that no man in the world has seen."

He claims that very short lines clustered in shoals can be clearly seen, although he believes they are not actually on the sun itself, but somewhere in space. He also says he saw an impression of Stonehenge on the sun, three days after the summer solstice. "I was amazed", he said. *Southampton Echo, 22 Dec 1992.*

BULL ABOUT A BEAR

A Norwegian university lecturer - trying to account for the savage deaths of 18 cows near the provincial town of Selbu - proposed that they had been raped and killed by a sex-crazed bear. News of this bizarre cross-species serial killing was flashed around the world on the newswires, for if true it would be astonishing. Within hours, a professor from Oslo University's Biology Institute was trotted out to confirm the very idea of a bear raping cows was ridiculous.

The slaughter of (and implied sexual attack on) these Norwegian cows has remained unsolved. *[PA] 4 Dec; {Reuter} 5 Dec 1992.*

BLACK WIDOW

Egyptian-born Omaima Nelson, 24, was a rape crisis counsellor by day and a hooker by night. She had a row about money with her husband William, 54, hit him with a lamp and tied him to a mattress in their home in Santa Ana, California. She then donned red shoes, a red hat and blood-red lipstick, hacked the 16-stone body to pieces and skinned it.

She barbecued his ribs and ate them, grinding up the rest of the body in the garbage disposal unit. Before being sentenced to 27 years, she told the judge that she was "a warm person who wouldn't harm a mosquito". *D.Star, 15 Mar; D.Record, 22 Mar 1993.*

QUICK DRINK AND FLOOD

■ A man walked into a Nairobi supermarket, gulped down two bottles of whisky and put a third in his pocket. He lurched out of the shop without paying and was promptly arrested. His name was Charles Wanjohi Hiuhu – which means, in his native Kikuyu, 'Charles of the Quick Drink'. *Western Morning News, D.Record, 26 Feb 1993.*

■ Chris and Jackie Flood have drenched their home in Chesham, Buckinghamshire, three times in 18 months. Their 45-gallon tropical fish tanks burst twice. Then Chris, 36, split water pipes with a nail. "I think our name is jinxed", said Jackie. *Sun, 26 Oct 1992.*

Sidelines

In an item about attempts to breed potoroos in Blackpool Zoo, we learn that the rabbit-sized Tasmanian animal is a species 'at risk' because males left together unsupervised have a tendency to tear off each other's genitals. *D.Telegraph, 18 Feb 1993.*

● ● ● ● ● ● ● ● ● ● ● ● ● ● ●

Palle Birkelund, 62, was jailed for being drunk in charge of a lift. Shoppers in Aalborg, Denmark, complained when he kept yelling: "This is the captain of your aircraft – we will be landing in the next few seconds." *News of the World, 27 Dec 1992.*

● ● ● ● ● ● ● ● ● ● ● ● ● ● ●

Stopped for speeding at 80mph, Michelle Rardin told police in Indiana she had no oil in her car and was racing home as fast as possible before the engine blew up. *D.Record, 26 Mar 1993.*

● ● ● ● ● ● ● ● ● ● ● ● ● ● ●

Sri Lanka's state-owned radio company caused a mini-panic on 16 January when it repeated an 18-year-old news bulletin about a plane crash to convince listeners it was providing a good service. (What?!) *South China Morning Post, 17 Jan 1993.*

● ● ● ● ● ● ● ● ● ● ● ● ● ● ●

From a court report in the *South Wales Evening Post* in mid August 1992: "A disgruntled customer hurled a rubber plant at a Swansea takeaway food business window, but it bounced off."

● ● ● ● ● ● ● ● ● ● ● ● ● ● ●

A school in Florida has banned pupils from reading the fairy tale *Snow White*, after Christian parents complained of its 'graphic violence'. *Midweek, 1 Oct 1992.*

● ● ● ● ● ● ● ● ● ● ● ● ● ● ●

A company in California is about to market a hand-held device that will enable the user to pinpoint his location anywhere on Earth, by use of satellites, to within 10 yards. *Toronto Globe and Mail, 27 Jan 1993.*

EXTRA! EXTRA!

Fortean headlines from newspapers around the world.

LIZZIE BORDEN MUSEUM AXED Columbus (OH) Dispatch, 25 May 1988.

JELLYFISH SHUT DOWN NUCLEAR STATION Glasgow Herald, 13 Sept 1991.

SATAN ON WANTED LIST D.Mail, 20 Sept 1991.

HAMMER FALLS ON FISH D.Telegraph 23 Sept 1991.

ARSONISTS OR GOD HIT EX-WITCH'S OLD HOUSE Northern Echo, 11 Oct 1991.

LAIRD LIVED IN LAVATORY UNAWARE OF HIS WEALTH D.Telegraph, 9 Nov 1991.

PARROTS FLOCK TO SIDCUP Bexley Leader, 13 Dec 1991.

MAN IN HOSPITAL AFTER PIG EXPLODES Canberra Times, 21 Dec 1991.

DEMON SCRATCHER

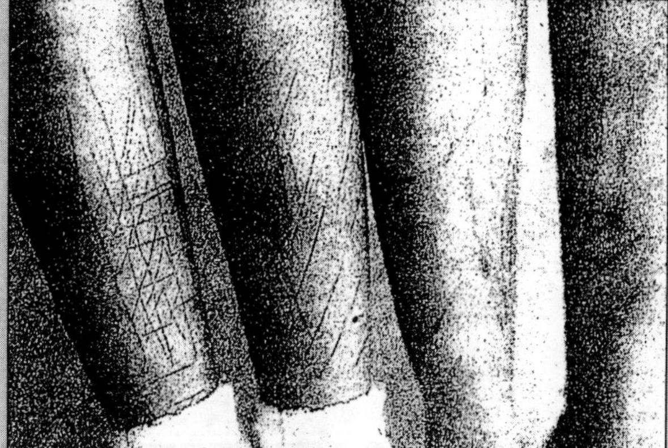

Girls in a small boarding school in Rietfontein, Botswana, have been the target of nocturnal attacks, increasing in frequency and severity since 1985. Every evening the nightmare resumes for the girls and their teachers. Entities assume both male and female forms and torture the girls by tearing their clothes, hacking off their hair and scratching their legs. X-rays taken by the school's physician reveal needles embedded beneath the skin and deep scratches. Baffled police have given up on any mundane explanations and declare the attacks to be supernatural. Despite their terror, none of the girls has left the school as they consider it their only avenue to a better life. *Eleftheros Typos (Greece), 19 Dec 1992.*

TRANS-SEXUAL TROUT

A Government report has discovered that male fish, particularly trout, are changing sex as a result of a hormone from sewage plants getting into rivers. The hormone is probably oestrogen either from the breakdown of detergents or from birth pills. Male trout exposed to effluent are producing an egg-yolk protein in their livers normally found only in fertile females. There are fears that all fish in affected rivers will become hermaphrodites, leading to a population crash. Thousands of trace organics are present in British rivers as a result of the chemical industry, but very little is known about their effects.

So far, human males seem to be unaffected. According to gynæcologist John McGarry, however, certain female hormones are so strong in the Thames during the summer low water period that tap water will sometimes give a positive result in a pregnancy test. *Guardian,D.Telegraph, 10 Feb; Brisbane Sunday Mail, 14 Feb; Guardian, 19 Feb 1993.*

POLAR PUPPY

A Hungarian couple bought a cuddly white stray 'puppy' at the Polish market in Budapest, a magical sort of place where they say you can get anything from Russian machine guns to bath towels. Taking their new pet for its vaccinations, they told the vet that it had a huge appetite and was getting vicious. The vet identified the animal as a polar bear cub.

"It's just possible for this to happen", Bruno van Puienbroeck, keeper of mammals at Antwerp Zoo, was quoted as saying. "There are a lot of polar bears on the market at present because many zoos want to get rid of them."

This yarn is intrinsically unlikely: polar bear cubs can fetch up to £10,000, so it would not be in the Budapest trader's interest to offload one for the price of a puppy. This is probably a Hungarian version of the Mexican Pet urban legend (American couple buy giant rabid rat, thinking it to be a puppy, ***FT47:13****). Wolverhampton Express & Star, 8 Mar; D.Mirror, 9 Mar; Guardian, 11 Mar 1993.*

GOLD CAPS

A goat slaughtered and cooked by aides to a Muslim cleric in the southern Iranian town of Lamard was found to have a 3mm coating of gold on its teeth, according to the Tehran newspaper *Salam.* Old people claimed a kind of grass growing in the region deposited gold on the teeth of grazing animals. Dr Ralph Kirkwood, of Strathclyde University's Bioscience Department, said: "There may be ions which are taken up by the grass and accumulated in some way. It has been seen with heavy metals like cadmium." *[Reuters], Scottish Daily Record, 29 Mar 1993.* For a Greek sheep with gold-plated teeth, see ***FT43:14***.

Mr Levent Süner bought Norwegian mackerel in some unspecified Turkish town and found a yellow stone in one of the fish which turned out to be pure 24 carat gold, weighing 4.5 grams. A jeweller offered him about £50 for it, but he wanted to keep it. When the news got around, there was a rush on imported mackerel. *Bugün (Turkey), 19 April 1992.* For a lump of gold in a chicken, see ***FT46:8***.

INDIAN INCIDENTS

Fortean Times's coverage of weird events in India is patchy as we have never had a long-term correspondent. The Indian press, particularly the local papers, teem with very strange stories, as we know from our forays there over the years. Here are a few stories which have trickled out recently.

BRAHMIN GHOSTBUSTER

The Foreign Correspondents' Club in Delhi opened in a government bungalow in September 1992, but no *puja* (ritual blessing) was made to purify the premises. Alarming testimony followed. Lights turned themselves on and off, and something pulled at the legs of Shakil, the *chowkidar* (night watchman). The steward, Rohil Malik, saw "a tall figure with a white beard in a long white robe". Rumour had it that a Nepalese couple had been employed in the building years ago. After constant quarrels, one burnt to death in a mysterious fire.

The servants declared that either the ghost went or they would. The Club called in Kuldip Sharma, Brahmin pandit and ghostbuster to make *griha shanti puja* (home and peace prayers). He marked the staff and correspondents with the vermilion *tilak* or third eye, lit incense and chanted mantras. He built a fire and added camphor, sugar and *ghee*. *The Times* correspondent and FCC president, Christopher Thomas, also added *ghee* on behalf of the club. Finally, the *puja* party was led round the club, scattering rose petals.

Mr Sharma was satisfied. "The spirit is now outside, but it will probably linger for a few days", he said. Unamused by the Brahmin's antics, the ghost continued its japes – until the steward left the club. *Guardian, 10 Feb; Sunday Express, 14 Feb 1993 + private communication.*

GANESH INCARNATION?

A baby boy with a long nose born at the close of 1992 drew large crowds who believed he was an incarnation of the Hindu elephant-headed god Ganesh, according to the United News of India. Priests recited prayers around the decorated cradle in the courtyard of his parents' house in the Sikh holy city of Amritsar. The boy had little if any upper lip and – months before dentition normally begins – two teeth that protruded like tusks. *Int. Herald Tribune, 5 Feb 1993.*

BREATHLESS FEAT

More than 5,000 spectators and devotees gathered in a New Delhi suburb on 8 November 1992 to see Kapil Adwait, an ascetic, emerge from a sealed tank, nine feet deep, where he had been roped to the bottom, under water, for four days "for the benefit of humanity". Adwait is known as Pilot Baba – he was a Wing Commander until the 1971 war with Pakistan. One of his plane's engines conked out and some unseen force (he claimed) guided him down. He became a religious recluse.

The crowd looked on apprehensively as the tarpaulin covering the tank was rolled back.

"I'm sure the pool's been empty until the last minute" said Sanal Edamaruku, leader of the Indian Rationalists' Association, to journalist Tim McGirk. "He's probably been down there sleeping and reading magazines."

The bearded yogi was floating face down in the water. He flopped over like a walrus and was dragged up the side of the pool. His skin was wrinkled only below the waist, throwing doubt on his claim to have been totally submerged. He changed into dry clothes, sprinted up a ladder and announced that his underwater meditation was intended to find India's future prime minister. He then endorsed a local politician of the governing Congress Party.

Meanwhile, Mr Edamaruku was examining two garden hoses in the tank, which might have been used to drain the water. He was spotted. "A rationalist!", someone cried, giving chase. Mr Edamaruku disappeared into the crowd. *Bangkok Post, 5+10 Nov; Independent, 10 Nov 1992.*

SIMULACRA CORNER

FANCY SEEING YOU HERE!
This look of surprise on the hood of a cobra was found in Valangaiman in Thanjavur district, India in 1991. We are always glad to receive pictures of spontaneous forms and figures, or any curious images. Send your snaps to the editorial address – with SAE – and we'll pay a fiver for any we use.

A NEW PRIMATE

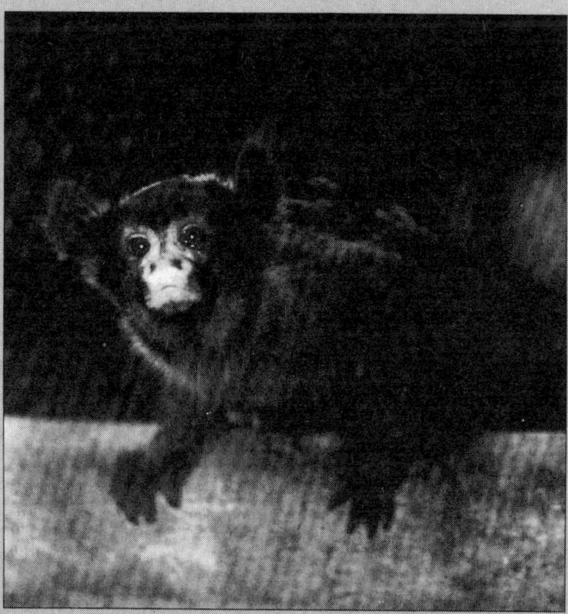

Swiss biologist Marco Schwarz travelled up the River Maués, a tributary of the Amazon, in 1985. Among other things, he was checking out native stories of a curious little monkey. He finally spotted some, 800 miles up-river from the Amazon delta, and returned to his wildlife breeding centre in Morretes, Brazil, with a single male and female. Eventually the female gave birth to two thriving infants.

It was not until 1991 that a visitor to the centre realised the creatures were unusual, and sent a snap of mother and children (the father had died) to Russell Mittermeier, a primatologist and president of the Washington DC based Conservation International. The moment he saw the photo, Mittermeier said: "Oops, we've got a new species here." Adding, "Oops doesn't have quite the ring of 'Eureka!'."

Christened the Maués marmoset, the pink-faced primate is eight inches long, weighs just 13 ounces and has faint zebra-like stripes in its dark fur. It was formally introduced to science as *Callithrix mauesi* on Columbus Day, 1992 – "A minor discovery to commemorate the discovery of the New World," said Mittermeier.

The Maués marmoset is the third new monkey to be found in Brazil since 1990, and is now the 244th member of the primate order and our newest relative.

Robert May, Royal Society research professor at Oxford University, reacted rather presumptuously, predicting this might be the last monkey species to be found: "Monkey species are very well-known. It's my guess that there are no more." Prof May – who has seemingly forgotten the recent discoveries of the Suntail guenon in Gabon, the Golden Bamboo lemur in Madagascar, the Black-faced lion tamarin in Brazil (see ***FT55:37***) and others – might discover that Nature has the capacity to surprise him yet.
[AP] 12 Oct; Times 13 Oct; Newsweek 26 Oct; D.Telegraph 2 Nov 1992 – etc.

'TRIANGLE' SWALLOWS AGAIN

Three French sailors and their brand-new 42-foot catamaran were reported missing after they failed to arrive at the Caribbean island of Martinique from Rhode Island on 23 December 1992. An intensive five-day air search of 7,200 square miles of ocean yielded no clue. No storms had been reported and the disappearance was a mystery. The area is known to maritime mystery buffs as 'The Bermuda Triangle', a label invented by Fortean writer Vincent Gaddis in 1965. The large number of disappearances in this area is not a statistical anomaly, given the volume of maritime traffic; however, many disappearances at sea all over the world remain a mystery. *D.Mail, 4 Jan 1993.*

FAST LANE TO HEAVEN

Last October, 25 mourners gathered on the central reservation of the North Circular Road at Golders Green in London to perform a nocturnal ceremony of exorcism designed to free the spirit of postman James Kwesi Simpson, 23, who was killed by a beer lorry.

The ceremony, for which the police diverted traffic, was conducted by Ghanaian spiritual leader Nana Duodo and attended by the victim's family from the Ivory Coast. "We needed to free his spirit", said the victim's sister, Gertrude. "Otherwise, drivers might have seen it on the road." *D.Telegraph, Sun, 17 Oct 1992.*

PIG VICIOUS

No-one is sure what attacked digger Roy Arrow in the outback of New South Wales. Was it a crazed pig or some sort of big cat?

PIG MUGS DIGGER

Nobody knows for certain what attacked Roy Arrow, 72, of Mt David, near Bathurst in New South Wales' Blue Mountains. On the evening of 14 July 1992, dressed only in his pyjamas, Roy went out into his yard to fetch wood from a shed, and in the darkness he was crash-tackled from behind by a smallish creature that began to bite and slash him all over.

"I didn't get a chance to see what hit me... It pinned me to the ground. I kicked at it until I got my bearings [and was] able to grab both its ears, giving it a good hard pull. I reached for a stick and pushed it in its mouth. Eventually it racked off and left me alone." Roy staggered to the house covered in blood and put himself to bed, deciding (like the stoic old Digger he is) not to worry. His daughter found him the following morning and drove him to hospital in Oberon. The various rips, bits, gouges and cuts needed 50 stitches.

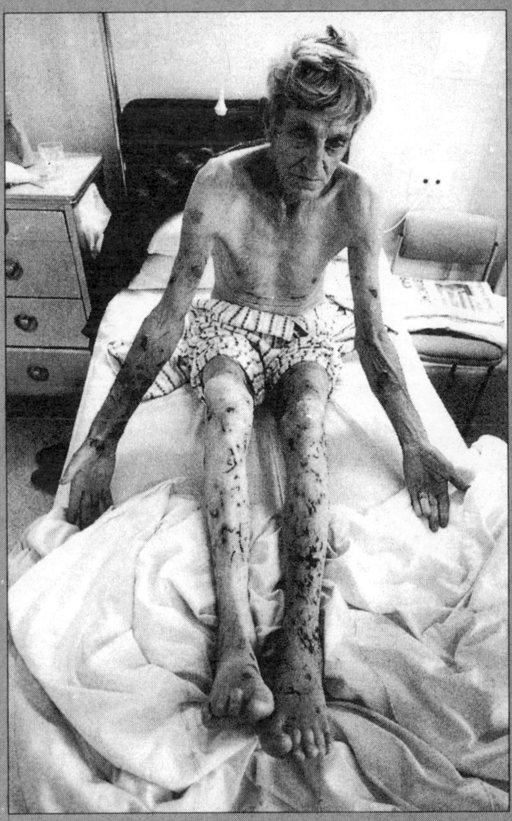

Roy Arrow - gnawed by a boar or attacked by a cat?

The attack became the talk of the region, with candidates ranging from feral pig or bandicoot to feral cat. Local cryptozoologist Rex Gilroy suggested the Oberon Panther (leopard-like and black), or the Mt David Lion (which he believes is a marsupial lion, *Thylacoleo carnifex*, supposed long extinct), or even the Tarana Tiger (a mainland survival of the normally man-avoiding, wolf-like marsupial thylacine).

At first, Roy was certain it was some kind of pig, but he changed his mind. "I remember the ears distinctly", he said from his hospital bed. "They weren't long and bristle-haired like a boar's [..] they were short and soft like a cat's. I reckon maybe I got hit by a big feral cat." However, our correspondent Paul Cropper investigated, telling us that the local ranger – who was well-aware of the local stories of 'big cats' – found only pig tracks around Roy's yard. *Sydney Morning Herald, 18 July 1992.*

Doris and her new owner Mrs Anne Thorpe.

1992 BOAR WARS: Recent porcine havoc

• ***Feb 1992*** – A boar escaped from Argyll Wildlife Park, near Inverary, Scotland, swam two miles across Loch Fyne and lived wild until shot near St Catherines, about 10 miles away and three months later.

• ***May 1992*** – A boar escaped from an abattoir at Dunblane, Perthsshire, and headed for foothills via a river. The search was called off.

• ***Nov 1992*** – Doris, a 15-stone pig, escaped from her orchard and caused havoc in the Gloucestershire village of Littledean. A deliveryman was trapped in a phonebox for over an hour (shades of *Cujo*) before Doris was trapped in a carpark. Owner Tim Pink said Doris "must have been feeling amorous. She usually enjoys sitting on the sofa in front of the fire."

• ***Dec 1992*** – A wild sow escaped from a 100-strong herd of boar kept by Chris & Janet Pinder at Newfield, near Bishop Auckland, Co Durham. One farmer blamed it for attacking one of his sheep. Still free, as far as we know.

Times, D.Telegraph, 28 May; Scotsman, D.Telegraph, 29 May; Sun, 3 June; Independent, Western Daily Press, 30 Nov 1992; D.Telegraph, 21 Jan 1993.

NOWT SO QUEER...

■ A young man pulled the emergency brake on a high-speed train in Sweden and handed out pamphlets protesting against the excessive pace of everyday life. "The cult of speed is an evil influence spreading across the world. Harmony is finding the right tempo, not speed", bewildered passengers read. Swedish railways reported the incident to police. *Eve. Standard, 10 Feb 1993.*

■ A family of four, including two children aged nine and seven, told their neighbours they were heading south to the sun, then locked up their house in Steinfort, Luxembourg, hid the car in the garage and spent the next fortnight camping in their damp cellar. In this way they avoided the shame of admitting that they could not afford to go away for their annual holiday.

They might have got away with it if police had not spotted light through a chink in the shutters and burst in, thinking it might be burglars. *[Reuters] 21 Aug 1992.*

■ Police in Baton Rouge, Louisiana, charged Redmond McGee, 25, with breaking into a woman's house and brushing her hair against her will. *[AP] 2 Aug 1992.*

■ Joseph W. Charles, 82, retired in October 1992 from his 'job' as the Waving Man in Berkeley, California. He stood in his front yard every day during morning rush hour for the last 30 years and waved to motorists. *[AP] 8 Oct 1992.*

■ Leroy Wilkinson, 46, of Cambria Heights, Queens, pleaded guilty last June to animal cruelty charges for blowing up a goat. He was arrested on 27 November 1991 after reports of an explosion at his house. Firemen found body parts of a goat and dead carcasses of other animals. Wilkinson told authorities he was "performing a religious ceremony". *NY Post, 6 June 1992.*

■ An Australian woman who said a furry toy penis kept by a female colleague in a plastic cage on a filing cabinet at her workplace had caused her stress lost her claim for sickness benefits.

The woman, who worked for the Federal Community Services and Health Department in Adelaide, said that she and her husband, the office supervisor, were made physically and mentally ill by the toy when it first appeared in February 1989.

Since leaving work in August 1989, she had received $14,500 in rehabilitation expenses, including counselling, gymnasium membership and money for an interior decorating course. Her husband had already won $45,000 in benefits for anxiety and depression. *[Reuters] 30 April 1991.*

SEEING IS BELIEVING

■ A dog walker spotted a man throwing something into a lake at Bewbush in Sussex. He took the man's car number and alerted the police, who called in frogmen while they went to interview the man. Reluctantly he told them that his son had been cursed and to remove the curse he had thrown a plate, a chicken and some rum into the water. "A likely story!" they muttered (no doubt). Then the divers emerged with...a plate, a chicken and a bottle of rum. *Crawley Observer, 11 Dec 1991.*

■ A woman came home to find her husband frantically shaking in the kitchen with what looked like a wire running from his waist towards the electric kettle. She picked up a heavy piece of wood and smashed it into him to jolt him away from the current, breaking his arm in two places. Then she discovered he was listening to his Walkman and having a jig. *Southport, Ormskirk and Formby Star, c.7 Oct 1992*

■ People were worried that an owl perched on a pylon at Johnstown near Wrexham, North Wales, never flew away, so someone called the RSPCA. An official spent an hour trying to coax the bird down before a neighbour told him "You're wasting your time. It's made of wood." The electricity firm Manweb had installed the decoy to discourage nest building. *D.Mirror, 18 Nov 1992.*

■ Terrified post office workers in Longsight, Manchester, hit the panic button and dived for cover when they saw an 'armed raider' loitering outside with a plastic bag over his head. Armed police discovered it was a labourer from a nearby building site sheltering from the rain. His 'weapon' was a French loaf for his mates' lunch. *D.Mirror, 1 Dec 1992.*

NEST FOILS PLANE

David Leslie, of Hartsdale, NY, was forced to land his single-engined plane at Danbury Municipal Airport in Connecticut, when fire erupted from his engine and smoke filled the cockpit. He was flying from Hartford to White Plains, NY.

By the time Leslie, 28, had landed, the fire was out and the danger passed. It was traced to a bird's nest lodged inside the casing. How it came to be there is one puzzle – how he could have taken off at all without noticing the problem earlier is another. Newark (NJ) *Star Ledger 22 May 1992.*

TIGHT ASS

Short-sighted miner John Bloor, 38 or 43, went to the bathroom in search of haemorrhoid cream but smothered his bum with superglue which his wife Carol had left there for mending her shoes. It took only seconds to realise he was in a sticky position and hours of sitting in a bowl of warm water to come unstuck. The story, which appeared in the *Sun* on 18 November under the headline 'Our John's Gone Potty and Glued Up His Botty', was cited by Labour MP Joe Ashton in the Commons debate on press intrusion. *D.Telegraph, 20 Nov 1992.*

HOT FOOT

Fire crews from St Neots and Papworth dashed to a house in Graveley, Cambridgeshire, when a pair of socks caught fire in the bathroom at about 5:15am on 13 January. They were too late – the fire was out. *Cambridge Evening News, 13 Jan 1993.*

TELECOM TERROR

Simon Wadland's phone calls to lonely, isolated rural housewives began deceptively – but half an hour later (longer in some cases) he had made them strip, describe their bodies and sexual experiences, push pins through their nipples and set fire to their pubic hair as he listened to their sobs.

Simon Wadland - smouldering stubble

He told them he had their husbands or children hostage, and would only stop torturing them if the women obeyed his demands. Eleven women and a girl aged 14 testified to this remote-controlled humiliation, but the prosecution mentioned at least 350 calls to 270 women in three counties around Wadland's home, near Banbury, Oxfordshire. The police suspect there may be many more who were too embarrassed to come forward.

Torture sessions

Wadland's convincing act began with his study of local newspapers for likely targets; many of the victims said he seemed to know all about them. He began his campaign in December 1988, ringing mothers to boast that he was beating and sexually assaulting their daughters. He claimed they owed him thousands of pounds for drugs and was sending a motorbike courier to their door to collect the money and to deliver photographic proof of the torture sessions. No messenger ever turned up and no money was ever handed over.

In April 1991, Wadland changed tack, inspired, he says, by a porn video. This time his goal was to force his victims into injuring and humiliating themselves. Wadland confessed that he got pleasure from controlling women in this way. One girl thought she was saving her father from being killed. Other women – including one six months pregnant – were told their husbands would be killed, or that two of Wadland's friends were outside, waiting for a signal from him to burst in and rape them. Some were told to lie naked on the floor to await his friends, anyway.

Naked wife

Some of Wadland's victims alerted the police immediately; others when they contacted their children or spouse and finally realised they had been duped. One husband came home to find his naked wife in shock, still holding the phone; while another intercepted a call and recognised Wadland's voice. The police tapped the phones of a number of likely victims and finally got the goods on him.

Wadland – a 29-year-old married man, who farmed at Woodford Halse – was described as "friendly, likable and respected". (You never can tell!) Despite Wadland's statement of remorse to the court at Northampton, the judge referred to the trauma of the women – many of them now terrified of ringing phones – and jailed him for five years on 5 October 1992. *(Sources on file)*

FOOTNOTE
We have two other cases of similarly cruel nuisances on file. An AP report of 12 June 1992 describes a phone-pest who talked at least 40 Californian women into destroying their shoes while he listened (see ***FT65:15****). Then – according to the Daily Record, 19 Sept 1992 – a woman in Hameln, Germany, was told, over the phone, to burn her house down or her daughter would be killed. Her daughter was safe, of course, but by the time the woman discovered she had been hoaxed, her home was a smouldering ruin.*

ELECTRIC FARMING

The problem with stray voltage in agriculture has long been underestimated. Cows have less resistance to electrical currents than humans, and feel the effects before we do.

A few months ago, farmers in New Zealand's Taranaki district were trying to find out why their cows frequently went berserk, leaping fences, bolting and charging through sheds. They suspected the cows were being spooked by electric shocks travelling through the ground, but the local electricity company said its system did not carry enough power to affect the livestock. *Independent on Sunday 29 Dec 1991.*

Farmer Adrian Fry of Manor Farm, Hutton Cranswick, near Driffield, Yorkshire, believes that electric shocks are giving his cows fatal heart attacks. Seven had died in a year. Once, 12 cows in the process of being milked collapsed, "shaking like jellies". Driffield vet Keith Dalby said there was "fairly strong circumstantial evidence" that the cows were suffering heart attacks caused by electrical shocks. Yorkshire Electricity tried unsuccessfully to rid the farm of the problem. *Yorkshire Post 5 Mar 1992.*

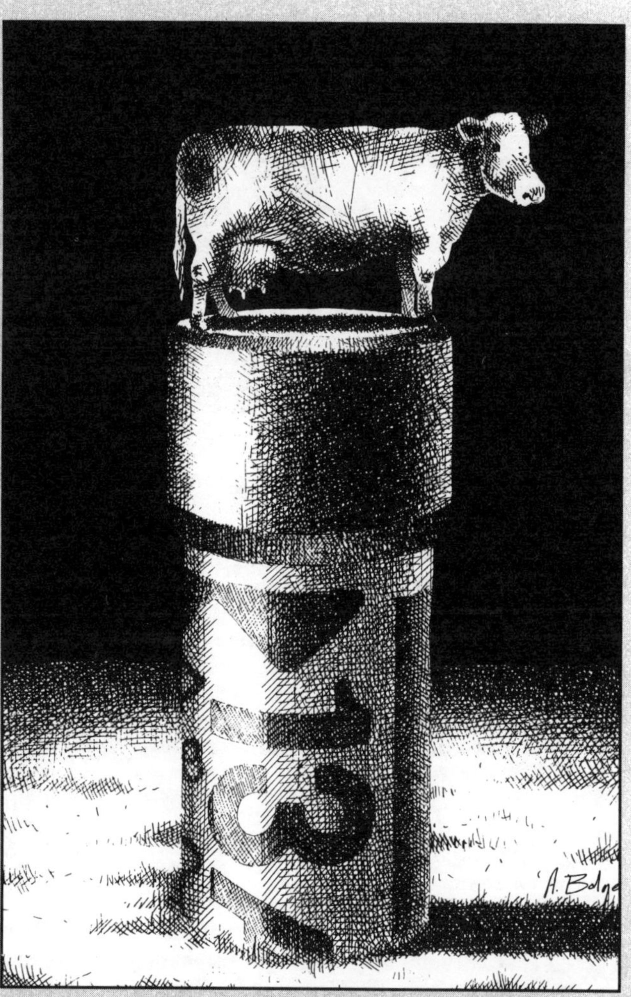

Something was spooking Keith and LeAnn Cook's cows in Kenyon, Minnesota. Some nights, the animals were so upset they couldn't be milked. It took two years and a jolt to a creamery worker to determine that electricity was leaking from power lines through the steel walls and metal pipes in the barn, giving the herd two- or three-volt charges every time they were brought in for milking. In June, the Cooks won a $405,000 judgment against the Goodhue County Cooperative Electrical Association, the second major stray voltage verdict in favour of Minnesota farmers in 1992. The co-op was planning an appeal.

Cows have lower internal resistance to electrical currents than humans, making them more sensitive to stray voltage, which shocks them through the ground. The problem has been recognised, in the US at least, since the 1940s. It has been estimated that 11% of Minnesota dairy farms and 30% of Wisconsin dairy farms are affected. In Wisconsin, the maximum stray voltage allowed is half a volt, while the US Agriculture Department recently lowered its allowable standard to two volts. "The cows have to light up in the dark" before the federal guideline triggers any action, according to the attorney that won the other 1992 Minnesota voltage victory against a power company. *[AP] 17 Aug 1992.*

Sometimes the electrocution is more dramatic than a slow leakage. Thirteen Holstein cows were killed at Maple View Farm in Avon, Maine, on 5 January 1993 when a pole mounted transformer burned up and is believed to have sent a wild surge of power through a breeding barn. Co-owner Wendell Cook speculated that the electricity "could have either come through a water pipe or through the cement floor and up their feet", although a vet pointed out that electrocution is almost impossible to prove. *Lewiston (ME) Sun-Journal, 6 Jan 1993.*

Farmer Ron Turner, 64, of Westfield Common near Woking, watched helplessly as his hay field went up in flames on 29 June, engulfing a new £14,000 tractor which he had borrowed, and his £8,000 baler. Two dead starlings at the foot of an electricity pylon were thought to be a clue to the fire. Electricity board officials believe the birds, part of a large flock that caused an electric short, were electrocuted by the 11,000-volt current jumping between connections. Their burning bodies fell to the ground, igniting the tinder-dry hay. Mr Turner was half a mile away on his lunch break when the fire started and was thus unable to drive the tractor and bailer to safety in time. *Woking Informer, 3 July 1992.*

OFFICER NOT A GENTLEMAN

General Tito Anibal da Paixao Gomes lived happily enough for 18 years, mainly on cash lent to him by his Lisbon neighbours against his military pension - until the secret of his smart Portuguese army uniform came undone. In February, the general they all thought was a deeply dignified, if slightly hard-up, highly-decorated war veteran went on trial for fraud.

Police arrested the general in 1992 for failing to repay loans amounting to £11,000. Checks with the military showed he had no record of service in the army, and he was asked to undergo physical and psychological examination. The truth was soon out: the general was in fact Maria Teresinha da Jesus Gomes, a woman of 60, who had disappeared from the island of Madeira after a broken romance.

During the Madeira carnival in 1975, Maria hired a general's uniform for three or four days to join the parades. During that time she met Joaquina de Conceicao, a retired nurse and widow 15 years her senior, whom she captivated with tales of CIA missions and gallantry in African wars. They married and resurfaced in Lisbon. Joaquina, who had agreed to a celibate life, was married for five years before wandering into the bathroom one day and discovering her partner's true gender.

Gomes was given a three-year suspended jail term in Lisbon on 29 April. We are reminded of the strange case of 'Colonel Barker' a leader of the 'Fascisti' who ran a restaurant in London's West End, unmasked as a woman during bankruptcy proceedings in 1929. *Guardian, 25 Feb; Telegraph, 26 Feb + 30 April 1993.*

Not Geoffrey Howe, but Maria Gomes, known as 'General Tito Gomes', awaiting trail on swindling charges in Lisbon.

SEEDS OF TIME

Hiroshi Utsunomiya of Yamaguchi University in Japan claimed in April to have raised a white eight-petal magnolia from a seed found in a 2,000 year-old-tomb. The seed was among hundreds found in a food-storage chamber about six feet underground in a tomb in Yamaguchi prefecture, 490 miles southwest of Tokyo. He said he put all the seeds in water shortly after the discovery in November 1982. Three months later, one seed swelled, he put it in a flower pot and it grew into a magnolia plant more than seven feet tall. *[AP] 7 April 1993.* For Chinese tomatoes grown from 2,000 seeds, see ***FT44:13***.

WITH THIS RING...

Romeo Sal Aspione watched in horror as his fiancee Sara Rizzi choked to death - on a diamond engagement ring he slipped into her champagne glass. Sal, a salesman in Sassari, Italy, said: "I wanted to do something special for the woman I loved."

■ Curt Crew, 22, asked the waitress in an Omaha, Nebraska, restaurant to serve up a $2,000 surprise engagement ring with his girlfriend's desert - then watched as she gave it to the wrong woman. Even worse, the other woman pocketed the ring and quickly left with her own boyfriend. *D.Mirror, 11 July + 15 Oct 1992.*

IRELAND'S FIRST OIL?

Johnny Bradley, 53, and his wife Carmel, 45, suffered headaches for months, as a pungent smell filled his house in Dundalk, Co Louth, Ireland. Environmental officers lifted part of the floor in the sitting room and oil welled up. A trench dug outside the 90-year-old house soon filled with bubbling crude too. It is generally thought that there is no oil in Ireland. Louth County Council said that the black stuff was not lubricating oil, diesel or petrol; scientists don't know what it is. An official report confirms the presence of 'hydrocarbons of unknown origin'. *D.Mirror, 26 Feb 1993.*

EYE EYE

Israeli police said a 50-year-old man restrained during a furniture-smashing rampage at his home was so enraged he plucked out his glass eye and hurled it at officers. He spent the night in the cells and was given his eye back the next morning.

■ Water authorities had to send 10 men to search sewage pipes after a woman blew her nose in her office lavatory in Bulawayo, Zimbabwe, and lost her glass eye down the pan. A monkey in Berlin zoo, fed up being teased by Erik Heineger, plucked out his eye. *Edinburgh Eve. News, 18 Feb; Sunday Mail, 14+28 Mar 1993.*

COUTTS HAUNTED

The Queen's bank, Coutts & Co., secretly enlisted the services of 'ghostbuster' Eddie Burks after four receptionists at the head office in the Strand had separately described a ghostly black headless figure in the atrium and a chilling drop in temperature that followed him. Coutts, founded in 1692, has occupied the Strand site since 1904, rebuilding its offices in the late 1970s.

Candidates for the Coutts ghost: Thomas Howard, 4th Duke of Norfolk (1536-72); and Robert Devereux, 2nd Earl of Essex (1567-1601).

Mr Burks, 70, a retired civil engineer, is an unpaid clairsentient (able to sense spirits) who specialises in 'earthbound spirits'. He came up from Lincoln last August and conjured up the ghost, whom he said was an Elizabethan nobleman, this time with head intact. "He was wearing a dark doublet and hose and a ruff round his neck. He was tall and slim, aged around 40, with a thin face and aquiline nose. He wore jewelled rings."

"He told me, 'I have been waiting a long time. I've practised the law. I would not bend to the Queen's command. By this time I knew too much. I could threaten Her Majesty, so a case of treason was trumped up and I was beheaded not far from here on a summer's day, which made me loath to depart. I have held much bitterness and am told that if I am to be helped I must let this go. In the name of God, I ask your help. I cannot do this alone. The memory is still strong.' He did not give a name."

Mr Burks heard the ghost's 'confession' and the necessary link with the other world came in the form of the unburdened man's daughter who materialised before the two disappeared. There have been no sightings at the bank since.

Paul Slack, fellow of Exeter College, Oxford, believes the ghost is the Earl of Essex who was beheaded in 1601 after attempting to start a popular rebellion. Another candidate, put forward by the Rev Francis Edwards, is Thomas Howard, 4th Duke of Norfolk, suitor of Mary Queen of Scots, executed on a trumped up charge of treason. His age and physical appearance match that of the ghost.

The Elizabethan is not the first apparition to be seen at Coutts. The late critic Alan Dent repeatedly saw the apparition of Angela Burdett Coutts, grand-daughter of Thomas Coutts and friend of Dickens and Henry Irving, who always disappeared into the building. *Sunday Telegraph, 21+28 Feb, 7 Mar; D.Mail, 22 Feb 1993.*

SPRING FEVER

Egypt set up an emergency ministerial committee on 7 April 1993 to investigate the wave of mystery nausea and fainting fits which had felled about 1,300 girls, mostly between nine and 16 years old, and closed at least 32 schools. The epidemic began on 1 April in a small village in the Nile Delta province of Buheira, 75 miles north of Cairo. A teenage girl, reading out loud in class, swooned and others followed suit.

It spread to rural areas and to Cairo, Alexandra and Ismailia. A rumour that a girl died after fainting led to 150 more fainting at a railway station in Damanhour on 6 April. Further faintings in the three days after 7 April brought the total affected to more than 1,500. Ministers, MPs and pundits blamed everything from food poisoning to nuclear contamination and a plot to make Egyptian girls infertile.

"They are more dizzy spells than actually fainting and losing consciousness" said Health Minister Ragheb Dewidar in a televised interview. "All results of medical and environmental tests are negative. They were conducted by senior doctors around the country and even by military chemical warfare experts."

"In my 32 years of experience I have never known anything like it", said Ahmed Rashid, medical director of Cairo's large El Agouza Hospital, after its gates were besieged by hysterical, weeping relatives of scores of schoolgirls in comas brought in by private car and ambulance, who obviously disagreed with the Health Minister's talk of 'dizzy spells'. Many of the girls affected claimed to have smelled something distinctive before they passed out.

Long-term readers of *Fortean Times* will be familiar with the phenomenon of mass hysteria. One factor in the enigmatic stew might be political tension. For instance, there was an outbreak among Arab schoolgirls in the Israeli-occupied West Bank in March and April 1983, and another among Albanian schoolchildren in Serbia's Kosovo province in March 1990, before the Balkan civil war started. *[AP], Times, Guardian, Independent, 8 April; Mail on Sunday, 12 April 1993. See* **FT33:22-27, 55:24, 57:22.**

SILENCE OF THE LAMBS

Sixty lambs were found dead in a field in Germany after they had been attacked by hundreds of crows. In scenes reminiscent of Hitchcock's celebrated movie, the crows perched on the lambs' heads and scratched their eyes out. *Aberdeen Press & Journal, 26 Mar 1993.*

THE ANDRONOV CURE

One Moscow doctor has a spine-chilling cure for alcoholics. "I simply inject a special serum into the top of the patient's backbone", explained Dr Andronov. "Mixed with alcohol, it causes paralysis – one drink too many and you're a cripple." He claimed a 100% success rate in the second half of 1992. *Guardian, 29 Dec 1992.*

EAR TROUBLE FORESEEN

Elaine Eames made regular trips to a psychic at the Spiritualist Church, James Street, Burton upon Trent, since the death of her mother. On one occasion, she said "I was asked if I had a son with dark hair and if so, was he having trouble with his ears. When I said 'no', I was told that he would do."

A week later, Mrs Eames's son Craig, 19, of Meynell Street, Castle Gresley, experienced a frightening flapping in his ear. He had it syringed with methylated spirits, which flushed out a pregnant house spider. Craig retained the spider in a bottle as a souvenir. *Burton Herald & Post, 14 April 1993.*

CRYING BOY RETURNS

The bad luck associated with that notorious kitch picture, the Crying Boy, apparently returned after six years [see *FT46:22, 47:36*]. Angela Worthington, 33, suffered three fires in one day at her council house in Middlesbrough, and suspected that her Crying Boy reproduction was to blame. At about 5:30pm on 8 March 1992, Angela and her daughters, Gemma, 5, and Sharon, 4, returned home to find smoke coming out of the coal house. Less than an hour after firemen had dealt with that, she had to call them back again when bedding in the washroom caught alight. Later that night, fire broke out a third time, again in the washroom.

"I've been here eight years and I've never had a fire before", Angela told *The Middlesburgh Evening Gazette* (9 Mar 1992). "Then on Saturday I went to see an aunt, who was moving house and she gave me this picture. I only put it up yesterday and then all this happened. It's spooky. Now I'm flinging it; I just don't want it any more."

'EDOUARD', THE SECRET WINE DRINKER

Last year saw a sudden epidemic of dwindling alcohol content in France's wine barrels, reported mainly in the Loire region. The virus/bacterium/enzyme or whatever, the greatest secret drinker in French history, has been dubbed Edouard by scientists on his trail. One thing they've noticed is that he doesn't like sparkling wine. A few isolated cases were noted after the 1988 harvest. Some growers who had aimed for 12.5 or 13% alcohol found themselves with wine of 10 or 11% or even less when it came to bottling. One of the most puzzling features of the phenomenon is that the only characteristic of the wine that changes is its alcohol content. If it were merely a case of ethanol being oxidised, that would produce acetic acid and the wine would taste of vinegar. The search for Edouard is organised by ITV, the Institut Technique du Vin, in Angers. "What we have is a map restricting his activities to a triangle covering the Loire-Atlantique, Vendée and the Maine-et-Loire", said Pierre Enjuabenés, ITV's assistant director. "He isn't quite a plague yet as we have found only 20 substantiated cases." However, producers are often reluctant to report the problem, which might be much more widespread. It has been suggested that the highly unusual weather of 1991 might be responsible: a late frost and fine pre-harvest weather left both mature and immature grapes in the same bunch, which may have affected fermentation. *New Scientist, 4 July; Guardian, 7 Sept 1992.*

IT'S A CRIME

A 17-year-old girl attempted to pass a cheque, backed up with ID, for $184 at a supermarket in Saanich, British Columbia, on 19 August 1992. The cashier called the manager to approve the payment. "Is this you?" he asked. "Of course it is."

"Well", said the manager, "then you're my ex-wife, but you don't look anything like her." The purse belonging to the manager's ex-wife had been stolen earlier in the day at Durrance Lake. *Victoria (BC) Times-Democrat, 21 Aug 1992.*

Suspected drug dealer Alfred E. Acree, 20, tried to evade capture in Charles County, Virginia, by running into a wood at night. But sheriff's deputies had no trouble following him – he was wearing L.A.Gear's new 'Light Gear' trainers, with battery-powered lights that flash when the heel is pressed. He had cocaine worth more than £500 on him. *[AP] 8 April 1993.*

Bank raider Rolf Horne escaped with £3,000, but was arrested two hours later trying to open an account at the same bank in Oslo, Norway. Teller Wilhelmina Elden said, "I couldn't believe my eyes when the same guy asked to deposit the money he'd stolen that morning". He told police he was afraid of being robbed and wanted to put it somewhere safe. *D.Star, 18 Feb 1993.*

Bank robbers in Cooperville, Ohio, drilled through a safe door, hit a brick wall, carried on drilling – and found themselves outside in the street again. *D.Record, 20 Feb 1993.*

Dennis Quigley was inside his motor home one morning parked in Seattle when he heard strange noises outside. He found sewage and what looked like vomit on the ground. Nearby was a 14-year-old boy curled up ill next to a car. "Apparently, the suspect was attempting to steal gasoline and got the sewage tank instead", said Officer Tom Umporowicz. He had siphoned not wisely, but too well. Quigley declined to press charges, figuring the boy had been punished enough. "It's the best laugh I've ever had", he said. *Lincoln (NB) Journal, 7 Aug 1991.*

Thieves broke into John Ashcroft's pigeon loft in Mere Brow, Lancashire, and stole 12 homing pigeons. A few days later, another 40 were taken, as well as 10 top breeding birds worth £100 each. Within days, all but 19 of the birds had flown home. *Guardian, 9 Feb 1993.*

After he had been robbed of $20 in Winnipeg, Canada, Roger Morse asked for his wallet back. The mugger agreed, handed over his own wallet by mistake, ran off – and Roger was $250 better off. *D.Record, 13 Mar 1993.*

BURIED ALIVE

According to Cairo's *El Gomhoria* newspaper, Hamid Afifi, 72, was entombed alive by his four children in the family vault on 8 July 1991 as none of them wanted to be responsible for his upkeep. Gravediggers rescued him after 45 days. When he returned to his house, his children feared that their father's ghost had come back to haunt them. *National Enquirer, 5 Nov 1991.*

The *Beijing Evening News* carried a grim tale on 24 June 1992. An 18-year-old youth from Hubei province, identified only by his family name, Chen, drank too much alcohol and was unconscious for 10 hours. His family thought he had stopped breathing, but more likely his breathing was so shallow that they were unable to detect it. The father didn't want his only son to be cremated, as required by Chinese regulations, and did not report the death. Instead, the family bought a coffin and secretly buried the youth.

Three days later, officials heard about the burial and persuaded the family to cremate the body. When they opened the coffin, they found the body in a sitting position, with arms pushed against the sides of the coffin. Chen's fingertips were bloodied from trying to claw out, his body covered in blood and his clothes in shreds. A doctor who examined the body said Chen had regained consciousness about 24 hours after burial. *[AP] 25 June 1992.*

THE FAR SIDE By GARY LARSON

Hours later, when they finally came to, Hal and Ruby groggily returned to their yard work — unknowingly wearing the radio collars and ear tags of alien biologists.

GELLER GETS RANDI

Berkshire-based Israeli spoon-bender Uri Geller (pictured centre) has won one of his legal actions against US magician James Randi. The action stemmed from an interview by Randi in the Japanese magazine *Days Japan* in 1989, published by Kodansha, one of the country's largest publishing houses. Geller, who was awarded costs, said the allegation was defamatory and damaging to his business and his family.

Randi, said Geller's attorney Yoichi Kitamura, had asserted that metallurgist Dr Wilbur Franklin, who had endorsed Geller's metal-bending feats, became so ashamed when Randi 'discredited' Geller, that he shot himself. In fact, Franklin died from natural causes.

Geller has other suits pending against Randi, including one in Washington DC. "Randi has claimed that I was convicted for the work I did in Israel. You can imagine how harmful that is to me and my family," he said. "I have never been arrested, let along convicted, of anything, anywhere in the world. [..] The amount of the settlement is not important. It was my name and my vindication." *[Rex], 22 March; D.Star, 3 April 1993.*

DAMNED MUMMY

Sinister occurrences associated with the filming of Professor Christopher Frayling's BBC2 series 'The Face of Tutankhamun' in 1992 gave further anecdotal support to that hoary old rumour about the mummy's curse. Frayling and producer David Wallace almost died when a hotel lift crashed 21 floors to the ground after a cable snapped.

Then, inside the boy-king's grave, two crew members were left in darkness high on a platform after the lights fused. Later, as the crew re-enacted a play meant to raise the spirits of the dead, they were blinded by a sandstorm which left almost all of them with conjunctivitis. After the film unit returned to Britain, a sealed canister containing a print of the series arrived at the BBC from a laboratory covered in fresh earth.

"I was extremely sceptical when I went out [to Egypt]", said Frayling, who is Professor of Cultural History at the Royal College of Art. "Now, I'm not so sure. I know this sounds like hype, but I promise you that I don't come from the sort of academic background where we get involved in hysteria." *Today, 17 Nov 1992.*

STRANGE DEATHS

✝ Commodities dealer Tim Brockman, 32, killed Sophia Keen, the lover who had spurned him, by hugging her to death in the flat they had shared in Fulham, west London. He may have begun out of affection, but carried on after she passed out. Coroner John Burton said he had "never heard of anyone dying like this" except for the victims of the 19th century body snatchers, Burke and Hare. We also recall the Children of God hugged to death in Belgium in 1975 and 1976 (see **FT21:10**.)

✝ Josephine Turner, 17, collapsed on 1 February 1992 at Marlborough College, Wiltshire, after eating a peanut-filled pretzel at her housemaster's cocktail party. She died 50 minutes later. A few months later, Kerry Foster, 18, a first-year student at Kent University, died after eating a vegeburger containing walnuts in her college canteen. In both cases, an allergic reaction to nuts caused fatal choking. *D.Telegraph, 4 Feb + 12 Dec 1992.*

✝ Clinton Richard Doan, 35, died on 27 January 1992 when he opened the fridge in his garage in Ketchum, Idaho. A beer keg ruptured, shot upwards and hit him in the head. *[AP] 2 Feb 1992.*

✝ Registered nurse Betty Niemi, 46, rushed to the aid of Judge William Mallen, 55, who had a fatal heart attack on the bench in San Francisco on 31 January 1992 while hearing a lawsuit challenging the nurse's 1988 dismissal from nursing school for allegedly not reacting properly to emergencies. *[AP] 2 Feb 1992.*

✝ Off-duty bus conductor Abdul Fadli Talib, 24, died after swallowing his dentures while sleeping on the back seat of a bus as it travelled from Kuala Lumpur to Seremban in western Malaysia on 21 September 1992. *[Reuters] 23 Sept 1992.*

✝ Cabbie Alla Dalhanna's habit of chewing his sunglasses had fatal consequences. His car was rammed by another in El-Alamain, Egypt, and he choked to death. *Sunday Mail, 28 Mar 1993.*

✝ Auxiliary nurse Dinah Rea, 58, of Belfast, was found standing doubled over, propped against her washing machine with her head touching the floor and arms passed backwards between her legs. She was dead. She had four times the legal drink drive level of alcohol in her blood. The weight of her trunk on her head prevented or interfered with her breathing, causing her death. *Belfast Telegraph, 4 Mar 1993.*

BLOODY MARY

Reports of Marian images weeping or growing hair are not uncommon in Catholic Chile, but what is said to be the first Chilean BVM bleeder occurred recently.

On 14 November 1992, the Nunez family smelt roses and then incense in the bedroom of their small wooden house in the southern Santiago suburb of La Cisterna. Then the two children discovered that a six-inch-high porcelain statue of the Blessed Virgin had started weeping red tears, according to their uncle Gonzalo Nunez.

"We're simple Catholics and never expected the word to get out like this", said Gonzalo. "We believe the Virgin is anguished by the convulsions of the world and with much love we just want people to open their hearts to this message."

Within hours of the first report, the Santiago coroner's office took samples of the red liquid staining the image from eyes to feet. The following day, it announced that it was human blood, type 0.4, so rare that it could only belong to six or seven people in the whole country. It proposed to run DNA tests on the sample for further information.

La familia que reza un
permanece unida

The bleeding Virgin Mary statue of Santiago.

The church was more cautious. Mgr Carlos Oviedo, Archbishop of Santiago, said that a priest would be sent incognito to gauge the ambiance. The number of visitors grew rapidly and by the beginning of December the Virgin was moved to the tiny front yard. She stood on a homemade altar amid flowers and candles with piped church music.

On 17 December, the result of the DNA tests was announced: it showed a "99.99995 per cent likelihood of coincidence with Mr Renato Nunez's blood" according to forensic scientist Nelida Chacón. A reporter broke the news live on peak-hour TV. "If it's my blood it's a divine miracle" said Renato, who is Gonzalo's brother (and, one presumes, the father of the two children).

The family has reported healings, and says there are medical certificates to prove two babies suffering from cancer were healed. "People have returned to the faith here", said Gonzalo. "It's the church which must decide." *Guardian, 4+19 Dec 1992.*

SPECIAL CORRESPONDENTS

AFRICA Cynthia Hind (Zimbabwe), Ion Alexis Will (Roving). **AUSTRALIA** Greg Axford (Vic), Paul Cropper (NSW), Arthur Chrenkoff (Qld), Rex Gilroy (NSW), Tony Healy (ACT). **BELGIUM** Henri Prémont. **CANADA** Brian Chapman (BC), Dwight Whalen (Ont.). **DENMARK** Lars Thomas. **ENGLAND** Claire Blamey, Bruce Chatterton, Peter Christie, Mat Coward, Hilary Evans, Peter Hope-Evans, Neil Frary, Alan Gardiner, Mick Goss, Chris Hall, Jeremy Harte, Ronnie Hoyle, Dionne Jones, Jake Kirkwood, Alexis Lykiard, Nick Maloret, Valerie Martin, Kevin McClure, John Michell, Ralph Noyes, Nigel Pennick, Andy Roberts, Tom Ruffles, Paul Screeton, Karl Shuker, Ian Simmons, Bob Skinner, Anthony Smith, Paul R. Thomas, Nigel Watson, Owen Whiteoak, Steve Wrathall. **FRANCE** Jean-Louis Brodu, Bernard Heuvelmans, Michel Meurger. **GERMANY** Walter J. Langbein, Ulrich Magin. **GREECE** S.C. Tavuchis. **HOLLAND** Robin Pascoe. **HONGKONG** Phillip Bruce. **ICELAND** V. Kip Hansen. **INDONESIA** Alan M. Stracy. **IRELAND** Peter Costello, Doc Shiels. **JAPAN** Masaru Mori, Shigeo Yokoyama. **NEW ZEALAND** Peter Hassall. **NORTHERN IRELAND** Caryl Sibbett. **PHILIPPINES** Keith Snell. **POLAND** Leszek Matela. **ROMANIA** Iosif Boczor. **RUSSIA** Vladimir Rubtsov. **SCOTLAND** David Burns, Stuart Herkes, Roger Musson, Roland Watson, Jake Williams. **SWEDEN** Anders Liljegren, Sven Rosén. **USA** Larry E. Arnold (PA), Loren Coleman (ME), James E. Conlan (CT), Karma Tenzin Dorje (CA), David Fideler (MI), Mark A. Hall (MN), Myron S. Hoyt (ME), John Keel (NYC), Jim Lippard (AZ), Kurt Lothmann (TX), Barbara Millspaw (CO), Ray Nelke (MO), Jim Riecken (NY), Ron Schaffner (OH), Chuck Shepherd (FL), Dennis Stacy (TX), Joseph Swatek (NB), Joseph Trainor (MA), Jeffrey Vallance (CA), Robert Anton Wilson (CA), Joseph W. Zarzynski (NY). **TURKEY** Izzet Goksu. **WALES** Janet & Colin Bord, Richard Holland, Joe Kelly.

CLIPPINGS & TRANSLATIONS FOR THIS ISSUE

Ian Abinnett, Dr Gail-Nina Anderson, Bruce Baker, Sherry Baker, Lisa Ann Barnes, S. Beckett, K.A.Beer, Lionel Beer, Bhaskar Bhattacharyya, Claire Blamey, Janet & Colin Bord, Murray Bott, Richard Bowden, Linda Brown, David J.Burns, ByRon, Cain, Stephen Castell, Brian Chapman, Steve Chilton, Arthur Chrenkoff, Peter Christie, Adam Clark, Regina Clarkin, Terry Colvin, Jim Conlan, COUD-I, Mat Coward, Tom Cridland, Paul Cropper, Mike Dash, Karma Tenzin Dorje, Jill Doubleday, Peter Hope-Evans, George Featherston, Larry Fiander, Neil Frary, Alan Gardiner, Mark Gillings, Ian Glasby, Izzet Goksu, Mark Greener, Mike Griffin, Dennis Griffiths, Peter Hassall, Stuart A.Herkes, Toby Howard, Myron S. Hoyt, Chris Jeffs, Dionne Jones, Dale Kaszmarek, Jake T. Kirkwood, Jenny Lawes, Jim Lippard, Alexis Lykiard, Ulrich Magin, Dave Malin, Nick Maloret, Valerie Martin, Lawrence T. May Jr, Barbara Millspaw, Cynde Moya, Jan Mura, Roger Musson, Ray Nelke, Roger O'Donnell, A. Parrish, Robin Pascoe, Nigel Pennick, Robin Peters, Chris Phillips, John Price, David Rider, Jim Riecken, Beth Robins, Brian Rogers, Sven Rosén, Tom Ruffles, Tom Salusbury, Paul Screeton, Nigel Searle, Keith Seddon, Ian Sherred, Doc Shiels, Karl Shuker, Ian Simmons, Andy Smith, Anthony Smith, Peter Stallard, Alan M. Stracy, SubGenius Digest, Joe Swatek, Dr Steve Tavuchis, Paul R.Thomas, Fred Thomsett, Mike Travers, Richard Turner, UFONS, Nicholas P. Warren, Cath Watkins, Christine R. Weiner, John Whiskin, Owen Whiteoak, Ion Will, Jan Williams, Jason Winter, Ron Wollaston, Susan Wood, Steve Wrathall, Chris Wren, Carl Wyant.

THERE ARE THOSE WHO SAY THAT NATURE CANNOT LIE...
PHENOMENOMIX
...AND THERE ARE OTHERS WHO SAY IT'S ALL ONE BIG FIB...
GOOD EVENING!
GREAT SCOTT! IT'S...IT'S A LONG-EXTINCT LYING MOA!
SO IT IS...
THE AMAZING FLIGHTLESS TALKING BIRD OF THE ANTIPODES!
THAT'S ME!
BE CAREFUL, CARRUTHERS, REMEMBER THAT ALTHOUGH THE MOA TALKS– IT INVARIABLY LIES!
NO I DON'T!
YOU SEE?
ANYWAY, WE THOUGHT YOU WERE EXTINCT!
I AM!
IS THAT A LIE? DOES THAT MEAN IT'S NOT EXTINCT?
IF YOU'RE EXTINCT, HOW COME YOU'RE HERE NOW?
SIMPLE! WHEN WE APPEARED TO BECOME EXTINCT, WE ACTUALLY LIED ABOUT IT...
YOU LIED ABOUT YOUR OWN EXTINCTION?
YES! ...er... THAT IS–NO, IF YOU SEE WHAT I MEAN...
SO, EVEN THOUGH YOU'VE BEEN EXTINCT FOR YEARS, AND NOBODIE'S EVER SEEN ONE OF YOU, YOU REALLY EXIST IN GREAT NUMBERS?
WELL... ...er... NO!
YOU SEE, WE'VE ALL CAUGHT A RARE MOA DISEASE AND DIED, SO WE ARE EXTINCT NOW!
THAT'S WHY YOU CAN SEE SO MANY OF US...
...BECAUSE I'M LYING AGAIN...
I CAN'T HELP IT– I'M A LYING MOA!
?
?
I'M TOLD THEY WERE EDIBLE...
I'M TOLD THEY MADE VERY GOOD HATS...
AMMO
HUNT EMERSON ©93

FORTEAN FANCIES

T-SHIRTS

**100% COTTON
T-SHIRTS, ONE SIZE
XL.**

NEW!
Italian Martians T-shirt 100% cotton, good quality heavyweight T-shirt in dark green. One size XL £9.99. Illustration by Walter Molino of Rosa Lotti's experience with the 'men from Mars'.

Charles Fort T-shirt - 100% white cotton T-shirt, one size XL £7.99 Charles Fort's Portrait and the slogan "One Measures a Circle Beginning Anywhere".

BOOKS

FORTEAN TOMES is a series of facsimile reprints of early issues of The Fortean Times (formerly simply titled The News). Each book covers a wide range of fascinating subjects from feral children to spontaneous human combustion to UFO abduction.

FORTEAN TIMES 1 - 15
Yesterday's News Tomorrow **£19.99**
ISBN: 1 870870 263 400 page paperback, colour cover, illustrated throughout.

FORTEAN TIMES 16-25
Diary of a mad planet **£19.50**
ISBN: 1 870021 258 416 page paperback, colour cover, illustrated throughout.

FORTEAN TIMES 26 - 30
Seeing out the seventies **£14.99**
ISBN: 1 870021 207 320 page paperback, colour cover, illustrated throughout.

SUBSCRIPTIONS

If you have enjoyed this issue, why not make sure that you receive a copy on a regular basis? Order a year's supply of Fortean Times for yourself or a friend and get it delivered direct to your doorstep. And that's not all: every new subscriber receives a FREE copy of Doc Shiels' Monstrum book (DIY monster hunting - worth £8.95). Fortean Times back issues also available (see below).

BACK ISSUES

FT51 - South Carolina's Lizard Man, albino frog fall and Yorkshire's water wolf.
FT53 - Crop circles, invasion of the slime creatures and Islamic simulacra.
FT58 - Lesbian vampires, trepanning today and alien abduction.
FT60 - Alpine ice man, Father Christmas as Odin and the Lake Erie monster.
FT61 - Homing treks by cats, everlasting light bulbs and social panics.
FT62 - The Piltdown Hoax, World's Heaviest Man dies and puddle -creating poltergeists.
FT63 - Crop Circle colour pull-out, acid tattoo panic and British alien big cats.
FT64 - Spielberg, Satanic witch hunts and the pregnant male hoax.
FT65 - Colour pull-out on Martian monuments, kidney kidnapping rumours and blood miracles.
FT66 - Florida's penguin panic, bogus social workers and horse-ripping.
FT67 - BBC's Ghostwatch hoax unravelled, plus Italian Martians.
FT68 - Cattle Mutilation in America, ESP Orgasms, Vampire at Croglin Grange.

Please send me the following items:

Item	UK Price	US Price	Overseas	Qty	Value
Yesterday's News Tomorrow	£19.99	$44.00	£22.00		
Diary of a Mad Planet	£19.50	$44.00	£22.00		
Seeing Out the Seventies	£14.99	$34.00	£17.00		
Italian Martians T-shirt	£9.99	$23.98	£11.99		
Charles Fort T-shirt	£7.99	$19.00	£9.50		

Postage and packing free.

Total £ ______

I would like to subscribe to Fortean Times from issue ______
***Please tick for free Monstrum book** ☐

For one year (6 issues) £12 ☐
Overseas inc USA £15 US$30 ☐

For two years (12 issues) £20 ☐
Overseas inc USA £26 US$50 ☐

Back issues £2 each (£2.50 overseas or US$5.00) Please circle your selection:

36	37	38	39	42	43	44	46	50
51	52	53	54	55	56	57	58	59
60	61	62	63	64	65	66	67	68

Name: Mrs/Miss/Ms/Mr ______________________

Address ______________________

____

______________________ Postcode ______________

I enclose a total payment of £______ made payable to: John Brown Publishing Ltd, or debit the above amount from my Access/Visa/Amex/Mastercard/Eurocard (delete where applicable) account.

Account No ☐☐☐☐

Expiry Date ☐☐

Signature ______________________

Date ______________________

**Please return this order form to:
Fortean Times, Freepost SW6096, Frome, Somerset BA11 1YA, U.K. or Freephone credit card details on 0800 581409**

**FREEPOST AND FREEPHONE SERVICES AVAILABLE TO UK RESIDENTS ONLY. OVERSEAS CUSTOMERS PLEASE ADD POSTAGE STAMPS TO POSTAL APPLICATIONS.
FOR TELEPHONE ORDERS PHONE (44) 0373 451777**

FT69

HOT STUFF

Dreams of cheap power received a major setback in 1989 when scientists failed to reproduce the Cold Fusion effects claimed by professors Martin Fleischmann (above right) and Stanley Pons (above left). Following a disastrous press conference during which they were accused of "inventing data, breaching ethics, violating scientific protocol and fraud", they fled from the university of Utah. More recently they have been continuing their research at a science park in the South of France founded by Technova, a Japanese scientific think tank itself financed by several big Japanese companies including Toyota. CHRIS TINSLEY reports....

Cold fusion died in 1989! Even a quite assiduous follower of science in the UK might well believe this. So what were about 300 scientists doing at a 'Third International Conference on Cold Fusion' in Japan last October? Only two of the delegates were from Britain; but there were 55 from the USA, 20 from Italy, and a dozen or so from Russia and from China.

Was this 'a seance of true believers' as some described it? Or did this conference herald the end of coal, oil, acid rain, fission power, the fusion programme, and much of the world's pollution – and perhaps even the distribution of electricity on the present scale?

A year ago, I'd have laughed at such a question. Now, I'm pretty certain that the answer is 'yes'. Perhaps a qualified 'yes', but I must agree with some eminent Japanese scientists: it really is the beginning of the end of the kind of world we know.

> "One of the problems the Fusioneers have faced is that their experiments last far longer than the media's attention span."
> **Dr Eugene Mallove**

The reasonable response to such an outrageous statement is to dismiss it. If the writing were on the wall for the energy industries, if there were solid scientific evidence for a new form of cheap power, we would all know about it – wouldn't we? – unless it were hidden in secret laboratories. In fact, while there may just possibly be classified work on Cold Fusion going on somewhere, as far as I know the only secret work is that of exploiting perfectly public and published research.

It is the Wright Brothers all over again. They first flew in 1903, and for a few years after, flew in full public view... there was a tramway nearby. Their efforts to interest the press or their government fell on stony ground, probably because heavier-than-air flight was – like Cold Fusion – 'known' to be theoretically impossible.

THE NEW POWER AGE

"I have now seen so many positive reports about – perhaps misnamed – Cold Fusion, from highly respected organizations that, after initial scepticism, there can be no further doubt that excess energy is being produced by some previously unknown process, which, I am sure, will be elucidated in the fairly near future.

Twenty years ago, when OPEC quadrupled its prices, I remarked: 'The age of cheap power is over – the age of *free* power is still fifty years ahead.' I may have been too pessimistic... Coal and oil will always be essential raw materials for chemicals, plastics – even synthetic foods. Oil is much too valuable to burn – we should eat it! If Cold Fusion can be scaled up for industry, the consequences are immeasurable. It will mean the end of the Fossil Fuel Age, CO_2 build-up and acid rain. If a plasma fusion rocket could be developed, it would open up the solar system.

Throughout history, crackpots have predicted the imminent end of the world. I have about 90% confidence that I'm now doing something very similar.

And this time, it's good news."

— From an address by Arthur C. Clarke (pictured right) to a US military seminar in Colombo, Sri Lanka, 29 March 1993.

It took five years for their triumph to be recognised, and even then the first two Wright factories opened in France and Germany before their American enterprise was able to get off the ground. Even then, after many years of demonstrable success, the Smithsonian Institute did not want to exhibit their original Wright Flyer, so the brothers let it be shown in London's Science Museum until 1948, as a constant reminder of the way their own country had treated them.

But what of Cold Fusion? There are two known ways of getting power from the atom: by the splitting (fission) of very heavy atoms like those of uranium; or by the fusion of very light ones, like those of hydrogen. Either method releases energy because they both produce middle-weight atoms, which have less energy than the very light or very heavy varieties.

The problems of fission power are well known, and commercially viable fusion power is generally regarded as being decades away. Fusion is not a completely clean source of energy – the fast neutrons produced tend to damage the reactor, making it radioactive. Nor is it easy – it requires the sort of conditions found in an exploding atomic bomb. Even in the sun's interior, less fusion energy is produced per litre than by the human body. But whereas the sun fuses hydrogen atoms (which have a single proton for a nucleus), it is easier to fuse one of the two isotopes of hydrogen – deuterium (which has a neutron as well as the proton), and tritium (which has two neutrons and the proton). Tritium is also unstable and therefore radioactive.

Early in 1989, there was great excitement when two very reputable chemists – Professors Martin Fleischmann of Southampton University and Stanley Pons of the University of Utah – claimed to be able to cause deuterium fusion, not under explosive conditions, but in a glass jar on a bench.

It has long been known that the metal palladium will absorb extraordinary amounts of hydrogen (or deuterium). The idea was that the resulting 'compression' would raise the chances of fusion to a useful degree. Both Fleischmann and Pons knew that this was extremely unlikely, but they had been experimenting with the idea for several years. They might well have abandoned their work – it was, after all, a crazy idea that they were funding themselves – had it not been for a singular event.

One of their electrolytic cells exploded with sufficient force to make a hole four inches deep in the concrete floor. The source of the blast was the small block of palladium which they were using; there was little of it left. This energy had to come from somewhere, and there was no obvious way in which it could have been stored in the metal and then released so violently. (It should not be forgotten that the British scientist Andrew Riley was killed in January 1992, during an experiment at the Stanford Research Institute. As he lifted a cell from its water bath, its base blew off "turning the rest of it into a rocket which shot upward striking Riley in the head." *New Scientist* 27 June 1992.)

Fleischmann and Pons continued their research and went public – see ***FT52:12*** – claiming that their cells produced far more energy (in the form of heat) than was being supplied to them as electricity. They also claimed evidence suggesting that this was due to fusion.

There was an immediate worldwide rush to duplicate Fleischmann and Pons' work, and it soon became clear that something was wrong. The amounts of heat reportedly produced should have been accompanied by a lethal flood of fast neutrons, but there was little, if any, detected radiation and hardly anyone found any excess heat. Also, there should have been noticeable amounts of helium or tritium, but where this was detected it was less than the expected amount. Arguments raged – and are raging still – about both the positive and the negative experiments, but there was no clear-cut confirmation of Fleischmann and Pons' original findings.

In a flurry of anger, accusations and threats of legal action, the whole affair died. The prestigious science journal *Nature* sought to bury the subject in an article entitled 'Farewell (Not Fond) to Cold Fusion'. As far as I know, no further work on Cold Fusion has been done in Britain: most people are not aware of just how much clout *Nature* has.

To outsiders, the bizarre history of this research holds up a mirror to science. There seems to be a distinct pecking order in science, in which physics outranks chemistry, and cosmologists stand far above those who made it possible to grow two heads of grain where previously there was only one. Even the famous palæontologist Stephen Jay Gould has complained that his subject stands low in the estimation of other scientists. A physicist, quoting Lord Rutherford, once told me: "There are no 'sciences', there is only physics; the rest is stamp collecting."

MILLS CELLS

Dr Randell L. Mills *(left)* – who runs HydroCatalysis Power, an experimental lab in Lancaster, Pennsylvania – developed his breakthrough cell *(see diagram at right)* in August 1990. His cell has functioned successfully since October 1991, delivering 100 watts for every 10 watts put in. Thermacore – a respected high-tech company, also in Lancaster – is attempting to develop a commercial unit. Mills said, confidently: "This is the last hope for a sustainable society. Thank God we found it before we ran out of fossil fuels."

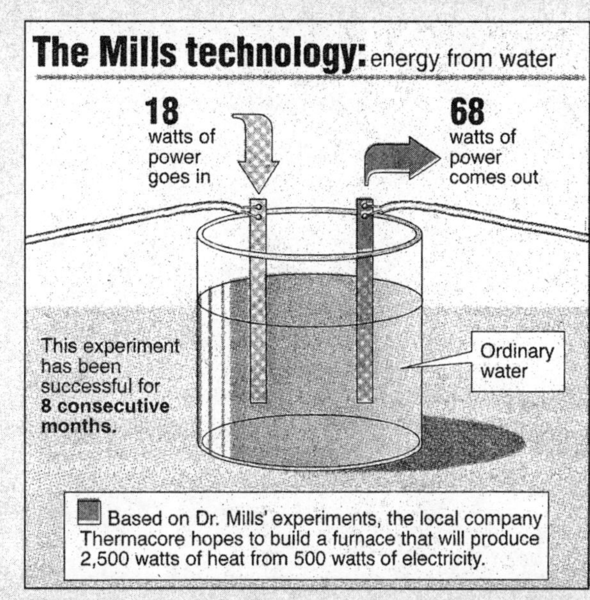

The Mills technology: energy from water
18
watts of
power
goes in
68
watts of
power
comes out
This experiment
has been
successful for
8 consecutive
months.
Ordinary
water
Based on Dr. Mills' experiments, the local company Thermacore hopes to build a furnace that will produce 2,500 watts of heat from 500 watts of electricity.

Elsewhere in the world, it was a different story. Too many people were intrigued by the strange data yielded by these apparently simple cells. There was little consistency between the results found by different groups, and often the same group would find that seemingly identical experiments gave completely different results. Reports of excess heat were generally dismissed as experimental error; and reports of the production of helium (which would be proof of fusion of some kind) were discounted as contamination. Dozens of reports of the finding of tritium were harder to explain away, though some critics said they were evidence only of fraud.

One especially odd discovery was that palladium sheets, used in some of the experiments, were found to fog photographic film, indicating the possible presence of radioactivity previously absent. This effect has now been shown to be the result of unstable isotopes of silver and rhodium in the palladium sheet – proof that some nuclear reactions had been occurring.

> "If you gave someone a dollar and they gave you back $10, couldn't you tell the difference?"
> **Dr Randell L. Mills**

But why the hostility from so many scientists? Firstly, many thought they had been hoaxed by Fleischmann and Pons to check-out a crazy idea which they *knew* to be theoretically impossible. Secondly, it was because mere chemists had dared to step onto the sacred soil of physics. It is bad enough (and conveniently forgotten) that two bicycle mechanics founded the science of ærodynamics, or that a meteorologist first proposed the notion of 'continental drift'. It irked nuclear physicists that someone from outside their well-established field should suggest it was seriously flawed.

More to the point was the issue of the non-reproducibility of results. Perhaps too much was made of this when it is well known that poorly understood experiments are very difficult to copy – but it remains a cornerstone of science that unreproducible results must in the end be discounted. What is not clear is why, now that results *are* solid and widely reproducible – at least to the degree that the same work can usually be replicated – and the yielded heat values are so great, the hostility should still be so strong.

Research continues into electrolysis of heavy water with palladium cathodes. Fleischmann and Pons – now in a Japanese-funded lab in France – can make their cells boil pretty much on demand. At SRI International in California, after several years of funded research, researchers have finally succeeded in defining the conditions required for excess heat. Meanwhile, in Japan, Dr Akito Takahashi of the University of Osaka (once an adversary of Cold Fusion) has devised a variant of the original experiment which has proved to be fairly easy to reproduce, though it is still not clear how he got lucky for a month and produced much more heat than usual. It was his work which decided the Japanese on increasing the level of their funding.

In Japan, Cold Fusion is accepted as fact by many scientists. A variant of Cold Fusion is done without electrolysis, using a number of methods for loading palladium with deuterium gas. This is being pursued vigorously in Japan, Russia and elsewhere. The most striking results come from Nippon Telephone and Telegraph (NTT), whose shares went up by 10% when their Dr Eiichi Yamaguchi announced that his experiment yielded large volumes of helium and much heat, and that he could reproduce this easily. NTT has tackled the problem of replication head on by offering 'DIY kits' for this experiment at around half a million dollars each.

In a way, this experiment encapsulates the whole Cold Fusion story. *Nature* reported it as almost a joke, claiming (wrongly) that abstracts of the paper were not available, and suggesting contamination as the source of Dr Yamaguchi's helium. Study of his paper shows that Dr Yamaguchi took great care to avoid this, and that helium was not detected when ordinary hydrogen was used instead of deuterium. What it did say was that even with ordinary hydrogen, heat was obtained, indicating that the energy did not come from fusion (because fusion is much harder with hydrogen). More mystery!

There is also a third kind of Cold Fusion, first reported by a doctor of *medicine*, Randell Mills, in 1991. It originated outside the Cold Fusion 'community' and is still viewed with disfavour by some 'traditional' Cold Fusioneers. Incredibly, it does not even use expensive palladium or deuterium, and is more easily reproducible. Instead of a delay of weeks or months followed by erratic bursts of heat, it is claimed that there is a steady flow of excess energy starting almost at once. Up to 20 times more heat has been reportedly produced than is input as electricity – although three to ten times is more common.

Furthermore, the excess heat keeps on coming month after month. These cells simply electrolyse a solution of ordinary potassium carbonate in ordinary water with a nickel cathode, with material costs of mere pence. To the increasing number of respectable institutions now checking this out, we must add the famous Lincoln labs in Massachusetts and in Canada, the Chalk River Nuclear Facility.

Dr Robert T. Bush, a theoretical physicist at California State Polytechnic University, has been involved with Cold Fusion research for some time, and holds the current record for heat production per gram of palladium. Moving his attention to Mills-type cells, he has found that he can obtain the effect with other solutions, and proposes that the heat is coming from a nuclear reaction between the potassium and hydrogen atoms, and that the deuterium Cold Fusion is the same sort of process, using lithium salts dissolved in the heavy water. He believes he now has solid evidence for the right kind of products, in the right kind of quantities. But – and there always seems to be a but – others have had similar cells running for a year or more and have seen no such products.

All these theoretical problems will have to be solved. It may not be possible to get the best from these cells until what is going on inside them is understood... as was true of the similar situation in the early days of transistors. It may even be that the heat is not of nuclear origin at all, despite the occasional sign that nuclear reactions have taken place, but a strange form of chemistry. There are dozens of theories, and scores of new results, surfacing with each passing month. The whole subject is in the sort of ferment which might be expected at the birth of a new branch of science.

There can be little doubt that there will be self-sustaining cells, with output in the kilowatt range, by the end of this year (1993). These could be scaled up for home generators of electricity. The 'fusion'-powered car – which Richard Petrasso of MIT wishes to see before he accepts all this – is a distinct possibility. It is exciting to speculate on what sort of world might have developed if Michael Faraday – who said: "Nothing is too wonderful to be true." – had noticed and developed the Mills effect. Great nuclear-powered steam locomotives of iron and brass could have thundered through the Victorian night.

Here and now, there are still many technical problems that need good engineering solutions; for example, what if a low-powered domestic cell suddenly came on strong and produced radioactive tritium? Fortunately, the amount of tritium does not square with the heat, and could perhaps be 'tuned out'.

Nevertheless, with money moving into Cold Fusion, and with the solid experimental base now available, we should very soon see the start of an extraordinary revolution. Shares in conventional oil or electricity may now be a poor long-term investment.

And no... the foundations of science are *not* going to crumble. The chaos will eventually be resolved, and peace will reign... until some new Fleischmann and Pons upset the established theories of what we now, perhaps wrongly, call Cold FT

SOUND + LIGHT = HEAT!

As we were working on this article, we received news (via Chris Tinsley and Dr Eugene Mallove) of the ex-periments of photochemist Roger Stringham (formerly of SRI International) in San Francisco. Stringham has spent years studying a phenomenon called *sonoluminescence*, in which tiny bursts of light are produced by collapsing microscopic bubbles in liquids bombarded by ultrasound.

Following the Pons-Fleischmann debacle in 1989, Stringham decided to attempt the triggering of Cold Fusion with ultrasonic energy in heavy water cells pressurised with deuterium gas. Experiments have successfully produced excess heat and nuclear products. In fact, so much heat was produced that the main problem is to *prevent* damage to the metal parts of the equipment. String-ham has determined that this excessive heat occurs only when heavy water is used; and because *no* lithium salts are involved, he believes lithium can be ruled out as an ingredient of the reaction.

Dr Mallove, who resigned his position as chief science writer for the MIT News Office over the unprofessional hostility of some physicists towards Cold Fusion experiments, says: "SLCF (sonoluminescence triggered Cold Fusion) though not yet confirmed, seems to be a demand phenomenon. It turns on *instantly* and shuts off *instantly* with the toggling of the acoustic energy [..] No such melting or vaporisation occurs in light water. This offers stunning visual proof of a fantastic difference in the behavior of the two hydrogen isotopes... equivalent to what the skeptics in 1989 said would be a convincing indication of Cold Fusion (ie. no effect in light water with palladium and an effect in heavy water with palladium) [..] I want this replicated in dozens of places. It should not be hard to do with the available information [..] These results, confirmed by others, would constitute irrefutable proof of Cold Fusion."

Patents have been applied for and Stringham is preparing for publication.

– THE EDITORS

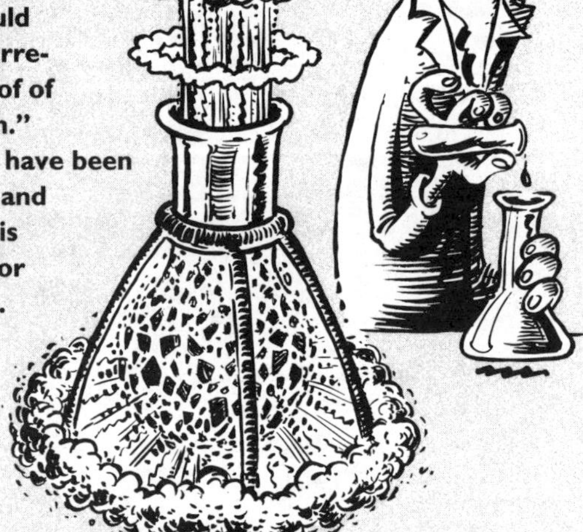

HEAD TO HEAD

SECRET INVASION

"All they want is our sperm and eggs." TIM COLEMAN talks to UFO abduction researcher DAVID JACOBS

Dr David Jacobs is one of the key proponents of the 'alien abduction' belief. In 1973 he gained his PhD with his dissertation *The UFO controversy in America* (Indiana University Press, 1975). It remains the only book on the subject, published by an academic press, which takes a 'pro' attitude to UFOs.

In 1992, he worked with 'missing time' colleague Budd Hopkins and the Roper Organization on a national US survey to determine the extent of the 'abduction' problem. The construction of the questionnaire and the interpretation of its responses were severely criticised when the eventual report concluded that about 2% of adult Americans – corresponding to an incredible 3.7 million people – believed themselves to have been abducted. Jacobs and Hopkins have also been criticised for offering seminars on the treatment of 'self-reported abductees' using hypnotism, when neither have any qualifications for teaching hypnotherapy.

Dr Jacobs is a professor of history at Temple University in Pennsylvania, and teaches the only known accredited course on UFO studies. His latest study of abduction experiences, *Secret Lives: Firsthand Accounts of UFO Abductions* (Simon & Schuster, USA, 1992), was published in Britain in March by 4th Estate. FT spoke to this controversial ufologist when he visited Britain last summer.

FT: Your *1975 dissertation The UFO Controversy in America* is reckoned to be one of the important studies in the history of ufology. Can you say what it was that your book changed?

DJ: It showed that the US Air Force and the scientific community had never really understood what the phenomenon was. The USAF, for example, thought it was just a public relations problem. Between 1948 and 1969 – when the USAF closed down Project Bluebook – no headway had been made in the subject whatsoever.

The other big problem was 'contactees': a group of people who, in the 50s and 60s, claimed that they had taken rides in flying saucers and had on-going contact with benevolent Space Brothers. They turned out to be mainly charlatans, which in turn allowed ridicule to be the appropriate reaction to *all* UFO witnesses. All the major UFO organisations at that time spent most of their time combating the contactees, and not shedding any light on the UFO problem itself.

My book explained why, after 20 years of UFO research, the world still knew so little about it. The US media, the government, the CIA, the UFO research organisations, and the lunatic fringe had all done a strange dance with each other while the subject stagnated. My case was that without a serious professional research network which could draw the disparate strands together and set new standards of behaviour and research, there could be little progress in understanding the phenomenon.

Dr. David Jacobs at MUFON UFO Symposium, 1988.

FT: How does the 'abduction' experience differ from the 'contactee' phenomenon?

DJ: The abduction phenomenon is very different from what we had previously imagined. It is basically a situation in which one species is exploiting another, physiologically.

The public's idea of contact with aliens is the culturally conditioned product of science-fiction – this is usually a magic moment, in which the aliens reveal themselves to us (or vice versa), and which will change us forever and for the better. This is *not* what we see in the abduction phenomenon, which is far more mundane.

FT: What are abductions, then?

DJ: Briefly, beings come down and take people... take sperm or eggs from them... sometimes implanting fertilised eggs into women... re-ab-

The invasion of Earth as imagined in early SF films was a much more public affair than the alien intrusions presented by Jacobs. A scene from *Earth Versus The Flying Saucers* (1956).

ducting them after a short time and removing the foetus for external gestation. Once it has grown into a baby, the woman is again abducted and asked to hold or touch the baby. Some of these events are accompanied by mental manipulation – the insertion into the mind of false memories of sexual intercourse or of giving birth; in other accounts these seem to be real experiences.

The whole focus is on the reproductive function, to produce babies which are hybrids – part-human, part-alien. We don't know why. We don't know what they do with these hybrids; since they are significantly different in appearance to normal humans, we know that aren't brought here.

In essence, we have been invaded, but not in the way depicted in science-fiction. These beings, neither malevolent nor benevolent, are just getting on with a job in a very clinical, routine way. It is a distressing scenario which has taken us totally by surprise. It suggests that technological superiority does not automatically mean moral superiority. Sometimes an abductee is healed of a life-threatening disease, but it's my opinion that this is not real benevolence, but simply to keep the abductee healthy during their experiment.

FT: Who are these abductors?

DJ: There are four distinct types of beings involved. About 90% of cases involve the notorious 'greys', described as small and hairless with thin limbs, a large bulbous cranium without nose or ears, big black eyes, and a slit for a mouth. The others are said to be reptilian, insect-like, and even humanoid. Who knows whether they come from the same place or not? They all do the same things.

FT: How long do you think this has been going on?

DJ: We have cases dating back to the turn of the century; however, we believe this is a 20th century phenomenon which began in earnest just after WW2.

We used to think this phenomenon was a rare bird. In the 70s we knew of maybe ten cases. In the 80s that increased slightly, but now the extent of the abductions is staggering.

You know Budd Hopkins and I worked with the Roper Organization to poll 6,000 people in the USA. The replies suggest that the number of abductees in the US alone reach into the millions... but of course we can't be sure because most people don't remember what happened to them seconds after it occurred.

FT: How many have you dealt with personally?

DJ: Personally? ..... about 70 people. I have had around 350 hypnotic regressions with them – which takes up a lot of time. Between Budd and I... perhaps 500 cases.

FT: When someone contacts you for help, how do you distinguish between a genuine abductee and the mentally ill?

DJ: I begin by asking them a series of 25 questions, which is aimed at screening out the seriously mentally ill. I talk with them on the phone, sometimes for up to two hours – this is usually enough time to tell whether they are suffering from a mental disorder. If so, I usually tell them this falls outside my area of expertise and refer them to a psychologist. Sometimes an abductee will be seriously mentally ill also, so it is possible to make mistakes. Mostly I deal with perfectly average people who have no major problems apart from the fact that they have been abducted.

FT: What ethical safeguards do you have, especially when the recollection of a trauma might actually *increase* their anxieties?

DJ: When they first come to me, I warn them strongly about the consequences of finding out what has happened to them. Abduction turns their lives upside down – nothing is the same afterwards. There are some positive aspects, but I emphasise the down-side of finding out. I also give them a pamphlet, written by Budd and myself. At this point, some say they don't want to continue, but if they do, I warn them again. If they are having a bad time once we're under way I refer them to a psychologist who can help them deal with the trauma. Most feel some gradual benefit, and begin to sort out their lives.

FT: Why are some people saying they have been visited or abducted many times throughout their lives? Is there a 'victim mentality', or some form of collusion?

DJ: We don't know why some people are picked over and over. It starts in infancy and continues into old age. It's not so much that people are 'picked' but that they can't stop it. Anyone who becomes aware of what has happened to them wants it to stop. They have slept with guns and knives, but no one has yet been able to prevent what has happened to them. We don't know why a technologically superior race would need to continue abducting people and taking sperm and eggs when, logically, they should be able to manufacture what they need genetically.

There is no collusion, but there *is* a victim mentality. Over the years, the abductees feel they are being victimised. They have low self-esteem and are frequently depressed. Once they learn what has happened to them, they usually get extremely angry – this is cathartic and improves their condition.

FT: If, as you say, Earth has been infiltrated, can we fight back?

DJ: We have found no way of preventing an abduction. One person reported abductions as frequently as twice a week; their life was disintegrating. We installed a video camera, which didn't prevent abductions but reduced them to a minimum. It was the best we could do. Whenever there *was* an abduction there was a power outage, so the camera never recorded anything.

FT: The accounts on which you base your book are mostly recovered through hypnosis, but hypnosis is well-known to be a flawed tool for recovering subconscious memories exactly. How do you resolve this difficulty?

DJ: Many people remember without hypnosis; but yes, hypnosis *is* a problem. Numerous studies have shown it is not a royal road to the truth; yet other studies have shown that hypnosis recovers memories better and more accurately when those memories are of a traumatic nature. In fact, it is an excellent tool for this job – it seems to act as a release mechanism and the memories just flow out.

The real problem is not that the abductee is telling the hypnotist what he wants to hear, but that the hypnotist does not know the right questions to ask.

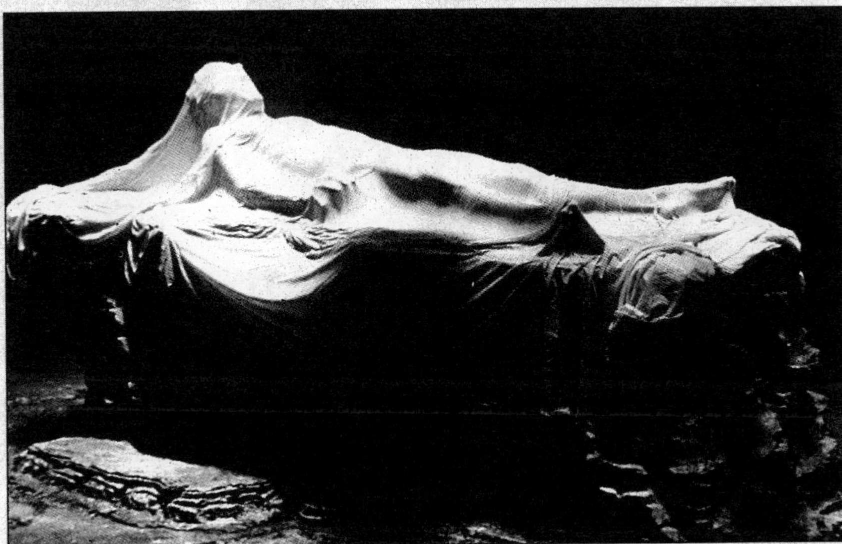

A recent portrayal of an abduction: Travis Walton wakes up in a space craft in *Fire In The Sky*.

FT: These are pretty fantastic ideas. Where is the hard evidence?

DJ: When people talk about hard evidence, they usually mean artifacts... like stealing an alien ashtray and presenting it to us. This kind of evidence is very hard to come by. With abductions, though, there is physiological evidence to back up the anecdotal kind. I can attest to this myself, having seen people develop scars within a few days. Natural wounds could not heal and scar in such a short space of time.

There are also implants – objects that have been placed inside the abductees. We have seen little white dots on MRI and CAT scans, and an X-ray of a very complex object lodged inside a woman's nose. The problem is that I can't force someone to have an X-ray. These objects are also hard to spot because they are usually radio opaque.

Sometimes the aliens will use a brownish liquid which will fall on the abductee's clothes, and we are able to study the stain using sensitive spectrum analysis. Although we have found unusual elements, they have so far been inconclusive as evidence.

FT: But surely, even people who are not necessarily hostile to these notions will need a reasonable level of proof?

DJ: Originally, I would have fallen into that category myself. This is not a subject to believe lightly. I am impressed by the preponderance of accounts – over and over again with the same precision and convergence of detail. Many details have not been published and could not have been picked up by such a wide variety of people.

Eventually you have to agree that something is happening. There is no comparable psychological model which can account for the phenomenon as well as the abductees' belief that they have been abducted.

FT: Some ufologists believe they are being manipulated – fed 'strange' data as part of a CIA disinformation campaign. What's your view?

DJ: It is possible, of course, but neither Budd nor myself, nor any of our abductees, have ever been interfered with by any official of any kind. I have heard classic abduction accounts from children who were not under hypnosis and who could not have been 'got at' by the CIA or anyone.

Abductees come from every conceivable type of background and race. The CIA would have to be inventing these stories and working night and day in every area of society all over the world. It seems so implausible... I believe that this subject is, at best, regarded with indifference by the government because the scientific world is generally sceptical.

FT: How has all this affected you personally?

DJ: It has been an enormous strain on both my time and my emotions. Dealing with abductees is terribly difficult – you become a *de facto* therapist.

In the old days it was a tremendous intellectual challenge which took you to the farthest reaches of knowledge and beyond. For 25 years, sightings were the passion of my life – but now that I believe that close encounter sightings are masking memories of abduction events, it has taken all the fun out of UFO research.

What I see now is a phenomenon which causes pain, brings catastrophe to peoples lives, and affects children's development. It is a toll of suffering which I never expected to see. I get hundreds of letters from all around the country, and reading them is, as Budd says, "a daily dose of pain". We all feel helpless in the face of it, and for all those involved, we want it to stop. **FT**

GOLDEN

KARMA TENDZIN DORJE GIVES US THE LOWDOWN ON THE H THE NEW KARMAPA IN TIBET. IT IS A FAR FROM SPIRITUA

H.H. the 16th Gyalwa Karmapa in Rumtek, Sikkim, demonstrating true emptiness. It is widely believed that this photo was taken shortly before he died, and he appears to be phasing in or out of solidity.

It was surprisingly hot in Tibet. Lhasa is on the same degree of latitude as Cairo, albeit 3,000 metres higher. That's 3,000 metres less protection from the sun's rays. My scalp became sunburned in no time.

I was there for the enthronement of Karma Ugyen Tinley, the 17th incarnation of His Holiness the Gyalwa Karmapa. It would take place in Tsurpu monastery, the traditional seat of the Karmapas, 100 km west of Lhasa. It is not the original structure; the present buildings were built with funds from western Buddhists after the original was demolished during the Cultural Revolution.

Karma Ugyen Tinley's enthronement as the 17th incarnation of H.H. Gyalwa Karmapa.

And I do mean demolished; the Red Guards did a very thorough job. It seems the Chinese were miffed that the 16th incarnation, demonstrating uncanny prescience, had decamped just prior to their 'peaceful liberation' of Tibet in 1959, taking his monks to a new home in the Himalayan kingdom of Sikkim. He also took most of Tsurpu's treasures, both material and spiritual, like the famous hat woven from the pubic hair of 108 *dakinis*, a sword with its blade tied into a knot, and, my favourite, the marble pebble which the Karmapa had squeezed like putty showing the imprints of his fingers. Some, however, like the great statue of Buddha Shakyamuni, had to be abandoned. This statue was said to contain relics of all the previous Karmapas, of Shakyamuni himself and even of the Buddha of the previous æon. This splendid monument was singled out for special attention by the cultural revolutionaries who packed it with massive charges of dynamite. Pilgrims still scour the earth where it stood in the hope of finding any remaining holy shards, no matter how microscopic.

The Chinese are still in control, of course, and it was they who decided on the date for the enthronement – 27 September 1992. A strange choice, considering that it was upon this date in 1987 that a peaceful demonstration for Tibetan independence was savagely repressed and about 90 unarmed people, including monks and nuns, were shot on the streets of Lhasa. Perhaps the rulers were trying to use the popularity of the enthronement to neutralise the bitter memories of the incident?

CHILD

NKS SURROUNDING THE ENTHRONEMENT OF
ALE OF INTRIGUE, SPANNING CONTINENTS.

The abysmal quality of petrol available in Tibet made jeep travel to Tsurpu painfully slow as well as simply painful. We had to stop every ten minutes or so for my driver to clear the accumulated crud and water from the carburettor. The six young monks we had picked up on the way saw nothing unusual in this. After all, they had never been in a motor vehicle before. Along with thousands of other pilgrims, they had started walking to Tsurpu as soon as they heard the news of the ceremony. They were from Kham, they said, and had been walking for two months, sleeping under the stars and begging for food along the way.

Having set out before dawn, it was mid-afternoon by the time we arrived and a queue was forming in the courtyard outside the main *gompa* (meditation hall). It was the queue to receive the blessings of the new Karmapa, an eight-year-old boy. Put another way, one could say that this boy was merely the latest vehicle for an enlightened consciousness which had chosen rebirth as a human on this planet since the first Karmapa was born in 1110 AD. Legends speak of even earlier lives – one taking place 15,000 *kalpas* ago – and of his exploits in other 'universes', such as the 'Very Clear and Light-Filled' world-system. [1] As one *kalpa* lasts for 4,320,000,000 years [2], give or take a few days, the Karmapa could be said to be eight years old, 883 years old, or quite possible ageless.

A friendly monk insisted I stand at the head of the queue. No one minded; it gave them a chance to practise patience. "Look," said the monk. "There's the Karmapa's family." Sure enough, the 'great mother' and 'great father', along with an assortment of their other children, had joined the queue for their son's blessing. The family is not a rich one, and until now had been simple nomads – but there they were, splendidly attired, especially the women, who wore huge pieces of amber and turquoise in their elaborately braided hair.

I thought I knew what to expect. I had acquired some photographs of this young boy with a pleasant smile before I left my home in California – incidentally, these made great gifts to the barmaids at the Lhasa Hotel, where I never had to pay for another cup of *ch'ang* – but to meet him in person was another matter. Even if he is *not* the Karmapa (and I will return to this matter later) he has such natural dignity and poise that one is forced to concede that he is no ordinary child. As I bowed and presented my greeting-scarf his eyes raked me from head to foot with keen interest. He touched my head and returned my scarf. A moment later I was back outside in the bright sunshine, calm, contented and just a little dazed. Although I stayed at Tsurpu for a week and saw Ugyen Tinley several times, that briefest of meetings is my most vivid recollection of him.

The eight-year-old Karma Ugyen Tinley arriving in procession at Tsurpu.

"Everywhere, one heard the sound of mantras, ritual bells and skull-drums. Near my tent, a Khampa dance troupe was rehearsing. A lama with an outlandish dialect taught me magic knots; another sold me an ancient copper bracelet (he said it had fallen from the sky)."

Over the next week, the pilgrims poured in. A small town of traditional white and blue tents appeared almost overnight, complete with tea-shops and market stalls. Estimates put the number of visitors somewhere between 10-20,000. Everywhere, one heard the sound of mantras, ritual bells and skull-drums. Near my tent, a Khampa dance troupe was rehearsing. A lama with an outlandish dialect taught me magic knots; another sold me an ancient copper bracelet (he said it had fallen from the sky).

The day before the enthronement, Chinese officials announced that admission would be by pass and that only 100 passes were to be issued. Curiously, a brisk black market blossomed and by mid-morning several hundred were in circulation.

Many of the pilgrims were content to watch the folk-opera in the courtyard, but a large, noisy, jostling crowd of hopefuls gathered around the steps at the entrance to the *gompa*. At the end of the entrance hall, a pair of young monks guarded the huge wooden doors to the meditation hall where the ceremony was taking place.

Tsurpu Monastery, hidden by formidable mountains, the spiritual home of the Karmapa.

They were armed with fresh willow branches and drove back the mob by lashing out at random, frequently drawing blood – some of it mine. The crush was so great that a stone balustrade, weighing several tons, was pushed into the courtyard below. Miraculously, no one was injured. I still can't figure out how I got inside – I was into my second hour of being painfully squashed against the *gompa* doors when they opened a crack, a monk's hand grabbed my jacket and pulled me through.

Of course, it's great to be able to say that I was there, with all those famous lamas, but the TV crews from China, Japan, Taiwan and Germany eroded what was left of any spiritual atmosphere. Just when I was concluding that I had been crushed, trampled and beaten over the head to hear three tedious hours of speeches, it was suddenly gift time. The newly enthroned Karmapa rose to his feet to receive a steady stream of presents: bolts of rich silk brocade, simple monastic clothing, gilded statues and even the latest Gameboy were handed over. I joined the line of lamas and well-wishers to give the Karmapa a crystal rosary I had made for him. In return I was presented with a damask silk greeting-scarf, a packet of photographs of the Karmapa, two protection ribbons and six packets of various magic pills. What a haul!

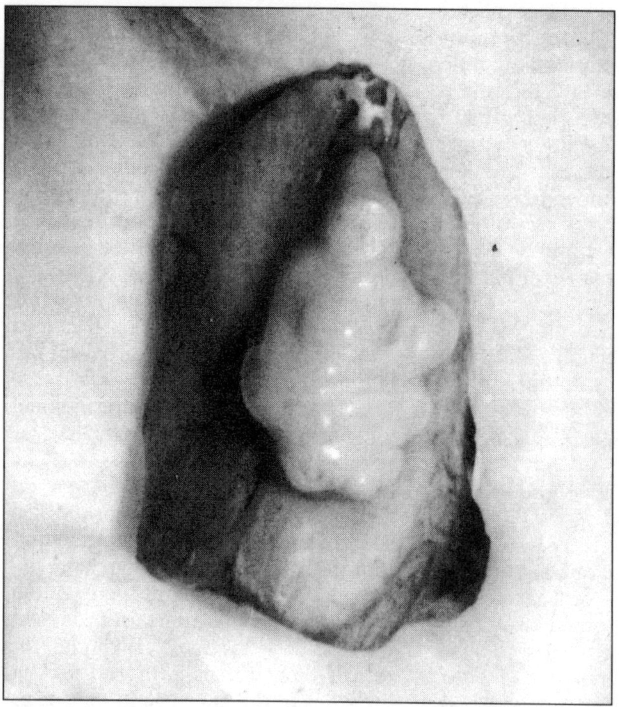

An alleged fragment of the shin bone of the late H.H. 16th Gyalwa Karmapa, given to Tsurpu Monastery by the Sharmapa shortly after the death of the Karmapa in 1981. The bone appears to bear the image of a meditating Buddha.

Back outside again, my mood lightened further when, out of a clear deep-blue sky, large fluffy snowflakes began to fall. As soon as the flakes touched the warm ground they vanished. This phenomenon is known as 'flowers of the gods' and is considered highly auspicious.

Scarcely two weeks later, I found myself at Rumtek, in Sikkim, world headquarters of the Kagyu order. It was buzzing with rumours... stories of labyrinthine intrigue and intimations of murder. But before I proceed, some background might be helpful.

Through his practice of the 'dream yoga', a monk called Drubtob u-Se (1110-1193) attained the final stage of realisation known as 'beyond meditation', and he came to be called Dusum Khyenpa ("he who knows past, present and future") or Karmapa ("he who performs Buddha-activity"). [3] He founded Tsurpu monastery and a new teaching lineage, the Karma Kagyu. Several years after his death, the precociously-gifted monk Chodzin (1206-1283) was declared to be the reincarnation of Dusum Khyenpa, and became the first officially-recognised reincarnation in Tibet, setting the precedent for the whole *tulku* tradition. [4] This monk is better known as Karma Pakshi, renowned for his supernatural powers. His fame as a wonder-worker occasioned a summons to the court of Kublai Khan, where he engaged Taoists in magical battles and entertained Marco Polo with cunning stunts.

Eventually, the Karmapas came to head the entire Kagyu order and, briefly, enjoyed temporal rule of Tibet. Unlike other reincarnate lamas, each Karmapa left a 'letter of intimation' predicting his next rebirth, which was used to identify his successor. Until the 16th, that is.

When the 16th Karmapa died in a Chicago hospital in 1981, he did leave a letter which the four young regents, now in charge of the order, assumed to be his 'letter of intimation'. Unfortunately, when opened, it was found to be a short poem about meditation which did not help the process of identification. There were also political considerations; any Karmapa born in modern Tibet would be vulnerable to Chinese control and manipulation. Add to this the machinations of various factions of Tibetan and Bhutanese aristocracy, and the mutual antipathy of two of the regents, and you can understand why the world had to wait so long for the announcement of a new Karmapa.

After the disappointment of the 'letter', the Sharmapa, one of the regents, had a dream which gave details of the Karmapa's rebirth. He even travelled to Tibet but... nothing. Ever since childhood there had been no love lost between Sharmapa and another regent, Tai Situpa. Once more, they found themselves in opposition. Of the remaining two regents, Gyeltsap sided with Tai Situpa and Jamgon Kongtrul attempted to mediate between them all. The stalemate lasted until March 1992, when Tai Situpa revealed a letter to the other regents, ostensibly in the handwriting of the 16th Karmapa and bearing his signature

Ole Nydahl poses with a statue of the first Karmapa. A Danish ex-boxer, he has proclaimed himself to be an emanation of the 17th Karmapa.

and seal. He told them how the Karmapa had given him a protective amulet which he had worn ever since and only recently discovered it to contain the letter of intimation.

The letter gave precise, if veiled, references to the names of the parents and the location of his next birth. The Sharmapa was openly sceptical of its authenticity and urged that its existence be kept secret. Tai Situpa went against the custom of unanimity and published the letter, forcing Sharmapa to express his doubts. Amid pressure from outside factions the tensions mounted. Then tragedy struck. The one person who might have successfully resolved the conflict – the much-loved Jamgon Kongtrul – died on April 26, 1992 in a car accident near Rumtek, just before he was to lead a search party in Tibet. The circumstances surrounding this tragedy are mysterious and there are many versions of the tale, each with its own villain. I do not intend to compound the confusion by adding my own ill-informed opinions to the list.

Despite the great loss, the expedition went ahead and had no difficulty in locating the child. It is said that various auspicious signs and miraculous circumstances surrounded his birth, and that when the search party arrived, four suns were seen to rise over the town of Chamdo. [5] Anyone who has witnessed a parhelion or 'sun dog' will not scoff at this claim. This ærial phenomenon is most often seen, as in this instance, early in the morning when the sun's rays are refracted by prismatic ice crystals in the upper atmosphere. Sun dogs are frequently bright enough to cast shadows – but that's as much as I'm inclined to explain away. When it comes to the accounts of the sounds of conch and cymbals being heard to emanate from the sky three days after Ugyen Tinley's birth, I claim Fortean neutrality.

Back at Rumtek, the unseemly displays of animosity between Tai Situpa and the Sharmapa were coming to a head. A large party of hot-headed Khampas (renowned throughout central Asia for their ferocity) left Kathmandu intent on persuading the Sharmapa of the error of his opinions. The Khampa style of debating includes arguments both weighty and pointed; so, fearing their methods of persuasion might be too forceful for comfort, the Sharmapa summoned an Indian army unit to Rumtek for his protection. The Khampas never arrived, but the army did, much to the annoyance of monastery officials and lay Tibetans. An ugly skirmish ensued in which a few people were injured. The Sharmapa left Rumtek soon after and has not yet returned. Ugyen Tinley has since been recognised by the Dalai Lama as the 17th Karmapa despite the Sharmapa's objections.

Meanwhile, a propaganda campaign is being waged in Europe. Since the late 1970s, Ole Nydahl, a Danish ex-boxer and former student of the 16th Karmapa, has set up Karma Kagyu centres (with himself as head) in Denmark, Germany, Poland and Russia. It is difficult to describe the excesses of Ole's bullying, bragging, racist style of machismo without risking your disbelief – better that you sample any page of the latest volume of his autobiography [6], and let him speak for himself. The Sharmapa astonished many by conferring the title of lama (spiritual guide) upon Ole. Perhaps he had hoped for Ole's allegiance and support. Well, Ole and his wife, Hannah, have certainly been tireless in their denunciation of Ugyen Tinley, but Ole has recently extended this to include all Tibetan lamas, *including* the Sharmapa. He now says that he himself is an emanation of the Karmapa and that he is creating a new 'pure' Buddhism suitable for Europeans. I give him two years either to create a brand new religion or to go barking mad. [7]

Doctrinally, there are any number of loopholes which could be used to resolve the mess. For instance, it is possible to recognise multiple reincarnations. There have been other cases in which, for instance, three candidates are taken to be reincarnations of the body, speech and mind of the deceased lama. Indeed, a Karmapa once said that there are, in fact, 8,000 Karmapas abroad in the world, working for the benefit of all sentient beings, but only one chooses to reveal himself.

As for Ole and Hannah, the head monk at Tsurpu says that their trouble-making and slander will be purified only if they complete ten *Ngondro* (each one involves 100,000 full-length protestations, 100,000 mantras, 100,000 mandala offerings and 100,000 guru-yoga practices) followed by a three-year retreat. Until then, the monk writes, "I ask both of you not to visit Tsurpu monastery. Your negative karma is so severe that it will contaminate this sacred place; anyone who drinks the water that springs from here, all the way to the ocean, will be contaminated by it." [8]

I have yet to hear of anyone who has met this remarkable child, Karmapa Ugyen Tinley, who has not been profoundly impressed with his lively intelligence and his mature, dignified presence. After all, if he is not the *real* Karmapa, then he has sufficiently good karma to be accepted as such by four million Tibetans and the great majority of Kagyupa around the world. Surely that's good enough. **FT**

NOTES

1 – H.H. Gyalwa Karmapa (tr. K. Holmes): *Dzallendara and Sakachupa* (Scotland, 1981).
2 – J. Dowson: *A Classical Dictionary of Hindu Mythology* (London, 1968).
3 – J. Thaye: *A Garland of Gold* (Bristol, 1990).
4 – K. Thinley: *The History of the Sixteen Karmapas of Tibet* (Boulder, 1980).
5 – K. Dowman: in *Tricycle: The Buddhist Review* (Winter 1992).
6 – O. Nydahl: *Riding the Tiger* (Blue Dolphin Publishing, 1992).
7 – There is, incidentally, a pseudo-Karmapa sect already in existence – the Purple Lotus Society of Taiwan.
8 – Drupon Dechen: 'An open letter to Ole and Hannah Nydahl' (October 1992).

Lunchtime at the PHANTOM DINER

We ate in silence, almost with an air of reverence, and finished the meal with Turkish coffee drunk in a glow of contentment. The atmosphere was hazy, almost unreal. At last we felt it was time to go. I asked Mr Hovanessian how much we owed. He told us shyly and the price was astonishingly cheap. "A fantastic meal", I said. "Quite the best I have ever eaten"

TONY CLARK recalls a mystery of gastronomic proportions in the wilds of central Asia

Some years ago, I was working as a civil engineer in Iran. In about 1956, I had to make a visit to Manjil in the north-west in connection with the construction of a cement factory and went up with an Iranian engineer. Manjil, the centre recently of a disastrous earthquake, is on the road to Rasht and about 150 miles from Tehran. At the time of my visit, it was very isolated and all that we had been able to eat was some unleavened bread and *dugh*, a type of liquid yogurt.

We were in consequence very hungry as we drove back to Tehran. From time to time we met a lorry and would slither past each other. We were fortunate to be travelling in the summer, as the road was quite often impassable with snow in the winter. Eventually we reached a plateau and, as we were still 120 miles from Tehran and 50 miles from Qazvin, the nearest town, any hope of eating was remote.

"Nothing much we can do", I said, "unless we can find a *tchae-khana*." This was the equivalent of a road-side café where we were unlikely to get anything more substantial than a glass of weak tea, strained through a lump of sugar held between the teeth.

Just then, we came to a village with some single-storey mud huts, permanently dusty from the continual passage of lorries and cars, and with a very distinct and unmistakable landmark in the shape of a pile of rocks with one balanced precariously on top.

"Looks promising", I said to my Iranian companion as we pulled up behind some lorries. "Should get some tea at any rate." We got out of the car and walked through some scattering, squawking chickens to the long, low building in front of us. After the brilliant sun which had been shining on us all the way from Manjil, it took us some time to get accustomed to the gloom; but how wonderfully cool it was! Round the walls were rows of charpoys, those essentially functional beds made from rope and wood. Some of these were occupied by drivers who were drawing sporadically on a hubble-bubble. There were a few carpets and in the middle some chairs and rough wooden tables. The walls were bare, apart from a highly stylistic picture of Hussein the Martyr.

From the back, the proprietor hurried up. "Good afternoon", he said nervously, but in flawless English. "My name is Hovanessian...Armenian of course and", he added with a touch of

Tony Clark in Tehran, 1958, with some of his English-language pupils at the British Council.

pride, "my wife is a White Russian. What can I get for you?"

"My friend and I are very hungry", I answered. We've had nothing to eat all day. Perhaps you can help us."

The Armenian smiled. "It is not often we have ferenguays...excuse me, I mean foreigners here", he said, "and it will be a great privilege and honour to prepare a meal for you. My wife and I are not unaccomplished as cooks. Please leave it to us." He ushered us to one of the wooden tables and swept imaginary dust away.

After a while, a beaming, moon-faced woman came in with a tablecloth and some cutlery which she laid out very carefully. The lorry drivers examined us incuriously and the gurgle of the hubble-bubble echoed rhythmically as the stem was passed from one cupped hand to the next.

Presently, Mr Hovanessian came in himself with two bowls of soup. And what soup! The basic ingredients were cucumber, raisins and yogurt, served ice cold. I don't know what else had been added, but it was quite the most delicious soup I had ever tasted.

When we had finished, Mr Hovanessian asked me confidentially if I would like some wine. "We have two types", he said, "Rezayeh or Qazvin." I chose the red Qazvin and we drank it very cold. The next course was dolmas (stuffed vine-leaves), which were delicious with a delicate flavour all their own. I asked for the recipe, but Mr Hovanessian was politely vague. "Oh, just vine leaves...rice, that from Rasht is particularly good...some meat and onions and a few herbs. This is not really an Iranian dish", he added, as if to justify his reticence.

The next course was Chelo Kebab, which I suppose can be called the national dish of Iran. Prior to grilling, the meat is marinated overnight in a special mixture of yogurt and spices. The Chelo part is rice prepared in butter so that a brown crust forms on top. In addition, a raw egg yoke is served and mixed with the rice just before eating.

We ate in silence, almost with an air of reverence, and finished the meal with Turkish coffee drunk in an glow of contentment. The atmosphere was hazy, almost unreal. At last we felt it was time to go. I asked Mr Hovanessian how much we owed. He told us shyly and the price was astonishingly cheap. "A fantastic meal", I said. "Quite the best I have ever eaten."

Mr Hovanessian's face flushed with pleasure. "I'm so glad to have served you something you enjoyed", he said. "As I said before, it is unusual for us to see a foreigner. Do call again and tell your friends to look in." He and his wife saw us to our car and as I drove off I made a note of the mileage.

Of course I told many people about this meal. "Impossible!" I was told. "How could you get a meal like that in such a remote place? What traffic is there on the road, apart from lorries bringing in caviar from the Caspian Sea and troops moving up to the Russian frontier?"

It so happened that three months later I had to make another visit to Manjil, this time with an English engineer who had been one of the biggest sceptics. The circumstances were identical. We were both tired and hungry and reached the plateau at about the same time.

"Here we go then", I said, looking at the mileage. "Just another five miles."

Sure enough, after five miles, we reached the village unmistakably the same one because of the pile of rocks with the one balanced on top. But of the *tchae-khana* there was no sign, nor was there any evidence of such a building having ever existed. I asked one of the villagers. "Tchae-khana? There's never been one in all the time I've been here and that's 40 years."

We drove disconsolately away. Naturally, my companion scoffed, but there was a hint of doubt, even fear, in his voice.

I can offer no explanation. I only know that I definitely had a meal in this village in a *tchae-khana* which I have ever since called the world's best restaurant. **FT**

The author in Manjil, Iran, in 1956.

FESTIVAL OF WARMINSTER

CENTRE FOR UFO STUDIES

Presents a second showing of the much acclaimed Warminster UFO and Corn Circles Exhibition and Video Show. Original reports from the sixties through to the present day.

TO BE HELD AT

The Old Bell Hotel

Market Place
Warminster
Wiltshire
Tel: 0985 216611

11am - 7pm Mon - Sat
from July 12th
to August 27th

PLUS: Lectures and Skywatches to be announced. UFO and Corn Circle Books, Magazines, T-shirts and Badges available.

Continuous showing of the latest UFO & Corn Circle videos.

ADMISSION £1.50 Refreshments Available

PICK OF THE CROPS

The Fortean Times Field Guide to English Circlemakers compiled by Jim Schnabel

AS THE CROP CIRCLES roll through their fourteenth consecutive summer in the public eye, the debate over the phenomenon continues. Flying saucers, whirlwinds, Gaia, hedgehogs, Robin Goodfellow, rabbits, Pan, whirling devas, Archon, plasmoids, Old Nick and miscellaneous field-sprites remain in contention for the honour of top Circlemaker, while the human artificers are almost universally reviled as mischief-makers, government spies, disinformation-spreaders, and annoying obscurants of the genuine, hauntingly beautiful, and (for some) deeply meaningful and supernatural phenomenon whose epicentre is England.

YET DESPITE THESE ATTEMPTS to marginalise the role of human circlemakers, it has increasingly been argued by a few bold cerealogists – and by the circlemakers themselves – that such mundane artistry, far from being incidental and obscurantist, IS the real phenomenon. At the CEREALOGIST's circlemaking competition last year, in Buckinghamshire, one judge was heard to remark that the top five teams – most of whose members had little or no prior experience – would have fooled the so-called experts under ordinary conditions. Such statements are echoed by the circlemakers themselves, who claim to have been fooling the same experts summer after summer. So... just who are these circlemakers? HOW do they do it? WHY do they do it?

THE SHORT ANSWER IS that throughout England each summer there appear to be as many as several dozen groups active, using a variety of methods and with a variety of motives. A description of every group would be impossible here: because of lack of space, because very few groups have made a major impact on the subject, and because little or nothing is known about most of them. With apologies to those who have been left out – eg the Burford Group, the Silbury Group, and Mr Sinister – here is a run down of some of the most interesting English teams.

Photo by Robert Irving (Spiderman). Pete Rendall of CERES finds footprints while George Wingfield of the CCCS looks for evidence of other energies at Overtown Farm, Wiltshire 1992.

DOUG AND DAVE

- **NUMBER OF MEMBERS:** 2
- **AGES:** Sixtysomething
- **FIRST CIRCLES:** Approx 1975
- **BASE:** Southampton
- **ALLEGED CONSPIRATORIAL AFFILIATION:** *Today* newspaper; MBF Services (MI5)
- **CEREALOGICAL BELIEFS:** All but a relatively few rough circles are man-made. Even rough circles might be man-made.
- **MOTIVES:** Originally to wind-up UFO buffs. Later, to wind-up New Agers and to wreck the meteorological theories of Dr Terence Meaden. Artistic pleasure throughout.
- **PREFERRED TECHNIQUE:** The 'stalk-stomper' (below), a plank held beneath one foot with a loop of rope. Enables upright circlemaking and authentic swirling effects. (Can quickly cause foot cramps in beginners.) Special techniques include cross-piece and torch signalling for spacing quintuplet satellites, and cap-mounted wire sighting device (above) for pictogram avenues and sidebars.
- **SCHNABEL'S GUESSTIMATE OF FORMATIONS ACTUALLY MADE:** Most formations in Hampshire, Oxfordshire, Sussex, Dorset and south Wiltshire from 1975 to 1992.
- **SAMPLE PRAISE:** "Augghhh!" (Pat Delgado, thrown to the ground by energies in a split-ring pictogram at Longwood Estate, near Winchester, 1990.)
- **SAMPLE COMMENT ON CEREALOGISTS:** "These people are crazy!"
- **BACKGROUND:** Doug Bower and Dave Chorley (below), the grand old men of the circlemaking underworld, met in the late 1960s. Both were artists, pranksters and UFO enthusiasts. In the mid-1970s, inspired by a famous 1966 'saucer nest' case in northeast Australia, they made their first circle in Strawberry Field, near Cheesefoot Head, west of Winchester. When the public failed to notice these and other designs, the duo nearly gave up – but significant press coverage of the Cheesefoot Head formations in 1981 inspired them to continue. Bower and Chorley were known between the mid-1980s and 1991 to be crop circle enthusiasts. Their circlemaking claims, published in *Today* on 9-11 September 1991, were widely disbelieved; although Terence Meaden, after confronting them with unpublished data on early circles, became convinced of their veracity. Bower and Chorley were filmed making a number of formations in the summer of 1992. These formations were widely agreed by circles experts to be 'genuine'.

THE BILL BAILE

- **NUMBER OF MEMBERS:** 3
- **AGES:** 14-18
- **FIRST CIRCLES:** 1990
- **BASE:** Northamptonshire
- **ALLEGED CONSPIRATORIAL AFFILIATION:** None
- **CEREALOGICAL BELIEFS:** Some circles are made by people, while others might have other causes
- **MOTIVES:** Curiosity about how circles are made. Pride in artistic achievement. Lack of circles in Northamptonshire.
- **PREFERRED TECHNIQUE:** Doug-and-Dave-style stalk stompers. Group also uses collapsiblefishing rod device with affixed wooden stake to form pivot for large rings without damaging central crops.
- **SCHNABEL'S GUESSTIMATE OF FORMATIONS ACTUALLY MADE:** About a dozen major and minor formations in Northamptonshire and Cambridgeshire during 1990-92, including the Woodford Rings and a massive complex with a five-pointed star at Cranford St Andrew.
- **SAMPLE PRAISE:** "It's impressive. It's wonderful." (George Wingfield on the Cranford St Andrew's complex.)

GANG

- **SAMPLE COMMENT ON CEREALOGISTS:** "They're running in circles."
- **BACKGROUND:** The majestic Woodford Rings of 1991 inspired Hertfordshire circles sceptic Michael Inns to search for the responsible artists. House-to-house enquiries in Woodford flushed out a 16yr-old with the *nom de plume* of 'Bill Bailey', who had made the formation with two accomplices. It had taken them six hours on hands and knees, using planks to push down the stalks. A year later, having gleaned the stalk-stomping method from the media coverage of Doug and Dave, the Bailey gang created the 160-metre wide formation at Cranford St Andrew.

During the execution of this masterpiece, at midnight, Bailey saw an orange ball of light over a field a quarter-mile away, imming rapidly into invisibility. Some of the more mystically-inclined cerealogists – who, despite having been kept informed of Bailey's activities since 1991, had seldom mentioned him publicly – began to spread the story that a team of hoaxers had been visited by the *real* circlemakers. Bailey is getting his driving licence soon, and will be able to venture further afield.

I KNOW THE DESIGN'S RATHER SIMPLE BUT I CAN TELL YOU IT WASN'T SIMPLE TO DO!

MERLIN AND CO

- **NUMBER OF MEMBERS:** 1-13
- **AGES:** Up to approximately 900
- **FIRST CIRCLES:** 1980 (claimed)
- **BASE:** Bristol
- **ALLEGED CONSPIRATORIAL AFFILIATION:** The *Sunday Sport* newspaper
- **CEREALOGICAL BELIEFS:** Merlin and his followers believe that they have made all of the English crop circles using "white magic"
- **MOTIVES:** Merlin (that is, the original Arthurian one) told them to do it. Enchantment of the world. Promotion of various enterprises.
- **PREFERRED TECHNIQUE:** Ritual magic while seated at the centre of a 16-foot diameter occult boardgame. More prosaic methods rumoured. Occasionally leaves one of his boardgames in circles for promotional purposes, and to enlighten cerealogical masses.
- **SCHNABEL'S GUESSTIMATE OF FORMATIONS ACTUALLY MADE:** At least several in Bristol, Avon and Wiltshire during the late 1980s and early 1990s. Possibly the Blackbird hoax, 1990.
- **SAMPLE PRAISE:** "We have indeed secured, on high quality equipment, a major event." (Colin Andrews, at Operation Blackbird.)
- **SAMPLE COMMENT ON CEREALOGISTS:** "Merlin is very alien. He can't relate to any of them."
- **BACKGROUND:** Better known to West Country local newspaper reporters as George Vernon, Merlin received his calling after a head injury during an auto accident in 1980. A vision of the ancient magician appeared to him and explained that he, Vernon, was the reincarnation of Merlin. Since then, he has embarked on a career of ritual magic and occult boardgame design – the latest version being 'Crop Circle Mysteries'.

Merlin swept onto the cerealogical scene in 1990, when copies of his 'Zodiac' boardgame were found within the hoaxed formation at Operation Blackbird, near Westbury. Merlin claims that other copies were left within many other circles, but were never reported by cerealogists. Merlin also claims to be the spiritual leader of 12 Bristol-area 'Druids' who aid his various activities.

THE WESSEX SKEPTICS

- **NUMBER OF MEMBERS:** 5-10
- **AGES:** 30s-40s
- **FIRST CIRCLES:** 1991
- **BASE:** Southampton University
- **ALLEGED CONSPIRATORIAL AFFILIATION:** Channel Four TV, CSICOP
- **CEREALOGICAL BELIEFS:** All circles are man-made
- **MOTIVES:** To demonstrate the plausibility of their belief and the ineptitude of their opponents
- **PREFERRED TECHNIQUE:** Garden roller. Sometimes, cardboard mats to avoid leaving footprints.
- **SCHNABEL'S GUESSTIMATE OF FORMATIONS ACTUALLY MADE:** Clench Common, Lurkeley Hill, Shaw Farm, Baltic Farm, all in Wiltshire (the last two overtly), 1991.
- **SAMPLE PRAISE:** "It's really a cracker!" (Busty Taylor, CCCS, on Clench Common.)
- **SAMPLE COMMENT ON CEREALOGISTS:** "I see no indication that there has been any attempt to apply the scientific method."
- **BACKGROUND:** The Wessex Skeptics' hoaxes, created for the *Equinox* TV documentary in 1991, were the first in a series of major embarrassments of cerealogists that year. The revelation of their work led meteorologist Dr Terence Meaden (with whom the WS had been briefly allied during 1990) to abandon all complex formations as hoaxes.

UNITED BUREAU

THE SNAKE (or The Flake)

- **NUMBER OF MEMBERS:** 1
- **AGES:** Twentysomething
- **FIRST CIRCLES:** 1992
- **BASE:** Oxford
- **ALLEGED CONSPIRATORIAL AFFILIATION:** MI6, CIA, Vatican, Trilateral Commission
- **CEREALOGICAL BELIEFS:** All but a few rough circles are man-made
- **MOTIVES:** Artistic pride. Fun. Technical curiosity. Irrational compulsion.
- **PREFERRED TECHNIQUE:** Doug-and-Dave-style stalk-stomper for small jobs and circle centres. Garden roller for large jobs and circle peripheries. Feet and hands for grapeshot. Defensive equipment rumoured to include thermal infrared night-sight and tracer-firing Uzi.
- **SCHNABEL'S GUESSTIMATE OF FORMATIONS ACTUALLY MADE:** Numerous pictograms in north Wiltshire and Oxfordshire in 1992.
- **SAMPLE PRAISE:** "The most important crop formation of 1992." (Michael Green, CCCS chairman, on formation near Silbury Hill.)

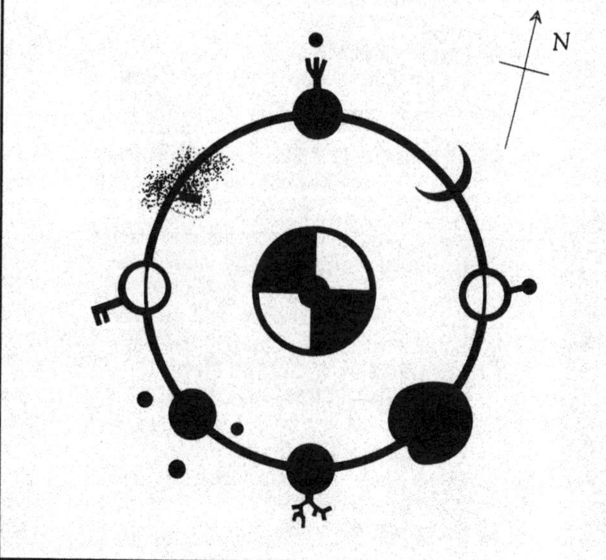

- **SAMPLE COMMENT ON CEREALOGISTS:** "A few are genuine; but most are fakes."
- **BACKGROUND:** Nicknamed 'the master of grapeshot' after his perfor mance at the *Cerealogist*'s competition in 1992, this young journalist was subsequently renamed 'the Snake' by George Wingfield for his apparently serpentine ability to slip into and out of fields without leaving a trail. ('The Flake' is an obscure reference to a past piece of journalism.) Excepting two or three collaborations with other circlemakers, including asuccessful UFO hoax with the Spiderman/Catwoman team near Alton Barnes, the Snake/Flake worked alone. Virtually all his creations were declared genuine. The eight-element 'Charm Bracelet' or 'Dharmic Wheel' pictogram at Silbury Hill, mid-August 1992, inspired a lengthy dissertation on Indo-Aryan mandala symbolism by CCCS chairman Michael Green. It was also the first formation ever to incorporate a water-trough symmetrically into its design.

Hoax!

OF INVESTIGATION

- **Number of members:** 5-10
- **Ages:** Approximately 15-30
- **FIRST CIRCLES:** 1991 (as a group; individual members believed to have been active from mid-to-late 1980s).
- **BASE:** Trowbridge, Devizes, Avebury, Alton Barnes area
- **ALLEGED CONSPIRATORIAL AFFILIATION:** Centre for Crop Circle Studies (CCCS). Circles Phenomenon Research Group (CPR). Centre for the Search for Extraterrestrial Intelligence (CSETI).
- **CEREALOGICAL BELIEFS:** UFO-millennarian. View circles phenomenon as a sign of approaching apocalypse.
- **MOTIVES:** Hastening apocalypse. Establishing communications with aliens. Something to do after a few pints of cider.
- **PREFERRED TECHNIQUE:** Garden rollers, plus special instruments resembling small surfboards. Also (bare) feet and hands, especially for small formations. Occasionally crystals are buried in formations to increase dowsable energy.
- **SCHNABEL'S GUESSTIMATE OF FORMATIONS ACTUALLY MADE:** Numerous major designs in north Wiltshire between 1988 and 1992.
- **SAMPLE PRAISE:** "These are as good as you're ever likely to see." (George Wingfield, CCCS, on the grapeshot at Bishops Cannings, Wiltshire, June 1992.)
- **SAMPLE COMMENT ON CEREALOGISTS:** "We're working with Colin Andrews again, and also with Erik Beckjord who's teaching us to communicate properly."
- **BACKGROUND:** The United Bureau of Investigation (UBI), aka the 'United Believers in Intelligence', are a highly fluid group drawing members and associates from the Trowbridge-Devizes-Beckhampton area, and as far away as Berkshire, Hampshire, Sussex and Wales. Although the group was not officially formed until 1991, its individual members have been circles activists in Wiltshire and Hampshire since the mid-1980s, and assisted such cerealogists as Pat Delgado and Colin Andrews (pictured left) at various cropwatches. At least one of the group's core members and several of the group's associates are also close to Isabelle Kingston, a medium based near Marlborough, who apparently predicted the arrival of crop circles at Silbury Hill in 1988 – the first major circles infestation in north Wiltshire.

UBI member Matt is said to have been making formations since 1989, at least. His colleague Paul made 'additions' to a circle near Avebury Trusloe in 1991. Matt, Paul and associate Bart were seen in June 1992 emerging from a field near Lockeridge in which several new 'grapeshot' circles had formed. At Urchfont, near Devizes, in June 1992, Matt and Paul made a rapeseed pictogram with motifs similar to the famous 1990 formations at Alton Barnes. UBI member John – an old Etonian dubbed 'the Weasel' by CCCS's George Wingfield – is the current keeper of the CCCS database and is widely rumoured to be a master-circlemaker, although he denies ever having made a formation.

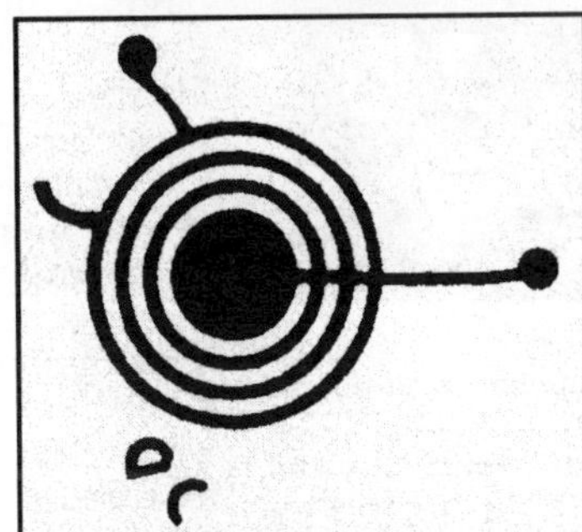

SPIDERMAN & CATWOMAN

- **NUMBER OF MEMBERS:** 2
- **AGES:** Classified
- **FIRST CIRCLES:** 1992
- **BASE:** Bath, Reading
- **ALLEGED CONSPIRATORIAL AFFILIATION:** MI6, CIA, Vatican, Beckhampton Group.
- **CEREALOGICAL BELIEFS:** All but a few rough circles – or possibly all – are man-made
- **MOTIVES:** Artistic pride. Fun. Curiosity about how circles are made, and their effects on people.
- **PREFERRED TECHNIQUE:** Great reliance on garden roller. Tend to roll circles from outside in, creating elliptical centres and oddly splayed bouquets of central stalks.
- **SCHNABEL'S GUESSTIMATE OF FORMATIONS ACTUALLY MADE:** Numerous pictograms in north Wiltshire and Avon in 1992.
- **SAMPLE PRAISE:** "Ohhh!" (Woman healed of arthritis pain in formation near Lockeridge, May 1992.) "If this is a hoax, I'll eat my shirt in public." (George Wingfield, on formation in barley near Wroughton, Wilts, June 1992.)
- **SAMPLE COMMENT ON CEREALOGISTS:** "They think that art is something that has to sit in a frame with a label underneath it. Circlemaking is all about broadening horizons."
- **BACKGROUNDS:** The artistry of Spiderman and Catwoman, cropwatchers turned circlemakers, was praised by cerealogists in 1992. Spiderman – so -called because, according to George Wingfield, he "sat at the centre of a web of intrigue" – originated the 'alpha' or 'fish' signature, and made frequent use of the 'scroll' motif.

With Catwoman – who dressed in cat-burglar black for circlemaking – Spiderman preferred large, simple for mations; nevertheless the duo created a 400-foot six-circle linear pictogram in 90 minutes one night in August 1992. Although widely rumoured to be associated with other circlemakers, collaborations with other groups or individuals were rare.

TOLD YOU THEY WAS A HOAX! CAUGHT THE LITTLE PEST UP THE TOP FIELD WITH A GARDEN ROLLER!

The placing of circle diagrams is purely for decorative purposes; creation by the hoaxer in proximity is not necessarily implied

Jim Schnabel's book *Round In Circles: Physicists, Poltergeists, Pranksters and the Secret History* is published by Hamish Hamilton at the end of June, price £16.99. FT

THE CASE OF THE MISSING MOA

KARL SHUKER evaluates recent sightings of big birds in New Zealand

ABOVE: Giant Moa and Kiwi.
BELOW: Beverley McCulloch, head of the prehistory department of Canterbury Museum and its moa expert, was unimpressed by Freaney's photo. "History is littered with possible moa sightings, none of which has been verified."

Just after 11:00 on 20 January 1993, following four hours of hiking through Canterbury's Craigieburn Range in the South Island of New Zealand, Paddy Freaney encountered a creature that, if correctly identified, could be the greatest cryptozoological discovery since the coelacanth.

Freaney (formerly an SAS instructor, now a hotelier) and gardener Rochelle Rafferty, had paused by a Harper Valley river bed while the third member of their party, Sam Waby (Aranui High School's Art Department Head), took a drink. Suddenly, Freaney spied a very tall bird by a bush about 40 yards away. Sporting reddish-brown and grey feathers almost down to its knees (but with unfeathered lower limbs and feet), it was approximately six foot tall from its huge feet to its small head. Its long, thin neck accounted for about half the creature's total height.

Hardly believing his eyes, Freaney whispered to his companions to take a look. Waby immediately identified it as a moa – a member of that famous family of flightless, ostrich-like and decidedly extinct birds exclusive to New Zealand. Although some zoologists believe that one of the smallest species – the turkey-sized upland moa *Megalapteryx didinus* – survived into the mid-1800s, all of the larger ones supposedly died out 400-500 years ago. Little wonder, then, that Freaney and company were so astonished.

The bird fled across the stream, Freaney pursued with camera, and before his quarry vanished in dense foliage, he took a single, hasty colour snap. He also photographed what he thought might be its wet footprint on a rock, and another in shingle nearby.

These photos were submitted to New Zealand's Department of Conservation (DOC), and the story of the sighting attracted media attention around the world. The Christchurch *Press* began its consistently detailed coverage on 25 January with a front page colour reproduction of Freaney's first photo, which was blurred in true cryptozoological tradition. The alleged moa is little more than a fuzzy brown blotch, out of which only a thickset horizontal body and a sturdy neck can be distinguished. Even more frustrating is that its limbs (the crucial feature for determining whether the creature was a biped or a quadruped) are obscured by a rock formation – and upon (or directly above) the creature were dark horizontal markings that could be shadows, background detail... or antlers!

Initially, the DOC regarded the episode with a mixture of bewilderment, interest and a degree of optimism. Its Protection Officer, Dr Ken Hughey, seemed ready to accept that the Cragieburn forestlands concealed a moa, or something very like one. As the only plausible moa-lookalike was an escapee Australian emu, checks were made around Canterbury to discover whether any had absconded from captivity – but none was reported.

Heartened by this, on 26 January the DOC announced plans to send a team to the sighting locality to search for droppings, feathers or any other signs of the bird's presence. Then it all went sadly wrong. That same day, in a Christchurch *Press* interview, Dennis Dunbar (owner of the Moana railway station) disclosed that he and

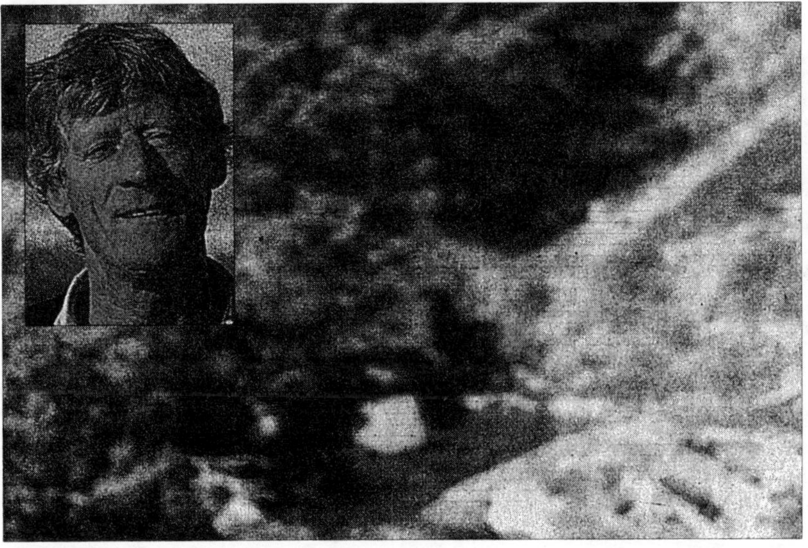

Port
Royal

Fuzzy moa photo (right) taken by Paddy Freaney (inset) and above, what might be its wet footprint in a river bed.

Freaney had been waging a year-long competition to see who could come up with stories that would attract media attention. According to Dunbar, Freaney had told him a few months earlier that his next feat would outdo anything either of them had done.

By the following day, the DOC had withdrawn its plans, saying it would consult with the Freaney trio further before deciding whether to continue. Dunbar then retracted his allegations, and Freaney said he would conduct his own search; meanwhile, his moa picture had undergone computer enhancement analysis at Canterbury University's electronics department. The results, released on the 28th, yielded a slightly 'cleaner' photo, but, of course, could not remove the obstructing rock. Nevertheless, its principal analyst, Kevin Taylor (a postgraduate student), was sufficiently impressed to opine that the object was indeed a bird – but of what species?

Even those scientists willing to consider that the brown smudge was a bird fell far short of favouring a moa identity. Among the more orthodox alternatives proffered were a Cape Barren goose, a weka (near-flightless relative of the corncrake and water rail), and even a kiwi – all difficult to reconcile with Freaney's estimate of a bird six foot tall. Others suggested it was not a bird but a model, or two hikers, a llama (!), or simply a red deer stag (this species being first introduced onto South Island from Europe in 1851 and now well established). The stag was the idea of palæoecologist Dr Richard Holdaway – who believes the neck of the creature was too thick to be that of a moa, and that the wet 'footprint' was nothing like a bird's – but it was rejected outright by Freaney and Waby, who both have considerable deer-hunting experience.

The DOC withdrew completely from the matter, and little additional news emerged until an extraordinary revelation about some German tourists and a visitors' book. As revealed by the Christchurch *Press* on 18 February, Bruce Spittle and his son Malcolm were visiting the Craigieburn area and stayed in the Bealey Hut (which provided accommodation for hikers). In the Hut's 'intentions' book, they noticed an entry for 19 May 1992, made by two German tourists, Franz Christiansen and Helga Umbreit. They wrote that they had been exploring the Cass-Lagoon Saddle area of Harper Valley, where they "were very surprised to see two moas".

A Christchurch hiker, Geoff Goodhew, who had used the hut a few days after the Germans, confirmed the existence of the record, made eight months earlier than that of Freaney's party. However, while Freaney was delighted with this apparent vindication, the DOC decided there was still insufficient evidence to warrant spending tax-payers' money on a moa hunt. In another surprising development, Freaney announced that he now had backing from an anonymous businessman to launch his own search. Attempts to locate the German hikers have so far been in vain.

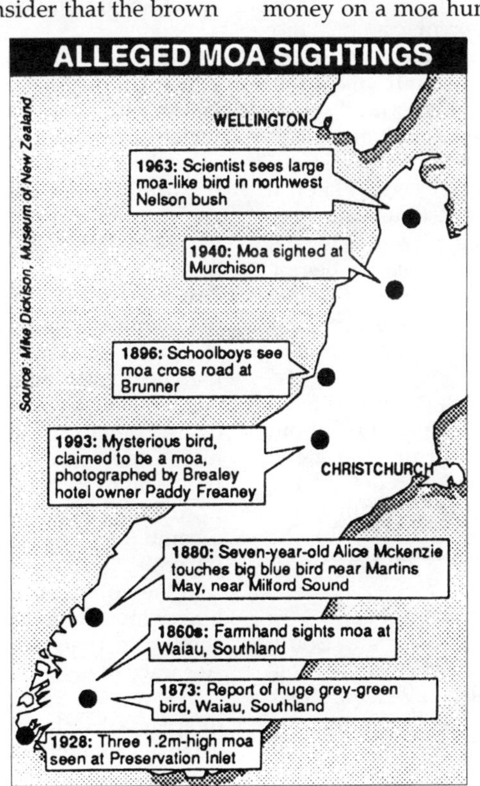
ALLEGED MOA SIGHTINGS
Source: Mike Dickison, Museum of New Zealand
WELLINGTON
1963: Scientist sees large moa-like bird in northwest Nelson bush
1940: Moa sighted at Murchison
1896: Schoolboys see moa cross road at Brunner
1993: Mysterious bird, claimed to be a moa, photographed by Brealey hotel owner Paddy Freaney
CHRISTCHURCH
1880: Seven-year-old Alice Mckenzie touches big blue bird near Martins May, near Milford Sound
1860s: Farmhand sights moa at Waiau, Southland
1873: Report of huge grey-green bird, Waiau, Southland
1928: Three 1.2m-high moa seen at Preservation Inlet

The case of the missing moa stands uncertainly amid speculation and scepticism. Is it really conceivable that a viable population of 6ft-tall moas (as opposed to the relatively smaller and inconspicuous *Megalapteryx* kind) could have survived, undetected and unsuspected by science, in an area regularly traversed by hikers?

Freaney estimates that his search will involve eight volunteers, take up to 10 days, and cost around AU$2,000. If he can raise that amount and find an obliging octet, the hunt will continue. If not, then cryptozoology has just added yet another initially promising but ultimately unfulfilled episode to its backlog of near-misses and might-have-beens. To be continued...? **FT**

Deadly Alchemy

PAUL SIEVEKING examines the rumours of red mercury, an elusive substance said to be useful in nuclear weapons, medicine and voodoo

Alan Kidger, 48, international sales director of British-owned Thor Chemicals, which imports mercury waste into South Africa for recycling, hung up the phone in early November 1991, told his wife he would be back shortly, and slipped out of his Johannesburg home. Several days later, he was found stuffed into the boot of his BMW saloon by two car thieves. His arms, legs, buttocks and head had been sawn off and covered in a black mercury compound.

As Thor Chemicals had long been accused of polluting the soil and ground water, his killing was initially blamed on eco-terrorists; then someone whispered the words 'red mercury' and soon the South African press was off and running with its version of this intriguing mystery.

The murder, as far as I am aware, remains unsolved.

The Roman god Mercury not only presided over orators and merchants, but also over thieves, pickpockets and villains of all stripes. He could make himself invisible or assume any shape he desired, and gave early proof of his craftiness by robbing Neptune of his trident, Venus of her girdle, Mars of his sword, Jupiter of his sceptre and Vulcan of many of his mechanical instruments.

How appropriate, then, that red mercury, a substance whose very existence is doubted by many Western scientists, should be touted by shady conmen from Nairobi to Baghdad, fetching up to a million pounds a pint.

When the stuff first appeared on the international black market in 1977, the supposedly top secret nuclear material was 'red' because it came from the Soviet Union; later, it actually took on a red colour. A report last summer from the US Department of Energy, compiled by researchers at Los Alamos, entitled *Red mercury: caviat emptor* began: "Take a bogus material, give it an enigmatic name, exaggerate its physical properties and intended uses, mix in some human greed and intrigue, and voilà: one half-baked scam."

The report said that the wonder substance was offered as a modern philosopher's stone that can do just about anything: it makes stealth aircraft stealthier, infra-red sensors more sensitive, counterfeits harder to detect, and atom bombs smaller and easier to build. Sometimes it is said to be radioactive, sometimes not. It might be the densest compound known to science, but then again, it might not.

All the samples recovered by official agencies – in countries as diverse as Ethiopia, North Korea and South Africa – had failed to have any special military application. They had included pure mercury, mercury tinged with brick dust, depleted nuclear reactor fuel, a mercury-antimony compound, mercuric iodide, mercuric oxide and mercuric cyanate. The last mentioned was at least reddish and explosive, but had been used for decades in artillery shells. "There is a report of one lazy con artist trying to sell mercury in a bottle painted red with nail polish", noted the DOE.

Noah Technologies Corporation, one of the largest suppliers of mercury chemicals in the United States, was telephoned in 1984 by someone claiming to be 'Prince Shami, the financial minister of Nigeria'. He said he needed red mercury liquid in order to colour Nigerian money. He also needed it to stop fungus growth on this money. Bob Blumenthal of Noah Technologies met the Nigerian in Manhattan and tried to convince him that the substance didn't exist. But 'Shami' insisted he wanted it and waved a very thick wad of high-denomination dollar bills around. Two weeks later, Blumenthal rang the Nigerian Embassy, but no-one had heard of 'Prince Shami'.

Since then, Noah Technologies has received about five calls a month from people all over the world wanting to buy red mercury liquid for voodoo, medicine or nuclear business. In the mid 1980s, scores of prospectors rushed to West Pokot District in Kenya, where red mercury was allegedly 'oozing from the hills'. Official denials only strenthened popular belief.

According to one version of events, red mercury is an antimony mercury oxide developed in the Soviet Union as a simple trigger for atom bombs. Such triggers, which surround a core of plutonium or enriched uranium, must be shaped so precisely that when exploded they uniformly compress the core, setting off a chain reaction; and they must provide an adequate supply of free neutrons to sustain that reaction. Red mercury supposedly combines both functions within one substance, and enables the construction of bombs using smaller quantities of fissionable material than standard atomic warheads.

Small wonder, then, that Third World demand for red mercury is red hot – or that Russia's economic chaos has encouraged strenuous efforts to satisfy it. Such a substance could transform the regimes of Saddam or Gadaffi into nuclear powers overnight. According to Evgeny Korolev, a politician in Ekaterinburg, a Russian centre of red mercury trafficking: "With red mercury, Saddam Hussein can make a bomb the size of a grenade that could blow a ship out of the sea."

One American nuclear expert said that size was no longer important. Nato already possessed nuclear artillery shells and there were small, handy-sized nuclear mines. Accuracy of delivery was today the paramount concern.

However, red mercury might be a real substance, despite all debunking efforts. There is said to be an extensive smuggling network that stretches from the Urals through Romania and Bulgaria to Austria, Germany and

From the top: Iraqui dictator Sadam Hussein, a customer for red mercury; Russian President Boris Yeltsin, who allegedly signed an export license for the stuff; Russian Vice-President Rutskoi and Attorney-General Stepankov, who both called for an investigation.

Italy. In 1991 Bulgarian police seized beer-bottle-sized flasks of red mercury bearing Soviet military symbols. In April 1992, Ukrainian police arrested thieves near the border attempting to smuggle out 180kg of the stuff. In Poland, eight kilos were found in a Lada car belonging to some Russians. Tass reported that two Armenians went to Siberia and kidnapped the son of a red mercury dealer to ensure delivery of their order. In November 1992 a Czech reporter said that he had become the first journalist in the world to buy red mercury on the black market... in Vladivostok. His assertion that it was used "mainly for the nuclear submarine programme" was apparently a first in red mercury lore.

The Russian government seems schizophrenic on the issue. In August 1992, Security Ministry spokesman Andrei Chernenko reported to the media on the success of Operation Tral, designed to combat the illegal export of strategic raw materials. He stated that red mercury "does not exist at all". Two months later in another press conference, Chernenko said that "no major leaks" of red mercury had occurred. In December, Russian Vice President Alexander V. Rutskoi told the Seventh Congress of People's Deputies that the inventors of red mercury had obtained the necessary export documents and were selling it abroad in great quantities and at astronomical prices. He called for an urgent investigation, as had Valentin Stepankov, the Russian attorney-general, some time earlier. In January 1993, the Security Ministry referred to the 'phantom product' and predicted that "the search for the non-existent substance has no prospects." It was possible that the export licences referred to by Rutskoi were simply a cover for smuggling other precious materials such as uranium, plutonium, gold, osmium and irridium.

Ramaz Tadeyev is scientific director of Alkor Technologies, a flourishing company in St Petersburg that says it has developed the technology to make liquid red mercury. "It can be used to make a nuclear weapon", he said categorically. "That is why the prices are so high." Oleg Sadykov, president of Promecology, a large company based in Ekaterinburg and Moscow with official permission to sell red mercury, is equally certain about the potentially lethal nature of the substance. "The black market in red mercury for nuclear weapons is a real threat to all countries and Russia cannot stop it alone. The West needs to get organised."

A list of officially sanctioned red mercury export orders compiled for Russian deputies in Moscow records 30 separate applications. Companies in Germany, Britain, the US, Liechtenstein and Hungary are mentioned, but it has proved impossible to trace them. President Yeltsin, Premier Gaidar and atomic energy minister Mikhailov are all mentioned as having granted permission for export.

British nuclear weapons expert Frank Barnaby found the subject of red mercury far-fetched, but pointed out that quite senior Russian politicians, who were unlikely to be involved in a hoax, had claimed that the substance existed. He postulated a liquefied form of a mercury-antimony compound to which is added, in a reactor or particle accelerator, a transuranic actinide such as californium 252, 'an extremely good emitter' of neutrons.

John Hassard, lecturer in nuclear physics at Imperial College, was also uncertain. He mused that antimony and mercury were both very heavy atoms which, when joined, created a lattice of 'boxes' just about the size of plutonium atoms, "and that makes me think that you might be able to drift plutonium into it. Do that and you overcome, in one stroke, the problems of thermodynamics in the implosion of your nuclear weapon."

Given world demand for a nuclear short-cut, Russian thirst for hard currency and an anarchic economy, ripe for scam artists and grifters – and red mercury seems heaven-sent. The vexation of experts, east and west, is understandable. Hoaxes usually die away, but this has been chugging along for 15 years or more. The CIA continues to keep a wary eye on the trade; offers of red mercury have been accompanied by offers of enriched uranium, small quantities of plutonium and a conventional warhead from an SS-19 missile. Other US agencies see red mercury as only the latest version of alchemy's perfervid dreams.

Sources: The Nation (Nairobi) c1986; Manchester Evening News, 15 Oct 1991; Bangkok Post, 2 Feb 1992; New Scientist, 6 June 1992; Sunday Times, 18 Oct 1992; Barron's (USA), 15 Feb + 1 Mar 1993.

UNEARTHED

1. MINI MAMMOTHS LINGER LONGER

STEVE MOORE delves into recent archæological curiosities

It used to be fairly simple: mammoths were enormous hairy pachyderms that died out at the end of the last Ice Age, about 10 12,000 years ago (although outsider betting is on 7,500 years ago). The biggest question seemed to be 'why?'. Maybe it was the changing climate that made their usual habitat, the fertile steppe-tundra, disappear (although mammoths had survived previous climate changes by simply moving north when it got warmer and south again when the cold returned). Maybe they were hunted to extinction by palæolithic humans (although hunter-gatherers tended to husband their main food-animals and not wipe them out). Maybe it was both, or neither...

Wrangel Island lies in the Arctic Ocean north of Siberia, near the Bering Strait. Not a lot of people go there – but mammoths did about 12,000 years ago when the sea was still frozen and they could reach it from the mainland. Their remains have been found and dated, and they were enormous hairy pachyderms standing ten feet high at the shoulder.

So far, so good. However, more anomalous mammoth remains have also been found there, according to Andrei Sher, of the Institute of Evolutionary Animal Morphology and Ecology in Moscow, and Lev Sulerzhitsky, a radiocarbon dating specialist. The oddities were rather small hairy pachyderms, standing just six feet at the shoulder. Their tooth-fragments date from just 4,000 years ago, while tusk and bone samples give dates of 3,700 years.

This appears to be a case of 'island dwarfism' – cut off by the rising sea-levels, the mammoths reduced their bulk in accord with their shrinking habitat. Similar processes have happened elsewhere: the pygmy hippos of Cyprus and the dwarf elephants of Malta, for example. What is not clear, though, is why these mini-mammoths died out. The reports imply that these remains are of the last survivors, while humans are not thought to have reached Wrangel Island before 3,000 years ago, by which time the diminutive mammoths were already extinct.

And yet... northern and eastern Siberia is still a largely unexplored wilderness, populated by hunter-herder tribes. One such tribe, the Evenks, were not contacted until the beginning of this century, and were reported to have well-preserved mammoth skins and quantities of ivory. In 1922, the Evenks claimed to have 'recently' come across a lone mammoth on the coast of the Arctic Ocean. So, perhaps somewhere, tall or small, mammoths still thunder across the tundra...

Meanwhile, in Japan, archæologists have found the remains of 28,000-year-old ovens and evidence suggesting they were used to roast the flesh of Naumann elephants, a kind of woolly mammoth. *Independent on Sunday, 7 Mar; [AP], Guardian, D.Telegraph, 25 Mar; New Scientist, 27 Mar 1993; Independent, Guardian, 17 Dec 1992.*

2. FOOTPRINTS IN THE SANDS OF TIME

The tabloids had a lot of trouble trying to describe it... 'crocodile-like', 'an enormous newt', 'an ancestor of the frog', 'a slimy killer' and 'the monster from the Black Lagoon'. *It* was actually a Temnospondyl (drawing, right), a 6ft-long amphibian that came ashore at Howick, Northumberland, 300 million years ago, and (far right) 8x4-inch footprints on the sea shore to prove it. The Temnospondyl is thought to be among the first creatures to migrate from sea to land, and these could be the oldest prints in Britain.

The set of 20 footprints, with a trail left by the creature's dragging belly, were found by David Scarboro on the surface of a sandstone bed after its covering of river-sand had been eroded by the sea. Unfortunately, it's proved impossible to cut them from the rock, and what the sea has uncovered is likely, within a year, to be destroyed by it too. *New Scientist, 13 Feb; D.Telegraph, 23 Feb 1993.*

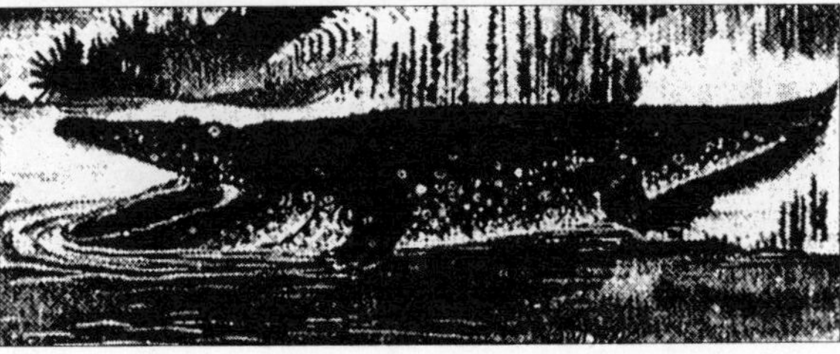

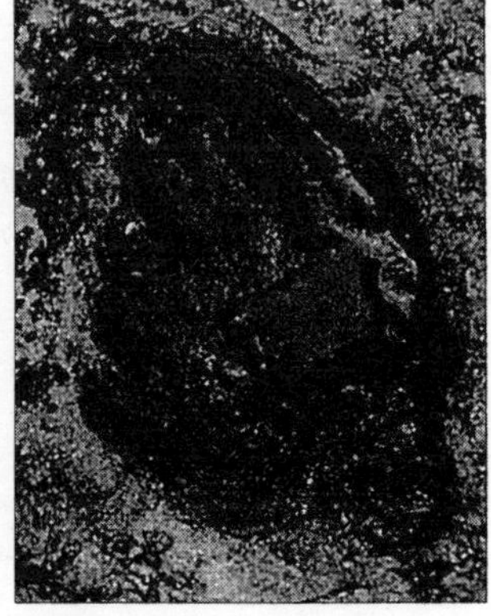

Hard To Swallow

Eating people may be wrong, but it has its uses. BOB RICKARD looks at some new entries in the 'Long Pig' cookbook

In the last days of 1992, Zheng Yi, one of China's ten most-wanted "counter-revolutionary criminals", escaped to the USA via Hong Kong, carrying official documents describing how hundreds of political prisoners were killed and eaten by Red Guards during the Cultural Revolution of the late 1960s. Thousands colluded in the cannibalism, said Zheng, to prove their political purity and enthusiasm.

Zheng Yi, the Chinese writer, who escaped from China with alleged evidence of widespread ideological cannibalism.

Zheng Yi, now 45, is a well-known writer in China and one of the leaders of the 1989 uprising who went into hiding after the Tienanmen square suppression. At a press-conference in New York, Zheng displayed his evidence, which also told of schoolchildren encouraged to murder and eat their school principals, and bodies displayed on meathooks at government cafeterias.

Although Mao wanted a lot of people killed, said Zheng, he certainly didn't endorse cannibalism. "Terrible things happened all over China, but in the province of Guangxi it was cannibalism," he said. The atrocities were common knowledge in Guangxi, but hardly known outside the province except by "disaffected intellectuals".

They became an issue in 1979, when the people of Guangxi, in southern China, posted their grievances on Beijing's Democracy Wall, saying they wanted compensation from the government. The posters had blamed Wei Guoqing, the Party Secretary for Guangxi during the Cultural Revolution, and friend and supporter of Party chief Deng Xiaoping. However, it now transpires that the upper echelons closed about Wei not so much to protect him as to prevent the matter getting out of control and becoming a brush with which to further blacken the reputation of the great founder of Chinese Communism, Mao himself.

Liu Binyan, China's celebrated investigative reporter (now resident in Princeton where he is host to Zheng and his wife), described Wei's downfall: "In 1983, he tried to overthrow Party General Secretary Hu Yaobang, who was very close to Deng. Wei was removed from office, and top officials in Guangxi, who had participated in the cover-up, were removed too. Hu saw to it that the cannibalism was investigated."

The enquiry uncovered the documents that, somehow, Zheng was able to photograph. Zheng Yi believes that many hundreds, possibly thousands, were eaten in Guangxi. His own investigation into just one county revealed that 137 people were devoured. "I think thousands participated in the cannibalism," he said, yet none was ever charged or tried. Official action fizzled out as less than 100 cannibals were expelled from the Party, some with their pay or rank reduced.

Historically, this kind of ideological cannibalism is a rare thing, but a letter to the *Times* (15 Feb 1993) by Pierre-Antoine Bernheim, author of a book on the subject, pointed out that it is not unprecedented in China, where the ancient chronicles record a number of accounts of "revenge, hatred [..] medical and 'gourmandaise' cannibalism". For example, says Bernheim, "defeated Emperor Wang Mang was killed and partly eaten by his opponents in AD 28." *Int.Herald Tribune + [R] 7 Jan; D.Telegraph 8 Jan; Observer 10 Jan 1993.*

In a curious parallel, another ex-patriot scholar – Toshiyuki Tanabe, an academic from western Japan – claims to have found documentary evidence of 100 cases of cannibalism amongst Japanese soldiers abandoned in New Guinea at the close of WW2.

Former Chinese Communist Part General Secretary Hu Ysobang. He lost his post amid student demands for democracy.

Tanabe, unlike Zheng Yi, is not a fugitive, but works as an associate professor at Melbourne University, delving into Australian military archives. This is the first formal proof of a subject that has spawned an informal canon of heated public accusations, TV documentaries and at least one successful film (*The Emperor's Naked Army Marches On*, 1987). *[AFP] Bangkok Post 11 Aug 1992.*

DIARY OF A MAD PLANET

February — March 1993

This diary aims to record, in two-month segments, the geophysical highlights of our planet: the tempests and tantrums, the oddities and extremities. Compiled by the editors and various correspondents.

ERUPTION **2 February PHILIPPINES:**
The almost perfectly conical, 7,940ft high Mayon volcano, 200 miles SE of Manila, dormant since 1984, erupted at 1:11pm, hurling ash 10km, turning day to night and killing at least 68, mostly with scalding mud flows. Over 57,000 were evacuated from the area. The eruption came 20 months after Mount Pinatubo exploded in the most violent eruption of the century, cooling the Earth's surface by an average 0.5C. Mayon continued to rumble and splutter in the following days; there were seven eruptions on 21 March, with plumes of ash two miles high.

HEATWAVE **3 February SOUTH AUSTRALIA:**
Temperatures up to 45C (113F) killed at least 23. The hottest place was the outback town of Tarcoola. Conditions in Adelaide and Melbourne were made worse by power failures caused by excessive demand, leaving many homes without air-conditioning. Meanwhile, snow gripped much of the Middle East; the hills of the Holy Land were blanketed with white.

FLOOD **5 February JAVA:**
The death-toll from flooding reached 60. Thousands of houses were destroyed and 250,000 evacuated. Record high February temperatures were recorded in Colombo, Sri Lanka (36.2C) and Muscat, Oman (34C).

VOLCANOES **16 February SOUTH PACIFIC:**
Announcement of discovery by sonar scanning of the greatest concentration of active volcanoes on the planet – on the sea bed 600 miles NW of Easter Island. Some of the 1,133 mountains and volcanic cones, covering 55,000 sq miles, were almost 7,000ft high. There could be two or three eruptions there at any given moment.

RAIN **26 February FIJI:**
Heaviest rainfall since 1942 – Nandi Airport reported over 11in in 24hrs – only 0.15in less than the whole February average. Bhuj-rudra-mata, near the Gulf of Kutch in India, which expects significant February rain on one day every 120 years, had 0.8in.

ARIZONA: About 3,500 were evacuated from the town of Roll after billions of tons of water spilled over the Painted Rock Dam, flooding the Wellton-Mohawk Valley. Record rainfall in the previous month led to flooding of the Gila River. Up to 14,000 hectares of farmland were at risk.

EARTHQUAKE **18 March GREECE:**
(38.346N 22.114E) Depth: 52km. Magnitude: 5.6R. Felt strongly throughout the Gulf of Corinth and in Athens.

STORM **20 March EASTERN USA:**

'Storm of the century' roared north from the Gulf of Mexico, closed down every city from the mouth of the Mississippi up to Maine and killed at least 184. Birmingham, Alabama, had 13 inches of snow in one day, more than had ever fallen before in an entire winter, while Florida, still recovering from Hurricane Andrew last August, was swept by 50 killer tornadoes.

■ The lowest barometric pressure of the century was recorded and there were 30ft waves along part of the east coast. People skied down 5th Avenue in New York. At its zenith, the storm reached from Cuba, where banana and tobacco crops were devastated, to the Canadian Maritimes. The storm struck on the anniversary of the infamous Blizzard of 1888, which killed more than 400 people when it blanketed the east coast.

AVALANCHE **24 March AFGHANISTAN:**
About 100 died of cold and thousands were trapped in savagely cold conditions after an avalanche of snow and ice blocked the main northern highway in the Hindu Kush mountains.

EARTHQUAKE **26 March SOUTH GREECE:**
(37.221N 21.568E) Depth: 10km. Magnitude: 5.2R. There were four quakes within 15 minutes today in southern Greece. One death, 12 injuries and extensive damage in the Amalias-Pirgos area.

Special thanks to the Global Seismology Group of the British Geological Survey for the earthquake data.

The MIA

Every picture tells a story but, as RICHARD HALSTEAD discovers in the case of relatives of US soldiers still missing in Indochina, it may not be the obvious one.

Americans can't stop thinking about the Vietnam war, two decades after their official involvement ended. Indeed some, such as Walter Capps in his book *The Unfinished War*, would say they're still fighting it. This phenomenon has sparked whole hosts of anomalous ripples in the American consciousness – Sylvester Stallone's improbable success as 'Rambo', for instance – but its most curious effect must be the persistent and tantalising rumours about The Ones They Left Behind: the 2,266 servicemen listed by the US government as Missing In Action (MIA).

A rash of photos continue to surface from Southeast Asia, claiming to show Americans still being held by the Vietnamese in labour camps. Reuters distributed one in early July 1991, allegedly showing three US pilots, Colonel John Robertson, Major Albro Lundy and Lieutenant Larry Stevens, shot down during the war and listed as MIA. A tourist had been given it in Cambodia. Newspapers printed it, and the reaction was amazing: not only did the families of the pilots come forward and positively identify them and Veterans groups dust off their protest statements about GIs being abandoned, but Congress launched a full-scale inquiry into the possibility that MIAs were still alive and in Vietnamese hands.

FAT, HAPPY CAMPERS

Doubts about the photo's authenticity were legion: the shot was very poorly exposed, black and white, and retouching experts confirmed that it had been substantially altered. The three pilots were holding up a sign between them, showing a date (May 25, 1990) and some unidentified letters and numbers, and the retouchers viewed this part of the photo as particularly suspicious. There seemed to be anomalies in the depth of shot: Major Lundy, the middle of the three, appeared to be standing a few feet behind Robertson and Stevens, yet the size of his head and features should have placed him equidistant from the camera. The Vietnamese authorities had produced the remains of Robertson a month before the photo had allegedly been taken (though oddly, the remains turned out to be "not human"). Most striking of all, according to former US intelligence analyst Sedgwick Tourison, the figures didn't look genuine: "I'm looking at a picture of three fat, happy campers with trimmed moustaches and nice haircuts. I'm not looking at a picture of three 'prisoners' here. I don't know *what* I'm looking at."

A 1988 enhanced ærial photograph of a rice paddy in Laos shows the letters 'USA' with a 'K' below. These could be distress signals from American POWs or doodles by a rice farmer's son, according to conflicting US Senate testimony in 1992.

Indeed, the Pentagon didn't know what it was looking at either. The media stepped into high gear: the pictured men's families held televised press conferences; experts, including British writer Nigel Cawthorne, author of *The Bamboo Cage*, a study of MIAs in Indochina, were wheeled out to pronounce the photo 'thoroughly convincing,' and most significant of all, Colonel Millard Peck, director of the Pentagon's POW-MIA office, resigned. He said he couldn't keep using his office as a 'black hole' where reports of MIA sightings routinely disappeared. Senator John Kerry announced he would chair a Congressional investigation at which Cawthorne, Peck and Nixon's Defence Secretary James Schlesinger, among others, would testify. Kerry, a Vietnam veteran, paid an 8-day visit to Hanoi in August to check out the 'hot leads'. He came home empty-handed.

POORLY MANIPULATED FAKE

By this time the picture itself was old news: every expert consulted declared it a poorly-manipulated fake (though interestingly it took the Pentagon until mid-1992 to declare it so). *Guardian* picture editor Eamonn McCabe said his paper wouldn't go near the photo. *XYZ Magazine* ran the shot in a story in their September issue about retouching. Some of the men's features had been added by hand, and the sign's writing was almost certainly new, it said.

It turned out to be a picture of three Russian farmers, taken in 1923 and reproduced in an article on collectivised farming in a recent issue of the magazine *Soviet Union*. Copies were available at the Phnom Penh library, and it had apparently been used before for hoax pictures. The phenomenon, however, showed no signs of collapsing. The families of the MIAs put it best: the picture, fake or not, "only raises more questions," they said.

WORLD WAR TWO PRISONERS

A few days later, on July 31 1991, they received support from an unlikely source. Former KGB general Dmitri Volkogonov, advisor to President Yeltsin, writing in *Izvestia*, claimed that American POWs from World War Two had been shipped off to the Soviet Union at the end of the war and forced to renounce their citizenship. Those

Photo Mystery

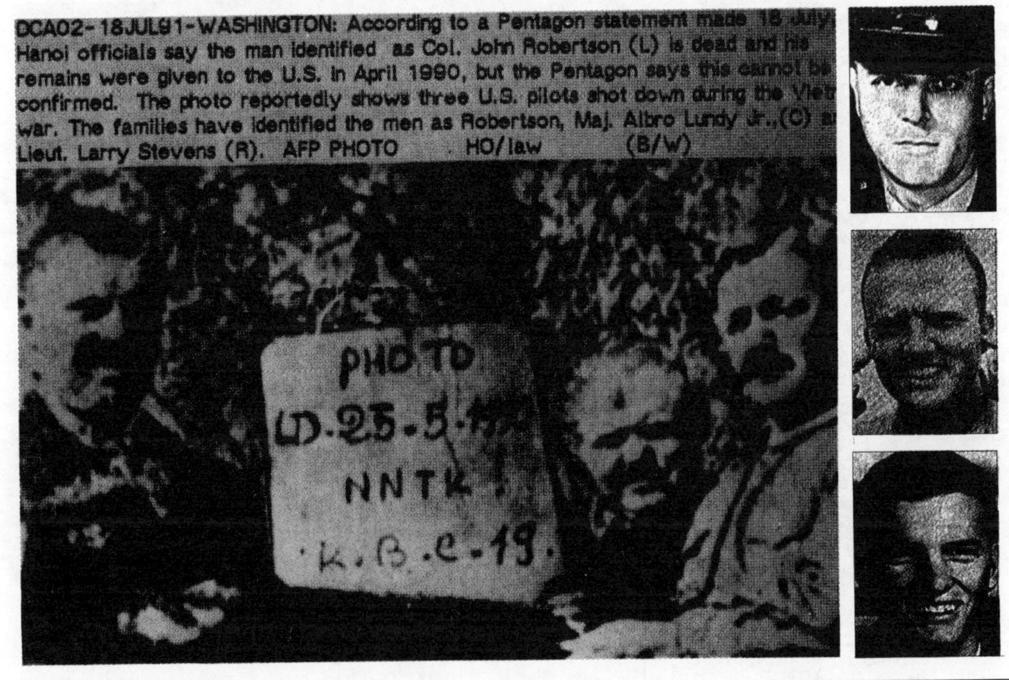
DCA02-18JUL91-WASHINGTON: According to a Pentagon statement made 18 July, Hanoi officials say the man identified as Col. John Robertson (L) is dead and his remains were given to the U.S. in April 1990, but the Pentagon says this cannot be confirmed. The photo reportedly shows three U.S. pilots shot down during the Viet war. The families have identified the men as Robertson, Maj. Albro Lundy Jr.,(C) a Lieut. Larry Stevens (R). AFP PHOTO HO/law (B/W)
PHOTO
NNTK
K.B.C-19.

This doctored 1923 photograph of Russian farmers was distributed by Reuters in 1991 as evidence of the survival of three American pilots posted missing in Vietnam.

Inset portraits show (from top) genuine likenesses of Colonel Robertson, Major Lundy and Lieutenant Stevens.

who pledged to remain US citizens had been imprisoned in the gulag. He denied that any were still alive. (In November 1992, *Pravda* reported that four Americans trapped in Soviet-held territory after the war had been found living in western Ukraine. One of them wanted to go home, it said, though nothing more was heard.)

Reuters ran a story on August 2 that claimed the 70 Americans who chose to remain in Vietnam after the war were the source of 'MIA sightings.' The story came from the Vietnamese, who were perhaps trying to throw more cold water on the persistent rumours. To no avail – on 21 September, just as Senator Kerry's committee was taking its first evidence, another photo came to light. It was a colour, focused shot, allegedly of a Captain Donald Carr, shot down over Laos in 1971 and listed as missing. The Pentagon said it was "taking the Carr photo seriously." "Of all the photos we've received, it's quite the most striking" said Carl Ford, their east Asia expert. He was giving the case top priority.

THE MYTH OF SURVIVAL

Over in Senate committee room 3, former Defence Secretary James Schlesinger said: "American prisoners were almost certainly left behind when President Nixon withdrew US forces from Vietnam." "How many?" asked Senator Kerry. "About 135, but I didn't know this at the time." The committee wound up in early October, after some testimony from veterans groups, but the media could already hear the choppers warming up: a joint US-Vietnamese group of investigators would go to the jungle camps where the MIAs were allegedly held and try to come up with some hard evidence. The media would go too.

They found nothing. In fact, not one American has emerged from the camps in Vietnam, Laos or Cambodia for 20 years. No Robertson, no Lundy, no Stevens, no Carr, nor any of the other MIAs whose alleged likenesses wash out of Indochina every year. The only activity, it seems, is that of gullible Americans being relieved of their dollars by former Green Berets, mercenaries and Southeast Asian 'guides' who all promise "to find their son/husband", and of course never do.

Yet the MIA myth goes from strength to strength. The Vietnamese won't release secret prisoners until 'war reparations' have been paid; they're holding thousands of servicemen's remains for the same reason; GIs are still fighting, isolated in the jungle; MIAs are in Chinese labour camps; these are just some of the more resilient myths. It was rumoured last year that the Administration's Vietnam policy was largely responsible for Ross Perot's presidential campaign. Apparently Perot, a long-time campaigner on behalf of the MIAs, had been deliberately thwarted in his efforts by President Bush and labelled a 'wacko.' It has not been denied.

The next batch of photos should be arriving soon. Get your airbrushes ready.

Vietnam yesterday handed over seven boxes of recently discovered remains for US forensic experts to determine whether they are those of Americans killed in the Vietnam War. A total of 2,261 Americans are listed as missing in action.

Daily Telegraph, 9 February 1993

SECRET COUNTRY

Mysterious places to visit in Great Britain compiled by Janet & Colin Bord

9: Cerne Abbas, Dorset

The 200-foot Cerne Abbas Giant is unique among British hill figures. His ancestry is unknown – the first written record of him was in 1751 – but it seems likely that he has been around for far longer than 250 years. In 1764 the antiquarian Dr Stukeley announced that the giant was Hercules, a legendary hero who, like the giant, was depicted brandishing a club. A Roman sculpture found at Corbridge shows Hercules nude with upraised club. But we can't be sure that the Cerne Abbas Giant was intended to represent Hercules; he may indeed have originated in pre-Roman times, and his erection suggests he was part of some phallic cult.

On the hill above his head is a small earthwork of bank and ditch called the Trendle or Frying Pan, where a Maypole used to be erected every year. The Maypole symbolises both tree and phallus, and the festivities were part of a fertility rite. Women would sit on the giant in hopes of bearing a child; unmarried girls pray at his feet for the gift of a husband; and married couples copulate on the figure to ensure pregnancy.

The giant may be linked to the nearby ruined abbey of Cerne Abbas. Legend has it that pagan practices based on a god called Helith, Helis or Heil were followed here, until St Augustine came and smashed Helith's idol and founded the abbey. The giant may have been part of the pagan practices; the figure was certainly important to the local community, who saw to his upkeep. A hill figure left untended soon becomes overgrown and disappears.

It has been suggested that the monks may even have made the giant. Elsewhere in England in the 13th century, a community of monks made a representation of Priapus, the pagan god of fertility, to help the country people whose cattle were diseased. However, it seems unlikely that monks would have constructed such a large and blatantly sexual figure; they probably tolerated its presence because of strong local feeling.

The giant's value as a tourist attraction must be something of a mixed blessing to Cerne Abbas; but few visitors know of this pretty village's other 'earth mysteries'. It is said that when St Augustine arrived, his followers were tired and thirsty, so the saint stuck his staff into the ground and clear water flowed at the spot. St Augustine's Well can now be found beyond the burial ground near the abbey.

An underground passage is said to run from the abbey to the site of St Catherine's Chapel on Cat-and-Chapel Hill. Few of the hundreds of rumoured underground passages in Britain actually exist. The straight line of the passage is echoed in the straight line of the ley. Paul Devereux noted a ley at Cerne Abbas in *The Ley Hunter's Companion* (1972). It links St Mary's church, St Augustine's Well, the abbey ruins, the giant, the Trendle and several other antiquities, making a seven-mile line. **FT**

ABOVE: The Cerne Abbas Giant, with the Trendle earthwork above his head.

BELOW: Some remains of the former abbey buildings

ASTROLOGY: Mike O'Neill, a computer programmer, has been convener of the Astrological Investigation & Research (AIR) group for eight years.

EVOLUTION: Colin Wood specialises in researching the origins and original meaning of the early texts of *Genesis*, specifically the *'Adam and Eve'* temptation narrative.

PSYCHICAL RESEARCH: Ralph Noyes is the Honorary Secretary of the Society for Psychical Research and the Centre for Crop Circle Studies.

CRYPTOZOOLOGY: Loren Coleman is an experienced cryptozoologist and Fortean, living in Portland, Maine, with eight books under his belt.

Astrology

The Importance of Timing

Mike O'Neill outlines the recent advances in astrological research through the study of twins

Until now, the most dramatic results in astrology research have been the work of the Gauquelins. Their most famous result is that sportspeople tend to be born when Mars is rising or overhead, but their work extends to most professions and associated planets. Their data and results have now been scrutinised for 40 years without any faults being found. Independent replications by sceptics have shown the same effects. Recently, Professor Suitbert Ertel has found eminence sub-effects in the data which remove any last doubts about the work (*Skeptical Inquirer*, Winter 1992). So, incredible though it is to current scientific understanding, the moment of birth has now been proven to correlate with human potential and a growing band of scientists worldwide are quietly following up what must be among the great scientific breakthroughs of the century.

The results are so well accepted that even most 'skeptics' concede their validity, but dismiss their importance either because their percentage variations are too small or because they are only found in eminent people. New research answers these objections and is even more significant than the Gauquelins' results. It is by Dr Suzel Fuzeau-Braesch, director of research at the respected National Centre for Scientific Research (CNRS) at Orsay near Paris, and was written up as "An empirical study of an astrological hypothesis in a twin population" in the October 1992 edition of the psychological journal *Personality and Individual Differences* and the book *Astrologie: la Preuve par Deux*. The book also covers the history of astrology, and the latest research and theories that try to explain how and why such effects operate.

> "The moment of birth has now been proven to correlate with human potential."

The research design was straightforward: two short character descriptions summarising the astrological differences between twins' charts were sent to their parents, who were asked to decide which description best fitted which twin. Chance would suggest equal numbers right and wrong; however, of 218 who made a decision, 153 picked correctly and only 65 were wrong. The probability of this is around **one in a billion**! (p=1.16 x 10-9 one-sided binomial). The results were equally strong for natural or induced births and there was little variation based on gender or zygosity (identicalness).

Of course, one cannot accept any research breakthrough without a replication, but this one looks very promising and so the AIR group is starting one. If you have any twins' birth details (date, place and **two** times – which should be on birth certificates) and the address of a parent (or family member or twin) who is prepared to complete a short questionnaire, please forward it to me at Flat J, 14 St Albans Road, London NW5 1RD, or phone 071 267 6354.

If it does replicate in the same way, then the consistent message of these two studies is that the time of day, not the day itself nor the month, is the most crucial astrological timescale. It also suggests that astrological influences lie dormant in most people. They are apparent in eminent professionals because success requires that potentials be optimised, and in twins because they have an increased need to individuate and yet insufficient environmental and hereditary differences to exploit. To explain how astrology operates it has been suggested that the personality is inherent and leads to the child choosing the appropriate moment of birth; however, if the twin result continues with induced births, then this idea seems to be outmoded and the mechanism of astrology remains as mysterious as ever.

Evolution

Missing Links

Colin Wood finds weaknesses in the arguments of a Darwinist guru

Last February, I attended a talk by Dr Richard Dawkins, entitled "How to deal with 'Creationists'". Dr Dawkins, an avid atheist and author of *The Selfish Gene* and *The Blind Watchmaker*, is widely seen as the top 'evolutionary' guru.

While identifying myself with the 'Creationist' label, I cannot defend the fundamentalist cause. I accept that the fossil record has great antiquity and that evidence of Modern Man has been found at many locations around the world dating tens of thousands of years before Adam and Eve were supposed to have lived in their earthly paradise, and I agree with Dr Dawkins in disregarding the 'six day creation' model. Where I disagree with him is about interpreting the fossil record.

The idea of 'evolution' is that species are supposed to change through minute adaptations to environmental and physical pressures, with the Darwinian qualification that only the best adapted survive. Accordingly, as an evolutionist, Dr Dawkins stated, early on: "By evolution, I mean that everything came from a common ancestor."

This is indeed what the fossil record was expected to prove. Darwin himself thought it was just a matter of time before the appropriate finds would be made. Today, after considerable investment of time and money, the fossil record is reckoned to be 99% *incomplete* – ie, only one percent of that which could be expected if evolutionary processes accounted for life on Earth.

More to the point, when fresh fossils are found, they tend to confirm previously discovered specimens, and are never of an identifiable intermediary or transitionary stage. Occasionally a 'new' find is made, such as the recent discovery of the world's smallest dinosaur - but an undeniable dinosaur it proved to be, not some evolutionary link.

Gaps abound between the major classes in the fossil record, and have been documented by the proponents of evolution. So, I wondered, how was Dr Dawkins going to explain these anomalies? He fielded an absolute master stroke, saying: "The fossil record is *not* important for the theory of evolution." This recalled a statement by Robin Dunbar, Professor of Anthropology at University College London, in a letter to me: "I keep reminding you that the fossil record is quite irrelevant to the truth or falsity of the theory of evolution."

> "Dr Dawkins wrote to me: 'If one were to scour the fossil record for smooth transitions, it would be harder to find a smoother transition than that leading from *Homo erectus* to *Homo sapiens*.'"

In theory, good science dictates that when a mismatch occurs, the theory should be modified or changed for one that *does* match the evidence. In practice, it seems, when the evidence is not seen to match their theory, the evolutionists are prepared to dismiss the evidence.

To his credit, Dr Dawkins is aware of the gaps in the fossil record, but explains them with some highly creative 'evolutionary' reasoning. In the talk, he acknowledged that the fossil record showed a development of life complexity in stages, and that "evolution accounted for the 'sensible steps' taken". (NB: evolution acquires a new property; the fact that a species survives shows that a 'sensible' choice had been made.)

Dr Dawkins was adamant that the gaps in the fossil record did *not* imply any missing links; a position he justified with imagination and ingenuity. According to him, evolution did not occur within the existence of a species for vast tracts of time. Then, all of a sudden, because of sudden environmental changes, the species evolved so rapidly over such a relatively short period that *no* evidence of the transition has been located.

The list of transitions is comprehensive: from 'no life' to single-celled (but scientifically very complex) bacteria; from single celled creatures to multi-celled invertebrates; from primitive plants to modern plants; from invertebrates to fish, to amphibians, to reptiles, to birds and mammals; land mammals to sea mammals; non-flying mammals to bats; apes to hominids; and from *Homo erectus* to Modern Man (the last 'link' in the chain).

Dr Dawkins stated, quite categorically, that *no* missing link existed that separated Australopithecus (man-like ape) from *Homo erectus* (ape-like man) – yet the fossil record gap between the two covers a considerable period of time. About the last link in the chain – the jump to Modern Man – Dr Dawkins wrote to me: "If one were to scour the fossil record for smooth transitions, it would be harder to find a smoother transition than that leading from *Homo erectus* to *Homo sapiens*." As expected, there is no fossil evidence of this transition at all.

In conclusion, Dr Dawkins said: "We *must* have descended from fossil man." To support the concept of 'evolution' this *must* have happened. All transitionary stages *must* have occurred for us to have evolved from our common ancestor, a primordial blob. For the evolutionist this *must* have happened, and therefore "evolution is a fact" ... a fact of which the fossil record does not appear to be aware.

Afterwards, I asked Dr Dawkins how he defined a 'creationist'. He replied: "Somebody who believes in a supernatural architect." I invite you to decide who is relying on 'special pleading'.

FORUM is a column in which anyone with something to say about a particular field, theory or incident can share their thoughts with our readership. If you'd like to join in with an opinion on any area of Forteana, send it in to the editorial address. Ideal length: 500–1000 words. Please enclose a three-line biography and head and shoulders photo of yourself with all Forum submissions.

The Id, the Ego and the Supernatural

Ralph Noyes looks at the parallels between sexuality and the paranormal

In *FT61* I outlined the engaging suggestion of Dr John Beloff that various weirdities act like intruders into a healthy system which then develops antibodies and throws them out, remaining largely immune to further 'infection'. This entertaining speculation certainly has the great merit that it could be applied as much to Mothman as to Mother Shipton. But I would now like to suggest that his metaphor, drawn from immunology, may be less helpful than one which leans on classical Freudian psychoanalysis.

Freud has had a bad press in recent years. New Agers prefer Jung, who sounds more 'spiritual'; Old Agers attack him for lack of scientific rigour; and most agers now somewhat deplore his preoccupation with the wicked Id in us, particularly his seemingly obsessive concern with the steamy jungle of human sexual peculiarity. Yet as Brian Inglis reminds us in that indispensable book, *The Paranormal: An Encyclopædia of Psychic Phenomena* (1986), Freud is on record as saying, "If I had my life to live over again, I should devote myself to psychical research rather than psychoanalysis." This is the same Freud who elsewhere writes with distaste of "the black tide of occultism". Curiously, he never seems to have explored in much depth a possible link – a very 'Freudian' connection – between the occult and the Id, both 'hidden' (because repressed by the needs of reason and social harmony – 'damned' in Fort's sense), both likely to erupt at any time without warning, and both likely to be thrust firmly back into their underworld by 'pure' and 'reasonable' men, sometimes with the kind of brutality which marked the historical witch hunts, sometimes by the gentler, though more devious, methods of self-styled 'skeptics'.

In Freud's model, the frail Ego is forever engaged in an attempt to make sense of, and to survive within, a material world which (as it seems) harshly punishes those of its creatures which ignore the local 'rules of the game'. This little daylight Ego, carried atop a biped of apparently recent and hasty evolution whose sheer survival as a species depends upon social consensus and harmony, is endlessly beset by threats to its 'rational' intentions, not the least being the rich absurdities of its ever-demanding sexuality.

This 'handling' of sexuality takes several forms. Some people simply lie back and enjoy it, anyway in private. I will hazard the hypothesis that none of these ever suffers an intrusion of the paranormal; collecting the evidence by a door-to-door canvass should be an enjoyable means of earning a doctorate in the social sciences.

Others, among them the Victorian researchers, have allowed a degree of what Freud called 'the return of the repressed', meaning that the sexual elements were never directly acknowledged, but peeped through and were passed off as part of the vicissitudes of research. To appreciate the point, one has only to read the accounts of that short-lived phenomenon, ectoplasm, an unappealing substance which emerged from all orifices of the ladies concerned, involving intimate physical examinations which the researchers often felt obliged to undertake to exclude fraud.

> "We can flex our muscles as we wish, other parts (as Joe Orton once put it) appear to have a mind of their own."

Others again have noted a connection, more or less direct, between human sexuality and paranormal phenomena. Poltergeist manifestations are often associated with young people at the stage of early puberty. Many accounts of the behaviour of witch covens and other esoteric groups include elements of sexual conduct, often of a kind which the nervous Ego calls 'perverse'. UFO lore dwells increasingly on the kitchen-table gynæcology practised on their victims by grey dwarves who pretend to come from other worlds. Bernini's sculpture of the paranormal ecstasies of Saint Teresa of Avila in the Cornaro Chapel of the church of Santa Maria della Vittoria at Rome is notoriously associated with the lineaments of orgasm, often with the snigger of those who feel they are making a bar-room point, sometimes with the recognition that sexual orgasm may be the nearest analogue our species has of union with the para-human. There is a multiplicity of other, similar connections.

Of all human capacities, the sexual faculty – like any paranormal phenomenon – is the least under conscious and deliberate control. We can flex our muscles as we wish, other parts (as Joe Orton once put it) appear to have a mind of their own. As Shakespeare expresses it in his 151st sonnet:

"My soul doth tell my body that he
may
Triumph in love: flesh stays no further
reason,
But rising at thy name doth point out
thee
As his triumphant prize."

In short, sexual response happens whether we like it or not; and so do our paranormal experiences. What's more, both kinds of experience often contain elements of the grotesque, the jokey, the wholly unpredictable, the far-from-socially-acceptable. In sex, as in the paranormal, we seem to be in the presence of forces – sometimes 'dark', sometimes more jocular – which thrust themselves upon the Ego willy nilly, suggesting that we inhabit a world which, in its hidden aspects, the anxious Ego can merely stifle (or from time to time supinely yield to) rather than control.

On this kind of model, the paranormal represents the 'return of the repressed', frequently containing elements of sexual fantasy if we care to look for them, and always reflecting those things which are forbidden or damned by the Ego, which rapidly chucks them out again as quickly as possible, using whatever means are to hand – the Inquisition, the sceptical press, CSICOP, the Amazing Randi, Mrs Mary Whitehouse.

However, sex and the paranormal always come back again, changing their shape if necessary. As the ancients put it, you can turn Nature out with a pitchfork, but the old bitch always returns. All we can do is to await – with hope or anxiety – her next Protean trick. One day, perhaps, we shall psychoanalyse her – or ourselves.

Really Out-of-Place

Loren Coleman asks Forteans to distinguish between real and imaginary animals

Last year, England seemed to be in the throes of its *usual* unusual wave of out-of-place animals. For instance – thanks to ***FT65:14*** – we learned that coatimundis, native to semi-tropical and tropical areas of the New World, turned up at least twice in eastern England. Two weeks after the capture of the second one, alive, at Wrawby, farmers in Lincolnshire were warned to be on the lookout for a South American tapir. This set me thinking about the need to define just what we mean by 'out-of-place' and 'phantom' animals.

A real distinction must be made between the two types: on the one hand we have 'real' zoological specimens which have been caught, killed, photographed and catalogued, and on the other we have those which exist only as vague rumours or unsupported *sightings*, but which are interpreted as evidence of real out-of-place animals. A third type of mystery animal report is generated by the truly cryptozoological creature – one that might be real but which has not yet been discovered, such as the Bigfoot of California.

Real out-of-place animals are largely accounted for by the importation and escape of exotics, and by some animals extending their range. Whether or not the coming and going of these exotics is, in part, the result of *teleportation* is an interesting topic, and deserves to be taken up another time.

A whole shadowy zoo exists in the landscape – for example there are the 'kangaroos' which featured in dozens of reports across the USA in the 1980s – of which no specimen was ever caught or definitively photographed. Many writers have muddled real out-of-place animals with imaginary phantoms and cryptozoological creatures. George Eberhart, in his classic reference work *A Geo-Bibliography of Anomalies* (Greenwood, 1980), catalogued most reports of the second kind under such headings as 'phantom baboon' or 'phantom panther'; however, in reports of the first type (classed as 'erratics') we find some phantoms (like the kangaroos) alongside real armadillos and a peccary.

> "There's a world of difference between two coatis in the hand and a 'tapir' in the bush."

Take, for instance, Eberhart's 'erratic giant anteater'. At face value, one would assume that a flesh and blood anteater had turned up in Harrisburg, Illinois, in August 1963... but if we trace the story to its source in *Fate*, in an article on a series of UFO sightings in that state, we find mention only of the sighting of a large animal *resembling* an anteater. It is a vague sighting, and not, strictly speaking, anything to do with cryptozoology. In this sense, the Lincolnshire tapir alert belongs firmly in the 'phantom' category, while the more tangible coatis were definitely 'real'. This becomes important when otherwise 'normal' cryptozoological investigations are interrupted by captures of 'real' exotics in the midst of a flap of sightings.

The *procyonids* – including racoons, ringtails, cacomistles, kinkajous, and the coatimundis – particularly, form a regular part of my Fortean files, often caught as real out-of-place animals. Among many incidents, a tropical cacomistle was found in a hen house in Washington DC at the turn of the century; a ringtail was shot near Niagara Falls in 1912; a coatimundi was in a South Bend, Indiana, basement in January 1923; another was shot near Woodward, Oklahoma, in November 1950; and in late August 1970, a kinkajou was found wandering in Denver, Colorado.

During the 1974 flap of kangaroo sightings in the vicinity of Chicago, a kinkajou was caught. The papers claimed this finished the wave of kangaroo sightings, but it did not. During 1981, the area around Tulsa, Oklahoma, experienced its own kangaroo sightings, during which (in September), a Patagonian cavy or mara was found in Tulsa itself and used by the media to explain all the 'roo reports.

In the summer of 1974, the Four Mile Run area of Arlington, Virginia, was terrorized by a mystery creature dubbed 'The Screamer', blamed for the deaths of two dozen cats, dogs and rabbits. A very rare Malay civet (*Viverra tangalunga*) was found by police, three miles away from the killings. Its origin was unknown, but that did not prevent the media positively identifying it as The Screamer.

Exotic animals out-of-place *should* be chronicled – but we must begin to make distinctions between those 'real' animals and the 'phantoms' of rumour, misperception and misidentification. There's a world of difference between two coatis in the hand and a 'tapir' in the bush. **FT**

DREAMACHINES

A comprehensive range of strobe mind-machines for self-development and visionary experience.

Many optional features and accessories inc biofeedback audio sync., phase oscillation, alpha and theta driving.

For catalogue (out mid-July) 2 x 1st class stamps to:

HIGHLAND PSIONICS,
SCORAIG, GARVE, ROSS-SHIRE IV23 2RE

Crop Circle MYSTERIES BOARD GAME

INCLUDES P&P

ORDER FORM
(Please tick boxes as appropriate)

I would like to receive:

☐ Advanced £26

☐ For ages 7 to 70 £17

join the UK HUNT

THE BOARD GAME WITH A TREASURE HUNT

ADVANCED Game only

PAYMENT by postal order.
Make payable to:
G. T. Vernon
16 Beggarswell Close
St Pauls
Bristol BS2 9JH

signed Merlin

Please allow 28 days for delivery

KHAT!

REDISCOVER THE DRUG OF OUR ANCESTORS

At the dawn of the human race, the holymen, writers, painters and poets of North East Africa explored KHAT to enhance spirituality and creativity. KHAT awakens primal sexual instincts, lightens the spirit and focuses energy.

The fresh KHAT plant is a stimulant which is chewed. A social catalyist similar to the coca plant, KHAT is wild, organic and renewably harvested from the Kenyan mountains.

MIRAH TEA is roasted KHAT and acts as a "pick-me-up" free of caffeine. The active constituent has been widely prescribed as a dietary suppressant. Sweet tasting it is a renowned aphrodisiac.

Fresh KHAT £6.50, MIRAH TEA £2.65, P&P 40p per item (80p non Europe). Cheque/PO's to RUNDALL addressed KHAT, 95 Ditchling Rd. , Brighton, E. Sussex.

MASS UFO SIGHTINGS

The largest mass UFO sightings ever recorded have been occurring in Mexico since July 1991. The facts are clearly presented in the riveting video documentary "MESSENGERS OF DESTINY". From the first major sighting on July 11th 1991 when a silvery disk-shaped object hovered for 23 minutes beneath the eclipsing sun (filmed from 17 different locations around Mexico City), to the regular sightings which continuously led to the volcanic region of Mexico.

"MESSENGERS OF DESTINY" contains an incredible amount of UFO footage (including daytime sightings), and the first ever filmed UFO "Hyper-Jump", and points to the strong connection between UFO's, Ancient Prophecy and Earth Changes.

Available for £21.15 from: ARK SOUNDWAVES (FT), P.O. Box 1395, Glastonbury, Somerset BA6 9FE, U.K.

Bungee Jump, Parachute or **Tandem Skydive** FREE

You can be sure of the experience of a lifetime, and it's free if you meet your sponsorship target figure. Ring **061 228 3777** or send a stamped addressed envelope. We will send you all you need to know about Skyway Events and MENCAP.

Skyway Events Ltd
Bridgewater House
58-60 Whitworth St.
Manchester M1 6LU
Tel: 061 228 3777
Fax: 061 228 2111

mencap
making the most of life
Mencap is a registered charity
Registered in England No.222377

WATERPIPES, GLASS, CERAMIC, PLASTIC, PIPE & CONE, WOOD PIPES , PESOLA'S etc, etc,

send S.A.E. for FREE catalogue or call:-

"WICKED" 47, The Grove, Uplands, Swansea. SA2 0QR

tel:0792 648009/201819

REVIEWS

THE MATTER MYTH
BEYOND CHAOS AND COMPLEXITY
by Paul Davies and John Gribbin

Penguin, 1992, pb £6.99, pp314, bib, index.

A paradigm shift is replacing the 19th century scientific view of the universe as a vast machine with a 21st century one of the universe as information. Davies, a physics professor, and Gribbin, a science writer with an enviable track record of explaining the inexplicable, report from the crest of this wave.

This book, basically a 'spotters' guide' to the science frontier, explodes the idea that scientists lack imagination and cannot deal with the truly bizarre. The authors concentrate on physics and cosmology, but they tip a nod to the life sciences in the final chapter.

The universe Davies and Gribbin present not only appears to contradict common sense, but can only truly be described by the kind of hellbastard mathematics that gives you a headache just to read, let alone try to understand. The authors admit that it will often be very difficult to visualise what is being discussed (11 dimensions are required in one theory).

Miraculously, a chapter explaining how Paul Davies grasped relativity as a student avoids screeds of mathematics completely. By taking such care in dealing with their readers, they have produced a book which manages to communicate some seriously difficult science to a wide audience. It is certainly clearer than the mystifyingly successful *Brief History of Time*, although not quite up to the fast-paced lucidity of Rudy Rucker's *Fourth Dimension*. However, the authors do tend to take a good basic grasp of science for granted.

The picture Davies and Gribbin paint is fascinating and breathtaking. The universe is no longer seen as a dull machine, but teems with surreal entities like superstrings with extra dimensions wrapped up inside them; virtual particles and antiparticles popping in and out of existence; black holes, worm holes, and new universes budding off from ours; chaotic systems where prediction fails; matter which becomes less solid the closer you look until it more or less vanishes, and so on. They conclude that Ryle was right to reject Descartes' view of the human as a discorporate mind in a corporeal body, deriding it as 'the Ghost in the Machine' - not because there's no ghost, but because there's no machine.

The universe of *The Matter Myth* is richer and more complex than the Newtonian one science is leaving behind. With the tools and viewpoints this paradigm provides, areas that science has previously scorned as 'irrational' may soon become amenable to scientific investigation, perhaps even 'undamning' some of the outcasts Fort brandished in the face of mechanistic science.

Ian Simmons

DEMONS, DOCTORS AND ALIENS
by James Pontolillo

INFO, Box 367, Arlington, VA 22210-0367, USA. 1993, $10 (inc postage), pp22, bib.

The subtitle declares this slim monograph to be "An exploration of the relationships between witch-trial evidence, sexual-medical examinations and alien abductions". After a rapid survey of the source material, Pontolillo, an American Fortean, concludes that "no credible evidence exists to support the objective reality of alien abductions". Instead, he confidently asserts that the potent subjective nature of these experiences lies in the recollections of frightening physiological experiences - including medical examinations, child abuse, and birth trauma.

Pontolillo argues that the theme of sexual abuse by aliens of unwilling and largely female humans is but the latest variation in an ancient tradition of misogeny which can be traced back to the earliest lore and codes of most influential cultures, particularly in the traditional literature about encounters with fairies, demons, and night hags.

There are indeed analogies to be drawn from this variety of material, but does, for example, the fairy changeling really equate with an alien hybrid foetus? No distinction is made in Pontolillo's usages of the reliability or colouring of the narratives he cites; for example, the agonised confessions wrung from 'witches' under torture, which owe more to fantasies of their persecutors than they do to the actual beliefs of the victims, are here on an equal footing with folk-narratives of fairylore and with the voluntary recollections of UFO abductees - three very different origins. Likewise, a distinction between the pre-Christian origin of most fairylore and Christian demonology is briefly made then effectively ignored. Important critical studies of the primary source material about the mediæval obsession with attack by supernatural forces – by Keith Thomas and Norman Cohn, for example – are not even mentioned.

Pontolillo cites many accessible sources second-hand, and this doesn't inspire much confidence in the rigour of his research. For example, instead of quoting Hilary Evans's important studies of claimed contact with supernatural entities directly, he quotes via Philip Klass's sceptical work; and for John Keel's article on Ray Palmer, he goes to Ted Schultz's *Fringes of Reason* instead of its original appearance in *Fortean Times*.

Other, similar comments could be made, but I don't wish to detract from Pontolillo's obvious seriousness and delight in his own discoveries and conclusions. His commentaries on the medical concomitants to the sexual symptoms reported by abductees (phantom pregnancy, extra nipples, genital warts, bodily fluids, scars etc) are most interesting. He has gone further than many other American analysts of this modern American phenomenon, and these ideas deserves proper consideration.

A separate letter from INFO explained that this publication was published before the ruling committee could approve it. It will certainly be of interest to Forteans and ufologists, but whether it is "the most complete interpretation and understanding to date of [alien abductions]" whose publication is, according to a foreword by INFO president Ray Manners, "a pivotal event in the annals of ufology" is open to doubt.

Bob Rickard

ROBIN HOOD
THE SPIRIT OF THE WOOD
by Steve Wilson

Wisely avoiding the generally futile and unproductive question of 'Who was the real Robin Hood?', Steve Wilson concentrates on the mythical aspects of the character, presenting a broad overview of the 'Spirit of the Forest', with a commendable range in time and space. When we realise that certain motifs in the story can be traced as far back as the period of Neolithic hunter-gatherers, or that others can be found in the Indian epic *Ramayana*, it becomes obvious that the mythic figure of the forest archer is by far the most important element of the tale. Any 'historical' person linked to this is merely an appendage to the greater theme.

Wilson provides an excellent compendium of Indo-European myth and culture, and traces the mutations of the character through ballads and literature, May-day celebrations and Morris dances, TV and film - for the spirit of Robin is still with us, currently incarnating in the modern pagan and ecological movements. Learned, green and passionate, with a thought-provoking and context-setting foreword by comics-writer Alan Moore, this is essential reading whatever your approach to the subject. ***Neptune Press, London. 1993, pb £7.95, pp133, illus, bib, index (£8.50 inc p+p from Atlantis Bookshop, 49a Museum St, London WC1A 1LY.)***

Steve Moore

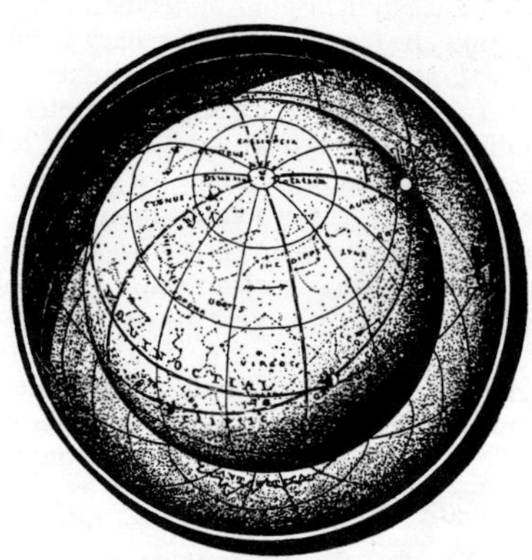

ARKTOS
THE POLAR MYTH IN SCENCE, SYMBOLISM AND NAZI SURVIVAL
by Joscelyn Godwin

Godwin has descended into the psychic underworld to seek out the meaning of the archetype of the Poles, both North and South, both celestial and terrestrial. It is an extraordinary journey though ancient cosmology, fragmented myths, obscure occultism, eccentric scholarship, cranky geography, exotic esotericism, and even classic Forteanism.

Godwin identifies a spiritual tradition in the West, parallel to Christianity (but more ancient), that he calls the 'Polar Tradition' - referring to the origin of the Arctic, Nordic or Aryan race, which inhabited a hospitable polar Hyperborea before the poles shifted altering the climate of this Earth, scattering the polar people and culture. It is a tradition related to the loss of the Golden Age, the Hollow Earth, Atlantis, UFOs, Ultima Thule, and the hidden kingdoms of Agartha and Shambhala, which found its lowest expression in the sinister mystical ideology of the Nazis, and its highest in the mystical philosophy of mediæval Persia. All of these are dealt with in detail.

Godwin is a professor of music at Colgate University, New York State, and author of a number of valuable studies of mystical philosophy, and as one would expect, this is far from the being the semi-literate ravings of a paranoid, rightwing lunatic. On the contrary, Godwin finds an astonishing balance between his fascination with the evolution of complexity in the archetype, and his desire to shine a little light into its darkest and sometimes repugnant corners. He also realises that the tradition is alive today in the arcana of many New Age interests including UFOs, channelling dubiously ancient entities, alchemy, and even such myths as secret Nazi bases in Antarctica.

This is a profound essay in spiritual symbology that is easy to read and exciting in its range of insights. Highly recommended. ***Thames & Hudson, London. 1993, pb £10.95, pp260, illus, refs, bib, index.***

Bob Rickard

FRACTALS
by John Briggs

If your sole interest in fractals – "the patterns of chaos" – is in the curiously organic forms which emerge from the iterative algorithms of fractal maths then this book is for you. It delights the eye with its sumptuous graphics. The text, on the other hand, has far less value. The print is large; Briggs is no mathematician; and the technical background is skimpy and vague. In some cases it is just wrong – one, admittedly beautiful, illustration is described as part of the Mandlebrot set explored by "Newton's Method". (I can hear hardcore fractal freaks falling about laughing.) Newton's Method is, of course, a technique used to solve polynomial equations and has no direct relevance to the Mandlebrot set. A book to look at, not to read. ***Thames & Hudson, London. 1992, pb £12.95, pp192, 256 illus (178 in colour), index, bib.***

Karma Tendzin Dorge

THE GODDESS HEKATE
edited by Stephen Ronan

A collection of pieces about Hekate in her various disguises. The ancient Great Goddess of Hesiod, the Græco-Roman deity of the underworld, magic and the Moon, the 'Chaldean' Hekate of NeoPlatonic philosophy and theurgy appears in late antiquity. The first

two aspects are dealt with in the opening half of the book, which consists of valuable reprints of work by earlier scholars (Farnell, Rohde, etc) – then, after a translation of four hymns to the goddess, the Chaldean Hekate receives a lengthy treatment from Ronan himself.

Obviously the book's major contribution, this new material collects and discusses the Hekate references in the fragmented Chaldean Oracles, probably the only body of esoteric doctrine to come down to us from the Classical World. Ronan builds up a more fully-rounded image of the goddess, her functions, and her history. Learned, detailed and often complex, it's not light reading - but this sort of material is essential for an understanding of ancient philosophy, religion and occultism. Recommended. ***Chthonios Books, 7 Tamarisk Steps, Hastings TN34 3DN, (Tel: 0424 43302). 1992, hb £24.50 (post free), pp166, illus, index.***

Steve Moore

THE YEAR OF THE SORRATS
by John Thomas Richards

The author is a long-standing member of the Society for Research Rapport and Telekinesis (SORRAT) in the States. He has chosen the fictional approach in his attempt to publicise the extraordinary phenomena triggered by the SORRAT team. His novel, though competently written and readable, fails to make the phenomena more believable. Richards has already written a history of the first 20 years of the SORRAT experiments (1961-81). It is time to update this survey. ***BookMasters, 638 Jefferson St, Ashland, OH 44805, USA. 1992, pb $10 (inc. overseas postage), pp242, illus.***

Janet Bord

AMERICA'S FIRST CROP CIRCLE
edited by Donald Cyr

The catchy title refers to a rather well-known (to scholars) folktale of the Algonkin Indians. This is the second collection of articles relating (directly and indirectly) to the crop circle phenomenon, from Cyr's own periodical *Stonehenge*

Viewpoint. Much here that is interesting - especially about electrical and optical phenomena in the atmosphere. *Stonehenge Viewpoint (UK agent: Leonard Smith, 16 Solstice Rise, Amesbury, Salisbury, Wilts SP4 7NQ). 1992, pb £7 (inc p&p), pp96, illus, index.*

Bob Rickard

THE AFTERLIFE

by Jenny Randles & Peter Hough

A competent and encyclopædic survey of beliefs about the Afterlife, nicely presented, illustrated and designed, including reincarnation, hauntings and the modern incarnation of what used to be called 'astral travel', so-called Near Death Experiences (NDEs). The authors present interviews with a variety of leading mediums, researchers, the haunted, and people who have had NDEs and other experiences which have convinced that they will survive death with their personality intact. Randles even tries out 'life regression' therapy, a sort of guided daydreaming.

No matter how interesting, detailed or scholarly books on this topic are, there is, ultimately, no definitive proof one way or the other – this is a tantalising meal that fails to satisfy one's hunger. Despite peppering the book with personal experiences, the authors maintain a healthy scepticism; for example, listening to medium Bill Tenuto channel John Lennon, Randles finds it "impossible to decide if this is clever mimicry". However, to help the reader make up his or her own mind about the data presented there is a running scoring system, leading to an evaluation of the score as an indication of your level of belief. *Piatkus Books, London. 1993, hb £16.99, pp240, illus, refs, index.*

Bob Rickard

MISSING PIECES

by Robert A. Baker and Joe Nickell

This guide to investigating "Ghosts, UFOs, Psychics and Other Mysteries" is written by two members of CSICOP (the Committee for the Scientific Investigation of Claims of the Paranormal), but don't let that put you off; it is highly informative if you make allowances for the shortcomings of their absolutist 'skepticism'.

The two best chapters deal with 'Investigatory Tactics' and 'Getting at the Truth', emphasising that "there is no record of a ghost ever harming a human being". There are useful hints on how to handle interviews and how to avoid the problems of libel and copyright infringement. *Prometheus Books, Loughton, Essex. 1992, hb £17.50, pp339, index.*

Andrew Green

MAGWATCH

The 'abduction case of the century', as MUFON called it, has occasioned open feuding among top US ufologists as articles on the alleged levitation of Linda 'Napolitano' over the rooftops of Manhattan into a UFO appear in many current issues.

***UFO JOURNAL*, the revamped organ of Mutual UFO Network (MUFON), reaching its 300th issue (April 1993), includes a defense of the case by MUFON chief Walter Andrus, and introduces a new medical-sexual abduction case involving four campers on the Allagash River, Maine, investigated by veteran Raymond Fowler.**

The *INTERNATIONAL UFO REPORTER* #100 – edited by Jerry Clark for the Hynek Centre for UFO Studies (CUFOS) – usually firmly pro-ET/'missing time' abductions, has allowed two critical articles in the March/April 1993 issue alongside a spirited defence of the 'Napolitano' case by Budd Hopkins and David Jacobs.

Nor can John Rimmer, editor of *MAGONIA* – the wasp that stings the assholes of ufology – resist having his say about the 'Napolitano' case. Fed up with entrenched 'experts' bickering for want of tangible evidence, he offers to send readers photocopies of the material so they can decide for themselves. Issue #45 (March 1993) also has Peter Rogerson laying into David Jacobs; Martin Kottmeyer on 1960s paranoid ufology; and Christopher Allan assessing the current state of 'crashed saucer' research.

The case crops again in Robert Sheaffer's column in *SKEPTICAL INQUIRER* v17n3 (Spring 1993), but this is overshadowed by a critique of the successes claimed for the 'Facilitated Communication' method of teaching autistic children. Some 'zealot' teachers, it seems, have been pretending success where there was none. Also noteworthy is Martin Gardner trying to explain the semantics of Korzybski.

***WONDERS* #4 (Dec 1992), the quarterly journal from Fortean cryptozoologist Mark Hall, carries a detailed analysis of sightings of what seemed to be a dinosaur in the St Johns River, Florida in 1975.**

If you're interested in mazes, get lost in *CAERDROIA* #25, Jeff Saward's annual round-up of labyrinth research.

Bob Rickard

ADDRESSES

Caerdroia: ***53 Thundersley Grove, Thundersley, Essex SS7 3EB.***
CUFOS: ***2457 W. Peterson, Chicago, IL 60659, USA.***
MUFON: ***103 Oldtowne Rd, Seguin, TX 78155, USA.***
Magonia: ***John Dee Cottage, 5 James Terrace, Mortlake Churchyard, London SW14 8HB.***
Skeptical Inquirer: ***Box 703, Buffalo, NY 14226-0703, USA.***
Wonders: ***9215 Nicollet So. 104, Bloomington, MN 55420, USA.***

FILM

FIRE IN THE SKY

An allegedly true story of a backwoods abduction by aliens

What happened to Travis Walton at 5:49 pm on 5 November 1975 in Arizona's Sitgrave-Apache National Forest? Was he truly abducted and examined by aliens? Or was the story concocted by him and fellow timber-workers because they were unable to meet the deadline on their wood-cutting contract? *Fire in the Sky* is an even-handed look at the facts, fraud, and fantasy surrounding this extraordinary encounter case.

On their way home after a hard day's logging, the crew were attracted to a fiery light in the forest. Investigating, they are all frightened except Travis (D.B. Sweeney), who rushes out of the pick-up truck. A bright beam of light blasts him across the clearing. Thinking him dead, the terrified loggers drive off at high speed back to the small town of Snowflake.

The forest is searched for five days without a single clue being found or any sign of Travis dead or alive. His friends are simply unable to say what happened to him, so Lt Watters (James Garner), a hard-bitten state investigator who doesn't believe in UFOs, presumes that Travis has been murdered. Then, unexpectedly, Travis is found – crouching, naked and semi-conscious. He recovers in hospital, but is still dazed when released. Later he has a vivid recollection of his time with the aliens.

In the forest, Walton is struck by a powerful beam of light

The abduction sequence is the most interesting and shocking part of the whole film. Travis wakes inside a slime-filled cocoon. Forcing his way through a membrane, he falls towards the centre of a cylindrical room lined with other cocoon-niches. Falling into one, he stumbles over a seemingly half-eaten human corpse. He flees into a room full of inert *Communion*-type aliens and realises they are hollow space suits.

He is seized by half-glimpsed aliens with potato-like skin, long arms and legs and thin bodies, rushed along a corridor to a table, and subjected to a horrifying and meaningless examination or operation. This includes black slime and a tube forced into his mouth, a cable poked into the side of his neck, being shrink-wrapped in a rubbery membrane, and an intimidating drill-like probe lowered down to his right eye. This image of imprisonment and torture is genuinely disturbing.

Travis Walton (left) and Mike Rogers, after the abduction

In an epilogue, set two and a half years later, we are shown Travis happily married and seemingly prosperous. In contrast, his best friend and team leader Mike Rogers, (played by Robert Patrick), is shown to be adversely affected; his marriage has broken up and he has become a recluse.

The viewer can accept Lt Watters' opinion that it was a clever hoax, or believe that the loggers really did encounter ETs. Another plausible interpretation is that Travis the dreamer had some kind of fugue; lost, dazed, starving, and bruised, he wanders for five days, interpreting all that happens to him through a vision of an ET abduction.

Travis and the others involved were consulted by the scriptwriter Tracy Tormé (who had worked on the *Intruders* TV series) – nevertheless there are many significant departures from the earlier published accounts of the incident. Travis's own book describes the aliens as white-skinned with tan-brown robes. Travis said he was led (not dragged) to a chair (not an operating table) where nothing particularly horrifying happened to him. Later, he was found fully clothed. Unlike his portrayal in the film, earlier accounts say Walton failed his first lie-detector test, used hypnotic regression to recall his abduction, and was a broken man afterwards.

Can we write off these discrepancies as dramatic license? True, some of the differences are due to Paramount's desire to distance the 'product' from images of abductions, aliens and UFOs that would be familiar to US audiences from *Communion* and the *Intruders* series – but this does not explain why Walton's own account has developed a wealth of new details.

Tormé tried to explain the confusion elsewhere: "I don't think the Travis case is an abduction case. I think of it more as a hit-and-run accident... it doesn't fit any of the other patterns that we explored in *Intruders*." At best we have to agree with Travis when he says: "I think most people know better than to expect a documentary."

Presented as a mystery story in the documentary-drama style, this is more like a superior TV movie than a spectacular myth-making Spielberg-type production. Director Robert Lieberman is obviously constrained by some of the essential "facts", but he intelligently invests the film with visual references to other films and to ufology. For example, when first we see Lt Watters there is an immediate joke reference to a similar scene in Spielberg's *Close Encounters*.

UFO experts, investigators, believers and sceptics should not miss this film, nor should anyone who likes a thoughtful mystery film. It is a convincing dramatisation of what an abduction experience might be like, and the impact such an event has on the people, their families and their community.

Nigel Watson

Director: Robert Lieberman (Paramount, 1993; Cert. 15; 110 mins).

DEAR FT...

A Russian sturgeon (or Beluga) 14ft 2in long. Photograph from the Gerald Wood Archives, provenance unknown.

LARGEST FISH CLARIFICATION

■ With regard to your report 'Chinese fish was a red herring' ***[FT67:10]***: it is correct to describe the rare pla beuk (*Pangasianodon gigas*) as the world's largest freshwater fish (maximum 3m, 240kg) because its whole life is spent in fresh or brackish waters.

The sturgeon, on the other hand, is usually found in temperate seas and only enters large rivers for spawning. The 13ft specimen claimed to be displayed in China's Sturgeon Artificial Reproduction Institute, Wuhan, is only a tiddler in record terms. According to Russian ichthyologist Dr Leo S. Berg, the largest known specimen of the Russian sturgeon (*Huso huso*) was a gravid female taken in the estuary of the Volga in 1827. She measured 24ft in length and weighed an astonishing 3,249lbs.

Susan Wood
The Gerald Wood Archives Whitham, Essex

PRUDES FROM SPACE

■ Why don't extraterrestrials sprout any genitals? In the reports of alleged encounters – even those with dead ETs recovered from crashed saucers – the aliens either lack genitals altogether, or have them demurely hidden under spacesuits of some kind. The only exception seems to be the interstellar bimbo who seduced Antonio Villas Boas in Brazil in 1957. Is there a Freudian significance to all this?

David Keyworth
Tasmania

BOLLOCK!

■ There are limits to what one can consider believing, and 'Dogged by Misfortune' ***[FT67:19]*** passes them. A grown man who has never been in a changing room or an art gallery, and is unaware of his deficiency in the scrotal department until he notices his dog's! No, there's a leg-pull somewhere; the story's bollock.

David Gamon
Wells, Somerset

TROLLEY TRAVEL

■ I was overjoyed to see you have joined the debate on shopping trolleys ***[FT67:19]***. Whilst travelling by train between Plymouth and Cardiff recently, I noticed a large number of these errant vehicles lying on embankments next to bridges. Could it be that railway bridges are favoured suicide spots for trolleys who see no future in the carting life?

Aldo Z. Picek
Plymouth

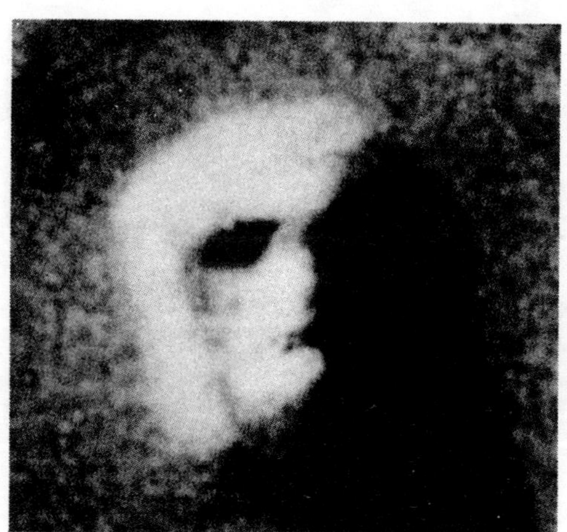

Primary face

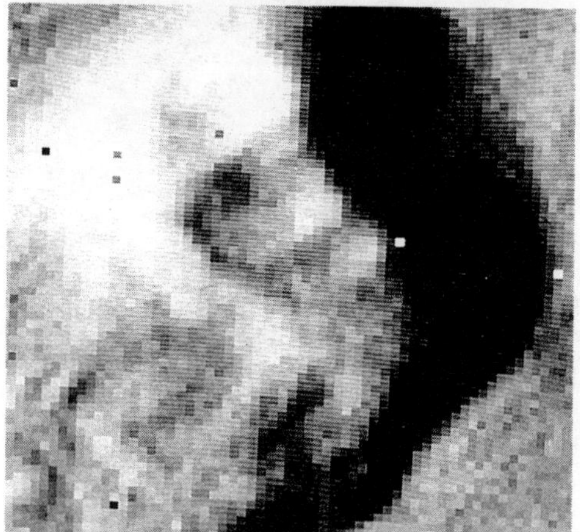

Secondary face

ANOTHER FACE ON MARS

■ Your insert on the 'monuments of Mars' – ***FT65*** – drew attention to the enhancement of the 1976 Viking images of Mars to reveal seemingly intentional structures known as the Primary Face, the Fort, the D&M Pyramid, the City and so on.

As the focus of these Cydonia studies had been to the east of the D&M Pyramid, I began a survey of the images to the west of it, resulting in the discovery of a feature I call the Secondary Face, best seen on frame 70A11. Barely three Martian miles from the Secondary Face is a peculiar star-shaped formation on a ledge.

The Secondary Face is approximately twice the distance from the apex of the D&M Pyramid as the Primary Face. Both Faces are of almost identical size, and both are aligned at more or less the same angle with respect to north on Mars.

The Secondary Face appears to be more eroded than the Primary Face, suggesting that it may have been 'made' first, especially as it seems to have been carved into a ledge. The top surface of the ledge shows what seems to be 'furrowed ground'. Other researchers have noted the presence of such 'ploughed-field' areas in the vicinity of many of the anomalous features. Dr Mark Carlotto, in his book *The Martian Enigmas: A Closer Look* (1991) relates that this has fuelled speculation about 'quarrying' on the surface of Mars.

FT readers may like to know that I have a few copies for sale of *Unusual Mars Surface Features* by Vincent DiPietro, Gregory Molenaar and Dr John Brandenburg (privately published in 1988 by Mars Research). This fourth edition has colour enhancements. Price postpaid: £13.00.

Ananda Sirisena
Unisys Europe Training Centre, Fox Milne, Milton Keynes, MK15 0DN

■ The FT Martian Sphinx pullout supplement claims that the 'mirrored halves' of the Face resemble the faces of a human and a cat. Humans don't have long floppy ears, extended snouts and split lips; but dogs do. Far from being a sphinx, the Face is a representation of the alchemists' *rebis hermaphrodite*, the union of male and female. The dog and cat are, traditionally, symbols of the masculine and feminine aspects of humanity.

Then again, seen from a distance, the whole thing looks like a cyberman from *Doctor Who*. Perhaps that's it.

Bobby Spiromat
Uxbridge

AGE OF THE EARTH

■ Jim Lippard accuses me of dishonesty in his letter [***FT68:65***] about my article on the age of the Earth [***FT66:24***], which he also calls 'highly misleading'. Yet his arguments fail to address any of the issues I raised.

It was not me, but Funkhouser and Norton themselves, who urged caution in the application of potassium-argon dating in their study of Hawaiian lavas. When Lippard says that the Hawaiian anomaly "is the sort of thing that is allowed for in radiometric dating", he is falling into the very fallacy I have exposed: there is *nothing* in potassium-argon dating that would have disclosed the anomaly. We know the age of the lavas in this case by accident because the eruptions happened in historical times.

Regarding meteoric dust, he has missed the point. Even taking his lowest possible estimate of dust entering the atmosphere, there would still have been 73 million billion tons of dust with highly distinctive nickel content (about eight million billion cubic feet) deposited on the Earth's surface if the Earth were 4,600 million years old, yet there is no trace of any such deposits (and only one inch of dust on the moon). Lippard offers no explanation for this absence.

He also repeats the often-made claim that different dating methods yield concordant dates. This is simply false. Even different radiometric methods yield discordant dates that have to be 'harmonised' in the laboratory (that is, they are fiddled with until they look 'right'). Carbon dating is 'calibrated' by reference to tree rings (is fiddled with until it looks 'right').

Lippard urges readers to turn to the orthodox dating texts so that they can absorb the received wisdom on dating; I am urging readers to examine dating methods critically and reach their own conclusions.

Richard Milton
Tonbridge, Kent

■ As someone trained in geology, I am disappointed in Lippard's response, which is far from adequate. To take one example with which I am personally familiar: the Borrowdale Volcanic Group of the Lake District is conventionally supposed to represent about 10 million years of volcanic activity. However, the rock types present in this 6,000-metre-thick volcanic sequence are known to accumulate quite rapidly. It is clear that the bulk of the 10 million years is simply not recorded in the sequence.

The only answer that an Old-Earther can give is to claim that the 'missing' time is accounted for by erosional gaps in the sequence, but this is simply a *belief* and cannot be demonstrated scientifically. In fact, in many instances of 'missing' time, this explanation is untenable since the strata have undergone little appreciable erosion during the supposed lapse in time.

Paul Garner
Littleport, Cambs

SAI BABA'S MIRACLES

■ John Keel is quoted in your interview with him [***FT65:27-30***] as saying that no one has "come up with a real exposé of Sai Baba". This is incorrect. Dale Beyerstein's *Sai Baba's Miracles: An Overview* (US$10 from Dale Beyerstein, Apt A, 1267 W.70th Ave., Vancouver, BC, Canada V6P 2Y4) points out that sleight-of-hand by Sai Baba can be seen in Richard Bock's videotape, "Christ in Kashmir, The Hidden Years", which is circulated by Sai Baba devotees. A 'thumb-palmed' necklace is visible on the tape at the 44-minute point before Sai Baba 'materialises' it, and at the 45-minute point another necklace is bunched up in his right hand and he uses his left hand to free it. Beyerstein also points out several other places on the videotape where evidence of conjuring tricks may be seen.

Jim Lippard
Tucson, Arizona

MUSIC TO OUR EARS

■ I recently picked up my first copy of ***Fortean Times.*** There are just *no* magazines that are *this* interesting, well done, *and* fun to read. You have made a loyal reader out of me – even if I *do* have to pay five bucks an issue. Thanks.

Anthony Hayes
Los Angeles

GIVEN THE BIRD

■ Your tale of Mollyhawk, the confused albatross of the Shetlands, is strange and interesting [*FT64:12*]. I saw this bird the first time I was in Scotland, back in 1977. The bird is, as you have stated, a black-browed albatross. However, your picture shows another species, either a grey-headed or a yellow-nosed albatross.

Lars Thomas
Valby, Denmark

[Editors' note: Mollyhawk resumed his lonely vigil at Hermaness at the tip of Unst, the most northerly of the Shetland Islands, in April 1993. He has been looking in vain for a mate for a quarter of a century. The nearest nesting colony is over 7,000 miles away in the Falklands.]

PARROT CHICKEN MINDER

■ Last December, a few weeks before I received your magazine with Karl Rowley's letter on the parrot chicken minder [*FT66:64*], I sang, for the first time in many months, the 'Parrot Song' which has been part of my folk song repertoire since the 1950s. I learnt it from Vic Neep, who lived at Buntingford at the time. I have no idea where he got it from, but it is extremely unlikely that he knew about John Locke's essay.

It is sung to the tun of 'Making Whoopee':

The parrot is the strangest bird
In words as wise as most you've heard
He says it's normal to be informal
When making whoopee.

He tells his friends, 'Just look at me,
They caught me in a mango tree
While I was dizzy and very busy
Just making whoopee'.

He used to raise the dickens
Way down in *old Brazil;*
He used to keep six chickens,
Who always paid the bill.

But in his cage now, our feathered friend
Is out of luck, for to the end
He'll have his heart in, but can't take part in
Just making whoopee.

Ken Woodward
Wrexham, Clwyd

BIRD DEATH MYSTERY

■ I was particularly interested in your item about the 300 birds found dead and dying near Bodedern, Anglesey, last year [*FT68:6*]. A similar phenomenon took place at Pwllheli in the same county in 1904, and this may be the Llyn Peninsula reference from ADAS. It was reported in the *Oswestry Advertizer* on 30 March 1904:

"An extraordinary event is recorded from Pwllheli. A number of men were working in the early morning at Gimlet Rock, when an immense number of birds, attracted perhaps by the lights, dropped upon them and the shipping and the beach. They found heaps of all sorts of birds lying dead or dying on the ground, whilst as many had dropped into the sea. This was the case for a great distance along the shore; some of the fields immediately adjacent were also strewn with thousands of feathered creatures in like stricken condition. The birds included starlings, blackbirds, thrushes, and robins, and several snipe were also said to be among the victims. The event has caused quite a stir in the district."

Bye-Gones also informs us of considerable UFO activity around Pwllheli 30 years previously, so perhaps they were zapped!

Richard Holland
Clwyd

THE FACE(S) IN THE WINDOW

■ It was New Year's Day 1968. A friend, Colin Crabbe, was staying for the festivities at Tyninghame, our family home in those days, and on our exploring the garages, Colin took a shine to the old Brougham that sat forlornly in one of the bays. Being an antique car dealer, he asked my father if he would do a deal on the unloved coach. Rather surprisingly, my father agreed to sell it to Colin.

Saddened by this impending loss to the family's former mode of transport, I decided to make a final record of its final years at Tyninghame. Colin and I pushed it out into the centre of the yard that evening at about 6:30pm. There was a light sprinkling of snow on the ground and the air was frosty. I had a Nikon 35mm SLR camera and was using a flash. I took one or two photographs from different angles and we returned the Brougham to its bay in the garage. We may have sat in it in the yard for a while before taking the photographs, and examined its condition outside in better light, but had no unusual experience at the time.

I went to Switzerland a week later and had the film developed there. When I saw the photograph [*reproduced above*] it was a great surprise. I have never seen anything so bizarre in a photograph before, apart from those photos of cotton wool ectoplasm issuing from the mouths of phony mediums. Is it a trick of the light or are the faces in the window something else?

The Earl of Haddington
Berwickshire

[Editors' note: SPR Hon. Secretary Ralph Noyes discerns a small 'laughing cavalier' and – larger – the face of a woman.]

VON DANIKEN GOT THERE FIRST

■ Caroline Menis points out that Assyrian gods carried 'wristwatches' [*FT66:64*]. Erich von Däniken drew attention to this in 1973 in his photo-book *Meine Welt in Bildern* (pp18-20). Similarly, Graham Hancock was not the first to trace the lost Ark of the Covenant to the Church of St Mary of Zion in Axum, Ethiopia [see review of his book *The Sign and the Seal*, ***FT68:59***]. Von Däniken revealed the secret in *Prophet der Vergangenheit* in 1979.

Walter J. Langbein
Lügde, Germany

[Editors' note: Irritation with von Däniken's wild assertions has sometimes obscured his many contributions to original research.]

noticeboard

EXCHANGE & MART

● **UFO AFRINEWS** edited by Cynthia Hind. The only UFO magazine in Africa. Write: Gemini, Box MP49, Mt Pleasant, Harare, Zimbabwe.

● **FORTEAN PICTURES** The Fortean Picture Library is a self-funding project for the rescue and preservation of valuable documentary material, photographs and drawings etc. If you have anything of this nature, please let FPL look after it. 50% of the revenue from the commercial use of the material (in books etc) could come back to you. FPL covers all expenses from its half. Contact Janet Bord, FPL, Melysfan, Llangwn, Corwen, Clwyd, Wales LL21 ORD. Fax 049 082 321.

● **WANTED** – Send, gratis, old Fortean and paranormal magazines to a new (but impoverished) Romanian UFO and paranormal group. Contact Mr Manea Maius, Str. V. Lupu 88, bl.Z.sc.C.ap.3, Issi 6600, Romania.

● **EARTH CHANGES REPORT** details of recent and impending earthquakes, volcanoes etc. Unavailable in any shops. Beware – contains disturbing information. Cheques for £4.95 includes PP to A.J.D(F) 64, Bove Town, Glastonbury, BA6 8JE.

● **FREEDOM OF INFORMATION CAMPAIGN** Everything you need to know, but were never told about. For info contact:- Rev Anthony G Pike, 141 Austen Rd, Sth Harrow, Middx, HA2 OUU. Tel 081-426 8758.

● **APHRODISIACS?** Ritual Herbs? Magical Mixes? We supply the goods and the info. Catalogue £1.50 refundable on first order. Hi-Spirits, 118 St Mary St, Southampton.

● **UFO NEWSCLIPPING SERVICE** – UFO reports from the world's press reproduced facsimile, along with news-wire items and foreign reports in translation. 20 pages monthly, strong on Cryptozoology. Highly recommended by FT. For information and sample pages write to UFONS, Lucius Farrish, Route 1 – Box 220, Plumerville, AR 72127 USA.

● **THE SKEPTIC** takes an entertaining rational and humourous look at pseudoscience and claims of the paranormal. Articles, reviews, columns, cartoons and much more. Sample issue £1.85; annual sub (6 issues) £12. The Skeptic, PO BOX 475, Manchester M60 2TH.

● **UFOS: FACT, FRAUD OR FANTASY?** Indeptndent UFO network international conference. Speakers include: Budd Hopkins, Jenny Randles, Cynthia Hind, Paul Devereux, Hilary Evans, Dr Sue Blackmore and others. 14-15th August 1993, Sheffield Polytechnic. For full details send SAE to: Stu Smith, 15 Rydal Street, Burnely, Lancs BB10 1HS. Phone 0282 24837.

● **A TRUE MYSTERY** written by F Russell Clampitt, geocryptologist. "The Coldrum Line" may be the strangest ley line in Britain, stretching from an ancient burial mound in Kent to the far depths of the North Sea. Maps, diagrams and photographs. Price £3.95 inc p&p. Cheques/ PO's payable to Akelarre, PO Box 3 Llandeilo, Dyfed SA19 6YJ. USA dollar bills only. $10 surface mail, $13 air.

● **ORACLE ANSWERS** 4 questions £10.00 SAE "OM" 41 Terminus Drive, Herne Bay, CT6 6PR.

● **WANTED** anything relating to the visionary, occult artist AUSTIN OSMAN SPARE (AOS). In particular, original artworks depicting satyrs, witches, ghosts and elementals, astral and arboreal landscapes, self-portraits etc. Good prices paid, telephone 081 742 7347/ Fax 081 9952 2961. Attention John Balance or write to BM Codex, London, WC1N 3XX.

● **MAD COLLECTORS** – see FT62:34 – writer seeks information. Julian McKenny, 7 Alma Rd, Levenshulme, Manchester, M19 2FG.

● **FIRST TRANSMISSION** (Ex-Topy) A synthesis of occult/performance/enlightenment, as misused by CH4's 'Despatches'. Essential one hour edit. VHS. £12 payable M.A.S. BcM Em Comm, London WC1N 3XX.

● **HANDMADE WOODEN RUNE** sets in red velvet bags, complete with instructions £10.50 including P&P. Also wooden witch stones available £6.50. Payments to: P Jones 22a Marion St, Hendon, Sunderland, SR2 8RG.

● **LEGAL HIGHS** A detailed study of over 70 plants with hallucinogenic, stimulant and tranquillising properties. Don't buy expensive pre-mixed preparations of anonymous herbs, send for this book and explore the world of botanicals. £7.50 or SAE for more details: Sirus(F) PO Box 524, Reading, Berks, RG1 3JY.

● **UFO BOOKS, MAGAZINES, VIDEOS** Lists SAE SR Stebbing, 41 Terminus Drive, Herne Bay, Kent, CT6 6PR.

● **PORTRAITS OF ALIEN ENCOUNTERS** UFO case histories and much more! Hardback £12.00, Valis Books, 52a Lascotts Road, London N22 4JN.

● **STREET LAMP INTERFERENCE.** Can some people make street lamps switch off without physical contact? A new 52 page book, published by ASSAP, is the result of what is probably the first ever detailed examination of this subject. To obtain the "The SLI Effect" by Hilary Evans send £3.35 (of $7 from abroad) – cheques payable to ASSAP – to: SLI Effect, ASSAP, St Aldhelm, 20 Paul Street, Frome, Somerset, BA11 1DX.

● **THE C.I.B REPORT.** A quarterly newsletter on crop circles and related phenomena. Published by Circles Investigation Bureau. Write: C.I.B, The Cottage, Hollis Street Farm, Ninfield Road, Bexhill-on-Sea, East Sussex, TN39 5JS.

RESEARCH

● **DOWSING** – researcher seeks stories, anecdotes, references to successful finding of oil, water, fractures, faults etc, including methods and interpretations (aura, vibrations, signatures etc). Peter Aristedes, 810 N. Elmwood, Oak Park, IL 60302, USA.

● **HELP!!!** Anyone knowing details about circles of 6 red carnations please contact:- H.U.R.G, c/o P.S. John, 6 Whitehouse Drive, Kingstone, Hereford, HR2 9ER.

● **WRITER WOULD LIKE TO HEAR FROM** anyone who has had a genuine experience of the supernatural in past 30 years. Sarah Hapgood, 47 Sharland Close, Grove, Wantage, Oxfordshire, OX12 OAF.

● **SACRED RELICS RESEARCH GROUPS** Aim – Quest for The Ark of the Covenant. Anybody interested in joining the group contact Jonathon Boulter, 4 Huntington House, St Pauls Ave, Willesden Green, NW2 5SR.

● **ATLANTIS** Astonishing new theory in illustrated first edition booklet £2.95. J.M Allen, 36 Scotland Rd, Cambridge, CB4 1Q6.

MISCELLANEOUS

● **YOUNG UNEMPLOYED MAN** 30, would like a career working in the field that this magazine deals with. Anything considered, please write, with offers to: Mr Russell Horne, 16 Arundel Close, Stratford London, E15 1UH.

● **HOUSE FOR SALE** 5 bedroom stone house in North Wales, spacious but cosy, with outbuildings, in 2.5 acres including organic veg garden, fine trees and rich in birdlife; quiet location near village in South-west Clwyd – £120,000. For more details phone 049 082 472 or fax 049 082 321.

● **GLASTONBURY COTTAGE** Forget expensive hotels & B&Bs, Charming 2 bed house to let in mystic Glastonbury town centre. Central-heating, fully furnished with necessary utensils, crockery etc, and unique view over Abbey grounds. Tel:0234 211606 (answerphone) for leaflet.

● **WELSH HOLIDAY COTTAGE.** Self-catering accommodation in historic North Wales town of Denbigh. For further details, contact Janet Bord, Melysfan, Llangwm, Corwen Clwyd LL21 ORD. Tel:049 082 472 Fax:049 082 321.

● **TEMS** social and study group for paranormal phenomena and earth mysteries. For details phone Lionel Beer 081 979 3148

EVENTS

● **ANSWERING SPIRITS.** A new play about Spiritualism by Stephen Volk, author of BBC's 'Ghostwatch' and Ken Russell's 'Gothic', premieres at The Glynne Wickham Theatre in Bristol on 31 July – and at The Rondo, Larkhall, Bath on 5-7 August. Tel Antidote Theatre on 0225 862281 or 0225 722262 for more details.

● **SOCIETY FOR PSYCHICAL RESEARCH** Lectures: 17 June 'A Psychophysics Approach to PSI Research' (Peter Maddock). 15 July 'Who are the Falsifyers? The Paranormal in Print' (Melvin Harris). Venue: the Lecture Hall of Kensington Central Library, Campden Hill Road London W8, at 6.30pm. Non-members £3, student cards £1. Further information from the SPR at 49 Marloes Rd, Kensington, London W8 6LA. Tel 071 937 8984.

● **LONDON EARTH MYSTERIES CIRCLE.** Evening meetings in St Andrew's Seminar Room, Maria Assumpta Centre, 23 Kensington Square, London W8, at 6.30pm. 22 June 'The Mysterious Caves of Europe' (Clive Gardener). 13 July 'Sacred Greenwich' (Jack Gale). 27 July, social evening. Members £1.00, non-members £2.00, unwaged £1.50. All welcome. For other info send SAE to: Rob Stephenson, PO Box 1035, London W2 6ZX.

TO ADVERTISE ON THE NOTICEBOARD OR BOOKMART

simply fill in the form below and send it,

together with a cheque made payable to JOHN BROWN PUBLISHING LTD, to:

FT Classifieds, John Brown Publishing Ltd. The Boathouse, Crabtree Lane, Fulham SW6 8NJ.

Classifieds cost £15 for the first 30 words, 50p for each additional word.

I enclose my message of __________ words plus payment of £__________

Message reads: ____

____

____

____

Preferred section: ❑ **Exchange & Mart** ❑ **Research** ❑ **Bookmart** ❑ **Miscellaneous** ❑ **Events**

Classified adverts should reach us by 15th July 1993.

ILLUSTRATION COPYRIGHTS

5 New England Journal of Medicine **6** Associated Press (AP) **7** Southampton Newspapers **9** Indian Express **10** (l) (AP) (r) Arthur Chrenkoff **11** (t) John Fairfax Group, Sydney (b) Bristol United Press **12** Merrily Harpur **14** Alan Bolger **15** Popperfoto **16** (b) Peter Poole **17** Middlesboro Eve. Gazette **18** Intercontinental Features **19** (t) Fortean Picture Library (FPL) **21** Hunt Emerson. **23** Dr Eugene Mallove **24** Topham **25** Lancaster (PA) New Era **26** Hunt Emerson **28** FPL **29 (T)** UIP, **(B)** sculpture by Mars Effects, Granada Hills, CA. **31-34** Tsurphu Foundation, Hawaii. **33-36** Tony Clark. **37** Robert Irving. **38 (both)** Matthew Polak/Sygma, **(B)** Pete Loveday. **39** George Vernon. **40 (T)** Press Association. **41** Pete Loveday, D Scarboro/M Tucker **42 (T)** Karl Shuker, **(B)** Christcgurch Press, NZ. **43 (T)** Paddy Freaney. **45 (T)** Topham, (rest) Popper. **47 (BR)** Scarboro **50** AP. **51** Reuters. **52** Janet & Colin Bord **62** (t) Dennis Stacy/FPL (b)Paramount/UIP **63** Gerald Wood Archives **64** A Sirisena/Nasa **65** Earl of Haddington

ALIEN ABDUCTION
NOVEMBER 5, 1975
5:49 PM
WHITE MOUNTAINS
NORTHEASTERN
ARIZONA

FIRE IN THE SKY

BASED ON
THE TRUE STORY

PARAMOUNT PICTURES PRESENTS
A JOE WIZAN/TODD BLACK PRODUCTION
A ROBERT LIEBERMAN FILM
"FIRE IN THE SKY" D.B. SWEENEY
ROBERT PATRICK CRAIG SHEFFER
PETER BERG AND JAMES GARNER
MUSIC BY MARK ISHAM
EDITED BY STEVE MIRKOVICH
DIRECTOR OF PHOTOGRAPHY BILL POPE
CO-PRODUCERS TRACY TORME AND ROBERT STRAUSS
EXECUTIVE PRODUCER WOLFGANG GLATTES
SCREENPLAY BY TRACY TORME
PRODUCED BY JOE WIZAN AND TODD BLACK
DIRECTED BY ROBERT LIEBERMAN

A PARAMOUNT COMMUNICATIONS COMPANY

LANDS JUNE 18th
IN THE WEST END AND AT CINEMAS ACROSS THE COUNTRY

NUMBER 70

UK £2
USA $4.95

FORTEAN TIMES

THE JOURNAL OF STRANGE PHENOMENA

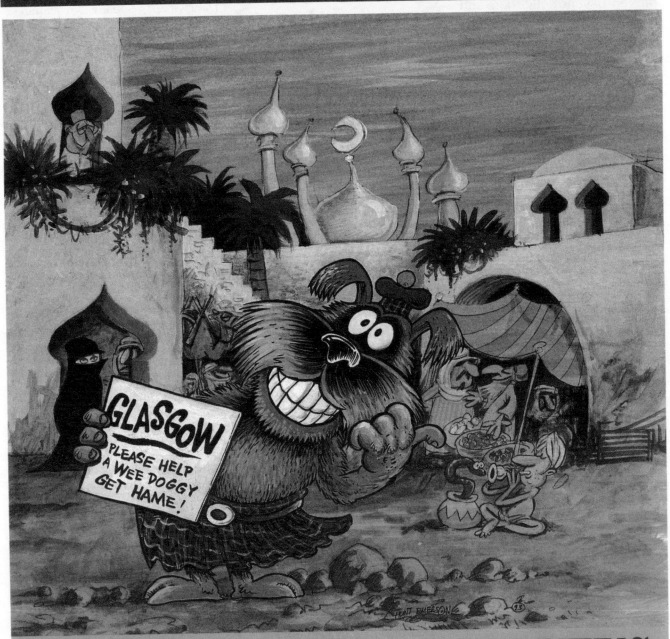

INCREDIBLE DOG JOURNEYS

MÜNCHAUSEN'S SYNDROME

The Link Between a Child-Killer and a Princess?

Butterfly Alphabet • John Blashford-Snell Interview • Egg Voyagers
Guru on Ice • The Vancouver Dragons • Three's a Shroud

Contents

ISSUE 70 AUGUST/SEPTEMBER 1993

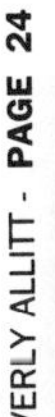

BEVERLY ALLITT - PAGE 24

EDITORIAL 4

Impostor syndromes • Indian Forteana • Pets' mammoth journeys

STRANGE DAYS 5

Guru on ice • Electronic abnormalities • Chinese chimeras • Fainting Swedes • White hind shot • Meteor news • Amazing Randi litigation • Ayers Rock curse • Deliverance from bullets

PHENOMONOMIX 21

HUNT EMERSON'S humorous look at the world

THE MÜNCH BUNCH 23

JIM SCHNABEL on Beverly Allitt, Princess Diana and the connections between shamanism, Münchausen's Syndrome, poltergeists and alien abduction

THE FT INTERVIEW: JOHN BLASHFORD-SNELL 30

BOB RICKARD talks to the seasoned explorer, Britain's answer to Indiana Jones

I-CON MAN 35

In the wake of 'Three's a Shroud', the recent exhibition by Jeffrey Vallance in Los Angeles, EDWARD YOUNG considers the significance of faking religious relics

JOHN BLASHFORD-SNELL - PAGE 30

ROVERS' RETURN 38

PAUL SIEVEKING reviews some of the epic canine walkabouts of the 20th century

FROM OUR FILES 42

- HOAX: Faking fossil skulls on Java
- EGG VOYAGERS: Monstrous eggs washed up on Australian beaches
- THE DRAGONS OF VANCOUVER: sea serpents off Canada's west coast
- DIARY OF A MAD PLANET: Weather watch April/May 1993
- UNEARTHED: The hidden 'chamber' in the Great Pyramid
- SECRET COUNTRY: Trellech, Gwent

FORUM 53

Martyn Kollins • Lynn Picknett • Alan Mitchell • Stephen Volk

REVIEWS 59

Round in Circles • Magical Elements of the Bible • Urban Myths • The Struggle to Understand • Blast Your Way to Megabucks • Superstitions

BUTTERFLY ALPHABET - INSERT

LETTERS 63

Lenticular cloud • Black Lagoon revisited • Elephant sits on mini • Devil's hoofprints • Albino lobsters • Brush with the Black dog

NOTICEBOARD 66

Fortean meetings, lectures, events, research, products and offers

COVER BY HUNT EMERSON

WHY 'FORTEAN'?

CHARLES FORT (1874-1932)

Fortean Times is a bi-monthly magazine of news, reviews and research on all manner of strange phenomena and experiences, curiosities, prodigies and portents, formed in 1973 to continue the work of the iconoclastic philosopher CHARLES FORT. Fort was sceptical about scientific explanations, observing how scientists argued for and against various theories and phenomena according to their own beliefs, rather than the rules of evidence. He was appalled that data not fitting the collective paradigm was ignored, suppressed, discredited or explained away (which is quite different from explaining a thing).

Fort was perhaps the first to speculate that mysterious lights seen in the sky might be craft from outer space. He coined the term 'teleportation' which has passed into general usage through science fiction. His dictum "One measures a circle beginning anywhere" expresses his philosophy of Continuity and the 'doctrine of the hyphen', in which everything is in an intermediate state between extremes. He had notions of the universe-as-organism and the transient nature of all apparent phenomena. Far from being an over-credulous man, Fort cut at the very roots of credulity: "I cannot accept that the products of minds are subject matter for beliefs ... I conceive of nothing, in religion, science, or philosophy, that is more than the proper thing to wear, for a while."

Fort was born in Albany, New York, in 1874 into a family of Dutch immigrants. Beatings by a tyrannical father helped set him against authority and dogma, and on leaving home at the age of 18 he hitch-hiked around the world to put some "capital into the bank of experience." At 22 he contracted malaria, married his nurse and settled down to 20 years of impoverished journalism in the Bronx. During this time he read extensively in the literature of science, taking notes on small squares of paper in a cramped shorthand of his own invention, which he filed in shoe boxes.

In 1916, when he was 42, Fort came into a modest inheritance, just enough to relieve him of the necessity of having to earn a living. He started writing *The Book of the Damned*, which his friend, the novelist Theodore Dreiser, bullied his own publisher into printing in 1919. Fort fell into a depression, burnt all his notes (which numbered some 40,000) as he had done a few years earlier, and in 1921 set sail for London, where he spent eight years living near the British Museum (39 Marchmont Street) and wrote *New Lands* (1923). Returning to New York, he published *Lo!* in 1931 and *Wild Talents* in 1932, shortly before he died. He left 60,000 notes, now in the New York Public Library.

THE GANG OF FORT
EDITORS:
Bob Rickard & Paul Sieveking
CONTRIBUTING EDITORS:
Steve Moore,
Mike Dash & Ian Simmons

ISSN 0308 5899

EDITORIAL ADDRESS
Fortean Times:
Box 2409, London NW5 4NP, UK.
Tel & Fax: 071 485 5002 or 081 552 5466.

CAVEAT
The opinions of contributors and interviewees are not necessarily those of the editors. FT itself has no corporate view except to bring the widest range of interpretations to stimulate discussion.

SUBMISSIONS
Submissions are invited of suitable articles, news, art, cartoons, letters and reviews. Preliminary discussion with the editors is advisable. Text can be submitted on floppy disks, but check with the editors first. Submissions may be edited.
FT assumes no responsibility for submissions, but all reasonable care will be taken while they are in FT's possession. Requests for return of material should be accompanied by stamped addressed envelope.

CLIPPINGS
All clippings, references, etc, should be identified by source, date and clipster's name. Mail or fax them to the editorial address (above).

SUBSCRIPTIONS - UK
One year (6 issues). £12. Two years (12 issues) £20. For payment and inquiries by phone, ring FREEPHONE 0800 581409. Major credit cards accepted – or make cheques/ money orders payable to: **JOHN BROWN PUBLISHING, and send to Freepost SW6096, Frome, Somerset BA11 1YA.**

SUBSCRIPTIONS - OVERSEAS
One year (6 issues). £15 or US$15. Two years (12 issues) £26 or US$50. For payment or inquiries by phone, ring (+44) 373 451777. Major credit cards accepted – or make sterling cheques/ money orders drawn upon a London bank payable to: **JOHN BROWN PUBLISHING, and send to Fortean Times, 20 Paul Street, Frome, Somerset BA11 1DX, UK.**

ADVERTISING ENQUIRIES
DISPLAY or CLASSIFIED:
contact **Ronnie Hackston** or **Dan Squirrell** at John Brown Publishing Ltd: The Boathouse, Crabtree Lane, Fulham, London SW6 6LU, UK.
Tel: 071 381 6007 or Fax: 071 381 3930.

PUBLISHER
John Brown Publishing Ltd, The Boathouse, Crabtree Lane, Fulham, London SW6 6LU, UK.
Tel: 071 381 6007 or Fax: 071 381 3930.
MANAGING EDITOR: Fiona Jerome.
PUBLISHER: Vic Lime.

DISTRIBUTION
UK trade distribution by UMD, Castle House, 37/45 Paul Street, London EC2A 4PB Tel:. 071-490-2020 Fax: 071-490-1239 USA newsstand distribution by Eastern News Distributors Inc, 2020 Superior St, Sandusky, OH 44870, USA.

Bob Rickard

Paul Sieveking

Will the Real Impostor Please Stand up!

● In a profile of Norma Major by Caroline Phillips and Tom Leonard (London *Evening Standard* 11 June 1993), the Prime Minister's wife was described as suffering from "impostor syndrome". Referring to Mrs Major's well-known dislike of the political limelight, the authors explain this as a type of anxiety that afflicts people who are forced, by obligations or circumstances, to play a role for which they feel they are not suited.

Our lead article, this issue, discusses a quite different kind of 'impostor syndrome' – one that is just as neurotic, perhaps, but, being outwardly directed, is capable ultimately of a lot more mischief. This is 'Münchausen's syndrome', a complex type of behaviour that has distinct links with hysterical and dissociative disorders (such as anorexia and Multiple Personality syndrome). Münchausenians typically injure themselves and others, or pretend to have done so.

Contrary to popular belief, the condition is not rare. On the contrary – as Jim Schnabel's article (p23) argues – through a number of variations it seems to play a significant part in the phenomena of shamanism, mediumship and spirit possession, poltergeists and the mortifications of religious mystics. These phenomena share many characteristics, indicative of a more common, fundamental psychic disorder whose presentations must be extended now to include the growing phenomenon of 'survivors', whether they be from alien abductions, Satanic child abusers, or abusive secondary personalities.

If researchers such as Schnabel are correct, we are moving into an exciting period of progress in understanding the genesis of some of the bizarre experiences of the kind we chronicle. Schnabel's second article, on the related topic of 'False Memory syndrome' follows next issue. Who knows. We may yet see poltergeists and alien abortionists becoming a branch of psychology!

● Having said last time that our coverage of weird events in India was 'patchy', we find that a lot of Indian Forteana has found its way into this issue. We have the drama of the unburied Bengali guru (p8), a clutch of elephant stories (p16), and two exceptional Indians in the 'Medical Bag' (p18). Elephants also figure in our interview of Colonel John Blashford-Snell (p30), who had just returned from an expedition to a remote part of Nepal. He is the leading light of a small group of British explorers (including Bill Gibbons and Benedict Allen) who keep an eye out for Forteana on their wanderings. If the elephants of the Royal Bardia Park turn out to be of a kind previously unknown to zoology, they scotch, enormously, the belief that the only animals left to discover are tiny ones.

● Paul Sieveking returns to a popular subject – long journeys made by domestic animals. In ***FT61*** he told of the cats that came back – this time it's the turn of dogs who have trekked, sometimes over thousands of miles, back to their owners (p38).

● There is still time for you to send in you completed questionnaires, if you haven't already done so – but **please** send them to the Frome address.

The Editors

STRANGE DAYS

16 pages of worldwide weirdness

NICE TO SEE YOU

The French National Front leader, M. Jean-Marie Le Pen, is greeted in Nice on 14 March 1993 by 'a supporter' (according to Reuters). To our untutored eye, it looks more like the Wild Man of Borneo about to bite off the fascist's nose while disgusted supporters look on.

EXTRA! EXTRA!

Fortean headlines from newspapers around the world.

UNKNOWN SOMETHING SEEN PULLING COSMOS
Cleveland (OH) Plain Dealer, 7 Dec 1986.

BLESS ME FATHER FOR I HAVE A GUN
Today, 11 Jan 1992.

SNAKE FORCES WOMAN TO QUIT COMPOST HEAP
Daily Telegraph, 16 Jan 1992.

£8.5M FALLS DOWN BACK OF SOFA
Today, 17 Jan 1992.

AFRICA USES KIPPERS AS IVORY WAR SMOKE-SCREEN
European, 17/23 Jan 1992.

MOUSE-POISONING VEGAN BECOMES HUMAN SACRIFICE
Observer, 19 Jan 1992.

SACKED SOLICITOR 'FROGMARCHED OUT BY OFFICE TOADS'
Daily Telegraph, 28 Jan 1992.

MISSING CONTACT LENS FOUND ON EYE
Independent, 24 Feb 1992.

Although an unexplained phenomenon, there is a place on the outskirts of Mayfield, Neb., where the sun does not shine.

BLOODY ANTS

Large blood-seeking ants, of the genus *Solenopsis*, began besieging the town of Envira in the Amazon jungle about 5 March. In the following weeks, the 10,000 residents were forced to wear permanent plastic bags around their ankles and fought back with poison and boiling water, but the ants kept spreading. Seeking out meat, salt and blood, they devoured cats, chickens and turtles, leaving only the bones. There were also reports of attacks on children. People who died in Envira were taken for burial to Feijó 40 miles away, because the ants concentrated some of their assaults on the local graveyard.

A physician said the ants only appeared in areas cleared of jungle, which eliminates their natural enemies such as birds and spiders.

Seventy per cent of the town had been invaded, with low ant-hills every four yards.

D.Telegraph, 12 Mar; Rocky Mountain News, Independent, 23 Mar; Guardian, 26 Mar 1993.

NAFF'S THE WORD

Many foreign products have decidedly odd names from the English-speaking viewpoint. In Sweden you can find Fartek babywear, Krapp lavatory paper, Bums biscuits and Nora Knackers crackers; Italy offers Dribly lemonade, Mental breath fresheners, Mukk yogurt and Smeg kitchen appliances. In Holland you can buy Poxy (a floor surface), Prik (a fizzy drink), Vaccine and Gammon (aftershaves) and Glans (a shampoo). In Japan, the shops sell Skina Babe baby lotion and Cow shaving foam.

Then there are Spain's Bonka coffee and Arses red wine, Greece's Zit lemonade, Cyprus's Cock Drops cocktail bitters, Portugal's Atum Bom tuna, Mexico's Bimbo biscuits, France's Crapsy high-fibre breakfast cereal and another cereal called Plopsies, Germany's Plops savoury snacks, Denmark's Sorbits chewing gum and England's own Foul Medames tinned beans.

New Scientist, 27 Feb, 27 Mar, 29 May 1993.

ELECTRONIC DEMONS

The trouble at Broward County Governmental Center, Fort Lauderdale, Florida, began in October 1992 after contractors gutted the Records Division and refitted it with new rugs, furniture, computers and telephones. Shortly after they returned, office workers wewere greeted with an electronic horror show of blips, glitches and conniptions. The copy machine turned itself on and off and spewed paper like a possessed Linda Blair launching lunch. Computer screens would convulse and black out. The electric typewriter in the corner clacked away – unplugged.

"So far, we don't think it has any supernatural origins", said records controller Sue Baldwin. In January 1993, the authorities brought in Mark Tatum, a trouble-shooter on electromagnetics working for BWS Architects and Engineers. "He's looking at everything", said Baldwin. "Bouncing microwaves from another building, stray radio signals, electrical interference. We're not having any trouble anywhere else in the building."

Columbus (OH) Dispatch, 13 Jan 1993.

SIMULCRA CORNER

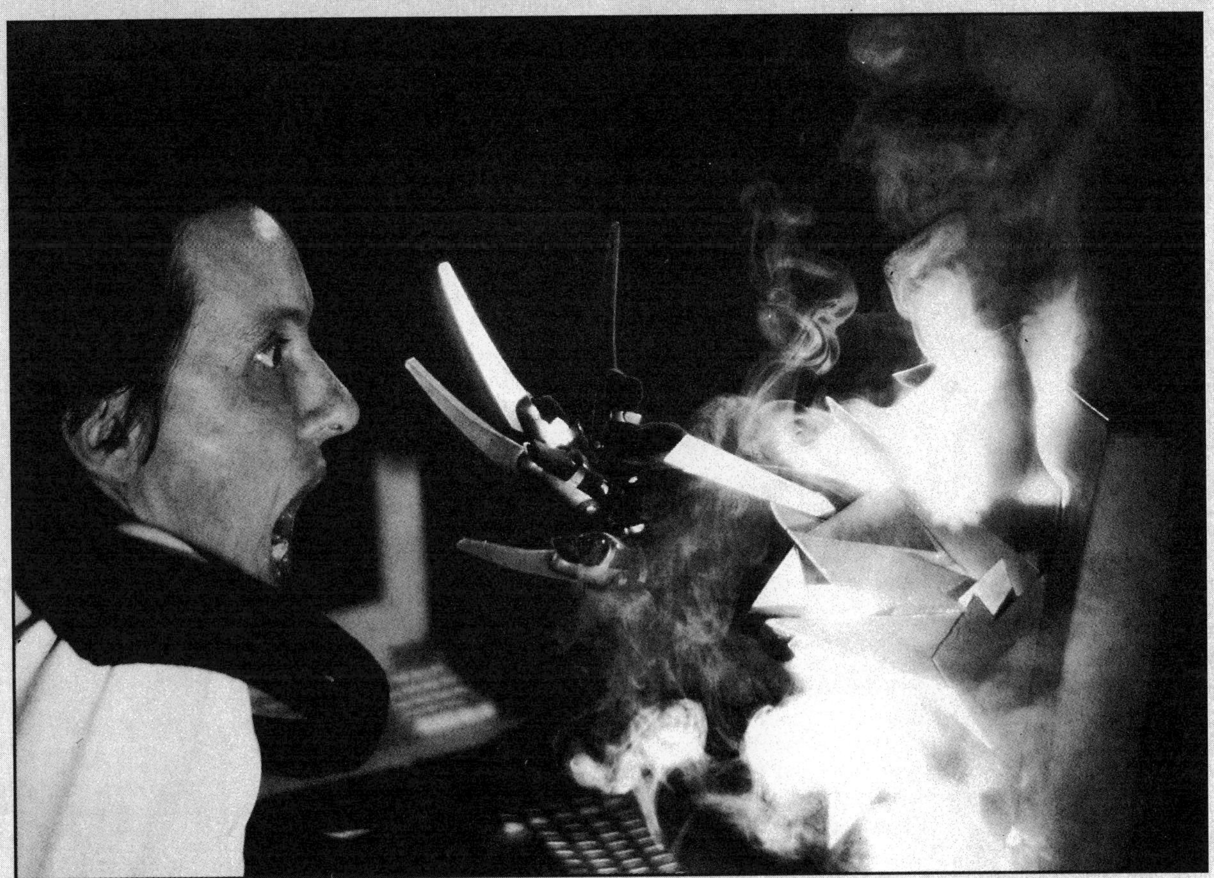

Ewing-Reeson Photography was contracted to illustrate the 'fear of technology' for a trade magazine dealing in telecommunications. Their idea was to have the character Freddie Krueger (from *Nightmare on Elm Street*) bursting out of the commuter screen, and they made use of an ordinary theatrical smoke machine.

It was only when the shots came back from processing that the eerie simulacrum of Freddie's face was spotted. Our thanks to Mark Ewing for sending it in.

We are always glad to receive pictures of spontaneous forms and figures, or any curious images. Send them to the editorial address – with SAE – and we'll pay a fiver for any we use.

FAX FROM LIMBO

Corporate affairs consultant Anne Forrest of Ice House Street, Hong Kong, got a stray fax last May. It was sent by Mr Phil Cross of Dorset on 18 January 1972, and addressed to Phil Cundall of Mining Surveys Ltd. The terminology and contents suggested that it really was 21 years old. The word 'facsimile' was used for 'fax' and the writer carefully explained how a fax worked ("A photocell is caused to perform a raster scan over the subject copy… which is transmitted to a remote destination"). While fax machines were first mass produced in the 1930s, it wasn't until the late 1970s that they really caught on in the UK. *South China Morning Post, 28 May 1993.*

CROSSED WIRES

Last February, The Nepal Telecommunications Corporation warned people not to pick up the telephone if there was a long, insistent ring. Anyone who did could get zapped by "an accidental connection between the telephone and a power line" of more than 600 volts. Shyam Krishna Dawadi received such a voltage; he managed to drag himself to a nearby temple before he died.

In the weeks up to 10 February, five other telephones and a fax machine were burnt. The telephone company was unable to explain why these rogue connections were happening after many years of painless telephone calls. *Independent, 10 Feb 1993. For lightning strikes down the phone, see* ***FT45:8***.

WAKEY! WAKEY!

Police battle devotees to bury a dead guru

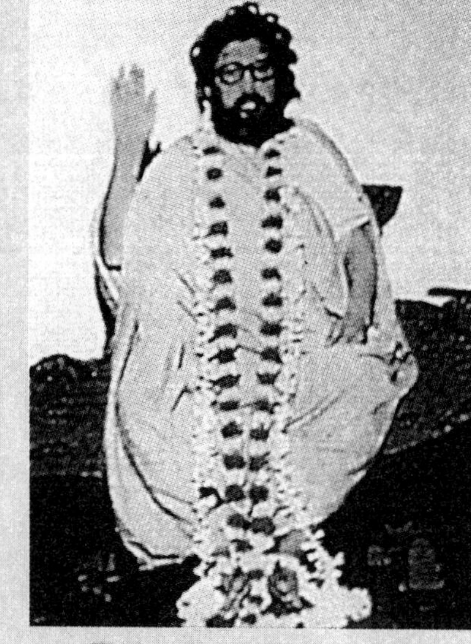

Thakur Balak Brahmachari

Thakur Balak Brahmachari, 73, reputed to have 50 to 70 million followers in India's West Bengal state, was pronounced dead from heart failure on 5 May. His disciples and aides, convinced that he was in *samadhi* and would return to them, put his body on ice slabs in an air-conditioned room of his ashram by the Ganges in Sukhchar, about 24 miles north of Calcutta.

Thousands of pilgrims, haggard farmers, widows in white saris chanting mantras and poor families kept vigil in the scorching summer heat outside the ashram, waiting for a miracle. Their numbers were swelled by curiosity-seekers and sceptics from the Indian Rationalists Association. Kiosks selling food, drink, portraits of Brahmachari, cassettes of his speeches and products from the ashram's ayurvedic laboratories were open day and night for the roaring trade.

Every day at 1:30pm, Chitta Sikdar, general secretary of Santan Dal, the guru's 29-year-old Hindu sect, together with a few acolytes, bathed their master's body and laid out a clean set of clothes for him. Resurrection was confidently expected on 25 May, but the day came and went. Aides collected water from the melting ice slabs under Brahmachari and distributed it as *prasad* (holy food) to devotees. The practice ended at the beginning of June, when a newspaper condemned it as a health risk. The body according to one visitor, was looking "like a fish in a deep freeze". The skin had turned black and was beginning to flake.

Sikdar said that in 1960 Brahmachari spent 21 days in samadhi, with no detectable heartbeat or pulse and without food and water. The feat, celebrated in the media, established the guru's reputation and he began to attract a huge following. Sikdar said he was prepared to keep the body uncremated for as long as six months.

Brahmachari was known as the 'Marxist Godman' because he preached 'vedic communism' or spiritual equality, which found resonance in West Bengal, ruled by the communist-led Left-Front government for the past 15 years. The law requires bodies to be disposed of within 24 hours – but the state government refrained from storming the ashram, wary of alienating the substantial Santal Dal voting block.

Hygiene finally prevailed over politics and religion on 30 June with 'Operation Holy Rite'. More than 1,200 Calcutta police armed with clubs stormed the ashram after overcoming 4,000 devotees armed with tridents and throwing acid-filled light bulbs and fistfuls of chilli powder. Sixty police were injured and 950 disciples arrested. The fly-blown swami was seized after 56 days on ice, and rushed off to an electric crematorium.

Independent, 13 May, 1 June, 1 July; [Reuters] 12 June; India Today, 15 June 1993.

DRAMATIC REUNION

Cpl. Robert C. McDonald Jr, 21, a maintenance repair technician at El Toro Air Station, California, went to hospital at nearby Camp Pendleton on 1 June to check up on a knee injury. A nurse called his name and two men started to follow her until the younger one noticed the mixup and held back. Later he discovered that the other man had the same middle initial and was the father he hadn't seen in 16 years.

Robert C. McDonald Sr, 59, said; "He's the spitting image of some of my military photos. I was just speechless and happy." Both men have the same hairline, blue eyes and slight pigeon-toes gait.

The McDonald family dissolved in divorce in 1977. The son, who hadn't seen his mother since he was 12, was raised by foster parents in the Los Angeles suburb of Garden Grove. His father said that after a stint in jail, judges repeatedly denied him access to his son and two daughters. He served in the Navy and Air Force and had lived on the northern San Diego County base for two years, working as a security guard. He awoke with flu on 1 June and went to the hospital for treatment. *[AP] 3 June 1993.*

THE BLUE FLASH

In a letter to *New Scientist* (3 April 1993), Celia Jeffrey declared that she had observed tiny blue flashes of light when opening the flap of a self-sealed junk-mail envelope. She called her husband and they continued their observations in the dark, noticing that "the blue flashes were more spectacular, tinged with yellow at the edges [and] appeared to come from the glue."

Two replies on the subject – *New Scientist,* 24 April 1993 – both identified the phenomenon as a type of triboluminescence or crystalloluminesence in which the excess energy released when the crystalline structure of the glue is cleaved shows in tiny cold flashes of excited molecules. Gary Evans of the Science Photo Library said he had seen a similar effect in a darkroom while opening a new pack of photographic paper. Andrew Alexander of the University of Edinburgh said that "there are millions of light-emitting reactions occurring around us each second" only a few of which might be visible to the careful observer. Paul Devereux attributes flashes of light around standing stones to a related effect. We'd be interested to hear of other examples, domestic or otherwise, from our readers.

CHINESE WHISPERS

As a quarter of the world's population live in China, it's not surprising that reports keep rolling in from there. But the tales seem to get stranger as the years pass – as this selection shows...

CHICKEN AND EGG

Zhang Jing, 65, a collector of the stone nodules known as 'egg stones', shows off a strange 'chicken simulacrum' found inside one of the items in his 200-strong collection. Zhang, an engineer in the jade trade, planned to donate his find to the nation to mark the current Chinese 'Year of the Rooster'. Which came first, the chicken or the egg? In this case, it seems they both arrived simultaneously! *China Daily, 21 Jan 1993.*

ROBOTS, WORMS AND SPIES

The following tangled tale from Chongqing in SW China was first reported by that city's *Legal News.* A rumour spread among primary and middle-school students that an American robot had gone out of control and escaped to their city, which swiftly developed into a panic affecting kids and parents alike. More precisely, it was reported as a `robot zombie', and it was said to specialise in eating children wearing red clothes; several youngsters were said to have been devoured.

Rather than simply wearing different coloured clothes, we next hear that many children refused to go to school unless their parents made crosses out of chopsticks and put garlic in their book-bags, causing a garlic shortage in the local markets. Rumours seem to boil down to a child-eating robot zombie vampire ogre. Chongquing's municipal education commission was said to be doing 'good ideological work' on teachers and students alike. Let's hope it worked. *Independent, South China Morning Post, 22 March 1993.*

★ More hysteria in Wen County, Henan province, when 40,000 school students were given a medicine to prevent intestinal worms. Soon afterwards, up to 20,000 of the victims complained of nausea, stomach pains, dizziness and headaches. Some had fevers, others were unable to walk or control their limbs. Hospitals overflowed and rumours spread that several children had died. Fake medicine and overdoses were posited, but testing by the authorities ruled out both possibilities and 'experts' concluded that the whole thing had been a case of mass hysteria. The victims returned to normal after a few days. *South China Morning Post, 4 Feb 1993.*

★ And from Yunnan, in SW China: foreign spies, disguised as high-class tourists, were said to be scouring China's rubbish dumps, bins and recycling centres for state secrets. 'It is very difficult to smell them out as spies,' said the *Yunnan Legal Newspaper. Edinburgh Evening Argus, 6 April; Brisbane Courier Mail, 7 April 1992.*

SHANGHAI SKYLARKS

Something very strange appeared in the skies over Shanghai, China's largest city, on Tuesday 2 March 1993. According to the *Xinmin Evening News*, at 7.05pm an orange-red man-shaped object appeared and "filled the sky", which makes it sound quite large. The sky-hanging man-thing alternately moved and stopped for 20 minutes and then its head began to emit red light (or red flashes) and its body glowed with a yellow aura as it sent out green tendrils.

Then, "slowly the man transformed himself into a giant mushroom which hung in the northeastern corner of the sky, then the mushroom shrank until it became the size of a soybean and then disappeared" ... apparently at about 8.15pm. And that, alas, is all we have. If any readers happen across more details, we'd love to hear them. *Irish News, Rocky Mountain News, 5 March; Straits Times, 6 March 1993.*

EAT THIS...

Liu Deshun, 26, was a fourth-grade teacher at the aptly named Niulu (Cow Road) Village elementary school in Hubei province, China. When his pupils failed to hand in homework, fought, or didn't pay attention, he forced them to eat cow dung as punishment (make up your own jokes here...this is a nice magazine). The punishment was administered 56 times to 27 students in two months. Of the class of 34, only two with good grades, and five who were related to him, escaped. "Some of the students began vomiting without stop after they ate the cow dung, which affected the normal studying process." Hardly surprising, really. Liu was jailed for two years on 20 March 1992, for "subjecting others to indignities". *Globe & Mail (Toronto), 16 May; Bangkok Post, 8 Aug 1992.*

Sidelines

A busload of Russian shoppers refused to break off their trip to Poland when one of them died of a heart attack. They tried to get the man buried on the spot, but the Polish authorities wouldn't allow it; so they continued bargain-hunting for days, leaving the corpse on a back seat. *[Reuters] 11 Jan 1993.*

• • • • • • • • • • • • • • •

A man using a donkey to carry hashish was arrested near the northern Moroccan town of Al-Hoceima. While police waited for a car to take the man to prison, the donkey ate the evidence and the man was released. The donkey was found in a coma. *Western Morning News, 5 April 1993.*

• • • • • • • • • • • • • • •

A French-Italian scientific expedition to Mt Everest has returned with the news that the world's highest mountain is two metres lower than commonly believed. For the record, the new measurement is 8,846.10 metres (29,022.6ft)… until the next revision.*[R] 21 April 1993.*

• • • • • • • • • • • • • • •

A Canadian survey has shown that 50% of anglers who fall out of boats have their flies undone, as they were relieving themselves at the time. In America the coastguards have a term, FOA, for dead bodies they recover – Flies Open on Arrival. *Midweek, 11 Mar 1993.*

• • • • • • • • • • • • • • •

A 6yr-old girl in southern Israel was taken to a doctor suffering from severe earache. Examination in a Beersheba hospital revealed that a tree seedling had sprouted in her ear, and had even produced a tiny leaf. *[DPA] 16 April 1993.*

SWEDISH STUNNERS

Why are women passing out across the country?

In early March 1993, *Hallandsposten*, a local paper in Halmstad, Sweden, warned women to beware of knock-out drops in their drinks. "It happened to me twice", said Jenny Hofvander, 23. "I suffered a total black-out. I have no idea what was put in my beer or who did it." On both occasions she just sipped one beer and had no recollection of what followed. Several of her friends had been knocked out as well. One ended up on a park bench, where some men tried to abduct her before she was rescued.

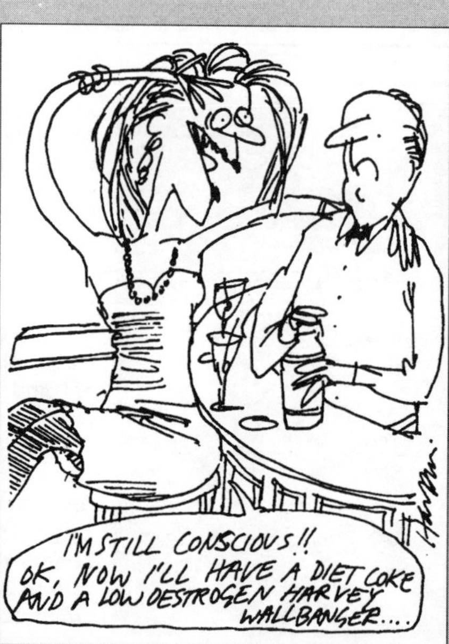
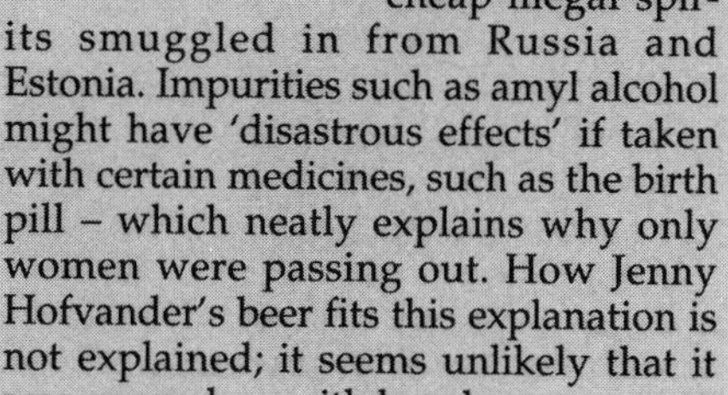

I'M STILL CONSCIOUS!!
OK, NOW I'LL HAVE A DIET COKE AND A LOW OESTROGEN HARVEY WALLBANGER....

Immediately after this news report, the Halmstad police received a flood of calls from women (mostly in their 30s and 40s) claiming to have been drugged and in some cases sexually abused. One married middle-aged woman said she had been abducted and "raped for hours" before being thrown out in the street with her clothes torn to shreds. "She was fully aware of what happened, but couldn't lift a finger to prevent it", according to police investigator Lars Tore Svensson, who was convinced that all the reports were true. He said they had at least one suspect, but he could not be arrested, as no-one had made a formal complaint. As no particular bar in Halmstad had been singled out by the victims, police mounted a watch on all of them.

The phenomenon spread like wildfire. In early April, some 50 women had formally reported to police that they had been drugged, probably only a small proportion of actual incidents. At Easter, 'hosts of women' were knocked out, mostly in Strömstad and Boras, where police received about 30 reports, but also in Karlstad and elsewhere. Two unconscious women were hospitalised in Boras, and blood samples were sent for analysis in Linköping.

The motive became a lot less clear-cut. Inspector Rolf Rosholm of Boras said that "the motive is a mystery. None of the victims was robbed, nor was there any attempt at sexual abuse." According to narcotics agent Bo Delberger, the phenomenon was confined to towns in western Sweden; but by mid-April it spread south into Scania. The Link-öping lab did not found any drug traces in the blood samples.

Delberger and other investigators now advanced the hypothesis that, because of the recession, pubs and restaurants were buying cheap illegal spirits smuggled in from Russia and Estonia. Impurities such as amyl alcohol might have 'disastrous effects' if taken with certain medicines, such as the birth pill – which neatly explains why only women were passing out. How Jenny Hofvander's beer fits this explanation is not explained; it seems unlikely that it was pepped up with hooch.

According to the local Eskilstuna paper *Eskilstunakuriren*, quoted by Radio PL on 2 May, several women had been drugged in pubs and discos in Eskilstuna, west of Stockholm. One had her stomach pumped in hospital after two glasses of wine at a disco, while another, Sarah, said she had only drunk half a glass of beer when she became dizzy, went into a cold sweat, and "everything became black. A doorman helped me out into the street, where I vomited incessantly. It was horrible." The local police suspected that LSD had been slipped into her beer – a very odd speculation, considering the symptoms. Further incidents were reported in Linköping on Sweden's east coast, so the enigmatic 'druggings' covered the whole country.

Expressen, 10+11 Mar, 3 May; Idag, 14+20 April 1993.

WHO KILLED BAMBI?

The savage death of a Quantock deer

For 19 years, Snowy, the white hind, was one of the chief and best-loved attractions of Somerset's scenic Quantock Hills. Now, for residents and visitors of the area around the quiet village of Bagborough, near Taunton, the familiar fleeting glimpse of white amidst the bracken is no more.

Snowy was last seen on Monday, 15 February, sometime after which she was brought down by a poacher's lurcher dogs and shot on the outskirts of the village. Particularly distressed was Roly Ford, former hunt master of the Quantock Staghounds, from whom she had special protection. "She bled to death within 100 yards of a house," he said. "She was a legend in her own lifetime. Everyone here is devastated."

Peter Sealy, a local deer expert, said: "There's no doubt she has been taken, from all the white hairs and blood in the mud. You can see where she was dragged over a hedge. It's a damned shame."

Confirmation of their worst fears came on 25 February, when fishermen on the Taunton and Bridgwater canal recovered Snowy's head. Following the posting of a £1000 reward by The League Against Cruel Sports for information leading to the conviction of Snowy's killer, the Avon and Somerset police received a number of leads. One of these led them, on 23 March, to a house in South Somerset where they found Snowy's distinctive hide. No arrests have been made because of insufficient evidence.

Snowy was believed to be one of the oldest red deer in the country, and the only known white one. She was not a true albino – a rare recessive gene coloured her white but allowed her brown eyes and some patches of red or brown – she had a normal-coloured calf every year since she was three years old in 1977.

White deer have figured prominently in symbolism and folklore. Aristotle describes a veritable cervidian Methuselah, dedicated to Diana the Huntress by Diomedes at the siege of Troy and killed a thousand years later by Agathocles, King of Sicily. Pliny records that a white stag caught by Alexander the Great was released with a gold collar – mediæval English legend tells of similarly collared stags being caught in the great forests. In the 15th century, Henry VII spared the life of a white deer while hunting in the New Forest and commemorated the event by renaming an inn in Ringwood 'The White Hart', since when this has been a popular pub name throughout England. *Western Morning News 22+23+26 Feb, 26 March; D.Mail 23 Feb 1993.*

Top left: Snowy, in her heyday. Above: Sgt Tony Booker at Taunton police station, with Snowy's hide.

Sidelines

Malaysian Prime Minister Mahathir bin Mohamad declared at a recent political gathering that too much democracy leads to homosexuality, moral decay, racial intolerance, economic decline and single parent families. *Int. Herald Tribune, 31 May 1993.*

• • • • • • • • • • • • • • •

Two Mormons knocked on a door in St Albans, Herts, and asked if the woman who answered "knew about God". Hearing that it was the house of Lord Runcie, the former Archbishop of Canterbury, the baffled Americans asked: "What church would that be?" *Sun, 28 April 1993.*

• • • • • • • • • • • • • • •

Bertha, believed to be the world's oldest cow, celebrated her 48th birthday on 22 May with two bottles of whiskey from farmer Patrick O'Connell, of Tipperary in Eire. *D.Record, 22 May 1993.*

• • • • • • • • • • • • • • •

A ground-to-air missile, covered in Cyrillic inscriptions, complete with launcher and in perfect working order, was found by a motorist in a highway parking lot near Osnabruck, western Germany. Police mystified. *Europa Times, June 1993.*

• • • • • • • • • • • • • • •

Judy Clarkson, 45, bought a dozen eggs at Tesco in York and found that *all 12* had double yolks. The odds against this occurrence are astronomical. *D.Mirror, D.Record, 3 Mar 1993*

• • • • • • • • • • • • • • •

A naked man running across New York's Brooklyn Bridge singing "Oh what a beautiful morning!" was run over by a car and killed. *D.Mirror, 18 May 1993.*

BAR CODE MADNESS

The latest in a baffling series of bogus charity drives involved bar codes off packaging. Appeals were made across the country by leaflets and posters. As one would expect with such folklore, the details varied considerably from report to report. One letter received by Brighton Council in November 1992, headed BARCODES, read: "A five-year-old boy is in Queen Mary's Hospital, Roehampton, suffering with a kidney failure and will die early in the New Year unless a kidney or a dialysis machine can be bought for him. Please save bar codes from food wrappers, sweet wrappers, cigarette boxes, cat food etc." It said a research company had agreed to supply a machine if 1,500,000 bar codes could be collected by 15 December.

Some versions called the Roehampton hospital 'St Mary's' while others targetted the Royal London Hospital in Whitechapel. Children from as far away as North Yorkshire started collecting after posters appeared claiming a firm in Chelmsford, Essex, would donate a penny for each code collected. Both hospitals said the appeal was a hoax and no-one could find the dying five-year-old boy.

A similar rumour had swept New Zealand in the first half of 1992, except there the dialysis machine was to be procured with ringpulls from aluminium cans (or 'tear-tops' as they call them). Thousands of ringpulls were collected over six months, in spite of the fact that kidney dialysis is provided free in New Zealand. *Wellington (NZ) Eve. Post, 28 Aug; 11 local English papers, 26 Nov-10 Dec 1992.*

BAR CODE COLLECTION
NO, ACTUALLY I'M JUST A BAR CODE SPOTTER
Harpini.

LOVE 'S LABOUR LOCKED

A Simunye woman from Swaziland took advantage of her husband's absence on a weekend trip to entertain her lover in the conjugal house. After a bout of love making on Friday, 4 December 1992, the couple fell victim to the condition known locally as *likhubalo* – translatable as 'dog-knotting' or 'love-lock'. Yells for help went unheeded. According to the *Times of Swaziland*, it was not until Monday morning that a woman neighbour discovered them.

The naked duo were being taken away on (one) stretcher by police when the husband met them on the road. According to the news report, the 'dog-knotting' was caused by a *ulunyoka* spell which he had cast, suspecting his wife's infidelity. The ritual involves opening a pocket knife, which if not closed with the proper charms, locks the two lovers together until they die. The husband agreed to perform the releasing ritual.

The incident recalled a 1992 case in Lagos, Nigeria, in which an adulterous couple was found locked together and dead on the floor of the husband's battery-charging shop. Police believed that during love-making the wife had accidentally touched a live wire, causing fatal electrocution. But rumour held that blood and a worm were found oozing from the lover's mouth, the sign of a 'magum' spell that fatally locks unfaithful lovers together. *Guardian, 9 Dec 1992; New African, Oct 1992 + Mar 1993.*

WATER TOO CLEAN

A battle to eliminate pollution from Lake Vänern, Sweden's biggest and Europe's third biggest lake, has been so successful that the water is in danger of becoming sterile; fish are unable to survive in the ultra-clean water. The lake is the source of one third of Sweden's drinking water, but suffered badly from a cocktail of heavy metals and organic compounds discharged by factories over many years. In the past two decades, a string of water purification plants has been built and the guilty factories forced to share the cost of the clean-up. Water clarity rose 100% and mercury levels plummeted. There is now a move to close one or more of the cleaning plants and allow more phosphates into the water to aid plant and fish growth. *European, 12 Nov 1992.*

FISH FALLS

On 25 February 1993, senior constable Eric Asjes flew to isolated areas of North-West Australia affected by floods. On a visit to Sturt Creek homestead, 112 miles from Halls Creek, he was rained on by two-inch-long freshwater bream. Those that fell into puddles swam around quite happily, while those that fell on the ground flopped around until they died. The Weather Bureau in West Perth gave the conventional (though undemonstrated) explanation: whirlwinds.

A few days later, Carl Smith of Oklawaha, Florida, was driving home from a restaurant when a 17-inch, two-pound white bass fell from the sky and landed on the roof of his car. He was miles from the sea. He assumed it was dropped by a bird. *The West Australian 26+27 Feb; South Wales Echo, 1 Mar 1993.*

METEOR NEWS

A round-up of crumbs that have fallen recently from the celestial table

● Astronomers at the European Southern Observatory have found what appear to be the oldest rocks on Earth in a remote region of Chile's Atacama desert – meteorite fragments that made a 30ft crater about 3,500 years ago, scattering debris over eight square miles. The previous record holder – a meteorite fragment found in 1984 in northwestern Canada – dates back 3,900 million years, while the Chilean specimens have been dated to 4,500 million years.

The 77 stony iron fragments – darker than other rocks – were found near the Dead Cow (*Vaca Muerta*) river, in a barren region where there is no rain or other forms of erosion. The original meteorite was once part of an asteroid "perhaps 60 miles wide", which collided with another, partly molten, before becoming part of a cloud of debris that sweeps past the Earth in long elliptical orbits. *[ESO] D.Telegraph, 29 July 1991.*

● Stories of meteorites hitting ships are quite rare, but something which may have been a meteorite crashed onto the deck of a Japanese ocean-going car-transporter moored in the Bay of Minawa in April 1992. The object cracked into pieces, but crewman Hidenobu Minao managed to rescue a 15-ounce chunk, which is being studied at the National Museum of Science. *[Kyodo] 27 Dec 1992.*

● A huge meteorite, estimated to have been a metre across, exploded about 10 km above the Dutch town of Joure, on the evening of 19 (or 26?) August, in the northern province of Friesland, rattling doors and windows. Despite heavy cloud cover, at least 10 people said they saw a huge flash or fireball. *New Scientist, 29 Aug 1992.*

● Another Japanese meteorite fell on 10 December, punching a hole through Matsumoto Masaru's house in Mihonoseki. The 14.3lb rock fell through his mother's bedroom; luckily, she was out at the time. Compensation will be paid – a first in Japanese insurance history. Examination of the 10x4" missile by Tokyo's Natural Science Museum revealed that its composition included rare radioactive scandium 44 and masses of small stones. *[PA] 17+18 Dec 1992; London Eve.Standard, 10 Feb 1993.*

● The Della Marna brothers, Ivan (81) and Martin (68), died when a meteorite hit their house in Istria, northern Italy, and exploded. "There was a blinding flash," said a neighbour. *Today, 21 Jan 1993.*

● Thai authorities seized a football-sized meteorite weighing 37lbs which villagers regarded as a good-luck omen after it landed in Petchabun Province on 13 June. Thai law states that all objects fallen from the sky are state property. *[AP] 20 June 1993.*

Above right: ESO astronomer Harri Lindgren with fragments of the Dead Cow meteorite in the Atacama desert, Chile. Above left: Through the kindness of the *Peekskill Herald*, we have obtained photos of the 22-pound meteorite which smashed through the trunk of Michelle Knapp's 1980 red Chevy Malibu on 9 October last – see *FT67:49*. The meteorite – seen here with police Sgt. Karl Hoffman – and, allegedly, the car, were eventually sold to collectors for about $69,000.

Sex, Libels and Audio Tape

The continuing trials of James Randi

A jury in the US District Court of Baltimore has ruled that the 'Amazing Randi' defamed scientist-turned-parapsychologist Eldon Byrd by referring to him as a "convicted child molester" in a magazine, and saying, in a speech in 1988, that Byrd was known to the police in the Washington DC area as "the shopping market molester". In the speech Randi also alleges that Byrd used his children and stepchildren to lure other youths to his car.

Eldon Byrd, of Finksburg, near Fort Washington, wrote articles in the mid-1980s which wholeheartedly endorsed the reality of paranormal phenomena. Byrd's lawyer said that Randi set out to discredit his client after "failing to disprove a scientific metal-bending experiment in which Byrd was involved". The jury deliberated for three days, trying to disentangle the mud-slinging between Randi and Byrd, and cleared the other defendant, the Committee for the Scientific Investigation of Claims of the Paranormal (CSICOP).

The 'Amusing' Randi was once a specialist in impressive Houdini-type illusions, but has since made a second career of discrediting those who claim to have supernatural powers, which group seems to include anyone he disapproves of. This rare picture shows Randi, then aged 30, being helped from a submerged steel coffin after 1 hour 58 minutes imprisonment underwater, during a visit to London in 1958.

Mental anguish

In their verdict, given on June 4, the jury said that Eldon Byrd, 53, had suffered humiliation, mental anguish, and damage to his reputation because of the false statements. However, they also ruled that Byrd was not entitled to any monetary damages after hearing that he had sexually molested and later married his sister-in-law.

The long-standing dispute between the two continued mercilessly in the court. Randi's lawyer clarified things by saying Byrd was a child molester who had never been convicted. To back this up he produced evidence to show that Byrd collected pornographic pictures of young girls, and that he had sexually abused his sister-in-law for 13 years, beginning when she was 12 years old. Outside the court, Byrd insisted the girl had been 16 when they first had sex and that he married her after she turned 18.

Byrd was arrested in 1986, in Virginia, for child pornography, and by pleading guilty he seems to have avoided the more serious charge of sexually abusing a minor. He did, however, lose his job with the UN Navy because of the pornography conviction. Technically then, if Randi had evidence sound enough to secure a conviction for molestation, he failed to produce it and therefore libelled Byrd. Randi's lawyer admitted that her client had been wrong to libel Byrd, but that his statements were "substantially true" and made "in good faith".

Teenage boys

Byrd's lawyer fought back by playing to the jury audio tape recordings of what appeared to be Randi in conversation with teenage boys who were calling his number for sex. Randi said the tape was made from edited recordings to make it appear that Randi was molesting young boys. Byrd attempted to "blackmail" him, Randi said, by threatening to distribute the tape.

James Moseley – who publishes *Saucer Smear*, a private and often hilarious commentary on the UFO scene – calls the 64yr-old illusionist "the Amusing Randi". Moseley says he's heard the tape, bootleg copies of which have been circulating for some time, and that it didn't seem to have been obviously doctored. More damning for Randi, Moseley recalls that on winning a tax-free award from the MacArthur Foundation in 1986, Randi boasted: "It's so wonderful... No one can take [the money] away from you... You don't even have to continue in the same field. You can announce you are a communist, transvestite, child molester, and no one can touch the money..." This kind of "good faith" makes a convincing case for atheism.

Randi claims that he is being forced to defend the fight against pseudo-science and fraudulent paranormalists on behalf of the Truth and us all, and that it has broken him financially. As Moseley points out, Randi has brought his legal woes upon himself by being very free with ill-advised remarks (often to the embarrassment of his CSICOP chums).

Sources: Baltimore (MD) Sun, 23 May, 5 June. Saucer Smear, 10 June 1993.

A CAPTIVE AUDIENCE

A fully clothed, but badly decomposed corpse was found in the northern French town of Croix, near Roubaix, on 23 March 1993. Neighbours had complained of a putrid smell coming from the house. Former street sweeper Eloi Herbaux, 55, was sitting on a sofa in front of the TV, which was still on, with a 'snowy' screen. By examining the pile of mail and overdue electricity bills by the front door, investigators determined that Herbaux had died sometime in June 1992, 10 months earlier. The divorced father of two had been living alone for 15 years and had no contact with his neighbours.

Three weeks later, we heard of another corpse watching TV. George Carver, 76, sat dead in front of a month's broadcast entertainment in Weymouth, Devon. Neighbours could hear the sound and thought he was OK. The truth was discovered after a friend spotted a pile of newspapers in the letter box. *[AP] 25 Mar; D.Mirror, 17 April 1993.*

LOST IN ROMANIA

The Baci forest near the city of Cluj in central Romania is the focus of many UFO reports. Sometime in 1992 (*Romanul Magazin*, 16 April 1993 is not specific), Zoltan Frenc and his son-in-law visited this forest. Although the sky was cloudless, the sun suddenly grew pale. The son-in-law quickened his step and Frenc lost sight of him. A wind began to blow, a thick fog descended and Frenc's eyes began to sting. The fog lifted very quickly and the sun shone again – but the son-in-law had vanished. A search by villagers and police turned up no clue.

SHOES THAT PASS IN THE NIGHT

Someone should write a history of science from the point of view of footwear. We remember a story about a nuclear reactor leak being plugged by socks – and now Nike trainers are helping to verify and calibrate computer models of the off-shore currents off America's north Pacific coast.

It began in a storm on 27 May 1990, when 80,000 trainers were lost overboard some 800km southeast of Alaska. No one thought anything of this until reports of trainers being washed up on beaches in British Columbia, Washington and Oregon after eight months were noticed by Curtis Ebbesmeyer of the US National Oceanic and Atmospheric Administration (NOAA). He and colleague James Ingraham realised they had been handed a unique opportunity to test their virtual currents against the real thing. Their predictions have been fairly accurate, but sightings of beached Nikes (about 1,300 have been recovered) are proving invaluable in revealing shifts and reversals of currents that they had not even foreseen.

Many of the shoes have been wearable, and beachcombers have held 'swap meets' to find matching pairs. Some have reached the Hawaiian islands, and might reach China and Japan eventually. We wonder if the NOAA boys have a model that can explain eggs floating from Madagascar to Western Australia (see p44). *New Scientist, 31 Oct 1992, 9 Jan 1993; Scientific American, Nov 1992.*

BLIND FAITH

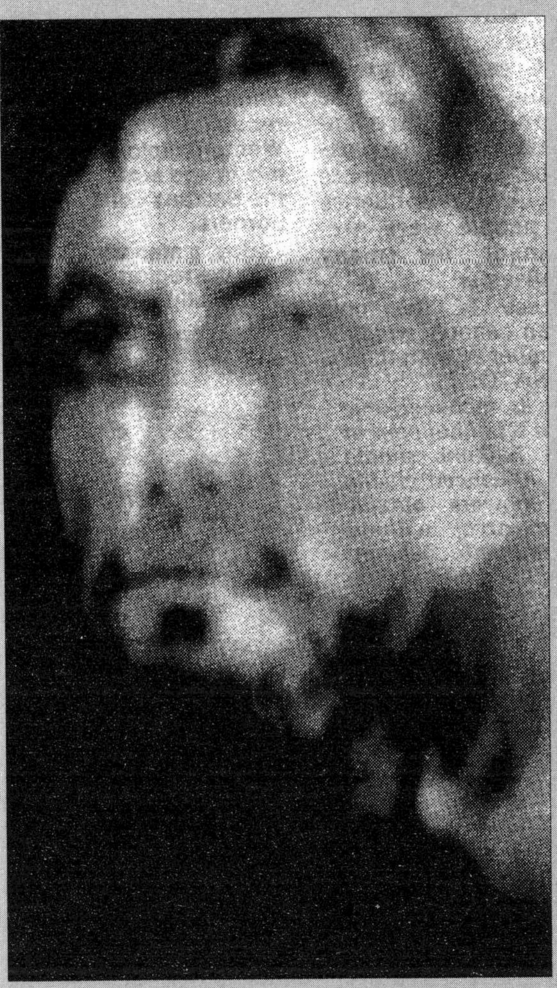

This picture of Christ was said to have appeared in the sky near Genoa in Italy. It was photographed by Pino Casagrande, 69, who claims to have dozens of prints showing Jesus and the Virgin Mary. Four people staring at the sun in search of the 'vision' have seriously damaged their sight and could lose it altogether. *Sunday Express, 4 April 1993.*

DEATH TO CANNIBALS!

A cemetery attendant, in the Highfield area of Harare, Zimbabwe, was shocked to come upon two men and a woman, all naked and devouring the breast and head of an exhumed corpse.

If this wasn't true, it is typical of the sort of story that periodically spooks African crowds, and sure enough, as news spread, a crowd gathered outside the cemetery demanding to be allowed to stone the cannibals to death. The riot police had to be called. Later a similarly murderous crowd, or the same one, was dispersed when it besieged a police station believing the cannibals were being held there. *[AFP] Bangkok Post, 16 Oct 1992.*

ELEPHANT NEWS

RUM DO IN JUNGLE

In recent years, elephants have regularly made off with scores of bottles of rum from a supply base in the jungle area of Bagdogra, north Bengal, by dousing fires lit to scare them away and short-circuiting electrified fences with uprooted trees. Once inside the depot, the huge raiders make short work of the thin steel railings and wooden windows to get at the rum, sugar, flour and bananas inside.

They brake the bottles by curling their trunks around them and smashing off the necks. The pesky pachyderms then sway around enjoying themselves before returning to the jungle. Woe betide any soldier who offers resistance. One elephant never forgot the man who poured hot water on him one night – and returned regularly to demolish his hut. The loss of rum is a sobering prospect for the soldiers, who are given daily quotas to help them keep warm in winter. *D.Telegraph, 14 Dec 1991; South China Morning Post, 13 Jan 1993.*

THE ELEPHANT'S REVENGE

An elephant whose calf was knocked down by a locomotive in the Sylhet region of Bangladesh on 21 February 1993 blocked the next train that passed an hour later and banged her forehead against the engine for 15 minutes, until it could no longer run. She then walked off into the jungle, leaving about 200 passengers stranded for over five hours. The extent of the baby elephant's injuries were not known. *[AP] 22 Feb 1993.*

TUSKER ROAD BLOCKS

Elephants in the north-east Indian state of Assam have taken to highway robbery. They stop trucks and cars passing through the Garampani wildlife sanctuary and have to be bought off with sugar cane or fruit. Most drivers are happy to oblige – Ganesh, the elephant-headed Hindu god, is a symbol of prosperity – but those who refuse to pay the 'toll' risk having their vehicles pushed off the road. A truck driver's hand had to be amputated after a large male elephant wrenched a bunch of bananas from his grasp.

It all started with truck drivers throwing cane to baby elephants. Tourists started to arrive, fruit and cane stalls sprang up, and soon the jollity turned sour. The Assam government has started to tackle the problem by posting tame elephants along the highway to chase off their wild counterparts. There are plans to ban industrial deforestation and sugar-cane plantations, and to discourage any further contact between man and elephant. *Independent, 5 July 1991; D.Telegraph, 9 Nov 1992.*

FUNNY MONEY

In early 1992, the Swedish government issued a new 1000-kronor banknote with a portrait of the 16th century rebel Gustav Vasa against a background drawing of old Stockholm featuring some impressive 'sun dogs' or parhelia – based upon a famous painting of mock suns over the city in 1535.

In their February issue, a satirical magazine called *Gazette* printed a reasonable facsimile of the note in colour on their cover, inviting their readers to "cut it out and go shopping". Within a week, police said, 200 of the joke-notes had been found in circulation, and at least 100 people were in custody, arrested while trying to spend their cut-outs. Some people had been seen buying bundles of copies; and they even turned up in Denmark.

Mock suns on the new 1000 kroner note

The Attorney General, Harald Dryselius, failed to be amused: "It wasn't funny", he griped. "We will have to put up with these counterfeits for years to come". The government decided to act on it, ordering the police to seize remaining unsold copies, and to prosecute *Gazette's* editor Sten Hedman. One paper-mill owner – to whom 22,000 copies were sent for pulping – made a further mockery of the affair by allowing his workers to take some home. It was their usual perk, he explained. *Sydsvenskan, 17,21,23,27 Feb, 2,24 Mar; Expressen, 11 Mar 1992.*

SNAKE REMOVAL

During the filming of *Suicide Commando*, Turkish actor Sönmez Yikilmaz slept in a tent with the film crew. One night a black snake crawled into the tent and into Mr Yikilmaz through his open mouth. An X-ray proved that the snake was alive in his stomach, but he refused an operation to remove it. Instead, he tried out an ancient method of snake removal. He was hung upside down form a tree with a pot of steaming milk below him on the ground. The smell of the hot milk lured the snake out. *Bugün, 29 July 1991.*

Mr Yikilmaz

THE CURSE OF ULURU

Hundreds of tourists who have chipped pieces from Ayers Rock are sending them back to Alice Springs National Park to avert a supposed aboriginal curse, and asking rangers to replace them in their original position. They believe that the stones have brought them bad luck, marriage break-up or ill-health. The rocks had been coming back in ones and twos for a couple of years, but the spring of 1993 saw a sudden upsurge.

Ayers Rock is an oval dome-shaped mass rising 1,110ft above the flat, arid plain 100 miles south of Alice Springs in central Australia. It is considered sacred by the nearby aboriginal community who call it Uluru. They attribute spirits to various geographical features of Uluru, but most are said to be friendly. They deny there is any particular curse.

One Arizona man sent back a small stone with a note: "Please return it to its place of rest as I have suffered a lot of sickness since I removed it." The stone was taken near a spot where five tourists had fallen to their death in the past 15 years. An Australian woman admitted taking a piece in 1968 and said she had subsequently developed diabetes and had a stillborn baby.

Ayers Rock, known to the Aborigines as Uluru

Meanwhile in Hawaii, sack loads of lava are sent back every day to the ranger station on the edge of Kilauea, one of the most active volcanoes in the world. It comes from tourists desperate to lift the 'Curse of Pele', a Hawaiian goddess who supposedly inflicts legendary doses of bad luck on anyone who removes even a speck of lava. Some even try to bribe Pele with Jim Beam whisky, candy and, once, a black nightgown. Incoming lava started as a trickle in about 1976 and has increased every year since. Nothing in Hawaiian legend mentions a curse on souvenir hunters. *Hong Kong Standard, D. Telegraph, 21 April 1993; [Knight Ridder] 6 Oct 1991. See also* ***FT28:42***.

ATTACK OF THE EIGHT FOOT BIRDS

Farmers around Chinnor, in Buckinghamshire, put out a general alert on 21 February 1992 for the public to be wary of a huge golden eagle. It had plucked a day-old lamb from a field and killed it nearby. It also tried to snatch a Jack Russell terrier being walked by sheep-breeder Colin New. He managed to kick the eagle, which let go of the dog and swooped on him. "It looked very hungry," he said. The bird is believed to have escaped from captivity, because Mr New noticed a leather thong or jess still attached to one of its legs. *D.Mail, 22 Feb 1993.*

Rummaging through the files for signs of large exotic birds on the loose, we found:

In March 1992, a spokesman for Windsor Safari Park revealed that a two-year-old bald eagle, on a training flight, was 'blown away in strong winds' *(Today, 23 Mar 1992)*. Could this be the same 'large, unidentified raptor' spotted near Spurn, Humberside, a couple of weeks later *(D.Telegraph, 10 April 1992)*? Or was that the huge white-tailed eagle spotted by twitchers in a tree by the busy A1 motorway at Belfond, Northumberland, just up the coast? This eagle, with an 8ft wingspan, also had a strap dangling from one leg *([PA] 11 April; S.Mail, 12 April 1992)*.

Through May to July 1992, there were reports of at least 150 red-footed falcons seen in various parts of Britain, which greatly exceeds any previous annual total of these rare visitors from eastern and southern Europe *(D.Telegraph, 18 May 1992)*.

What else is out there, with straps dangling from legs?

MEDICAL BAG

TRIPLET TREK

A Congolese woman, apparently unaware that she was pregnant with triplets, gave birth in three different villages during a three-day walk over 60 miles, according to the country's health ministry.

Bernadette Obelebouli, 34, had the first child in Otslaka on 5 April with the help of a midwife. Then she and her husband headed south. After walking 30 miles, she bore a second child in Lekana the next day. Sensing something was wrong, She visited a hospital the following day in Djambala and gave birth to the third child after walking another 30 miles. *[AP] 10 April 1993.*

LIZARD EGGS

S. Adinrayanan went to hospital in Kuala Lumpur, Malaysia, with severe stomach pains. After doctors removed three spherical objects from his stomach, he was arrested and handcuffed to his hospital bed, as it was thought the objects were condoms containing heroin. The man was released when they were found to be lizard eggs. *USA Today, 10 Jan 1992.*

BABIES IN BABY

Three undeveloped foetuses were removed from the stomach of a five-month-old boy in Batra Hospital, New Delhi, on 12 June 1992. "The baby after the operation is hale and hearty", said hospital spokesman V.N. Seth. The extremely rare condition of *foetus in fetu* (baby inside baby) was discovered when the baby was two months old. There are only 31 cases recorded this century worldwide and only four or five involving multiple foetuses. The foetuses occupied half the infant's stomach and were inside "a lumpish grey sac weighing 17 ounces". They had umbilical cords but undeveloped limbs and features. One had a skeleton but all were headless. *[Reuters] 16 July 1992.*

SELF-REPLICATING (ALMOST)

Jang Bahadur, 30, a farmer from Faizabad, India, had a pain in his scrotum which was keeping him away from work. Married for ten years, Bahadur was infertile, although he had normal genitalia. A swelling in his left groin gave him pain fo rhe last siz years.

After an ultrasound test, doctors in New Delhi discovered that Bahadur had a fully-developed, three-inch-long uterus between his testes. He also had Fallopian tubes, and a sperm duct opening into the vagina, raising the possibility of 'self-impregnation' if ovaries had been present.

Dr Usha Maheshwari of Sujan Mohinder Hospital operated on 18 February 1993 and Bahadur was home convalescing at the end of April. Dr Maheshwari said he would be fertile within two weeks. *Independent, 30 Mar; The Pioneer, New Delhi, 23 April 1993.*

BEST FEET FORWARD

Last summer, two New Zealand climbers found a boot containing a human foot on K2 in the Himalayas. They believe it belonged to American Dudley Wolfe, who disappeared in 1938. *D.Telegraph, 3 Aug 1992.*

A similar relic was washed up on a South Australian beach last November. A pair of running shoes with feet still inside them were found on Adelaide's Henley beach. A week later, an object found on a beach 220 miles south of Sydney was identified as a human penis. Shortly before this, police in Sydney collected a right and a left leg, an arm and a male torso, all from the same body. The penis is from another body. *Cambridge Eve. News, 26 Nov; [Reuters] 3 Dec 1992.*

A left foot in a navy nylon sock and size 10 Nike training shoe was washed ashore at Clevedon in Somerset on 15 June 1993. It was thought to have been in the water at least two months. A plastic canoeist's helmet inscribed with the name Nicky Lewis was discovered about 400 yards from the foot. Missing persons files revealed no-one of that name. *Western Daily Press, 16 June; South Avon Mercury, 17+24 June; Western Morning News, 18 June 1993.*

PROFESSIONAL WAIF

Officer William Tatro discovered a lost boy outside the police station in Bennington, Vermont, on the night of 26 May. He said he was 12 years old, came from Alabama, and had been abandoned in Maine. "The kid's had a raw deal", Tatro told the *Bennington Banner*. "He played rough, but he looked like a little kid – very sad and shy." The public response was good: many people wanted to adopt or foster him.

The boy was taken to hospital for a routine exam, where 'he' was discovered to be a 23-year-old woman. An Illinois picture ID with the name Birdie Jo Hoaks was found hidden in her clothing.

It was discovered that Hoaks had been pulling similar scams all over the country. Previous stops for the Hoaks hoax included Idaho, Texas, Maine, New Jersey, West Virginia and New York.

"She's just a transient", said Sgt. Ron Elwell. "She knows the system, knows how to get into it to get free lodging and food and that type of stuff." She was jailed with bail set at $1,000. *[AP] 30 May 1993.*

LUNCH ON THE WING

Lepidopterists introduced two 18-month-old cotton-eared marmosets to Butterfly World, in Stockton, Cleveland, to add authenticity to its jungle setting. The rare South American monkeys, bred in Britain, were released at the end of May in the huge glasshouse where 3,000 butterflies live. They were thought to pose little threat to the 60 species of butterfly because their normal diet is fruit and nuts; but within a week they had caught and killed more than 50 winged snacks, including at least six Charaxes butterflies, a species facing extinction in Malawi. Lepidopterists were having second thoughts... *D.Telegraph, 2 June 1993.*

QUAKE GODS

Folk tradition in Japan blames earthquakes on the wriggles of the giant subterranean catfish *Namazu*, and, by a type of sympathetic magic, it is also believed that ordinary catfish behave excitedly just before an earthquake. In recent years, geophysicists have taken an interest in the idea that animals reacting to the build up of electrostatic forces, or perhaps even the release of unusual gasses, hoping to find a way of predicting quakes.

We have a note that in 1991, the Pavlov Institute of Physiology in Leningrad was studying catfish from the murky Mississippi, but the *Guardian* (29 April 1993) reports that the Japanese themselves are abandoning their own catfish studies – after 15 years they still have no reliable method. Instead, the Marine Science and Technology Centre is to focus its attention on the behaviour of clams in Sagami Bay, near Tokyo. If that disappoints, they will work doggedly through the remaining sushi ingredients.

DIALLING THE DEAD

A new fad in Malaysia has callers attempting to reach the spirits of the dead by ringing 999998, 999444 and 999999. The calls are automatically routed to fire, police and ambulance services. When the calls are answered, some believe they have reached 'the other side' and start chanting incantations or asking questions about heaven and hell. A telephone company spokesman said thousands of such calls were received in May and early June, and the origins of the fad were being investigated. *[Reuters] 14 June 1993.*

GUN HO!

BANG!

James Janecke, 25, was shot above his right eye during a traffic dispute in Chandler, Arizona, on 20 December 1992, while riding in his girlfriend's car. His nose began bleeding in hospital, he blew it, and out came a .22-calibre bullet. He was treated and released. *Lewiston (ME) Sun-Journal, 23 Dec 1992; Olympian, Jan 1993.*

BANG!!

Rafaela Ramos, 33, was standing with friends a short distance from where a traffic dispute led to a shootout between rival gangs in Torrance, California, on Saturday night, 25 May 1993. Her life was saved when a stray .22 calibre slug embedded itself in her wide, choker-type gold necklace. *[AP] 25 May 1993. The Sun (26 May)* moved the shooting to Los Angeles, aimed the bullet at her heart and stopped it with a medal of the Virgin Mary given to her by her mum when she was 15. How's that for creative journalism?

BANG!!!

Ava Donner was in her kitchen in Pittsburg, California, when a .45-calibre bullet flew through the window and struck the stainless steel spoon she was holding. An inch either way and it would have hit her in the chest. Youths were randomly firing from wasteland 125 yards away. *Victoria (BC) Times-Colonist, 1 Mar 1993.*

BANG!!!!

When a mugger blasted Herb Kravitz, 62, in the chest in North Brunswick, New Jersey, the bullet ricocheted off his wallet, crammed with plastic cards. He escaped without a bruise. *People, 18 April 1993.*

BANG!!!!!

Nightclub boss John Monzouros, 30, was shot in the mouth by a crazed drinker in London's Ferdenzis Club in March 1992. The bullet passed in and out of his jaw, neck, shoulder and back without hitting any vital organs. *D.Mirror, 25 March 1992.*

BANG!!!!!!

Two men burst into a post office in Battersea, London, and opened fire. A 9mm bullet went through an armoured glass screen and hit postmistress Bharti Patel in the mouth just two feet away. It ricocheted off her teeth and spun out through her cheek. She was badly injured, but was expected to survive. *D.Mirror, 19 Mar 1993.*

BANG!!!!!!!

An unnamed 29-year-old Ulster loyalist was shot repeatedly by an undercover soldier on Belfast's Shankhill Road on 31 March. He cheated death when one bullet shattered a brass Chubb door key in his jacket pocket, deflecting it away from his body. *Belfast Telegraph, 2 April 1993. [For similar escapes, see **FT64:21**.]*

FORTEAN ALMANAC 19 August – 11 October 1993

Notable feasts and anniversaries in the coming weeks

THURSDAY 19 AUGUST:
In 1972, a strange creature – about five foot tall, silver coloured, bipedal, with enormous ears and scaly skin – emerged from Thetis Lake, British Columbia, and chased two boys.

SATURDAY 21 AUGUST:
In 1879, 'shining statues' of the Virgin Mary, St Joseph and a bishop appeared, floating two feet off the ground, to a group of witnesses by the church wall in Knock, County Mayo, Ireland.

TUESDAY 24 AUGUST:
St Bartholomew's Day. Bartholemew comes from Bar-Tholomeus, "Son of Ptolemy", a regal name. The Bartholomew Fair was held on this day in West Smithfield, London, from 1133 to 1855

SATURDAY 28 AUGUST:
Feast day of St Hermes, probably a Christian version of the Greek god of magic, medicine and occult wisdom. In 1883, Krakatoa (*west* of Java) erupted, killing 35,000.

WEDNESDAY 1 SEPTEMBER:
Feast day of St Fiacre, who intercedes for hæmorrhoid sufferers, and of St Giles, patron saint of cripples.

WEDNESDAY 8 SEPTEMBER:
The Nativity of the Virgin Mary. Mary's mother was St Anne, patron saint of midwives and miners. The Roman *Anna Perenna* was Grand-mother Time, mother of the Aeons.

SUNDAY 12 SEPTEMBER:
In 1880, many reputable witnesses on Coney Island saw a man with bat's wings and 'improved frogs' legs' flying towards New Jersey at an altitude of 1,000 feet.

THURSDAY 16 SEPTEMBER:
Rosh Hashanah (Jewish New Year 5754).

FRIDAY 17 SEPTEMBER:
St Lambert of Maastricht's Day.

SATURDAY 18 SEPTEMBER:
St Joseph of Cupertino's Day. Joseph (1603-63) was one of the church's most famous levitators. Witnesses included Pope Urban VIII, the Infanta Maria and the patron of Liebnitz, the mathematician. (See picture page 28).

TUESDAY 21 SEPTEMBER:
In 1823, the Angel Moroni appeared to Joseph Smith in Palmyra, New York. Later, he directed Smith to some buried gold plates, on which was written *The Book of Mormon.*

THURSDAY 23 SEPTEMBER:
Mabon, or Autumnal Equinox. Sun enters Libra 00:23 GMT. Birthday of Victoria Woodhull (1838), banker and US Presidential candidate, known as 'Mrs Satan'.

SATURDAY 25 SEPTEMBER:
Teleportation Day, in honour of St Cadoc (the Welsh abbot who was transported in a cloud from Llancarfan to Benevento in Italy) and St Finbarr (who crossed the Irish Sea on horseback). Today is the feast day of both saints. Today is also Yom Kippur.

MONDAY 4 OCTOBER:
Feast day of St Francis of Assisi. In 1224, after a vision of Christ crucified, he developed the full stigmata – bleeding holes in his hands and feet.

MONDAY 11 OCTOBER:
In 1973, fishermen Charles Hickson and Calvin Parker were abducted by aliens off a pier on the Pascagoula River, Mississippi, and subjected to medical examinations.

SPECIAL CORRESPONDENTS

AFRICA Cynthia Hind (Zimbabwe), Ion Alexis Will (Roving). **AUSTRALIA** Greg Axford (Vic), Paul Cropper (NSW), Arthur Chrenkoff (Qld), Rex Gilroy (NSW), Tony Healy (ACT). **BELGIUM** Henri Prémont. **CANADA** Brian Chapman (BC), Dwight Whalen (Ont.). **DENMARK** Lars Thomas. **ENGLAND** Claire Blamey, Bruce Chatterton, Peter Christie, Mat Coward, Hilary Evans, Peter Hope-Evans, Neil Frary, Alan Gardiner, Mick Goss, Chris Hall, Jeremy Harte, Ronnie Hoyle, Dionne Jones, Jake Kirkwood, Alexis Lykiard, Nick Maloret, Valerie Martin, Kevin McClure, John Michell, Ralph Noyes, Nigel Pennick, Andy Roberts, Tom Ruffles, Paul Screeton, Karl Shuker, Ian Simmons, Bob Skinner, Anthony Smith, Paul R. Thomas, Nigel Watson, Owen Whiteoak, Steve Wrathall. **FRANCE** Jean-Louis Brodu, Bernard Heuvelmans, Michel Meurger. **GERMANY** Walter J. Langbein, Ulrich Magin. **GREECE** S.C. Tavuchis. **HOLLAND** Robin Pascoe. **HONGKONG** Chris Williams. **ICELAND** V. Kip Hansen. **INDONESIA** Alan M. Stracy. **IRELAND** Peter Costello, Doc Shiels. **JAPAN** Masaru Mori, Shigeo Yokoyama. **NEW ZEALAND** Peter Hassall. **NORTHERN IRELAND** Caryl Sibbett. **PHILIPPINES** Keith Snell. **POLAND** Leszek Matela. **ROMANIA** Iosif Boczor. **RUSSIA** Vladimir Rubtsov. **SCOTLAND** David Burns, Stuart Herkes, Roger Musson, Roland Watson, Jake Williams. **SWEDEN** Anders Liljegren, Sven Rosén. **USA** Larry E. Arnold (PA), Loren Coleman (ME), James E. Conlan (CT), Karma Tenzin Dorje (CA), David Fideler (MI), Mark A. Hall (MN), Myron S. Hoyt (ME), John Keel (NYC), Jim Lippard (AZ), Kurt Lothmann (TX), Barbara Millspaw (CO), Ray Nelke (MO), Jim Riecken (NY), Ron Schaffner (OH), Chuck Shepherd (FL), Dennis Stacy (TX), Joseph Swatek (NB), Joseph Trainor (MA), Jeffrey Vallance (CA), Robert Anton Wilson (CA), Joseph W. Zarzynski (NY). **TURKEY** Izzet Goksu. **WALES** Janet & Colin Bord, Richard Holland, Joe Kelly.

ILLUSTRATION COPYRIGHTS

5 Eric Gaillard / Reuter / Hulton Deutsch. **7** Ewing-Reeson Photography. **8** Intercontinental Features. **9** Xinhua News Agency. **10** Merrily Harpur. **11(both)** Somerset News. **12** Merrily Harpur. **13(t)** European Southern Observatory, **(b)** Richard Huff / Peekskill Herald. **14** Topham. **17** Hulton Deutsch. **19** Martin Impney. **21** Hunt Emerson. **23(tm)** Central TV / PA. **24** David Jones / PA / Topham. **25** Malcolm Croft / PA. **26-29** Mary Evans Picture Library. **30-31** Nick Brown. **32(t)** Nick Brown., **(b)** Julian Freeman Attwood. **33(both)** John Blashford Snell. **34(t)** John Blashford Snell, **(b)** Fortean Picture Library. **35-37** Jeffrey Vallance. **41(t)** H. Armstrong Roberts. **42** Alan Walker. **43(t)** Nationaal Natuurhistorisch Museum, Leiden, **(b)** Alan Walker. **44** Peter Ramshaw / Sunday Times, Perth. **46** John Yanshin / Vancouver Sun. **47(t)** Provincial Archives of British Columbia. **49** Ken Howitt / Northwich Chronicle. **52(both)** Janet & Colin Bord. **59** John McNish / CircleVision. **63** Eric Brady. **64** Ralph Noyes. **65** Anon. **All others:** unknown or see caption.

CLIPPINGS & TRANSLATIONS FOR THIS ISSUE

Jayne Amat, Dr Gail-Nina Anderson, Larry E. Arnold, Mike Avis, Sherry Baker, Lisa Ann Barnes, Jon Barraclough, K.A.Beer, Bhaskar Bhattacharyya, Pierre Bonello, Janet & Colin Bord, Iosif Boszov, D.M. Bozzom, Linda Brown, David J.Burns, ByRon, Cain, Brian Chapman, Danny Cheveaux, Arthur Chrenkoff, Peter Christie, Loren Coleman, Mark Conti, James Conway, COUD-I, Mat Coward, Joy Critchley, Paul Cropper, Mike Dash, Scott Deschaine, Karma Tenzin Dorje, John De Vos, Jill Doubleday, Martin Eads, Bill Ellis, Peter Hope-Evans, Lucius Farish, Larry Fiander, Neil Frary, Jon Fry, Robert Gifford, Ian Glasby, Matthew Goulding, Mike Griffin, Mark A. Hall, Peter Hassall, Tony Healy, Stuart A.Herkes, Steve Hexter, Myron S. Hoyt, Christopher E. Iles, Dionne Jones, Roger Laidlaw, Chris Lonsborough, Alexis Lykiard, Ulrich Magin, Nick Maloret, G. Markie, Valerie Martin, Mike Meakin, Barbara Millspaw, Ian Morgan, Cynde Moys, Jan Mura, Ray Nelke, Caroline Norris, Ralph Noyes, Roger O'Donnell, Nigel Pennick, John Price, Andrew Rawlinson, Jim Riecken, Peter Rogerson, Zvi Ron, Sven Rosén, John Rowe, Tom Ruffles, John Sappington, Tom Salusbury, Paul Screeton, Ronnie Scott, Dr Karl Shuker, Ian Simmons, Arthur Smith, Richard Smith, Peter Stallard, Alan M. Stracy, Joe Swatek, Dr Steve Tavuchis, Paul R.Thomas, Pam Thornton, Fred Thomsett, Richard Turner, Dr Mark Tyrrell, UFONS, Sarah Walsh, Nicholas P. Warren, Nigel Watson, Dwight Whalen, John Whiskin, Owen Whiteoak, Ion Will, Jan Williams, Chris Williams, Simon Harvey-Wilson.

PHENOMENOMIX·

HUNT EMERSON. 1993

ANOTHER LAKE SERPENT DISCOVERED - THIS TIME IN CANADA!

AT ONE TIME THE ONLY LAKE WITH A MONSTER WAS LOCH NESS...

...BUT MORE AND MORE ARE REPORTED FROM ALL OVER THE NORTHERN HEMISPHERE...
..WALES...
...RUSSIA...
...AMERICA...
...FINLAND...

"WHERE ARE ALL THESE LAKE-SNAKES COMING FROM?" THE WORLD ASKS ITSELF...
?

AT LAST I CAN REVEAL THE TRUTH! ALL THESE SIGHTINGS OF LAKE MONSTERS ARE IN FACT DIFFERENT PARTS OF THE SAME CREATURE!..

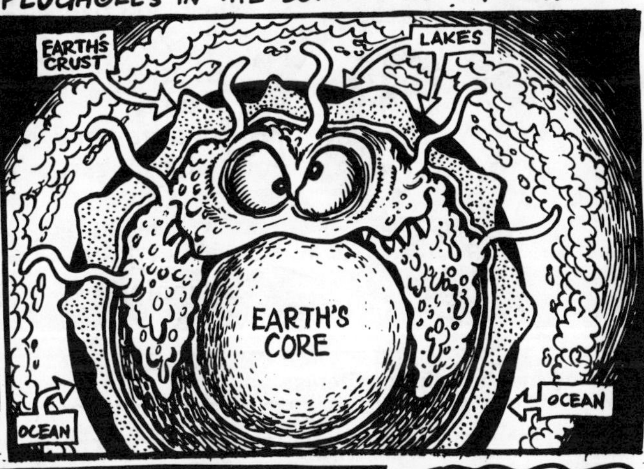

...A HUGE LIVING THING IS GROWING INSIDE THE EARTH, A SORT OF CANCER BENEATH THE NORTHERN HEMISPHERE... AND AS IT GETS BIGGER, IT POKES FINGERS THROUGH THE PLUGHOLES IN THE BOTTOMS OF LAKES...
EARTH'S CRUST
LAKES
EARTH'S CORE
OCEAN
OCEAN

...FINGERS THAT ARE TAKEN FOR LAKE SERPENTS!
The Head is a sort of finger puppet!

BUT WHY, YOU ASK, IS THIS VILE AND DISGUSTING CREATURE DOING THIS?

WELL, IT'S GETTING A GOOD, STRONG HOLD READY FOR WHEN IT'S FULLY GROWN, AND CAN RIP THE TOP OFF THE WORLD IN ORDER TO FREE ITSELF!

AND IT'S THERE, UNDER OUR FEET! GROWING! GETTING BIGGER, AND POKING IT'S FINGERS IN OUR LAKE BOTTOMS!!
Don't worry - he's harmless ...He doesn't get out very much...

FORTEAN FANCIES

T-SHIRTS

**100% COTTON
T-SHIRTS, ONE SIZE
XL.**

NEW!
Italian Martians T-shirt 100% cotton, good quality heavyweight T-shirt in dark green. One size XL £9.99. Illustration by Walter Molino of Rosa Lotti's experience with the 'men from Mars'.

Charles Fort T-shirt - 100% white cotton T-shirt, one size XL £7.99 Charles Fort's Portrait and the slogan "One Measures a Circle Beginning Anywhere".

BOOKS

Check out more fascinating reports, from spontaneous human combustion to UFO abduction, in this collection of facsimile reprints of early Fortean Times (formerly simply titled The News).

FORTEAN TIMES 1 - 15
YESTERDAY'S NEWS TOMORROW **£19.99**
ISBN: 1 870870 263 400 page paperback, colour cover, illustrated throughout.

FORTEAN TIMES 16-25
DIARY OF A MAD PLANET **£19.50**
ISBN: 1 870021 258 416 page paperback, colour cover, illustrated throughout.

FORTEAN TIMES 26 - 30
SEEING OUT THE SEVENTIES **£14.99**
ISBN: 1 870021 207 320 page paperback, colour cover, illustrated throughout.

NEW! FORTEAN TIMES 31-36
GATEWAYS TO MYSTERY £19.99
ISBN: 1870870 379 400 page paperback, colour cover, illustrated throughout, published end of August. Order now.

SUBSCRIPTIONS

If you have enjoyed this issue, why not make sure that you receive a copy on a regular basis? Order a year's supply of Fortean Times for yourself or a friend and get it delivered direct to your doorstep. And that's not all: every new subscriber receives a FREE copy of Doc Shiels' Monstrum book (DIY monster hunting - worth £8.95). Fortean Times back issues also available (see below).

BACK ISSUES

FT52 - Lizard Man, albino frog falls and Yorkshire's water wolf
FT53 - Crop circles, invasion of the slime creatures and Islamic simulacra.
FT58 - Lesbian vampires, trepanning today and alien abduction.
FT60 - Alpine ice man, Father Christmas as Odin and the Lake Erie monster.
FT61 - Homing treks by cats, everlasting light bulbs and social panics.
FT62 - The Piltdown Hoax, World's Heaviest Man dies and puddle -creating poltergeists.
FT63 - Crop Circle colour pull-out, acid tattoo panic and British alien big cats.
FT64 - Spielberg, Satanic witch hunts and the pregnant male hoax.
FT65 - Colour pull-out on Martian monuments, kidney kidnapping rumours and blood miracles.
FT66 - Florida's penguin panic, bogus social workers and horse-ripping.
FT67 - BBC's Ghostwatch hoax unravelled, plus Italian Martians.
FT68 - Cattle Mutilation in America, ESP Orgasms, Vampire at Croglin Grange.
FT69 - Who are the Circlemakers? Chinese cannibalism, lama drama.

Please send me the following items:

Item	UK Price	US Price	Overseas	Qty	Value
Yesterday's News Tomorrow	£19.99	$44.00	£22.00		
Diary of a Mad Planet	£19.50	$44.00	£22.00		
Seeing Out the Seventies	£14.99	$34.00	£17.00		
Gateways to Mystery	£19.99	$44.00	£22.00		
Italian Martians T-shirt	£9.99	$23.00	£11.99		
Charles Fort T-shirt	£7.99	$18.00	£9.50		

Postage and packing free. **Total £ ______**

I would like to subscribe to Fortean Times from issue ______

***Please tick for free Monstrum book** ☐

For one year (6 issues) £12 ☐
Overseas inc USA £15 US$30 ☐

For two years (12 issues) £20 ☐
Overseas inc USA £26 US$50 ☐

Back issues £2 each (£2.50 overseas or US$5.00) Please circle your selection:

37	38	39	42	43	44	46	50	51
52	53	54	55	56	57	58	59	60
61	62	63	64	65	66	67	68	69

Name: Mrs/Miss/Ms/Mr ______

Address ______

______

______ Postcode ______

I enclose a total payment of £ ______ made payable to: John Brown Publishing Ltd, or debit the above amount from my Access/Visa/ Mastercard/Eurocard (delete where applicable) account.

Account No ☐☐☐☐

Expiry Date ☐☐

Signature ______

Date ______

**Please return this order form to:
Fortean Times, Freepost SW6096, Frome, Somerset BA11 1YA, U.K. or Freephone credit card details on 0800 581409**

**FREEPOST AND FREEPHONE SERVICES AVAILABLE TO UK RESIDENTS ONLY. OVERSEAS CUSTOMERS PLEASE ADD POSTAGE STAMPS TO POSTAL APPLICATIONS.
FOR TELEPHONE ORDERS PHONE (44) 373 451777**

FT70

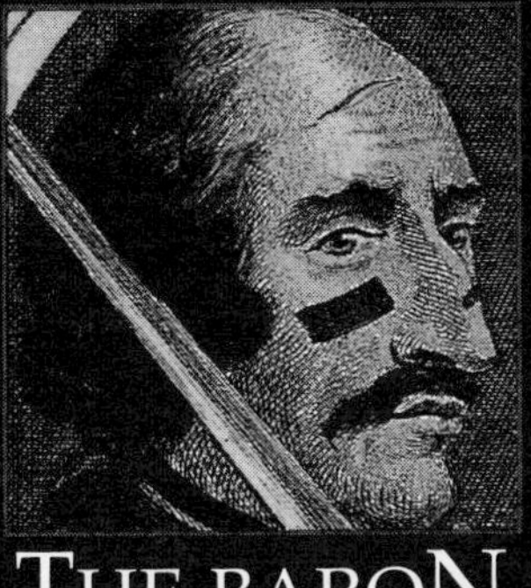

THE BARON

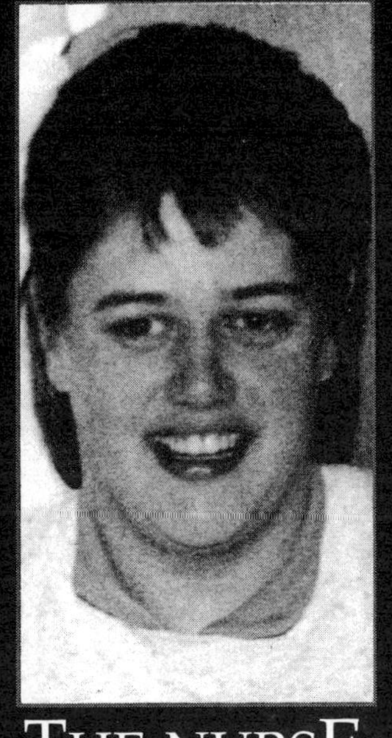

THE NURSE

THE PRINCESS

THE MÜNCH BUNCH

THE NUN

THE SAINT

After the trial of the child-killing nurse Beverly Allitt earlier this year, it was with an almost palpable sense of relief that the British press and public learned that she had been suffering from a 'rare personality disorder' – indeed, two rare personality disorders, known respectively as Münchausen's syndrome and Münchausen's syndrome by proxy (MBP). JIM SCHNABEL argues that the adaptive psychology which links Allitt to a diverse group of characters including the Princess of Wales can be traced back to ancient shamanism and may cast new light on reports of strange experiences ranging from poltergeist manifestations to alien abductions

Beverly Allitt A CASE HISTORY

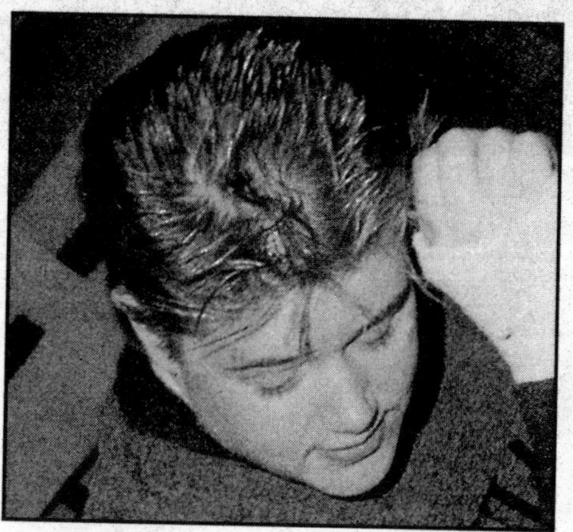

Part of Beverly Allitt's condition – some say the heart of it – was a cripplingly low level of self-esteem. "I know I am not competent," she once shouted at friends. "I am one of the crappiest nurses out. I am the lowest of the low."

Between 1985 and September 1991, Allitt made over 40 visits to the casualty department of the same hospital in which she murdered and attacked 13 children – 20 of these 'emergencies' were before her induction there as a trainee nurse in 1988. They actually stopped during the period she attacked the children – between February and April 1991 – and resumed while she was on bail. Even in prison, awaiting trial, she managed to scald herself with hot custard.

THIS MEDICAL HISTORY IS SUMMARISED FROM A NUMBER OF SOURCES:

Sept 1985 – Injury to toes.
Feb 1986 – Injury to finger.
July 1986 – Worried about missing two periods. Referred to obstetrician. Pregnancy test negative.
Aug 1986 – Injury to toes.
Oct 1986 – Three separate complaints of abdominal pain. Claims she has two ulcers. Admitted for gastroscope examination; no sign of ulcer. Produces green vomit. Staff believe she is making herself vomit.
Dec 1986 – Injury to hand. Claims problems eating fat. Claims gall bladder problems. Surgeon writes; "My feeling is symptoms are psychosomatic..."
March 1987 – Hæmatoma on hand. Claims hand is stiff before and after physiotherapy during which it moves normally.
June 1987 – Another hæmatoma on same hand. Days later, another bruise to same hand.
July 1987 – Injury to other hand.
Aug 1987 – Doctors puzzled by recurring hæmatomas on hand; recommend no further X- rays.
Nov 1987 – Five more injuries to hand. Denies to suspicious doctors that she did them deliberately.
July 1988 – Goes to different hospital complaining of wrist fracture. Nothing found.
Sept 1988 –Shortly after beginning training, two separate complaints of muscle strains.
Jan 1989 – Claims to have hit head in a fall. Subsequent separate complaints of double vision and protracted headaches.
March 1989 – Referred to surgeon for back strain. More headaches and blurred vision. Complains of urinary infection and blood in urine. None seen by doctors.
Aug 1989 – Two separate injuries to foot.
Oct 1989 – More complaints of glass in foot. None found. Minor injury to leg.
Jan 1990 – Training at different hospital. Injuries to hand.
May 1990 – Claims urine retention; admitted for tests.
July 1990 – Complains of severe colic. Urologist writes: "Hysterical symptoms. Shown how to catheterise herself. Hoped this would discourage her, instead she thrives on it."
Aug 1990 – Injury to ankle.
Oct 1990 – Separate complaints of stomach pains and blood in urine. Urine noted to be clear. Complains of appendicitis; appendectomy done; appendix appears "grossly" normal. Later wound is found open and bleeding in way that suggests tampering.
Nov 1990 – Complains of cystic lump in right hip. No pathology.
May 1991 – Injury to foot. Claims urinary infection, but tests reveal nothing. Doctor writes: "Pattern of symptoms extremely odd and gruesome vicissitudes of self-treatment." First arrest and interview.
June 1991 – Complains of acute retention of urine and temperature of 41° which drops to normal in seconds. Doctor suspects thermometer was warmed; writes "A very strange lady."
July 1991 – Right breast swollen. Three puncture marks found, suggesting injection of liquid.
Aug 1991 – Urine retention. Breaks catheter. Breaks catheter again days later. Nurse attempts removal, notes tip is left behind in bladder. Hospital pointedly makes no follow-up appointment. Complained of brain tumour; scan is negative. First mention of Münchausen's. **BR**

THE MÜNCH BUNCH

Diana, Princess of Wales. Could her neurotic behaviour be a form of Münchausen's syndrome?

Beverly Allitt had for years been feigning and self-inflicting illness and injury in the classic Münchausenian manner, smashing her hand with a hammer, pushing glass into her feet, injecting one of her breasts with liquid, feigning appendicitis until her healthy organ was removed, plucking at her surgical wounds, breaking off a catheter within her urethra, and even eating her own fæces.

When, in early 1991, she began to direct such behaviour, with substantial medical technology at her disposal, towards half a dozen helpless children on her ward in Lincolnshire's Grantham and Kesteven hospital, she earned the additional diagnosis of Münchausen's by proxy.

Of course, the point of such disclosures, and of such epithets as 'rare personality disorder', was that Nurse Allitt was not like you and me; she was instead, as the *Independent*'s Jonathan Foster put it, "an extraordinarily disturbed psychopath".

In fact, there is reason to believe that Münchausen's and Münchausen's by proxy are not terribly rare or necessarily psychopathic, and belong to a fairly common group of behaviours and phenomena including ordinary hysteria, shamanism, mediumship, poltergeists, spirit-possession, multiple personality disorder, the ecstatic self-mortifications of the saints and mystics, and even the alleged propensity of the Princess of Wales to hurl herself down flights of stairs.

CONVERSION NEUROSES

The connection between Münchausen's and these other psychological phenomena begins with its links to hysteria, a complex of behaviours which involves the unconscious rather than the conscious and deliberate fabrication of illness. Orthodox manuals of mental disorders isolate Münchausen's-type behaviour from hysteria and from other categories of strange behaviour, but a number of medical commentators on Münchausen's have noted a general similarity of behaviour between Münchausenians and hysterics.

Richard Asher, the physician who described the syndrome in 1951 guessed that some Münchausenians might simply be hysterics, presumably acting out their manipulative urges in a conscious manner. Herzl Spiro, a psychiatrist at Johns Hopkins University in Baltimore, noted in 1968 that several cases on his files involved individuals who exhibited not only Münchausenian deception but 'conversion neuroses' – a psychoanalytic term for the hysterical conversion of emotional turmoil into physical pains or disorders. One such disorder, the eating disorder anorexia nervosa, is said to have been responsible for Beverly Allitt's enormous loss of weight since her arrest last year.

Indeed, it may be that Münchausenians, as contrasted with hysterics, are merely those who do not always have the ability to fabricate medical problems unconsciously. As such, they may be as common as hysterics – who are very common indeed – and may overlap behaviourally to such an extent that exclusive definitions become misleading. Consider the case of the Princess of Wales. According to the numerous books about her, she was fantasy-prone and manipulative in childhood, and in adulthood responded to the turmoil of her marriage with eating disorders such as anorexia and bulimia. She also reportedly employed less unconscious but no less dramatic attempts to manipulate her husband, wounding herself with various household items, and, most famously, throwing herself down stairs while pregnant – the latter behaviour, perhaps, being susceptible to diagnosis as simultaneous Münchausen's and Münch-ausen's by proxy!

ALTER EGOS

The next link in the chain is represented by the dissociative disorders, of which hysterical illnesses are often a major feature. In fact, early psychologists simply considered these disorders to be variants of hysteria. The best known dissociative disorder is Multiple Personality Disorder, or MPD – whose sufferers are renowned for the injuries they either imagine or inflict upon themselves. Oddly, despite the frequency of such injury, Münchausenian behaviour is seldom diagnosed in MPD patients, and dissociative hysteria seems to be assumed instead.

However, there are several reports in the literature of cases in which MPD patients have clearly exhibited classic Münchausenian behaviour, repeatedly injuring themselves or feigning illness, and wandering from hospital to hospital seeking treatment. In one such case, the self-injection of insulin to bring about hypoglycæmia (a standard Münchausenian technique later used by Allitt) was admitted by one of a patient's alters, who claimed he had been under stress; the other alters all claimed amnesia about the source of their various ailments.

Jean Goodwin, a psychiatrist and dissociative disorder specialist at the Medical College of Wisconsin, noted in a paper in 1988 that the behavioural parallels between MPD and Münchausen's include frequent self-abusive actions, feigned or imagined physical symptoms, histories of childhood abuse or trauma, histories of apparent

MÜNCHAUSEN'S SYNDROME

"Few doctors can boast that they have never been hoodwinked by the condition," wrote the Central Middlesex Hospital physician Richard Asher in his seminal article in the Lancet in 1951. "Often the diagnosis is made by a passing doctor or sister, who, recognising the patient and his performance, exclaims, 'I know that man. We had him in St. Quinidine's two years ago and thought that he had a perforated ulcer. He's the man who always collapses on buses and tells a story about being an ex-submarine commander who was tortured by the Gestapo.'"

Asher named the condition Münchausen's syndrome, after Baron Karl Friedrich von Münchausen, an eighteenth-century character who was alleged (in a book whose contents were later said to be substantially false) to have wandered from tavern to tavern throughout his life, telling tall tales. The individual with Münchausen's, according to Asher, typically bore scars from numerous prior operations, and presented with a medical condition which was acute but not obviously confirmable or convincing, and was often attributed to unusual or fantastic causes.

Since Asher's time, Münchausenians have been reported to have feigned or fabricated (by injuring themselves or by tampering with laboratory samples) the symptoms of a great variety of disorders including AIDS, allergies, cancer, depression, epilepsy, hallucinations, kidney disease, paraplegia, suicidal ideation, and several new and controversial conditions such as post-traumatic stress disorder following satanic ritual abuse. A letter to the New England Journal of Medicine in 1980 even described a man who had falsely presented with Münchausen's syndrome (his scars washed off with soap and water) although that letter was later retracted as a hoax.

Münchausen's by proxy (MBP), described by Leeds pædiatrician Roy Meadow in 1977, is a term intended to cover the behaviour of an adult – almost always a mother – who turns her Münchausenian urges upon a proxy victim, usually her child. Typically the child is artificially made to suffer from actual symptoms which suggest an underlying disease. Suffocation of the child is probably the most common technique – it was part of Beverly Allitt's lethal repertoire – while others include poisoning, deliberate malnutrition, and scarring. Such children may go on to develop Münchausen's syndrome themselves, and MBP mothers – as the Allitt case illustrated so well – typically have a history of Münchausen-type behaviour directed against their own bodies.

Münchausen's syndrome and MBP occur relatively frequently in pregnant women and in nurses, which suggests that these syndromes, even if based upon genetic factors or adverse childhood experiences, may be triggered by a stay in hospital during which the soon-to-be Münchausenian is given a pleasurable amount of attention by both parents and hospital staff, or after working in a hospital and envying the attention enjoyed by patients. **JS**

Two illustrations by O. Herrfurth for Raspe's edition of *The Travels of Baron Münchausen*, which have unexpected shamanic overtones. Above left, the tall-tale-teller climbs to the moon on a rope, recalling the shamans' own ascent of the *axis mundi*, the path that links the terrestrial with the celestial, and which is echoed in the infamous 'Indian rope trick'. Above right, the Baron discovers the reason for his horse's mighty thirst; it has been sliced in two. Inadvertently, perhaps, it reminds us that the relationship between genital mutilation and its proxy, the mutilation of the genitals of animals (the back half), may be as close as that between Münchausen's and its proxy.

lying, active imaginations and changeable life stories, the use of different names, and sudden, fugue-like disappearances. Goodwin proposed that Münchausen's syndrome, currently classified as chronic factitious (ie. false) disorder, should be re-classified as a dissociative disorder alongside MPD. Goodwin might also have noted that Münchausenian patients have presented falsely with war-related and satanic abuse-related post-traumatic stress disorders – disorders which have been associated with reports of prior dissociative experiences.

Münchausenian behaviour, hysteria, and the dissociative disorders thus appear to be interconnected. Hysteria and the dissociative disorders have long been implicated in paranormal-type experiences and claims, including UFO abductions, spirit-possession, mediumship, and shamanism. These in turn have often been connected to deceptive behaviours, from the tricksiness of poltergeists, to the outrageous frauds of mediums, to the sleight-of-hand gimmickry of shamans. We might therefore suspect that Münchausen's-type behaviour too is linked to the paranormal.

A Mongol shaman levitates a stool, witnessed in 1854. Shamanic rituals, as Mircea Eliade puts it, are "archaic techniques of ecstasy". Many commentators have been confounded by the facility with which seemingly genuine phenomena appears alongside barely-concealed sleight-of-hand. This ambiguity also appears in today's Münchausen-like phenomena, including claims of satanic child abuse and alien abduction. Sexual ambiguity was also the mark of the shaman who has a cultural licence to bridge many different worlds simultaneously.

PIOUS FRAUD

Jean Goodwin in her 1988 paper briefly cited the case of Benedetta Carlini, a nun who lived in a Tuscan convent during the late Renaissance, and despite a promising career as a visionary and a stigmatic, was jailed as demonically-possessed after accusations of fakery and lesbianism were levelled against her. Goodwin, who retrospectively diagnosed Carlini with both Münchausen's syndrome and MPD, wrote little about the case, noting only that Carlini had been seen wounding herself to create and maintain stigmata, and had occasionally manifested alter personalities including Jesus and a lusty young cherub named Splenditello.

However, Goodwin's source for this material – *Immodest Acts: The Life of a Lesbian Nun in Renaissance Italy*, by the historian Judith Brown – makes clear that the young nun, and perhaps many more who were reported to have perpetrated similar deceptions, was a classic illustration of the deep relationship between deception and the paranormal. Carlini's self-reported childhood history had included harassment by the devil in the form of a black dog which disappeared when her parents responded to her cries, and encouragement by God in the form of other animals. She had been sent to live in the convent in 1599, at age nine, and during her early twenties became the focus of an extraordinary wave of supernatural phenomena.

One of the first instances occurred when the convent's Mother Superior, responding to Benedetta's screams, found her beside a fallen statue of the Virgin Mary; Carlini claimed that the statue had been bending to kiss her. Later, Carlini began to report visions of demonic figures, and therefore asked that she be provided with another nun, one Bartolomea, as a companion, to give her solace during these nocturnal attacks. Bartolomea, reassured by Carlini (who when she wanted sex would enter a trance and channel Splenditello or Jesus) that she was committing no sin, became Carlini's more or less enthusiastic lover (*Immodest Acts*, incidentally, is kept in a special cage for obscene books at Oxford's Bodleian Library).

On other occasions, however, Carlini's thoughts and visions were of a congenial Christ, and as time went on, Carlini began to seem like a saint in the making. With the help of a knitting needle, she developed the stigmata, painting her scalp with blood from her hand to simulate the wounds from an ethereal crown of thorns. Blood from her stigmata was also put to use on statues of the Virgin Mary, which tended to weep red tears when she was around. Despite occasional secret bingeing on salami and mortadella, she insisted that Christ had forbidden her to eat meat or dairy products. With the help of some saffron, she painted a yellow 'ring' on her finger to symbolise her 'sacred marriage' to the Son of God.

One night before the marriage ceremony, while Carlini lay in bed beside Bartolomea, Christ visited her and, explaining that he wished to prepare her for her sacred marriage, reached into her and pulled out her heart, three days later replacing it with his own much grander one. (Bartolomea dutifully reported to the authorities the fantastic details of these operations.) As Judith Brown noted, the heart exchange motif was common in the lore of the female saints of the time (it has been reported too in a satanic abuse claim published recently in the psychiatric literature); it also had obvi-

THE MÜNCH BUNCH

ous links with the imagery of shamanic initiation, in which wounding features heavily, and ordinary vital organs are often replaced by supernaturally-derived ones. Indeed, Benedetta Carlini, who could channel otherworldly entities so convincingly that when she did so she could speak other languages and dialects and could take on a distinctly new appearance, appears to have been a classic example of a Renaissance shamaness.

THE SHAMANIC REFLEX

The shamanic experience, which can elevate the lowliest member of society to a position of substantial power, is one whose central features include a long prelude of oppression or illness, and a crisis involving possession or wounding by otherworldly entities. Illness and wounding, of whatever origin, are so important to this process that the shaman is often referred to as the 'wounded healer' – or the "wounded surgeon" as T.S. Eliot once put it. Being ill or wounded was once, and to a certain extent still is, highly adaptive. In some cultures, children with frequent epileptic seizures were marked for a life of shamanism. Sometimes, shamanic initiates were separated according to whether they could undergo their initiatory injuries by 'the spirits' (ie, while left alone by themselves) or required help from other shamans. Needless, to say, the latter were considered second-rate.

The faking of illnesses which were popularly believed to predispose to shamanism – especially epilepsy – might also have been quite adaptive. Like obtaining admission for one's child at a posh school, they virtually guaranteed a bright future. Is it a coincidence that 'pseudoseizures' – ie. hysterical or feigned epileptic fits –

St Joseph of Cupertino (1603-1663) inflicted gruesome injuries and austerities upon himself to "subjugate the flesh". His spontaneous ecstatic levitations were often well and reliably witnessed, including one, depicted here, in the presence of Pope Urban VIII.

VENUS UNHINGED

In his column last issue (FT69:55), Ralph Noyes reminded us of the sexual overtones of the ectoplasmic mediumship of yesteryear – indeed, the seance allowed a level of eroticism that would ordinarily be scandalous. In a darkened room neurotic women gained the rapt attention of eminent medical and scientific gentlemen by abandoning themselves to the direction of their impulses and 'spirits'.

However, the prelude to these experiments was sometimes even more dubious. To allay the suspicion that 'ectoplasm' was just muslin swallowed and regurgitated, or smuggled in any orifice, researchers – as reported by Richet and Schrenck-Notzing, for example – often insisted upon a thorough rectal and vaginal inspection prior to the seance; some even administered emetics to make the medium vomit. Humiliation and attention – Münchausenian heaven!

Beverly Allitt, too, engineered several intimate examinations. She went to hospital claiming that she could not urinate; she was catheterized by nurses, but promptly broke off the catheter, necessitating a delicate removal operation which involved much handling of her genitals by medical staff.

The abusive alters of Multiple Personality Disorder patients also seem prone to inflict injury upon their (or their core personalities') genitals, as if driven by the same dark impulse which lies behind the mare-slashing horse-rippers. Similarly, women who claim to be victims of UFO abduction have been known to report alien examinations and inseminations so violent that their blood spatters the decks of the spaceships which imprison them.

The same rape-and-wound motif is also found in satanic ritual abuse claims and in claims of demonic harassment (although the victims of demonic possession four hundred years ago were sometimes known to consort very satisfyingly with the devil and his well-endowed minions, even writhing in public ecstasy as they did so).

Do these anecdotes represent merely the random surfacing of the baser, weirder, instincts amidst a dissociative maelstrom? Or is sexual angst and frustration – made worse when one's proclivities are unorthodox – the stressful spur to dissociation-related behaviour? Or are unorthodox sexual appetites and dissociative tendencies somehow inherently linked? Psychiatrists don't seem to know.

Meanwhile, anthropologists puzzle over the fact that shamans, from the Palæo-Siberian 'soft men' to the cross-dressing Joan of Arc, are disproportionately likely to be bisexual or homosexual, with transvestitism a common feature. **BR/JS**

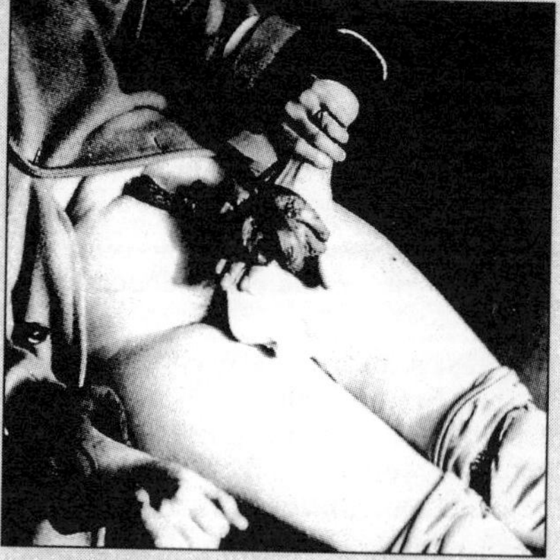

Margery Crandon was a physical medium from Boston, Massachusetts, who flourished in the 1920s, producing a whole range of phenomena from levitating tables, voices, lights and hands that wrote in nine languages (including Chinese). She was investigated by Houdini and a *Scientific American* team for whom she produced an ectoplasmic hand from between her legs. Our picture, from a seance in 1925, shows the extent of her exhibitionism – as ectoplasm exudes from her navel, her pubic region is barely concealed by an investigator's handkerchief. An easy target of character assassination and *a priori* accusations of fraud, she was never really given a fair investigation.

are extremely common both in MPD and in Münchausen's syndrome? A report in the journal *Archives of Disease in Childhood* in 1989 noted the case of a young boy whose mother, acting out Münchausen's by proxy, had taught him to fake seizures so well that at age four he was mimicking them without prompting, and thus represented perhaps the youngest Münchausenian ever diagnosed.

The anthropologist I.M. Lewis has made a similar suggestion about spirit-possession, which apparently originated as a shamanic sub-phenomenon but now, like all other dissociative phenomena, has become primarily the province of women (although it should be noted that shamans themselves were and are often bisexual, homosexual, transsexual, or female). Lewis argued that the diagnosis and treatment of spirit-possession among women in certain African societies...

"...gives women the opportunity to gain ends (material and non-material) which they cannot readily secure more directly. Women are, in effect, making a special virtue of adversity and affliction, and [are], often quite literally, capitalising on their distress."

St Teresa of Avila (1515-1582), foundress and mystic of the Carmelite order, was, unlike St Joseph of Cupertino, educated and intelligent. However, like him, she was frequently rapt in ecstasy and once experienced God's love as a flaming spear of divine love that pierced her heart. In this devotional portrait she is shown seeing a vision of Christ's bleeding heart while the mystical arrow transfixes her breast.

Compare this with the comment of an American UFO abductee who in the late 1980s, in an interview conducted by the sceptic Philip Klass, confessed to having invented her claims:

"...the only way [people who become abductees] can get any kind of satisfaction is to fabricate some sort of story to get the focus of attention that they need."

TRICKS AS RITUALS

Joseph Campbell, in his studies of shamans and mythology, also noted that medicine-men often perpetrated sleight-of-hand tricks and other frauds upon their audiences. Campbell assumed that such deceptions were sometimes necessary to maintain the shaman's spiritual and political authority, but, he also suggested, such deceptions might sometimes represent techniques, like eating peyote or chanting rhythmically, for elevating the shaman's consciousness into a genuine altered state. Sleight-of-hand tricks, according to Campbell's argument, could thus be hallucinogenic for the magician as well as his audience.

The stigmata of the saints, and their well-known obsessions with 'the mortification of the flesh' – ie. everything from fasting to freezing, to severe and prolonged self-mutilation – can obviously be seen in a similar light. St. Joseph of Cupertino, for example, wore an irritating hair shirt and several metal plates that cut into his skin, abstained from meat and frequently went without all food for days, sprinkled a mortifyingly nauseating powder on whatever he did eat, and flagellated himself with an ingeniously torturous whip, so violently that according to one authority the blood would spurt from his body and stain the walls of his ascetic cell. And it worked! Cupertino, a contemporary of Carlini, went into ecstatic trances very frequently, often (reportedly) levitating before large audiences, once during a visit by Pope Urban VIII.

One might even speculate, albeit somewhat hazardously, that the abuse of children by MBP mothers in modern culture echoes a similar but adaptive role in shaman-revering cultures. In particular, the induction of hypoxic seizures in children by partial suffocation is very common in MBP cases. Aside from the inherent trauma, partial suffocation would tend to establish in the child the neurological instability which is, on a biomedical level at least, the essential feature of shamanism.

SEXUAL AMBIGUITY

The apparent association between Münchausenian behaviour, Multiple Personality Disorder, mediumship, spirit-possession, and shamanism, suggests that all of the former might be outgrowths or atavisms of the latter. In fact, this has already been postulated by other writers for all of the above, save Münchausenian behaviour. If, as I suspect, Münchausen's and Münchausen's-by-proxy also spring from an ancient shamanic reflex, we might expect to see in Münchauseians the sorts of things one sees in dissociative, more obviously shamanic individuals – such as an interest in alternative religions, claims of harassment by obscure or demonic forces, hysterical eating disorders, and even the confusion over sexual identity that is so common among medicine men and women.

Of course, investigating the background of Münchausenians is inherently problematic, given their notorious reluctance to tell the unvarnished truth, but it seems worth noting that at the trial of Beverly Allitt, it was revealed that she was a closet lesbian with a serious eating disorder, who on several occasions before becoming a nurse had indulged in mischievous behaviour - setting curtains on fire, putting a knife through her bedroom pillow – which she afterwards had attributed to oppressing poltergeists. **FT**

Jim Schnabel is a freelance journalist whose history of alien abduction research, *Dark White*, will be published by Hamish Hamilton in 1994. An earlier version of his Münchausen's-and-mysticism thesis appeared in *MUFON UFO Journal* (May 1993).

"Get a photo of it and I'll investigate it."

BOB RICKARD talks to JOHN BLASHFORD-SNELL, the man who's most at home when he's heading for terra incognita

THE EXPEDITION

Without a doubt John Blashford-Snell is Britain's nearest equivalent to Indiana Jones – he seems to have stepped out of the pages of Rider Haggard, lacking only Alan Quartermain's leopard skin hatband. A soldier-traveller, he has packed more adventure into his life than most us even read about. Everything about him underlines this impression; for example, when I asked Carol Turner at Expedition Base – his current headquarters, where he's known as JBS, or Colonel John – for any maps of where JBS has been, she sighed: "It's a tall order, because he's been pretty much everywhere."

Born in 1936, the son of a vicar, he became a commissioned officer in the Royal Engineers at the age of 20. He made the most of every opportunity to develop his talents for leadership and exploration and a spectacular string of successful ventures – including the Blue Nile (1968), the British Trans-Americas (1971-72) and epic Zaire River (1974-75) expeditions – earned him an MBE, the Livingstone Medal and the Segrave Trophy.

In 1969 he helped found the Scientific Exploration Society: "There were 10 of us who sat around a kitchen table in Camden in 1969 – so next year is our 25th anniversary." As well as writing a number of books on military matters, explorers and explorations, JBS put most of his adventures of Fortean interest into *Mysteries: Encounters with the Unexplained* in 1983.

During his 37 years in the British Army he ran Operation Drake (from 1978) to provide "inspiring challenges" for young people. In 1984 this gave way to Operation Raleigh which took over 8,000 youngsters on adventurous expeditions, conservation and community tasks. On retiring from the Army at the end of 1990, JBS promptly founded Discovery Expeditions to satisfy the adventurous spirit of the wrinkled over-25s.

"Older people now are fitter, live longer, have more leisure and are curious – they want to see what there is in the world that they can pit themselves against. They believe that youth is only a state of mind. So we take two or three Discovery Expeditions a year to various parts of the globe to investigate some mystery or to help the environment, the ecology or the people, or to do medical work."

John Blashford-Snell, Britain's Indiana Jones

JBS himself fits the prescription – an impossibly fit 56, this veritable dynamo still finds time to be a family man, chairman of the Scientific Exploration Society (SES), chairman of the British Chapter of the American-based Explorer's Club,

ST

and fit in "a spot of work for the Ministry of Defence".

"It's a very busy life," he says with typical understatement.

MAMMOTH FOOTSTEPS

We met in a private room at the Sheraton Park Tower in Knightsbridge, which the Explorers' Club use as their European headquarters. The association is symbiotic, as displays of the Club's memorabilia in the bar have become a great attraction. The hotel's generosity will soon stretch to a permanent suite with display cases on the first floor. "We're very grateful to the Sheraton for providing it," said JBS.

I asked how he first learned of the strange new elephants his team found in western Nepal. "I was on an SES expedition to Mount Xixabangma in Tibet, near its border with Nepal. We had stopped in Katmandu to get our stores, so I lunched there with a friend of mine, John Edwards, who runs Tiger Mountain, probably the premier organisation in Nepal for treks, sherpas and what have you… At the end of lunch he told of stories of a mammoth-like creature living in the jungles of west Nepal. I'd had a few beers by this point, and I rather laughed at him, saying something like: 'Get a photograph and I'll come and investigate it.'"

JBS didn't give it any more thought until two years later, when a young lady walked into his office in the MoD with three slides taken at long distance from a canoe moving down the Karnali River. They showed a very strange elephant-like creature, with an enormous bump on its large head, a huge, almost grotesque body, and what appeared to be a ribbed, almost reptilian tail. "They were clearly not a hoax," he said. He showed them to various experts and they all said that they'd not seen anything like it before.

The distinctive nasal ridge and twin-domed head are reminiscent of prehistoric drawings of mammoths. Just how the Bardia bulls relate to more primitive elephants like the extinct stegodon remains to be discovered. Inset: a mammoth from a cave wall at Les Eyzies, Dordogne.

The formidable wild tusker Rajah Gaj. Due to obvious difficulties, measuring his height taxed the team's ingenuity. They determined he was close to their original estimate at 11ft 3ins and 50 years old, while his companion Kancha was about 10ft 6ins and about 40 years old.

Colonel John and his colleagues took their first expedition to Nepal's Royal Bardia National Park in 1991. They found only footprints, but what footprints! They were 22 inches across. Following a reliable and well-known formula, they deduced that the creature was something over 11 foot, bigger than the largest known Asian elephant – a bull shot in Ceylon in 1882 – which stood 11ft 1in high.

MEETING THE GIANTS

The following year – 1992 – they went back again with Nepalese naturalists and biologist Mark O'Shea, the curator of reptiles at the West Midlands Safari Park. "He's a slightly mad Irishman, who's just been bitten on the wrist by a rattle snake." I was beginning to notice that JBS's narrative is peppered with characters – scientists become 'snake men' or 'plant people', while the lay members of the teams are introduced as "the publican of the Jolly Woodman at Slough who's a great man on dolphins", or "an engineer from Huddersfield who's an expert on moss". They tend to be exceptional, qualified people whose outside interests become an asset to their team. The kind of people, said JBS, "who would ask sensible questions about the odd things we find, and get pretty meaningful answers."

The Royal Bardia National Park is about 1,000 square kilometres of virgin *sal* forest lying in a huge valley. It was formerly a private hunting area for the King, who had kept everyone out. JBS sent word ahead to the people who live and work in the area to seek out some tracks in advance of their arrival. This paid off; on their first morning there, they set out on elephants and picked up some tracks without difficulty, following them to

"The only way to search the area was on elephant."

a small copse.

"The girls," as JBS affectionately calls the elephants, "all stopped, looked straight ahead to the trees and began purring. They were obviously talking amongst themselves and do this anyway with rhino or tiger. Of course you trust your elephants implicitly. They're damned nearly human. If you drop your lens cap they'll pick it up and hand it back to you. A relationship with an elephant is an amazing thing, and without a doubt they're my favourite animal."

David Warren ("a chief-inspector from Grimsby who's a keen bird man with damned good eyes") who shared JBS's elephant, shouted "Christ!" What looked like a pile of grey rocks began to move. "Suddenly this enormous head came out from behind the *sal* trees, and the girls started to shuffle back. For a moment there was chaos – we were all a bit perturbed. Then out of the trees came not one, but *two*, enormous elephants with these bumps or domes. They were gigantic bulls."

The smaller of the two – Kancha ('youngest') – was the more aggressive, and appeared to act as an escort to the older giant, who was called Rajah Gaj ('King Elephant'). Both were frequently seen tossing trees aside with frightening ease. There were many dangerous incidents, which, typically, JBS laughs off as marvellous photo opportunities – "Our cameras were going like crazy... Kodak made millions that day."

One night, Rajah Gaj slid noiselessly into the camp and stole Honey Blossom, JBS's elephant, snapping her tethering chains like a piece of string. Tracking them by torchlight, JBS stumbled onto Rajah Gaj himself. "You do feel slightly ridiculous, in a sarong, being chased around some trees by a randy elephant at midnight." This elephantine feat of stealth and strength impressed them greatly. "We knew then that we were dealing with a highly intelligent and sophisticated animal."

By the end of their stay the expedition had found no trace of any herd of cow elephants, despite the rumours of them. The film and photos they brought back were shown on CNN all over the world. A third expedition was arranged for Spring 1993. Dr Chris Thouless, an elephant expert ("who got the Queen's Gallantry Medal about 18 months ago for saving a woman who was skewered to a tree by an elephant in Kenya") accompanied them. This time the bulls were easy to locate because they had just destroyed a banana plantation and rampaged through a village. The team trailed the old tusker. "It was like following a council house on wheels as he rocked from side to side like a great ship. We got some of our best photographs about this time. He could turn very fast and could have outrun the girls – it was pretty scary."

MURDEROUS BULL

Again they found no sign of other elephants, although villagers remembered a herd of around ten animals with three massive bulls some years ago. Its matriarch had disappeared with the calves, and a year or two later a murderous bull called Milo vanished too. It is thought they went towards India to another area of forest. JBS said they learned of a big herd in that direction, at Sukla Phanta. Finding those cows will be the objective of future expeditions.

Chris Thouless went off to report to the Asian

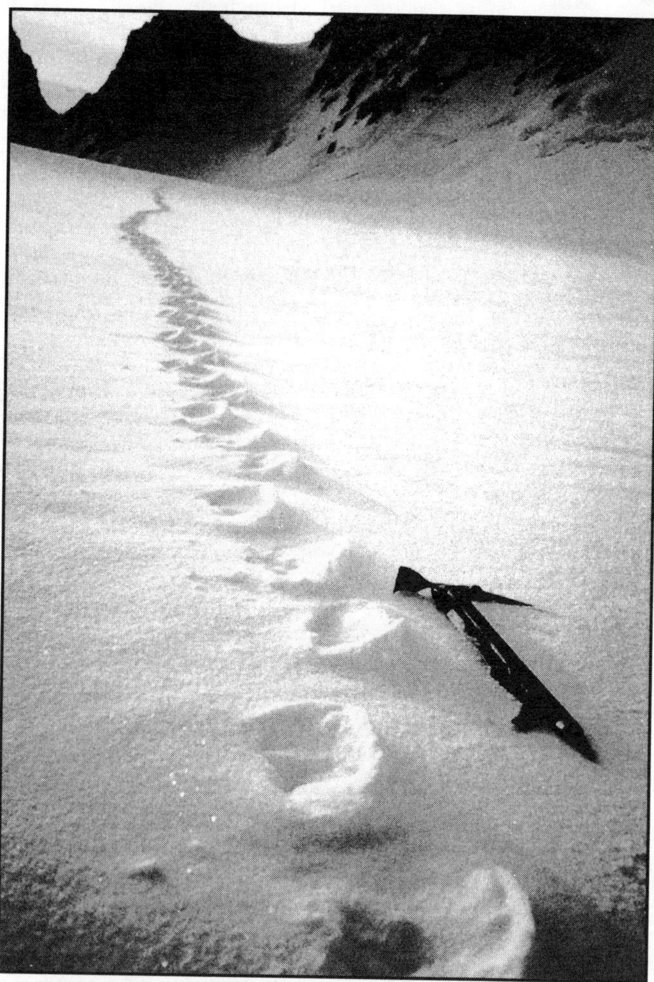

These still unidentified tracks, stretching for 1.5km across the Alexandroff Glacier, were photographed during the Mongolian Expedition in 1992 by mountaineer Julian Freeman-Attwood, in an area the Mongolians believe to be populated by wildmen they call Almas. The safe explanation is that they were made by a Siberian bear, but considered opinion points to un-bear-like features such as shape and gait.

elephant conference, while JBS went to Assam to speak to the elephant breeders there. Nobody had ever seen anything quite like these bumpy bulls. Meanwhile, Clive Coy of the Royal Tyrrell Museum in Alberta, studying the pictures, drew attention to the resemblance of the bulls to a stegodon. Further identification would need physical evidence, but then, said JBS, "A few weeks ago I heard that some have been found. They may be fossils, but one zoologist on the spot has examined them and said they were quite different from *Elephantus maximus* which is the normal Asian elephant."

JBS stresses that no one is saying these wild tuskers are living mammoths, but (and this is almost as exciting) they could be the nearest thing to it. "I don't want people to think I'm making any false claims... As far as I'm concerned it's a most extraordinary type of elephant. Of course they want you to say it's a mammoth... but I can't do that, and nor can anyone until we have more evidence. Chris Thouless, speaking as a zoologist, thinks its simply a big elephant at the extreme of its development. Until we see the herd of cows we won't know whether these are mutant features."

JBS turned the conversation towards the responsibility that such a discovery brings. "The most important part of discovery is to use it as a tool for conservation. Just imagine if a *mokele mbembe* was discovered by Bill Gibbons and then someone went and shot it... These wild tuskers may be the last two of their type in existence, because they have become separated from the main herd. So it is important now, to use this interest to conserve the remaining herds of Asian elephant, because there's no doubt the herds are declining as more of their habitat is threatened."

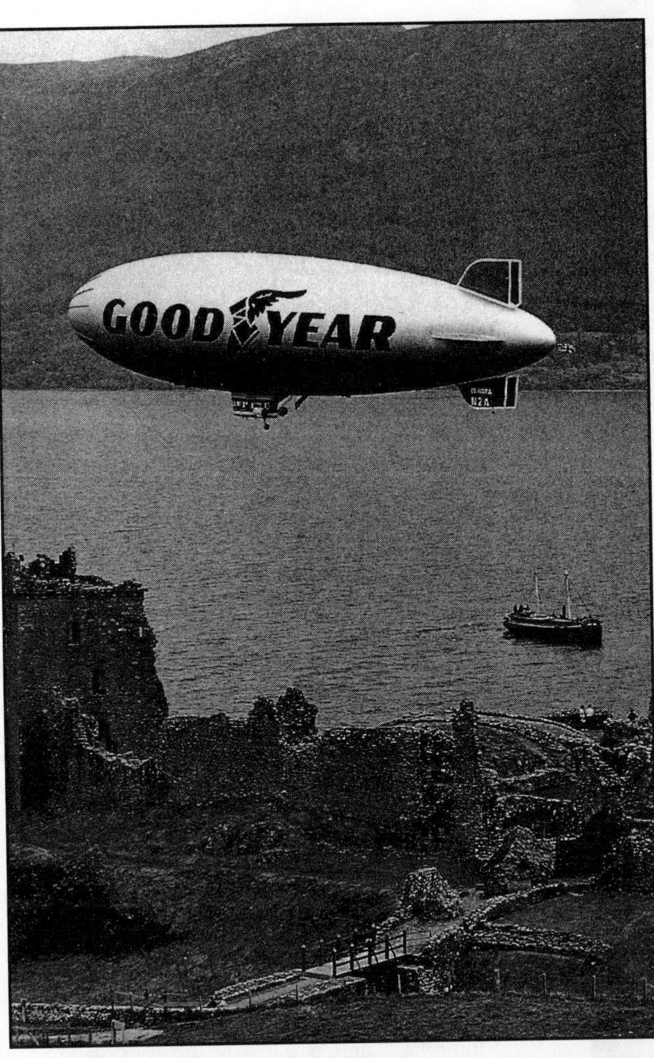

JBS joined the Loch Ness and Morar Survey teams in the summer of 1982. The latest Army sonar devices were deployed on the barge 'Phyllis' moored by Urquhart Castle as the airship 'Europa' monitored the loch from on high.

MONSTROUS PROJECTS

Had he ever thought of adding the *mokele mbembe* to his list of projects? "Well," he said, "Bill Gibbons has asked me several times if I'd be interested in coming to the Congo. I would, but I think I'd need a bit more substantial evidence before I can commit what are, after all, considerable funds to such a venture. As I said to John Edwards, get a photograph of the thing and I'll come with a team to study it."

Getting to the Royal Bardia National Park was itself an adventure, involving a 60 mile hike and a scary ride over the raging rapids of the Karnali River.

On the other hand, they occasionally add a hunt for a poorly-substantiated but interesting animal to their itinerary in a region they are already planning to visit. As preparation for a trip to Guyana in late August/September, JBS interviewed some ex-soldiers turned 'pork-knockers' (diamond miners). "With much swearing on their mothers' graves they talked about seeing this giant anaconda with horns – the *Camoodi* they called it." Twenty feet is not exceptional for an anaconda, but the horns are. Not surprisingly, Mark O'Shea, "the snake man", is in on this trip.

JBS revealed that they had outline plans for trips as far ahead as 2001. He is convinced that time put in on reconnaissance and planning is essential; it certainly paid off on his expeditions to date. On his last trip to Uttar Pradesh in India, he heard tell of an apparently prehistoric tribe that had no knowledge of fire, living in caves on the border. "The area was closed so I couldn't get up there. That is going to be a fascinating area to explore when it opens up."

Among the many exciting adventures during Operation Drake visits to Papua New Guinea in 1979, they investigated the local belief in a huge tree-climbing crocodile called the 'Artrellia'. It turned out to be a Salvador's monitor lizard. At six foot in length, this specimen is still a baby.

WILDMEN AND NESSIE

I asked him if there were parts of the former Soviet Union he'd like to visit. He seemed less than enthusiastic: "I went into Siberia a few years ago, and last year we had a big expedition to Mongolia, with Julian Freeman-Attwood. But Russia is becoming difficult. They want money for everything now."

But what about the wildman sightings there? He is no stranger to the subject – he has met many primary witnesses, talked to Dr Jeanne Kofman, and Odette Tchernine, the great pioneer of Yeti-searching, was once his literary agent. "I think that if the Almas, or Yeti, is ever found it will be in Mongolia. There is a greater proportion of people there who claimed to have seen it firsthand. I've never come across this elsewhere. They are regarded as not particularly unusual, just 'wild people'.

Knowing of his enthusiasm for the Loch Ness Monster in *Mysteries*, I wondered what he thought about Nessie now. "There's got to be an explanation", he said. "I've never seen anything there myself, but I went with Tim Dinsdale in 1982 to interview a few people who had seen something when I was a disbeliever. I do think there is something there, but I don't know what. I can't believe it's *all* a hoax. It's a pity the subject is fogged by hoaxes, just like Bigfoot."

"I've often wondered whether Nessie was supernatural. It depends whether you believe in ghosts... whether it could be a ghost. But that wouldn't account for the sonar echoes. I've seen it on sonar." JBS is partial to ghosts, "but I've never seen one myself."

BIZARRE BANQUETS

Out of curiosity, I asked JBS what was the most disgusting thing he'd ever eaten. He really had to think about that one. I had expected an answer on a level with Frank Buckland's legendary appetites, but he replied: "Monkey turns you off, it looks rank. I suppose Wichitty grubs..." Most explorers now are conservationists, he explained. "In the field you sometimes have to live on what you can get – but I wouldn't kill any endangered thing."

But what about the bizarre dishes, like rhino's pizzles, served at club and society dinners? "It's a spoof," he said. It seems that long ago the Aga Khan "or somebody" took exception to one of their "exotic hors d'oeuvres" and complained to Prince Philip that they were eating endangered species. JBS laughed loudly as he said that Prince Philip resigned on the spot. "The poor old club president, an eminent scientist, flew to London to explain that it was just a joke, but that was that. Now, when we have our Discoverers' Dinner, it's just a fun evening, with normal dishes given exotic names; for example, we'll call beef 'yak steaks' or something."

Rather sheepishly, I asked if he was getting tired and jaded. "Not at all," he fired back. "The world is still an exciting place, with lots of things still to be seen and done. I want to concentrate, in the years left to me, in getting like-minded people to come with me. That's the idea behind Discovery Expeditions Ltd, and I don't mind you saying we are always happy to hear from people who are interested. They can write to us at: Expedition Base, Motcombe, Dorset SP7 9PB – or phone 0747 54456." FT

At the earliest opportunity, a Discovery Expedition will investigate the contentious existence of Loys' ape, of which the only evidence is this photograph taken by Swiss geologist François de Loys, on the border between Colombia and Venezuela, moments after shooting it in 1917.

I-CON MAN

The holy relics of Christendom have been a byword for credulity and gullibility ever since the scathing commentaries of Erasmus and Calvin nearly 500 years ago. In 'Three's a Shroud', an exhibition held at the Rosamund Felsen Gallery in Los Angeles last April, American artist Jeffrey Vallance displays a range of objects and images based on the Shroud of Turin, the Veil of Veronica and the Holy Lance of Longinus. His deadpan commentary on the tradition of relic veneration bears directly on our perception of 'originality' and the nature of fetishism and physical evidence. EDWARD YOUNG considers the significance of faking religious relics

Jeffrey Vallance working at the Schosserei Eidherr in Klosterneuburg, Austria, 1992

Jeffrey Vallance likes to forge counterfeit artifacts *without irony*, wedding the ridiculous to the sublime. In a masterstroke of fraud, he has presented his own version of the Richard Nixon Library & Birthplace, a museum devoted to the former US president who was himself known for mixing truth and fiction. While it is commonplace to assert that history is a fiction, artifice parading as objective record, the message of Vallance is more subtle and elusive.

His phony relics expose the social mechanisms underlying belief of any kind, whether in history, art, ideology or religion. They also comment on a side-effect of our economic system: in the welter of perpetual novelty demanded by consumerism, the line between souvenirs and artifacts is inevitably blurred. His multiple copies of the holy lance (which supposedly pierced the side of Jesus) and the Veil of Veronica (which bears an alleged image of His face) – relics made venerable by their direct contact with the blood of Christ – continue the mediæval tradition of relic multiplication, as well as undermining our desire for the 'original' objects and amplifying their iconic power by repetition (a method popularised by Warhol). It was long believed that the sacred quality of a relic could be passed on by touching it to the original, a process of magical contamination.

His phony relics expose the social mechanisms underlying belief of any kind

Vallance's tone is described by Amy Gerstler in the magazine *Artforum* as approximately "the fusion of an overzealous, fixational seventh-grader's-international-affairs report; the knowing/naive diction of a 1956 World Book Encyclopædia entry; a rapt article in some fringe phenomena magazine like *Fate* or *UFO Digest*; and the travel notebooks of an eccentric uncle."

With their considered and elegant presentation, the Vallance 'relics' revel in their falsity, as if being counterfeit was no cause for embarrassment. They supersede Feuerbach's judgment that capitalist culture prefers "the sign to the thing signified, the copy to the original, fancy to reality", preferring, in the words of Ralph Rugoff, "not so much copy over original, as the equivocal tension between them".

Vallance's works are also documents, records of a performance lasting several months. He writes to myriad institutions and meets the relevant authorities, incorporating evidence of these activities in his presentations. An exhibition of his shroud drawings in Turin, for instance, included objects borrowed from the official shroud museum. This connection to recognised authority confers a certain legitimacy and in return devalues official rhetoric by pointing up its arbitrary nature. Giving symbols a life of their own is something Vallance has explored throughout his career. After all, he once transformed a frozen chicken into a universal icon of martyrdom (see 'Shroud of Blinky', *FT53:23*).

In presenting fake religious relics as art, Vallance implies that our relationship to representation – particularly the display of physical evidence – combines awe and misdirected faith. He

Above: 'La Santa Lancia' (the Holy Lance and leather.

counsels us against a metaphysics that pits the true against the false. In a world whose official surface is a tissue of lies and disinformation, uncertainty and doubt are far more appropriate attitudes than belief. As with the writing of Charles Fort, we can never really gauge to what extent Vallance is pulling our collective leg. Even though his exhibitions exude the air of a practical joke, many truths can best be imparted through humour.

The Spear of Destiny

Michaelangelo's dome atop St Peter's Basilica in Rome is supported by four colossal piers each containing the statue of a saint in a niche: Andrew, Helena, Veronica and Longinus. The statues display symbols of relics which were preserved in chapels high up in each of the pillars. Of the four relics, the head of St Andrew was returned in 1963 to the Greek Orthodox on the island of Patmos. The fragment of the cross is but one of the many from the discovery of the True Cross in Jerusalem by Helena, the mother of the Emperor Constantine. Veronica is *Vera Iconica*, the 'True Image' of Christ preserved on a cloth or napkin. The Veil of Veronica, also known as the Sudarium, Mandylion, Holy Handkerchief or Holy Vernacle, is the third relic. Longinus was the Roman soldier who converted to Christianity after piercing the crucified Christ with his spear, the latter being the fourth relic.

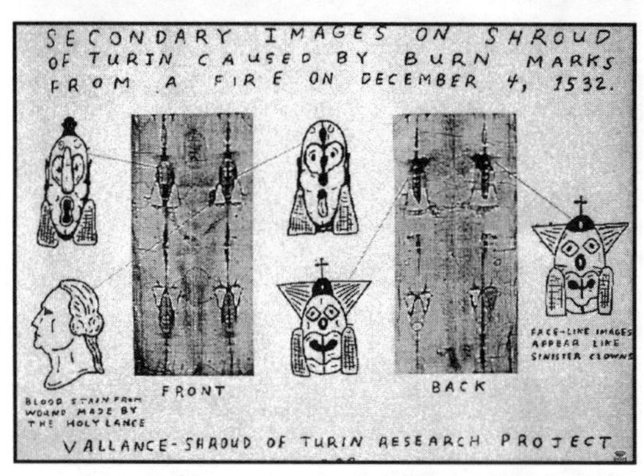

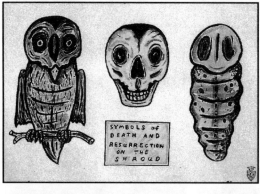

Symbols of death and resurrection – secondary 'accidental' images on the shroud of Turin – re-drawn by Jeffrey Vallance.

After it was thrust into Jesus, the Emperor Caligula used it to kill his pregnant sister

Saint John's Gospel tells us that as Christ hung on the cross, "one of the soldiers with a spear pierced his side, and forthwith came there out blood and water". The flow of blood that would have been caused by such a spear appears in the Turin Shroud image. The Roman soldier is traditionally known as the centurion Gaius Cassius Longinus, and his spear or lance immediately became invested with mysterious and awesome power. The sixth-century St Antoninus of Piacenza states that he saw it in the basilica of Mount Sion in Jerusalem. Tradition claims that to escape the plunder of Jerusalem by King Chosroes of Persia in 614, it was brought to the Chapel of the Virgin at Pharos, Constantinople.

Like the other primary Christian relics – the crown of thorns, the true cross, the holy nails, and Christ's seemless robe – the holy lance had the gift of duplicating itself. In 1098, the crusaders conquered Antioch. St Anthony appeared in a dream to Peter Bartholomew of Provence and revealed that the lance was buried in St Peter's Cathedral there. It was unearthed and carried into victorious battle, later ending up in Constantinople like the Jerusalem relic. A third lance, known as the Spear of St Maurice, appeared in the imperial treasury in Vienna and became part of the insignia of the Holy Roman Emperors. A fourth, kept at Etchmiadzin, belongs to the Armenian church, to whom (according to a 13th century chronicle) it was given by Jesus's disciple Thaddeus.

ey Vallance (1992). Iron, brass, steel

One of the Byzantine lances was given to the French king Louis IX by Baldwin II in 1241, while the other reached Rome, a gift of Sultan Beyazit II to Pope Innocent VIII, in the 1480s, and is allegedly the one now kept in the Longinus pillar in St Peter's, sculpted by Bernini. The French lance disappeared during the Revolution. Many copies were made over the centuries, the last documented being a replica of the Spear of St Maurice allowed by the Emperor Franz Joseph of Austria in 1913.

Fantastic legends accrued to the lance of Longinus. It was forged from meteoric iron by Tubal-Cain, born to the seventh generation of Adam and the last generation of Cain, which naturally tainted the weapon with the Mark of Cain. It belonged to Kings David and Solomon, was jabbed into Julius Caesar by Brutus, and into the first-born of Judæa by order of King Herod. After it was thrust into Jesus, the Emperor Caligula used it to kill his pregnant sister. It subsequently passed through the hands of Constantine, Attila, Saint George, Sir Lancelot, Charlemagne, Frederick Barbarossa.... You name him, he had it. Hitler swiped the Spear of St Maurice in 1938 (along with the rest of the Hapsburg regalia) and kept it in Nuremberg, until the Americans seized it on the very day that he (allegedly) committed suicide in the bunker. The whole occult farrago can be read in all its dubious and delirious detail in Trevor Ravenscroft's *Spear of Destiny* (1972).

The Spear of St Maurice, *die Heilige Lanze,* is on display at the Schatzkammer (Treasure Chamber) of the Hapsburg Palace in Vienna. It is just over a foot long. At some point, a nail from the crucifixion was added. The centre of the spear was hollowed out and the Holy Nail inserted, and bound into place with gold wire. The spear had been broken and the two halves joined by a sheath of silver, while two gold crosses were inlaid into the base near the haft.

The four clowns of Turin – secondary images on the Shroud – re-drawn by Jeffrey Vallance.

The Clowns of Turin

Besides the image of a tortured and crucified man, some have claimed to see 'other' images on the Shroud of Turin such as coins on the eyes, chin bindings, packets on the forehead called 'phylacteries' and cryptic words and letters.

A group of secondary images caused by burn marks from the fire of 1532 (and subsequent patching by Poor Clare nuns) produced what appear to be sinister clown-like faces. Some believed that the devil tried to burn the Shroud, and when this proved unsuccessful he created the scorch marks (which are actually darker than the Holy Face) in an attempt at mockery. People have also claimed to have seen symbols of death, resurrection and procreation, including likenesses of owls, skulls, cocoons, atomic weapons, as well as the reproductive organs of both sexes.

In the *Three's a Shroud* exhibition, Vallance had a series of drawings of these secondary 'accidental' images, some of which are reproduced here. These images call to mind the way researchers studying the Virgin of Guadeloupe shroud have found countless pictures concealed in the Virgin's eye.

The bloodstain allegedly made by the Holy Lance forms a profile that has been likened to that of President Washington [see ***FT65:64***]. The Shroud owl resembles the North American barn Owl *Tyto alba pratincola (Bonaparte),* also known by the French-Canadian name of *Læffraie* ('the frightener') because during nocturnal flight the white underside can be perceived as a ghostly spectre. The Shroud's cocoon image resembles the chrysalis of the Death's-head Moth *Acherontia atropos,* which shrieks and feeds on deadly nightshade. **FT**

ROVERS RETURN

Dogs and other household pets sometimes make extraordinary – almost unbelievable – journeys to their old homes or to rejoin human companions who have since moved house.

***Paul Sieveking** reviews some of the epic canine walkabouts of the 20th century*

The phenomenal journeys of cats and dogs were cited by Charles Fort as examples of the magic which surrounds everyday life. He witnessed one such journey while he lived in Marchmont Street, London. The dog who lived in the house "had frenzies. Once he tore down the landlord's curtains. He bit holes into a book of mine, and chewed the landlord's slippers." The landlord dumped him out of London about ten miles, but he found his way back. "I cannot accept that the magician [as Fort called the dog] smelled his way home, or picked up a trail, taking about two weeks on his way. The smelling played a part, and was useful in a final recognition: but smelling indiscriminately, he could have nosed his way, for years, through the streets of London, before coming to the right scent." (*Wild Talents*, chapter 27.)

Fort gives two other instances of canine journeys: a large mongrel, taken 340 miles in a baggage car, found his way home (*New York Sun*, 24 April 1931); and a Canadian dog found his way home over 400 miles away (*New York Herald Tribune*, 4 July 1931.)

Some time after its arrival in India the dog disappeared, and a few months later it bounded into the house of its master in Inverkeithing. Evidently, it had stowed away at Calcutta on a ship bound for Dundee

Our latest prodigious canine journey comes from an Associated Press wire of 1 September 1992: "A dog swam three rivers, walked eight miles and then kept a week's vigil outside a jail until his master, held for assault, was released", according to the Bangladeshi *Sangbad* newspaper. Sohrad Ali was arrested for critically wounding a neighbour in a land dispute in the village of Nakla, Sherpur district. His dog swam behind the boat that ferried him across the first river, braving blows rained on his head by the boatman.

Perhaps the most celebrated travelling dog was Prince, the collie/Irish terrier crossbreed who joined his master in the trenches during World War I. James Brown went to France with the 1st North Staffordshire Regiment in September 1914, leaving Prince with his wife in Buttevant, Ireland. She took him to Hammersmith, London, where he disappeared. After a fruitless search, she wrote to tell her husband the sad news; but the following day she heard that Prince was with him in France, where he had turned up two weeks after disappearing.

Brown, then Adjutant's servant, was returning to his quarters near Armentières on horseback when a friend in his battalion called out to him: "I've got your dog here, Jimmy". Brown took it as a joke, but he dismounted and found that it was indeed Prince. The regiment adopted Prince as mascot and he stayed in France throughout the war. He learnt many tricks and was a champion ratter, once killing 137 rats in one day. Prince returned to England in May 1919, and he was much feted; but his years of war service wore him out prematurely and he died on 18 July 1921, two years after his discharge. He was lying beside his kennel when he saw a mouse and gave chase; he caught it, but the exertion was too much for him. He crept away into a cellar and died.

Some odd cases of dogs finding their way home by public transport are given by Edwin Arnold in *The Soul of the Beast* (1960). One is of a terrier which travelled by train from London to its old home in Staines, Middlesex, where it was caught and returned to its master. The guard of an early morning train at Bishop's Road station saw it entering one of the carriages. It alighted at West Drayton, where it was necessary to change for Staines, and went to the correct platform where it caught another train.

The most wonderful of such cases is of a collie sent off by its owner, living near the small port of Inverkeithing in Scotland, to a friend in Calcutta. Some time after its arrival in India the dog disappeared, and a few months later it bounded into the house of its master in Inverkeithing. Evidently, it had stowed away at Calcutta on a ship bound for Dundee. There it had disembarked and proceeded on a coastal vessel to Inverkeithing. It was suggested at the time that the collie had been attracted to the right vessel at Calcutta by the Scottish accents of the sailors!

We have on file the curious story of Spot, an eight-month-old cross-bred sheepdog, that made a 300-mile round trip to see the bright lights of London. He jumped a queue of 28 passengers and boarded a National Express coach at Cardiff bus station. He refused to budge and growled fiercely at inspectors and drivers who tried to coax him off with biscuits.

Driver Alan Watkins, 23, eventually set off 15 minutes late with his non-paying passenger curled up in the front seat. When the coach arrived at Victoria coach station, Spot jumped off and disappeared. Half an hour later, he reappeared, only minutes before the coach set off on its return journey. "He just settled back in the same seat", said Watkins, "and I explained to the passengers who made a great fuss of him." Spot was met by staff from the Cardiff RSPCA, who took him to their dogs' home.

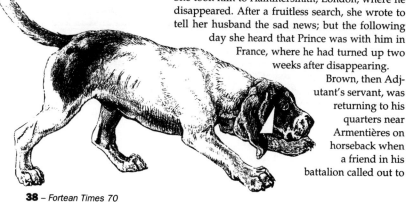

FORTEAN TIMES LEAGUE TABLE OF CANINE TREKKING

Each journey is headed by the name of the dog, the distance travelled and the year of departure. There are two categories: journeys to old homes and journeys to new homes to rejoin old human associates (indicated with an asterisk). Both types of journey show great fortitude and unexplained navigational abilities; journeys to new homes, however, are the more extraordinary and defy ready explanation, suggesting paranormal abilities. [For a corresponding League Table of Pussy Trekking, see FT61:46.]

1 BOBBIE, 3,000 miles, 1923

This dog was immortalised in Charles Alexander's Book, *Bobbie: A Great Collie of Oregon.* Bobbie belonged to a restaurant owner called Brazier from Silverton, Oregon, who in August 1923 was visiting relatives in Wolcott, Indiana. On 15 August, Bobbie got chased away by a pack of dogs while the owner was at a garage and could not be found. Six months later, on 15 February 1924, he arrived back at Silverton, dazed, hungry and exhausted. He had crossed the White River, the Wabash River and the Tippecanoe River, Iowa, Nebraska, the Great Plains and the Rocky Mountains.

On his return, he reverted to his days as a puppy, and made for an old farmhouse where he had been raised. There he was found by the farm tenants, asleep, on top of the grave of a fox terrier, his puppyhood companion. After he had been revived with food and drink, he hurried to the restaurant, and leapt onto the bed where his master was taking a nap. There was no doubt that he was the same dog; Mr Brazier recognised a scar and an injured hip sustained when he was a puppy. Thousands flocked to see the wonderful dog, for whom a model bungalow was built. He received a gold collar and a handful of medals and lived for another twelve years after his return.

From the statements of people with whom Bobbie stopped or by whom he was seen on his trip, it seems that at first he cast about in a wide arc of almost 1,000 miles before he could get his bearings and start on a straighter line for home.

2 NICK, 2,000 miles, 1979

This five-year-old Alsatian bitch got lost on a camping trip in the southern Arizona desert with her owner Doug Simpson of Selah, Washington. Mr Simpson searched for two weeks without success and then drove home. Four months later, Nick turned up, bloody, battered and emaciated. A familiar scar on her head confirmed her identity. Her journey had encompassed "some of the roughest terrain on earth" – scorching desert and – assuming she went in a straight line – the Grand Canyon, icy rivers and the snow-covered, 12,000-foot-high mountains of Nevada and Oregon.

3 JIMPA, 2,000 miles, 1978

Jimpa, a Labrador-boxer cross, was one of a litter sired by a dog bought by Lord Snowdon while making a film at Alice Springs. Snowdon sold Jimpa (Aboriginal for 'Little Dog') to motor mechanic Warren Dumesney, who in March 1978 took him to a farm at Nyabing, south of Perth, where he was working. A neighbour threw stones at the dog and he ran away. Fourteen months later, in May 1979, Jimpa turned up at Dumesney's home in Pimpinio, in Victoria. He must have walked across the almost waterless Nullabor Plain.

4 WHISKY, 1,800 miles, 1973

Truck driver Geoff Hancock lost his fox terrier when he stopped off at a cafe near Darwin, Australia, in October 1973. Whisky turned up at his owner's Melbourne home nine months later.

5 BARRY, 1,200 miles, 1973*

Armin da Broi, 23, sold his Alsatian, Barry, when he became too big for his flat in Bari, southern Italy. Armin then moved to Solingen, West Germany, and a year later, on Christmas Eve, the dog was found whimpering outside his flat. Armin vowed they would not be parted again.

6 SPOOK, 1,000 miles, 1976

In December 1976, Christine and Michael Rowe were taking the night ferry through the Haro Strait a mile off the coastline of British Columbia on their way to Alaska, where Mr Rowe was taking up a new job. Spook, their Alsatian, was nowhere to be found, and it was concluded that he must have fallen overboard. The captain said it would be useless to turn around and search for him in the dark; in any case, the water was so icy that the dog would not survive more than a few minutes.

Seven months later, they returned to their old home in Sacramento, California, to see relatives. Mrs Rowe went to the town's dog pound to collect her brother's terrier which had been picked up by the local dog patrol. In a nearby cage she saw Spook, looking emaciated. He howled until his cage was opened and Mrs Rowe clasped him in her arms.

James Camberton, the pound warden, told her that he had been picked up 100 yards from his old home, and that the dog pound staff had never seen an animal with such worn down paws and nails. Spook was due to be put down the following day if no-one had claimed him. The Rowes flew back to Alaska, taking Spook with them.

7 VESNA, 1,100 miles, 1979*

Viktor (or Vyacheslav) Strupovets (or Stupovyets), 45, a Russian engineer, had to leave his pet German shepherd dog Vesna behind in Kuybyshev in the Urals when he moved to a better job in Mozyr in Byelorussia, because no animals were allowed in his new flat. Vesna was left with friends of the family, but she broke her chain and wandered off in April 1979. One evening, nearly four years later, as he was walking home from work, Viktor felt something nudging the back of his legs. It was Vesna, tired, bedraggled and thin. The council of the block of flats where the Strupovets family lived were so impressed by the amazing journey that they allowed the dog to stay with the family.

8 FIDO, 1,000 miles, 1989*

Lise Deremier put her sheepdog in a boarding kennel when she moved from Mons in Belgium to Gijon in northern Spain. When Lise and her Spanish husband Jose sent for him, they were told he had been given to new owners. Two years later, she opened her front door to go shopping and tripped over Fido on her doorstep. He had a distinctive white patch on his nose and only answered to French.

   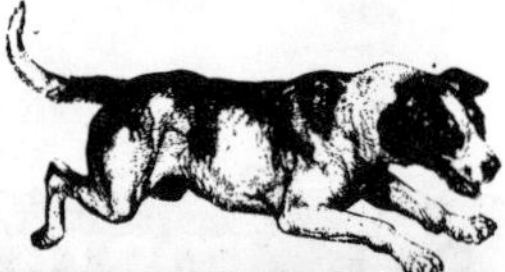

FORTEAN TIMES LEAGUE TABLE OF CANINE TREKKING

9 SAM, 840 miles, 1983*

Debbie and Ray Foltz sold their six-year-old terrier-poodle cross before moving from Montrose, Colorado, to Santee, California, in January 1983. Ten weeks later, they found the dog on their doorstep, very weak and covered with grease. His paws were blistered and he was suffering from malnutrition and muscle spasms.

10 REX, 750 miles, 1977

Suzanne le Goff, 56, lost her brown Alsatian while visiting her daughter Liliane in Roscoff, Brittany, in the summer of 1977. During the subsequent eight months, she made several trips back to Roscoff from her home in Toulon, in search of her pet. Then her grandson, Pascal Peron, called, not knowing she was away in Roscoff. Rex was lying on the doorstep, painfully thin, his fur matted with mud and dried blood, and his paws badly torn.

11 JESSE, 650 miles, 1977

Jack Millikan, 23, driving from Illinois to California, pulled off the Interstate highway in July 1977 to take a rest. When he pulled back on the highway he was stopped by police, who told him he had been in an accident, was swerving all over the place and was apparently suffering from sunstroke. Witnesses to the accident said they saw his four-year-old Irish setter, Jesse, limping away from the car towards the North Platte River, near Lincoln, Nebraska. Millikan organised a hunt, but all that was found were a few traces of fresh blood.

Six months later, on 5 December, Millikan opened his front door to go shopping in South Elgin, Illinois, and there was Jesse, scruffy, matted, dirty and skinny. A wound on her right leg had healed remarkably well. She had no address tag on her collar and she had never been anywhere near Nebraska before.

12 REX, 620 miles, 1990

The owner of this seven-year-old Belgian sheepdog left him in September 1990 with relatives in Nimes to be trained, but he escaped and made his way home to Metz several weeks later. His master declared himself to be 'very moved' by the dog's exploit, but he left Rex with a friend 'for the weekend' in late July 1991, and never returned. By the time of the news report in August, Rex was being held in the local dog pound.

13 BEDE, 300 miles, 1976

This grey-haired setter got lost while on holiday in Cornwall with its owner, Father Louis Heston, a Roman Catholic priest from Braintree in Essex. Six months later, Bede turned up in Braintree, half-starved and scruffy and was given refuge by a householder. He mentioned the dog to the postman, who was one of father Heston's parishioners. The priest took his dog on a convalescent holiday – to Cornwall.

14 DOMA, 300 miles, 1982

This German shepherd disappeared from the home of her owner, Rick Sellard, in Yuma, Arizona, just after she had bred her second litter. Four months later, she turned up with a new puppy on the porch of Rick's parents, Virgil and Vicki Sellard, near the Mexican border. Duma had a scar on her rump from being hit by a car, which confirmed the identification of the dog.

15 VIXEN, 250 miles, 1990

This white husky trekked 250 miles along the Siberian coast, from Provideniya to Uelen, with her owner, Sue Steinacher, an artist and teacher from Nome, Alaska. A plane carrying her, two Soviet mushers and about 30 sled dogs crashed after takeoff from Uelen on the Bering Strait, on 13 April 1990. A Soviet musher died, along with two of Steinacher's dogs. Vixen and another dog couldn't be found. "I saw her running around outside the plane. She was in bad shape", said Steinacher, who suffered four broken ribs and bruises.

Later, she had a report that Vixen had been shot by Siberian Eskimos defending wild reindeer herds from wolves; but it was her other missing dog which was shot and killed. Then Asanassi Makovnev, the leader of an earlier dog sled expedition, flew to Provideniya to check out another white dog report. It was Vixen, who had taken up residence in a half-buried pipe. He coaxed the frightened animal from her lair, and she was flown back to Nome on 1 July.

16 SANDY, 240 miles, 1942

Sandy was a barracks mongrel with the Royal Signals Company in Egypt during World War II. He had long hair, short legs and was of uncertain age. Posted from Alexandria to Mersah Matruh, Sandy had to be evacuated when Rommel drove the Eighth Army back to El Alamein. The truck Sandy was in was intercepted, the crew was taken prisoner and Sandy got a German boot. A few weeks later, he turned up at the barracks in Alexandria. He had crossed 240 miles of desert in the midst of intense fighting.

17 GUARD, 225 miles, 1977

Bernard Parks, 26, left Chula, Missouri, for a part-time job in Springfield, taking Guard, his five-year-old English sheepdog. Guard disappeared two days later. Parks returned to Chula 16 months later, having crossed the rugged peaks and dense wilderness of the Missouri Ozark mountains. He was tired, dirty and 20 pounds lighter.

18 HENRY, 100 miles, 1980

When Mrs Ruth de Savary sold her hotel in Chedington, West Dorset, she left her cocker spaniel with people in Devon. Three years later, the dog turned up at the hotel, then owned by Hilary and Philip Chapman. He was filthy, starving and ill, with a big sore on his head. He was allowed to stay on at the hotel.

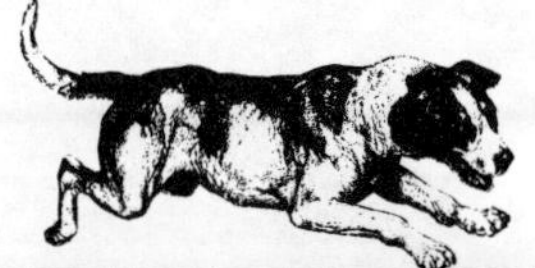

FORTEAN TIMES LEAGUE TABLE OF CANINE TREKKING

19 ANNI FANNI, 100 miles, 1983

Paula Kerslake left her 14-pound Lhasa Apso dog, Anni Fanni, at the home of a relative in Apple Valley, California, hoping that the desert dryness would rid the pooch of fleas. Two months later, the tiny dog turned up at Miss Kerslake's house in Orange County, tired – and still flea-ridden.

20 RALPH, 60 miles, 1987

The black-and-tan hound wasn't wearing a collar when he took off after a deer during a rabbit hunt between Decatur and Arab in Morgan County, Alabama, on 3 January 1987. Six days later, he was found sitting in the Morris, Alabama, yard of owner Randy Hughes.

21 KEENO, 50 miles, 1977

Rancher Van Price from Darlington, Idaho, was out rounding up cattle in the desert with his pet Australian dingo, Keeno, during one of the hottest summers on record. Keeno got lost. "There's nothing out there but sage, lava, rattlesnakes and coyotes", said the rancher. "The only water is the Lost River." He got some calls from ranchers who had seen the dog here and there. Finally, 120 days later, Keeno made it the 50 miles to Butte City, which was about 20 miles from Price's ranch. She had caught her foreleg in a coyote trap, but had managed to break the chain that held it to a stake and dragged the trap after her. Her leg had to be amputated. The mayor of Butte City contacted Price's brother Blaine, who took Keeno home.

22 MICKY, 5 miles, 1979

Not a long journey, granted, but Micky was 15 years old, blind and almost stone deaf. For three years since the death of his former master in King's Langley, Hertfordshire, he had lived at Hemel Hempstead with his new, kind owners, Victor and Moira Philips. Micky disappeared over Easter, and the police discovered him outside his old, derelict home. He had a crushed paw, having apparently been run over during his trek which took him across many busy roads.

REFERENCES

Anni Fanni, Omaha World Herald, 2 April 1983; **Barry,** S.Mirror, 30 Dec 1973; **Bede,** D.Mirror, 4 Jan 1977; **Domo,** Weekly World News, 28 Dec 1982; **Fido,** Reuters, 5 April 1991; **Guard,** Houston Chronicle, 23 Nov 1978 + Lincoln (NB) Star, 9 Jan 1979; **Henry,** News of the World, 13 Feb 1983; **Jesse,** Lincoln (NB) Star, 13 Dec + S.Express, 18 Dec 1977; **Jimpa,** D.Mail, 14 May 1979; **Keeno,** National Enquirer, 20 June 1978; **Micky,** S.People, 29 April 1979; **Nick,** S.Express, 22 July 1979; **Prince,** Animal War Heroes (by Peter Shaw Baker, 1933); Ralph, Huntsville (AL) Times, 13 Jan 1987; **Rex** (1977), S.Express, 12 Feb 1978; **Rex** (1990), San Francisco Chronicle, 10 Aug 1991; **Sam,** Niagara Falls Gazette, 26 Mar + Northwest Arkansas Times, 3 April 1983; **Sandy,** D.Telegraph, 27 Oct 1992; **Spook,** S.Express, 26 June 1977; **Vesna,** Reuters, 24 Jan 1983; **Spot,** D.Star, 25 Mar 1983; **Vixen,** San Jose (CA) Mercury News, 3 July 1990; **Whisky** (1973) D.Express 5 July 1974.

Top: Bobbie the all-time champion trekker. Bottom left to right: In fifth place, Barry who walked 1200 miles to find his new home. Eighth, Fido after his 1000 mile trek. Fourteenth, Doma, who gave birth during her four-month trip.

Hoax!

BONEHEADS

Pat Shipman – an anthropologist and writer living in Maryland – investigates the unusual Indonesian industry of skull faking

Forged relics have not commanded very much attention from palæoanthropologists since the highly publicised unveiling of the Piltdown fakes [see ***FT62***] back in 1950. The story of how the Piltdown remains distorted scientists' views about human evolution in the subsequent 40 years serves as a moral tale, a warning to the over-confident. Other forgers are active today.

They first came to notice in 1989, when the National Geographic Society contacted my husband, Alan Walker, who is known for his work on African *Homo erectus*. They wanted his help in responding to a letter from some Australians who were offering to sell a Javanese *Homo erectus* skull for $2.6 million. The sellers believed that the skull had originally been collected by Dutch anatomist Eugene Dubois.

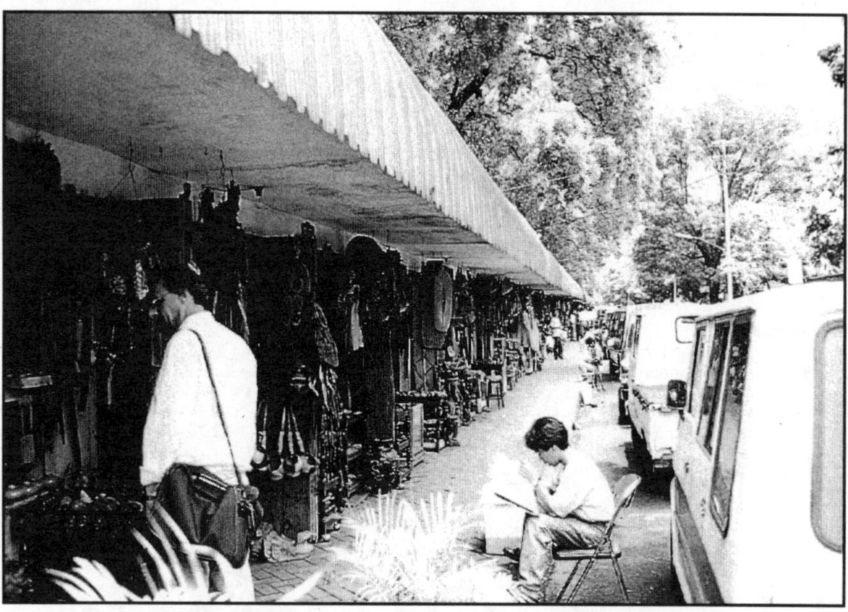

The antiquities market in Sangiran in which the skulls are sold, with John de Vos in the left foreground

Dubois pulled off one of the most remarkable fossil discoveries of all time between 1891 and 1893. After predicting, from theory, the location of the 'missing link', Dubois resigned his promising position teaching anatomy in Amsterdam, enlisted in the Royal Dutch Navy as a physician and sailed, with his new wife, for the Dutch East Indies (now Indonesia) in 1887. On time begged or stolen from his professional duties, he searched Sumatra for fossils.

By 1889, he had found enough animal fossils to enable him to convince the government to release him from service to pursue the 'missing link'. He was even supplied with a budget, two civil engineers and a work-force of convicts. They shifted operations to Java, and in 1891 his gamble was rewarded; he found the first ever fossils of *Homo erectus*. This should have ensured Dubois' scientific fame; instead, he faced a tidal wave of scepticism, and for the rest of his life stood alone, disbelieved and discredited. At the time, few fossil humans were known whose anatomy was different from that of people today, and their existence was still controversial. Dubois' find was the most primitive and ape-like yet, and thus the least credible.

As credentials, the Australians sent photographs of two skulls. There was no clear link between Dubois and the sellers – however, some accounts of Dubois' work mention a second skull, whose whereabouts are now unknown. One, brown-coloured, had a complete brain case and an impossible face – it was patently a fake. The second skull was hauntingly plausible, even with its face broken off below the orbits. It had a strong brow ridge and was unmistakably fossilised grey bone; even the cranial sutures – the complex zones where vault bones interfingered with their opposite partners – could be seen.

> "Psst! Come over here!" one youth hissed furtively. "Be careful... no one must see," he added, clutching a small backpack to his chest. They followed him down the lane away from the market to the shade of an abandoned hut, where the youth extracted his prize – a *"Homo erectus"* palate.

Alan consulted John de Vos, curator of the Dubois collection in Leiden. After studying the photos, de Vos exclaimed: "I have their brothers in my office." They were fakes brought to him by a conscience-stricken priest, and were so similar to the Australians' brown skull that they were surely the work of the same man.

Who made these skulls? Was the grey skull genuine but 'touched up' by a skilful hand? To solve the

Eugene Dubois in 1902.

mystery, we travelled to Australia in October 1991. The owner of the skulls showed up in a tropical print shirt, carrying a lumpy cloth satchel that clunked slightly as he set it down. He unwrapped its contents slowly.

The brown skull was surprisingly small: about the size of a large monkey cranium. It had been carved from the highly weathered, fossilised ball of the femur of a buffalo-sized animal. The man's face fell when we showed him that it was an undoubted fake.

The grey skull *was* a skull, but it was not *Homo erectus*. Its artisan had taken the cranium of a large animal – perhaps a hippo – and had reversed it. The brow-ridge, orbits and upper face were all carved out of the sloping plane at the back of the animal's head, where powerful neck muscles were once attached. The original face was broken away to reveal a convincing (if oddly-shaped) brain case. The cranial sutures remained, but were backwards. It was a masterpiece of forgery.

Our admiration for the forger's skill did little to assuage the disappointment of their owner, a reputable antiques dealer. Where had the skulls come from? The dealer had brought them from a secretive man, who had conducted him into a large, darkened room, its floor littered with bones, skulls, stone tools and other antiquities. Many items were clearly of Javanese origin; they were said to be from the estate of an elderly man whose family had lived in Java for several generations. The secrecy was necessary, it was implied, because some of the rarer objects might not have been exported from Java legally.

Although the dealer was not knowledgeable about fossils, he had sensed the potential. This was exactly the sort of circumstance in which the missing Dubois skull – if there ever was one – might turn up; in a jumble of curiosities collected and passed down from some ex-colonial to his descendents. Unfortunately for the dealer, who was now several thousand dollars the poorer, the skulls were forgeries. He smiled at us ruefully and left.

We, on the other hand, were elated, for his information linked the skulls more firmly to Java; but could we find the forger? In March 1992, Alan went to Java with Richard Potts (of the Smithsonian Institution) and John de Vos. John took them to an outdoor market in Sangiran, the antiquities row of which featured mythical items such as "fossilised rhinoceros horn" (keratin does not fossilise) and skulls of fabulous animals. The shadow play – a traditional Javanese art form that celebrates the illusory nature of life – began when they asked for human fossils.

"Psst! Come over here!" one youth hissed furtively. "Be careful... no one must see," he added, clutching a small backpack to his chest. They followed him down the lane away from the market to the shade of an abandoned hut, where the youth extracted his prize – a "*Homo erectus*" palate.

"It's a fake!" the anthropologists responded, grinning and pointing to the mixture of upper and lower milk and adult human teeth.

"No, no, it is genuine," the youth insisted solemnly, then scuppering his credibility by giggling. In time, many 'fossils' were produced with dramatic flair and enormous price tags. After bargaining, the scientists bought an antelope cranium and two allegedly-*Homo erectus* skulls for $60.

Our *erectus* skull is the more winsome, with close-set orbits and a charmingly skewed face that suggests its tongue is firmly in its cheek. The skull bought by Potts has a homelier face but boasts chalk teeth, complete with crude, demarcating cusps. The antelope cranium is a testament to the Javanese mastery of cement.

Between the wars, Sangiran was the headquarters of the German palæontological expedition led by anthropologist Gustav von Koenigswald – the fakes can probably be traced to his influence. However, unlike Dubois, who used convict labour, von Koenigswald simply paid local people to bring him specimens. The enterprising soon learned to break once-whole specimens and apparently skilful carving followed behind, after von Koenigswald's death. Today, the museum in Sangiran displays helpful models (casts of real specimens) and fossil fakery has become an indigenous handicraft.

The magnitude of this cottage industry is difficult to ascertain. Shown photographs of the fakes, Christopher Stringer of the Natural History Museum, London, commented: "Oh yes – I get someone coming in with one of these about once a year."

Will the Javanese fakes provoke an outbreak of Piltdown-like confusion? Not likely; although the 'discovery' of the two new *'Homo erectus'* skulls provided a barely-resisted opportunity for an April Fool's Day release, they are too inaccurate to have any impact on science.

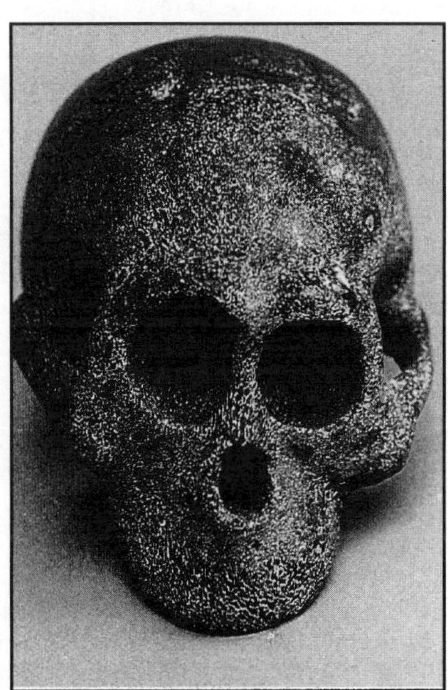

The skull we bought, carved from the cranium of a large animal.

Yet these skulls are poignant testimony to the impact of science on a local community. Scientific expeditions create new job opportunities, foster education, and may promote a new sense of pride. The cruelty of their transiency is revealed only when the expedition leaves; the immediate good leaves a long-lasting shadow that may manifest in overt hostility to foreigners.

The Javan response was gentler, confounding reality with illusion. If outsiders want these things, they will provide them.

This article first appeared in New Scientist, the weekly review of science and technology, and has been updated by the author.

EGG VOYAGERS

A monstrous egg has been discovered by three children close to a beach in Western Australia. Dr Karl P.N. Shuker investigates.

In March 1993, Jamie Andrich (9), Kelly Pew (8) and Michelle Pew (6) (pictured from left to right) were walking amid sand hills near the beach at Cervantes, 150 miles north of Perth, when they saw what appeared at first to be a smooth rock, partially buried in the sand. After digging it up, they realised it wasn't a rock, and decided to break it up with a tomahawk in order to make a fishing float from it. Fortunately for science, the Pew duo's father realised it was an enormous fossilised egg and prevented its demolition. It had a circumference of 80.5cm (32.2in). [1] By comparison, the circumference of an average-sized ostrich egg – the largest egg laid by any species of animal alive today – is a paltry 14 inches.

Dr Ken McNamara, senior curator of palæontology at the Western Australian Museum, described the find as 'extremely important'. There were only two birds who could have laid such an enormous egg.

One was an ostrich-like species called Newton's mihirung (*Genyornis newtoni*), which became extinct around 15,000 years ago, the last surviving member of a long line of giant flightless birds called dromornithids. [2] Native to Australia, they are known both from their fossilised skeletons and from fragments of fossilised eggshells found in coastal sand. [3] No intact eggs have ever been found – they would need to survive water percolating through the sand for several millennia. If the Cervantes specimen was a *Genyornis* egg it would be unique and, according to Dr Paddy Berry of the WA Museum, 'a priceless scientific find'.

The other candidate for laying the egg might seem at first sight highly unlikely – the great elephant bird *Aepyornis maximus* from Madagascar. This creature inspired the legends concerning the mighty roc of *Arabian Nights* fame. Its eggs, some of which exceeded 30 inches in diameter, were the largest ever laid, but it became extinct more than 200 years ago. A number of well-preserved *Aepyornis* eggs have since been excavated in Madagascar, but for one to be washed ashore in Australia it would have to float across 4,000 miles of ocean. There is a notable precedent for this.

In 1930, rancher's son Vic Roberts and his friend Chris Morris discovered a huge egg in some coastal sand dunes at Nannup, near Augusta in the Scott River region of Western Australia, about 195 miles south of Perth. With a circumference of roughly 26.75in and a capacity of almost 12 pints (equivalent to about 135 chicken's eggs!), it remained a family curio until 1962, when it was examined by Australian naturalist Harry Butler. Recognising its similarity to a large *Aepyornis* egg, he arranged for it to go to the WA Museum on permanent loan. Butler suggested that it had floated to Australia, pointing out that the Indian and Southern Oceans happen to converge at the very coastal point where it had been found. [4]

Some media accounts implied that the Nannup egg was fossilised [5], which opened up the possibility that it was a dromornithid's. However, I have learned from Ron Johnstone of the WA Museum's Department of Ornithology that it is of geologically Recent date, thereby supporting the æpyornid identity. [6]

Another precedent for long-distance egg floating occurred in January 1991, when Ongerup farmer Kelly O'Neill discovered a 4.4in-long, barnacle-encrusted egg washed ashore near Bremer Bay on Australia's south coast. It was identified at the WA Museum as that of a king penguin *Aptenodytes patagonica*, a species native to Kerguelen and other sub-Antarctic islands off the southeastern coast of Africa. Ornithologist Geoff Lodge had found a similar specimen 17 years earlier... washed ashore near Nannup! [7]

The Cervantes egg is currently the subject of negotiations between its owner and the WA Museum, which hopes that it will be donated or presented on permanent loan as with its Nannup predecessor.

REFERENCES

1 - Bill Thompson: 'Roc of ages unscrambles egg mystery', *Sunday Times* (Perth), 21 Mar 1993; 'Fossil egg of Madagascar elephant bird found on beach', *Bangor Daily News* (Maine), 22 Mar 1993.

2 - Pat Rich: 'Feathered leviathans', *Hemisphere*, 1981, v25, pp298-302.

3 - D.L.G. Williams: '*Genyornis* eggshell (Dromornithidæ; Avis) from the Late Pleistocene of South Australia' *Alcheringa*, 1981, v5, pp133-140.

4 - Harry Butler: 'Australia's embarrassing egg', *Science Digest*, Mar 1969, v65, pp70-73; and Ivan T. Sanderson: *Investigating the Unexplained* (Prentice-Hall, 1972), pp80-86.

5 - 'Giant egg sets a problem for science', *Western Australian* (Perth), 3 May 1962.

6 - 'The Scott River Egg', 1991 information sheet from the WA Museum, and personal communication from Ron Johnstone, 13 Sept 1991.

7 - Pat Fraser: 'Ongerup farmer's egg find sheds light on old mystery' *Great Southern Herald*, 19 June 1991.

THE DRAGONS

MIKE DASH uncovers a tale of mangled carcasses, baby

The name's LeBlond... Paul LeBlond. And though this Vancouver-based marine biologist may not spend his time foiling the plots of evil master-spies, he's in search of an equally elusive quarry – Caddy, the sea-serpent of the Pacific coast.

LeBlond – head of oceanography at the University of British Columbia – and fellow-scientist Ed Bousfield – a semi-retired former chief zoologist from the Canadian Museum of Nature – presented a 28-page academic paper to the American Society of Zoologists (ASZ) when that august body held its annual conference in Vancouver (December 1992). In the paper, the two men summarised more than 50 years of sighting reports and evidence from Canada's west coast and concluded that a colony of sea-serpents – animals nicknamed Cadborosaurus, or Caddy for short – probably does live in the rich waters of the north Pacific.

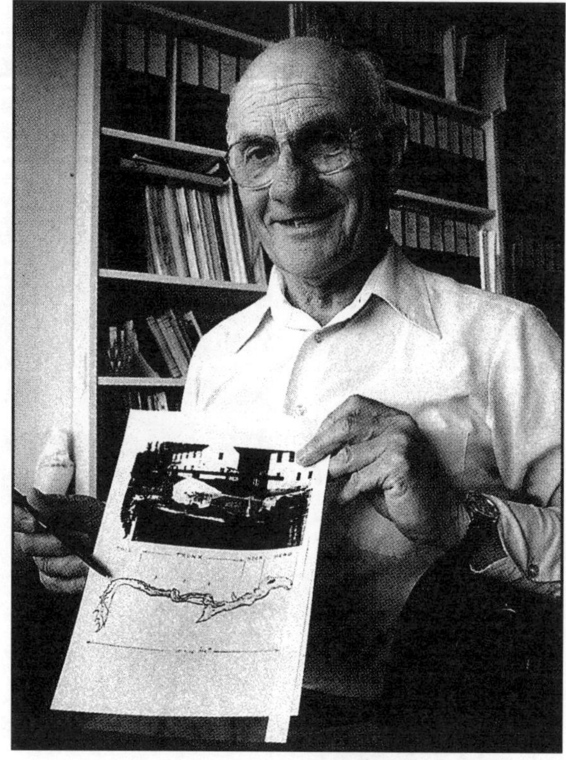

Ed Bousfield and his interpretation of the Caddy carcase photo. "I knew I had found scientific evidence."

There is, in fact, a wealth of evidence – some 80 sightings at least – that something serpentine has been paddling around the waters off Vancouver Island. Typical reports describe Caddy as snake-like, with a horse's head and a surprising turn of speed. As the monster swims, witnesses say, it shows coils or humps. It can reach speeds of up to 25 miles per hour.

Typical reports describe Caddy as snake-like, with a horse's head and a surprising turn of speed

Take the report of John Celona. The University of Victoria music don claimed one of the most recent Caddy sightings in May 1992 and reckoned the multi-humped creature was at least 25 feet long.

"I was standing on the deck of my friend's sailboat, gazing out at the water, when I was suddenly startled by what I saw," Celona said. "There was this serpent-like creature swimming along about 50 yards ahead of us. I've been sailing for many years, and I knew from experience that this wasn't a sea lion or any other recognisable animal." [1]

Celona's report was just one of 12 made in 1992 [2], which proved – thanks to the advance publicity surrounding LeBlond's and Bousfield's report – to be the best year for Caddy sightings in decades, and the first in five to generate fresh accounts. Altogether, the two scientists collected "dozens" of sightings dating back at least to 1905, when two fisherman at the mouth of the Adams River reported a six- to eight-foot (2-2.5m) head-and-neck surfacing among a school of salmon. But Caddy really came to prominence in the autumn of 1933, when a Major Langley and his wife allegedly spotted a huge olive green hump while sailing off Discovery Island and the Chatham Islands [3]. Sceptics observe that this was about the time that the Loch Ness Monster was making its first headlines around the world.

Similar reports continued in succeeding years, at one time "at the rate of almost one a month", according to Bousfield. But the most dramatic claim was undoubtedly made by a former sea captain, William Hagelund, in the book *Whalers No More*. He asserted that while fishing in Pirate's Cove, De Courcy Island, one day in 1968, he caught a baby Cadborosaurus in a dip net [4].

The animal was still alive when it was hauled aboard, and according to the sailor, "his lower jaw had a set of sharp tiny teeth and his back was protected by plate-like scales, while his undersides were covered in a soft yellow fuzz. A pair of small, flipper-like feet protruded from his shoulder area, and a spade-shaped tail proved to be two tiny flipper-like fins that overlapped each other." Hagelund's sketch of the animal – see page 48 – shows the latter feature as a characteristically mammalian bilobal tail.

Not realising (rather astonishingly) what he had netted, Hagelund left the 16-inch (40cm) creature swimming around a bucket on deck. When he came up the next morning, though, he "felt a strong compassion for that little face staring up at me. I lowered the bucket over the side and watched him swim away quickly."

Pooling all the information, LeBlond and Bousfield came up with a Caddy composite to put to the ASZ conference. The animals, they wrote, have reptilian

)F VANCOUVER

pents and some all-too-close encounters off the west coast of Canada

features, but appear to be warm-blooded. They probably spend most of their time far out to sea, but move inshore each summer to bear young. They are carnivores, and capable of diving to great depths.

"Evidence strongly supports recognition of this animal as a distinct vertebrate species, of presently indeterminate class," their paper concluded [5].

Attempts to lump a century of Caddy sightings together nevertheless seem to have caused problems for the two men. Their composite has a curious mix of reptilian and mammalian features, and though he toed LeBlond's warm-blooded line at the ASZ conference, Bousfield had had his doubts six months earlier, telling *The Economist* he favoured a 45-foot (15 metre) cold-blooded serpent; its shape, he correctly pointed out, would not hold body heat well. Speaking to the *New Scientist*, Bousfield also hypothesised an elaborate (and hitherto quite unknown) respiratory system: tubercules lining the animals' back acting as gills to pass water over highly vas-cularised tissue beneath. LeBlond, meanwhile, had had a change of heart since authoring a 1973 report on *Observations of Large Unidentified Marine Animals in British Columbia and Adjacent Waters*. Then, he identified two different creatures from Caddy reports, one with a short neck and horse's head, the other, less common, with a similar head but a much longer (6-9ft, 2-3m) neck [6].

The mangled remains allegedly removed from a whale's stomach and displayed at Naden Harbor whaling station, Queen Charlotte Islands.

The scientists' conclusions were based on years of work by a predecessor, Clifford Carl, director of the Royal British Columbia Museum [7]. It was the discovery of his research – including musty piles of press clippings and interviews – that spurred the previously uninterested Bousfield into examining monster reports. But what the men see as their most persuasive piece of evidence was unearthed elsewhere, in the provincial archives. It is a photograph of a reputed Caddy carcass taken in 1937.

The carcass lies stretched out on a series of packing cases and appears to be in an advanced stage of decomposition. A contemporary report submitted to fisheries officials described it as "having a head similar to a large dog, animal-like vertebræ and a tail resembling a single blade of gill-bone as found in whales' jaws." [8]

According to Bousfield, the picture shows the remains of an adolescent, 10- to 12-foot long Cadborosaurus cut from the belly of a sperm whale and put on show at Naden

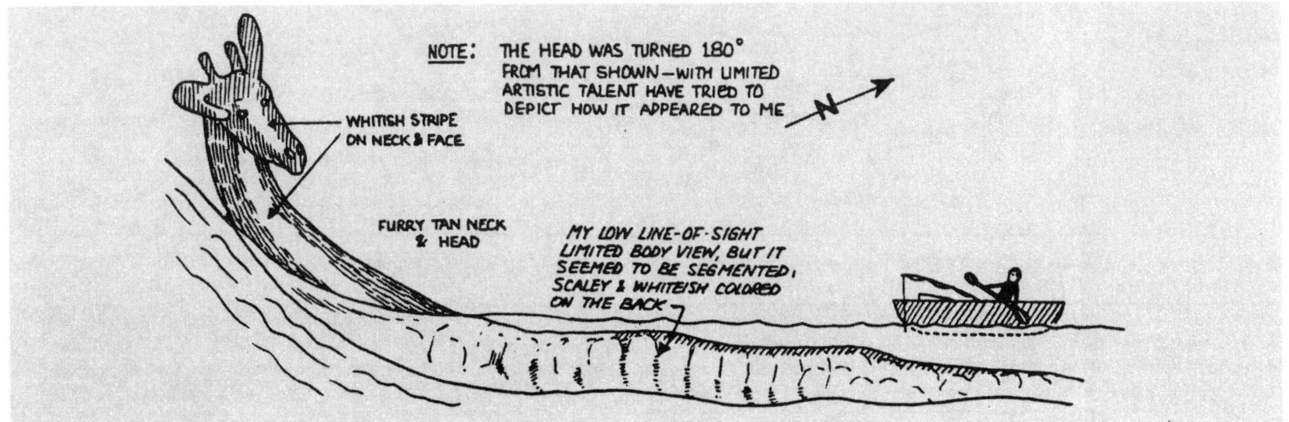

The Spanish Banks sea-serpent of 1984. From a drawing by witness Jim Thompson (in Bright).

Harbor whaling station in the Queen Charlotte Islands.

"Right then, I knew that I had found scientific evidence", the excited scientist said. "It's an entirely authentic picture. This photograph is almost three-dimensional. You can even see the creature's coils behind its neck. Nothing ever known to science has three coils behind its neck. The only thing it compares to is the dragon of mythology. This is some kind of missing link. Also the morphology of the animal exactly fits the known profile of Cadborosaurus." [9]

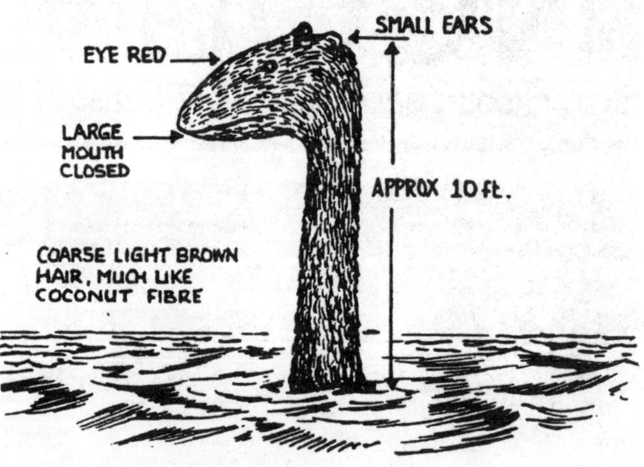

The Discovery Island creature of 1959. From a drawing by David Miller (in Bright).

So far, so good – but like much of the supposedly hard evidence secured by cryptozoologists, the Naden Harbor carcass has vanished. The remains were allegedly shipped to the Field Museum in Chicago, where no record of their arrival exists. [10]

There are, in fact, six other reports of alleged Caddy carcasses [11], two of them well-documented – and while one presumes doctors LeBlond and Bousfield have ruled out any confusion between their supposed 1937 serpent and the others, curious parallels exist.

In 1947 a very similar-looking beast was hauled off the rocks at Effingham, on the west coast of Vancouver Island, by a timber merchant named Henry Schwartz and three others. Overall, the body was at least 40 feet long, but when lifted it fell into three sections, one of which (the tail) was left in the water and the other two taken ashore. Photographed, the horse-like head of the Effingham beast bears a decided resemblance to that of Bousfield's 1937 Caddy. It was later identified as a very badly decomposed basking shark – that most common culprit in supposed sea serpent strandings. [12].

Thirteen years earlier, an even more closely analogous case occurred at Henry Island, where a 30-foot long carcass covered in hair and "quills", and bearing four fins or flippers, was cast up on a beach. It was hauled up on a quay and photographed. Witnesses described it as "slender and sinewy". Samples of the skeleton were sent to the government biological station at Nanaimo. They too were identified as parts of a basking shark. [13]

Yet sighting reports continue to come from the Cadboro Bay and Georgia Strait areas of British Columbia. One recent author, collecting new accounts, notes the story of two fishermen, David Miller and Alfred Webb, who claimed in 1959 they had come within 30 feet of a long-necked creature whilst out boating off Discovery Island. They were close enough to describe its coarse brown fur, red eyes and small ears. Much more recently, in 1984, a mechanical engineer named Jim Thompson was canoeing in Vancouver's outer harbour when he paddled to within 200 feet of a furry, long-necked animal with two horns surmounting a head much like a deer's. It swam rapidly out towards the Pacific. [14]

Sceptics have a ready explanation for the typical Caddy sighting of a horse's head plus coils. Former Vancouver Island resident Robert Adamson, writing to *The Economist* [15], records his own experience of finding himself in "the coils of such a creature. Schooled in the legend, I was convinced my time had come... [But] the head was a sea lion sentinel who alerted his feeding mates with their arched backs (the coils). All suddenly poked their heads above water, then dived *en masse* leaving me, thankfully, to continue on my way."

An increasingly frustrated Bousfield is well aware of the need for more concrete evidence. Hearing of another possible Caddy stranding, in Washington State – where a high school teacher supposedly buried some bones to be retrieved later, before inconveniently dying – he sighed: "All we need is a bone. Then we'd be home free." [16]

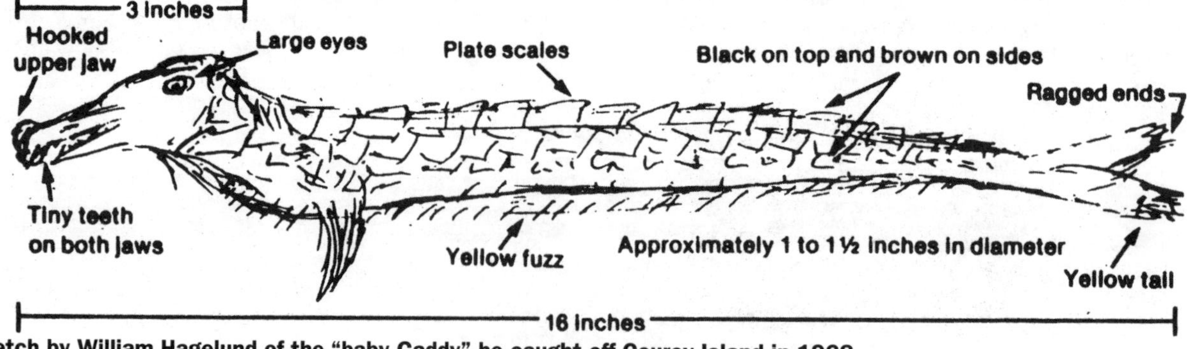

A sketch by William Hagelund of the "baby Caddy" he caught off Courcy Island in 1968.

References: 1 – Victoria (BC) *Monday Magazine*, pp14-20 Jan 1993. 2 – Tacoma, Washington *News Herald*, p28 Dec 1992. 3 – Heuvelmans, Bernard, *In the Wake of the Sea Serpents*, London 1968, pp441-3. Bright, Michael, *There are Giants in the Sea: Monsters and Mysteries of the Depths Explored*, London 1989, p81. 4 – Bousfield quoted in Victoria (BC) *Times Colonist* 16 Aug 1992. Hagelund info in Vancouver *Sun*, 17 July + Vancouver *Province* 2 Aug 1992. 5 – *Ibid*. 6 – *The Economist*, 29 Aug 1992. *New Scientist*, 23 Jan 1993. Bright *op-cit*. pp95-6. 7 – *The Economist*, 29 Aug 1992. 8 – Vancouver *Sun*, 17 July 1992. 9 – Victoria (BC) *Monday Magazine*, 14-20 Jan 1993. 10 – *The Economist*, 29 Aug 1992. 11 – Tacoma, Washington *News Herald*, 28 Dec 1992. 12 – Heuvelmans, *op-cit*. pp474-6. 13 – *Ibid*. pp131-2. 14 – Bright, *op-cit*. pp89-94. 15 – *The Economist*, 14 Nov 1992. 16 – *The Economist*, 29 Aug 1992.

DIARY OF A MAD PLANET

April - May 1993

This diary aims to record, in two-month segments, the geophysical highlights of our planet: the tempests and tantrums, the oddities and extremities. Compiled by the editors and various correspondents.

EARTHQUAKE 18 April PERU:
(11.611S 76.552W) Depth: 90km. Magnitude: 6.1R. Six killed, including three by quake-induced landslides in Lima. 30 houses destroyed. Felt throughout the western coastal region of Peru.

TORNADO 25 April OKLAHOMA:
This twister killed seven and injured over 90 when it tore through Tulsa (where it wiped out a church) and moved on to Cartoosa, seven miles to the east. Cars and trucks were blown off Interstate 44 and 242 houses and mobile homes were destroyed. An area a mile wide and two miles long was completely flattened. Damage was estimated at $100 million.

SANDSTORM 5 May CHINA:
The province of Gansu in northwest China was hit by a cataclysmic sandstorm, dubbed 'the black wind', killing at least 43, mostly children, drowned after being blown into water channels and pools. "It whipped up sand and pebbles, turning day as black as night", said the China News Service. The winds damaged 200,000 hectares of farmland and destroyed 99,400 trees.

LANDSLIDE 9 May ECUADOR:
Weeks of torrential rain caused up to 15,000 tonnes of rock in the remote Nambija region to crash down on the gold-mining settlement of Las Brisas, on the border with Peru. 200-400 feared dead. Another landslide 250 miles further north on 29 March killed about 300.

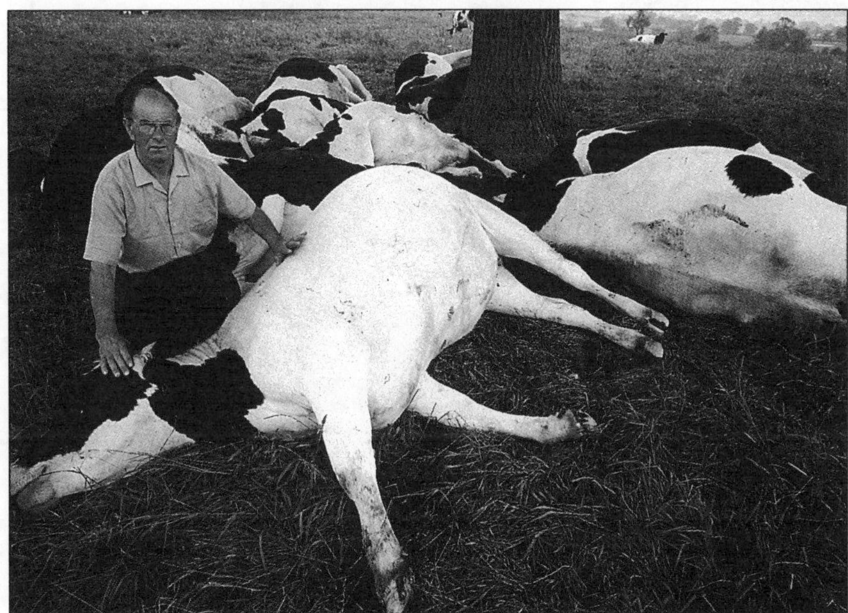

A bolt of lightning at dawn on 15 June on New Farm, Occlestone, near Middlewich in Cheshire, struck an oak tree and killed the 12 pedigree dairy cows sheltering beneath it. Farmer George Yoxall, 57, said: "They would have been dead in the blinking of an eye, before they even hit the ground." He estimated his losses at £20,000. Four days earlier, four cattle were killed in Leicestershire after lightning struck a tree and passed along a barbed wire fence. [For 13 cows struck down under an oak tree on the Isle of Wight in 1988, see *FT51:24*]

SANDSTORM 11 May CHINA:
Force 12 winds in the remote western province of Xinjiang buried seven sections of the only railway, along a 100km corridor in the Gurbantunggut Desert, stranding 34 freight trains and 14 passenger trains, with over 10,000 passengers. The storm hampered emergency distribution of food and water.

WHIRLWIND 17 May WALES:
A whirlwind ripped through Pantydwr, Powys, carrying a flock of sheep half a mile over stone walls, a river and across five fields. About 20 survived while at least a dozen were killed. Ned Jones found the stray sheep, owned by Dilwyn Rees of Pentalcae Farm, mixed up with his own flock, while sheep carcases were found nearby. Mr Rees had the roof ripped off his farmhouse and his outbuildings flattened.

According to tradition, a flock of sheep was blown from the Gwithian Sands over into St Ives Bay in Cornwall, where they were caught by fishermen. We have no recent flying sheep data, though last year a twister near Mason City, Iowa, carried a horse two miles and dumped it unhurt into a river while in China a girl was transported a similar distance, landing unhurt in a tree. See ***FT68:14.***

Special thanks to the Global Seismology Group of the British Geological Survey for the earthquake data.

PEACE TOGETHER
CD • CASSETTE • LIMITED VINYL
THE PEACE TOGETHER ALBUM IS RELEASED ON JULY 19th
FEATURING EXCLUSIVE, NEVER BEFORE RELEASED TRACKS BY -
U2 featuring LOU REED Satellite Of Love - live
CARTER USM Peace In Our Time
BILLY BRAGG, ANDY WHITE & SINEAD O'CONNOR Religious Persuasion
YOUNG DISCIPLES Bad Weather
MY BLOODY VALENTINE We Have All The Time In The World
POP WILL EAT ITSELF Games Without Frontiers
BLUR Oliver's Army
THERAPY? Invisible Sun
ROLF HARRIS & LIAM O'MAONLAI When We Were Two Little Boys
CURVE & IAN DURY What A Waste
FATIMA MANSIONS John The Gun
PEACE TOGETHER featuring PETER GABRIEL, SINEAD O'CONNOR & FEARGAL SHARKEY Be Still
+ ROBIN GUTHRIE REMIX featuring ELIZABETH FRAZER
PEACE TOGETHER
ALL PROFITS RAISED BY PEACE TOGETHER WILL BE USED TO CREATE A TRUST FUND IN SUPPORT OF CROSS-COMMUNITY ACTIVITIES FOR YOUNG PEOPLE IN NORTHERN IRELAND
ISLAND

bufora

NUMBER EIGHT 1993
Steamshovel Press
"...happily wallowing in the conspiracy scene." -FATE Magazine
Lars Hansson on J. Edgar Hoover
Sean Morton: UFOs at Area 51 & Moonbases
Jim Martin: Quigley, Clinton, Straight, & Reich
Stephanie Caruana: GEMSTONE
Secret Service Files on Mae Brussell
Philip K. Dick & The Illuminati
A. J. Weberman: JFK & Hunt the Tramp
Tool of the Rockefellers
Bill Clinton's Mentor
Wall Street Soviet Spy
Queen of Conspiracies
Family Couldn't Alibi

MYSTERY OF THE PHARAOHS

What lies behind the recently-discovered hidden chamber at the Great Pyramid of Cheops? STEVE MOORE considers the possibilities

One might have thought that after 4,500 years, the Great Pyramid of Cheops at Giza would have had no further secrets to reveal; but that doesn't seem to be the case. Apart from a stone sarcophagus, it appears to have been empty since antiquity, which has led to speculation that somewhere within *must* lie a hidden chamber ... and this sort of thinking seems to have coloured the interpretation of the events recorded here.

The tale begins ordinarily enough with a project to improve the ventilation within the pyramid, carried out by the German Archæological Institute in Cairo. Each visitor to the pyramid leaves behind 20 grams of water from breath and perspiration, which is threatening the limestone fabric of the monument. The idea was to clear two small passages leading from the King's Chamber to the outside, which had become clogged by rubble.

A 19th century view of the Great Pyramid of Cheops and environs.

German engineer and roboticist Rudolf Gantenbrink was given the task, achieved by the simple expedient of attaching a point to an old lorry axle and dropping it down the shafts; after which he used a small, tracked robot with a video-camera to study the shafts before fans were installed. He next requested permission to use his robot to explore a similar passage leading from the Queen's Chamber, which lies lower down in the pyramid. And this is where the story gets interesting.

The passageway is 20cm square and rises from the Queen's Chamber at an angle of 45 degrees. It was previously thought to extend no more than eight metres, but Gantenbrink sent his robot up and it just kept on going (very slowly) for 65 metres. Over the last couple of metres, the walls of the passage changed from rough to finely polished limestone, and then the robot came to a door. This is possibly of alabaster or yellow limestone, with tongue and groove fittings suggesting that it might be raised or lowered.

The door has two copper fittings near the centre, which have been variously described as handles or just plain strips. A gap exists at the bottom of the door, too small for the camera to see through, and in front of this lies a scatter of black dust. The robot is to be refitted with a fibre-optic lens and light-source later this year, which should be able to peer through the gap and show what lies beyond the door.

That's basically the story so far; now the speculation starts. The black dust is thought to be the decomposed detritus of wood or other organic remains, and the fact that it's apparently come through the gap to the passage side of the door suggests that if there is a chamber on the other side, it's large enough to allow some air circulation.

The instant conclusion leapt to was that here must lie the hidden burial chamber of the pharaoh Cheops, packed with treasure to match the tomb of Tutankhamun, followed by talk of tunnelling through 25 metres of solid limestone to reach it. Backing this up, we're told that the putative new chamber is 21.5 metres above the large King's Chamber, which is the same distance above the Queen's Chamber; it's thus presumed that the new chamber will be of similar size. This is what we can call the unrestrained hypothesis.

The restrained hypothesis comes from Dr Ivan (or Eiddon) Edwards, formerly of the British Museum. It appears that the two passages from the King's Chamber aligned with stars: to the north, the passage would have pointed to what was then the pole-star, Alpha Draconis, identified with the hippo goddess Rer; the southern passage to the belt of Orion, representing Osiris.

The newly explored passage seems to align with Sirius, representing Isis, and the idea is that the passages were built to allow the pharaoh's spirit to escape to the stars and union with the gods. Edwards's notion is that behind the door there probably lies a small chamber containing a statuette of Cheops gazing toward the heavens, or a protective charm or emblem.

Finally, we come to no hypothesis at all. Presumably working on the same information as everyone else, the archæologist in charge of the Giza plateau and the pyramids, Zahi Hawass, has declared of the door 'there is no way they will find anything behind it'. Best of all, though, is the quote from Rainer Stadelman, head of the German Archæological Institute in Cairo. He described the whole notion of a hidden chamber as 'very annoying'. *Independent, 16 + 17 Apr, Today, D.Mail, 17 Apr, Hong Kong Sunday Standard, 25 Apr 1993, etc.*

SECRET COUNTRY

Mysterious places to visit in Great Britain compiled by Janet & Colin Bord

10: Trellech, Gwent

The three tall standing stones in a field on the outskirts of the small Welsh village of Trellech are obviously of prehistoric origin, but their purpose is far less obvious. At least three stories explaining the origin of the monoliths have come down to us.

One tells how they were thrown there by a local giant called Jack o' Kent. He jumped from one mountain, the Sugar Loaf, to another, the Skirrid, where he played quoits with the stones, tossing them to Trellech. Or he was at Beacon Hill, engaged in a throwing match with the Devil.

No one is quite sure about the true identity of Jack o' Kent. He might have been based upon John Kent, an astrologer and writer on witchcraft in the 15th century. Stories about Jack o' Kent were widespread in Herefordshire and Gloucestershire, as well as Monmouthshire (now Gwent). He was said to have made a pact with the Devil, besting him in numerous trials of strength like this stone-throwing.

The standing stones at Trellech are today known as the Harold Stones, because another story claims they are a memorial to a battle in the 11th century in which the Welsh were beaten by the English led by King Harold Godwinson. All who fell in the battle are said to be buried in a huge mound called Tump Turret, which stands in a farmyard in the village. A footpath leads to it, and it's worth a look. In the village church not far away is a 17th-century sundial carved with the main features of this legend – the stones and the tump – and also the holy well just outside the village.

This well – called St Anne's Well or Virtuous Well – is protected by an old stone building. Steps lead down to a pool where the spring water collects. There were once nine wells at Trellech, according to tradition, and each cured a different disease. They were very popular in earlier centuries, and reputed to cure "the scurvy, colic and other distempers".

St Anne's Well is also a wishing well; you just drop a pebble into the water and a plentiful uprush of bubbles signified that the wish was granted. A few bubbles meant a delay, and none meant the wish failed.

Fairies were said to dance at the wells on Midsummer Eve, and to drink water from harebells, which would be found strewn around the next morning. Once, when a farmer closed the wells, a "little old man" appeared and told him that, as a punishment, no water would flow on his farm. He quickly reopened the wells and his supply returned.

In most areas of Britain, tales of underground passages are found in the local folklore, and at Trellech it is said that the nuns from Tintern Abbey three miles away would travel through a tunnel to bathe in the medicinal pool (presumably St Anne's Well). Alas, no such tunnel has been detected, and there were never nuns at Tintern Abbey!

Another legend tells of music heard underground below a meadow at Trellech. The ground was excavated to reveal a cave in which two old men were playing harp and violin. They said they had been there for many years, taking turns to venture out for food; they died shortly after. This is similar to other tales of fiddlers vanishing – usually in a place said to be an entrance to fairyland – and thereafter faint snatches of their music might be heard. Many elements of the stories around Trellech seem to be fragments of forgotten tales of times when the fairies frequented the village wells. **FT**

Harold's Stones. Tossed by a giant?

Janet and Colin Bord are authors of Mysterious Britain, The Secret Country, Alien Animals, The Atlas of Magical Britain, and Modern Mysteries of Britain among many others

Virtuous Well, also called St Anne's Well

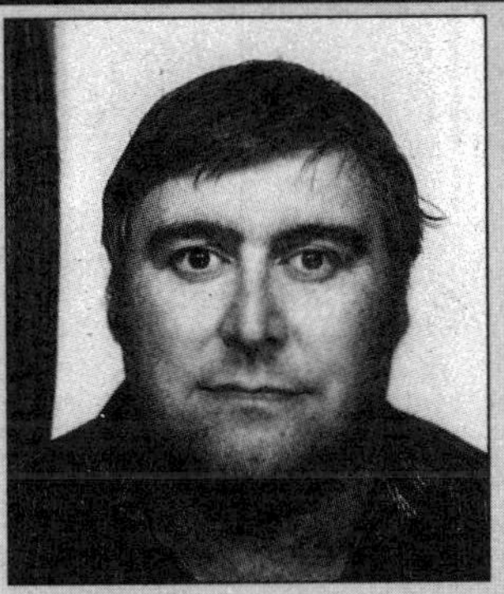

BIOLOGY:
Martyn Kollins is a botanist and playwright with a side interest in mythology.

RELICS
Lynn Picknett, author of *Flights of Fancy?* (1987) and Macmillan's *Encyclopædia of the Paranormal* (1991,) is LBC Radio's paranormal agony aunt.

DENDROLOGY
Alan Mitchell is a reseracher for the Forestry Commission. His many years of data gathering led to the Tree Register of the British Isles (TROBI), a registered charity.

THEATRE
Stephen Volk is a playwright and screenwriter living in Wiltshire. He wrote the Ken Russell film *Gothic* and the controversial BBC Hallowe'en play *Ghostwatch*.

Biology

Evolutionary Fast Food

Martyn Kollins puts the debate about evolution into its global context

One factor seems to have been forgotten in the recent wave of FT articles and letters on fossils, evolution and the age of the Earth.

Evolution, both biological and geological, is dependent on ecology, the overall balance in the system. All living things, as well as the mineral matrix of the earth, are part of great food cycles. Each species eats and, in its turn, is eaten by something else. Even those species at the top of food chains such as lions and humans are eventually eaten by worms, bugs and fungi. It is the way that nature has ensured that we are not up to our eyes in carcases, and that the finite resources available are recycled. Because of these food cycles, fossilisation is a very rare event. Even where large numbers of fossils have been found, these represent only a tiny fraction of what was going on in the biosphere.

Genetic mutations happen all the time. However, if the environment doesn't change to favour them, their traits will not be expressed in the species. Environmental changes which *do* favour mutations would, by definition, be unfavourable to the non-mutated population, whose numbers would rapidly decline. This would provide a large assemblage of non-mutated bones, a very small proportion of which might get fossilised.

Because of the crash in numbers, the food resource which the species represented within the food cycle would be at a premium. Other species in the cycle could not afford to waste this dwindling resource or they would be threatened themselves. Carcases, including bones, would be picked clean, making fossilisation even rarer. Because of this, the chances of finding transitional species in the fossil record are vastly reduced.

> "Does it matter whether we came about 3,000,000 years ago, 30,000 years ago, or even a week last Tuesday? The important point is that we are here."

Given time, the remaining, mutant, population will either be eaten into extinction or increase in sufficient numbers to establish a genetically stable population. In either case, the relatively small population of transient species would be put to better use by participants in the food cycles than being left around to be fossilised. The fact that we have not found large numbers of transitional fossils is an argument for evolution happening over very large time periods. Short time periods would not be long enough for the transient species to be cleared out of the system. Not only would many transient species have been found in the fossil record, but there would be many of them still walking around.

So far, most of the argument has been about fossil bones. This is hardly surprising, since the most spectacular fossils are those of bones. Soft, fleshy bits of plants and animals don't mineralise in the same way that semi-mineralised bone does, and consequently turn up even less frequently as fossils. There is far more soft tissue than hard tissue (bone or calcareous shell) in the biosphere. Large numbers of mutations in this soft tissue could have occurred and been expressed without any reciprocal effect on the bone structure. How could the development of the elephant's soft tissue trunk be traced in the fossil record?

I sometimes wonder why we should even bother with all this anyway. A question that never seems to be asked is what relevance does it have to us, here and now? Studying the genetics of living species is fine. There may even be some point in dragging ancient genetic material out of fossils and reviving it. But does it matter whether we came about 3,000,000 years ago, 30,000 years ago, or even a week last Tuesday? The important point is that we are here. The past may be interesting, but it cannot be changed. The mechanisms of genetics today are what matter. Our future is still out there waiting to be moulded... always supposing we do not become extinct first.

The Answer's in the Negative

Lynn Picknett on fear and loathing among the 'Shroudies'

In September 1988 the Holy Shroud of Turin – long believed to be the actual winding sheet of Jesus – was carbon-dated, showing it to be a mediæval/Renaissance fake. Yet it has now become very hot property indeed, as I and my colleague Clive Prince hope to show in our forthcoming book *In His Own Image* (Bloomsbury, autumn 1994).

We have concluded that the Shroud is a self-portrait of Leonardo da Vinci, circa 1492. It is not a painting (although there is some paint on it), but an image made on cloth with chemicals and light...In other words, a 500-year-old *photograph*. Our attempts to bring this exciting idea into the forum of 'Shroudies' was greeted with savagery and bigotry.

There exists an organisation called the British Society For the Turin Shroud (BSTS), which claims (falsely) to welcome all shades of opinion. As the latest victim of its ethnic cleansing, I was held up to ridicule for the suggestion that I give my talk 'Did Leonardo fake the Turin Shroud?' to the membership. It was alleged that I got my information from none other than the Renaissance polymath himself, through some form of mediumship.

Later, when Clive Prince and I gave an interview to Ysenda Maxtone Graham for an article in the *London Evening Standard* last March ('The Turmoil That Is Tearing Apart The Shroud Crowd'), I was expelled for 'bringing the society into disrepute'. The only reasons given were, quaintly, that I had mentioned the date of the society's meeting to the Press, and that I had talked 'about people'. When I tried to get into their next meeting, I was grabbed bodily and chucked out. "We do not have to give a reason", said the Chairman.

Now the French equivalent of the BSTS' Newsletter (*La Lettre Mensuelle du C.I.E.L.T.*) is saying that we have colluded with Maria Consolata Corti of the Italian research group LUCE. She too is saying that Leonardo did it and put his own face on it... (That old Fortean/Sheldrakean phenomenon strikes again. We had never heard of Ms Corti previously.)

A word of explanation is needed here, although (despite rumours to the contrary) I wish it were not. In 1988 I began a two-year, on/off relationship with Ian Wilson, author of the 1978 bestseller *The Turin Shroud*, (the research for which converted him to Catholicism). He it was who suggested the carbon-dating; which he now regrets, quoting 'Thou shalt not put the Lord thy God to the test'.

> "While other Shroudies moan that no publisher will touch the subject any more, we were snapped up one hour after the *Evening Standard* article hit the newsstands."

During the course of this relationship, I was consultant for the Royal Photographic Society's exhibition 'The Unexplained', which boasted the full-length transparency of the Shroud. Clive and I (who had been co-researchers for some time) chatted to visitors and heard hints of something we'd been told months previously – that Leonardo faked the Shroud. Intrigued, we did some months' research and concluded that it checked out.

What did Ian Wilson think of the Leonardo theory? All he said was: "1492? Yes, the Shroud did disappear around then". Unfortunately, I also told him about some of my 'automatic' scribbles during a parapsychological experiment. I laughed that they had been signed 'Leonardo'! Well, they would be, wouldn't they? I was eating, sleeping and breathing him by then.

Time passed. Our relationship ended mysteriously. Clive and I joined the BSTS – of which Ian is Vice Chairman and Newsletter Editor – hoping to get some dialogue going with Shroudies here and abroad. Instead, Ian went into print mocking my sources as being 'mediumistic' and stressing that the BSTS only deals in 'scientific, checkable facts'. (Later, the Society gave space to a member who claimed to channel Jesus).

I have been accused of the hysteria alleged to be rampant in every 'woman scorned'. Attempts to get the BSTS to take the theory seriously have met with such responses as "Come on, Lassie, the man on the Shroud looks nothing like Leonardo". (This from Secretary Michael Clift, who wrote to Ysenda Maxtone Graham: "There is only one possible use for your article, but I do not want to insult my perineum".)

The row has been savage and ongoing for the last year, although not mentioned in the Newsletter. While other Shroudies moan that no publisher will touch the subject any more, we were snapped up one hour after the *Evening Standard* article hit the newsstands. Wilson sneers: "No doubt your Leonardo theory will appeal to *Sun* readers...".

Clive Prince has now been expelled from the BSTS for writing 'tiresome correspondence' and not behaving like 'a normal member'.

It will be interesting to see how – or if – BSTS reports Corti's Leonardo theory. Unless their Vice Chairman has been particularly nimble, it's unlikely that they can accuse *her* of being motivated by 'woman scorned' bitterness.

Lynn Picknett is available for lectures on Leonardo and the Turin Shroud. (071 624 0284)

FORUM is a column for anyone with something to say about a particular field, theory or incident. If you'd like to join in with an opinion on any area of Forteana, send it to the editorial address. Ideal length: 500-1000 words. Please enclose an SAE, a three-line biography and a head-and-shoulders photo of yourself, preferably in black and white.

Tricks of the Trees

Alan Mitchell reminisces about trees that appear to come and go at will

Trees have a practical magic all their own. By practical magic I exclude the miasma of myths and old-fashioned witchcraft that clings round some species and is recounted in that kind of book. I mean the ability to appear suddenly, to move, to disappear and reappear again.

It was possible to believe, as my colleagues did, that the vast Drumtochty Sitka spruce, one of the biggest trees in Britain, had not moved or been moved across the road between my first two visits and to insist that I had come up to it from the opposite direction without realising the fact.

It was possible that, on four occasions, several of us had walked between, and almost beneath, a Sitka spruce and a Grand fir at Inveraray, both nearly the size of Nelson's column, without noticing them, avid to find big trees as we were. But next time they beckoned from afar, and I measured them, and a few years later they had gone again. I rather expect them to be back next time.

Then, at a local talk, I showed my slide of a weeping beech in the district, hanging over a gate lodge of distinctive design, and a lady from a nearby village said how sad it was that this had been blown down in recent gales. For a few years, when I showed that slide, I said it was *in memoriam* for a lost tree. No one queried it. Then at last I went down that road again. There the tree was as prominent as ever. It had grown very well too, during its absence.

Similarly, I passed the finest Swedish whitebeam I knew, in the last mile of a regular journey to Westonbirt. Then, to my dismay, it was no longer there. I mentioned this at the arboretum. Yes, they said, a great pity, but it was very close to the house in a tiny front garden, so it was understandable. Maybe. But the tree did not think so. Next time I passed, it was back again.

Then there are the trees which never were. The first three larches in Scotland were, according to an 1813 account, raised in 1680 in a glasshouse and soon became sickly and were thrown out with the rubbish into a hollow nearby, wherein, the account continues, they flourished and had become quite big trees by 1813. In 1954 I found three obviously very old, although not enormous, larches in a dip not far from the house. I measured all three and was thrilled to have found such notable veterans.

I returned in 1970 to photograph and re-measure them. There were only two. I knocked on the door and said what a shame the third tree had gone.

> "For a few years, when I showed that slide, I said it was *in memoriam* for a lost tree. Then at last I went down that road again. There the tree was as prominent as ever. It had grown very well too, during its absence".

"What third tree?" I was asked.

"In 1954, perhaps before you came here, there were three."

"I have been here all my life, and there never has been more than those two."

But I have the measurements in my diary.

Worse, though, in 1983 one of the two had been blown down and crosscut. The rings showed clearly that it dated from only 1740, thus rubbishing my various writings about Scotland's first larch.

The Zelkova is a relative of the elm which grows into enormous trees. In this country, mysteriously, it usually takes the shape of a vast brush with a hundred or more stems, although it remains a normal tree in its home woods in the Caucasus and Elburz mountains. One of the biggest in Britain was measured in 1904 by a house near Hereford. I was delighted to find it, twice as big, in 1962. In 1973 I could not find it. In the rose garden where it had been there was no sign of a stump eight feet across, nor of the disturbance of removing one. I asked the gardener. Never heard of it.

"Ah", I said patronisingly, "before your time; it was here in 1962."

"So was I", he said, "and have been for twenty years". It was the biggest tree for miles. I returned last year, but the tree has not come back yet.

The owner of one of two nearly adjacent estates of big trees told me she could no longer enjoy visiting her neighbour since his superb tulip-tree had gone. I knew the tree well, hugely prominent on a lawn, and we bemoaned its loss since I had seen it. Next time I was there, however, it was there again in all its magnificence, and remained so until the Great Storm of October 1987. She lived across the road, made frequent visits and knew the garden well, so I believed her implicitly.

The Crom Castle yew in County Fermanagh is a prime piece of evidence. There have been descriptions of it for 150 years, of how the branches were trained over a great area, supported by 100 oak posts, and shading tea parties of 200 guests. There are engravings of it and even an early photograph, when it was in a well-kept garden, although half a mile from the castle, away out on a slight eminence along the side of a vast area of lake and bog. It was suitably eerie in swirling mist and rain when I was taken there.

However, we found that there are now two Crom yews. They are only about ten yards apart, of the same age, same size and same once-trained branching, uniting to make the arbour. How could anyone, observer, artist or photographer, contrive not to see or picture this other half of the remarkable pair? It demonstrably was not there. It has suddenly appeared, ready matured, and long trained.

[Editorial note: While typing up this article, we received the following clipping: "Conservationists have discovered giant Californian redwood trees thriving in Sheffield. Although about 100 years old, the 150ft trees have never been noticed by botanists." Yorkshire Post, (22 Oct 1992).]

Theatre

'Foxing the Public'

Stephen Volk raises the curtain on the interchangeable worlds of actors and mediums

I saw Joan of Arc the other day, in Bath. Not so long ago I saw Richard III. I've also had a moving experience in the company of Jesus Christ. Superstar, that is.

The dead are all around us, earning Equity rates and inhabiting the nether world between happy hour and chucking-out time in the West End – or more probably, haunting the dole office. What makes me feel in my bones that, in essence, actors are mediums and mediums are actors?

It started in 1986 when I began to research my current play *Answering Spirits*, about the Fox sisters, the originators of Spiritualism. I spent long hours in the SPR library weighing the evidence of different biographies: some flatly contradicted others, some were horrifyingly biased. Of course, they were all the truth.

In 1848, Maggie and Kate Fox – two farm girls in Hydesville, New York State – began to hear rapping noises which they identified (they said) as the spirit of a pedlar murdered in the cellar. News spread like wildfire. Contact with the dead.

Before they knew it, they were carried along by a tide of public reaction. Spirit circles were set up. Their eldest sister Leah joined in. The three of them were hailed as 'The Mothers of Spiritualism'. By 1854, there were ten million Spiritualists in the USA. By the 1860s mediums were being entertained at the White House, and before long by Gladstone and Queen Victoria.

But the story was to take a wonderfully ironic turn. On 21 October 1888, Maggie Fox stood on the stage of the New York Academy of Music and, before a packed house, launched into a confession, saying that the religion they had founded had all been a hoax and a fraud from beginning to end.

It was the idea of Maggie's outrageous confession that convinced me that the dramatic story of the Fox sisters had to happen in a live theatre – in a way, just as it did in 1888. Then the connections became more and more fascinating.

> "The dead are all around us, earning equity rates and inhabiting the nether world between happy hour and chucking-out time in the West End"

What are sæances, in fact, if not 'theatre'? As Alex Owen says in her excellent book *The Darkened Room*, "the entire business of mediumship was pure theatre, using as it did the creation of atmosphere, its suspension of disbelief, the use of identification, timing – and fakery..."

Of course, whilst the clever Foxes played it straight, mediums like the Davenport Brothers had posters that looked like Vaudeville playbills, advertising conjurors and escapologists. This was the company in which spirit mediums found themselves. Show Biz.

Victorian actors and mediums also shared something else – ill repute. What happened when the lights were turned down reflected in the general opinion that the acting profession was similarly 'of loose morals'.

They also shared the same tools of the trade. Tricks with mirrors. Flying wires for levitation. Optical illusions. Special effects.

But is it all the same thing, play-acting and possession? Contact and curtain calls? Ectoplasm and grease-paint? Or is there a deeper connection than the surface fakery and lies?

Theatre and Spiritualism both require the audience to believe in what they are offered – to a point. We *want* to believe, *need* to believe. We meet in the dark to opt out of the real world and contact something different and elusive. The medium/actor has total control of us; and if they are good, by losing control of themselves. Letting 'another' take over – the character or the ghost.

Anyone watching an actor 'psyching up' before a performance could be forgiven for thinking a medium was testing the vibes. Channelling? Acting? Or the real thing? Do we believe that Maggie Fox created Spiritualism, as she claimed, by making raps with her knee-bone, convincing countless millions to take up her faith? Or that there really is a Summer Land we go to when we die?

All I know is, that's entertainment.

And I can say honestly, in the knowledge that all writers are liars, that everything in my play *Answering Spirits* is absolutely true. **FT**

More details about the play 'Answering Spirits' can be had from Antidote Theatre, c/o 9 Coppice Hill, Bradford-on-Avon, Wiltshire BA15 1JT. Tel: (0225) 862281.

REVIEWS

PLAYING WITH OUR FOOD

ROUND IN CIRCLES

by Jim Schnabel
Hamish Hamilton, London, 1993, hb, £16.99, pp295, photos.

Was it Shakespeare who said "what fools we mortals be"... or was it *Mad* magazine? Either way, it's all too applicable, for tragedy and comedy abound in Jim Schnabel's insider history of crop-circles and the crop-watchers. And yet... somehow, Schnabel's heroes and anti-heroes remain magnificent in their folly and pathos, their ardour and their humanity. For this, more than anything, is the human story of the crop-circle phenomenon.

Schnabel arrived relatively late on the circle scene, in 1991, but has somehow, miraculously, managed to provide a convincing history of the phenomenon from its first intrusion into public consciousness in 1980 which reads as if he was an eye-witness to every event. All the major players are here: Meaden, Andrews, Delgado, Taylor and others, as well as innumerable lesser members of the cast. The 'explanations' are present too, and we can watch Meaden's whirlwind theory develop into plasma vortex, see UFOs pass by to be replaced by 'higher intelligences' and observe Mother Nature in all her New Age finery... until finally the infamous Doug and Dave burst cataclysmically upon the scene. But far more interesting is the jockeying for position: the setting up of organisations, the welcoming and exclusion of members, the disputes, the rivalries, the solicitor's letters, the rumours, undercurrents and threats. And, still more, the way that individuals react to the unexplained, seeming to draw to themselves yet more mystery, until their interaction with it becomes a strange phenomenon worthy of study in itself. Here, if anywhere, is the tragi-comic heart of the matter.

Obviously, the way the story is presented is moulded to a certain extent by Schnabel's selection of material, but generally his attitude seems eminently Fortean. Strange tales (mysterious lights, poltergeists, psychic communications, 'black magicians', etc.) are presented without comment or explanation, and the protagonists present their theories, opinions and scandalous jibes largely in their own words... it's then up to the reader to form his own opinion as to the sense or foolishness displayed. Similarly, it's the reader who's left to speculate on certain other curiosities: if the entire phenomenon was a hoax, it still seems to have attracted a certain amount of inexplicable anomalies... and if there is some core

Jim Schnabel and hoaxer's equipment caught on infra-red film one night this summer

anomaly, what are we to make of the way it was handled, of the theories built upon it, of its attraction to pranksters and so on?

Whatever your view on crop-circles, this is essential reading. As the phenomenon fades from public attention, it leaves us with material for a perfect, self-contained case-study of the way such things develop: how mysteries are reported, how theories develop into explanations, how fantasies develop into cults and disagreements into quarrels, and how, as usual, the dreaded words 'mystery explained' leave us eventually with yet more to think about than we had before.

Apart from anything else, though, this is a gripping read. To say 'highly recommended' hardly does it justice...

Steve Moore

SUPERSTITIONS

by Peter Lorie

Simon & Schuster, London. 1992, hb £14.99, pp255, illus.

Did you know that eating pigs' brains is supposed to render you incapable of telling a lie? I think it would render me incapable full stop! Although the blurb says this is a book of ancient lore, it is in fact a handy compendium of over 200 old wives' tales, folklore and daft beliefs and practices with which the ignorant, the gullible and the fearful, the pagan and the religious, have fended off ill fortune or divined the good. Most are familiar – but there were a few delightful and amazing ones which were not. All are organised in five major groupings with a detailed contents list and a sparse preamble. Each 'entry' is divided into a description of the act or belief and a general discussion of its 'lore and sources'. It has to be said that scholars will find it almost useless, lacking any critical analysis or referencing.

Where the book comes into its own is as a visual reference. It is a feast of lavish illustrations (mostly in colour), superbly designed. The picture researcher should be commended for seeking out new and unfamiliar material. Would make an interesting gift.

Bob Rickard

SPACESHIP CONSPIRACY

George Knap

George Knap Publishing, 4408 Wildwood Crescent, Burnaby, BC V5G 2M4, Canada. 1991, pb $8.95, pp90, illus.

In 1968, while daydreaming before his fireplace, George Knap invented a new form of propulsion for spaceships using a combination of rocket and centrifugal forces. He already had a history of really useful inventions – new kinds of hairpin, concrete post, and bottle cooler; a powered potato-peeler; a self-cleaning comb; a phone-book index; a rivet sorter; and so on.

This is the self-published story of how he tried to bring his orbital propulsion system (fully explained) to the attention of various government and public institutions, including – à la Henry Root – all the correspondence with uncomprehending authorities. It is a stereotypical story of an eccentric inventor taking on a system, with Knap's enthusiastic idealism, frustrated hope, anger and disappointment lighting every page. He stays true to his vision of "deep space liners" plying between the stars, powered by Knap engines.

In one episode he tried to interest the Chinese in his ideas, and when they tried to recruit him as a spy, he fled to the Canadian Intelligence and Security Agency, only to be told they knew all about him. Little wonder then, that Knap concluded there was a conspiracy against him. At one point, a government scientist agrees that Knap's device – which was granted a US patent in 1978 – would indeed produce thrust, but that there were cheaper and more effective ways of doing so. End of interest. Knap believes he has been fobbed off as a crank. He deserves a proper hearing.

Bob Rickard

THE PLAINS OF SAN AGUSTIN CONTROVERSY

prepared by George Eberhart

Jointly published by the J. Allen Hynek Center for UFO Studies &the Fund for UFO Research, PO Box 277, Mount Ranier, MD 20712, USA. 1992, pb price unknown, pp88, illus.

The alleged recovery of unusual debris from a remote sheep ranch near Corona, New Mexico, in July 1945 has been the focus of one of ufology's long-standing disputes about whether it was the remains of a crashed UFO. The arguments are further complicated by an additional claim that an intact craft and several alien bodies were recovered from the Plains of San Agustin, about 150 miles to the west of Corona.

This is a collection of papers presented at a special conference on the subject held in Chicago in February 1992. There is so little tangible evidence from so far back, that investigators are having to make elaborate deductions from imperfect memories of people who may or may not have been there. Bloody battles are still raging in which every iota of each opposing argument is dismembered. Picking over the remains is both daunting and, in the end, fruitless. Nothing concrete has been proved so far, and most pro-crash claims are in doubt if not actually disproved... and here is all the documentation in considerable detail.

Bob Rickard

BLAST YOUR WAY TO MEGABUCK$ WITH MY SECRET SEX-POWER FORMULA

by Ramsey Dukes

Revelations 23 Press, Sheffield, 1993, pb £10.95, pp230, illus.

If you're outraged to find a book with a title like this reviewed in FT, you've already fallen into the first trap (the second one is trying to read the book from the front!). The third one is to think that the book isn't to be taken seriously. Coming from (and transcending) an occult background, these essays, mostly from the early 1980s, range through the nature of reality and virtuality, psychological typing, sexual stereotypes, the value of charlatanry, and much more. Overall, it's witty, charming, humorous and thought-provoking. And how could any Fortean resist an article entitled "A New Muddle of the Universe? A delight.

Steve Moore

UNUSUAL PERSONAL EXPERIENCES

Bigelow Holding Corp., 4640 S. Eastern, Las Vegas, Nevada 89119, USA. (Available FREE from Fund for UFO Research Inc., Box 277, Mt Ranier, MD 20712, USA, for the cost of postage $5.00.)

This is not a sex-contact publication in the usual sense, but the now-famous analysis of the data from three surveys in the USA of UFO/abduction-related beliefs and experiences. Conducted by the Roper Organisation in 1991, nearly 6,000 adults were sampled for evidence of "UFO abduction syndrome", and the results are discussed here by leading proponents of the abduction idea: Budd Hopkins, David Jacobs (interviewed last issue of ***FT***), and Ron Westrum.

Apart from asking about UFO sightings, the questions cover some interesting subjective ground – the feeling of flying, seeing a ghost, dreams about UFOs, feeling paralysed or that someone was in the room while you lay in bed, missing time, unusual balls of light, puzzling scars, and seeing a terrifying figure ("a monster, a witch, a devil") in your room or cupboard as a child.

Whether or not you agree with the interpretation of the replies – and there has not yet been an impartial or hostile analysis – there does seem to be evidence of a 'syndrome'. However, a great deal of further research, surveying and thinking has to be done before the idea of UFO abduction can be distinguished from the imaginative dramatisation of stress, anxiety and trauma, albeit in the unusual forms of alienation and vulnerability. This series of surveys ought to be continued so that we have a growing database to help us understand a very human nightmare.

Bob Rickard

HEALEY AND GLANVILL'S URBAN MYTHS

by Phil Healey and Rick Glanvill

Virgin Books, London. 1992, pb £3.99. pp212.

The fantasy writer Terry Pratchett has a theory about urban legends – they are not so much stories that are repeatedly told, but archetypal events having their own morphogenic fields which allow them to actually happen over and over to different people in different places. I don't know, perhaps it is true. My mum used to work with someone who swears 'The Hairy Hand' incident really happened to him in Croydon. But there we go! Urban myths are like that – so tantalisingly real. It's always the second cousin of a bloke in the pub, or a friend of a friend (foaf)... good tales balancing on the edge of plausibility.

Many of the classics are here – the microwaved poodle, the horror of the Hook, Granny's corpse, but where's the Mexican pet or LSD tattoos? – loosely grouped under such headings as Technophobia, Man's best friend, or Car trouble. There's also a selection of those suspect 'facts' *everyone* knows to be true, such as sparks from underground train tracks wiping your credit card data, or crocodiles thrive near power station waste outlets on the river Trent because of the hot water. These are all the more plausible because some are actually true – there *are* wallabies in the Peak District.

The authors limit their depth analysis to the occasional conversational aside, allowing the stories to roll on thick and fast, indulging their cheerful obsession with injury, death, sex, fæces and embarrassment. My only cavil was the vast number of typos in the unbound proof I had for review, which I hope will be corrected before publication. Undeniably lightweight, but nicely complements the serious stuff. Read, enjoy, then tell them to your friends in the pub.

Ian Simmons

AN INTRODUCTION TO THE MAGICAL ELEMENTS OF THE BIBLE

by Margaret Stutley

Weavers Press. 1991, pb, pp224, refs, bib. (From Janet Bord, Melysfan, Llangwm, Corwen, Clwyd LL21 0RD – UK £9.50 inc p&p, elsewhere £10, airmail £12.50.)

Margaret Stutley is an expert on Hinduism and has written on aspects of Indian magic and folklore. Here, she transfers her attention to the Christian tradition, and specifically to the supernatural aspects of the Bible. It is surprising how much occult material there is in the Bible, and her texts range over magic, circumcision, the significance of blood, divination (by a variety of methods including dreams and astrology, water and conjuration of the dead), oracles and prophecy, curses and blessings, amulets and talismans, sex, demonology and possession, exorcism, miracles, taboos, the virgin birth, the dead, and so on.

One particularly interesting discovery is that the belief in demonology, which passed from Judaism into Christianity (becoming more extreme in the process), led to the widespread irrational fears of Satan and his minions in the Middle Ages, which led in turn to the torture and burning of so-called witches. Some of the beliefs have also survived into the 20th century, making unexpected links between the present day and biblical times. The magical aspects of the Bible have rarely before been gathered together, making this a welcome reference work a rich and available source of esoteric lore.

Janet Bord

Extending the Frontiers

THE SCIENCE GAP

by Milton A. Rothman.

Prometheus Books, Buffalo, NY. 1992, hb £15.95, pp254, notes, index.

THE CHARACTER OF PHYSICAL LAW

by Richard P. Feynman.

Penguin, London. 1992, illus.

THE STRUGGLE TO UNDERSTAND

by Herbert C. Corben.

Prometheus Books, Buffalo, NY. 1992, hb £15.95, pp398, bib, indexes.

Science is a big problem. Everyone knows how it works and (perhaps) knows what a theory is, an experiment is, and sometimes feels confident enough to realise that scientists get some things wrong, or have missed something and yet when they come up with their own theories or explanations, they can find themselves ignored or ridiculed as a 'lunatic fringe', or as Milton Rothman prefers, "paradoxers". Science is a bit like a Rubik cube, easy to twist in any direction, but an awful lot harder to get back into the correct pattern unless you know the rules. It is the ground rules of science that are the subject of these books.

Rothman is sufficiently confident to write *The Science Gap* in order to dismiss the creators of unorthodox theories as scientific "paradoxers" with a caricatured view of science. He sets out various popular myths about science – eg "nothing is known for sure", "nothing is impossible" etc – and attempts to refute them methodically in order to show how science and thinking about science works.

Unfortunately Rothman is also a CSICOP hardline debunker who falls into the very error of which he accuses his "paradoxers", namely caricaturing his opponents and then believing the caricature. For him, all UFOs are nuts and bolts machines from Mars, telepathy is totally impossible because it can't work, and Cold Fusion is nonsense because Pons and Fleischmann didn't play by the rules and publish their data in a peer-reviewed journal first. Anyone who even considers these ideas might be worth investigating is automatically a crank.

Rothman's technique of assuming that the most extreme position held by a single opponent is the norm across a (usually) heterogeneous group of opponents is not really conducive to dialogue and understanding. To be fair, he does include some scientists in this group, and he does not shy away from admitting that science may be fallible, and if you can stomach the arid and tedious tirades against representative opponents that punctuate this book, it is nevertheless a good introduction to the workings of science and tackles head-on the rhetoric of many pseudo-beliefs.

It might be an idea to read Rothman's book in tandem with the late Richard Feynman's *Character of Physical Law*. Feynman was one of the 20th century's more extraordinary scientists – an artist, bongo player, topless bar aficionado and Tuvan throat-singing enthusiast, he won a Nobel prize for his work on quantum electrodynamics. This cheerful book is based on a series of lectures given in 1964 and covers similar ground to Rothman's, but is wider ranging and less immediately accessible for non-physicists. Using description and analogy, Feynman analyses basic scientific laws, showing how we know what we know about them and what that means for our understanding of the world. In this, it is more practical than Rothman's book; so read Rothman first for clarity, then Feynman for humanity... *then* go off and create your theory of antigravity.

Ian Simmons

Herbert Corben's *Struggle to Understand* came to us late, but it is right to include it here. It is a momentous study of the history of wonder and discovery, rich in detail, illuminating in its insight, and thoughtful in its analysis. Corben's range is vast, covering four millennia of ideas, controversies, suppressions, and breakthroughs, with special attention given to the contributions to Western scientific culture from other civilisations (Islam is well discussed here, while China is oddly absent).

Mostly the book is arranged in thematic discussions – eg 'Witches, Devils, and Lunatics', 'Birth, Death, and Resurrection', 'Matter, Atoms, and Vacuum' – but towards the end is a biographical list of those who were persecuted because their ideas or discoveries drew the (often fatal) attention of the (then) establishment; and another list of despots who used their authority to encourage emerging sciences. Corben writes passionately: "If science were superstition these people would be gods; if a religion they would be saints."

If it were not so obviously 'on the side' of science against the iniquities of religion, mysticism and superstition, it would be almost Fortean in tone, but even this bias is gentle, recognising that great discoveries may come from almost any direction. If only they could put books like this on the school curriculum – not only would the discussions be *interesting*, but students would be more aware of the fundamental problems of scientific 'progress' and the innate power of thinking properly and clearly. Highly recommended to all.

Bob Rickard

MAG WATCH

Paul Fuller, editor of *THE CROPWATCHER*, took me to task for implying (MagWatch FT68) that *CW* was "increasingly partisan and directionless". I am happy to say that recent *CWs* (#15, Jan/Feb;and #16, March/April 1993) show how wrong I was. Fuller's feisty magazine is fiercely independent and determined to uncover what's going on, fact or fiction. Fuller even beat us to a feature on hoaxers. Each issue is solid with insider information about individual formations, meetings, disputes (including the latest invective) and personalities on any related topic.

ASSAP – the Association for the Scientific Study of Anomalous Phenomena, the UK's only general investigative outfit – publishes a bi-annual report called *ANOMALY*, the latest issue of which includes a report by Hilary Evans on the 'Street Light Interference' project.

The Society for Psychical Research, besides producing a very scholarly quarterly *JOURNAL* containing research papers and reviews, also publishes *THE PSI RESEARCHER*, a well-laid-out lively newsletter accessible to anyone.

Mark Hall has published another two cryptozoological essays in *WONDERS* series: on 'Giant Bones' (March 1993), and 'Lake Michigan Monsters' (June 1993). This is Fortean research at its best, with tight writing, lots of fresh case material and good references.

FOAFTALE NEWS is the quarterly newsletter of the International Society for Contemporary Legend Research, edited by Bill Ellis, with contributions from leading folklorists and urban legend researchers worldwide. It is essential for up-to-the-minute monitoring of the latest preposterous stories in circulation, packed with references, and often hilarious. The May 1993 issue reports on political stories in Mongolia, poisoned burgers, and Bill Clinton as AntiChrist.

One of the USA's longest-running periodicals on New Age type 'fringe science' topics has been impressively re-designed. The *Journal of Borderland Research*, founded in 1945, has become *BORDERLANDS*, still under Thomas Brown's editorship and still covering "the crossroads of science and spirit".

If strange libertarian existentialism sounds interesting, check out *CROATOAN*, whose recent contents have looked for philosophical gold in *The Prisoner* and *Kolchak, The Night Stalker*. Edited by Abbo and Nikira, it shows what can be done with home-DTP, intelligence, sincerity and humour.

Bob Rickard

ASSAP: St Adhelm, 20 Paul St, Frome, Somerset BA11 1DX, UK. Borderlands: Box 429, Garberville, CA 95542, USA. ***Croatoan:*** 9 Navarre Gardens, Collier Row, Essex RM5 2HH, UK. ***Crop Watcher:*** 3 Selborne Court, Tavistock Close, Romsey, Hampshire S051 7TY, UK. ***Foaftale News:*** c/o Paul Smith, Dept of Folklore, Memorial University, St Johns, Newfoundland A1C 5S7, Canada. ***SPR:*** 49 Marloes Road, Kensington, London W8 6LA, UK. ***Wonders:*** 9215 Nicollet So. 104, Bloomington, MN 55420, USA.

ALSO RECEIVED

THE SILBURY TREASURE by Michael Dames.

First published in 1976 and now available in soft cover, this is an excellent piece of archæological and mythological detective work. Dames takes apart all the old notions about Silbury Hill as a burial mound and reveals it to be, instead, a representation of the Neolithic Great Goddess. More astonishing still, he also manages to reconstruct its ritual usage. Well illustrated, and required reading for Earth Mysteries buffs. *Thames & Hudson, London. 1992, pb £8.95, pp192, illus, refs, bib, index.*

THE DEVIL'S NOTEBOOK by Anton Szandor LaVey.

More 'wit and wisdom' (ho hum) from the Hollywood Satanist. If you're convinced by the argument that the publishing industry ignores LaVey because it's afraid of him, this is probably for you. *Feral House, Oregon, 1992, pb $10.95, pp147.*

COLUMBUS WAS LAST by Patrick Huyghe.

A round-up of putative settlers in, and visitors to, the American continent before 1492. Wide-ranging, but none too critical in its use of sources. *Hyperion, New York, 1992, hb $22.95, pp262, bib, index.*

ON JUNG by Anthony Stevens.

Potential students of Jung often feel intimidated both by Jung's style and the sheer bulk of his collected works. They should turn to this book, an admirably clear survey of Jung's thought and development. *Penguin, 1991, pb £6.99, pp402, bib, index.*

IN SEARCH OF THE DEAD by Jeffrey Iverson.

The book of the engrossing BBC TV series, it provides a cautious survey of various ideas about what happens during and after death, in which personal experiences are balanced with medical and psychological research. The sections dealing with unexplained mental powers and experiences, visions, apparitions, reincarnation and the alleged inheritance of fears or physical characteristics from previous lives, are well written and sensible. Iverson says his search began in personal doubt and confusion, and ended with the conviction that death is the "next stage in the evolution of human consciousness". *BBC Books, London. 1992, hb £11.95, pp212, index, bib, plates.*

JUNG FOR BEGINNERS by Maggie Hyde and Michael McGuinness.

For those who like picture books, this is even more accessible than Stevens's book on Jung. The general exposition appears to be reliable and occasionally quite witty. *Icon Books Ltd, Cavendish House, Cambridge Rd, Barton, Cambs, 1992, pb £7.99, pp176, illus.*

THE WHOLE PERSON CATALOGUE edited by Mike Considine.

Modelled on the hugely successful post-Hippy *Whole Earth Catalog*, this is essentially a huge classified list of communities, courses, centres, services, publications, theories, therapies, foods and drugs, and music etc, covering the whole spectrum of New Age merchandising (from crop-circle t-shirts to tipis, and incence to water-birthing pools). Practical sections include advice on starting your own therapy business, how to prevent financial bad luck by correctly siting your toilet the Feng-shui way. Claims to be the "ultimate sourcebook" but falls far short: eg. omits *Fortean Times* but includes New Age-bashing *Skeptical Inquirer;* and omits *The Ley Hunter*, despite including an article by its editor Paul Devereux. Nevertheless, it has been well produced with some humour. *Brainwave, London. 1992, pb £14.95, pp248, illus, index.*

THE UNIVERSE AND I. Text by Timothy Ferris, Illustrations by Ingram Pinn.

From Gaia to the greenhouse effect and from nanotechnology to Nostradamus, Ferris summarises, without condescension but with admirable clarity, the major issues which exercise the world's leading scientists. Pinn's drawings, as readers of *New Scientist* will know, are full of whimsy and strangely enlightening. A beautiful and useful little book for readers of all ages. *Pavilion Books, 1993, hb £9.99, pp88, illus.*

PASSPORT TO MAGONIA by Jacques Vallee.

A welcome new edition of the 1969 (long out-of-print) classic work by pioneering ufologist Vallee. This was one of the few key books that broke out of the ET straightjacket and demonstrated the close parallels between the accounts of UFO contactees and abductees and stories of encounters with fairies, demons, elementals and other entities of legend, fantasy, folklore and supernatural beliefs, and even of fiction. It comes with a new preface and the full 'Century of UFO Landings' listing that was omitted from some early editions. *Contemporary Books, Chicago. 1993, $14.95, pp372, index, notes, plates.*

DAO DE KING by Lao Tzu.

A well-produced, large format edition of the Taoist classic, each chapter accompanied by a full-page photo. More startling, it's produced by Taoists who want to give it away for nothing. So now's the time for you to be obligingly receptive..! *The Daoist Foundation, P.O.Box 93, Penzance, Cornwall, TR18 2XN, 1992, pb, free (+ £2.25 p+p), pp164, photos.*

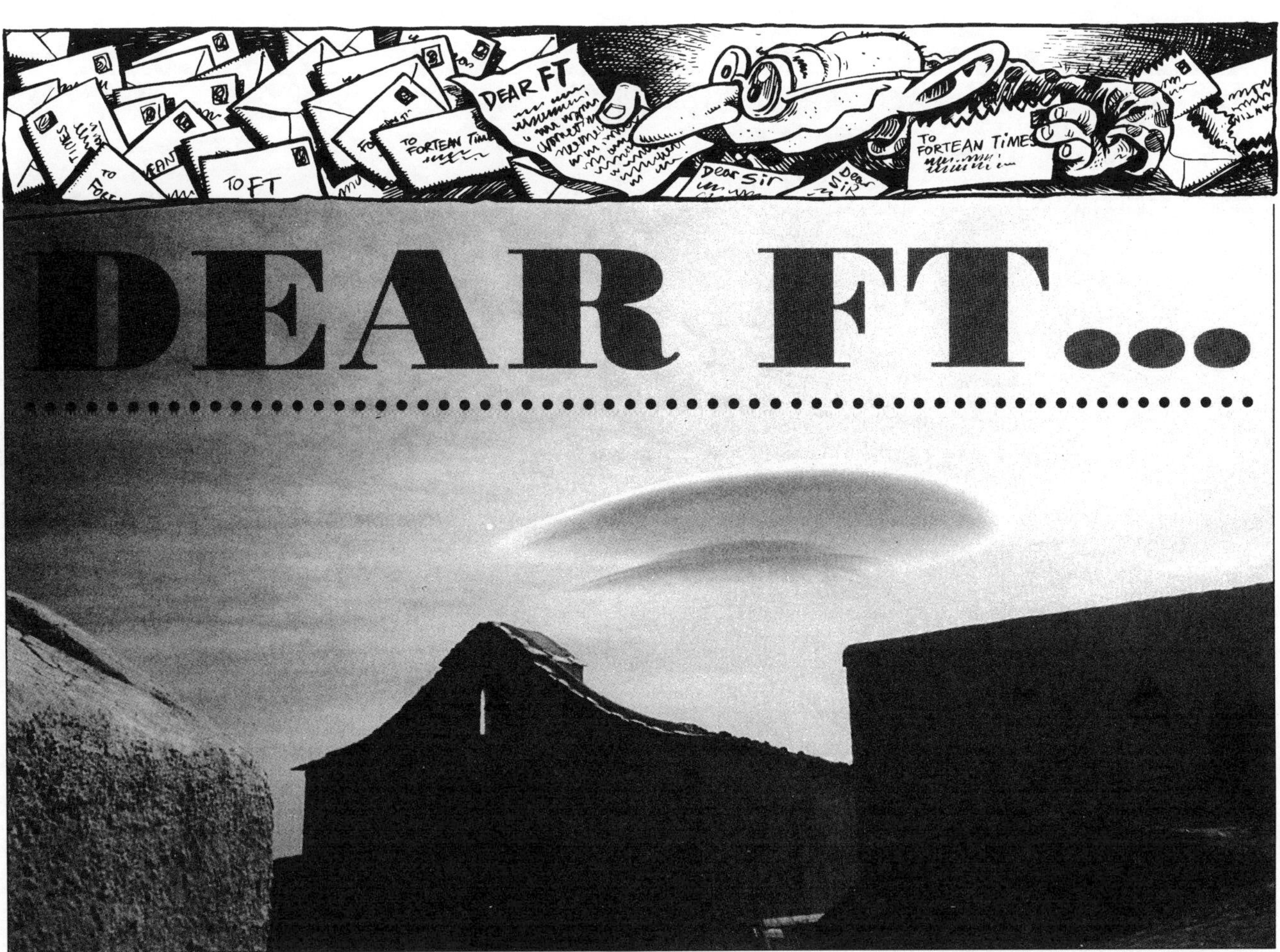

DEAR FT...

LENTICULAR CLOUD

■ I photographed this fine lenticular cloud, which looked like a huge flying saucer, on 15 November 1991 in the village of Los Llanos between Orjiva and Trevelez in the Sierra Nevada region of Spain. I watched it with my wife for a long time. It gradually assumed a more normal cloud shape.

Eric R. Brady, *Staffordshire*

BLACK LAGOON REVISITED

■ I was pleased to see Ulrich Magin's *Scaly Horrors* [***FT63:40***]. The public doesn't realise the numbers of these entities being reported, so it was great to see a roundup. I tend to see a more direct connection than he does between the 'gill-men' of folklore and similar forms in fiction and modern sightings. He uses my ***FT40*** discussion of the 1972 Thetis Lake (not 'Lake Thetis' as in the article) 'monster' to support his notion that this sighting is linked to Jack Arnold's 1954 movie *The Creature from the Black Lagoon* – a tenuous link in my view.

As I have pointed out (*Curious Encounters*, p71), the area is not lacking in indicator folklore. The Kwakiutl Indians have tales of a fish-faced, paired incisored merman, *Pugwis*, which must have resembled Jack Arnold's creature on some metaphorical level. Among the Micmac here in Maine and eastern Canada the mermen and merwomen are called 'the halfway people', not seen as supernatural beings, but merely another tribal group. In some ways, all of these 'lagoon creatures' are halfway people – caught between ancient folklore and modern sightings, but most graphically captured for modern *Homo sapiens* in the cinema.

The folklore, fiction and tales may indicate a genuine phenomenon. Magin may wish away these gill folk as mere 'reptilian nightmares', but I think he's mixing apples and oranges to win his argument. As Mark Opsasnick, Mark Chorvinsky and I tried to show in some articles [*Strange Magazine* #3, 1988] these creatures could be anything from 'skunk apes' to 'reptilian bipeds'.

Incidentally, I notice you credit the drawing of the Thetis Lake creature to 'unknown'. It is in fact my drawing, enhancing the faded sketch accompanying the article "Battle of the Uglies?" by Walter McKinnon (Victoria (BC) *Victoria Times*, 24 Aug 1972).

Loren Coleman
Portland, Maine

OF CATS AND SHOPPING TROLLEYS

■ Regarding your discussion of six-toed cats [***FT26:10***]: a friend of mine has a cat with at least six toes per paw. It is totally black and has a satanic temperament. I have a framed photograph of a winged cat at home; it lived in Somerset at the turn of the century.

Another back issue featured a wallaby loose in the area round Wallingford, in the mid-1980s. I lived in Wallingford then and remember it well. It 'disappeared' in typical fashion, but was shortly afterwards found drowned in a garden swimming pool in Benson.

Your recent notes on shopping trolleys [***FT67:19, 69:63***] reminds me of one I saw driving down Oxford Street about midnight, against the traffic, one wet and windy November evening last year.

Christopher Iles
Shillingford, Oxon.

CABIN FEVER

I don't believe in UFOs, I still don't, I don't know what I saw on Saturday, May 1 1993, around six o'clock, while spending a weekend in my cabin. I don't know where it came from, it wasn't even moving and it just gave me enough time to reach for my camera, take a shot and in a matter of seconds it was gone. I don't want any publicity. For personal reasons I wasn't supposed to be there.

Anonymous
Postmarked Van Nuys, California

[Editors' note: you don't have to 'believe' or 'not believe' in UFOs: some flying whatsits are undeniably unidentified, like this one. It looks to us like a soup bowl flung from behind the cabin... but, there again, it might have travelled many light years to greet us.]

ALBINO LOBSTERS

As a regular FT reader and healthy sceptic, I am surprised to be able to report my own Fortean occurrence. I live in a terraced house in Kentish Town, north London. Some while back, over a period of months, I found what appeared to be lobsters in my garden. They were quite large and albino. No-one believed me, and I didn't think to keep them – they weren't too fresh. One night, a friend who was visiting for dinner stumbled upon one of these creatures by my back door. We concocted a number of implausible theories for their presence, including seagulls snatching them from market stalls.

Finally, he posted the specimen to the Natural History Museum, where the Crustacea Section was able to help. The aggressive Turkish Crayfish (*Astacus leptodactylus salinus*) have turned up in Camden's canal system. The road next to my own is called Angler's Lane. The river for which this road was named went underground long ago, but still links up with the drains between my road and the canal. The crayfish appear to have crawled out of my uncovered drainage outlet and onto the lawn. I am now beginning to appreciate the thin line between the commonplace and the absurd…

Christopher Fowler
Kentish Town

THE END WAS NOT NIGH

I wonder if any FT readers can help me. One of the things that profoundly affected me as a 10-year-old boy was an 'End of the World' scare in, I think, 1958. I have subsequently spoken to several people from different parts of the country who remember this event – one remembers the teacher herding the children out into the playground at the appointed time. (What good this would have done I am not sure!) I have looked in *The Times Index* for 1958 and 1959 with no success. Any ideas?

John Penderton
23 West Way, Banbury, Oxon.

FRACTAL FREAKS

I have not read *Fractals* by J.Briggs [Reviewed ***FT69:60***], but I doubt that 'hard-core fractal freaks' would have any good reason to 'fall about laughing' at a connection between Newton's method and the Mandelbrot set. Read, for instance, *Newton's Method, Circle Maps, and Chaotic Motion* by D.G. Saari and J.B. Urenko, American Mathematical Monthly, Jan 1984, p3. The point about Newton's method is that it is iterative. Anybody who has used the method will be familiar with the fact that it frequently fails (to converge) if the starting conditions are ill-chosen. The Mandelbrot set helps to rationalise and identify those sets of conditions under which iterative procedures will succeed. By the way, it was only recently proved that the Mandelbrot set *is* a fractal.

On the subject of 'red mercury' [***FT69:44***]: I have checked the scientific literature for the past 90 years and have found only a handful of papers on this material. Nearly all of them concerned its crystal structure and none of them indicated any special properties. I suspect that belief in its nuclear properties may stem from the daft theories of Louis Kevran – the man who once claimed that lobsters could manufacture gold and who believes that transmutations merely involve adding up the atomic numbers of elements.

Dr David J. Fisher
Cardiff

ICY MIST

The following incident happened recently to my Bridge partner, Bob Jones, who works as a security officer in Octel, a heavy chemical plant in Ellesmere Port. Early one morning at 2:45 he was in the Research and Development Plant checking the doors. One was open and he fell into the room. Turning round, he noticed that the bolt of the door was sticking out. He went into the new portakabin extension (built in about 1990) and locked the door behind him. There were three laboratories on either side of a narrow passageway, which ended in a blank wall. When he reached the end of the corridor and turned round, he was enveloped in an icy mist, so thick and white that he couldn't see through it. He took one step forward and the next thing he knew he was at the other end of the corridor – he couldn't recall taking the nine or ten paces to get there. He looked round and the mist was gone. He unlocked the door and went out.

In about 1967 an industrial chemist at the Research and Development Plant at Octel had committed suicide by drinking lead. Had Bob encountered his ghost?

Mrs C. Carr
Birkenhead

HIJACKED?

I was distressed to find the cover and five full pages of the last issue handed over to the crop circle debunker-in-chief, Jim Schnabel. What drives the obsessive Schnabel to produce his inaccurate, exaggerated and dishonest confections? And whatever possessed you to lower your usual consistent standards? You have allowed your pages to be hijacked by a clever propagandist.

Michael Glickman
London

*[Editors reply: Having given much space over ten years to the paranormal and meteorological approaches to crop circles, we felt it was time to shift our perspective and look at the artistic side of the phenomenon. No-one, as far as we know, doubts that many flattened crop patterns are man-made; whether **all** of them are, as Schnabel implies, is another matter. Considering the long pedigree of simple circles (see supplement in FT63) and the eye-witness accounts of circle formation accompanied by buzzing noises etc, we reserve final judgment – as usual.]*

ELEPHANT SITS ON MINI – AGAIN

Urban legends go in and out of vogue over the years: take the Elephant and the Red Car, once all the rage in the 1970s. An elephant has been trained to sit on a red box at the sound of its trainer's whistle. It takes part in a circus parade through some town, hears a factory siren (or a traffic

DEAD FUNNY

■ Forteans may enjoy the fact, exhibited in this photograph, that the Society for Psychical Research has now settled into new premises which it shares with a distinguished firm of undertakers. This was not by deliberate choice. We are treating it as an interesting synchronicity.

Ralph Noyes,
SPR Hon. Secretary
Chelsea

cop's whistle), spies a red car (a Volkswagen or a Mini) and sits on it, flattening the hapless vehicle.

In September 1975, the Swedish paper *Expressen* published a photograph of just such an event. A distraught driver gawps at an elephant which is sitting – or more correctly leaning – against the car's fender. It looks convincing, although it was obviously posed after the putative event. Plenty of *Expressen* readers would have been unaware of the legend at the time, so its presentation as news in a national daily served to strengthen the folkloric motif. Then Nellie the Elephant packed her trunk and said goodbye to the circus.

In September 1992, I was strolling down Doncaster High Street when I caught sight of a pink elephant flattening a red car in a window display at the local Automobile Association offices. The accompanying slogan was: *Don't be a Nellie – take out A.A. insurance cover against the unexpected.*

As a student of urban folklore, my curiosity was aroused. I phoned the headquarters of the AA's marketing division in Basingstoke and spoke to Lucy Shaw, marketing co-ordinator and originator of the 'Don't be a Nellie' campaign. "Well, we needed an eye-catching design for our stand at the Motor Fair at Earl's Court in October 1991", she explained, "so I sounded out an artist named Derek Matthews, who does a lot of work for us. He faxed over quite a few good cartoon-type designs, including the elephant squashing the car, which is the one I chose. It was very eye-catching and drew a lot of interest." She was quite certain that she had never heard of the old urban legend.

Derek Matthews had never heard the story either. "It just cropped up from my designs", he explained. "My brief was to show a car suffering some sort of accident, but with no serious overtones, such as a traffic accident or injury. Also, the car had to be parked. I thought about something heavy coming down on a parked car and the elephant seemed logical, as something heavy passing by."

There were several details echoing the urban legend. Apart from the elephant being pink (with possible connotations to the other AA and drink-driving), the design clearly shows the pachyderm in circus trimmings and, crucially, the car is red. "The car was coloured red to stand out", said Mr Matthews, "and in my original design the elephant is pinky-grey. As for the circus trimmings, I suppose it was a natural explanation for the elephant being in the vicinity of a parked car. Perhaps I *may* have heard the story somewhere before, a long time ago, and forgotten it, but I certainly didn't know of the urban legend."

This apparently spontaneous re-emergence of a folkloric motif seems to support the notion proposed by some folklorists that such stories originate in the collective unconscious. Now to see if the hairdresser of my electricity meter reader's aunt has *her* red car squashed by an unruly elephant...

Nick Mays
Doncaster

A BRUSH WITH THE BLACK DOG

■ A friend of mine, Dominic Gray, used to work at Tesco's in Great Yarmouth. I was talking about the couple of 'black dog' stories I knew about Great Yarmouth when he mentioned that he had had an encounter a few years back.

He was the last to leave the store along with the assistant manager at about 2am in the morning. It was pitch black on the rooftop carpark. As they approached their cars, they heard a dog running towards them. Dominic said that from the sound of claws on the tarmac he got the impression of a very large dog. As they turned towards the sound, they 'felt' the dog or whatever it was rush past them very close by. They ran to their respective cars to put on the headlights to see what it was, but there was no sign of any animal. There is only one way down from the roof and the 'dog' had been running away from this, and there was no cover for it to hide behind.

Claire Blamey
Great Yarmouth, Norfolk

WE STAND CORRECTED

■ You are well behind the times [*FT69:7*]. There are at least two machines which will provide your location within a few yards and/or OS reference, which have been on the market some time in the UK at about £600.

N.M.Howlett
Frome, Somerset

DEVIL'S HOOFPRINTS

■ I live in a small rural town near Albuquerque, New Mexico. In December 1985, while walking outside my house in the fresh snow from the night before, I happened upon some odd hoofprints. At first I took no notice; there are many horses in the area. When I looked more closely, however, I realised that they formed a nearly straight line. Vaguely remembering a similar curiosity, I ran into my room and got a book on mysteries, which included the famous Devil's Hoofprints of Devon in 1855. The drawings and measurements of the prints in the book were nearly identical to those in the snow. The hoofprints went about 15 feet in one direction, away from the property. I followed them back and found they passed within five feet of my bedroom window. I found no trace of them in the surrounding area.

I showed the prints to my father, who saw the similarity. I was only 14 at the time and didn't have the presence of mind to take photographs. I don't claim that the Devil walked by my house that night, but *something* left a few dozen aligned, cloven hoofprints in the snow. I promise photographs if they reappear.

Benjamin Radford
Corrales, New Mexico

[Editors' note: The FT Occasional Paper on the Devil's Hoofprints is still in preparation. To all those who sent us advance payment, we say: Don't give up hope. One day your prints will come.]

noticeboard

EXCHANGE & MART

● **FORBIDDEN MYSTERIES OF ENOCH** why Church Fathers suppressed the real story of the fallen angels. Send SAE details to Arcturus, The New House, East Grafton, Marlborough, Wilts SN8 3DB

● **FREEDOM OF INFORMATION CAMPAIGN** everything you need to know, but were never told about UFO's, aliens, cures, cover-ups,conspiracies. For free catalogue write to:- Rev Anthony G. Pike, 141 Austen Rd, Sth Harrow HA2 OUU Middx. Tel. 081-426-8758.

● **WINNING WITH MAGICK Are You? LOVE! MONEY! HAPPINESS! SUCCESS!** Guaranteed or your money back! The World's best loved psychic manual - Used successfully by 1000s. Katherine Sullivan & Daniel Goodman give you over 75 pages of safe & easy to perform mental rituals and techniques, never revealed before to: Bring Back A Lost Lover, Keep a Present Lover, Attract A New Lover. Plus! How to PREDICT accurately, Turn to page 45 to begin a whole new life, then use your 'Super Aura' to Zap! Whatever you want: Cash, Luxuries etc. Create a 'Thought Talisman' Discover the Lazy way to Learn and Earn! Make Money While You Sleep! Send £10 to: Thought Magick, Dept FT, 27 Old Gloucester St., London WC1N 3XX & 071-916-0133

● **WANTED** - Anything relating to the visionary/occult artist AUSTIN OSMAN SPARE (AOS). In particular, original artworks depicting satyrs, witches, ghosts and elementals, astral and arboreal landscapes, selfportraits etc. good prices paid. Telephone 081-742-7347 Fax: 081-995-2961. Attention John Balance or write to BM, Codex, London WC1N 3XX

● **A TRUE MYSTERY** written by F Russell Clampit, geocryptologist. "The Coldrum Line" may be the strangest ley line in Britain, stretching from an ancient burial mound in Kent to the far depths of the North Sea. Maps, diagrams and photographs. Price £3.95 inc p&p. Cheques/PO's payable to Akelarre, PO Box 3 Llandeilo, Dyfed SA19 6YJ. USA dollar bills only. $10 surface mail, $13 air.

● **LEGAL HIGHS** A detailed study of over 70 plants with hallucinogenic stimulant and tranquillising properties. Don't buy expensive pre-mixed preparations of anonymous herbs, send for this book and explore the world of botanicals. £7.50 or SAE for more details: Sirus (F), PO Box 524, Reading, Berks, RG1 3JY

● **INSTANT ENLIGHTENMENT** esoteric physical technique explained - free info' contact F.E.F. P.O. Box 37-217 Parnell, Auckland, New Zealand.

● **UFO BOOKS, MAGAZINES, VIDEOS** lists SAE SR Stebbing, 41 Terminus Drive, Herne Bay, Kent, CT6 6PR.

● **THE ENIGMA** articles on horror, politics, psychology, the occult and religion,plus subjects enigmatic for we are the ENIGMA. But not a puzzle. £1.50 UK, £2.00 overseas. Payment to: The enigma, 1 Austin Close, Ircester, Northants NN9 7AX.

● **NEW DIMENSIONS** the monthly magazine of esoteric information. The best occult articles, qabalah, metaphysics, psychology, book & music reviews. Dynamic in origin. The best all-rounder. Magic at its best £1.25 UK, £1.75 overseas. Dept. MS, 1 Austin Close, Irchester, Northants, NN9 7AX.

● **UFO NEWSCLIPPING SERVICE** keeps you up with the real 'close encounters'. Many fascinating UFO reports from the world's press are reproduced facsimile, along with news-wire items from the major agencies. UFONS is 20 foolscap pages monthly, with a Fortean section strong on cryptozoology. Foreign language reports are provided in translation. For information and sample pages, write today to: UFONS - Lucius Farrish, Route 1 Box 220, Plumerville, AR 72127, USA.

● **THE SKEPTIC** takes an entertaining, rational and humorous look at pseudoscience and claims of the paranormal. Articles, reviews columns, cartoons and much more. If you like FT you'll like The Skeptic. Sample issue £1.85; annual sub (6 issues) £12. The Skeptic, PO Box 47, Manchester M60 2TH.

● **COMMUTE REGULARLY** Into inner space? Mind machines take you places yet undreamt of. Money back if not mindblown. 2x 1st class stamps to: Highland Psionics, Scoraig Garve, Ross-shire 1V23 2RE.

● **UFOS:** Contact International has researched the subject for 25 years. Our magazine, "Awareness", pulls no punches, devastating new findings on origin of crop circles. Information: 11 Ouseley Close, Oxford, OX3 0JS

● **UFO AFRINEWS** edited by Cynthia Hind. The only UFO magazine in Africa. Write: Gemini, Box MP49 Mt Pleasant, Harare, Zimbabwe.

● **THE TOTALLY AMAZING "A-Z OF PSYCHIC SECRETS!"** Claire Abbots Reveals the "Tricks of the trade!" with over 80 pages of Palmistry, Astrology, Graphology secrets, plus over 30 full length Dynamic Money Spells & Potent Love Spells, Plus! Free programmed Brazilian Quartz Point Crystal Attuned to the book. Plus!! FREE Love & Money Talisman: also 'Astro-Love Match' chapter to guide you to the perfect love partner. Learn how to perform spells to change your love life forever! Discover the power of DESIRE BELIEF & EXPECTANCY! Learn how to 'read' someone's character from a glance at their palm! At last! - What the life line really means. Learn to assess someone's intelligence from a quick glance at their handwriting! Plus much more. Send £10 to: Claire Abbots', 27 Old Gloucester St., London WC1N 3XX. No quibble refund if not absolutely delighted. & tel: 071-916-0133

EVENTS

● **UFO '93** Nov 6/7 Hever Village Hall, Talks, Films, Slides, Abductions, Close encounters, M.I.B's Hilton Highland Glen, Graves End Ad Shurne, Kent, DA12 3JW

● **PUBLICISE YOUR EVENT HERE FREE** Fax us details on 081-552 5466.

● **ORGONE93** Conference on orgone, UFOs crop circles and earth mysteries. 4 Sept 1993 at Conway Hall, Red Lion Sq, London. Lectures, evening social & Sunday tour. Tickets £10. Details leaflet from Orgone93, SKS, 20 Paul St, Frome, Somerset BA11 1DX. Tel: 0373 451777.

● **CORNFERENCE** Cerealogist magazine's 3rd annual convention, at Corn Exchange, Dorchester, Dorset - 2-3 October 1993 - speakers, panels , latest videos exhibition - Tickets £25 & £40 from SKS, 20 Paul St, frome, Somerset BA11 1DX. Tel: 0373 451777.

● **SOCIETY FOR PSYCHICAL RESEARCH LECTURE** 6.30-8pm Kensington Central Library, Campden Hill Road, London N8 Nearest tube: High Street Kensington. Admissions: £3 (concessions £1). Phone: 071-937-8984. Thursday 16th September 1993. "WHITEMAN'S PHILOPSOPHY OF SPACE AND TIME". Professor John Poynton.

● **FRIDAY 10TH TO SUNDAY 12TH SEPTEMBER 1993** SOCIETY FOR PSYCHICAL RESEARCH 17TH INTERNATIONAL CONFERENCE with talks and discussion on all aspects of psychical research. Ingram Hotel, Glasgow. Registration + full-board £134; registration + lunches £46. Phone 071-937-88984 for further information and booing form.

● **CROP CIRCLE GEOMETRY & SYMBOLISM** with John Martineau, Micheal Glickman, Earl of Haddington, at The Priory, Wymondley, Herts, on 19 Sept 1993, Tickets £20.

● **FOLKLORE SOCIETY EVENTS** 'Women's Folklore Day School', 30 Oct 1993 at University of Kent, Canterbury - Katherine Briggs Lecture by Dr Ruth Finnegan 'The Poetic and the Everyday' 9 Nov 1993 at University College London. For details on these and other events, phone Steve Roud at the Folklore Society: 071-380 7095 (messages 071-387 5894).

BOOKMART

● **JONATHAN WOOD-LITERATURE & PRIVATE WRITINGS** Anything from Aleister Crowley to Arthur Machen and Ralph Chubb. Catalogues and No obligation booksearch. Write for latest catalogue: J.Wood, BM Spellbound, London, WC1N 3XX.

● **MIDNIGHT BOOKS** - Quality secondhand books on all aspects of the unexplained. SAE for 32 page catalogue: Steven Shipp, Midnight Books, The Mount, Aserton Road, Sidmouth, Devon, EX10 9BT. (0395) 515446

● **MILLENNIUM BOOKS** 2nd hand books on UFOs, and mysteries weird and wonderful. For free list, write, fax, phone - 9 Chesham Road, Brighton, Sussex BN2 1NB.- 0273 671967

● **EXCALIBUR BOOKS** New, secondhand and imported titles on folklore, paranormal and UFOs. Free lists - 1 Hillside Gardens, Bangor, Co Down BT19 6SJ, N.Ireland. (0247 458579)

MISC

● **ALETHIA, WHITE WITCH,** will cast spells for luck, love etc. Also dreams analyzed and lucky talisman sent on request. Dreams £5, Spells £10, Talisman £5. Send SAE to 50 Norn Hill, Oakridge, Basingstoke, Hants RG21 2HE.

● **CLASSIC ITALIAN RECIPES** 8 for £5.00, your family and friends will come back for more. Preston, 6 Cleveland Road, Ealing, London W13 8AU.

● **WELSH HOLIDAY COTTAGE** Self-catering accommodation in historic North Wales town of Denbigh. For further details, contact Janet Bord, Melysfan, Llangwm, Corwen, Clwyd LL21 ORD. Tel: 049 082 472. Fax: 049 082 321.

● **YOUNG MAN** desperately needs cures,advice,psychic information, prayers,love,techniques,healing,contacts,anything for stress related asthma, ulcers,psoriasis. Write P Younger, 21 Beeches, 200 Lampton Rd, Hounslow, Middx, TW3 4EH.

● **YOU CAN MAKE** a substantial extra income, in your own time, working from home. Low investment, superb potential! Write to: Eclipse Business Enterprises, P O Box 54, Birkenhead, Wirral, L43 7FD.

● **POSTAL TAROT READINGS** Full question & answer service., £5.00 per question, returnable photo and fee to Chris Donkin, 10 Crown Terrace, Scarborough, North Yorkshire, YO11 2BL.

● **INTERESTED IN A CREED OF IRON?** Read " THE ODIN BROTHERHOOD" (£6.95)from Mandrake Press , Ltd, Essex House, Thane OX9 3LS

● **POEMS** wanted on strange phenomena and inexplicable events. Send up to two poems, maximum 30 lines, to arrive before 14 Sept 1993, to POETRY NOW, Strange But True, 1-2 Wainman Rd, Woodston, Peterborough PE2 7BU, including SAE. All unused work returned.

● **CATALOGUE ZERO** Fifty items of literature and weirdness for sale. Also an essay on Arthur Machen. Write with unseemly haste for YOUR copy: Jonathan Wood, BM Spellbound, London WC1N 3XX.

RESEARCH

● **PRIMROSE HILL/UFO's** Information required on the connection: Personal experiences, newspaper clippings etcetera. Please write to: Daniel Gooding, 59b Pentonville Road, London N1 9LP.

● **MINOAN CRETE...** They seemed to have a way of experiencing life quite unlike any other people. Research Group into the First Europeans, contact: J. Douglas, 39 Sedgemere Avenue, London N2 OSY.

● **SOUTHEND** Any oddities or strange phenomena about this town or environs needed for book on Southchurch. Write: Marion K. Pearce, 78 Hamlet Road, Southend-on-Sea, Essex SS1 1HH

● **FORTEAN PICTURES** The Fortean Picture Library is a self funding project for the rescue and preservation of valuable documentary material, photographs and drawings etc. Contact Janet Bord, FPL Melysfan, Llangwm, Corwen, Clwyd, Wales LL21 ORD. Fax 049 082 321.

NUMBER 71

UK £2
USA $4.95

FORTEAN TIMES

THE JOURNAL OF STRANGE PHENOMENA

MEMORIES OF HELL:

Real-Life Trauma or Hysterical Hypno-Fear?

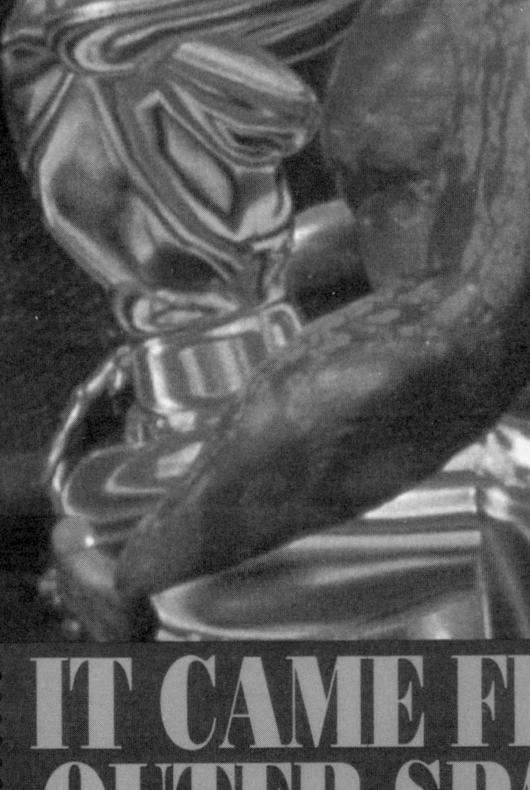

IT CAME FROM OUTER SPACE!

Full Colour Pull-Out Guide to 20th Century Aliens

Terence McKenna Interview • Balkan Spider Terror
Fairy Sightings in the UK • Peruvian Vampire Scare

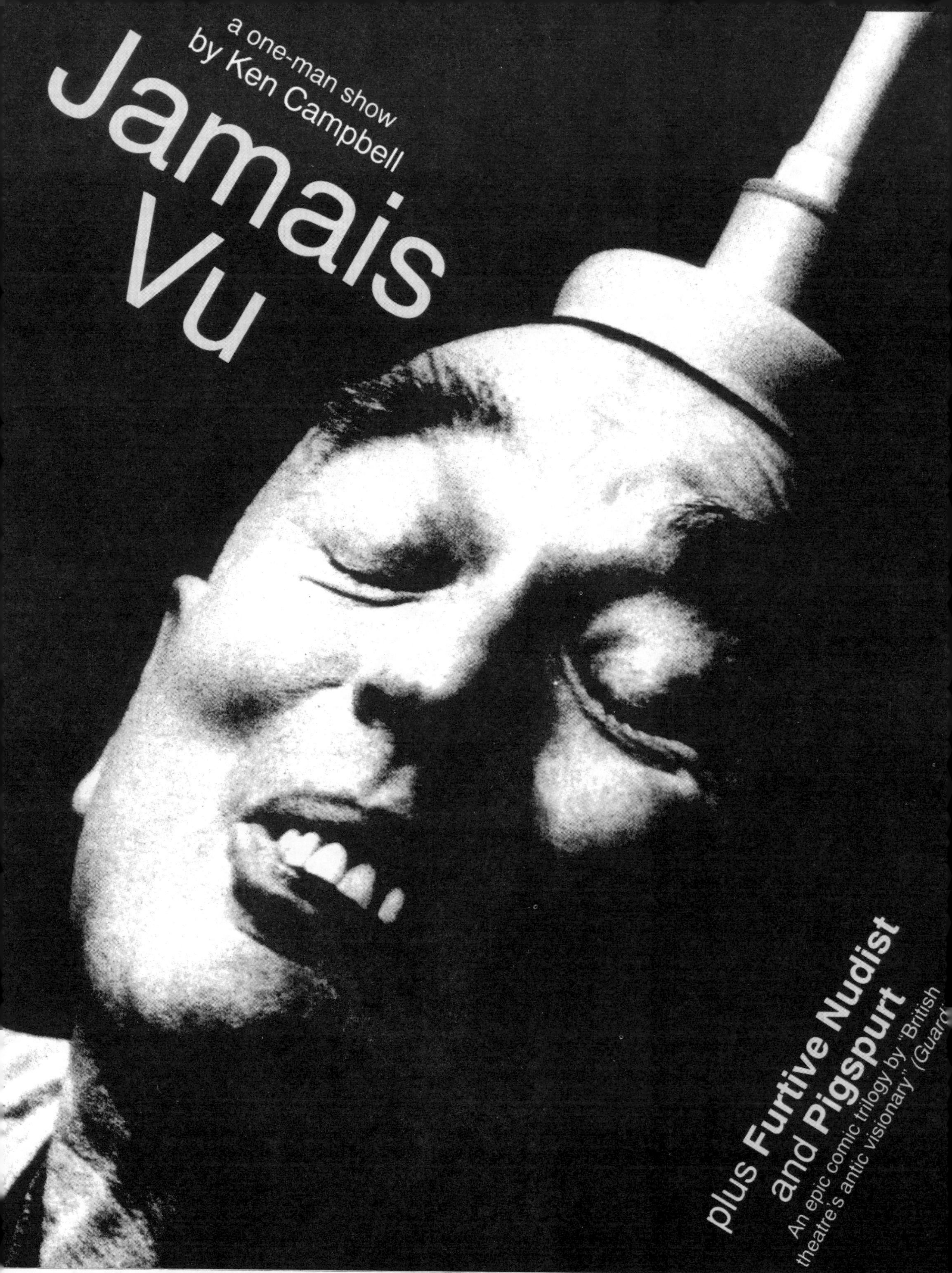

a one-man show
by Ken Campbell

Jamais Vu

plus **Furtive Nudist and Pigspurt**

An epic comic trilogy by "British theatre's antic visionary" (Guard

FIRST CALL
071-836 3464

riverside studios

Crisp Road Hammersmith W6 9RL • 081-748 3354

3-27 November

Direct from the Royal National Theatre

Jamais Vu
Tues - Sat 8.00pm
£9.50, £7.50 concs

Furtive Nudist
Sats 1.00pm

Pigspurt
Sats 4.30pm

Riverside Studios is a registered charity

Contents

ISSUE 71 : OCTOBER/NOVEMBER 1993

TERENCE MCKENNA - PAGE 35

EDITORIAL 4

Dissociation • False Memory Syndrome and Forteana • FT Reader Survey • Competition winners

STRANGE DAYS 5

Heretic dinosaurs • Talking Turkey • Peruvian vampire scare • Miraculous images • The Taos Hum Ghosts on TV • Loose lions • Organ kidnapping McDonald's and the IRA

PHENOMENOMIX 21

HUNT EMERSON'S humorous look at the world

MEMORIES OF HELL 23

JIM SCHNABEL on the questionable nature of 'repressed' memories, False Memory Syndrome and the role of hypnotherapists

THE WEBS OF WAR 34

Has the Serbian airforce being dropping synthetic spiders' webs laced with chemical weapons? PAUL SIEVEKING investigates

THE FT INTERVIEW: TERENCE MCKENNA 35

TOM HODGKINSON talks to the psychedelic philosopher from California

MODERN FAIRY SIGHTINGS 39

Encounters with fairies as told to the magazine *John o'London's* in the 1930s, presented by DAVID LAZELL

FROM OUR FILES 43

- HOAX: The levitation photo of Mirabelli *Guy Lyon Playfair*
- ARCHIVE GEMS: The Bowhead Incident
- DIARY OF A MAD PLANET: Weather watch June/July 1993
- FEELING CROSS: A modern stigmatic *Bob Rickard*
- SECRET COUNTRY: Callanish, Outer Hebrides *Janet and Colin Bord*

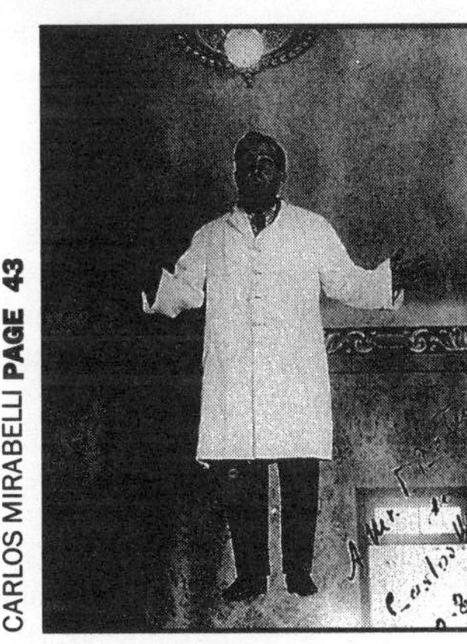

CARLOS MIRABELLI PAGE 43

FORUM 53

Yvonne Greene • Gerald Baker • Peter Carr Paul Sharville

REVIEWS 59

Encyclopedia of Strange Physical Phenomena • A Confusion of Prophets Video reviews • Biological Anomalies • Materialisations • Magwatch

LETTERS 63

Fainting goats • The Haunted Billabong • Randi replies • Shrouded retort Levitation • Jung's dream

NOTICEBOARD 66

Fortean meetings, lectures, events, research, products and offers

COVER : FROM THE LAWNMOWER MAN
INSET : AVELEY ABDUCTION : SEE CENTRE PULLOUT

WHY 'FORTEAN'?

CHARLES FORT (1874-1932)

Fortean Times is a bi monthly magazine of news, reviews and research on all manner of strange phenomena and experiences, curiosities, prodigies and portents, formed in 1973 to continue the work of the iconoclastic philosopher CHARLES FORT. Fort was sceptical about scientific explanations, observing how scientists argued for and against various theories and phenomena according to their own beliefs, rather than the rules of evidence. He was appalled that data not fitting the collective paradigm was ignored, suppressed, discredited or explained away (which is quite different from explaining a thing).

Fort was perhaps the first to speculate that mysterious lights seen in the sky might be craft from outer space. He coined the term 'teleportation' which has passed into general usage through science fiction. His dictum "One measures a circle beginning anywhere" expresses his philosophy of Continuity and the 'doctrine of the hyphen', in which everything is in an intermediate state between extremes. He had notions of the universe-as-organism and the transient nature of all apparent phenomena. Far from being an over-credulous man, Fort cut at the very roots of credulity: "I cannot accept that the products of minds are subject matter for beliefs ... I conceive of nothing, in religion, science, or philosophy, that is more than the proper thing to wear, for a while."

Fort was born in Albany, New York, in 1874 into a family of Dutch immigrants. Beatings by a tyrannical father helped set him against authority and dogma, and on leaving home at the age of 18 he hitch-hiked around the world to put some "capital into the bank of experience." At 22 he contracted malaria, married his nurse and settled down to 20 years of impoverished journalism in the Bronx. During this time he read extensively in the literature of science, taking notes on small squares of paper in a cramped shorthand of his own invention, which he filed in shoe boxes.

In 1916, when he was 42, Fort came into a modest inheritance, just enough to relieve him of the necessity of having to earn a living. He started writing *The Book of the Damned*, which his friend, the novelist Theodore Dreiser, bullied his own publisher into printing in 1919. Fort fell into a depression, burnt all his notes (which numbered some 40,000) as he had done a few years earlier, and in 1921 set sail for London, where he spent eight years living near the British Museum (39 Marchmont Street) and wrote *New Lands* (1923). Returning to New York, he published *Lo!* in 1931 and *Wild Talents* in 1932, shortly before he died. He left 60,000 notes, now in the New York Public Library.

THE GANG OF FORT

EDITORS:
Bob Rickard & Paul Sieveking
CONTRIBUTING EDITORS:
Steve Moore,
Mike Dash & Ian Simmons

ISSN 0308 5899

EDITORIAL ADDRESS

Fortean Times:
Box 2409, London NW5 4NP, UK.
Tel & Fax: 071 485 5002 or 081 552 5466.

CAVEAT

The opinions of contributors and interviewees are not necessarily those of the editors. FT itself has no corporate view except to bring the widest range of interpretations to stimulate discussion.

SUBMISSIONS

Submissions are invited of suitable articles, news, art, cartoons, letters and reviews. Preliminary discussion with the editors is advisable. Text can be submitted on floppy disks, but check with the editors first. Submissions may be edited.
FT assumes no responsibility for submissions, but all reasonable care will be taken while they are in FT's possession. Requests for return of material should be accompanied by stamped addressed envelope.

CLIPPINGS

All clippings, references, etc, should be identified by source, date and clipster's name. Mail or fax them to the editorial address (above).

SUBSCRIPTIONS - UK

One year (6 issues). £12. Two years (12 issues) £20. For payment and inquiries by phone, ring FREEPHONE 0800 581409. Major credit cards accepted – or make cheques/ money orders payable to: **JOHN BROWN PUBLISHING, and send to Freepost SW6096, Frome, Somerset BA11 1YA.**

SUBSCRIPTIONS - OVERSEAS

One year (6 issues). £15 or US$30. Two years (12 issues) £26 or US$50. For payment or inquiries by phone, ring (+44) 373 451777. Major credit cards accepted – or make sterling cheques/ money orders drawn upon a London bank payable to: **JOHN BROWN PUBLISHING, and send to Fortean Times, 20 Paul Street, Frome, Somerset BA11 1DX, UK.**

PUBLISHER

John Brown Publishing Ltd, The Boathouse, Crabtree Lane, Fulham, London SW6 6LU, UK. Tel: 071 381 6007 or Fax: 071 381 3930.
MANAGING EDITOR: Fiona Jerome.
PUBLISHER: Vic Lime.

DISTRIBUTION

UK trade distribution by UMD, Castle House, 37/45 Paul Street, London EC2A 4PB Tel:. 071-490-2020 Fax: 071-490-1239 USA newsstand distribution by Eastern News Distributors Inc, 2020 Superior St, Sandusky, OH 44870, USA.

Bob Rickard

Paul Sieveking

Are Memories Made of This?

● Readers will hardly have failed to notice the intensity of recent media discussions of False Memory Syndrome (FMS), in which fantasy memories are taken for real ones, Münchausen's Syndrome [see *FT70*] and various abuses of children (physical, mental and sexual). There is no doubt these sensitive issues upset many people – but why, we have been asked, should they interest us?

It is right that we should inquire whether these subjects have any basis in fact. If there is a possibility, however remote, that some of the more fantastic tales of gynæcological experiments by aliens, sexual assaults by devils, possession by demons and secondary personalities, and so on, are rooted in similar dissociative processes then we need to know how these unusual states of mind were brought about.

We all have the potential to isolate unpleasant experiences by dissociation, but that does not mean we all do it (even some of the time). FMS and Münchausen's tend to be initiated in a relatively small, but susceptible, section of the population when stress becomes persistent, damaging and unbearable – and the extreme forms that interest us occur in a sub-group of that. We are talking about a relatively small number of people, but what they do teaches us about imagination and belief.

In 1992, there were nearly three million official reports of child sex abuse in America alone. True or false, these allegations unleash forces which can be devastating for family and society alike (but for different reasons). We do not deny the real incidence of rape, incest and abuse of children, but turn our attention towards the weirder matter of people who claim falsely to be victims of these crimes, who confabulate stories and then believe them implicitly.

As we close this issue, police in Grays, Essex, have arrested a man who, just a week earlier, drew sympathy from the nation because his eyes were superglued together, he said, when he surprised two burglars. The attack, it seems, never happened (though he won't say how his eyes became glued). Did this man make a false claim to attract sympathy? Many other people have, and Jim Schnabel's important dissection of FMS (p23) provides more disturbing and relevant examples.

Of the American abuse cases, 60% could not be substantiated – which means that an awful lot of people were wrongfully accused. Add to this the harm of panics like the Cleveland fiasco; the increasing use of childhood abuse in criminal defences (see p28); and its use in blackmail and extortion (as in the murky Michael Jackson saga p30); and we are probably seeing only the tip of the iceberg. We are staring at a complex cultural problem, the true scale of which is unknown.

● The response to our reader survey was overwhelming at around 8.5% – which is almost unheard of. This unexpectedly high number, and the fact that many of you embellished the survey form with additional data, deserves a closer study – something we couldn't do in time for this issue. We'll present a detailed report next issue.

What we *can* do is announce the winners of the prize draw. First name out of the black hole is Jim Beckwith of Reading who becomes the owner of an amazing Amstrad Pen Pad. The runners-up are: Steve Bush of Nottingham; Andrew Emmerson of Northampton; S.H Joyce of Maldon, Essex; Tony Brennan of Stewarton, Ayrshire; Alan Mansfield of Hertford; and Dr Richard Brunt of Gelsenjirchen, Germany. Congratulations to them and thanks to you all.

The Editors

STRANGE DAYS

16 pages of worldwide weirdness

MENTAL FLOSS

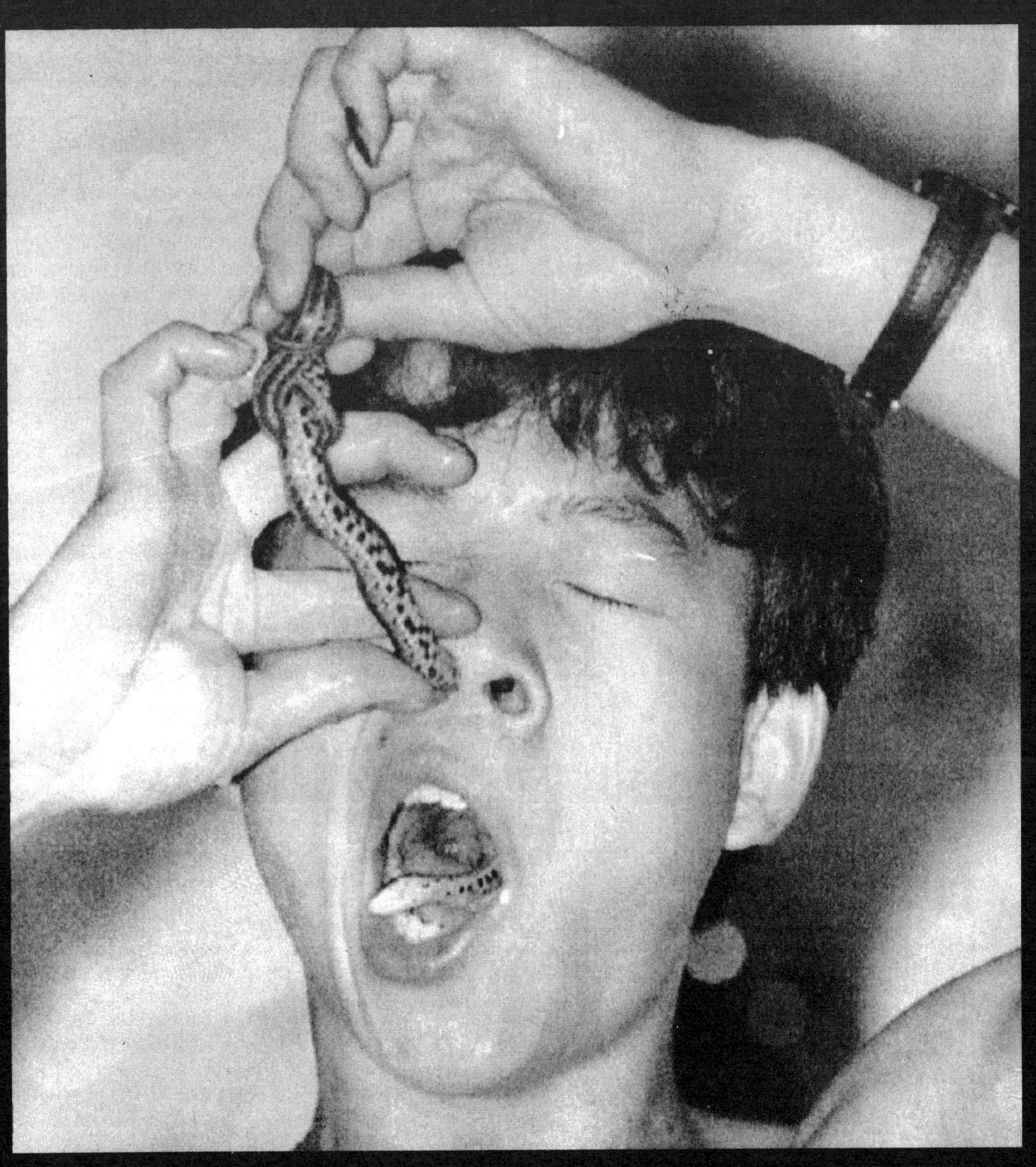

A snake handler in a street corner sideshow in north eastern Beijing threads a live snake into his nostril and out of his mouth during a daily performance. Our acquaintance, Matt the Tube from the Jim Rose Circus Sideshow, performs the same gag with a condom. *[Reuters]* *20 August 1993.*

EXTRA! EXTRA!

Fortean headlines from newspapers around the world

ENORMOUS VOID NOT AS EMPTY AS WE THOUGHT
Cleveland (OH) Plain Dealer, 11 Dec 1986

KILLER MOSQUITO TERRORISES DISNEY WORLD
Today, 6 Mar 1992

MAN CHARGED WITH DRUNKEN MOWING
Lewiston (ME) Sun–Journal, 11 Mar 1992

ASTRONOMERS SPLASH IN FOUNTAIN OF ANTI-MATTER
Guardian, 16 July 1992

DEAD SHEEPDOG LAYS GOLDEN EGG
Guardian, 2 Sept 1992

FOSSILISED RAT DUNG HELPS FIND NUCLEAR WASTE SITES
Independent, 9 Oct 1992

UNIVERSE MAY STILL HIDE A DARK SECRET
Times, 25 April 1992

SQUIRRELS FROM HELL
Today, 2 May 1992

THE FAR SIDE By GARY LARSON

"Gad, it gives me the creeps when he does that. I swear that goldfish is possessed or something."

MURDEROUS WATER GODDESS

Police in Yola, the capital of Nigeria's eastern Adamwa state, arrested a transvestite claiming to be a water goddess who had murdered 200 men and women. Alfred John was wearing women's clothes when he was collared on 14 April, reported the News Agency of Nigeria. He said he was a 'mammy water', a goddess in a local animist cult.

It seems that this water spirit was also a vampire. John said that he would disguise himself as a woman and, by invoking the aid of water spirits, would lure his victims to the banks of the Benue river, kill them and suck their blood. Last we heard, a cautious spokesman said John's claims would be investigated. *Thanks to Agence France Presse (15 April 1993) for help on this one.*

MISSED!

An asteroid a few metres across passed within 90,000 miles of the Earth on 20 May without being detected, the closest any asteroid has ever been known to come to our planet: less than half the distance from Earth to the Moon. The rock, designated 1993 KA2, was about 30ft in diameter with an estimated mass of 6,000 tons, about the same as a naval destroyer, and travelling at about 48,000 mph. Had it survived a fiery plunge through the atmosphere, it would have made a significant crater. It was only spotted several hours later as it whizzed away. It was the faintest asteroid ever observed, visible only because it came so close. *Washington Post, 21 June; New Scientist, 26 June 1993.*

BEAR–FACED CHEEK

A Russian bear was bought from a Russian circus by a tourist agent after he was asked to provide an American visitor with a 'wild bear hunt'. The tourist was set up in Moscow's Perdelkino Forest, and the bear was released. As the hunter closed in on his prey, a postman passed by on his bike, and tumbled off in surprise, according to the local newspaper, *Vecernaya Moskva*. The bear, recalling his Big Top training, grabbed the bike and pedalled off. The American was suing for fraud. *Sun, 21 June; Sunday Telegraph, 11 July 1993.*

EAGLE SNATCHES DOG

A Chihuahua-like dog was let out of a motor-home to run around at a gas station in Valdez, Alaska, while the owners, an unnamed couple from Georgia, cleaned the vehicle's windshield. Suddenly, a bald eagle swooped down from a nearby tree, snatched up the dog and flew off towards the harbour with the pooch in its talons.

"It was the damnedest thing I ever saw", said Dennis Fleming, a gas station attendant. "The dog gave one yelp and that was it." The woman owner clutched her hands to her face and cried, "Oh my God!". Fleming said the husband walked around the side of the motor home, out of sight of his wife. Chopping his hands in the air and grinning, he exclaimed, "Yeah! Yeah!". *[AP] 20 June 1993.*

MICKY FINN

Many hundreds of thousands of mice died mysteriously during May in the Altay grasslands of north-west China's Xinjiang province, puzzling Chinese scientists. Herdsmen said the plains were strewn with thousands of dead mice, and vast numbers more floated in lakes and rivers. At one river sluice gate alone, so many were found that they stopped counting at 300,000.

Some scientists said that the mouse population of the grasslands had been increasing in recent years and suggest that they became vulnerable to an infectious disease, but no-one has found any evidence of such a plague yet, nor has any possibly related illness been observed in other animals or humans in the area. The disaster seems to have afflicted only one species, known locally as "the big-eyed devil" because of its bulging eyes.

The Xinhua news agency quoted speculation that this might be "a premonition of an unprecedentedly drastic earthquake" – but as far as we know, there has not been one yet. *Guardian, Leicester Mercury, 12 Aug 1993.*

DON'T MENTION SEX!

An unnamed woman of 29, who says she faints at the mention of the word 'sex', took William Gray, 42, to court in Cincinnati, for felonious sexual penetration after he whispered the word in her ear on 9 April in the lobby of her apartment building, causing her to pass out. Gray pleaded not guilty by reason of insanity.

The woman's reaction was caused by an unusual psychological condition called conversion hysteria, which can cause paralysis, voice loss, seizures or fainting in response to a word. She fainted six times during preliminary hearings at the Hamilton County Court, and was revived each time with smelling salts. It was decided to substitute 'nookie' for the troublesome word so that the trial didn't drag on till Christmas. The prosecution wondered how the woman could recognise her attacker if she was unconscious at the time. *[UPI], D.Mirror, 15 July; Independent, 16 July 1993.*

BOTTLES TOPS WITH ISLANDERS

The Lamet group of islands – from the initials of Lavongai, Mussau, Emirau and Tench – off Papua New Guinea don't have much going for them: total population 16,000, widespread soil infertility due to the overuse of chemicals, coral beds ruined when they were plundered to make an airstrip – and the world's biggest mound of Coca-Cola bottles. Then came Michael Couch of the Waverley Rotary Club in Sydney, who visited Emirau in 1991.

The 100,000 bottles were dumped there by US troops in the 1940s, and the islanders had made an appeal for help in melting them down for recycling. "But I had a better idea," said Michael. He noticed that most of the bottles were of a classic design and colour prized by collectors, so he planned to ship, clean and package them for resale at around £14 a piece. The profits will be given back to the Lamet islanders in the form of industrial fish-processing equipment which will allow them to freeze and package their fish. It will also bring electric power generation to the islands for the first time. *D.Telegraph, 11 May 1993.*

HERETIC DINOSAURS

Sales of Tara dairy products in Israel are said to have tripled since they put a dinosaur on their cartons as part of the *Jurassic Park* media fever. Rabbi Zvi Gefner, head of the kosher certification department of the Agudat Israel ultra-orthodox party, issues the *kashrut* certificates without which no food can be declared fit for Jews to eat. He has threatened to withdraw Tara's kosher certificate unless they removed the picture.

"We as observant Jews count the beginning of the world from 5,753 years ago", said the Rabbi. "The dinosaurs symbolise a heresy of the Creation because they reflect Darwinistic theories." The giant creatures, if not actually a fraud, are at best the product of fevered imaginations. The Council for Freedom of Science, Religion and Culture (Hemdat) countered the kosher threat by urging the public to boycott any company which succumbs to rabbinical pressure. *Eve. Standard, D.Telegraph, 13 Aug 1993.*

ANCIENT GUM

In the summer of 1993, archæologists excavated a Stone Age village near Ellös on the island of Orust north of Göteborg in western Sweden. One of their most sensational finds was a piece of chewing gum 9,000 years old. Archæologist Bengt Nordqvist said that "the beautifully preserved toothprints proved that it was chewed by a teenager. Other finds have shown that the people of the Stone Age spiced their chewing gums and sweetened them with honey."

Nordqvist also said that the Orust chewing gum is the oldest found as far north as Bohuslän, apparently indicating that other chewing gums are even older. Eight years ago, a piece of gum with teenage toothprints was found at Segebro in Scania and heralded as the oldest ever found. This was, however, only 8,000 years old. *Sydsvenska Dagbladet, 14 Aug 1993. [See FT48:21].*

SIMULACRA CORNER

This face among the coffee grounds was taken about two years ago and was sent in by T. Williams of Datchet in Berkshire. We are always glad to receive pictures of mysterious forms and figures, or any curious images. Send them to the editorial address – with SAE – and we'll pay a fiver for any we use.

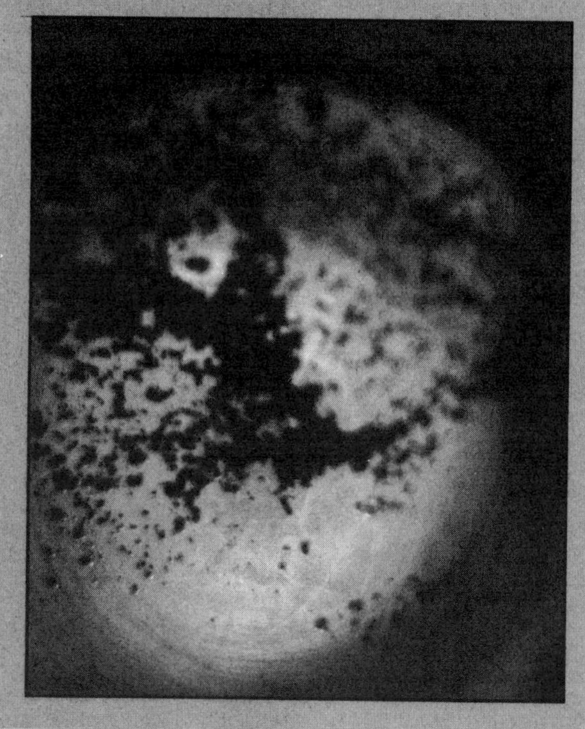

SECRET BLINDNESS

Rose Northmoor kept her virtual blindness secret for 70 years; even Norman, her husband of 48 years, and their three children, didn't know. The truth finally came out when she went to see an eye specialist with her husband, and was told she had only *one-and-a-half* per cent normal vision.

Mrs Northmoor, 73, of Doncaster, South Yorkshire, suffered damage to her optic nerves following an attack of whooping cough when she was three. In World War II, she fooled Army doctors by pretending her glasses were broken when she went for an eye test to join the Women's Auxiliary Army Corps as a cook. She rose to the rank of quartermaster.

"I have always done my cooking by guesswork because I can't read any scales", she said. "I have a terrific memory and I can make out shapes, so that I was able to get through my life without anyone suspecting, even though I could never read a book or newspaper. I never allow any of the furniture to be moved in the house. I keep all the food in exactly the same places. I know what my kids' faces look like because I have touched them. Now I have finally decided to tell the world. In a way, I am glad to get it off my chest." *D.Mail, D.Mirror, 18 Feb 1993.*

LOOK WHO'S TALKING

■ Ruth Durbin, 55, of Nailsea, near Bristol, found a budgerigar in a tree. He repeatedly told her in a West Country brogue: "My name is Pippy. I live at number seven Strawberry Close, Nailsea. Got that?" Owner Arthur Bendon, 72, who had lost Pippy the day before, was delighted to have him back. He had bought a replacement bird, which he gave to Mrs Durbin as a reward.

■ Pippy has a vocabulary of 50 words. According to the *Guinness Book of Records*, the most talkative bird is an African Grey Parrot owned by Iris Frost of Seaford, East Sussex, which can say 800 words. *Belfast Telegraph, D.Telegraph, 30 April 1993.*

■ Pastor Patrick from Texas is a Bible-bashing budgie who sits on his church perch saying things like "Praise be to Jesus" and "Walk in the light". His owner, Rev James Johnson, said: "He's very popular – not so long-winded as most of us." *People, 6 June 1993.*

■ A stolen parrot was returned to its postmistress owner after squawking "Bilsy and Beeby" (the names of her children) to a judge in Kerala, south India. *[AP] 4 June 1993.*

ANIMALS SERVE TIME

■ In the Middle Ages, animals were frequently tried in court for a range of crimes, from causing famine and disease to copulating on Sunday. (See *The Criminal Prosecution and Capital Punishment of Animals* by E.P.Evans, Faber 1987). This strange practice is not dead. In Cordoba, Argentina, a judge sentenced a dog to life imprisonment for killing its owner's three-year-old stepson. This was said to be the first such ruling in the country. *[EFE] Independent, 15 Aug 1991.*

■ A report from the official Tanzanian radio said that a court in the south-eastern Tanzanian town of Mtwara had jailed a goat for seven days for illegally grazing on a private farm. Another goat was jailed for two days in a remote Kenyan town for stealing £1.40 belonging to a fruit seller. *[AFP] 11 Jan 1992; Southampton Echo, 27 Feb 1993.*

■ A shopkeeper walked into the police station in Busia, Kenya, clutching four live rats and demanded that police arrest them for ruining his bread supply. "I want these rats put in the cells and charged in court for the damage", he said. He was found to be sober and of sound mind and was advised to contact the Public Health Officer. *[Reuters] 29 Jan 1993.*

FORTEAN FUNNIES

"Crikey, you look like you've seen a ghost"

TALKING TURKEY

More strange discoveries, odd events and weird coincidences from the cradle of civilisation

ANCIENT SPACE MODULE?
This object was excavated in the town of Toprakkale (known in ancient times as Tuspa). It is 22cm long, 7.5cm wide and 8cm high, with an estimated age of 3,000 years. To the modern eye, it appears to represent a space vehicle for one, with the pilot's head missing. Some scientists have cast doubt on its age. It is kept in the Museum of Archæology in Istanbul, but not exhibited. ***Bilinmeyen, vol.3, p.622.***

★ VENERABLE OLIVE TREE

An olive tree in the San Selim Mosque garden in the town of Payas, Hatey province, has been bearing fruit for almost 1,000 years. It was first mentioned in the Travel Book of Evliya Celebi. According to him, the tree was saved when the mosque was being built in 1574, because of its great age. Today, it bears plenty of olives. *Bursa Hakimiyet, 8 Aug 1991.*

★ MONSTER MICE

Residents of Göçkün, Doyran and Yenice villages near the town of Alaçam in Samsun province mount an armed watch round the clock because of attacks by giant white mice with webbed back legs, weighing four to six kilogrammes. These pests first appeared almost two years ago and their numbers have risen all the time. They are attacking chicken runs and eating 10 to 20 chickens every day. They also attack cats and even dogs. The total cat and dog population used to be 70 to 80, but they have now all run away. Even a villager, Mr Behram Pekgöz, was attacked and bitten. Poisoned food has been laid, but the canny critters have not been tempted. *Hürriyet, 6 April 1993.*

★ WORLD'S OLDEST CLOTH

A fragment of white cloth dating back to 7000BC has been found at Cayonu, a village near the headwaters of the Tigris about 30 miles from Diyarbakir. Measuring three inches by one and a half inches, the fragment was clinging to a handle believed to be a portion of antler, the calcium in which had caused the cloth to be semi-fossilised. It is probably a piece of linen and judging by the weave, was produced on a simple frame of four sticks.

The cloth was excavated in 1988, but was only definitively identified earlier this year. Its age was arrived at by radiocarbon dating. Although clay impressions of textiles of about the same age have been uncovered before in the region, no other piece of pre-historic cloth produced earlier than 6000 to 6500BC had been found anywhere in the world. Weaving fibres is one of the most important innovations associated with the beginnings of agriculture and the rise of civilisation. *New York Times, 13 July 1993.*

★ CATNIP

Mrs Ayse Yilmaz, from Bevealan village near the town of Vezirköprü in Samsun province, took the nappy off her one-year-old son, Osman, and left him on the bed naked, as it was a hot summer day. She left the room to do some housework, but rushed back a few minutes later when the baby screamed. She couldn't believe her eyes: a cat had come in through the window and was eating Osman's penis. She hurried to Havza State Hospital, where Dr Ibrahim Akpinar reassured her that her son was quite well, but had been given an expert circumcision. He had never heard of a cat doing this before. *Bilinmeyen, pp770-71.*

★ DOOM OF THE DENTIST

Onder Akgün, a dentist at Elazig State Hospital, was driving on a religious holiday with his wife and three children, when a truck crashed into his car repeatedly from behind and killed his son, sleeping on the back seat. The truck driver said it was an accident.

Years later, Mr Akgün drove to Bursa on the same religious holiday. Another car crashed into them repeatedly from behind and killed their daughter, sleeping on the back seat. The car driver said it was an accident. The dentist asked, if both were accidents, why they were crashed into several times on each occasion? *Hürriyet, 29 Sept 1991.*

Sidelines

According to the Vampire Research Center (Box 252, Elmhurst, NY 11373), there are 1,215 real vampires worldwide, up from last year's total of 810. Los Angeles remains the world's highest density area, with Dallas second. Japan is the lowest density area, and most vampires in Britain, Australia and Germany are in their teens. *Columbus Dispatch, 21 June 1993.*

A German firm is selling mints containing human blood. Heart Drops come in four flavours – types O, B, A and Assorted. Sweet firm boss Helen Wolfe prefers type A "because they taste like salty watermelon." *People, 8 Aug 1993.*

A disc jockey on an English provincial radio station introduced a record for a listener "who's 111 today". Pause. "Sorry. That's not 111. He's ill." *D.Telegraph, 26 June 1993.*

People Unlimited, that odd group of hopefuls who believe they can live forever by willing or wishing it, recently lost three members because they died. Spokesperson Beryl Gregory trotted out the explanation favoured by failed prophets in other circumstances: they simply didn't believe hard enough. *D.Star, 9 Aug 1993.*

Kuwait Airways is grounding nine new airbuses after finding that seat covers in first and business class compartments had a pattern 'similar' to the Arabic script for the name of God. To sit down on it knowingly would be blasphemous. *[AFP] 9 Aug 1993.* [For more on the 'Allah Problem' see **FT45:8, 53:8, 55:4.**]

THE LADY IS A VAMP

A small Peruvian fishing town awaits the vampire's revenge

Devotees place flowers and a cross on the tomb of Sarah Ellen Roberts, supposed third bride of Dracula, on the eve of her anticipated resurrection.

Around 1,000 people turned up at a small graveyard in Pisco, Peru, on the night of 8 June to witness the resurrection of an English vampire at midnight. But Sarah Ellen Roberts, billed by a US Spanish-language programme on vampires some months ago as the third bride of Dracula, stayed peacefully in her coffin, disappointing radio and television stations who transmitted live from the graveside. (In case you're wondering, the other two brides of the pointy-toothed Romanian are buried in Mexico and Panama.)

A British Embassy spokesman confirmed that an Englishman called John Roberts arrived by ship in Pisco about 80 years ago with a coffin containing the body of his wife after the authorities denied him permission to bury her in Blackburn, Lancashire. He paid five pounds to bury her and was never seen again. John Roberts had allegedly roamed the world for four years seeking some place that would allow him to bury his wife.

However, Blackburn reference librarian Ian Sutton found a death notice in a local paper dated 13 June 1913, saying that Mrs Roberts, formerly of 25 Isherwood Street, Blackburn, died in Pisco – not in England – four days earlier.

The actual inscription on the tomb leaves the place of death open: "In Memory of Sarah Ellen, beloved wife of J.P. Roberts of Blackburn, England. Born March 6, 1872 and died June 9, 1913."

Peru's *Expresso* newspaper said that she had been sentenced to death for murder and witchcraft and had been buried alive in a lead-lined coffin to avoid her escape, but had sworn to return for revenge on the 80th anniversary of her death. Excitement was increased a few days before the deadline, when a large crack appeared in the headstone.

Police broke up a group of people dancing and drinking at the cemetery gates to placate the Englishwoman's spirit and had to fire shots in the air to disperse the crowds after midnight. A small group of local witch doctors gathered near the simple grave, casting spells and splashing the tomb with water and white flower petals.

Houses in the small port town were festooned with garlic and crucifixes and £1.60 anti-vampire kits – crucifix, mallet, wooden stake and string of garlic – had sold out. Local women left the town to prevent the vampire being reincarnated as their new-born children. However, the mayor, Edgar Muñoz, pleased with the 60% jump in tourism, said he was going to celebrate the death of Sarah Helen every year and would twin Pisco with Blackburn. *[Reuters] 8 June; [AFP] 9 June; D.Mail, Independent, 10 June; [AP] 11 June 1993.*

JESUS IN THE DISHWASHER

Mysterious images appeared on Cyril Legge's glasses

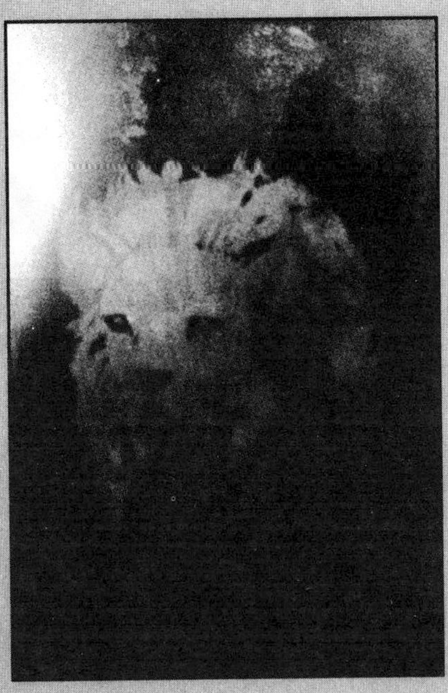

The images of a robed man (above left) and a lion's head (above right) that appeared on glasses belonging to Cyril Legge (below)

Cyril Legge, 55, who runs the Margaret Roper House for the mentally ill in Birkdale, Merseyside, recently took a holiday in Kenya, where he visited the Portrease mental hospital in Mombasa and was saddened by the awful conditions there.

Back home in Birkdale, he began to have dreams about Liverpool's Catholic Cathedral. "On Good Friday", he told the press, "I emptied the dishwasher as usual, and discovered that among the shiny, clean glasses was one dirty one. I held it up to the light and there was a clear image of a saint-like figure. Some say it is Jesus. I didn't know what to do, so I kept it in a box."

A few days later, a second image, of a lion's head, appeared on another glass from the same set, which Mr Legge had bought from a local hardware shop almost 10 years ago. He saw it as the Lion of Kenya, while friends told him it might represent the Biblical Kingdom of Judah.

Ten Liverpool University scientists studied the glasses and said neither had been tampered with. Dr Ronan McGrath said: "It seems to be some sort of freak grease stain. The figure of Christ appears to be in layers, so some parts appear more opaque than others. The lion is interesting because of the detail – but I can't comment on the religious significance."

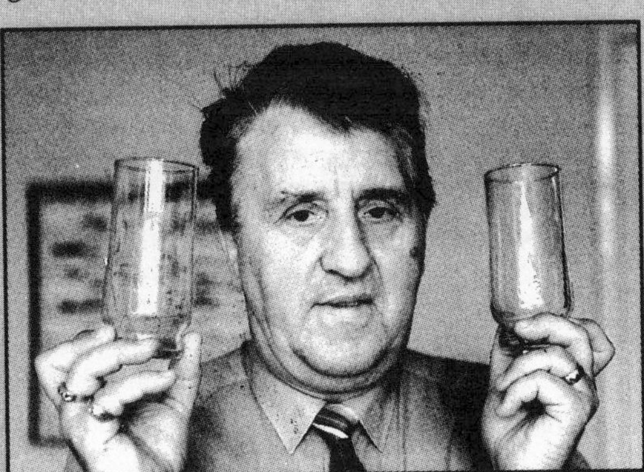

Mr Legge, a devout Catholic, believes the images are a Sign from God to set up a fund-raising committee to improve the lives of the patients in Portrease hospital and other underprivileged people in Kenya. *Liverpool Echo, 20 May; Sun, 21+22 May 1993.*

Sidelines

'Operation Right to Know' picketed the White House on 5 July to urge President Clinton to declassify all government documents about alien contact. Group spokeswoman Elaine Douglas declared: "You have to be brain dead if you don't have the faintest inkling that there are aliens operating on this planet." *Lewiston (ME) Sun–Journal, 1 July 1993.*

• • • • • • • • • • • • • • •

Another medical first! A paper in the *Journal of Genito-urinary Disease* has added inflatable sex-dolls to the list of ways in which venereal disease may be transmitted. The risk with pneumatic playmates was brought to light after a Greenland trawlerman secretly availed himself of a colleague's blow-up doll unaware its owner had contracted gonorrhoea. *Guardian, 13 Aug 1993.*

• • • • • • • • • • • • • • •

The 45ft trawler *Triumph* was returning to North Shields, Tyne & Wear, when it was torpedoed by a floating 50ft sycamore tree, 20 miles out to sea. A helicopter rescued the crew. *Today, 26 May 1993.*

• • • • • • • • • • • • • • •

Two walruses (native to Arctic waters) have been sighted off the north Donegal coast. Walruses have never been recorded off the Irish coast before. *The News (Portsmouth), 7 July 1993.*

• • • • • • • • • • • • • • •

A Colorado entrepreneur who says the idea came to him in a dream, has invented a machine that vacuums prairie dogs from their burrows and deposits them unharmed, "but somewhat confused", in a truck for relocation. His business, Dog-Gone, is booming. *Washington Post, 30 Dec 1992.*

THE TAOS HUM

A strange noise in a New Mexican town is driving people crazy

In *FT65:12* we reported on the eerie hum that plagues Hueytown, Alabama. Over a thousand miles to the west, another hum has been plaguing selected inhabitants of Taos in northern New Mexico. Catanya Salzman first noticed it one quiet night in May 1991 – a low, grumbling noise on the threshold of audibility. As persistent as a bee trapped in a jar and as irritating as fingernails scraping across a blackboard, it's driving many people nuts, not least because nobody can identify it. Saltzman had to give up her career as a dancer because the Hum affected her inner ear, throwing her off balance.

Speculation has ranged from secret underground testing at Los Alamos National Laboratory 60 miles away, to messages from space aliens. Last summer, an acoustical engineer captured the hum – or at least a hum – on an oscilloscope. The ultralow frequency (between 17 and 70 hertz) is audible only to the most sensitive ear. Another wave has since been detected, pulsing between 125 and 300 hertz. Auditory profiles made by James Garner, an Albuquerque microwave engineer, have eliminated as suspects power lines, natural-gas conduits, power plants, appliances and excavations in the desert.

In April 1993, Rep. Bill Richardson, a member of the House Intelligence Committee, asserted that the Hum was 'defence-related' and asked the Pentagon to 'shut it down'. The Navy is known to use extremely low-frequency waves to communicate with submarines through a buried power grid. However, in May, Under Secretary of Defence John Deutch said that "there is no program, classified or not, which would cause this hum".

Garner suspects the hum is caused by 'seismic slip', a small but steady movement of one tectonic plate against another, analogous to the 'singing sand' phenomenon sometimes heard in the desert. Taos sits atop the Rio Grande Rift, and some kind of hum has been reported in Albuquerque, Santa Fe and southern Colorado, all along the Rio Grande Rift. This is the explanation offered for the sounds heard for centuries in Moodus, Connecticut. But hold on: why is there no sound heard along the San Andreas fault? The rather unconvincing reply is that Californian tectonic plates move differently.

In June, we heard of another troubling hum, this time in Maine. It was variously described as a hum, a vibrating sound, heartbeat thump or generator rumble, and about two dozen claimed to have heard it, from as far south as York and as far north as Thomaston.

In July, engineers and physicists affiliated with the University of New Mexico lugged equipment to Taos for measuring acoustic, electromagnetic and seismic signals. A second team of ear specialists set about testing those who say they hear the sound. Although most people can't hear the Taos Hum, those who do are driven to distraction. K.C. Grams, 43, says the sound sometimes gets so loud that "my head buzzes as if it were a beehive". Finding the source is only the first step. What sufferers want is for the Hum to buzz off.

Wall Street Journal, 5 Aug 1992; Newsweek, 3 May; Lewiston (ME) Sun-Journal, 21 June; [AP] 22 June; [Knight-Ridder] 11 July 1993.

BECHSTEIN'S BAT

A woman in Taunton, Somerset, got into her shower and found one of Britain's rarest bats hanging from the curtain. It was the first Bechstein's bat found roosting in Britain since 1866, according to the English Nature Conservation Group. Four months later, celebrations by scientists who found another Bechstein's bat, at Carisbrooke Castle on the Isle of Wight, were cut short when a cat ate it. *D.Mirror, 12 Feb; IoW County Press, 18 June 1993.*

BAFFLING BEADS

Beads fell from the sky during a hailstorm over the northern English seaside resort of Redcar at some unspecified time early this year. Pensioner Eleanor Graham retrieved them from her shopping bag, believing they were hailstones. When they didn't melt, she contacted the *Northern Echo* (report 13 Mar 1993.) The Met Office was mystified. ICI experts identified the beads as amorphous silica, but had no idea where they came from.

NECROLOG

Recent fatalities among the eminent and the weird

AIMÉ MICHEL, 1919–1992

Michel (above) was the first successful populariser of the UFO phenomenon in France to become influential internationally. His first book, *Lueurs Sur Les Soucoupes Volantes* (1954), carried a preface by Jean Cocteau. In 1958, Michel's detailed study of the 1954 French wave of UFO sightings and landings, *Mystérieux Objets Célestes*, introduced significant new ideas about non-biological, non-human intelligences.

Michel's interests covered the Fortean canon – spontaneous combustion, religious phenomena, super-science – in fact, anything that presented a bold challenge to scientific dogma. In *Flying Saucers and the Straight Line Mystery* (1958) – he published his discovery of 'orthoteny' – a theory of UFO behaviour based on the alignment of UFO-related sites – which was enthusiastically received by the UFO and ley-hunting fraternities. He was profoundly disappointed when it was shown conclusively to be an illusion arising from errors in data and estimates of probability.

Born on 17 May 1919 into a farming family, his growth was stunted by severe polio in childhood which diverted him into an academic career, teaching and journalism. Michel lived all his life in the village of St Vincent-les-Forts, in the Alpes de Haute Provence, until he died aged 73, on 28 Dec 1992.

SUN RA, 1914–1993

To his parents he was plain Herman P. Blount, born in Birmingham, Alabama on 23 May 1914 – but according to himself, he was born on Saturn "about 5,000 years ago". An influential jazz pianist, Sun Ra and his band (below), the Arkestra, pioneered the use of electronic instruments. He adopted the persona of Sun Ra in the 1950s, a surreal integration of Western occultism, Egyptian spiritualism and science fiction.

An advocate of Black consciousness, Ra insisted on the provenance of Black culture long before the publication of *Black Athena*, proclaiming that Egyptian priests were the first jazz musicians and that they were black. He received 'space vibrations', and had a strong sense of his mission to save the planet. "People are being watched very carefully by other worlds who are surrounding them in spaceships," he said. "My music is a bridge to the change."

He was serious in his intentions, but with a veneer of wit which still confuses those who cannot penetrate it. In 1990, Ra corrected one interviewer: "I'm not a man ... I'm an archangel. I've been promoted recently." On 30 May 1993, Sun Ra received his final promotion.

DAVID BOHM – influential American physicist-philosopher, he worked on the Manhattan Project and quantum mechanics, was a victim of the McCarthy commie-hunt at Princeton University, and formulated the holistic notion of the 'implicate order' linking seemingly unconnected things. Died October 1992, aged 74.

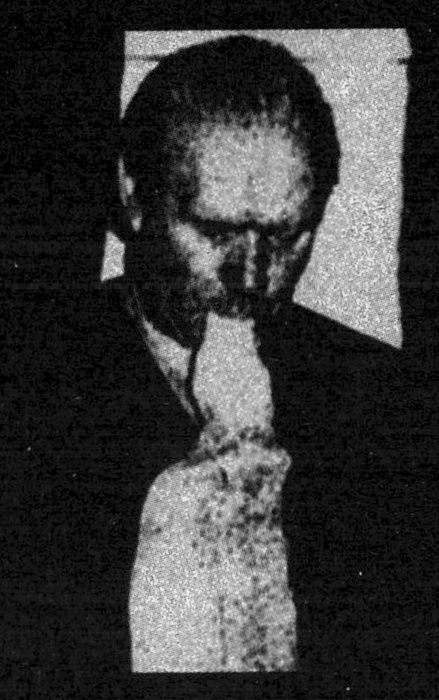

GORDON HIGGINSON – (above) son of a medium and a practising medium himself since the age of 12, he served as president of the Spiritualists' National Union for 23 years and his strength of character is credited with steering the SNU through damaging crises and declining morale. Died in late January 1993, aged 74.

JAN OORT – celebrated Dutch astronomer who discovered that the Milky Way rotated and that our system lies not at its centre but further out, and who gave his name to the Oort Cloud (a vast cloud of 100,000 million comets about one light year distant). Died November 1992, aged 92.

ISHIRO HONDA – the Japanese film director who created Godzilla and his rubberoid pals. Died 28 Feb 1993, aged 81.

MARGARET, DUCHESS OF ARGYLL – the feisty socialite whose promiscuity generated column yards of scandal through several decades. A stereotype of the romantic New Ager, she patronised many unusual causes, apparently on a whim. She called herself "gullible, impulsive and over-optimistic", while a reviewer of her memoirs observed: "Her father gave her some fine earrings but nothing to put between them." She was a subscriber to *FT*, having been recruited by the legendary Ion Will; who acted as her divination consultant. Died 26 July 1993, aged 80.

NOT THEIR DAY

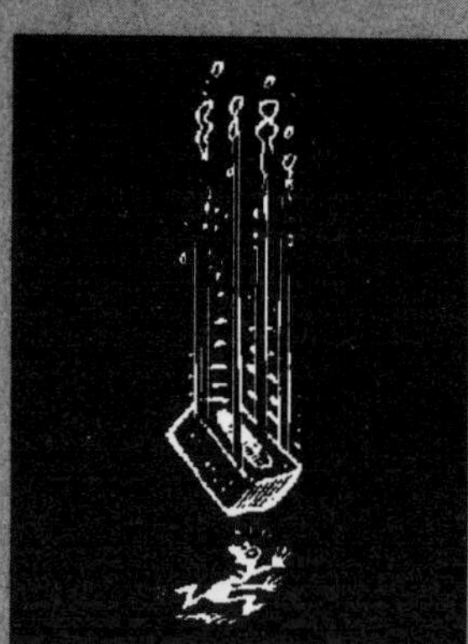

Joyce Rowsell refused to cut short her public telephone conversation so that a man could make an emergency call to the fire brigade. When she arrived back at her flat in Dartmouth, Devon, she found it well ablaze. The good Samaritan had been trying to summon fire-fighters to put it out. *Sunday Mirror, 20 Sept 1992.*

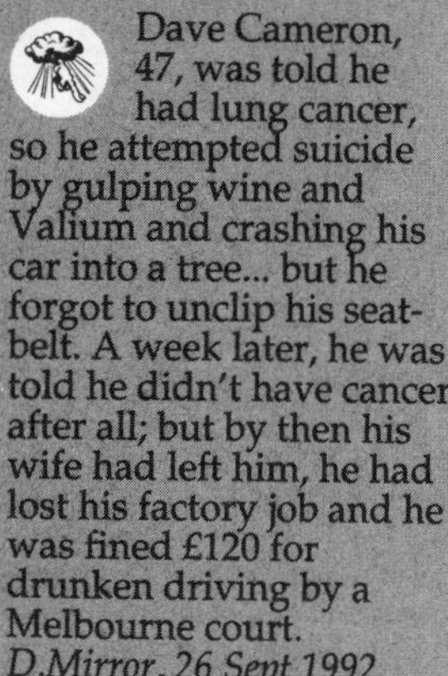

Dave Cameron, 47, was told he had lung cancer, so he attempted suicide by gulping wine and Valium and crashing his car into a tree... but he forgot to unclip his seat-belt. A week later, he was told he didn't have cancer after all; but by then his wife had left him, he had lost his factory job and he was fined £120 for drunken driving by a Melbourne court. *D.Mirror, 26 Sept 1992.*

Newsagent Dennis Brightey of Brandon, Suffolk, pinned up a 'No milk today' sign. Seconds later, milkman David Roberts lost control of his float after swerving to miss a car and crashed into the shop with 1,000 pints. *Sun, 23 Sept 1992.*

Fred Turner set out from Beaufort, South Carolina, on a cross-country walk to reassure himself that "99 per cent of the people in the world are generally good." After about 35 miles he encountered the other one per cent. Two men in a rusty pickup truck accosted him and asked if he was the guy walking across the country. He said yes, they demanded his wallet and threw him off a bridge into the Savannah River on the Georgia state line. The 53-year-old New York City native survived the 75-foot plunge and floated a mile and a half to an island where he spent the night. He was rescued by fishermen the next day. He nursed a black eye, wrenched back, turned ankle and twisted knee, but planned to hit the road again soon. His optimism was undimmed, he said. *Atlanta Constitution, 14 May 1992.*

It was not a good day for Norwegian dentist Arnt Helge Dybvik. His car skidded down an icy Oslo hill into another car. As he was inspecting the damage, a third car slid into his car and broke his arm. He hailed a taxi to get to hospital, but on the way it was wrecked in a three-car crash. *Mail on Sunday, 21 Feb 1993.*

Lilian Sokolowsky of New Hampshire hid jewellry worth £14,000 in a fake can of soup to fool thieves. She then absent-mindedly gave it away to the Salvation Army. *D.Record, 11 Feb 1993.*

A woman's plan to emulate Cleopatra by bathing in ass's milk backfired when she stole a donkey. It was a male and brayed so loudly that neighbours in Leipzig called the cops. *Sunday Mail, 8 Nov 1992.*

PROVIDENCE STRIKES

The life of Austria's top hostage negotiator was saved on 14 June when the mobile telephone in his breast pocket stopped a bullet fired by a bank robber who had already killed one policeman. Colonel Friedrich Maringer had just negotiated the release of two hostages who were holed up in a clothes shop after a botched bank raid, when the thief panicked. The bullet would have hit the Colonel in the heart, but all he suffered was some bruising.

In August, Bob Jones, 27, fixed a smoke alarm to a ceiling with sticky tape in his Halifax, West Yorks, basement flat. When the battery ran down, the alarm began to bleep as a warning. Bob removed the battery and forgot to get a replacement. A few days later, he fell asleep after friends had been round. A lighted cigarette is believed to have slipped between the cushions of an armchair. When flames reached the ceiling, the tape melted and the fire alarm fell on Bob's skull. He awoke to choking smoke and escaped just in time. He was treated in hospital for smoke inhalation. *[Reuters] 15 June; D.Mirror, Sun, 3 Aug 1993.*

IF YOU PARK HERE, YOU'RE DEAD

A Los Angeles County parking control officer who ticketed a Cadillac parked illegally on Piru Street at 9:46am on 11 September 1992 got no excuses from the driver sitting stiffly behind his steering wheel. He had to reach in the window right past the driver to put the $30 ticket on the inside of the dashboard.

The driver was, in fact, dead, shot in the head perhaps as long as 13 hours earlier. The stiff was noticed around 10:30 by a resident, who called the police. The driver had severe rigor mortis. He was slumped slightly forward with blood on his face, which was discoloured.

A dead man slumped in a van in Oklahoma City in 1989 wasn't noticed for at least three days, during which time 12 parking tickets were put on the windscreen. *Denver Post, 12 Sept; Int. Herald Tribune, 14 Sept; Sunday Times, 20 Sept 1992.* [See also **FT59:13.**]

THE MADNESS OF SEVENS

Brian Yinger, 42, a policeman in Dearborn, Michigan, was suspended in November 1992 and sent to a psychiatrist because he writes the number 7 in the European style, with a horizontal line through the downstroke. Six months earlier he was instructed to break the habit acquired when he was 12 and continued during his years in the Navy, the Naval Reserve and for more than 15 years on the Dearborn force, because "the way he was writing was confusing the typist". However, he forgot whilst writing some reports and as a result was suspended for three days without pay. Corporal Yinger then appealed to the city's Civil Service Commission to overturn the ruling. *[AP] 7 Nov 1992.*

GHOSTS ON TV

A strange fear gripped Hong Kong children last year when they saw more in a TV ad than others did

印象中,火車永遠美妙;
現實裏,我們全力爲您延續這份歡笑.

Apparitions on TV are not a common phenomenon, judging from the number of cases in the Fortean archives. One curious incident excited much press speculation in Hong Kong last autumn. Two commercials for the Kowloon-Guangzhou Railway Company were made in mainland China and aired on Hong Kong television in 1991 without controversy. The first featured a group of six children in single file imitating a train, while the second had the children mimicking traffic lights. The slogan went: "The train remains forever beautiful in our memory; in reality, we do our best to prolong this smile for you". (This might have lost some of its snappiness in translation.)

When the second commercial was broadcast for the last time in early October, it was said that ghostly figures appeared. Many pupils in one school were too ill to attend lessons after seeing it. Rumours proliferated: it was claimed that while only six children were filmed for the first ad, there were actually seven pairs of feet. A little girl in pigtails was seen by some viewers, but not others. Some said the young girl second in line had blood spilling from her mouth. A pale ghostly character was seen to fly off from behind a tree. Then there was talk of disappearing heads and organs, heads covered in blood suddenly appearing from trees and heads cracking open. Two of the children as well as the film director were said to have died after the filming.

Fog of rumour

Wu Gang, a popular Hong Kong television presenter, flew to Beijing in the hope of dispelling the fog of rumour that was sweeping over the young viewing public. He was able to show that all the children in the ads were in good health, as was the director. However, although a professed sceptic, Wu Gang armed himself with Buddhist rosary beads and a necromancer's compass when he visited the site where the ads had been filmed. There was nothing unusual about the place, he reported, except that it was near an old graveyard.

The two commercials were broadcast again to allay fears; while claims of ghost sighting continued, the railway company were pleased to learn that scepticism was growing among adults, although many children were still too frightened to watch television or sleep at night. The footage was studied frame by frame, and the 'dripping blood' from the little girl's mouth was explained as a twitch in her lower lip. There were no signs of any poltergeist characteristics.

Possessed by vampires

Meanwhile, a popular 'media spiritualist' said that the children in the commercials were possessed by little vampires. After performing a rite to 'open the heavenly eye', he was able to see one ghost on the left of the screen, one floating in mid-air and one resting on the last child, causing him to walk with very heavy footsteps. Reporters viewing the film with the spiritualist were unable to see any of this, as they lacked the benefit of 'heavenly glasses'.

■ On 19 April 1993, startled viewers jammed ITV switchboards claiming to have seen a phantom pirate glide across the *This Morning* studio and sit on the coffee table between Judy Finnigan and Richard Madeley. The couple were interviewing exorcist Graham Wyley, and the ghostly guest popped up just as he said "I don't sense anything here". TV spokesmen denied any technical trickery; perhaps an entity from the etheric bore a grudge against Wyley and was out to ruin the poor man's reputation. *ASEAN – Far Eastern Monitor, Feb; D.Mirror, 20 April 1993.*

LOOSE LIONS

Lions, or rumours of lions, have been spreading panic in Paris and Pennsylvania

Last April, the French newsagency AFP announced that a lion had escaped from Vincennes Zoo and was seen by several witnesses roaming around the motorhomes and merry-go-rounds of the Foire du Trône, a fairground in the Vincennes wood close to the 14th district of Paris. The fair was closed at 11:15pm on Thursday 29 April instead of 1:00am the next morning, while zoo keepers, policemen and firemen searched in vain for three hours. In fact, no lions were missing from the zoo.

FT correspondent Jean-Louis Brodu went to the fair to investigate. Monsieur Papin of the press bureau suggested three explanations: a hypothetical street peddler had lost a lion; a large dog had been misidentified; or it was a malicious hoax. He insisted it was not a publicity stunt – the fair had lost a lot of money because of the enforced closure. A story of a UFO landing at the fair had once been invented for publicity, and a lion used for promotion purposes had actually escaped for a while before World War II.

The hypothesis that most satisfied the fairground hands and the police was that an attraction owner, expelled from the fair for non-payment of rent, took revenge by concocting the lion story. Jean-Louis was told the name of a suspect; but in classic Fortean fashion, the case remains unproved.

A brown blur

When Greg Havican's chickens and turkeys disappeared from his farm in Erie County, Pennsylvania, he figured a fox or wild dog was to blame. He believes he met the real culprit on the morning of 31 May. His grandmother had fallen in the kitchen, and as he prepared to follow an ambulance to the hospital, he heard his dogs barking and saw a 'brown blur' outside. He grabbed a shotgun and went to his front yard, where he was confronted by a growling lion. He fired a warning shot, and the lion took off. He did too – back into his house.

Two hours later and a mile away, a motorist called police on a car phone to report a lion on Interstate 90 near a fast-food restaurant. State trooper said the male African lion weighed between 150 and 200 pounds and was wearing a red collar with gold bells, suggesting he was a pet or circus animal. He saw no need for more description: "If anyone sees a lion, it's probably the lion we're looking for." No paw prints or other evidence was found and there were no reports of lions missing from zoos or circuses. A review of state permits indicated there were no recorded lion owners in the Erie area.

probably let loose from a circus.
By a clown.

Our correspondent Robert Anton Wilson said the lion with bells "sounds like the work of the Committee for Surrealist Insurrection against Claims of the Normal (CSICON)."

Copycat reports

Two days later, reported lion sightings had risen to nine, and there were more suburban reports in the following two weeks. "We wonder if they are copycat reports", said state police. A chewed up wading pool was found, and two sets of tracks; these turned out to be those of a deer and a Great Dane. Game official Lorraine Yocum maintained that many reports of out-of-place animals had elements of exaggeration: a week before the first lion sightings, for instance, there had been a report of a kangaroo. It turned out to be a possum that had lost a lot of hair.

Two months later, on 5/6 August, there were three separate sightings of a full-grown lion near Lehighton, Pennsylvania, and the local police chief said that 10 'credible witnesses' had been interviewed. Carbon County naturalist Judy Wink found tracks at the various locations that looked to her like a bobcat's. A search by fire-fighters and police helicopters failed to find anything.

•••••••••••••••

OTHER LIONS

On 3 May, police had found a hungry male 150lb lion, eight months old, in a vacant Detroit house after neighbours reported hearing roars coming from the basement. Nine days later, on 12 May, another lion was waiting inside the Beulah Baptist Church in Calabash, North Carolina, when a church member unlocked the door to let an organ repairman in.

Detroit had been the scene of an earlier African lion discovery in November last year. Five-month-old Katie was found chained in the dank basement of a crack house and was taken to the Detroit zoo.

Today, 23 Sept 1992; [AFP] 30 April; [AP] 2 Jan, 4 May, 13 May, 2 June, 19 June; USA Today, 2 June ; Intelligencer Journal (PA) 7 Aug 1993.

FLOYDADA OUTING

Police in Vinton, Louisiana, stopped a 1990 Pontiac Grand Am on 19 August after reports that it contained naked people. The driver got out wearing only a towel, but then jumped back in and crashed into a tree. Officers looked on slack-jawed as 20 completely naked people, ranging in age from one to 65 and including three pregnant women and five children, piled out of the wreck and began religious chants.

The car was a write-off, but the injuries were all minor, as the passengers were packed in very tightly, cheek to cheek. This particular Pontiac has a small interior: two bucket seats in front and a rear seat not very suitable for adults. The children were stuffed in the trunk (boot).

The party were all Pentecostals from Floydada, a small Texas Panhandle town, on their way to a religious retreat somewhere in Florida. Driver Sammy Rodriguez, 29, and his brother Danny said they were preachers. The Floydada police had been looking for them for two days since relatives had reported them missing. The Rodriguez brothers had declared that the devil was after them and Floydada (love that name!) would be destroyed if they stayed there. The group, who were all related, left Floydada in five or six cars, abandoning them and their belongings along the way. They stripped because their clothes were possessed by the devil. *[AP] 20 Aug 1993.*

ORGAN KIDNAPPING

Honduran President Rafael Callejas said last April that the kidnapping of children for the purpose of selling their organs was taking place in Honduras. A UNICEF official cast doubt on this; however, according to a politician, some 600 children had disappeared in the preceding six months, while police said that various bands were also kidnapping children for adoption abroad. Rumours of kidnapping for the organ trade have surfaced before in Honduras and elsewhere in Latin America.

On 11 August, eight supposed baby traffickers were arrested at Rio de Janeiro airport, as they were about to hand over a 15-day-old baby to an Israeli couple allegedly ready to take the child to Germany on false papers. Police suspected the gang of selling South American babies to European organ transplant clinics for the last two years.

Also this summer, a doctor and mortuary worker were arrested in Cairo for stealing eyes from corpses, while the Deputy Minister of Public Works in the Kenyan parliament told his colleagues that bodies of Kenyans and foreigners had been turning up on roadsides minus eyes and genitals. In both cases, the motive was said to be exporting to the transplant trade, but we doubt that local gangs would have adequate technical ability and equipment to deliver useable body parts. Until we see some credible evidence to the contrary, we will place these tales in the scare-lore folder. *[Reuters] 19 April; D.Telegraph, 12 Aug; Sussex Eve. Argus, 7 June; Western Morning News, 3 July 1993. [See* ***FT59:63, 65:50.****]*

YO! BORIS!

ABOVE: Russian President Boris Yeltsin with rock musicians Boris Kinchev (centre) and Oleg Usmanov at the Kremlin on 21 April 1993. Yeltsin thanked the musicians for staging a concert in Red Square in support of the imminent referendum to decide the fate of his presidency. He is copying the musicians' gesture, which means "hang loose, or relax", according to Russian folklore.

Christian apoclypticists who were disappointed that Gorbachev was not the Antichrist they had predicted (the Mark of the Beast turned out to be just a birthmark after all) should delight in this proof of his successor's demonism. In the West, the sign is the satanic salute of the adolescent epigones of death metal bands, although, of course, the gesture has many meanings, such as warding off the Evil Eye. *[AP] 21 April 1993.*

BELOW: President Yeltsin tries to grasp his wife Miana's hands around the 800-year-old Iron Pillar at Qutab Minar in New Delhi on 28 January 1993. This is supposed to bring good luck. The pillar is believed to be immune from rust, and features in the work of Erich von Däniken as an extra-terrestrial object. *[Reuters] 28 Jan 1993.*

UNDERNEATH THE ARCHES

A bizarre and stubborn rumour has attached itself to a fast-food chain ...

The Mother's Day bombing of a shopping precinct in Warrington on 26 March, which killed two children, has revealed a peculiarly persistent piece of foaflore that is as crazy as the idea that Procter and Gamble are in league with the devil [see *FT59:17*], and will doubtless prove as hard to get rid of. The groundswell of ill-feeling towards the IRA generated by the murders has also made McDonald's fast-food chain its target.

Warrington has two McDonald's, one of them very close to the site of the explosion. In the panic following the blast, the story goes, a McDonald's manager rushed out to ask a police officer whether he should evacuate his staff only to be told to stay in the restaurant because "you lot support the IRA". Since the disaster, McDonald's staff at Warrington and their families have suffered abuse and threats, some in direct confrontations and some through the restaurant's suggestion box.

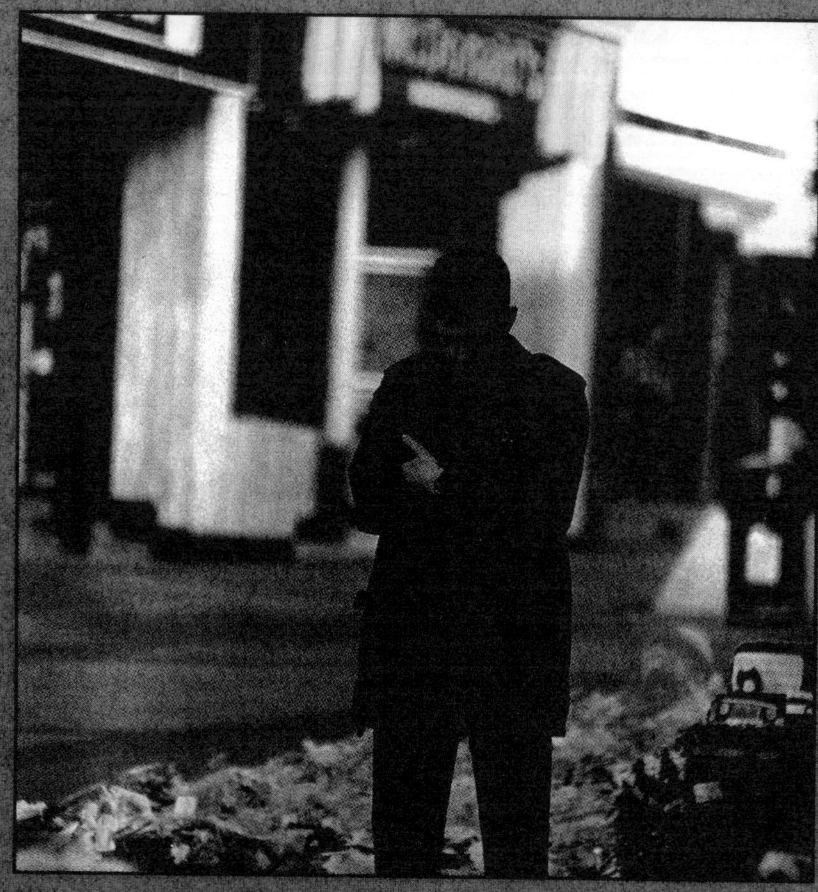

Warrington, March 1993 – A policeman contemplates the scene outside McDonald's where a bomb killed three-year-old Jonathan Ball.

Disgust

Mrs Corinne Reed Comfort, PR head for McDonald's, said she had "30 letters and some phonecalls from people expressing their disgust at us for supporting the IRA." One Warrington citizen was more specific, writing: "Most of your customers are children. How can you justify giving four percent of profits to the IRA?" In a small place like Warrington, said Mrs Reed Comfort, "everyone knows where you work", and she admitted that some staff are "on the brink of leaving".

US companies in Britain have always been at risk of being pilloried if they were suspected of contributing to NORAID, the US-based IRA fundraisers. This has not been the case with McDonald's, so how did they become tarred with this brush? Mrs Reed Comfort believes that it all began with a discussion on CNN, in 1989, of tax-free retirement funds on, in which "McDonald's was cited as an employer noted for its generosity in contributing to individual retirement accounts – or IRAs, for short." Some British viewers, she suggests, picking up the programme by satellite, came to a mistaken conclusion. Only a handful of UK employees are on the IRA scheme, and reference to it has been removed from their payslips, she said.

Outrage

Terry Carroll, an ex-Met chief superintendent and now head of McDonald's UK security, dates the rumour even further back: "It has been going around for about six years and has gathered momentum with each IRA outrage. It started off with a whispering campaign but we are not sure of its origins. We have strongly denied it, but once something like this starts it is very difficult to get rid of. People say 'There's no smoke without fire'."

Mr Carroll feels the macfoafs have been particularly prevalent among servicemen and their children. Staff have even been attacked by off-duty soldiers, he said. "What worries me is that it even seems to be filtering through to the police service." He has already heard talk of an entry in a station parade book "warning officers not to buy anything from McDonald's."

The company has conducted a low-profile campaign of letters to the Ministry of Defence, the authorities and local institutions, fearing that a more vigorous denial would "fan the rumour". *The Police Review, 23 April 1993.*

FORTEAN FUNNIES

"You look like a wise guy"

TAKING THE ASHES

Nathan Radlich, 74, returned to his house in Boynton Beach, Florida, on 13 May and found his bathroom window missing. None of the obvious things, like electronic gadgets, was stolen; but his fishing tackle box, lid open, was thrown on the bed. The box, which had held the cremated remains of his sister Gertrude, was empty. The brother and sister shared a house for 12 years until she died three years ago aged 70. Police guessed that the thief had mistaken the cellophane-wrapped, greyish-white powder for cocaine. We are reminded that cocaine sold in Egypt in 1986 was found to be cut with powdered human skull [see **FT46:13**]. *[AP] 4 June 1993.*

MANY HAPPY RETURNS

April 19 is a special day for the Novak family of Albuquerque, New Mexico: it's the birthday of seven of them. All the births were natural – no cæsarian sections or induced labours. The streak got a double boost in April with the arrival of Lucille and Ted Novak's newest grandsons, twins Matthew and Michael Cericola.

Novak's mother, Ann Koubsky, was born on 19 April 1901, and died in 1986. The Novaks' son Ric was born on 19 April 1951, and their daughter Karen on 19 April 1964. Exactly 24 years later, Karen and her sister Jean both gave birth to daughters, Tiffany Cericola and Aimée Fischer. *[AP] 20 May 1993.*

TOYOTA TWINS

Two cars operated by a single key rarely show up in the same part of the country, let alone in the same car park. It's rarer still to have identical 1984 Toyota Camrys painted the same dark brown parked within three spaces of each other. That's what happened in Stanton, California, last March when Lam Danny Nguyen stuck the key to his sister-in-law's Camry into the ignition of Alan and Rochelle Kantor's car and drove off.

Every 10,000th car has identical keys, according to a spokeswoman. With the millions of vehicles on the road, it would cost a fortune to make unique keys for each one. It took police six hours to unravel the mystery and get the two Toyotas back to their rightful owners. *Wellington (NZ) Evening Post, 27 Mar 1993.*

STRANGE DEATHS

✝ Ken Charles Barger, 47, accidentally shot himself to death last December in Newton, North Carolina. Awakening to the sound of a ringing telephone beside his bed, he reached for the phone but grabbed instead a Smith & Wesson .38 Special, which discharged when he drew it to his ear. *Hickory Daily Record, 21 Dec 1992.*

✝ In July, Stephen Cawthorne, 43, a former district engineer from York, died from head injuries when his Yamaha 600cc motorcycle was jumped on by an emu in a narrow cutting near Mount Surprise, Queensland. A week earlier, on 16 July, motorcyclist Kelly Cordry, 39, was killed when a 40-pound black dog fell on him from a railway bridge in Commerce City, Colorado. The motorcycle slammed into the crash barrier and Cordry was thrown into the path of oncoming traffic. *Sunday Express, 25 July; [Reuters] 26 July; Denver Post, 17 July 1993.*

✝ There was another odd death, also in Commerce City, a suburb of Denver, four days later. Derek Romero, 15, was found crushed to death on a bedroom floor with the family's 11.5ft Burmese python, Sally, coiled next to him. The snake, which belonged to the victim's elder brother, was quite agitated and hissed at the police. It had been in the house for eight years, and had no history of attacking people. Since Sally had been fed a rabbit about five days earlier, it was unlikely that she was seeking prey. The family's theory was that Romero forgot to wash his hands after playing with a pet rabbit – a definite no-no, since snakes hunt by smell. *[Reuters], Rocky Mountain News, 21+23 July 1993.*

✝ Jackie D. Johnson, 19, was killed in his mobile home at Adams Branch, near Elkhorn City, Kentucky, on 23 February. A 10-foot-square, 30-ton boulder fell about 500 feet from a cliff and crashed through the roof onto the sofa where he was sitting. Virgil Ramey, his grandfather, who was sitting beside him, escaped with a broken shoulder. Virgil's wife, Lucille, had just got up to let her little dog in, and was uninjured. *[AP] 25 Feb 1993.*

✝ Nanette Meech, 76, of Santa Fe, was canoeing down the Brule River in Wisconsin with her daughter Laurie on 15 July, when a 40ft poplar tree, about 18in diameter, that had been gnawed by a beaver, crashed down on her head with fatal consequences. *Denver Post, 17 July 1993.*

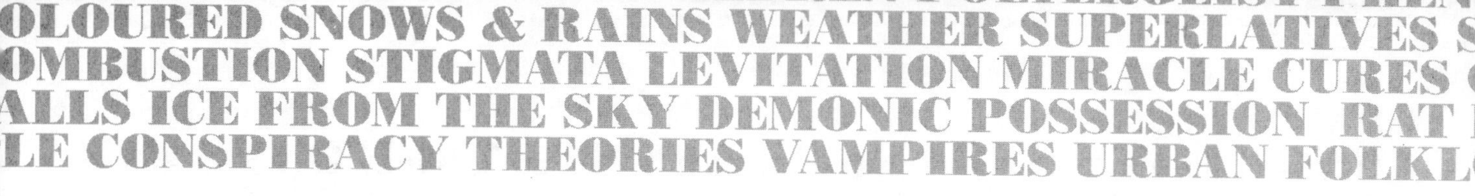

FORTEAN ALMANAC 12 October - 20 November 1993

Notable feasts and anniversaries in the coming weeks

TUESDAY 12 OCTOBER: Birthday of the magician Aleister Crowley (1875). Incidentally, he pronounced his own name like the bird (crow-ley), not crow as in 'crowd'. This info comes from Lance Sieveking, FT editor's father, who knew the man.

FRIDAY 15 OCTOBER: Feast Day of the stigmatic St Teresa of Avila (1515-82), foundress and mystic of the Carmelite order. In 1957 the Brazilian farmer Antonio Villas Boas allegedly had sexual intercourse with a fair-skinned alien woman in a flying saucer.

SATURDAY 16 OCTOBER: Feast Day of St Gerard Majella (1726-55), an Italian lay brother who had ecstasies, bilocation (apparently being seen in two places at once) and powers of healing, prophecy and ESP.

THURSDAY 21 OCTOBER: Feast Day of St Ursula, who was supposed to have been killed in Cologne with 11,000 other virgins. Ursula ('bear' in Latin) was a name of the goddess Artemis, one of whose shrines was in Cologne.

FRIDAY 22 OCTOBER: Happy 5,997th birthday, world! According to Bishop James Ussher (1581-1656), the Creation took place at 6:00pm on 22 October 4004BC.

SATURDAY 30 OCTOBER: The start of four days' penance for Aztecs. No mating, with ceremony or without. Today, we should also remember one of this century's greatest hoaxes, Orson Welles' broadcast of *The War of the Worlds* (1938).

SUNDAY 31 OCTOBER: Hallowe'en (All Hallows' Eve), once the Eve of Samhain (the Celtic New Year), named for the Aryan Lord of Death, Samana, the Grim Reaper. The fracture of space and time at the change of the seasons allowed contact between the worlds of the dead and the living.

MONDAY 1 NOVEMBER: All Saints' Day and the old fire festival of Samhain, the beginning of winter, when effigies representing the ills and sadnesses of the past year used to be burned (a rite preserved today as Bonfire Night on 5 November).

FRIDAY 5 NOVEMBER: In 1975 forestry worker Travis Walton was apparently abducted by a UFO near Snowflake, Arizona, an event which formed the basis of the film *Fire In The Sky*.

THURSDAY 11 NOVEMBER: St Martin's Day. Nothing involving a wheel should be undertaken before midday. The mild weather which sometimes occurs around this date is called a St Martin Summer.

FRIDAY 12 NOVEMBER: Hugh Gray allegedly took the first photograph of the Loch Ness Monster on this day in 1933.

SATURDAY 13 NOVEMBER: The Hindu festival of Diwali begins.

MONDAY 15 NOVEMBER: Birthday of William Herschel (1738), the self-taught astronomer who discover Uranus, which he wanted to call George in honour of his king. Herschel lived one Uranian year, 84 Earth years.

THURSDAY 18 NOVEMBER: Anniversary of the Jonestown Massacre (1978), when 914 followers of Jim Jones' People's Temple committed mass suicide in Guyana.

SATURDAY 20 NOVEMBER: Unsuccessful hot-dog salesman George Adamski claimed he met a Venusian called Orthon in the California desert on this day in 1952. Adamski became the most famous 'contactee' of the 1950s.

SPECIAL CORRESPONDENTS

AFRICA Cynthia Hind (Zimbabwe), Ion Alexis Will (Roving). **AUSTRALIA** Greg Axford (Vic), Paul Cropper (NSW), Arthur Chrenkoff (Qld), Rex Gilroy (NSW), Tony Healy (ACT). **BELGIUM** Henri Prémont. **CANADA** Brian Chapman (BC), Dwight Whalen (Ont.). **DENMARK** Lars Thomas. **ENGLAND** Claire Blamey, Bruce Chatterton, Peter Christie, Mat Coward, Hilary Evans, Peter Hope-Evans, Neil Frary, Alan Gardiner, Mick Goss, Chris Hall, Jeremy Harte, Ronnie Hoyle, Dionne Jones, Jake Kirkwood, Alexis Lykiard, Nick Maloret, Valerie Martin, Kevin McClure, John Michell, Ralph Noyes, Nigel Pennick, Andy Roberts, Tom Ruffles, Paul Screeton, Karl Shuker, Ian Simmons, Bob Skinner, Anthony Smith, Paul R. Thomas, Nigel Watson, Owen Whiteoak, Steve Wrathall. **FRANCE** Jean-Louis Brodu, Bernard Heuvelmans, Michel Meurger. **GERMANY** Walter J. Langbein, Ulrich Magin. **GREECE** S.C. Tavuchis. **HOLLAND** Robin Pascoe. **HONGKONG** Chris Williams. **ICELAND** V. Kip Hansen. **INDONESIA** Alan M. Stracy. **IRELAND** Peter Costello, Doc Shiels. **JAPAN** Masaru Mori, Shigeo Yokoyama. **NEW ZEALAND** Peter Hassall. **NORTHERN IRELAND** Caryl Sibbett. **PHILIPPINES** Keith Snell. **POLAND** Leszek Matela. **ROMANIA** Iosif Boczor. **RUSSIA** Vladimir Rubtsov. **SCOTLAND** David Burns, Stuart Herkes, Roger Musson, Roland Watson, Jake Williams. **SWEDEN** Anders Liljegren, Sven Rosén. **USA** Larry E. Arnold (PA), Loren Coleman (ME), James E. Conlan (CT), Karma Tenzin Dorje (CA), David Fideler (MI), Mark A. Hall (MN), Myron S. Hoyt (ME), John Keel (NYC), Jim Lippard (AZ), Kurt Lothmann (TX), Barbara Millspaw (CO), Ray Nelke (MO), Jim Riecken (NY), Ron Schaffner (OH), Chuck Shepherd (FL), Dennis Stacy (TX), Joseph Swatek (NB), Joseph Trainor (MA), Jeffrey Vallance (CA), Robert Anton Wilson (CA), Joseph W. Zarzynski (NY). **TURKEY** Izzet Goksu. **WALES** Janet & Colin Bord, Richard Holland, Joe Kelly.

ILLUSTRATION COPYRIGHTS

5 REUTER/HULTON DEUTSCH **6** INTERCONTINENTAL FEATURES **7(b)** HUNT EMERSON **8 (t)** T WILLIAMS **(b)** PAUL WOOD **9** BILINMEYEN **10 (l)** POPPERFOTO **11 (tl+b)** LIVERPOOL DAILY POST & ECHO **(tr)** MERCURY PRESS **12** MERRILY HARPUR **13 (tr)** FLYING SAUCER NEWS **(tl)** PSYCHIC NEWS **(b)** REDFERNS **15** ASEAN FAR EAST MONITOR **16** MERRILY HARPUR **17 (t)** ASSOCIATED PRESS **(b)** REUTER/HULTON DEUTSCH **18** PA **19** MAX STEIGER **21** HUNT EMERSON **24** SOUTH BEDS NEWS AGENCY **25** STEVE BLOOM/THE OLYMPIAN, OLYMPIA (WA) **26** FRONTLINE/PBS **27** WALTER SMITH **28 (t)** CHRISTOPER JONES **(b)** AP **29** MARY EVANS PICTURE LIBRARY **30** AP **32** FORTEAN PICTURE LIBRARY **34** ALAN BOLGER **35** EBURY PRESS **36** ANSEN SEALE **37-8** G M GILBERT **39-41** GREG BECKER **42** SOLO SYNDICATION **43-44** MEPL **45** JOHN BELOFF/CAMBRIDGE UNIVERSITY LIBRARY **46** MEPL **47** REUTERS/HULTON DEUTSCH **48** THIS SUNDAY/PA **49** FT ARCHIVE **52** JANET & COLIN BORD **56** PIERRE HOLLINS **63** TODD L PETERSEN **65** DAVID GREEN

CLIPPINGS & TRANSLATIONS FOR THIS ISSUE

Gail-Nina Anderson, Sherry Baker, Pierre Bonello, Janet & Colin Bord, Jean-Louis Brodu, Linda Brown, David J.Burns, Kevin Busby, ByRon, Cain, John Cannon, Brian Chapman, Danny Cheveaux, Mark Childs, Arthur Chrenkoff, Peter Christie, Adam Clark, Jim Conlan, James Conway, COUD-I, Mat Coward, Paul Cropper, Jim Darroch, Mike Dash, Karma Tenzin Dorje, Jill Doubleday, Paul Drennan, Bill Ellis, Peter Hope-Evans, George Featherstone, Larry Fiander, Neil Frary, Alan Gardiner, Robert Gifford, Mark Gillings, Ian Glasby, Izzet Goksu, Joan Good, Matthew Goulding, Lucy Hall, Peter Hassall, Stuart A.Herkes, Steve Hexter, Cynthia Hind, Toby Howard, Myron S. Hoyt, Dionne Jones, Alex Kashko, Grame Kenna, John J. Kohut, Heidi LaFleche, Roger Laidlaw, Jim Lippard, Su Llewellyn, Gerry Lovell, Alexis Lykiard, Dave Malin, Nick Maloret, Gary Mangiacopra, Dave McKinnon, Barbara Millspaw, Jan Mura, Roger Musson, Ray Nelke, Roger O'Donnell, Robin Pascoe, Nigel Pennick, John Price, Benjamin Radford, David Rider, Jim Riecken, Zvi Ron, Sven Rosén, John Sappington, Tom Salusbury, Charles Schwamb, Paul Screeton, Chuck Shepherd, Ian Sherred, Karl Shuker, Adrian Sill, Ian Simmons, Andy Smith, Ian S. Smith, Richard Smith, Sean Steele, Joe Swatek, Paul Thomas, Joe Trainor, Richard Turner, Jeffrey Vallance, Nicholas P. Warren, John Whiskin, Stephen C. Whitcombe, Owen Whiteoak, Ion Will, Chris Williams, Jan Williams, Robert Anton Wilson, Jason Winter, Gary K. Yates.

HUNT EMERSON ©1993

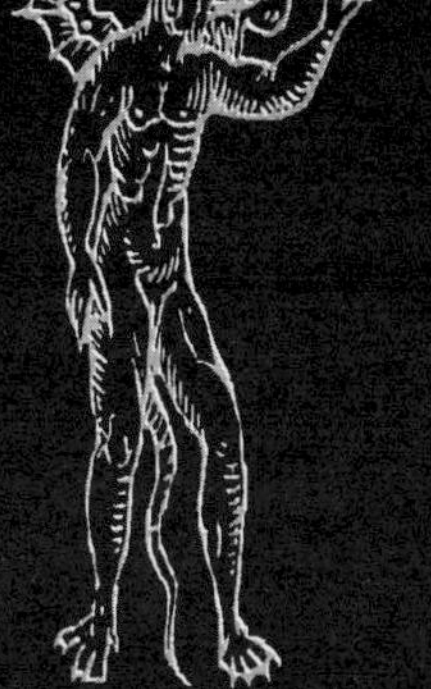

Memories

# of Hell

Tens of thousands of people, with the aid of hypnotherapy and other techniques, are retrieving 'repressed' memories of childhood trauma. **Jim Schnabel** wonders whether these memories are real, or are merely manifestations of self-victimisation.

HOAXED CRIMES: LYING FOR HELP

...a Grenside
...rates' court,
...her mother.
...al discharge
...g police time.

Writing in *Time Out* (5 May 1993), Denis Campbell drew attention to a new drain on over-stretched police resources, "a sudden spate of hoaxers who claim to be the victims of horrendous crimes". Professor David Downs, a criminologist at the London School of Economics, is quoted saying that hoax calls to the emergency authorities by children are an ever-present nuisance, "but adults making up stories isn't something I've heard much about until recently." These people should not be confused with 'professional victims' (who lie down in the wreckage of traffic accidents and sue for damages, for example). Here are a few recent cases ...

■ On 19 October 1992, a 19-year-old male hairdresser panicked the thousands of commuters who daily use the Northern Line underground by claiming he had been dragged off the train at gunpoint – *during the evening rush hour* – and taken up to Hampstead Heath by three men who raped him. Three weeks later he had to admit it was "a pack of lies". He had gone to the Heath to try out gay sex and lied to his girlfriend when she found out. She called the police to report the 'rape'. The man was cautioned for wasting police time.

■ On 15 December 1992, Joanna Grenside, a 25-year-old fitness instructor, staged her own disappearance from the carpark of the leisure centre in Harpenden, Herts. She turned up in the same carpark 36 hours later, dishevelled and in shock, claiming to have been abducted and raped – in fact she had taken a train to Heathrow airport and wandered there for the duration. Fearing she could be dead, police had wasted 1,800 man hours costing over £20,000 in extensive searches.

Four days later, she confessed to the hoax, but this was not a tale of malicious trickery. She had a history of eating disorders since her teens, hiding her eating and purging fits from friends and family. The approach of Christmas filled her with dread and anxiety, and what began with an impulsive flight, 'snowballed' until she could sustain it no longer. Her distress was so real, or at least convincing, that on her return, a psychiatrist ordered a two-day delay in interrogation so she could rest. In the meantime, police became suspicious when they learned that when Grenside had visited Sydney, Australia, a singer had staged a similar vanishing trick. When told they no longer believed her, she broke down and confessed.

Frances Heidensohn, a criminologist at Goldsmith's College, said that Joanna Grenside was typical of a great many adults who claim to be victims of crimes that never happened. "She *is* a victim, but not of a crime. These people are usually in some kind of distress – as she was. Perhaps they act to cover-up self damage or self-mutilation."

■ In March 1993, a French teacher in Southwark accused two pupils, aged 14 and 13, of raping her in school when she kept them back for detention. Police investigating the complaint said they were obliged to continue their inquiries, even though they privately admitted to reporters that the teacher's story was not credible. In the end, no charges were made and the case dropped.

■ In mid-April 1993, two frightened eight-year-old boys told police they had been attacked in King George's Park, Wandsworth – that he poured petrol on them, set it alight and ran off. For two days the police hunted the maniac, said to be a moustachioed black man with a zigzag haircut, a gold tooth and "probably under the influence of drugs". When a witness said he had seen boys fitting their description stealing a can of petrol earlier, the police denounced them as liars. The boys confessed they had been playing with matches and petrol. A detective said: "It turned out they were describing a man they had seen earlier, whom other people also remembered seeing in the area. We could have arrested an innocent man."

■ On 23 April 1993, the whole of west London was alerted to help police trace a four-year-old girl called Rachel who called the Samaritans to say her mother had collapsed bleeding and wouldn't wake up. Scores of officers spent an entire day knocking on nearly every door in Acton, until 'Rachel' was discovered and said to be an adult female who needed psychiatric help.

■ As we go to press, another kidnap victim has confessed that she had made up the allegation. The unnamed 33-year-old woman said a man wielding a knife clambered into her car when she stopped at traffic lights in Cardiff and forced her to drive 300 miles to north Wales, sexually assaulting her on the way. The two-week police investigation is reckoned to have cost over £100,000, and she may be charged with this waste of time. *Independent, 26 Aug 1993.*

Memories of Hell

Paul Ingram (left), a police detective in Olympia, Washington, accused by his children of satanic child abuse, listens in court to his sentence, with his attorney Monte Hester.

A few years ago in the sleepy, Edenic town of Edenton, North Carolina, a child care centre run by respected town citizens was shut down following allegations that over 80 children at the centre had been sexually abused by staff. Seven people were arrested, and so far two have received life sentences, while the rest await trial. Strangely, the child care centre was in the centre of town, subject to frequent unannounced visits by parents and other adults, but none of these potential witnesses had ever noticed anything unusual. The children's allegations, which were coaxed out by therapists and parents over a several-month period, also included tales of witchcraft, child-killing, being thrown into the water and surrounded by sharks, and travelling in hot-air balloons and spaceships. One of the defendants, the owner of a video store, had no connection to the childcare centre but was named by the children as the owner of the sharks. In a recent American PBS television documentary about the case [1], several jurors from the trials complained that they were forced by zealous colleagues to agree to guilty verdicts, against their better judgment. One of the jurors who had argued for conviction stated that he believed there might have been some truth to the story about the sharks.

> "Every time a train came by a whistle would blow and a witch would come in my window... I would wake up, but I couldn't move. It was like the blankets were tucked under and I couldn't move my arms."

In the town of East Olympia, Washington, at the same time that the Edenton case was brewing, a 22-year old woman named Ericka Ingram broke down during an all-female prayer meeting at her Christian fundamentalist church. Earlier, a woman who had been speaking to the group had sensed, via the "Holy Spirit", that one or more of them had been abused by a parent. Several young women had come forward in anguish. Ericka merely drew attention to herself by sobbing and becoming immobile, but readily accepted the diagnosis when the Spirit-filled speaker told her that she had been sexually abused by her father, Paul Ingram, a local deputy sheriff and the county chairman of the Republican Party. Ericka's 18-year-old sister Julie soon developed similar memories, and as the police became involved, Ericka, with Julie following her lead, began to tell stories of bizarre satanic rituals involving not only their father, mother and brother but several of their father's friends.

The girls' mother Sandy initially resisted these stories, but under prodding from prosecutors and therapists, she eventually produced her own detailed memories of satanic rituals, rapes and sodomies of which she too had been a victim. Her son Chad likewise initially denied that he had been ritually abused, but after encouragement from prosecution therapists, he recalled two childhood dreams: In one, 'little people' – who reminded him of Snow White's Seven Dwarfs – watched him through his upper-floor bedroom window and then floated into the room and walked on his bed. In another, he said, "Every time a train came by a whistle would blow and a witch would come in my window... I would wake up, but I couldn't move. It was like the blankets were tucked under and I couldn't move my arms." The witch, who was obese and wore a black robe, would sit on top of him. Therapists interpreted the dreams as actual memories of sexual abuse by cult members; Chad agreed with them, and more specific memories soon followed.

Most remarkably, Chad's father Paul Ingram seemed willing to confess to any charge put forward against him. Eventually, he agreed to, and even elaborated on, charges which were deliberately invented by a social psychologist and cult expert to test his memory's validity. The case soon collapsed, but by that time Ingram had pleaded guilty to six counts of third-degree rape. He is now serving a 20-year prison sentence, and will be eligible for parole in 2002.

Truth, Justice and the Salem Way

Last year, the USA's largest child sex abuse prosecution reached its first trial, resulting in the conviction of Robert Fulton Kelly (right, in cuffs) on 99 out of 100 counts. Kelly, who owned the Little Rascals day-care centre in Edenton, North Carolina, was sentenced to 12 consecutive life terms, one for each of the children he was found guilty of molesting. Six other people, including three of his staff, still face trial as a consequence of the original investigation and arrests in 1989.

The case has created an uncivil war in Edenton, the shock of the accusations and the legal quandaries leaving friends, families and the community itself divided. Some believe it began with a slap, or a rift between friends. Kelly's wife Betsy blames her former best friend for the earliest rumours of abuse at the centre. Soon there were rumours of rape, sodomy, and children hanging in trees or being thrown to sharks or cooked in microwave ovens. Townsfolk, who could not accept that their little children could invent such horrors, or who proclaimed "I can tell when a child is telling the truth," chose to believe them implicitly.

As more parents became convinced that "something had happened to their children", they involved police and therapists to draw out their stories. Some parents openly admitted to using stronger methods – such as withholding dessert at mealtimes (the child held out for three weeks) – until their child came up with a description of what was done to them and by whom.

In the end, most of the 90 children were interviewed by four therapists, yet these therapists were not called to testify "for strategic reasons". Doctors said there was no clear physical evidence for the sex crimes (including claims that cutlery and needles were poked into the children); however these 'expert witnesses' disagreed vehemently about why their examinations were so inconclusive. With this lack of tangible evidence and the lack of any adult witnesses, the court was obliged to place great weight upon the testimony of the children.

The accounts given in a closed court by the children – now three years older and probably well acquainted with what was required of them – often reduced the jury to tears. At first their testimony seemed consistent and unshakeable, but more people were noticing improbabilities. Some jurors even expressed doubts about the prosecution tactics of pursuing the same question from different angles until they obtained the response they sought. Kelly's attorney, Jeff Miller, was in no doubt about the central dilemma for the American legal system: "Science says that preschool children are at the most suggestible age, so it's dangerous to ask them leading questions. The law, however, says that *because* they are so young, it's appropriate to ask them leading questions."

The jury was out for three weeks. Mary Nichols, a juror, said she felt the children were doing their best to tell the truth, this commodity being what they though their seniors wanted to hear. "The kids said a lot of things," another juror said, "I mean, flying into space in hot air balloons... This is the same kid that said Mr Bob stuck a finger in their rectums and shot babies at the centre."

All of the remaining defendants are still adamant about their innocence having endured three years of prison and interrogation, but Kelly's conviction has severely eroded their morale. Most fear they don't have the stamina to fight the next dilemma – if they accept the offer to plead guilty to lesser charges they could avoid the increasing certainty that a jury will convict them and sentence them to life imprisonment. While one of the accused, Robin Byrum, is defiant – "If the good Lord means for me to sit in jail for something I didn't do, that's what it's going to be." – another, Dawn Wilson, was almost willing to accept anything to end the nightmare. "I'm being forced to make a decision I don't want to. Part of me wants to take the plea so that it will be behind me", she says, "the other part of me doesn't want to lie ... to say I'm guilty when I'm not."

Michelle Re-remembers

Michelle Remembers was written in 1980 by Michelle Smith (below) and her psychologist-counsellor Lawrence Padzer, whom she later married. Claiming to tell the story of how Michelle had been inducted into a coven as a child and made to participate in sexual abuse, murder and ritual cannibalism, culminating in a horrific encounter with Satan himself, the book was one of the first bestsellers of its kind, impressing credulous readers in the worst possible way.

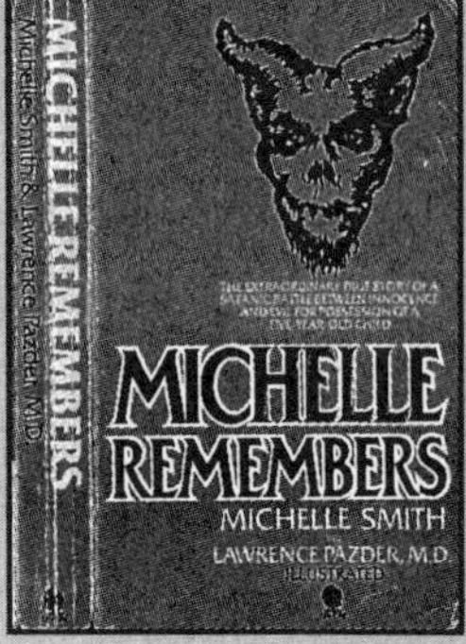

Such cases are now hotly debated in the media, especially in America. A number of high-profile publications including *Ms* and *Vanity Fair* have defended the notion that child-abuse and satanic ritual abuse are rampant, while many others have concluded that cases like the ones in Edenton and East Olympia are modern examples of mass hysteria. two, and that is the nature of the dissociation-prone personality. Dissociation-proneness is a relative term as there seems to be a fairly smooth spectrum of dissociative tendencies throughout the population – however pre-adolescents, as well as some 5-10% of adults report, a high number of 'dissociative' episodes, such as vivid daydreaming, periods of amnesia, and out-of-body experiences. In general, people who are dissociation-prone are very suggestible and are liable, particularly when under stress, to fall into trance states which make them even more suggestible. The existence of a highly suggestible section of the population helps to explain why numerous psychological experiments have shown how easily 'false memories' can be implanted, often merely by insisting that something happened and that the individual must have forgotten it. Once a false memory is implanted, it may be quickly connected with emotions and supplementary memories until it becomes an almost seamless and unshakeable part of a person's self-history and self-awareness.

Pamela Freyd, who founded the False memory Syndrome Foundation in Philadelphia, in March 1992, to help the victims of false accusations of satanic, sexual and other abuse of their children. They are currently helping about 3,700 families, mostly in the USA.

■ The FMSF can be contacted on (USA area code 215) 387 7944.

"People who are dissociation-prone are often highly creative and imaginative, and seem to account for a disproportionate number of poets, novelists, and entertainers."

The term 'False Memory Syndrome' (FMS) has been coined, and the False Memory Syndrome Foundation has been set up in Philadelphia by parents who contend that they have been wrongly accused of either prosaic or satanic-ritual abuse, or both.

Most criticisms of FMS-type cases have tended to focus on two factors: The first is the extraordinary zeal of the prosecutors and therapists involved, some of whom are unable to keep themselves from coaxing 'memories' out of alleged victims, usually because they themselves have a deep conviction that child sex abuse and satanic ritual abuse are widespread but hidden by their conspiratorial perpetrators. The second factor is a notion at the heart of the modern psychoanalytical paradigm – that traumatic memories can be 'repressed' for many years in one's unconscious and 'recovered' years later through hypnosis, intensive questioning, or similar techniques.

These criticisms are probably on target, but ignore another factor which is at least as important as the other

People who are dissociation-prone are often highly creative and imaginative, and seem to account for a disproportionate number of poets, novelists, and entertainers. Indeed, this talent for imaginative role-playing may indicate a fundamental psychological mechanism which enables the achievement of a wide variety of personal goals by other means – for example, an imagined ailment, or a dramatic but convincing story, may attract approval, admiration or other social resources. The more unconscious this deception is to the dissociator, the more credible he will seem to himself and to his intended audience. In some cases, the audience may be only the dissociator's own consciousness, as when dreams or visions, or other products of the unconscious, impart useful or behaviour-altering information.

Unfortunately, such imaginative behaviour doesn't always find socially acceptable outlets, and sometimes extraordinary episodes are triggered in which a dissociator may be inclined to manufacture supporting evidence in the form of scars, bruises, or mysterious and usually elusive ailments, or will continue to play out dangerous fantasies when other people's lives and livelihoods are at stake. In the Edenton case, the children initially denied ever having been abused by care centre staff, but after their parents and state-funded therapists began to assert to them that such abuse had occurred and that they need only remember it, they soon complied – not only with the requisite stories of pædophilia, but with a flood of increasingly bizarre and obviously fantastic tales [2]. Under cross-examination, the children attested to the truth of all of their allegations with unvarying fervour, whether these involved prosaic abuse or witches and spaceships. They showed no reaction at all to the fact that their testimony had ruined seven (probably innocent) people's lives.

In the East Olympia case, a similar pattern occurred, this time in adults who seemed unusually, and perhaps were to some extent genetically, dissociation-prone. Most family members, under questioning, appeared to go into a trance-like state which was specifically noted by their police interrogators. Paul Ingram even stated that he used a 'relaxation' technique, involving the visualisation of a warm

It happens in the UK too ...

'James' (right), a 57-year-old former ex-Royal Navy officer, was summoned by his 28-year-old daughter one afternoon in September 1991. When he arrived at her flat in London, she was sitting yoga-style on a dias. She read out a statement saying he was the cause of all her difficulties in life, concluding with a list of the sexual abuses James was supposed to have inflicted on her since she was a baby. Later she accused her grandfather of similar assaults, adding that at the age of four her father took her to satanic gatherings at which she was buggered by other men while he watched, and at which a baby was sacrificed, and that he forced her to eat his excrement.

The nightmare began when James' daughter went to see a specialist recommended by friends for treatment of vaginal thrush. The homeopath, who became her counsellor and goes by the palindromic name Melissa Assilem, also endorsed the daughter's claim of £70,000 in compensation from her father (for the pain of 're-remembering', losing her job, finding a 'safe' place to live and the cost of her therapy). Although James did not pay this, he did offer to pay for a qualified therapist at the London Institute.

James is still stunned by the accusations which, he says, came out of the blue and are completely untrue. He has two other daughters from his first marriage, the youngest of whom has chosen to believe the accusations. His first wife is guarded about what she says; already rejected by the accusing daughter for failing to protect her, she knows that any sign of disbelieving the accusations will end any hope of reconciliation with her daughter. James' second wife is standing by him, helping him "through fear and despair".

James was also helped by a new organisation called Adult Children Accusing Parents (ACAP), affiliated to the False Memory Syndrome Foundation in the USA, and like them founded to help families broken apart by wrongful claims of abuse and to raise public awareness of false memory syndrome. Organiser Roger Scotford told *FT* that 170 families have come to them for help since they were established. In almost every case the problem has originated with, or been made worse by, a hypnotherapist or counsellor who believed they could recover 'hidden' memories of child abuse and that these were the cause of present-day problems.

■ ACAP can be contacted on 0225 868682.
■ James' story is abbreviated from 'A child's memories and a father's nightmare' by Claudia Fitzherbert (*S.Telegraph* 7 March 1993), and 'Families haunted by accusations of childhood abuse' by Rosie Waterhouse *Independent* 24 May 1993).

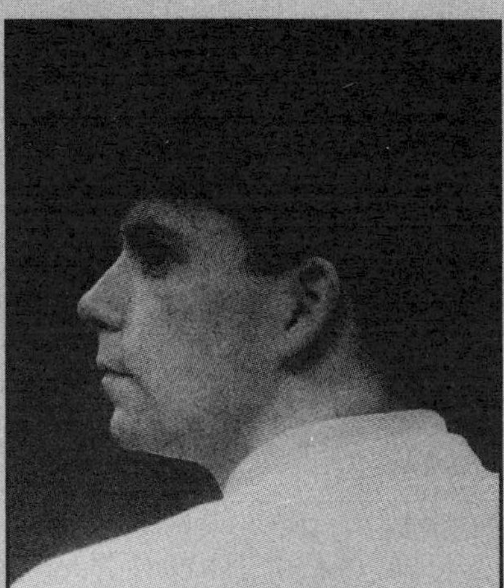

Abuse Excuse

Lyle Menendez (left), 21, and his brother Erik (right), 18, at their trial in Los Angeles for the brutal shotgun murder of their wealthy parents in Beverly Hills, California, after which they went on lavish spending sprees. The brothers kept silent for the four years they were in custody, then, on the eve of their trial, announced a sensational new defence. They killed their parents, they said, in self-defence after years of horrendous sexual and psychological abuse by their father Jose. The prosecution alleges they were impatient to inherit their estate, estimated to be worth £10 million.

white fog, whenever he needed to 'remember' something the prosecutors assured him he had done. He then would retire to his cell to meditate and pray to God to give him, spontaneously, an accurate memory of what had happened. His daughter Ericka, from whom the charges had originated, was moody and withdrawn, tore at her hair during interrogations, and sent a forged threatening letter to herself from "your ex-father," just when the prosecution case was beginning to weaken. With her sister Julie, she claimed to have numerous torture scars none of which were evident, and, it later emerged, had a history of making unsubstantiated claims of having been raped or sexually assaulted by various townspeople.

"Judges and juries, as well as therapists, were accepting the idea that some people could witness or experience events that were so traumatic that they would afterwards unconsciously repress the memories as a means of protecting the ego."

The current debate over 'real' versus 'false' memories should itself provoke a sense of *déjà vu* [3] among Forteans – at least those who are acquainted with the outbreaks of epidemic possession between the 15th and 17th centuries, the 19th-century disputes over the nature of hysteria and the neuroses, and, of course, the modern 'UFO abduction' phenomenon.

The possession epidemics usually began with one dissociation-prone and sexually-frustrated nun in a convent, whose own Dionysian antics would quickly be followed by those of dozens of other nuns unless the first nun was quickly isolated. In some of these cases, the possessed nuns exhibited symptoms which we now know to be consistent with Multiple Personality Disorder (MPD), but these symptoms also tended to evolve as the epidemics progressed. Indeed, the epidemics often seemed like competitions – one French nun topped her sisters with the revelation that she was possessed by 6,666 demons [4] – for the attentions of a monk or priest who perhaps had served as convent confessor, and who would often be enlisted as an exorcist.

As has always been the case with primitive magic, possession could be attributed not only to evil spirits, but also to other humans. These, as witches or sorcerers, could be men as well as women, but it was usually women who (sometimes without any more coercion than the ecclesiastical suggestion that such things sometimes happened) confessed that at night they flew from their beds, through the walls of their houses, to great witch conferences where they took part in various bizarre tortures and cannibalistic sacrifices.

In the 19th century, as psychology and psychiatry developed into institutional sciences, specialists marvelled at the wave of patients, again mostly female, who complained of pains and illnesses of undiscoverable origin, or other traumatic experiences. Often hypnosis was used to demonstrate that these patients were inherently prone to fall into trances and could be manipulated into believing almost anything. It was suggested by many eminent psychiatrists that these patients' mysterious ailments were simply unconscious expressions of sexual frustration.

The young Sigmund Freud, however, impressed by the remarkably similar stories of sexual trauma alleged by these patients, began to entertain the notion that they were telling the truth. In the mid 1890s, he put forward his 'seduction theory', according to which childhood sexual trauma of some sort accounted for all of the neuroses. His colleagues declined to take him seriously, though, and within a few years Freud found reason to recant. For one thing, he noted that his patients often developed an amorous attachment to him, as they did to other male psychiatrists. For another, he realised that if his theory were true, the prevalence of sex offenders among the fathers of Vienna would have to be nearly 100%, considering how many families were sending their hysterics and neurotics to see him.

Freud replaced the seduction theory with the Oedipus Complex and its corollaries, according to which hysterical neuroses were caused not by real events but, as his colleagues had long suggested, by unfulfilled libidinal urges. By World War I, the notion that psychological problems were rooted in early sexual trauma was all but dead, and it remained so for more than 60 years thereafter, thanks largely to the influence of Freud and the science of psychoanalysis which he had helped to found.

Sigmund Freud in 1891, aged 35. The absurd conclusion of his theorising was that most of the fathers of Vienna were guilty of incest.

That science, as Marx might have said, contained the seeds of its own destruction – or at least corruption – in the form of the concept of repression. Repression was a variant of the common belief – which extends back to primitive medicine – that some diseases are merely somatic manifestations of buried traumatic or embarrassing information which, when exhumed or confessed, will alleviate or terminate the symptoms. Freud had originally applied the concept not so much to hidden

memories as to hidden impulses and fantasies which, he believed, had been repressed into the unconscious because they were unacceptable to, say, the cultural mores of the day. Accordingly, these repressions could be revealed by analysing the symbolism of dreams and other products of the unconscious. Recovered memories of personal experiences were useful, but mostly as a guide to hidden impulses; Freud, who eschewed hypnosis, recognised that recovered memories could be a mixture of fact and fantasy.

By the 1980s, with the rise of feminism and the appearance of a number of horrendous child abuse stories in the media, it had become politically correct to take all such stories seriously, however they were obtained. Suddenly, the spectre of rampant childhood sexual abuse was abroad again. Self-proclaimed victims flooded the airwaves and the bookstore shelves with lurid tales of abuse and recovery. Judges and juries, as well as therapists, were accepting the idea that some people could witness or experience events that were so traumatic that they would afterwards unconsciously repress the memories as a means of protecting the ego.

In dozens of high-profile cases, the victims have gone first to a psychotherapist complaining of nonspecific anxieties or other problems, coming away convinced – usually after encouragement by the therapist – that their problems arise from childhood sex abuse. Then victims go to the police, or to a personal-injury litigation lawyer, perhaps sending one or both parents to jail, and perhaps collecting monetary damages along the way. Sex abuse allegations have become so powerful that they are increasingly used as a defence in criminal cases, for example in the recent trial of the Menendez brothers of Beverly Hills (see page 28). Even New Agers have jumped on the abuse bandwagon with claims that their current anxieties are caused by traumas suffered in *past lives.* In therapist-filled America, mental health professionals can be found who will validate almost any claimed experience or memory.

As always, some of the key evidence for a link between childhood sex abuse and later behavioural problems has come from studies of the dissociative disorders – which significantly became epidemic in America just as therapists were beginning to believe patients' stories again. Of patients with Multiple Personality Disorder, the best-known and most dramatic dissociative disorder, virtually 100% claim that they have been sexually abused in childhood. [5] Moreover, the gender ratio in those diagnosed with MPD is about 9:1 in favour of women, similar to the gender ratio found among child sex abuse claimants. Psychiatrists, at least in North America, now believe that many abused children learn to use dissociation, including the creation of alter personalities, as a defence against their traumas, and carried this talent into adulthood as a defence against almost any form of stress.

At about the same time that this view was taking hold, a rapidly increasing number of people with MPD began to claim that as children they had been victims of satanic ritual abuse (SRA). Some were so convincing that their therapists, including some well-respected psychiatrists, became vocal advocates of the existence of a wide-ranging and insidiously invisible satanic conspiracy whose members tortured and killed thousands of people every year, harvesting babies from young women specifically for the purpose of using them in sacrifices. The belief in an SRA conspiracy coincided with an increase in Christian fundamentalism in America, and intensified especially following the 1980 publication of a book titled *Michelle Remembers* by a Canadian ritual abuse 'survivor' and her psychiatrist husband. Other SRA bestsellers followed, including *Satan's Underground*, whose author, another self-described victim of satanic abuse, was later revealed to be a woman with a long history of self-mutilation and unsubstantiated claims of sexual assault. Ericka Ingram admitted having seen a copy of *Satan's Underground* just before making the claims against her father. She said that she was able to read only a few

The Showbiz Shaman

Michael Jackson has been accused of pædophilia by 13-year-old Jordan Chandler, one of many young boys who have stayed at the singer's houses. Chandler – described as "the subject of a bitter custody dispute between his parents" – is said to have admitted to Jackson's detective that the assaults "never happened", while Jackson's lawyers counter that the boy is being used by his father, dentist Evan Chandler, to extort money from the star.

This will eventually be settled in court, but Jackson himself presents a fascinating case, turning Münchausen-type behaviour into a multi-million

dollar business. This showbiz shaman – whose childhood was tyrannised by a brutal father and a calculating mother – submits to regular surgery; feigns wounds (turning casts and Band-aids into fashion accessories); is obsessed with cleanliness and food fads; displays ambiguous sexuality (both male/female as well as exaggerated innocence /eroticism) and ambivalent maturity (child/man); suffers rather convenient illnesses and collapses; craves sympathy and adoration; and adopts fantasy personas. Unlike most Münchausenians, Jackson is indulged in his excesses by dependent corporate sycophants.

chapters before throwing the book down in horror – having suddenly recognised, after so many years, that all this had happened to her, too.

At about the same time that therapists began to encounter satanic ritual abuse claims, they also began to hear from the victims of an even more bizarre form of abuse, perpetrated not by pædophilic parents or cloaked ritualists, but by little grey aliens. The aliens' rituals were for their own inscrutable scientific purposes, presumably, but they somehow involved the same torturous wounding and sexual-gynæcological manipulations that had mesmerised the SRA theorists. Instead of breeding babies for satanic rituals, women were being forced to breed hybrid human-alien babies. Instead of flying through walls to witch convocations, abductees were flying through walls to waiting spaceships. Just as SRA victims were often drugged, restrained, and warned to forget their experiences by their assailants, UFO abductees would typically report feelings of paralysis at the outset of their abduction episodes, followed by a telepathic hypnosis-like process with which the aliens kept them under physical and mental control and later suppressed their memories.

Again, just as SRA victims often 'suddenly remembered' their abuse when reading a book or watching a television programme about SRA, UFO abductees too would frequently experience an overpowering shock of recognition when confronted with pictures of aliens or descriptions of abductions. Some of the books about alien abductions, including the extraordinary bestseller, *Communion*, had been written by abductee 'survivors.' Other books were written by abduction researchers, who would place their addresses in their books so that abductees could contact them. Abductees began to flock around particular abduction researchers just as possession victims flocked around earnest father-confessors and witch-hunters of yore, and MPD sufferers proliferated among the patients of certain psychotherapists.

As abductees began to compete with one another for the attentions of their confessor-therapists, their reported experiences began to reach dizzying heights of absurdity and implausibility. Recently, one female abductee turned up at the house of a well-known male abduction researcher soaking wet and covered with sand and seaweed. She claimed, without the need for hypnosis, that she had been abducted by two men, government agents, who had taken her to a nearby beach house, had asked her to put on a white nightdress like one she had worn during many of her previous alien abductions, and then had tried to drown her in the sea. Additionally, this abductee has described herself, presumably without intending any irony, as a matrilineal descendant of Saint Joan of Arc.

"She claimed, without the need for hypnosis, that she had been abducted by two men, government agents, who had taken her to a nearby beach house, had asked her to put on a white nightdress like one she had worn during many of her previous alien abductions, and then had tried to drown her in the sea."

Extraordinary encounters and experiences, and claims thereof, seem designed to express or to satisfy a wide range of human needs, as some researchers have recognised [6]. It would seem that some or all cases of satanic ritual abuse, UFO abductions, spirit possession, multiple personalities, and perhaps many *prosaic* memories of childhood trauma, represent a subset of such experiences in which the dissociator assumes, perhaps unconsciously, the role of a victim. The precise nature of the central role in these 'self-victimisation syndromes' is probably determined largely by the cultural material to which the role-player has been exposed.

Other types of self-victimisation syndromes include some everyday psychosomatic disorders, as well as deliberately feigned ailments or injuries such as those produced by people with Münchausen's syndrome (see 'The Münch Bunch', ***FT70:23-29***). There are both historical and ontogenetic antecedents of such self-victimisation – for example, in the initiatory illnesses of shamans and in the demanding screams of infants. Tales told by shamans and children often exhibit a kind of fantastic, dissociative 'dream logic' which has also been known to pervade the stories of individuals with MPD and its variants.

For modern adults, self-victimisation may be a solitary preoccupation - as it is for Münchausenians – or it may inspire a flocking together into 'support groups', as is common among MPD sufferers, UFO abductees, and SRA and ordinary incest survivors. The anthropologist I.M. Lewis has noted similar psychosocial phenomena in the Third World in the form of peripheral possession syndromes and possession cults, which are usually the province of women, and usually have as their purpose the manipulation, subversion and/or humiliation of males. The fact that, as Lewis puts it, membership in a victim group is often itself "in the nature of a cure" of the victim's underlying psychological problem has been lost on many modern therapists, who complain in exasperation at the extraordinary tendency of their patients to prolong therapy indefinitely – for example, claiming further trauma just at the point when their other anxieties have been soothed.

Lewis has suggested that the reason for the preponderance of females in possession cults is sociological – women are often treated as second-class citizens, and therefore sometimes feel compelled to use extraordinary means to achieve their goals. However, there is also evidence from the literature of psychology and neurology that women are inherently more prone to severe dissociative behaviour than men, suggesting that male dominance and other sociological factors may have influenced the evolution of female psychoneurology. (Additionally, there is evidence to suggest that while women typically seem to use dissociative experiences and storytelling to express libidinal urges, men more often use dissociation to express violent urges; as a result, the numbers of male dissociators may be hidden by short life expectancies or long periods in jail.)

A few more points are in order. The first, as therapists from Freud and Jung to Budd Hopkins have noted, is that the imagery and experiences reported by victims of these ostensible traumas surface in victim after victim, even when there are no obvious cultural antecedents. Moreover, many of the motifs found in one variant of this syndrome may be found in some or all

Michael Persinger of Laurentian University, Ontario, who has induced epilepsy-related sensations in people by applying magnetic fields to the temporal lobe of their brains.

of the other variants. For example, Chad Ingram's 'little people' and 'fat witch' dreams are almost identical to those reported by Freud's hysterics, David Hufford's 'Old Hag' victims [7], and innumerable UFO abductees.

Other motifs which are found throughout these syndromes include bedroom or sleep paralysis; a sensed 'presence'; feelings of being hypnotised or drugged, floating or flying through the air and passing through solid structures; lying down on a table and being sexually or gynæcologically assaulted or manipulated; impressions of undergoing surgical operations, or the removal or replacement of organs; the assumption of the victim's role followed by that of the healer; an expanded consciousness; apotheotic themes of god-given destiny or survival of fantastic adversity; and a desire to tell one's story (the 'talking cure', as one 19th century hysteric termed it, or "healing through art, ie. mythology and song" as Joseph Campbell has said).

Many of these motifs are archæic, being found in the mystical traditions of virtually all religions, and can be traced back to shamanic lore. For example, in recent cases of satanic ritual abuse, SRA victims have claimed that their hearts had been ripped out and replaced with those of animals or of Satan. The same motif appears in Christian mysticism as part of the 'sacred marriage' – a claimed experience in which numerous female mystics swapped hearts with Christ – as well as in many shamanic initi ation rites.

Some of these motifs may be culture-bound 'archetypes' (complex images which have become embedded trans-culturally in human consciousness), but there is a growing body of evidence that many of them have an even more basic neurological explanation. For example, experiences such as sensations of floating, of feeling at one with the cosmos, sensing a nearby presence, and even of amnesia have been associated with temporal lobe seizures. Michael Persinger, a professor of psychology at Canada's Laurentian University, has been in the forefront of such research, and has even induced such sensations artificially by applying magnetic fields over the temporal lobes.

Persinger has argued that the types of sensations which are experienced may depend upon the portions of the temporal lobe and related brain structures which are involved in the seizure. The idea is that abstract sensations such as floating or a sense of some mysterious presence originate from fundamental neurological processes which are triggered during a seizure or other episode of neurological abnormality (which itself may be partially under the control of the percipient, or may occur in response to stress, or in altered states such as hypnotic trances) and then are dressed in the appropriate cultural garments by the mind, just as, for a dreamer, ordinary sensory inputs (eg. a train whistle, or the urge to urinate) are woven meaningfully into the dream narrative.

It is not yet clear that temporal lobe abnormalities can explain dissociation – indeed, the relationship between the two is controversial, because, for example, not all dissociators exhibit electroencephalographic abnormalities while in a trance state. But it should be noted that (a) the phenomenology of dissociative states is similar to that of temporal lobe seizures; (b) the shamanic vocation has often been heralded by a childhood tendencies to epileptic-like seizures; and (c) studies have shown that dissociative people do seem to show a greater than average number of neurological abnormalities. Persinger has argued that such abnormalities may operate below the threshold of EEG surveillance, thus masking the true neurological substrate of dissociative phenomena.

If he is correct, and dissociators are merely prone to temporal lobe micro-seizures, then the mass hysterias which these individuals spark and sustain with their created memories and fantastic experiences might simply be the analogues – social seizures, so to speak – of what is going on in their heads. FT

Jim Schnabel is a freelance journalist whose history of UFO abduction research, *Dark White*, will be published by Hamish Hamilton in 1994.

NOTES

1 'Innocence Lost: The Verdict', a 4-hour *Frontline* Special Report by Ofra Bikel. Part 1 broadcast 20 July 1993 on PBS; Part 2 on 21 July 1993.
2 The similar technique, used by social workers in the Orkney SRA case to 'disclose' hidden memories, was severely criticised and discredited by judicial authorities – see *FT57:50, 55, 57*. There, too, pressure from the inquisitors brought forth fantastic details, and any attempt by the children to retract their stories was ignored or resisted by the very people they were intended to please.
3 Incidentally, experiences of *déjà vu*, which are neuropsychologically probably similar to what is now termed False Memory Syndrome, were long-ago called *falsæ memoriæ* by Augustine in his *De Trinitate*.
4 Pastor Doug Riggs, of Tulsa, Oklahoma, subjected his congregation to individual 'counselling' sessions (sometimes lasting up to 19 hours) and discovered that over half of them had secondary personalities due to SRA trauma in childhood. His prize exhibit is a woman who has "several thousand personalities, each possessed by hundreds of demons". ('In Satan's Name', *Viewpoint*, ITV, June 1993.)
5 MPD is almost unknown in Britain, where many therapists consider it a form of deliberate deception practised by attention-seekers and malingering criminals hoping to avoid responsibility for their actions.
6 See, for example, Hilary Evans, *Visions, Apparitions, and Alien Visitors* (Aquarian Press, 1984).
7 See David Hufford, *The Terror that Comes in the Night* (Pennsylvania University Press,1975).
The source of most details about the Ingram case and the SRA craze was Lawrence Wright's lengthy article 'Remembering Satan' in The New Yorker, 17 May and 24 May 1993, which is highly recommended to anyone with an interest in this subject.

THE WEBS OF WAR

Some very odd weapons have been reported in the current Balkan conflict. PAUL SIEVEKING investigates.

Spider webs have been researched for possible military purposes at least since World War II, when the Germans tested the dissemination of anthrax with silk thread webs. In the 1960s, the US army explored the use of such webs as a less expensive alternative to the aerosol testing of biological agents, but in 1968 declared their inability to re-create the natural silk polymer produced by spiders. After the genetic engineering advances of the last ten years, such synthesis should now be possible. However, the US Army today is tight-lipped about web warfare. A spokesman at Edgewood Arsenal in Maryland said the subject was classified and he was unable to answer even simple background questions.

Radio Croatia first reported the release of "a mysterious weblike substance" over its territory on 8 November 1991 [see ***FT61:21***], and by the following November there had been over 200 reports of cobweb bombardment in Croatia alone. Croat scientists presented inconclusive evidence that "the material had produced chromosomal aberrations", according to Benjamin C. Garrett, writing in an August 1992 issue of the ASA (Applied Science Analysis) Newsletter.

Garrett, an analytical chemist and executive director of the Chemical & Biological Arms Control Institute in Alexandria, Virginia, visited Croatia in June 1992 with other scientists to examine 'cobweb' samples. There were two distinct types of very fine fibres, one being one-tenth of a micron in thickness and of a protein nature that could be natural or man-made; the other was four-tenths of a micron thick, and 'most likely' made of polyurethane. Both were thinner than anything manufactured by routine processes. There was no sign of viruses, bacteria, fungi, or chemical warfare agents.

Garrett pointed out that spiders were migrating naturally when the cobwebs was first noticed, but there was no evidence that spiders were with the material when it was dropped. In any case, he said, "no spider has yet been found to synthesize polyurethane." However, Radio Croatia also claimed that 'large quantities' of live, yellow-backed spiders had emerged from canisters dropped on the eastern Croatian town of Daruvar by the Yugoslav airforce in late 1991.

Video footage of cobweb bombardments exist. Some show a fibrous mass ejected from aircraft, changing from spherical to sausage-shaped before breaking up and hitting the ground. Some of the threads were as long as 164 feet. According to the Tanjug news agency in Belgrade, the Yugoslav airforce admitted dropping the substance, and claimed it was to counter anti-aircraft defence; but Garret pointed out that the threads were non-conductive and so their supposed purpose made no sense. Perhaps the web bombardment was a means of spreading fear and uncertainty; all the experts remained puzzled. One suggestion, made by David Huxoll, an associate dean of the School of Veterinary Medicine at Louisiana State University, was that the webs could be used to deliver biological agents that could degrade insulation in electrical wiring or cause a rapid breakdown of lubricants.

Like any war, the conflict in the Balkans has been a hotbed for exotic rumours. Serbia, in particular, exhibits a sensibility of magical realism. In 1991, there was a claim that Croats in the town of Osijek had freed tigers from the local zoo to roam the countryside lunching on Chetnik guerrillas. State-run television, the main source of information for most people in Belgrade, often features a chap who assures viewers that at the moment when final destruction threatens the Serbian nation, a fleet of vampires will arise from the cemeteries to overwhelm its enemies. He advises Serbs to stockpile garlic for protection.

Main sources: Washington Times, 28 Nov 1992; NY Times, 16 May 1993.

It came from Outer Space!

A chronological guide to 20th century aliens compiled by Mike Dash

The depiction of aliens in literature and the cinema has come a long way since 1900 – and so has the way in which UFO witnesses describe their close encounters.

At the end of the 19th century, the crews of the mystery 'airships' seen hovering over the American midwest appeared entirely human; the sole tinge of exoticism was their oriental features. The first 'spacemen' spotted during the great flying saucer wave that began in 1947 were also humanoid.

The 1950s, on the other hand, saw the reporting of a bewildering diversity of aliens, from robots and dwarfs to hairy monsters and giants. At the same time, cinema latched onto saucers in a big way, spreading the idea of alien visitors to audiences far larger than those weaned on the pulp science fiction magazine of the 1920s and 1930s.

The degree to which cinema influenced UFO witnesses (and vice versa) is hard to determine; probably each had an effect on the other. But certainly the extensive press coverage of certain key cases (and perhaps concepts firmly rooted in science fiction) may be behind the developing consensus that has led to the emergence of the ubiquitous 'greys' (left) – small, large-brained humanoids – as by far the most commonly reported Ufonauts of the last three decades.

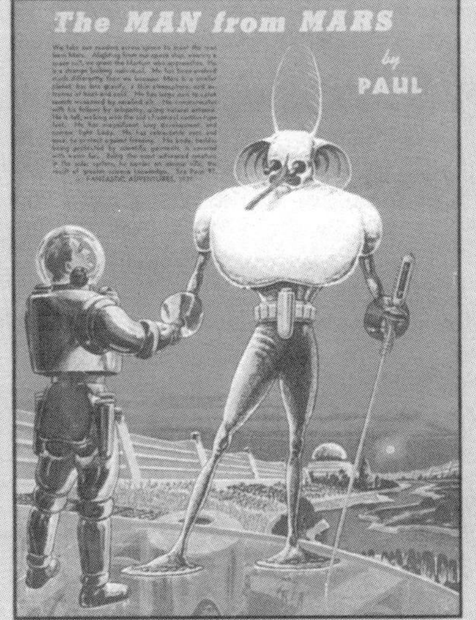

UFO witnesses rarely describe such exotic creatures as those envisaged by science fiction authors who have given serious thought to the living conditions on alien planets.

This Mercurian (top, from a 1939 issue of the pulp title *Fantastic Adventures*) is a hard-shelled insect evolved to withstand the intense heat of the planet, while the Martian (centre) from the same title has developed huge lungs to breathe the planet's thin air, and retractable eyes and nose to protect against freezing.

An alternative view of evolution on the Red Planet (bottom) was taken by *Fate* (Summer 1948), which kept the barrel chest but added fur to keep the Martian warm, webbed feet for walking on sand, eyes protected from the cold by natural goggles – and a jockstrap to protect the creature's modesty.

Picture credits. This page: top l. Mary Evans Picture Library; bottom l. Fortean Picture Library. Right t.& c. MEPL, b. FPL. Centre pages: 1901 FPL; 1918 & 1939 MEPL; 1953 National Pictures Corp.; 1954 MEPL; 1955 FPL; 1955 Cinemabilia; 1955/72 Ron Schaffner/FPL; 1957 Malibu; 1958 Paramount; 1961 Donn Davison; 1963 Saucerian Press; 1960s MEPL; 1970 & 1973 FPL; 1974 &1977 MEPL; 1992 Fox Video.

THE CHANGING SHAPE

MOON MEN (1901)

Belief that the Moon may be inhabited has persisted for even longer than the theory it is made of green cheese. The Greeks had a well-developed hypothesis that suggested Moon Men would be humanoid, but 15 times taller than anyone on Earth because the Moon day was 15 times longer than an Earth day [FT54:58–61].

At the turn of the century, the idea still held appeal for the early science fiction authors and film makers. Here an illustrator gives life to HG Wells' descriptions of *The First Men in the Moon*, a serial for the *Strand Magazine* in which intrepid (British) astronauts encounter a race of bipedal insects, the Selenites. The work subsequently served as an inspiration for Georges Melies' 1903 epic film *Le Voyage dans la Lune*, where the aliens are crustaceans living in a grotto of giant mushrooms.

MOON MEN (1918)

This illustration, from the French periodical *La Barionette*, is one of the first to show the classic motif of large-brained, hyper-intelligent aliens, in this case from the moon.

The creatures – who have evolved well beyond the stage of settling disputes by military means – are shown observing the closing months of the Great War and speculating that Earthlings use conflict as a means of preventing their planet cooling.

During the 1920s, the concept of moon-men gave way to Martians and Venusians and, as our understanding of astronomy has increased, the aliens encountered in both art and what passes for reality have hailed from progressively further into the void. This causes problems for those who believe in real-life aliens, as it is hard to explain why Earth is of such great interest to our intergalactic cousins.

KILLER 'CLOWNS' (1939)

The advent of pulp science fiction magazines in the 1920s lent enormous impetus to the spread of belief in aliens from other planets. Issue after issue featured spectacular encounters between bizarre humanoids or monsters from outer space and plucky Earthlings, many of them beautifully illustrated in colour on the magazine's cover.

This example, from a 1939 edition of *Fantastic Adventures*, shows the invasion of hostile creatures from Sirius, the Dog Star, in a story written by Leo Morey and illustrated by Ed Earl Repp. Apart from their eye stalks, they are human in appearance, and resemble nothing so much as killer clowns. The clown-as-villain has lately featured prominently in Fortean mythology, both as child abductor and cosmic joker.

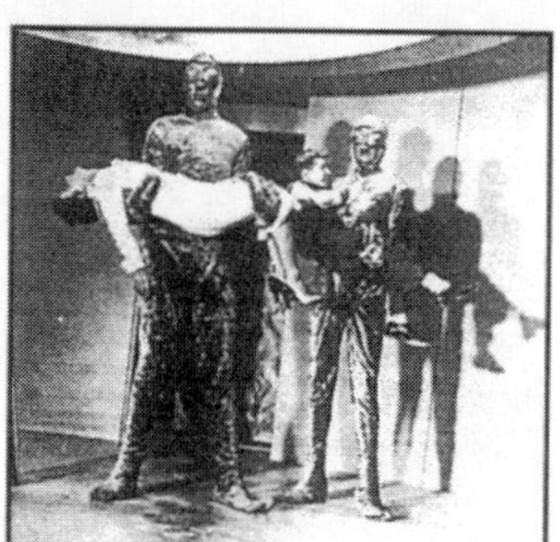

INVADERS FROM MARS (1953)

One of the most remarkable of '50s sci-fi films, *Invaders From Mars* features many motifs familiar to UFO investigators around the world. A boy awakened by the sound of a flying saucer sees his parents leave their house to investigate and return changed people. Investigating further, he discovers transmitters buried in his parents' necks which the aliens – depicted here as bug-eyed humanoid giants – use to control human behaviour.

Although the invaders hail from Mars, the red planet, they are portrayed as green (and, in the case of their leader, tentacled). Nevertheless, like many similar movies, *Invaders from Mars* can be seen as a comment on '50s fear of 'reds under the bed'. Not surprisingly, the aliens prove no match for the local militia in the climactic scene.

RADAR VALENCIENNES
RECONSTITUE LA FANTASMAGORIQUE APPARITION "MARTIENNE" QUI SIDÉRA Marius DEWILDE

QUAROUBLE, FRANCE (1954)

The French UFO wave of 1954 remains the greatest ever recorded, with sightings reported from from across the country over a period of months before saucer mania spread to other European territories.

Marius Dewilde, a metalworker from Quarouble in northern France, reported what became the most famous close encounter during the wave after encountering a UFO that had landed on a railway track near the town. Two small humanoid figures in 'diving suits' (but looking not entirely unlike George Lucas's later R2D2) approached, and he was paralysed by a green ray shot from the saucer itself.

French Air Force investigators later calculated that depressions in the railway track where the 'Martian' saucer had landed were made by something weighing at least 30 tons.

KELLY-HOPKINSVILLE, KENTUCKY (1955)

A group of bug-eyed aliens beseiged a farming family from Kelly, near Hopkinsville, Kentucky, in August 1955. This famous case is one of the very few featuring archetypal 'little green men', though the Kelly creatures glowed luminous silver and had bright yellow eyes.

Under repeated questioning, the Sutton family and their friends the Taylors stuck to the story that a group of three-foot tall creatures with big ears, long arms and talons had floated towards their home, and

were immediately fired on. Undeterred, they regrouped and were heard clambering over the roof; at one point one reached down to grab Billy Ray Taylor's hair. Taylor claimed to have seen the craft the aliens arrived in – a saucer that landed behind the farm.

THIS ISLAND EARTH (1955)

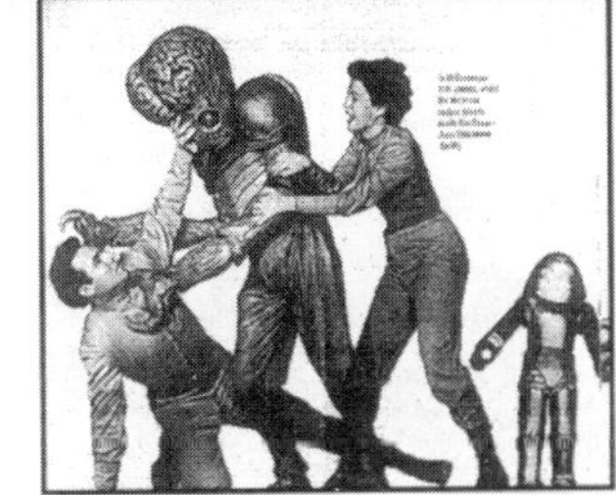

Despite its terrifying appearance, the Metalunan alien star of *This Island Earth* was one of the few friendly off-worlders featured in the cinema of the '50s.

The film's premise was equally unusual for the time, suggesting that nuclear power could have untold benefits. Certainly the Metalunans coveted it, kidnapping a group of Earth scientists in a doomed attempt to harness the power of the atom to repair the shield defences of their planet.

From a Fortean point of view, the Metalunans' chief interest lies in their greatly enlarged brain and eyes. This trait, suggestive of enhanced intelligence, has become a Ufological commonplace, and big-headed aliens are now by far the most common type of Ufonauts reported from around the world.

LOVELAND, OHIO (1955 AND 1972)

Tiny Loveland has generated four bizarre encounter reports, three in 1955 and one more recently.

The first, by a volunteer policeman, was of four malodorous "strange little men about three feet tall" spotted under a bridge a month before the Kelly sighting. Soon afterwards, a solitary and extremely smelly little man apparently covered in foliage appeared – like the Kelly creatures – in a garden one evening, looking into a house.

The third report, by a short order chef named Robert Hunnicutt, described a group of little men standing by the road late one night. Halting his car for a closer look, Hunnicutt saw "fire coming out of their hands" and smelled a foul odour.

Then, in 1972, this peculiar 'frogman', three to four feet tall, appeared near the Little Miami River and was shot at by policemen.

INVASION OF THE HELL CREATURES (1957)

The villains of this dismal would-be comedy bear a closer resemblance to the typical modern-day UFO occupant than do any of their predecessors. Little, green *and* male, the aliens land by a lovers' lane in middle America and encounter courting couples and pitchfork-wielding farmers before their spaceship is finally blown up by the US military.

The classic features of large heads and prominent eyes are present and correct, and were even more definitely emphasised in a '60s remake titled *The Eye Creatures*.

Director Edward Cahn's decision to play things for laughs symbolised the late '50s thaw in the Cold War which effectively killed off the alien invasion genre. Films made in the '60s, '70s and '80s were more likely to feature friendly aliens and environmental themes.

I MARRIED A MONSTER FROM OUTER SPACE (1958)

One of the last outbreaks of '50s Red paranoia occurs in this black & white B-movie, which features an intriguing memory-loss plot.

The hero is kidnapped by shape-shifting aliens who hook him up to a memory-transfer machine and give his personality and past history to a lookalike monster. It sets off in search of the earth women needed to save the alien planet from extinction. As usual, the day is saved when a posse of Earthling fathers discovers the creatures' spacecraft and rescue their female hostages.

The idea of aliens wiping abductees' memories became a Ufological staple shortly thereafter, with Betty and Barney Hill's 1961 "interrupted journey" sparking a continuing interest in hypnotic regression as a tool for exploring suppressed close encounters.

NEW HAMPSHIRE (1961)

The Hill's close encounter was the first and most celebrated UFO abduction in modern times and generated so much publicity over the years it has undoubtedly influenced more recent reports.

The abduction scenario now seems almost commonplace: the couple were driving through the White Mountains of New Hampshire when they became aware of a bright light following their car. A beeping noise from the boot of their car made them drowsy; another series of beeps awakened them and they realised they were 35 miles closer to their destination than they should have been.

Later, under hypnosis, the couple recalled an abduction and painful medical examination by large-brained and emotionless humanoids who communicated telepathically and told them they would not remember what had occurred.

USA (1963?)

A sharp escalation in the tension between the US and the USSR provided the backdrop for this terrifying encounter between New Zealander John Stuart, his attractive girlfriend Barbara, and an eight-foot-tall monster from another world.

Stuart, who had been researching UFOs since the early 1950s, had already received threatening phone calls telling him to lay off his investigation, while Barabara claimed to have been raped by an invisible, sandpaper-skinned monster.

This creature, while complete with fangs, saliva, and little piggy eyes, is a curious hybrid, combining a dense fur coat apparently suitable for cold, land-based climates with the webbed feet of a water-dweller. Whether it had any existence outside the imagination of the witnesses it is now impossible to tell.

SOUTH AFRICA (1960s)
Not all Ufonauts are so strange in appearance; a well-defined subset appear to be highly-evolved humans.

These are the aliens who make themselves known to 'contactees', frequently many times over a period of years. The earliest contactees (including the best-known, George Adamski), appeared shortly after the first saucer sightings, at a time when few if any 'flying disc' reports included mentions of occupants.

Typically, the aliens described by contactees bring messages of comfort, urge universal peace and spin homespun celestial philosophies to their Earth-bound friends. This one, named Akon, did rather more for his South African friend Elizabeth Klarer; she later claimed she had borne his child.

PENANG, MALAYSIA (1970)
Not all close encounters conform to Western stereotypes of alien appearance and behaviour. French Ufologists studying saucer sightings in Algeria have shown that reports from Arab cultures conform more closely to local folklore and tradition than they do to similar reports from Europe and the US. Similarly, the Malaysian schoolboys who sketched these star-spangled entities with tight-fitting suits and a saucer-shaped craft topped with a "Mr Kipling's Cakes"- style decoration may have been influenced by the conventions of Japanese *manga* comics, which are widely distributed in the country.

That said, one incongruous detail in the report is the aliens' size; far from being giants, like most Japanese comic characters, they were tiny, and so was their saucer.

FALKVILLE, ALABAMA (1973)
Photographs of alleged UFO occupants are thin on the ground, and this one, of an alien encountered by Police Chief Jeff Greenshaw in the early '70s, looks like nothing so much as a man dressed entirely in Bacofoil.

Greenshaw, however, believed the being might be a robot. It moved mechanically, he said, and had an antenna on its head. After taking four polaroids, the policemand turned his headlights on it and it ran off down the road so quickly his patrol car was unable to keep up. Several local residents later reported UFO sightings that coincided with Greenshaw's encounter.

The sighting caused considerable problems for the Alabaman, who was asked to resign by the local mayor within a month.

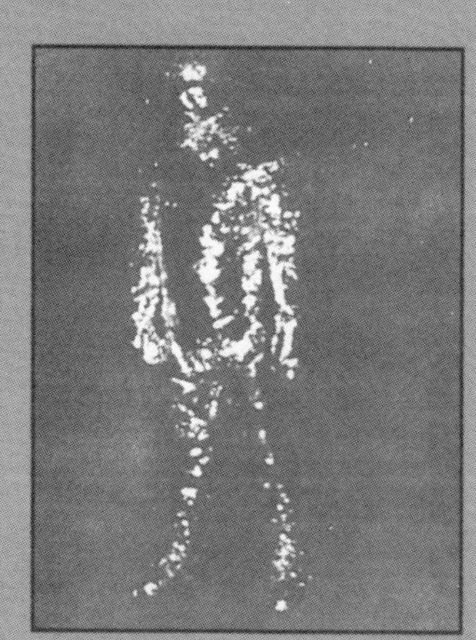

AVELEY, ESSEX (1974)
The Avis family's 1974 abduction experience was one of the most celebrated and hotly-contested UK cases of the decade – and also one of the most bizarre.

Recalling the experience later, under hypnosis, John and Elaine Avis described a classic abduction which featured an extensive medical examination. One particular peculiarity was the presence of two distinct types of aliens, one tall and humanoid, the other shorter, thicker-set and dog faced. The latter appeared to be medics and carried out the examination.

Proponents of the psychosociological school of Ufology have drawn attention to the Avis's admission that they had earlier watched a TV programme featuring the story of a similar abduction, and insist the experience was subjective in nature.

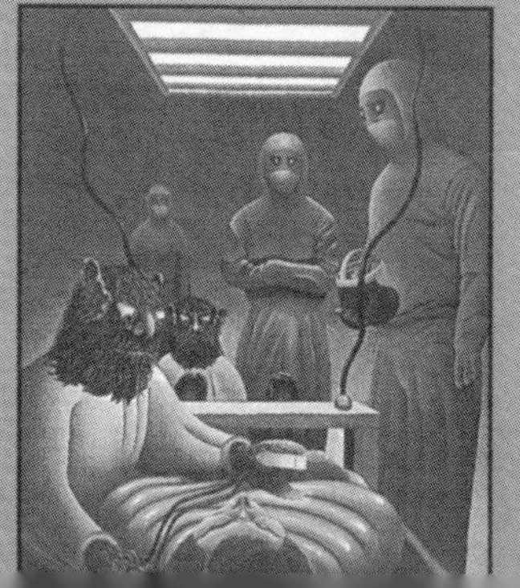

BRAZIL (1977)
These outlandish 'pogo stick' creatures were reported from South America by a witness named Antonio La Rubia. Sightings of such emphatically non-human creatures remain decidedly rare, however, leaving investigators to puzzle over the question of whether the proponderance of humanoids in UFO encounters suggests 'man' is the natural result of evolution on many different planets, or whether witnesses are moulding less tangible experiences in their own image.

Whatever the truth, the aliens' utility belts certainly seem to hint that extraterrestrials share one particularly Earthling trait – a love of superhero comics.

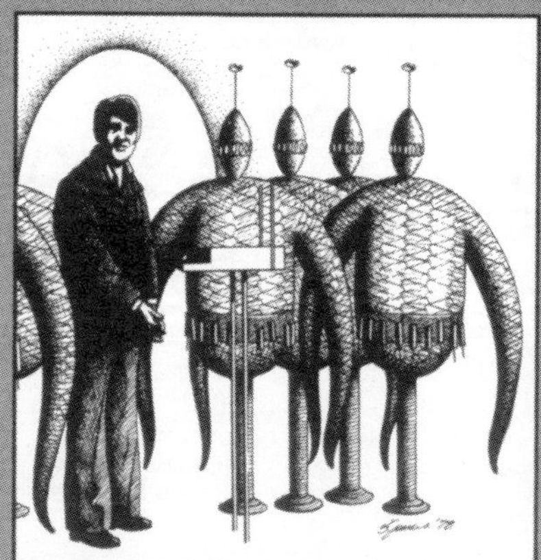

ALIEN 3 (1992)
Aside from their stunning special effects, the three 'Alien' movies reintroduced viewers to the concept of genuinely alien extra-terrestrials. Rather than apeing human behaviour patterns, the stars of these films have developed insect instincts, building large nests, each presided over by a giant queen.

In contrast, virtually all the UFO occupants described by witnesses display characteristically human behaviour and philosophy. Medical examinations, in particular, seem to reflect human experience, even though the purpose of some of the 'tests' administered remains obscure. Another example of man moulding aliens in his image?

Further reading: Isabel Davis & Ted Bloecher, *Close Encounter at Kelly and Others of 1955*, Center for UFO Studies 1978; Hilary Evans, *Visions, Apparitions, Alien Visitors*, Wellingborough 1986; Hilary Evans & John Spencer (eds) *UFOs 1947–1987*, London 1987; Phil Hardy, *The Encyclopedia of Science Fiction Movies*, London 1986; John Rimmer, *The Evidence for Alien Abductions*, Wellingborough 1984; Nigel Watson, *Portraits of Alien Encounters*, Valis Books, London 1990.

FT

interview

"Imagine living in a world with 10 billion people, a world of fascist hives, hideously minimal incomes, and nightmarish jobs."

TOM HODGKINSON talks to TERENCE MCKENNA about Virtual Futures and the End of History

RADICAL MUSHROOM REALITY

Terence McKenna, author of *Food of the Gods, The Archaic Revival* and *True Hallucinations*, is the most forceful advocate of psychedelics since Timothy Leary, combining ancient wisdom and Irish wit. Now 46, he first tried psychedelics in mid-sixties Berkeley. Unlike most of his generation, who buried their trips in a file marked Unidentified Youthful Indulgences, McKenna doggedly followed through and has been taking 'heroic doses' of natural hallucinogens ever since. He is particularly interested in the shamanic culture of Amazonia.

McKenna holds that magic mushrooms provide the key to spiritual reality, and regularly draws audiences of up to 3,000 in New York and Los Angeles, made up of psychonauts, cyberpunks and mycologists. He has a plan to found a Bohemian Institute in Prague. Tom Hodgkinson caught up with him in London, where he was publicising a single by The Shamen, which features his distinctive, dramatic, high-pitched Californian voice.

FT: Are we gearing up for some kind of change?

TM: I think that even the most sober observer of world culture would have to conclude that we have an appointment with transformation or extinction. There's no third possibility. Business-as-usual has been removed from the menu, and we're either going to run ourselves extinct, cut down the forests, pollute the ocean and destroy the atmosphere, or, within our lifetimes, do the most massive reorganising of human priorities in recorded history, because essentially we have to shed an entire culture, a thousand years of doing things a certain way.

It's very exciting and it has to come from youth because they still have the intellectual and social flexibility to create some kind of new world. It can't come from the banks, the manufacturing concerns, the major mass media;

they're too much a part of the old system. We have to dematerialise culture and limit population in very radical ways. It's heresy to say so, but capitalism is not a user-friendly way of doing things.

We cannot keep fabricating nature into products that are sold to those who have had bourgeois aspirations exported into their culture by world media. We need to create a virtual culture, in which products are made entirely of light.

TELEPATHIC WORLD

FT: If you imagine a future with limitless communication in hyperspace, it looks a bit like a telepathic world. It's almost like we're trying to recreate a half-remembered ideal of total telepathic communication between everybody, via technology.

TM: I think that's true. Essentially what technology may well be in the service of, or certainly should be, is a notion somewhat along the lines of turning the human being inside out. What we want to do is exteriorise the soul and interiorise the body, so that the body becomes a kind of freely-commanded image in the imagination.

The imagination is where the future lies; that's where we're all going to live. Is it going to be a virtual world, a nano-technical world, a pharmacologically maintained and delivered world à-la-Stanislav Lem, futurological congress ... ? There are different possibilities, but the kind of technology we have now can no longer be exercised on the surface of an ecologically dense planet like this.

FT: But isn't there a danger? I remember reading a story by Isaac Asimov in which there is virtually no physical contact between the inhabitants of a planet. They talk through videophones and find the idea of any physical contact utterly repellent.

TM: I think the way to go around that (and it's well understood by the technical community) is this: as technology becomes ever more pervasive, it should become ever less visible.

Here's one possible scenario: a world which appears to be a completely archæic world – people are tribal, naked, nomadic – but if you transpose yourself into one of these people's experience, you discover that technology has been reduced essentially to a pair of black contact lenses that are surgically planted at age three on the undersurface of the eyelid, so when you close your eyes, there are menus hanging in mental space ... computer menus. And by squinting or blinking you open menus, and the entire culture could be virtualised in this way.

So appearing to be primitive, we would actually have access to enormous databases, all kinds of situations of education, entertainment, personal interaction – but there would be no visible manifestation of technological involvement other than these contact lenses which could run off ambient static electricity and would be manufactured in a factory on the moon, or something. In other words, a complete abandonment of physical technology, but a complete maintenance of the capacity of physical technology.

Dr John E. Mack is one of the leading proponents of the Budd Hopkins-David Jacobs school which interprets tales of abduction by aliens as evidence of genetic experimentation with the human race. He is a professor of psychiatry at Cambridge Hospital, Harvard Medical School, Boston. He is now a full-time abduction researcher and has served as a consultant on the CBS-TV mini-series, *Intruders*.

> "We're dealing with something which disguises itself as an extra-terrestrial invasion in order not to alarm us."

FT: What happens to the difference between thought and action? Would you be able to tell the difference between kicking a tree and closing your eyes and going into the computer world? Will those two worlds be separate, in the way we recognise them as separate now?

TM: Probably the fair answer is no, that there will be a blending. We think in terms of reality and VR because we're just getting into the concept. But all kinds of bizarre situations and suggestions have been made. You could have yesterday running in virtual reality and today running in reality, and actually move between them mentally. Marshall McLuhan is the great proponent of the idea that technologies always carry hidden consequences that are never realised until the technology is already in place. I think VR would probably have the effect of breaking down our notion of reality pretty entirely. Causality can be fiddled with and the difference between memory and anticipation becomes less dramatic, and a number of things like that.

FT: Can you give us another example?

TM: Well... identity. I think that the human

self-image is dictated by the animal body, and as the animal body becomes less and less important, the human self-image will concomitantly evolve. In VR, if you're spending more than half of your time there, then are you who you are, or are you who you virtually are? And you may virtually be many people, or animals, or pieces of furniture or whatever.

MUSHROOM REALITY

FT: Your approach to UFOs is different from most other commentators.

TM: I see human history as a kind of alchemical conjuration, the purpose of which is the ultimate visible condensation of the soul, as a kind of dimension-roving lens-shaped vehicle. I can imagine in VR that we would transfer our self-identity to an image like that, in fact I really think that probably what is conventionally thought of as a flying saucer is in fact a kind of ricocheting mirage in time of a future state of transcendental unity that will come to typify the human experience.

"UFOs are the Overmind of the species at the end of human history ... It is the mysterious something that calls us out of animal nature."

I think that the mystery of what a human being is has to do with the fact that all primates have dominance hierarchies, but perhaps a million years ago or so, when we began to allow psilocybin in the diet, the ego was suppressed, which led to the collapse of the dominator-style behaviour of human beings. So, for perhaps as long as a million or a million and a half years, we literally pharmacologically inoculated ourselves against ego, reinforced through an orgiastic sexual and social style and the worship of a great goddess, visualised as a goddess of cattle with horns. It was in that interim period that we created language, community values, theatre, poetry, song, anticipation, analysis of past events – everything in short that defines us as human.

Well then, when the mushrooms disappeared, the ego (or the programmes that create it), which had always been there, were able to reassert themselves. The fall into history is very real; it actually happened. As soon as the mushrooms became scarce or unavailable, then suddenly you get intergroup struggle, standing armies, agriculture, the defence of surpluses, suppression of women, slavery – all of these things that are the root institutions of our own toxic culture.

FT: Wouldn't that imply that if everyone started taking mushrooms, the problems would be over?

TM: Well, it's not quite that simple because we are obviously in no position to start herding cattle around on the Sahara desert. Our dilemma is going to require a creative response. I mean, how do you back out of 5,000 years of monotheism, dualism, science, male domination, so forth and so on?

We need considerable imagination to make ourselves flexible enough to do what must be done. If nature is going to put us to the test – and we will find out whether our momentum for consumerism (what I call monogamy, hegemony and monotony) can be overturned, or whether in fact we're hard-wired for our own destruction. We may go to extinction, but not without certain voices being raised pointing out even in the final moments that it could have been done differently.

FT So how do you go about population reduction?

TM: Very simple. Ideally, every woman should bear only one natural child. The population of the earth would fall by 50% in 40 years without wars, epidemics, or catastrophe. If you think that's brutal, try a world with 10 billion people, a world where everyone lives in fascist hives on hideously minimal incomes, working at nightmarish jobs. There is no way out that isn't going to discomfort some people. What I like about the one woman, one child idea is that it still is a matter of individual decision, it's left up to women who have been up to this point left out of the process of political and cultural reform, and of the practical choices. I think it's probably the least brutal.

I mean, we could try and imagine totally science fiction possibilities: making everyone the size of a termite, we could then easily accommodate the human population; or downloading people into supercomputers, but no-one knows if these things can be done. I'm talking about something that we could begin this afternoon to implement. It's not hi-tech. It's not difficult to understand. Considering the other options, I think this would definitely be the way to go.

ALIEN ABDUCTION

FT: Let's talk about the subject of alien abduction.

TM: First of all, let me say that I do not believe that people are being taken into spacecraft from another star system and having fœtal tissue removed and examined. I don't know exactly what to make of John Mack. He's associated with Harvard and one expects a certain level of intellectual efficiency from someone in such a position. He was very puzzling to me.

"Can we overturn our momentum for consumerism – what I call monogamy, hegemony, and monotony?"

At one point in our interview he said, "I have reports from over 1,000 women of this fœtal removal and not a single one exhibits any sign of physical trauma whatsoever." And I said, "John, what does that imply to you?" and he said: "Advanced surgical techniques of which we have no knowledge." Well, that's not what it implies to me. What it implies to me is that these women are seriously deluded. I think it's a tremendously parochial, almost silly, view of extraterrestrial contact to think that it will have any interest whatsoever in human problems or fœtal tissue for that matter.

I think the universe is so vast and so strange that the real task is to recognise alien intelligence when it's in front of you because it's not going to stand up on two legs and have a keen interest in the Gross National Product of England, that's just preposterous to me. Nevertheless, something peculiar is going on, people are having a kind of experience that they download into this abduction metaphor because that's all they know what to do with it.

"The human self image is dictated by the animal body ... If you're spending more than half of your time in VR, you may virtually be many people, or animals, or pieces of furniture or whatever."

I have written a book that describes a serious of adventures I had in the Amazon and I dare say an epistemologically naive person who had gone through these experiences would say they had been abducted by flying saucers. But I paid very close attention and I love to say to my audiences, we're dealing with something which disguises itself as an extraterrestrial invasion in order not to alarm us with the implications of what it really is.

PSYCHEDELIC EPIPHANY

FT: What is it really?

TM: It's the Overmind of the species at the end of human history. Western science and philosophy has a very keen sense of causality – that the cause temporarily precedes the effect. And yet, there are many met with in the human world where processes are guided toward an end-state by a kind of homing process.

I think that human history is under the influences of a kind of strange attractor, to use the vocabulary of fractal mathematics. That the horse is not pushing the cart, the horse is pulling the cart. The cause of human history is not the sin of Adam and Eve, the cause of human history is a culminating transcendent event that lies ahead of us in time, and it has been exerting influence on our species ever since the first moment that we parted company with animal organisation.

When we seek to anticipate it through religious hierophony, psychedelic epiphany or poetic inspiration, we image it in various ways: as God the Father, or as concerned extraterrestrials come to help us out of our dilemma. It is none of these things; it's the atemporal portion of intelligent life on the planet that is communicating with us through the unconscious. Archetypal encounters are intimations of immortality.

As we get closer and closer to actual fusion with this transcendental object, things are going to get weirder and weirder. Ideas are proliferating at an ever-faster rate; peculiar religious intuitions, syncretic religions of all sorts are springing up. This to me indicates that we are very close to actually merging with the attractor itself. It is the mysterious something that has called us out of animal nature and is sculpting and moulding us to its image. And we don't know what its image is, or what its purpose is – why should we and how could we? We are, after all, advanced monkeys of some sort.

I'm not a reductionist, a rationalist, a materialist – I do think science has overlooked this teleological vector in organic nature and especially in the human species. I understand why this is; it has to do with Darwin and Wallace fighting free of the pervasive influence of deism in the 19th century, and so they absolutely eliminated *telos*, purpose, from their models. But we know a good deal more than they do, and we can see the acceleration of history, the compression of events, and you can draw these curves, and reach the conclusion that human history cannot possibly go on for centuries and millennia into the future – there's not enough wood-pulp and aluminium on the planet to permit that.

So instead history, which began, let's be generous, 15,000 years ago, is shortly to end. It is not a phenomenon once established that can be expected to persist for millions of years, it is in fact an incredibly quick phase transition, in which for a moment, in geological time, everything is up for grabs. But then there is a breakthrough into this transcendent realm.

I think this is what life has pushed for on this planet, that we are not enemies of biology or evolutionary process, we are the trigger species in the conquest of dimensionality that represents organic existence and that we – you, I, everybody – are in a position of being very close to the final act of the drama. It's going to happen in the first couple of decades [of the next century].

Our intellectual toolkit at this point is far too impoverished to allow us to anticipate the nature of the trans-cendental object. We can only approach it through poetical metaphors, like flying saucers, alchemical condensation, religious hierophony; but when we are finally face-to-face with the mystery, we will see that it was not any of those things. Those were masks, projections, facets, adumbrations, of what it is. But ultimately it's beyond rational apprehension.

Human history is not something that goes on endlessly into the future; so much novelty has accumulated that essentially every point in the system becomes co-tangent with every other. At that point, that's as much novelty as you can have and that's what I call the transcendental attractor, at the end of time. It's the novelty of novelty. It radiates its influence into the past, making historical time as we approach the transcendental object more and more novel and complex, and breakthroughs and so forth happen at an ever faster rate. And this has now reached the point at which it is asymptotically accelerating, and I believe sometime around the end of 2012 AD novelty will actually reach its maxima. FT

Tom Hodgkinson is editor of *The Idler*, 'the voice of the idle underground'. Issue 2 out now from 38 Aldridge Road Villas, London W11 1BW.

MODERN FAIRY TALES

Reports of fairy sightings in the 1930s were eclipsed by world-shattering events. DAVID LAZELL picks up the threads of a mystery that remains unsolved almost 60 years later.

Throughout the year 1936 a well-known English literary weekly, *John o'London's,* published a series of letters from people who had close encounters with fairies, elves, goblins and other Little Folk. The 1930s was a time of invasions and threats of invasions, including the famous broadcast by Orson Welles' Mercury Theatre Company about the menace from Mars – but these stories (some of them dating back to the First World War) related to something older and more profoundly eerie.

Given the controversy that had raged about the Cottingley Fairies in the 1920s – allegedly photographed by two girls, and accepted as genuine by Sir Arthur Conan Doyle [see ***FT43:48-53***] – one might have thought that most people would have kept quiet about any personal sightings. It is all the more remarkable that, at a time when the world appeared to be falling apart, so many shared personal recollections. Some are reported here, and are close to the original narrative.

Strange experiences reported years afterwards, often recalling childhood sightings of 'Little People', are sometimes dismissed as fantasy. What is interesting here is the number of similar accounts provided by 'sane and sensible grown-ups' who claimed their encounters happened recently. Such sightings – by people who had no reason to exaggerate, and who, in fact, seemed overcome by their experience – were probably more common than was supposed.

Some of the writers to the journal noted their original scepticism, and the sense of shock on discovering that fairies existed outside of the old stories and nursery rhymes. Given the reluctance of most Britons to confess experiences that they cannot rationally explain, the *John o' London's* mail was probably 'the tip of the fairyland iceberg', but eventually the theme of the letters moved to other matters as Europe moved toward hasty rearmament and war. There were – and no doubt still are – places where fairies were to be seen, and perhaps heard: a meeting of fairyland and the realm of mankind. Although I lived for many years in Wales, I did not encounter these remarkable characters, but, as the West Country and Wales abound in legends, it was hardly surprising that many of the letters in *John o' London's* came from the Celtic nations of olden time. I draw no conclusions on the matter, despite being an adopted Celt – but even as saintly a man as Rev. Samuel Chadwick, chided for writing fairy stories for children at Christmas time, responded: "Eyes that cannot see fairies cannot see anything". Perhaps, as some experts argue in respect of UFOs, a certain 'attitude of mind' is necessary before one can see fairies. But it seems true also that you need to know where to look!

Although rural folk had a proper regard for the Little People, and in some places still do – the Common Market has not yet, it seems, laid down any regulations on the subject – it is surprising how often sightings in the 1930s were thought to be fortunate. Perhaps in a blasé, over-sophisticated world, the sudden appearance of a pixie or elf, or even the hearing of fairy music, reminded men and women that humans did not 'know it all' by any means.

Some argued that there was good reason for believing in the objective existence of the Little People – by whatever name they were known. Edward Seago, a considerable artist of the day, noted, in a book of his experiences in Ireland, that he came to such belief when he saw how neatly the Little People plaited the horses' manes: "The braids consisted of only a few strands of hair and were far too small for any mortal hand to have made them".

I was evacuated from London on the day that war was declared, and could have used a good fairy or two at that difficult time. Some may explain that fairy stories relate to cultural disposition: that, for all our smart handling of technology and economic realities, we are what we are because of our beliefs, not our skills. Nature spirits are too deeply rooted in traditions, world-wide, not to have some original existence, but what that might be is beyond my modest wit. There are many classic works on the subject, and readers should not hesitate to ask local staff at public libraries if they have any good books on fairies and the Little People.

But watch who might be sitting on the top of the bookcase...

The Hearth Creature

One of the best examples of 'comings and goings' came from a woman of Nottingham called Marjorie, who wrote to *John o' London's* in March 1936, by which time the interest in fairy sightings had become considerable (it was to continue through the spring and summer). As a child, Marjorie had lived in a house surrounded by a beautiful garden and orchard in a rather lonely part of Nottingham.

One morning, as she sat in the early morning sunshine that streamed through her bedroom window, she stared toward the empty fireplace. There, on a filmy cobweb on the bars of the grate, sat a strange little creature, seemingly without fear, with a broad grin, apparently enjoying the bright morning too. She decided to take a closer look, but as soon as she left her bed, the elf disappeared. Once she had returned to bed, though, the personage returned. Disappearance and reappearance continued, until the young girl, almost absent-mindedly, brushed away the cobweb. This act seemed to prevent the elf returning; at any rate, it (he) was not seen again.

Marjorie described the visitor as being between four and six inches in height, with large ears and shimmering green body.

Roadside Glimpse

Sightings from cars were not unusual, and perhaps foreshadowed stories of UFO sightings observed from automobiles – however these experiences can be partly explained by driver fatigue and the sheer unpredictability of nature. In any case, such sightings were often momentary. Thus a correspondent of April 1936 recalled that he had been driving along a quiet lane in Hertfordshire, thinking entirely of the performance of the car and concentrating on his driving.

"Rounding a bend in the road, where the hedge and trees had been cut to the ground, I was suddenly surprised to see a little round-faced fellow, wearing a pointed cap, the peak of which fell over one side, in the fashion of a nightcap. He was sitting on a tree stump, and looking straight across the road in front of him. Standing, I judged he would be about 18 inches high, but he was gone in an instant, and though I slowed down at once, I did not get the chance to have a closer look at him."

Silvery Sounds

In March 1936, a native of Stirlingshire reported meeting a solitary fairy on the same hillside near Aberfoyle where Robert Kirk wrote his classic work, *The Secret Commonwealth* [see ***FT61:29***]. This fairy proved to be most friendly and showed the correspondent 'a wonderful sight'. One afternoon in Arran, he beheld ten fairies playing around the gorse bushes, and around grazing sheep who seemed to be quite placid – although the cattle edged away a little if the fairies approached too closely.

The same man also heard fairies in Arran, when their "silvery accents" led him to a group or clan of them hurrying along a path. They seemed angry about some matter, and ran away as he approached.

Tramping near Loch Rannoch, this same communicant, a man well used to observing the country scene, was attracted by some music – he described it as "tuneful tones" – coming from a clump of rhododendrons, and carefully advancing to the bushes, was captivated by the most beautiful dancing. Alas, within seconds, the fairies noticed him and disappeared into the bushes beyond. The first one to spot him impressed him considerably: "I shall never forget the glance she gave me, as she disappeared, and the gesture, the grace of her exit, I have seen approached only by Pavlova herself."

It would be interesting to discover if the revival in Greek classical dancing, so great a feature of the inter-war years, had something to do with the fairy dances – a common feature of these reports – the style of which, some might think, had classical forms.

Midnight Protest

In March 1936, an elderly woman in West Wales reported that she had watched a crowd of tiny men in a meadow one moonlit night. They were gathered round a little woman who sat on a stone. The 'small lady' addressed the gathering in Welsh, which, fortunately, the human viewer was able to comprehend. The message she gave, in no uncertain terms, was to the effect that they would not be able to use the meadow for much longer, because a wealthy man would buy it and he owned a carriage which would need no horses. Cars were then unknown in the locality, but within a year, the land was bought by a man who brought the first automobile to that part of the country.

Picking Berries

One correspondent from Pulborough, identified only by initials, told of her encounter during a blackberry-picking expedition at Cookham Dean in Berkshire during the summer of 1916. Although the blackberries were plentiful, most of them seemed to be small. Then the correspondent noticed some large berries on a bush which grew apart from the others.

"I was tugging at some berries, rather out of reach, when the whole bush seemed to shiver, the sprays parted, and from out of the centre of the bush darted a lean, brown man, dressed in brown, with pointed cap and straggly beard. He was solid as far as the waist, but his legs were transparent and shadowy. He slid away like lightning, and entirely disappeared. I regret to say that I was so startled that I dropped the fruit basket, took to my heels and ran all the way home. I never had the good luck to see another."

Goblin Shapes

According to a Welsh woman, there were local stories of "queer, round goblin shapes on high legs that escorted people along lonely roads after dark, hopping and skipping in front, and then leaping a high gate, and disappearing into the grounds of gardens or colleges".

Irish 'pixies' have a reputation for shape-changing, but this talent was observed in their Cornish cousins by a London woman who had visited the border country of Cornwall and Devon, where she saw the figure of a tiny man, dressed in black and "strutting about in a self-important manner". Being a sensible soul who did not 'believe in pixies', the woman felt sure that the figure would prove to be some trick of the light or a shadow, but he continued to remain a man, albeit a small one. Suddenly, he turned into something that looked more like a 'furry, long, black roll'.

A short time later, a matter of minutes, two more small shapes came into view, slightly larger and rather more rounded than the first pixie man. They were seated either side of a gorse bush making reciprocal movements as though they were operating an old two-handed saw. The woman, by now hastily revising her disbelief, attempted to get a closer view, but she stumbled over some stones and the noise seemed to prompt immediate disappearance. Examination of the site confirmed that the pixie on the seaward side must have been 'sitting on air' – or presumably was lighter than air itself – for the gorse bush grew at the cliff edge.

Shape-changing and weightlessness are not the expected properties of material biological life-forms; the exact nature of fairy bodies may be weirder than we can imagine. For example, Geoffrey Hodson, in his major study *The Fairies at Work and Play* (1925), wrote that "elves differ from other nature spirits chiefly in that they do not appear to be clothed in any reproduction of human attire, and that their bodily constitution appears to consist of one solid mass of gelatinous substance, entirely without internal organisation".

Pretty In Pink

A woman from Wigan, writing in May 1936, reported that when she was young she would never tread on daisies, because it was in a field of daisies that she saw her first fairies.

"There were usually seven or eight together, dancing in circles about three feet from the ground. They had long pointed caps, their bodies tapering off to very pointed feet. I remember their puckish grins, and seem to remember them as being dressed in brown. Then, just before I reached my teens, on many occasions, I kept tryst with a lovely fairy in a bower of wild roses near my home. Looking back now, it seems I was always aware of this fairy in that leafy nook. She was usually a few feet from the ground in shining pink raiment with long pink dresses and always in a pink aura. The fairy never stayed long in my presence but it seemed quite natural to me that she should be there."

This report neatly parallels one from a woman in south-west London, writing in June 1933. She reported that, during August 1931, she and her eldest daughter had seen 18-inch-high "females without wings, wearing some form of flimsy, transparent gown" on eight occasions, in their garden in Warwickshire, generally among flowering shrubs in an area bounded by a stream. "I saw the same little lady on three separate occasions ... she wore a pink gown while the others wore bluish ones. She was so shy that she only peeped at me around a bush and disappeared when I was about ten paces off." This correspondent, like others, was greatly impressed by their beauty of form and movement.

FAIRY TREE IN PERIL

One of the most famous sights in London's Kensington Gardens is the Elfin Oak by the Round Pond. In its heyday, an endless procession of nannies wheeled their charges up to it, pointing out the gaily-coloured tiny figures of elves clambering up the craggy trunk as miniature owls and animals peered from dark mysterious crevices.

Today, it is a sad sight – paint peeling from crumbling figurines which appear to flee from an encroaching sea of litter. The view is made more depressing by the spiked iron railings which seem more effective in isolating this piece of fairyland from the crass everyday world than it is in protecting it from vandals.

The Elfin Oak looks like an ancient pillar of some forgotten gateway to an autochthonic underworld; it beckons one downward, if only one could shrink to the size of those elves. This eerie atmosphere is a tribute to the Cornish sculptor Ivor Innes, for it is not a natural monument. The 800-year-old tree once stood in Richmond Park, and was moved to its present position by Innes in 1911. He would meditate on its gnarled trunk, calling, as perhaps only a Cornishman can, the tiny forms to reveal themselves to him.

The ex-Goon Spike Milligan led a publicised rescue of the tree in the 1960s, gaining the approval of the then Ministry of Public Buildings and Works to restore the decorations adding some cowrie shells from New Zealand (where Innes' widow lived at the time). Commenting on the need to restore the tree again, Spike says: "It will be a wonderful opportunity to encourage young craftsmanship ... It is much more attractive than some of the other things which eminent people try to save."

Responsibility for the landmark has been transferred through several agencies and rests today with the Royal Parks Agency (RPA), which told James Hughes-Onslow – writing in the *Evening Standard* (14 June 1993) – that it is well aware that restoration is overdue. The previous custodian, National Heritage, said the RPA receives near £23 million this year, but cannot insist the RPA spend it on specific projects. Spike Milligan said he'd seen it all before. "All this talk of millions has nothing to do with it. It would only cost about £1,000 to save this tree."

The RPA say that they are not held back by lack of money, but are planning "an exciting new children's adventure playground scheme which will include restoration of the Elfin Oak." They promise that park users will be consulted. Everyone entitled to should speak out for the best way of preserving this wonderful fairy relic.

Bob Rickard

Hoax!

THE GREAT MIRABELLI

Guy Lyon Playfair probes the rise and fall of Carlos Mirabelli, Brazil's most prodigious medium in the early 1900s

In 1927, news reached European psychical research circles of "a Brazilian medium, Mirabelli by name" whose reported "marvels" were considered "far too good to be true" in the journal (October) of the Society for Psychical Research. He was said to be churning out automatic writing in 28 languages, delivering trance speeches in 26 of them, also causing apports, dematerialisations, levitations, impressions in wax, strange light effects and – most marvellous of all – complete materialisation of identifiable people known to have died. There was more. He made things float off shelves in shops, he played billiards without touching his cue, and he could travel at a speed approaching that of light – he once vanished from a railway station and was reported as having arrived at another one 60 miles away two minutes later. He had been witnessed doing his various things by more than 500 people, invariably either in broad daylight or in well-lit rooms.

"It would be curious to know," sniffed the SPR journal, "to what modest dimensions these preposterous claims would dwindle, supposing Mirabelli were to appear at 31 Tavistock Square" (then the SPR's London home).

The president of the society did not share his colleague's attitude to events in a far-off country of which they knew nothing. Hans Driesch, the eminent Leipzig philosopher remembered today for his theory of 'entelechy', went to São Paolo the following year to check out Mirabelli for himself. Although he found him to be "quite a nice and jolly fellow", things got off to a poor start with a "very indifferent" discourse in Italian supposedly from the late Mirabelli senior, an Italian Protestant pastor who had emigrated to Brazil where Carmine (who later took the less androgynous name Carlos) was born in 1889.

There followed some dubious apports, Driesch wondering why the medium wore an overcoat "with enormous pockets" although it was quite warm indoors. Then things improved, with some close-range psychokinesis involving the movement of a mirror, a flower vase, a bottle and a kitchen pot. A double door closed on its own in response to a request for "a sign". All of this sounds rather like a hidden thread job to an experienced modern researcher, but Driesch found it "very impressive" and decided the man was worth inviting to Tavistock Square. Mirabelli accepted, provided he could bring his wife with him, also his friend and eventual biographer Eurico de Goes.

The trip was not to take place. Instead, the SPR sent off its research officer Theodore Besterman on a voyage of discovery in 1934 in the hope of solving the Mirabelli mystery once and for all, and in Besterman's opinion that is what he did. "Mirabelli left me in no doubt that he was purely and simply fraudulent," he wrote to me in 1973, shortly before his death. So he may have been in 1934, and Besterman seemed quite proud of his failure to verify any of the abundant testimony to the medium's earlier feats.

Carlos (Carmine) Mirabelli, 1889-1951

> He made things float off shelves in shops, he played billiards without touching his cue, and he could travel at a speed approaching that of light – he once vanished from a railway station and was reported as having arrived at another one 60 miles away two minutes later.

"Rumour, even printed evidence, about his earlier history is as plentiful as it is unreliable," he wrote in the SPR journal (December 1935), "nor have I thought it worth while to investigate it at all closely." So how did he know it was unreliable? No wonder Besterman was lambasted for total incompetence by his predecessor, anthropologist Eric J. Dingwall, whose own detailed account of the best of that printed evidence had appeared back in July 1930 in the journal of the American SPR.

Besterman did, however, manage to bring back one piece of useful evidence. He makes no mention of it anywhere in his writings and it lay undisturbed in the SPR archives until June 1990, when it was disinterred by visiting American researcher Dr Gordon Stein, a physiologist and historian of science and of magic. It is, I believe, the only primary evidence we have for deliberate deception by Mirabelli.

I am referring to a photograph showing him apparently poised in mid-air, arms outstretched, eyes upturned as if communing with spirits, and head almost touching the ceiling. It was taken in 1934, or earlier, in Mirabelli's house in the Tucuruvi district of São Paolo, which I visited in 1973. The room in question was at least at least 14 feet high, so that he must have been at least six feet from the floor when the picture was taken, I reckoned.

It now seems certain than when the picture was taken, Mirabelli was not levitating, jumping, or dropping through a hole in the ceiling. He was standing on the top step of a ladder.

The three pictures on this page are part of a series of photographs showing Mirabelli with one of his many remarkable full-body materialisations, an African-looking spirit. "If genuine", says Playfair, "they're the best ever." But that's a big if.

The photo has been reproduced several times. It was used as a frontispiece by Eurico de Goes for his book *Prodigios de biophysica obtidos com o medium Mirabelli* (1937), the most authoritative account of the medium's career. I included it in my book *The Flying Cow* (1975), because I thought it was a great picture (I still think so). I stated in my original caption that I was unable to authenticate it and that "it could have been faked". And faked it was.

The Besterman print measures 18x16cm and is inscribed "To Mr T. Besterman from Carlos Mirabelli" and dated 22 August 1934. It is a good deal sharper than the small and smudgy illustration which I used, and it shows clear signs of retouching either to the negative or to an earlier print which was rephotographed. The outline of the clothing and shoes has been sharpened, but it is just below the shoes that the evidence for fakery comes to light.

It now seems certain than when the picture was taken, Mirabelli was not levitating, jumping, or dropping through a hole in the ceiling. He was standing on the top step of a ladder. What gives the show away is the pattern of the wallpaper, which is in

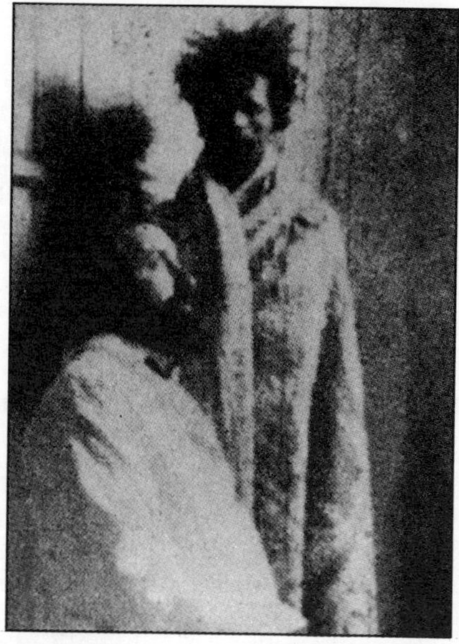

sharp focus all over the print except in one place: exactly where the step had been. On a photocopy, the phantom ladder effect is even more apparent. Under a magnifying glass, all doubts vanish.

Now, pulling a fast one on a visiting foreigner is fairly acceptable behaviour in Brazil. Deceiving your most loyal friend and supporter is another matter. Eurico de Goes knew Mirabelli well for more than 20 years, and by all accounts I heard he was, as Driesch put it, "very intelligent and educated" (he was director of the São Paolo public library). I find it hard to believe that he would have used the 'ladder' photo as a frontispiece to a book on which he must have worked for years knowing it to be a fake. On the other hand, it is almost as hard to believe how anybody could have seen an original print without spotting the signs of retouching as easily as Stein did. It is even harder to imagine that Mirabelli thought he would get away with it, and harder still that he very nearly did.

Once a fraud always a fraud? What are we to make of the rest of the evidence in favour of Mirabelli? Were all those splendid photos of full-form materialisations included in the de Goes book faked as well? We can be forgiven for suspecting this to be so. If somebody has been caught faking one photo, it becomes more likely that he faked more than one. If somebody has been caught playing other tricks as well, it becomes even more likely. Besterman was in fact sure that Mirabelli was using that old favourite, the Hidden Thread, though he never found one. This could of course mean either that

Mirabelli was not using one or that Besterman did not know where to look. One way or the other, what Besterman described in 1934 in his confidential report to the SPR, still unpublished, is consistent with the activity of a medium trying to keep his reputation going with some fairly

elementary conjuring tricks.

Yet let us not forget how Mirabelli came to earn that reputation. If he was always a fraud, he chose some unusual training methods – he lost his first job, in a shoe store, when the shoe boxes started flying off the shelves, and shortly after that he was briefly interned in a mental asylum, where two well-known doctors pronounced him sane but unusually gifted. Does a trainee phony medium walk out of a job and into an asylum where he risks being locked up for the rest of his life? Does he then demonstrate his abilities to as many people as possible in bright light? I think not.

The famous materialisation photos – if genuine, the best ever – were taken long before the phantom ladder one. To fake them would have involved a lot more than some retouching. There would have to have been several different accomplices to serve as models both for the 'spirits' and for the onlookers, who could not look as astounded as they do unless they were skilled actors or else genuinely astounded. And who would not be, by this sort of thing?

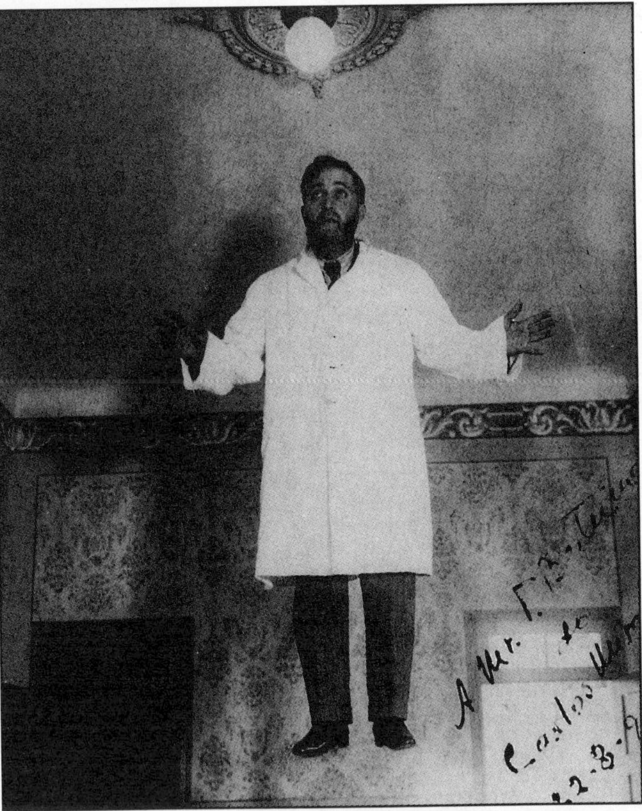

ABOVE: The infamous photograph showing Mirabelli aloft, rephotographed from the original in Cambridge University Library, courtesy of John Beloff. Previous reprintings were recopied from earlier books which tended to mask the signs of retouching. BELOW: An enlargement of the area beneath Mirabelli's shoes shows clearly an attempt to paint out a stepladder.

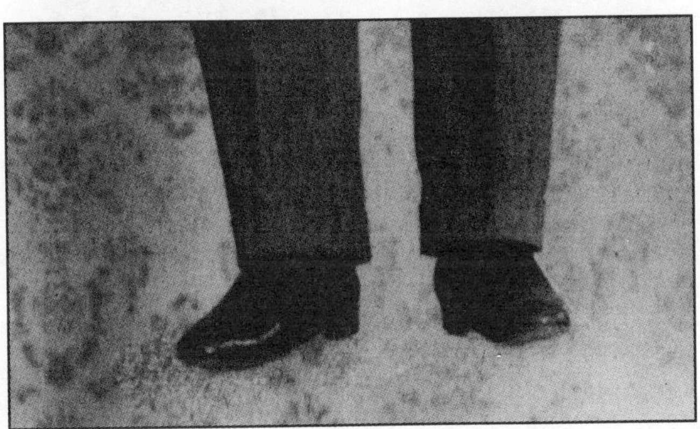

"...Photographs were taken and two medical men made a minute examination which lasted some fifteen minutes and as a result declared that the figure was that of a normally constituted human being of apparently perfect anatomical structure. After the examination had been completed the figure began to dissolve away from the feet upwards, and the bust and arms were seen floating in the air. One of the doctors who had examined the phantom was unable to contain himself. Rushing forward he exclaimed 'But this is too much!' and seized the half of the body which was still hanging in the air in front of him. Hardly had he done so than he uttered a shrill cry and sank unconscious to the ground whilst the phantom, or rather what was left of it, instantly disappeared."

When the poor fellow came round, he described feeling a "spongy, flaccid mass" and a violent shock before passing out. Commenting on the confederacy theory, Dingwall (from whose 1930 account the above is taken) noted that "confederates are human beings and human beings do not usually rise into the air, dissolve into pieces and float about in clouds of vapour". Never an easily-pleased investigator, Dingwall concluded of the reports of Mirabelli's early activities that "there is nothing like them in the whole range of psychical literature". They remain unequalled and unexplained.

Mirabelli was knocked down and killed by a car in 1951. Twenty years later, Hernani Guimarães Andrade, Suzuko Hashizume and I managed to put together a fat file of Mirabelliana for the archives of the Brazilian Institute for Psychobiophysical Research (IBPP). We located three of the man's sons and several people who had known him well. One described a partial materialisation, another assured me that Mirabelli once levitated in public while walking along a pavement. A third recalled that his father had seen the medium rise into the air plus the chair he was sitting in. Cesar Augusto Mirabelli, a detective in the São Paolo flying squad, recalled that life with father was one inexplicable phenomenon after another. "They just happened almost every day, any time and any place," he told us.

We collected our evidence in a few weeks with no difficulty at all. Had Besterman taken a fraction of the trouble we did, or Gordon Stein did in 1990, he might well have solved the Mirabelli mystery. It now seems unlikely that it will ever be solved.

Further reading:

Fate, March 1991 (Stein); Journal of the SPR, January 1992 (Playfair), and October 1992 (Stein & Playfair).

ARCHIVE GEMS

3: The Bowhead Incident

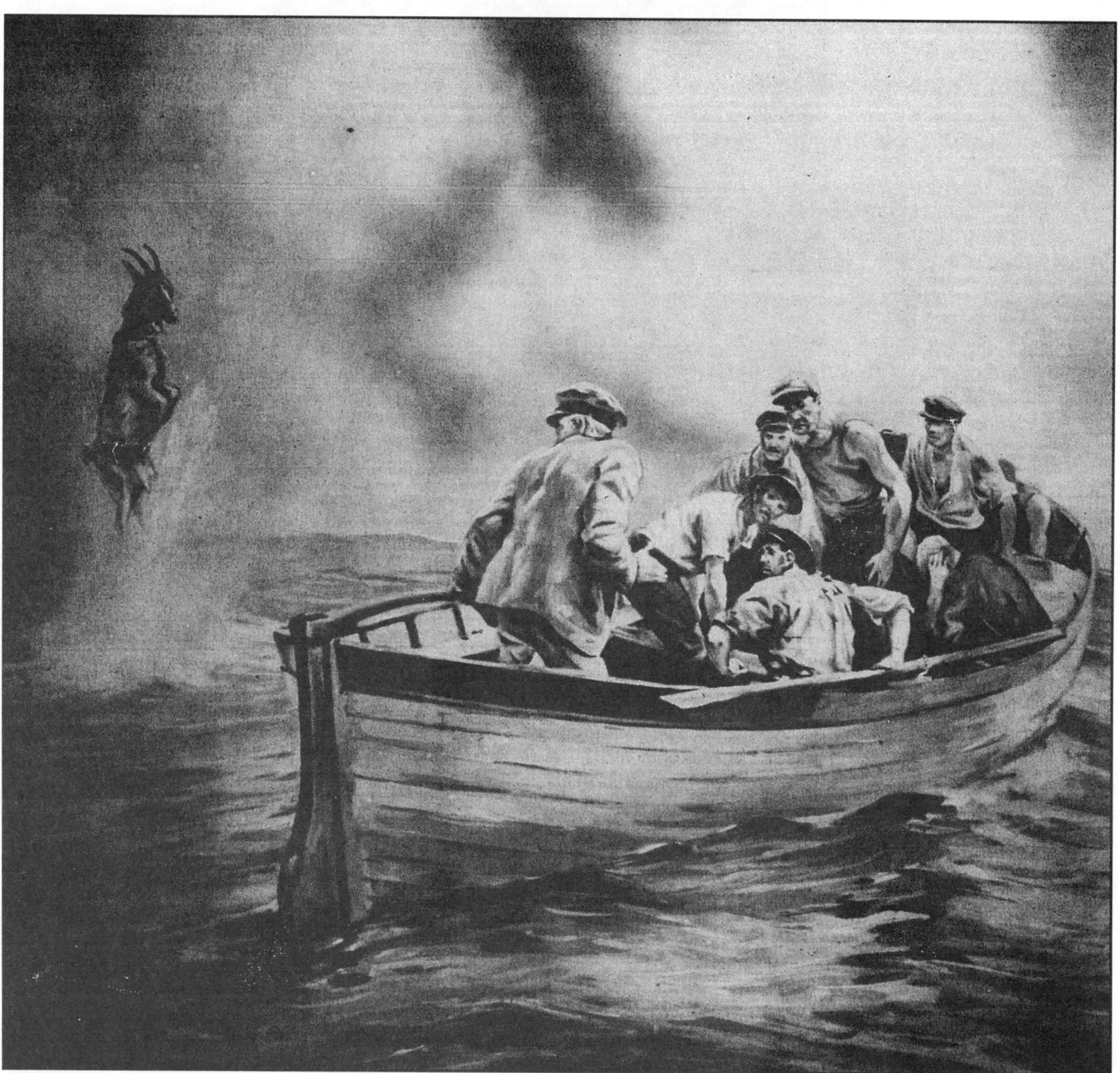

Our Gem, this issue, is accompanied by very little information. It comes from the excellent series of covers of war-time Italian periodicals in the Mary Evans Picture Library, Blackheath, and must qualify as one of the strangest scenes that have ever come to our jaded notice.

In 1938, an American whaler called 'Bowhead' struck an iceberg and sank in the northern Atlantic. As the survivors gathered themselves in their lifeboat, their attention was drawn to a tremendous eruption in the water alongside them. To their utter astonishment, a goat shot out of the sea.

The animal had been kept onboard and was trapped in a pocket of air as the ship went down. When the ship had sunk to a sufficient depth to pressurise the air, the bubble burst through the side of the wreck and blasted its eerie projectile to the surface. The colour illustration by Giacomo Avai (Jack Away) appeared in *Il Mattino Illustrato* (Naples) 25 July–1 August 1938.

DIARY OF A MAD PLANET

June - July 1993

This diary aims to record, in two-month segments, the geophysical highlights of our planet: the tempests and tantrums, the oddities and extremities. Compiled by the editors and various correspondents.

An exceptional Asian monsoon, the century's worst flooding in the USA, Cornwall's heaviest downpour in 500 years (3.6in in two hours on 9 June) and the 'storm of the century' in Wales (11 June) – the dominant element of this period was water.

A house normally near the banks of the Mississippi in Prairie du Chien, Wisconsin, surrounded by flood water six feet over flood stage level on 1 July 1993.

EARTHQUAKE 8 June KAMCHATKA: (51.386N 157.729E) Depth: 70km. Magnitude: 7.1R. Some damage. Minor tsunami detected on Hawaii.

SWARM 23 June HUNGARY: A swarm of locusts - the first for 60 years - wreaked havoc for several days before being checked by helicopters spraying insecticides. Meanwhile in northwestern Somalia, a moving band of locusts covered 23,000 square miles.

EARTHQUAKE 26 June CUMBRIA, UK: (54.209N 2.890W) Depth: 10km. Magnitude: 3.0R. Centred at Grange-over-Sands and felt from Barrow-in-Furness to Kendal and around Morecambe Bay.

FLOODS all July USA: The Mississippi, "Father of Waters", swollen by heavy rains since the middle of June, caused the worst floods of the century. On 16 July, the Mississippi joined the Missouri 20 miles up stream from their usual confluence. St Louis to the south was severely flooded, the waters reaching a peak of 47 feet on 20 July.

The 1927 lower Mississippi floods killed 217 people, after which the Army Corps of Engineers spent 50 years building 300 dams and reservoirs intended to make the river more tractable. Levees are both the solution and the problem: water dammed in one place breaks out at another.

By the end of July, 43 people had been killed, 50,000 evacuated and 16,000 square miles of cropland inundated in eight states. Flood damage was estimated at $10-12 billion, but total losses might exceed the $25 billion of Hurricane Andrew [see ***FT66:50***], which would make it the most expensive US disaster ever.

RAIN 11 July INDIA: The non-arrival of the monsoon in Andra Pradesh prompted the government to commission 11 days of rituals across the state to appease Varuna, the Hindu rain god. Dark clouds gathered and within two hours there was a downpour, which was still continuing five days later. The ceremony cost the Andra Pradesh government $166,666 in American money, which numerologists might find ominous.

By the end of the month, the monsoon had claimed more than 4,200 lives and left millions homeless, with nearly half of Bangladesh under water and vast tracts of Nepal and India devastated. Torrential rain in China killed 78.

EARTHQUAKE 12 July JAPAN: (42.841N 139.248E) Depth: 17km. Magnitude: 7.6R. The worst Japanese quake for 15 years. At least 200 killed and 39 missing in the Hokkaido region. Severe damage by fires, landslides and tsunami. More than 850 houses damaged or destroyed, at least 600 by the tsunami, which reached a wave height of 30.6 metres along the southwest coast of Okushiri Island.

HEATWAVE 14 July ALASKA: Barrow, 325 miles north of the Arctic Circle, sweltered under a record 79 degrees F as people picnicked by the Arctic Ocean.

LIGHTNING 19 July RUSSIA: Lightning struck a barn on a collective farm in the Urals semi-autonomous republic of Bashkortostan, burning 111 (yes, that's 111) bulls to death.

Special thanks to the Global Seismology Group of the British Geological Survey for the earthquake data.

FEELING CROSS

The manifestation of the stigmata – the wounds of Christ – is an age-old and truly mysterious phenomenon. BOB RICKARD looks at the latest example.

Heather Woods – a 43-year-old widow and mother of two from Lincoln – bears marks on her body in locations Christians associate with Christ's Passion. Those on her hands and feet relate to where Christ was nailed to the Cross; one on the right side of her abdomen corresponds to where Christ was pierced by a centurion's lance; and on her forehead a cross-shaped mark seems to represent Christ's crown of thorns.

A filmed interview, in which Mrs Woods' wounds are seen forming, was shown on ITV's religious programme *This Sunday* on 18 April 1993. Granada producer Colin Bell said: "The cross on her forehead came up like a welt, white and then red. The stigmata started as round marks which became moist and began bleeding as the day went on. It caused some pain, but this was mainly an emotional experience for her."

This dramatic broadcast is believed to be the first time that stigmata of this sort have been recorded as they happened. This was also the first time that Mrs Woods' story had been told. A devout and introverted woman, she is a deacon of a little-known mystical Celtic Christian sect based in the St Gregory Palamas Orthodox Church, Lincoln. They meet once a week for healing services at the home of Rev Eric Eades (whom one paper called 'a self-styled bishop').

It is believed that Mrs Woods had a vision that the marks would appear during Easter Week, and the TV journalists were there, on Good Friday, to record it. Cameraman John Brennan and Ted Harrison, a former BBC religious affairs journalist, said there was no suggestion oftrickery. "We have no reason to believe she deliberately

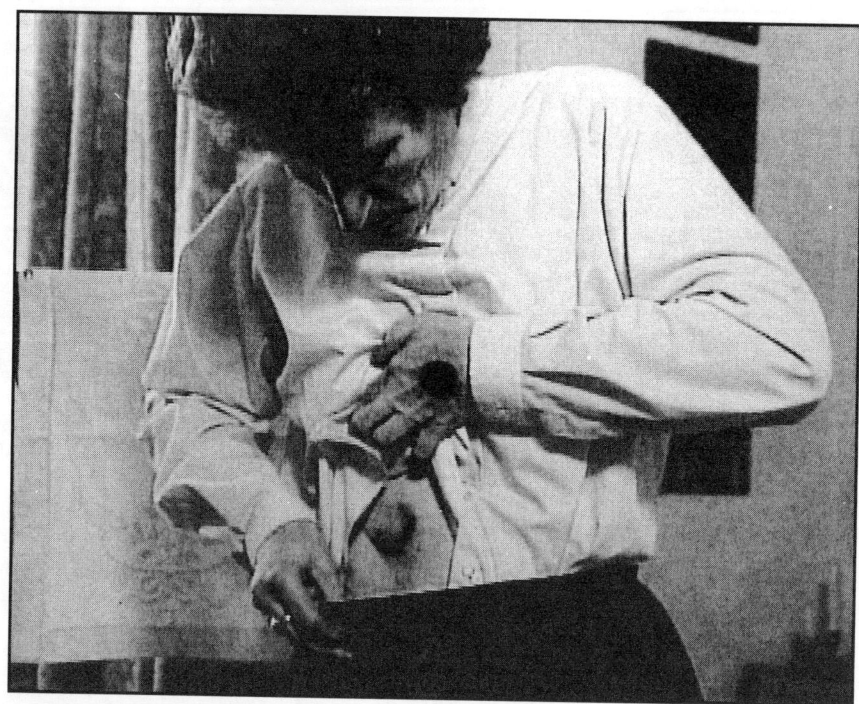

ABOVE: Heather Woods displays the wounds in her hands and sides – a detail from the documentary report by This Sunday (Granada TV) – and BELOW: those in her feet. The size and circular form of her wounds most resembles the marks manifested by Padre Pio (see opposite).

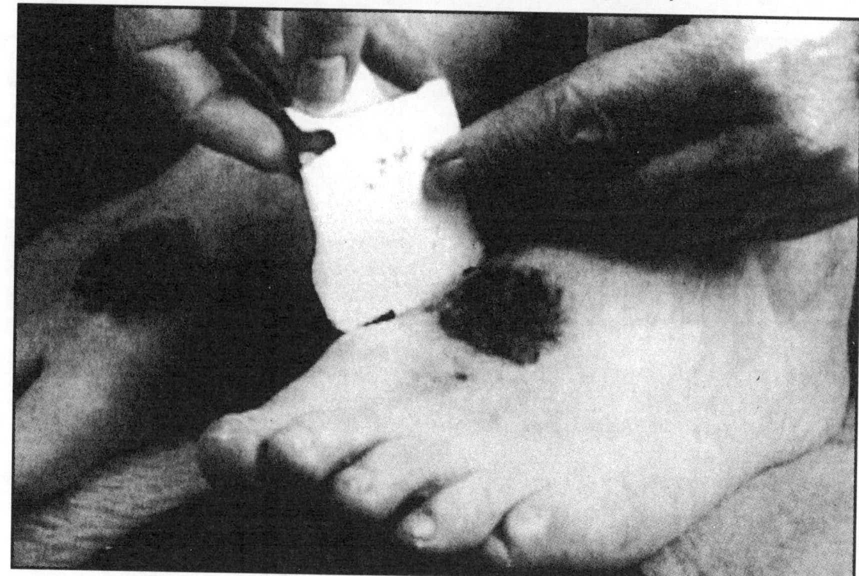

did this. It was a moving moment for the religious people around her."

Mrs Woods is believed to have had a similar experience four times since May 1992, at which time doctors believed she was in the final stages of cancer. She said it began with a strange feeling in her right hand. "I had been writing a lot. Later that evening I was watching the telly and felt as if ants were running across my ankle. I saw a large blister like a halo. Then I lifted my T-shirt and there was a big angry red mark shaped like a smile."

At some point, she showed the marks to Rev Eades who suggested to her they might be stigmata – this may or may not turn out to be an important point. To her surprise, the normally right-handed Heather began writing and drawing spontaneously with her left hand. She started having visions of the crucified Christ, and felt 'compelled' to record her experiences. "I had to stop whatever I was doing and write on anything to hand – the backs of envelopes, gas bills, even the wallpaper. I knew I was writing, but I didn't know *what* I was writing. I drew a picture of Christ on the cross and felt all the pain of the world. That's the only time I have been depressed." Ted Harrison said he has seen these writings: "They are not banal. They are mystical and literate."

Mrs Woods was in such pain her family became concerned that she might be dying. Her visions became more profound: "I can remember waking at 2:50am. I was in a room with ten men, one of whom was sitting down. As I went to hold his hand I believed it was our Lord. Then I found myself on the Cross alongside the Lord. I was looking down. There was no pain. I was out of my body and just felt calm, content and weightless as if in Heaven. The next thing I knew, I was cold and water was dripping from my head. I saw my hands and feet and they were pouring with blood."

Her GP was called, and she told him: "I'm healed. I feel no pain. I don't need the morphine any more." Mrs Woods plays down her own importance in this but is convinced that it is "an outward sign that miracles are not a thing of the past. Jesus is still among us." Rev Eades is in no doubt her remission from cancer was a miracle. "We have medical and hospital records," he said. "What we have seen is for real. She is a saintly person."

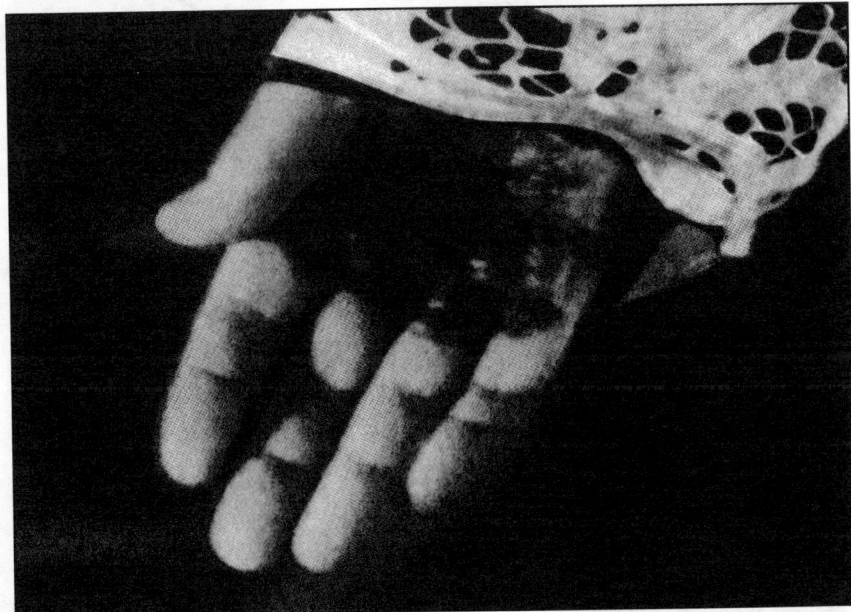

ABOVE: Padre Pio of Pietrelcina, Italy (1887–1968). His wounds were often at their bloodiest during his performance of the Eucharist.

The first stigmatic was St Francis of Assisi (1181–1226), depicted here receiving his wounds during a vision in 1224.

Colin Bell, who is currently researching a documentary on stigmatics, said:"There are clear psychological explanations for this phenomenon, although we are not ruling out the miraculous. There is a condition called 'psychogenic purpose' in which unexplained marks or bruises can be linked to traumatic experiences."

The Rev Dr Fraser Watts, a psychiatrist, concurred: "I know that there is an extraordinary range of physical displays of psychological conditions, but it is unlikely this lady would have willed this to happen. However, it could have developed from a preoccupation with the wounds of Christ. On one level it is a spiritual phenomenon – on another it could be seen as a psychosomatic disorder."

It is reckoned that there have been about 200 known cases of religious stigmata since the first known stigmatic, St Francis of Assisi, 800 years ago. In recent years there were two British stigmatics: Jane Hunt of Derbyshire, and Ethel Chapman, whose marks came every Easter until her death in the 1970s.

Official reaction has been frosty. A Roman Catholic spokesman at Westminster Cathedral said that "religious faith does not rely on miracles or proof"; and the Rev Keith Owen, vicar of the parish in which Mrs Woods and her Celtic Church live said, incredibly: "This does not interest us at all."

Sources: Press Association, 16 April; Sun, Leicester Mercury, 17 April; Observer, Sunday Mail, 18 April; D.Mail, 19 April 1993.

NB: We have not seen the broadcast film, and would welcome hearing from anyone who might have videotaped it.

SPECIAL READER OFFER
SAVE UP TO £65!

Give your home a Fortean theme with these beautiful hand-made crop circle tiles. Each tile is exquisitely detailed - you can even see the circular pattern of the flattened corn - and painted by hand.

There are five designs to choose from: 1. Silbury Hill, 2. Mandelbrot Set, 3. Three Satellites, 4. Church & Circle and 5. Pictogram. Each tile measures 132 x 90mm and comes complete with a felt underside, making it the perfect ornament for your mantelpiece or an ideal paperweight for your desk.

Makers Cropcraft of West Wickham, Kent, have been selling the tiles at £19.95 plus £2.50 postage and packing, but FT has negotiated a special price of just **£10.95** inclusive for readers - **a saving of £11.50.**

There are even better discounts for multiple orders. Choose any three tiles and you get them at less than half price: just £30 (saving 37.35). Or take all five for £47.95 and save a total of £64.30!

Each tile will be sent post free in secure packaging

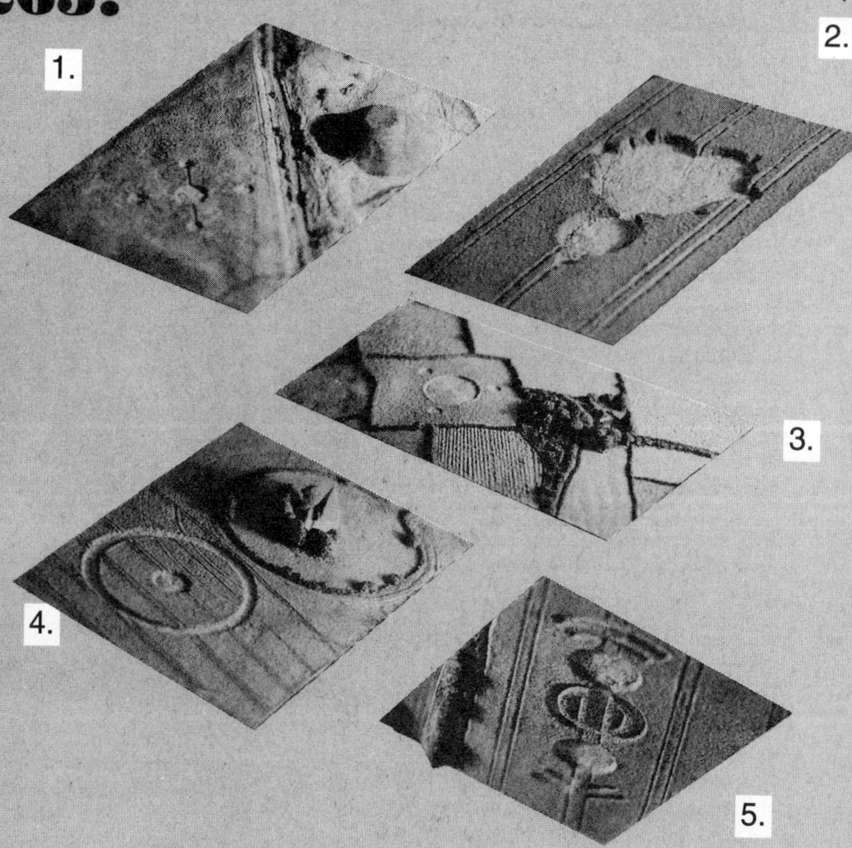

Please send me the following items:

Item	UK Price	US Price	Overseas	Qty	Value
Yesterday's News Tomorrow	£19.99	$44.00	£22.00		
Diary of a Mad Planet	£19.50	$44.00	£22.00		
Seeing Out the Seventies	£14.99	$34.00	£17.00		
Gateways to Mystery	£19.99	$44.00	£22.00		
Italian Martians T-shirt	£9.99	$23.00	£11.99		
Charles Fort T-shirt	£7.99	$18.00	£9.50		
Silbury Hill Tile	£10.95	$25.00	£13.50		
Mandlebrot Tile	£10.95	$25.00	£13.50		
Pictogram Tile	£10.95	$25.00	£13.50		
Church & Circle Tile	£10.95	$25.00	£13.50		
Three Satellites Tile	£10.95	$25.00	£13.50		
Set of Three Tiles	£30.00	$70.00	£36.50		
Set of Five Tiles	£47.95	$115.00	£58.50		

Postage and packing is free

Total £ ____________

Name:Mrs/Miss/Ms/Mr____________________

Address ____________________

____

____

____________Postcode ____________

I enclose a total payment of £ ________made payable to: John Brown Publishing Ltd, or debit the above amount from my Access/Visa/Mastercard/Eurocard (delete where applicable) account.

Card No

Expiry Date /

Signature ____________________

Date ____________________

For a set of three tiles, please circle the designs you require from the following list: 1. Silbury Hill, 2. Mandelbrot Set,3. Three Satellites , 4. Church & Circle or 5. Pictogram.

I would like to subscribe to Fortean Times from issue ________ *Please tick for free Monstrum book ☐

For one year (6 issues) £12 ☐ Overseas inc USA £15 US$30 ☐

For two years (12 issues) £20 ☐ Overseas inc USA £26 US$50 ☐

Back issues £2 each (£2.50 overseas or US$5.00) Please circle your selection: 35 36 37 38 39 43 44 51 52 53 54 55 57 58 60 61 62 63 64 65 66 67 68 69 70

Please return this order form to: Fortean Times, Freepost SW6096, Frome, Somerset BA11 1YA, UK or phone Freephone charge card details on 0800 581 409. Freepost and Freephone services available to UK residents only. Overseas customers please add stamps to postal applications. For telephone orders phone (44) 373 451777

F71

Check out more fascinating reports, from spontaneous human combustion to UFO abduction, in this collection of facsimile reprints of early Fortean Times (formerly simply titled The News).

FORTEAN TIMES 1 - 15
YESTERDAY'S NEWS TOMORROW £19.99
ISBN: 1 870870 263
400 page paperback, colour cover, illustrated throughout.

FORTEAN TIMES 16 - 25
DIARY OF A MAD PLANET £19.50
ISBN: 1 870021 258
416 page paperback, colour cover, illustrated throughout.

FORTEAN TIMES 26 - 30
SEEING OUT THE SEVENTIES £14.99
ISBN: 1 870021 207
320 page paperback, colour cover, illustrated throughout.

FORTEAN TIMES 31-36
NEW! GATEWAYS TO MYSTERY £19.99
ISBN: 1 870870 379 400 page paperback, colour cover, illustrated throughout.

100% COTTON T-SHIRTS,

There are two great designs to choose from -

Italian Martians T-shirt
Walter Molino's illustration of Rosa Lotti's experience with the 'men from Mars' portrayed on a 100% cotton heavyweight T-shirt in dark green (One size XL) - £9.99

Charles Fort T-shirt
Charles Fort's Portrait and the slogan "One Measures a Circle Beginning Anywhere". White, 100% cotton T-shirt (One size XL) - £7.99

SUBSCRIPTIONS

If you have enjoyed this issue, why not make sure that you receive a copy on a regular basis? Order a year's supply of Fortean Times for yourself or a friend and get it delivered direct to your doorstep. And that not all: every new subscriber receives a FREE copy of Doc Shiels' Monstrum book (DIY monster hunting - worth £8.95). Fortean Times back issues also available (see below).

BACK ISSUES

FT51 - Lizard man, albino frog falls and Yorkshire's water wolf
FT53 - Crop circles, invasion of the slime creatures and Islamic simulacra.
FT58 - Lesbian vampires, trepanning today and alien abduction.
FT 60 - Alpine ice man, Father Christmas as Odin and the Lake Erie monster
FT61 - Homing treks by cats, everlasting light bulbs and social panics.
FT62 - The Piltdown Hoax, World's Heaviest Man dies and puddle-creating poltergeists.
FT63 - Crop Circle colour pull-out, acid tattoo panic and British alien big cats.
FT64 - Spielberg, Satanic witch hunts and the pregnant male hoax.
FT65 - Colour pull-out on Martian monuments, kidney kidnapping rumours and blood miracles.
FT66 - Florida's Penguin panic, bogus social workers and horse-ripping.
FT67 - BBC's Ghostwatch hoax unravelled, plus Italian Martians.
FT68 - Cattle Mutilation in America, ESP Orgasms, Vampire at Croglin Grange.
FT69 - Who are the Circlemakers? Chinese cannibalism, Lama drama.
FT70 - Incredible dog journeys, Vancouver dragons, guru on ice.

SECRET COUNTRY

Mysterious places to visit in Great Britain compiled by Janet & Colin Bord

11: Callanish, Isle of Lewis, Outer Hebrides

This unique site comprises a roofless chambered cairn, another possible cairn, a formation of tall standing stones, and seven neighbouring stone circles. The standing stones – the most important visual component – are set out in a cross with a central circle of 13 stones and an avenue of 19 stones (some now missing), measuring 405ft north/south and 140ft west/east. The burial chamber, in the central ring, was possibly added later.

The standing stones may originally have acted as a prehistoric observatory, and survey work by Lockyer, Somerville, Hawkins, Thom and others has shown that Callanish is orientated towards the year's major solar events. At sunrise on Midsummer Day, according to folklore, the 'Shining One' would walk along the avenue, his arrival announced by the cuckoo's cry. The lunar cycle seems also to have been of importance, with especially dramatic events taking place every 18 years when the moon passes low over the horizon and appears to be among the stones. This happened in 1987 and will again in 2006.

Viewed from Callanish at the crucial time, the moon appears to rise out of the Pairc Hills, known as The Sleeping Beauty as they resemble a woman lying on her back. As Paul Devereux noted in *Symbolic Landscapes*: "It is as if the Sleeping Beauty, another name for the Earth Mother, gives birth to the moon at this key time in its cycle" (p.32).

Callanish standing stones, Lewis

Paul Devereux has also drawn attention (*Places of Power*, p.41) to the variety of crystals in the stones at

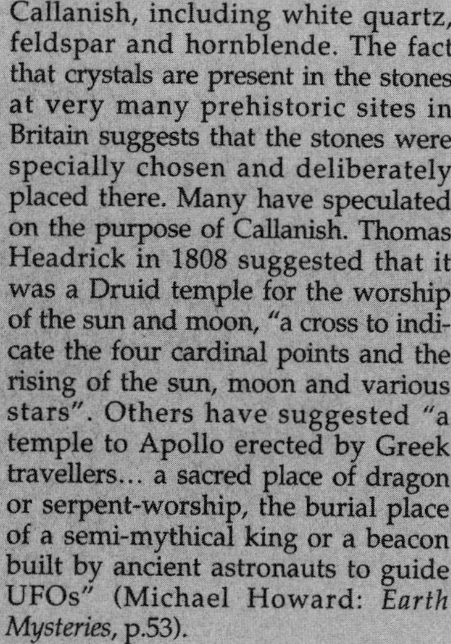

Callanish, including white quartz, feldspar and hornblende. The fact that crystals are present in the stones at very many prehistoric sites in Britain suggests that the stones were specially chosen and deliberately placed there. Many have speculated on the purpose of Callanish. Thomas Headrick in 1808 suggested that it was a Druid temple for the worship of the sun and moon, "a cross to indicate the four cardinal points and the rising of the sun, moon and various stars". Others have suggested "a temple to Apollo erected by Greek travellers... a sacred place of dragon or serpent-worship, the burial place of a semi-mythical king or a beacon built by ancient astronauts to guide UFOs" (Michael Howard: *Earth Mysteries*, p.53).

In the past, the Gaelic name *Fir Bhreig (false men)* was used for the stones, as they looked like human figures from a distance. There was also a legend that they were giants turned to stone by St. Kieran for failing to embrace Christianity whe he came and preached to them. It was at one time customary for men and women to exchange betrothal vows among the stones, and even to consummate their marriages there to ensure a happy future.

Local people have always visited the stones at Midsummer and on May Day, despite the disapproval of the church, for they instinctively knew they must not neglect them. It is as if a distant memory of the importance of the rites once performed had come down through the generations, though their purpose had long been forgotten. FT

HOW TO GET THERE
OS map reference: NB 214331
The stones at the southern end of Callanish village, which is 13 miles (21 km) west of Stornoway. The stones are well signposted.

Callanish standing stones, Isle of Lewis, with full moon

Janet and Colin Bord are authors of Mysterious Britain, The Secret Country, Alien Animals, The Atlas of Magical Britain, and Modern Mysteries of Britain among many others.

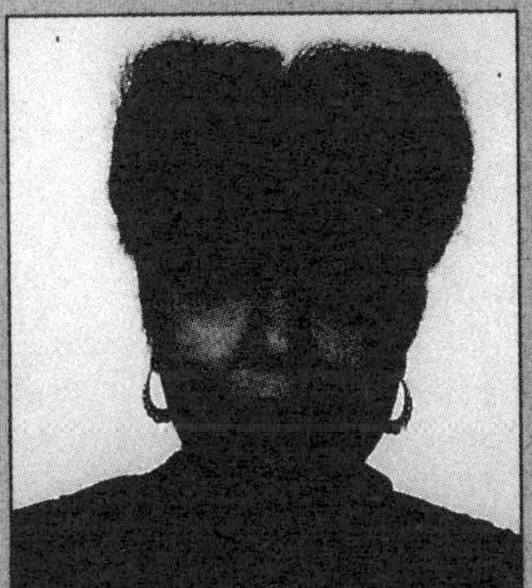

UFOLOGY
Yvonne Greene is a part-time lecturer in astrology and has run courses on the relevance and meaning of symbols. She has been interested in Forteana for over 20 years.

ASTROLOGY
Gerald Baker is a teacher of mathematics and science and is the Coordinator of *Science Frontiers*, a special interest group of Mensa.

BRAIN RESEARCH
Dr Peter Carr MA MBBS is a psychotherapist researching the visual imagery effects of stroboscopic light for exploring the unconscious. He is founder and director of Highland Psionics.

SPECULATION
Paul Sharville is 32 and lives in Kent. He commutes to London (by conventional transport) where he works as a marketing assistant and freelance journalist.

Ufology

Fœtal Memory Metaphors

Yvonne Greene proposes some analogies for alien abduction narratives

I was prompted to write after seeing *Fire in the Sky* [see review *FT69:62*]. The film is rife with symbolism, particularly in relation to the Birth Trauma Hypothesis of UFO experience. No doubt this is partly due to the film maker's artistic licence.

During what may be considered the most riveting part of the abduction sequence, Travis Walton breaks out of a cocoon after rupturing a membrane which surrounds him. This could be equated with the egg being released from the ovary. After falling, he climbs the side of a pit (the fallopian tube) towards the light. (This pit could also represent the womb/uterus). He sees the alien 'space-suits', one of which is apparently occupied. The white-suited aliens with their large heads and tapering bodies are unmistakably sperm-like in appearance; note also that Walton (the egg) and the alien (the sperm) 'collide' in a fight as he tries to defend himself. After that, Walton's body is 'invaded' by the aliens via examination. An 'umbilicus' is applied through which he is 'fed' and his body is immobilised by a 'caul'. When he is finally found back on the Earth, he is naked as the day he was born.

It appears that much of the abduction experience is indeed down to the artistic licence of the film makers and deviates from Walton's original – supposedly true – story. However, many abductees do present similar incidents to those depicted, which makes me wonder if this scenario is not so much one of Birth Trauma as of *Pre*-Birth Trauma. That is, a consciousness starting from the moment an egg is released from the ovary and commences its journey along the fallopian tube.

Another possibility occurred to me after seeing the film, triggered by a comment made by a friend I was with at the time. She said that the whole abductee/examination experience made her think of rape. This seems a pertinent observation and raises the question of the connection between the abductee experience and child sexual abuse.

> "I wonder if the abductee scenario is not so much one of Birth Trauma as of *Pre*-Birth Trauma."

At about the same time that *Fire in the Sky* was released, I saw the Viewpoint '93 TV programme on the so-called Satanic child abuse cases. I must stress that I am not a fundamentalist of any religious persuasion. The experience of those people who believed, after psycho- or hypnotherapy, that their parents had committed such abuse, reminded me of some abductee experiences, such as the insertion of tubes into various bodily orifices and the removal of fœtuses or new-born infants. The victim mentality and their inability to stop the abuse also seems relevant (see the David Jacobs' interview, *Secret Invasion FT69:27*) This correlation, of course, raises the 'demonic entity/possession' scenario as a possible answer to this type of experience. We can only wonder what the trigger could be; presumably the therapy session. Notice also that *Therapist = The Rapist*!

It is said that some 'abductees' have had UFO experiences intermittently since childhood and we know that child sexual abuse often continues with appalling regularity throughout childhood and adolescence.

Are abductees victims of early sexual abuse which they have unconsciously suppressed until it is released through therapy and translated into a UFO experience? Are abductees victims of traumatic birth, or are they reviving fœtal memories? Are they abducted by real extraterrestrial beings, or are they perhaps victims of demonic possession?

Do researchers ask enough of the right questions? I, for one, would like to have more information on what was going on in their lives at the time/s of their 'abduction/s'. Perhaps then we would have a clearer insight into this puzzling phenomenon.

Unexpected Birth Cycles

Gerald Baker on meteorite falls and the birth-dates of chess champions

In November 1982, a meteorite fell through the roof of a house in Wethersfield, Connecticut. It was the second such bolide to fall inside the town (population: 26,000) within a decade. My interest stimulated, I read T.R. Le Maire's *Stones from the Stars* during my Christmas vacation that year. This showed geometric and other non-random patterns of meteor and meteorite phenomena, in support of the author's thesis that at least some of these suggested a guiding intelligence. There appeared to be an 18-year cycle in meteor-related phenomena and I wondered whether such a cycle might also occur in human affairs.

Upon investigation, I found such a cycle in the birth-dates of world chess champions. Supposing a cycle of 18 years, always beginning in years divisible by 18, I divided people into four types: *W* – born in the 'warm' months (May-October) of the first half of the cycle (eg 1800-08); *X* – born in the 'warm' months of the second half of the cycle (eg 1809-1817); *Y* – born in the 'cold' months (November-April) of the first half of the cycle; and *Z* – born in the 'cold' months in the second half of the cycle.

It turned out that every world chess champion up to 1984, except Euwe, was either *W* or *Z*. My findings were published in 1984 in *Vidya*, the publication of the Triple Nine Society. The editor, Dr Norman Treloar, noted that Euwe was probably the weakest player of all world champions.

There is a lunar cycle of 18.03 years called the saros, associated with eclipses of the sun and moon. There is also a lunar cycle of 18.613 years, punctuated by the maximum and minimum northward swings of the full moon at the winter and summer solstices. The astronomer Gerald Hawkins found, many years ago, that the alignments at Stonehenge measured this cycle.

In 1985, *Chess Life* magazine informed me that Kasparov was born on 13 April 1963. By the 18-year cycle he was a *Y*, and thus unlikely to be a world champion. However, by the Stonehenge cycle, his birth-date was almost exactly on the regression line of the birth-dates of all world chess champions.

Here are the birth dates of the world chess champions:

Anderssen – 6 August 1818
Steinitz – 17 May 1836
Morphy – June 1837
Lasker – 24 December 1868
Capablanca – 19 November 1888
Alekhine – 18 October 1892
Euwe – 20 May 1901
Botvinnik – 17 August 1911
Smyslov – 24 March 1921
Tal – 9 November 1936
Petrosian – 17 June 1929
Spassky – 30 January 1937
Fischer – 9 March 1943
Karpov – 23 May 1951
Kasparov – 13 April 1963

> "Roman astrologers may have changed the recorded birth-dates of some of the emperors to make them conform with the Stonehenge cycle"

In the same year I read in *Nature* a report of a correlation between large southern Californian earthquakes and the major standstill of the Stonehenge cycle (when the full moons of winter swing furthest north).

I also read in *New Scientist* about correlations of drought periods with that cycle.

I then discovered that the birth-dates of ancient Roman emperors fitted the Stonehenge cycle. Those born near the major standstill tended to be born in the autumn. Those born several years before that standstill tended towards summer births, while those born several years after tended towards winter births. Those born at the opposite, 'minor', standstill tended towards spring births.

Roman emperor births had a slightly different phase from those of the chess champions, who, when born near the major standstill, tended to be born in the late summer, rather than in the autumn. Perhaps this can be put down to the procession of the equinoxes. My findings were published in *Science Quest* in 1986. Dr Hawkins suggested to me recently that Roman astrologers may have changed the recorded birth-dates of some of the emperors to make them conform with the Stonehenge cycle. That's a possibility to be considered.

Here are the known birth dates of some of the Roman emperors:

Augustus – 19 September 63BC
Tiberius – 16 November 42BC
Claudius I – 1 August 10BC
Galba – 24 December 3BC
Caligula – 31 August 12AD
Nero – 13 December 37AD
Titus – 30 December 39AD
Domitian – 24 October 51Ad
Trajan – 15 September 53AD
Hadrian – 24 January 76AD
Antoninus Pius – 19 September 86AD
Marcus Aurelius – 26 April 121AD
Pertinax – 1 August 126AD
Lucius Verus – 15 December 130AD
Commodus – 31 August 161AD
Caracalla – 4 April 188AD
Claudius II – May 214Ad
Contantine I 27 – February 286AD
Constantine II – February 317AD
Honorius – 9 September 384AD
Valentinian III – 2 July 419AD

In 1986 I also published in *Psychological Reports* my finding that, statistically, the ratio of births in May to births in November varies as a direct function of geographic latitude. For example, that ratio is higher in Canada than in the United States, and is even higher in Britain, where the demographic concentration is further north. I can send data or graphs about any of the above to those who request it.

FORUM is a column for anyone with something to say about a particular field, theory or incident. If you'd like to join in with an opinion on any area of Forteana, send it to the editorial address. Ideal length: 500-1000 words. Please enclose an SAE, a three-line biography and a head-and-shoulders photo of yourself, preferably in black and white.

Frankenstein Vibrations

Peter Carr explains the frequency on which we construct our world view

The experience of God and the experience of material reality both occur maximally on average at a frequency of around 18 cycles per second. This is the average clock frequency of the conscious brain. It is a relatively easy figure to remember, in Britain being the age of initiation into adult mysteries – the youth can buy beer legally in the pub for the first time. Stoned occultists with poor memories and triple vision might prefer the alternative mnemonic that 18 is 6+6+6.

The maximal experience of God in this context is not something to be too eagerly sought after or cultivated: it is the grand mal epileptic fit. In many languages, epilepsy is called the divine malady, the sacred disease, and many of its sufferers experience a seizure as an overwhelming influx of divine energy. It is a paroxysmal over-synchronisation of the brain's electrical rhythms, a mega-orgasm of the nervous system. Indeed, the Romans called the sexual orgasm a 'small epilepsy'.

In the relatively rare condition of photosensitive epilepsy, the fit is triggered by flickering light. In their book *Photosensitive Epilepsy*, Peter Jevons and Graham Harding give the results of their research into which frequencies of stroboscopic light over the range of 1 to 65 Hz (flashes per second) are most likely to produce seizure patterns in people prone to the disorder. They found that 96% exhibited maximum sensitivity to a frequency range of 15-20 Hz. Their results came out as a distribution curve with its peak around 16 to 18 Hz.

The average beta rhythm of the alert open-eyed awake cortex is around 18 to 20 Hz. One would expect the most convulsive frequency of flickering light to be that at which the brain is already operating, since this would be likely to possess the maximum capacity to over-synchronise or confuse. What is of more interest is the way in which this physiological data on the brain correlates remarkably well with psychological data on the mind.

It has always been a central tenet of the Buddhist faith that the mind, the ego, is discontinuous and therefore essentially non-existent, the sense of continuity of sense being an illusion. The Tibetan meditation master Chogyam Trungpa in one of his books puts it like this:

"The process which is ego actually consists of a flicker of confusion, a flicker of aggression, a flicker of grasping – all of which exist only in the moment. Since we cannot hold on to the present moment, we cannot hold on to me and mine and make them solid things. The experience of oneself relating to others is actually a momentary discrimination, a fleeting thought. If we generate these fleeting thoughts fast enough, we can create the illusion of continuity and solidity. It is like watching a movie: the individual film frames are played so quickly that they generate the illusion of continual movement."

> **"The nature of time remains a profound mystery to science, as does the nature of chance."**

What is of interest here is the particular speed or frequency at which these mental film frames are played. In his erudite and magnificent tome *The Natural Philosophy of Time*, G.J. Whitrow summarises the results of Western scientific research into this basic unit of perceptual time:

"J. Cohen [..] has drawn attention to the penetrating observation by the famous neurologist J. Hughlings Jackson that 'time in the form of some minimum duration is required for consciousness', the loss of consciousness in an epileptic seizure being due to the sheer speed of neural discharge. Cohen points out that our visual system normally acts as a protecting buffer for the brain by regulating the rate of information transmitted to it. The minimum duration of a visual experience can be defined in terms of the rate at which the successive presentations of static images is seen as apparent movement, particularly in the cinema. It is about 16 to 18 a second, each frame lasting about 0.06 seconds. For auditory sensation the minimum frequency is also about 16 to 18 cycles a second, and similarly about 18 tactile signals a second is the rate at which a clearly differentiated series of tactile impressions can be distinguished from an impression of tactile vibration. On this basis the duration of the unit of perceptual time would be of the order of 50 milliseconds. We may therefore take this as the approximate duration of the 'mental moment', i.e. the interval between distinguishable perceptions or decisions."

So, the flicker fusion thresholds of the three major human senses, sight, sound and touch, all overlap at around this magic number 18. It is at about this frequency that the average brain tends to fuse and synchronise all the flicker of its activity into that impression of continuous experience we know of as mind and world.

This data on perceptual processing correlates well with data on language processing. The average rate for normal speech is 18 binary bits of information per second. For those unfamiliar with the jargon, this means that normal speech involves about 18 yes/no decisions per second.

Some find a discussion of the brain as an electrical organ overly mechanistic and distasteful, if not downright disrespectful, to the human soul. However, a mechanistic model need not be exclusive and reductionist; mechanism can be open-ended. The nature of time remains a profound mystery to science, as does the nature of chance. Rhythms, frequency, vibe represent structures in time and may link in to many dimensions.

The horror of an exclusively mechanistic account of the human soul, as being no more than electrified brain, finds its most archetypal and powerful expression in the myth of Dr Frankenstein's monster. With a machine bolt through its neck, the creature is sparked to life with electricity conducted down a lightning rod. In daily reenactment of this myth, modern psychiatry uses rebirth by electroconvulsion as one of its standard healing rituals when confronted by what it deems to be psychic monstrosity.

Mary Shelley's masterpiece of Gothic horror, *Frankenstein*, was first published in the year 1818.

Speculation

Commuting at 186,000 miles per hour

Paul Sharville envisions some of the pitfalls of mass teleportation

In Star Trek's vision of the 23rd century, James T. Kirk and the crew of the Starship Enterprise could be beamed anywhere in seconds, thanks to the technology of matter transmitting. Back in 1931, Charles Fort wrote: "The look to me is that, in what is loosely called Nature, teleportation exists, as a means of distribution of things and materials."

Imagine you're living in the future. You've finished your day's work, washed out your sandwich box, and you're ready to go home. You step into the office transmat, dial your number and you appear in your hallway, 15 miles away. The journey took less than 10 seconds. There are no cars on the road. In fact, there aren't many roads. The M25 was ploughed up and landscaped 20 years ago.

Most of us would agree that this is the stuff of science fiction. Despite the accelerating pace of technological advance, we till find scientists' visions of the future hard to believe. Have you ever saved up for anything you've seen on *Tomorrow's World?*

Predictions often prove amusingly inaccurate. A UK Postmaster General once said that there would be no need for telephones as there was no shortage of messenger boys. A visionary American pundit disagreed and said that he could envisage a day when every town would have one. The Managing Director of IBM predicted in the early 1950s a total mainframe computer market of 30 machines. If he had been allowed to plan car parks, we might have had as many as 10 spaces in each one.

In fact, British Telecom and other communications companies are researching matter transportation – Beam Me Up Beattie, that sort of thing. Peter Cochrane, head of BT's Systems Research development unit, is enthusiastic, but realistic. He said: "A rough estimate for how much energy you would need to disassemble me, transport me over some distance and reassemble me in about 100 seconds is something in the order of 10 million power stations."

"You step in the booth, dial the number of your house in Surrey and you're transmatted to a small Albanian fishing village – the work of transmat vandals."

That's clearly some way off, but it will come, hopefully without us all living next door to a Sizewell B. The future massive public network of telephones and transmats will probably suffer the same problems as our current system.

There you are, watching telly, when a complete stranger appears, says "Sorry, wrong number" and disappears again, possibly to appear again moments later: "There seems to something wrong with my transmat. Sorry about this." A few of those and you'd be tempted to leave the transmat off the hook.

There will be those unfortunates whose numbers closely resemble those of major public venues. If you're one number away from the Earls Court Exhibition Centre when the Ideal Home show rolls round, you could come home to find 300 people wandering about your house, admiring your curtains and your avocado bathroom suite.

Public transmats will be as familiar as the present phone boxes – you step in the booth, dial the number of your house in Surrey and you're transmatted to a small Albanian fishing village – the work of transmat vandals.

Science fiction writer Larry Niven wrote a short story ('Flash Flood') in which looters used matter transmitters to 'flick in' to a riot, grab a telly and a handful of jewellry and 'flick out' again. The police got wise and redirected all the 'displacement booths' to a large police stadium. The looters, instead of arriving home, found themselves sliding down the wall of a huge stainless steel bowl, where they would muster until they were charged.

I envisage the portable transmat as a clear acrylic tube that folds up, concertina fashion, slipping neatly into the briefcase or pocket. The public transmat booth will be urine-proof and bolted firmly to the Earth's crust. A set of instructions and emergency transmat numbers will be fanned by a rosette of call-girls' business cards.

Still unconvinced? The video phone is out this year. No more answering the phone in your Y-fronts. Computer systems that lip-read, scan your retina for identification and recognise your face are not too far away. High-definition TV is here and will soon be hanging on your wall like a picture – you'll be able to freeze-frame a shot of Cliff Richard for when your granny comes round to see you. Transmats are just around the corner! **FT**

D.I.Y. Skeleton Keys

Step by step How to make skeleton keys for almost any lock

BEAT THE BANDIT

JACKPOT WIN

D.I.Y BANDIT JAMMER. EASY INSTRUCTIONS

FREE!!!

Yours absolutely FREE with every order. These 4 great titles are now banned from sale. As we are not allowed to sell them anymore, to get around the ban we are giving them away free with every order.

WARNING The contents of these publications are for information only and none may be used for illegal purposes.

Enquiries tel: 071 - 700 2021

ORDER NOW! Send to: CTX BOOKS (Dept 401) 302 Regent Street, London W1R 5AL. Please rush me all 10 amazing titles for just £19.95 + my 4 FREE Banned titles.

NAME..

ADDRESS..

....

....POSTCODE..................

All orders in strictest confidence I enclose CHEQUE/ P.O. PAYABLE TO "CTX BOOKS" for just £19.95

REVIEWS

SASQUATCH/BIGFOOT

THE SEARCH FOR NORTH AMERICA'S INCREDIBLE CREATURE

by Don Hunter with René Dahinden

McClelland & Stewart Inc., Toronto, Canada. 1993, pb, pp205, illus. Autographed copies available by air-mail (price $25.00 to UK, $17.00 to N.America/USA) from René Dahinden, 7340 Sidaway Road, Richmond, BC, V6W 1B8, Canada.

This valuable book on North America's hairy man-beast was first published as *Sasquatch* in 1973, but has long been unavailable and so this new revised edition is very welcome. René Dahinden has been on the track of the Sasquatch for almost 40 years, and his knowledge of the creature, and of the various characters who have been involved in the hunt for it, must be unsurpassed by any other researcher. His account, written with Don Hunter, covers numerous key cases, such as the 1924 Albert Ostman kidnap, the 1955 close sighting by William Roe on Mica Mountain, and of course the filming of a female Sasquatch by Roger Patterson in Bluff Creek, California, in 1967, this film remaining a controversial item 26 years later. *Sasquatch/Bigfoot* is an essential addition to the cryptozoology bookshelf, despite its lack of an index.

Janet Bord

HAUNTED NOTTINGHAMSHIRE VOL. 2

by Len Moakes

JH Hall & Sons, Derby. 1993, pb £2.95, pp63, index, illus.

Following the success of his first work dealing with the ghosts of the county, Moakes, chairman of the local Psychical Research group, has now produced this even better collection, offering a well-balanced and informative approach in an attractive little volume.

The foreword by Tom Perrott, chairman of the Ghost Club, emphasises the confusing attitudes sometimes taken by researchers and endorses the rational approach of Moakes and his team. Interesting new facts are revealed about some of the haunted properties featured, such as Wollaton Hall, Gelling House and Thrumpton Hall, whilst the well-placed photos make this one of the most attractive smaller publications for some time.

Andrew Green

Encyclopædia Forteana

ENCYCLOPEDIA OF STRANGE AND UNEXPLAINED PHYSICAL PHENOMENA

compiled by Jerome Clark.

Gale Research Inc. 1993, hb (US price unknown) £40, pp395, illus, refs, index.

UNEXPLAINED!: 347 STRANGE SIGHTINGS, INCREDIBLE OCCURRENCES AND PUZZLING PHENOMENA

compiled by Jerome Clark.

Visible Ink Press. 1993, hb $14.95, £12.50, pp443, illus, refs.

Both available from: Gale Research Inc, 835 Penobscot, Detroit, MI 48226-4094, USA. In the UK from Gale Research International Ltd, PO Box 498, Reading, Berks RG1 8QW.

Although Jerome Clark is better known these days for his involvement in ufology – he is editor of the important UFO bimonthly *International UFO Reporter* – he has also a long-standing interest in the wider sphere of Forteana. He was writing articles on strange animals for various magazines twenty years ago, and has co-authored with Loren Coleman books such as *Creatures of the Outer Edge* (on Bigfoot, manimals, phantom cats and dogs, winged monsters – 1978), and *The Unidentified: Notes Towards Solving the UFO Mystery* (on other worlds, fairyland, religion, airships and para-ufology – 1975).

There are today only a handful of true Forteans, by which I mean people who have embraced the *whole* field of Forteana rather than specialising in just one aspect such as cryptozoology or parapsychology. Jerry Clark clearly belongs to the former category, and is therefore better qualified than most other people to tackle such a wide-ranging project as a Fortean encyclopædia. Of course he is not infallible, for no-one could be aware of *everything* that has been written in this field. Even an encyclopædia cannot be 100% accurate, for there are always experts with conflicting views of the 'truth', because no event has one single 'truth'. But Jerry Clark can be relied upon to take a commonsense approach to a mystery and to be factual rather than indulging in flights of fancy.

An encyclopædia covering every type of strange event would be impossibly long, unless each entry were uselessly brief; so Clark has wisely restricted his coverage to 'physical phenomena' and omitted those happenings that are clearly non-physical, such as ghosts and poltergeists and the whole field of parapsychology. Despite this, he has managed to include a wide variety of topics and has devoted an essay to each, often several pages in length. To give a flavour of the book, here are a few of its topics: Alligators in sewers, Atmospheric life forms, Ball lightning, Bigfoot, Brown Mountain lights, Cattle mutilations, Champ, Devil's footprints, Entombed animals, Fairies, Flight 19, Giant octopus, Ice falls, Kraken, Mad gassers, Moving coffins, Noah's Ark, Springheel Jack, Tatzelwurm, Tunguska event, Ummo, Vile vortices, Werewolves, Yowie. People and organisations include: Tim Dinsdale, Ivan Sanderson, Brad Steiger, Fortean Society and SITU.

There are 152 topics in all, and each essay is followed by a list of sources. The *Encyclopædia* is a valuable reference tool which every serious Fortean must have on the shelf. It is readable and 'user-friendly' – items are easy to locate because the subjects are in alphabetical order and there is a full index. The book itself is large and pleasant to hold, and the two-columns text is in a clear typeface. The illustrations are sometimes not as good as they could be, and more photographs would have added to the value of the book. But this is a minor quibble. This is Jerry Clark's most important contribution to Fortean reseach so far, and it is impressive.

Because the *Encyclopedia* is not cheap, Gale made a decision to publish a cut-down softcover version for the popular market, omitting organisations, personalities, and theories, concentrating entirely on mysterious events. In its own right, *Unexplained!* is a worthwhile book, but if you can possibly afford it, you should buy the full version.

Janet Bord

A CONFUSION OF PROPHETS

VICTORIAN AND EDWARDIAN ASTROLOGY

by Patrick Curry

Collins and Brown, London. 1992, pb £18, pp192, illus, refs, index.

Not so much about astrology as astrologers, this is a perfectly accessible book about the men who, ultimately, gave us the form of today's popular astrology – brief lives of such as 'Raphael', 'Zadkiel', Alan Leo and others. Of these, the earliest, John Varley (1778-1842) is perhaps both the odd one out and the most interesting. A painter and friend of William Blake, with whom he collaborated on the 'Spirit Pictures' series, he was obsessively interested in astrology for its own sake, and his recorded predictions appear to have been remarkablyaccurate.

The rest, gradually fostering the commercialisation of astrology with their almanacs and magazines, come across as a bunch of mild eccentrics trying desperately to make a living. Were they to be faulted for this? They certainly were! Here is a sorry tale of persecution by the scientific and religious establishment, of prosecution under the Vagrancy Act (for "pretending or professing to tell fortunes"; a section not repealed until 1989), of ridicule and abuse that eventually changed astrology's emphasis from prediction to 'character' and 'tendencies'.

Curry's handling of his subjects is commendably even-handed, and it does have one great virtue – regardless of the 'truth of astrology' or otherwise, he has a compassion for his subjects as struggling human beings. Their opponents in the last century did not – and it has to be said, alas, that nor do their sceptical descendants today. This is an enjoyable, well-researched read ... if a little depressing when one realises how little has changed.

Steve Moore

THE BEAST OF EXMOOR

AND OTHER MYSTERY PREDATORS OF BRITAIN

by Di Francis.

Jonathan Cape, London. 1993, pb £7.99, pp150, plates, bib.

Di Francis' interest in British sightings of alien big cats (ABCs) has been a continuous obsession, which last saw public expression in her 1983 book, *Cat Country*. The intervening ten years have not dimmed her researches, nor her enthusiasm for her own explanation of the phenomenon, which was less than favourably regarded by professional zoologists.

Francis believes that the British landscape is dotted with small numbers of an undiscovered type of cat she likens to an 'indigenous panther'. Shy and solitary, it is not related to any known breed (such as wildcats, or feral domestic cats, or escaped exotic imports) but has descended from the

VIDEO REVIEWS

THE TERRESTRIAL CONNECTION

VHS, 93 mins. Available from its producer, David Percy, 25 Belsize Park, London NW3 4DU. £15.95 (inc p&p).

The Martian Face, the Sphinx at Giza, the megaliths at Avebury, the Mayan pyramids, and hyperspatial geometry, are all linked in this recording of a special presentation to the United Nations in New York by Richard Hoagland of the Mars Mission network. The event, on 27 February 1992, was unusual because Hoagland's avowed aim was to increase pressure on NASA to ensure the famous Face was photographed by the current Mars Observer craft. Perhaps the Martian engineers, he hints, intervened on Earth, changing the course of evolution and civilisation.

This video lecture is pretty much as summarised in *FT65*, but with the advantage of having details graphically explained by their chief proponent, aided by spectacular film and computer animations. Hoagland explains clearly and confidently until, near the end, he drags in crop circles to support his case. Most of his examples are now known to be man-made, but Hoagland dismisses the hoax theory on the grounds that the crop-glyphs contain the same tetrahedral geometry found at Avebury and Silbury, which appear to replicate the Cydonian complex. Hoagland's failure to recognise that the possession of similar geometries – many examples occur in natural forms – does not of itself imply a connection with Mars, and this error of logic makes one wonder what else has been glossed in the Martian thesis.

Despite this doubt, these are bold ideas – familiar from science-fiction but all the more exciting for being presented as a distinct possibility, and one which can be proved or disproved with the first good photo of the Cydonian Face. Either way, it is well worth a viewing.

Bob Rickard

THE WARP

VHS, six three-hour videos, £105 from Neil Oram, Goshem, Drumnadrochit, Invernesshire IV3 6XH.

This is a recording of the 1979 ICA performance of a play about one man's quest for self-discovery, which (at up to 24 hours) entered the *Guinness Book of Records* as the world's longest [see review in *FT28:31*]. Produced by Ken Campbell, *The Warp* takes us on a roller-coaster ride through the tortuous relationships and monomania of the 1960s, Bavaria in 1457, Beat poetry, Scientological auditing, psychotherapy, and meetings with Krishnamurti, Rajneesh and Buckminster Fuller, onwards to a final epiphany with a Californian psychic and recluse in Birmingham. The central character – Phil Masters (played by Russell Denton) – initiates John Michell's UFO quest and mints a few philosophical gems on the way.

In addition, playwright Neil Oram has added documentary footage of the production of *The Warp* and a tour around his Scottish retreat, including a generous dose of laughter therapy. The price seems enormous, but the cast (which includes Jim Broadbent, John Joyce and Bill Nighy) is excellent. Sheer bravura, weirdness and hilarity more than compensate for the occasional blips in recording quality.

James Nye

MESSENGERS OF DESTINY

VHS, 75 minutes. Produced by Genesis III (Box 25962, Munds Park, Arizona 86017, USA). Available in the UK for £21.15 (inc p&p) from Ark Soundwaves, Box 1395, Glastonbury, Somerset BA6 9FE.

This film by American ufologist Lee Elders and Mexican TV journalist Jaime Mausson, documents a UFO flap in Mexico, beginning with the total solar eclipse on 11 July 1991, during which at least 17 people, out videoing the eclipse at different locations around Mexico City, shot footage of hovering, silvery craft. Later analysis shows the objects were not stars (often real stars were identified as stationary reference points in the background) nor planes or balloons – in fact most of the objects appeared to be identical.

In the year that followed, Mausson and Elders – who produced the films about Billy Meier' 'UFOs from the Pleiades' – collected almost 200 video clips of similar ærial lights, many from professional cameramen, some seeming to hover for hours, and others leaving radar traces. The towns of Metepec and Atlixco, in Puebla state, seemed to have almost nightly visitations. They are joined by a Japanese TV team, and later have a collective sighting.

Elders and his wife Brit wax flowery when they link the UFOs to the reawakening of nearby Popocatepetl (4th largest volcano in the world), and with a prophecy in the Dresden Codex about the appearance of the 'Masters of the Stars' in the era of the 'sixth sun'. The arrival of the UFOs over the ancient city of the Aztecs during the eclipse, they argue, is a portent of great political change and geophysical catastrophe.

Whether or not you swallow this theory, the fact that so many seemingly independent recordings were made of seemingly similar objects in the Mexican sky raises real questions. Sadly, the production team leaves them unanswered in their dash for more marketable mysticism.

Bob Rickard

primitive cats of prehistory, surviving into the present era by mostly withdrawing to wilderness areas and keeping clear of man.

In the present book, Francis explains the diversity of modern ABC sightings as the novelty of the unexpected, "because what is seen has no exact comparison among ... known big cat species". Under this banner, she boldly annexes historical and folklore references to 'black dogs' (including Conan Doyle's *Hound of the Baskervilles)* and all manner of big cats from Cornwall to Caithness.

This is not an objective study or a scientific record, but a very personal account of her interviews with witnesses, her own sightings, her successful breeding of captured Kellas-type wildcats, her quest for specimens (eg. tales of an ABC hit by a car long ago and buried somewhere) and her forays into the academic world to get her evidence verified. It is the kind of book that makes scientists uneasy because her ideas and interpretations are invested in every line. Perhaps the most notable example of this is the chapter in which she proposes that Genette Tate (whose disappearance on the edge of Dartmoor in 1978 is still unsolved) might have been carried off by one of these leopard-sized cats. This may be her last word on the subject – fed up with the lack of interest from the establishment she is heading for France to breed lynxes.

Bob Rickard

BIOLOGICAL ANOMALIES

HUMANS 2

compiled by William R. Corliss.

Sourcebook Project, Box 107, Glen Arm, MD 21057, USA. 1993, hb $19.95, pp297, indexes. (Available in the UK from Midnight Books, Tel: 0273 671967.)

Corliss' incredible 'Sourcebook Project' rolls into its 13th volume, this being the second of three devoted to human anomalies. The formula of this series of ultimate Fortean reference books is now familiar: each topic is introduced by an assessment of its anomaly rating, followed by referenced examples – in this case, in the fields of chemistry and physics, health, bodily functions, internal structure and organs – ending with indexes of author, source, subject.

The only way to preview this remarkable work is to take a deep breath and rush through some headings: electric and magnetic people; anomalous human combustion; incorruption; nostril cycling; unusual objects in stomach; healing with electricity; limb regeneration; menstrual and other lunar cycles; astrology-type birth date correlations; coloured sweat; suspended animation; simultaneous deaths of twins; sleep oddities; epidemics and astronomical activity; longevity; AIDS- and cancer-related anomalies; the puzzle of pain and phantom limbs; anomalies of the bones, brain, eye, ear and neurological memory ... and many other subjects.

As working Forteans we find Corliss' compilations of original data-sources to be non-partisan and reliable, and an essential research tool. Every school and library should have this series.

Bob Rickard

MATERIALISATIONS

by Harry Boddington

Psychic Press, London, 1992, pb £6.95, pp116, plates, illus.

I have to confess that having little knowledge of Spiritualism I had always regarded it as slightly odd, so I expected this reprint from 1938 to be little more than a curiosity. Confronted by the quaint arcana of Spiritualist language, I wasn't disappointed: here are auras, ethers, rays, vibrations, Kilnascrenes and guides from beyond ... and the expected protests against sceptics, exposers and conjurers (some things never change!) There is also, of course, a strong message of survival of death and assistance from the otherworld. But having passed through the 'language barrier' I also have to confess that I found this little book on physical mediumship fascinating.

There's an obvious sincerity here – the argument is naturally one-sided and I can't buy the survivalist message – but there's also a laudable desire for investigation. The details are intriguing, with tales of mediums strapped down, caged, tied into muslin bags to prevent fraud (by Spiritualists, no less), weighed on scales and performing before flash cameras ... and still apparently producing 'psychoplasm', spirit-cloth, apports and fully materialised spirit-entities.

Frauds? Undoubtedly some were; but if only one was genuine, this is a phenomenon that deserves our attention. And if nothing else, this is certainly a worthy subject for the social and psychological study of human belief. Take it how you will: as an historical document, or a record of phenomena, or of human ingenuity and gullibility ... but do take a look anyway.

Steve Moore

THE HOLY PLACE

THE MYSTERY OF RENNES-LE-CHATEAU

by Henry Lincoln

Corgi, London, 1993, pb £4.99, pp176, photos.

"An immense geometric temple, stretching for miles across the landscape, a sparkling constellation of pentacles, circles and hexagons ... ", or just a load of old hogwash, fantasy and invention by a fading author trying to relive the glories of his bestseller *The Holy Blood and the Holy Grail?*

It has to be admitted Lincoln's book is very interesting, despite being sadly disjointed. The first half leads the reader up a series of blind alleys involving all the usual suspects (Priory of Sion, Knights Templar, etc.) before the second half unfurls an almost unrelated denouément detailing a series of quite fascinating natural and man-made terrestrial alignments in the Rennes-le-

MagWatch

This issue we turn the spotlight on the thriving occult/pagan magazine press (usually subscription only) which often contains material of considerable interest. Well-produced, enthusiastic, good-humoured and ranging from the weirdly serious to the seriously weird ...

AISLING is a Druid magazine with a strong historical interest; eg. the latest issue has material on 'Magic of the Druids and other Magic-workers in Celtic Ireland'. With a mix of new material and obscure reprint, it's consistently worth a look.

CHAOS INTERNATIONAL, like Chaos Magic itself, has broad interests, from the more traditional occult material such as Astral Projection to Satanism, Neo-decadence, pain. Always odd, sometimes surprising, occasionally baffling.

The **OCCULT OBSERVER**, with its colour covers and photos, is the most professional-looking of the bunch reviewed here. Non-denominational, it covers a wide field. No.4 has material on the Cosmic Mill, Hermes, Osiris, mazes, Cathars, magic in the formation of Surrealism, and Andy Collins' Orgone 93 project.

PAGAN NEWS combines news (both pagan and magickal) with articles, reviews and interviews. A little erratic of late, but No.36 had articles on Leo Taxil, 'inventor of Satanism', and the *iynx* magic wheel.

TALKING STICK, associated with a series of fortnightly talks in London, is probably the most consistently serious and well-written magazine in the field, again with a broad range of historical and contemporary articles. No.11 is a special thematic 'animals' issue, including Black Dogs. With a scholarly and disputatious letter-column.

Finally, a brief mention for **PSYCHIC NEWS**, now well past its 60th birthday and 3,000th issue. Weekly (how do they do it?), it's basically Spiritualist-oriented, but overlaps into psychic healing, clairvoyance and occasionally just plain weirdness. A little old-fashioned and strangely homely, it's truly a magazine from another world!

Steve Moore

■ *Aisling: PO Box 196, London, WC1A 2DY.* ■ *Chaos International: BM Sorcery, London, WC1N 3XX.* ■ *Occult Observer: 2 Tavistock Chambers, Bloomsbury Way, London, WC1A 2SE (Tel: 071 405 2120).* ■ *Pagan News: BM Grasshopper, London, WC1N 3XX.* ■ *Talking Stick: 117 Coteford Street, London, SW17 8MX.* ■ *Psychic News: Psychic Press, 2 Tavistock Chambers, Bloomsbury Way, London WC1A 2SE (Tel: 071 405 3340).*

Chateau area. The book ends with the construction of a huge edifice of speculation. "There must be no pursuit of 'possibilities', no drawing of hypothetical conclusions," says Lincoln. No indeed. Unfortunately what is already a brief book would become a large newspaper feature if Lincoln took his own advice. Still, for readers of his earlier works, this is probably a must.

There is probably enough material here to convince most doubters that Something Funny is going on at Rennes, even if the reader treats large chunks of what Lincoln says with appropriate scepticism. He is at his strongest when he gets out his ruler and compasses and starts drawing lines and circles on the map. His sense of awe and surprise at what the ancients constructed comes across strongly throughout the book. The Rennes temple is impressive, certainly, but not unique. *The Holy Place* is gripping in parts, vague and exaggerated in others. It's worth buying, but one wonders how much more he can squeeze out of this topic.

Richard Furlong

IN SEARCH OF THE NEANDERTHALS

by Christopher Stringer and Clive Gamble

Thames & Hudson, London. 1993, hb £18.95, pp247, index, bib, notes, illus, plates.

Like so many areas of research where the evidence is scanty and the subjects long gone, the study of Neanderthal man is riven with controversy. Were they direct ancestors of modern man, or were they replaced by our Cro-Magnon ancestors? Stringer and Gamble argue for the latter theory though, to their credit, they do give space to the proponents of the former. Still, there's far more here than just an academic argument.

This is a lively and absorbing account of both our knowledge of the Neanderthals, and the history of that knowledge, from their first discovery in 1856 to the present. Importantly, the authors look at how our conceptions of these early humans (as ignorant low-browed knuckle-draggers) shaped the way we research both them and human evolution generally. Only recently have these ideas begun to change, and we can now see the Neanderthals as a successful species that survived for 200,000 years, yet with very little cultural 'progress' or change.

Using both anthropological and archæological material, the authors attempt to build up a picture of Neanderthal life and physiology, habit and habitat, and eventual death and replacement. Yet they're also prepared to admit just how much we *don't* know about the subject, so the book has to be seen as a summary of what we know *so far*. On that basis, though, it seems to me to be a very good summary indeed, and well worth a look.

Steve Moore

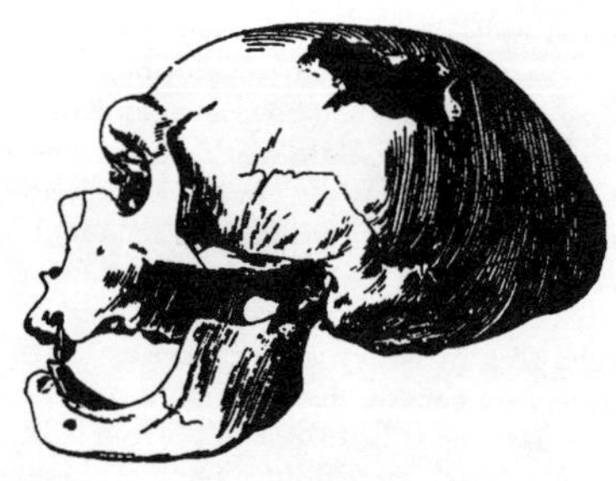

ALSO RECEIVED

THE SLI EFFECT compiled by Hilary Evans. Evans, one the most serious of Fortean researchers, has collected 77 accounts from people who say street light blink off whenever they pass, and, in connection with ASSAP, presents this analysis of the phenomenon. It is certainly a model of how research should be presented (great cover) – but is it, as I've heard suggested, a satire on the abstraction of sociological research? I can't tell. *$3.75 (US$7) by post, from ASSAP, 20 Paul St, Frome, Somerset BA11 1DX. 1993, pb, pp52.*

CROP CIRCLES: A MYSTERY SOLVED This is a new edition of the 1990 'classic' study by Jenny Randles and Paul Fuller. There is no sign or list of what may have been updated from the earlier text, but a new chapter tacked on to the end covers cerealogical developments between 1990 and early 1993. Still the best all-round overview outside of Schnabel's personalised chronicle. *Robert Hale, London. 1993, pb £6.99, pp256, plates, refs, index.*

WHERE SCIENCE & MAGIC MEET by Serena Roney-Dougal. If you want just one book to present the case for the New Age synthesis of traditional beliefs, intuitive and revealed knowledge, modern science and technology, and mystical philosophy, both personal and planetary, then this is the book you should read. Interdisciplinary discoveries in earth mysteries, the fairy faith, shamanism and natural magic, psychophysiology and meditation, and parapsychology are explained clearly and with scholarship. *Element Books, Dorset. 1991, pb £8.99, pp256, index, refs, notes, illus.*

THE TEMPLE: Meeting Place of Heaven and Earth by John M. Lundquist. The author claims to provide a *universal* key to understanding based almost entirely on Middle Eastern material (Mesopotamian, Egyptian and Judaic) with occasional reference to Central America and the Indo-Buddhist tradition. The result is one-sided and misleading, though the pictures are pretty. *Thames & Hudson, London, 1993, pb £6.95, pp96, 130 illus (15 in colour), bib.*

ATLANTIS: Lost Lands, Ancient Wisdom by Geoffrey Ashe. A short but excellent summary of the Atlantis mythos, with its resonances in 'Ancient Wisdom' and the lost 'Golden Age'. Plato, Donnelly, Blavatsky, Cayce – they're all here, and treated with great kindness, even if Ashe does sink Atlantis without trace. Lots of good illustrations. *Thames & Hudson, London, 1992, pb £6.95, pp96, plates, illus, bib.*

ULTIMA THULE, the Vanished Northern Homeland by Bernard King. The legend of Thule and its alleged influence on north European culture and thought. Discusses the early Greek descriptions, Norse magic, the 20th century German occult groups and their influence on Nazi ideology. Whether there's actually a body of 'Thulian doctrine' handed from antiquity seems arguable, though. *Asatru Folk Runic Workshop, 1992, pb £3.OO + 50p p+p, pp44, illus, bib. (Cheques to Freya Aswynn, BM Aswynn, London, WC1N 3XX).*

FEARFUL SYMMETRY: IS GOD A GEOMETER? At first sight, symmetry would appear the complete antithesis of chaos, but authors Ian Stuart and Martin Golubitsky reveal this is not so. In a meticulously clear and well-illustrated account, they subject the seemingly simple and familiar idea of symmetry to merciless scrutiny, revealing some unusual aspects. They concentrate on pattern-making and symmetry-breaking – the latter a phenomenon which they use to conjecture a very elegant origin for cropcircles. *Penguin, London. 1933, pb £6.99, pp287, index, bib, illus, plates.*

HECATE'S FOUNTAIN by Kenneth Grant. Anyone searching for evidence of the existence of alien beings should not forget to explore the realms of Hermetic thought and experimental occultism. Kenneth Grant, long-time writer in this field, had picked up on the possibility of entities who 'really do exist somewhere and at some time, and that they occasionally put in an appearance here on earth'. Rewarding reading for those who are on the right wavelength. *Skoob Books Publishing, London, 1992, hb £24.99 (USA $39.95), pp288, index, bib, illus.*

DOWSING: NEW LIGHT ON AN ANCIENT ART Author Tom Williamson supplemented his career as a geologist and geochemist with an extensive research into 500 years of commentaries, theorising, experiments and practice. He concludes by giving a dowser's overview of the 'earth energy' field, crop circles, and a wholistic interpretation that he calls 'geopsychology'. The curiosity is that with most crop circles turning out to be man-made, the dowsers are still getting reactions. A sensible and informed view of a maligned subject. *Robert Hale, London. 1993, hb £16.99, pp218, refs, bib, illus, plates, index.*

Janet Bord, Steve Moore, Bob Rickard, Ian Simmons

DEAR FT...

FAINTING GOATS

■ The American Tennessee Fainting Goat Association currently has about 100 members and slightly more than 1,000 goats registered. We generally hold a show in Boonville, Missouri, in September. Fainting goat contests were held once [see **FT58:18**], but so much flak was received from animal rights activists that it has not been done again. Two fainting goat organisations exist; the one in Iowa prefers black-and-white goats, while I tend to prefer brown ones. The ATFGA has no colour preference.

You might be interested in a story about General Patton's troops and fainting goats. In the 1930s, when Patton's tanks were on manoeuvres in Tennessee, they had occasion to drive past the farm of a man who owned a flock of fainting goats. When the goats saw the tanks, they immediately keeled over. The farmer, being a shrewd man, approached the Captain in charge and demanded payment from the Army for having killed his goats. It is said that he was paid several times, as each time the tanks went by, the goats fainted.

Todd L. Petersen
Minden, Nebraska

EDITORS' NOTE: *The Nervous News, The Official Publication of the American Tennessee Fainting Goat, is available from Pam Santorelli, 7300 Ridge Rd, Lockport, NY 14094, USA. Subscription plus membership of the ATFGA is $25 per annum outside the US.*

From a leaflet, we read: "Fainting Goats can be traced back to the 1880s to Marshall County, Tennessee. A man by the name of Tinsley drifted into town, bringing along a few goats and a sacred cow. No one knows where this man came from or where he went. He stayed long enough to help a farmer harvest a crop, marry a local woman, then leave. He sold his goats to a gentlemen by the name of R. Goode, who was fascinated with these goats. Tinsley also left his bride of only six months. He did take his sacred cow with him.

"From these first few goats, the Fainting Goat grew over the years. Many farmers kept them to save their sheep from coyote and dog attacks. After many years of sacrificing, the Fainters were almost extinct." Since the foundation of the two associations a few years ago (the ATFGA in 1987), the Fainters' future is assured.

FAX NOT FROM LIMBO

■ The fax received in Hong Kong ['Fax From Limbo' *FT70:7*] was an internationally used facsimile test document, known as the SLEREXE letter. It never was a real letter, but has been used as a test sheet for as long as I have been involved with fax machines (about seven years). Sorry, *South China Morning Post*, you've been scammed!

Slim Haines
Bromley, Kent

CROP CORRECTION

■ In your reply to Michael Glickman's letter about me – [**FT70:64**] – you say that I imply that all crop circles are man-made. For the record, I think there is a genuine but rare and relatively simple and rough circles phenomenon, which seems to be related both to wind vortices and UFOs (ie. luminous unidentified flying objects); although I think that humans account for most or all of the photographed post-1976 formations.

Jim Schnabel
Chevy Chase, Maryland

RATIONAL DEBATE

■ In your Magwatch [**FT69:61**] you say that IUR (International UFO Reporter) is "usually firmly pro-ET/'missing time' abductions" and now its editor "has allowed two critical articles" to appear in a recent issue. IUR and CUFOS (The Hynek Center for UFO Studies) have no editorial/corporate position on UFO origins or the reality status of abduction reports; our sole commitment is to rational, scientifically based inquiry and debate wherever they lead. We are, however, entirely unsympathetic to occult and/or conspiratorial theories about UFOs.

Jerome Clark
Canby, Minnesota

CHE IN THE CLOUDS?

■ I reckon that vision in the Italian clouds [**FT70:15**] isn't Christ at all, but Che Guevara. It's a pity no-one mistook the Cuban revolutionary for Christ while he was alive. Still, if Che is now appearing in the heavens, it's surely a sign for this Pope to curb his anti-radical strictures.

John Billingsley
Mytholmroyd, W.Yorkshire

BIRDS, SHEEP AND CREMATION ACCIDENTS

■ The report about crows who pecked out the eyes of sheep in Germany [*FT69:17*] reinforces my opinion that there is a fierce antipathy between birds and sheep. Of course, every sort of devilry can be expected from crows, but even a normally mild-tempered parrot can turn vicious when provoked by the presence of woolly gribblers, as the following extract shows.

"The Australian *kea*, a vegetarian parrot [..] became carnivorous with a particular addiction to the kidneys of grazing sheep, which it attacks with its powerful beak. It seems to have started the new habit by settling on the backs of sheep that had grown verminous and by feeding on their parasites, before it finally attacked the host itself." [Robert Eisler: *Man Into Wolf*, p123.]

The battle is not one-sided, however. On the Shetland island of Foula, sheep have been known to attack the nests of ground-nesting birds, biting off and eating their legs, wings and heads. (*Economist* 11 Feb 1989.)

As if crematorium operators didn't have enough to worry about – shrapnel from exploding heart pacemakers, toxic mercury vapour released from dental fillings, silicone from breast implants leaving gooey blobs – now they might also have to deal with UFO abductees whose bodies conceal artifacts of an alien technology. This is one of the implications of David Jacobs's interview [*FT69:27-29*], but for some reason he fails to acknowledge the possible danger. Is he hoping for a crematorium meltdown to validate his paranoia?

Brian Chapman
British Columbia, Canada

BIBLIOMANIA

■ I was interested to learn that Loren Coleman is a cryptozoologist "with eight books under his belt" [*FT69:53*]. Surely this must make walking and other physical activities rather difficult – or does he only keep the books there when he's sitting down?

James Nye
Isle of Wight

IT WAS CRAP

■ I am writing to correct the *Western Daily News* report you quoted about the mysterious oozing in the cellar of a Glastonbury shop [FT66:15]. The 'water' is in fact raw sewage. Complaints to the owner by the people living there resulted in the substance being pumped out when the Environmental Health Officer got involved – but it is seeping back in. Unfortunately for those renting rooms there, the fuse box is situated in the cellar. Replacing a blown fuse at the height of the flood involved paddling across on an upturned cupboard, like an Outward Bound course in Hell.

Mary Hallam
Somerset

Tom Jackson, putative Director of *The Haunted Billabong*

THE HAUNTED BILLABONG

■ I've done a bit of research on the history of Australian SF movies and discovered what must be the first SF movie ever made anywhere. It was called *The Haunted Billabong* and appears to have been about the strange mutilation of sheep on a station in Connabarabran. It was made in 1911 and was actually shot in the old Padstow Studios in Sydney, which have long since been demolished.

From what I can gather, the sheep were mutilated by visitors from outer space, and this is only revealed at the end of the movie. Before that, it was assumed that it was the work of rabid dingoes, but at the end you learn that a flying saucer had landed in the billabong and was using it as a base.

Needless to say, all surviving prints of the film have vanished, but I got this info from an old paper which reviewed the movie. I dug around a bit and found in the Archive a shot of the director, Tom Jackson. I think it's all that survives of the movie.

Bruce G. Kennedy
Yagoona, Australia

EDITORS' NOTE: *This is quite fascinating, and, if true, is probably the first association between animal mutilation and extraterrestrials. We are a bit suspicious of the term 'flying saucer' in this context. Can anyone throw additional light on this topic?*

BIRD RAINS

■ Today (10 June 1993), on the morning radio talk show of Gay Byrne, listener Antoinette Daly rang in to report that over the Bank Holiday Monday (8th June), she and neighbours in the Swords area of County Dublin found that hundreds of birds were plummeting from the sky – some dead, others seriously sick and barely able to move – into back gardens and on roadsides. Some were seen to fall in flight.

Being a Bank Holiday (NB: a different day from the British one) it was difficult to find any official to investigate the phenomenon, but the local TD (Member of the Irish Parliament) managed to contact a wildlife organisation in Ballsbridge, in the Dublin city area, to whom specimen birds were sent for examination. Although these tests have not been completed, the opinion was ventured that the cause might be poisoning. However, many different kinds of birds were involved – sparrows, pigeons, crows, finches, etc.

The area, normally rich in birds, is now very quiet, and the problem remains of disposing of hundreds of dead and dying birds. I have not yet seen any press coverage of this story. [For a similar event in Anglesey, see ***FT68:6***.]

Leslie Shepard
Blackrock, Co Dublin, Eire.

RANDI REPLIES

■ I would like to comment on your recent article 'Sex, Libels and Audio Tape' [***FT70***].

First, you state that I have "made a second career of discrediting those who claim to have supernatural powers, which group seems to include anyone he disapproves of." This is a sweeping statement for which no evidence exists. I personally disapprove of Nazis, terrorists and bigots, and they have never been my targets. My intention is to investigate claims of supernatural, occult or paranormal powers ... I have never yet failed to show that the claims I investigate do not stand such examination.

You quote Byrd's lawyer as saying that I failed "to disprove a scientific metal-bending experiment in which Byrd was involved." That is not true; I was not concerned with that activity of Byrd's. However, it most certainly was not 'scientific', and it was blown away by the investigation of others.

The jury did not say, as you report, that Byrd "had suffered humiliation, mental anguish, and damage to his reputation" as a result of my statements; they said exactly the opposite. My lawyer – she, not he – established that Byrd was a child molester, not by showing "that Byrd collected pornographic pictures" as you report, but by producing the victim herself to testify to that fact. There was never any attempt by me to "secure a conviction for molestation". I had nothing to do with the matter, which was handled entirely by the local police in Maryland. My only error was in saying, in good faith, that Byrd had been "convicted" of that crime ... I was wrong, and admitted it.

It was not Byrd's lawyer who "fought back by playing to the jury tape recordings of what appeared to be Randi in conversation with ... boys ... calling his number for sex." It was my lawyer who insisted on playing that tape, which had been made by me at the instruction of the investigating police to trap (successfully!) kids who were plaguing me with those calls; we got a conviction as a result. Byrd introduced the tape as a ploy, representing it as a 'tap' that had been placed secretly on my phone by police. The Inspector from the Post Office verified my statements in court [and] we de-fused Byrd's ploy by playing it for the jury. They left the room, and returned to give Byrd nothing. The blackmail attempt is still under investigation.

I am not being "forced to defend the fight against pseudo-science ... on behalf of Truth and us all", nor have I ever implied that. I have said that defending myself against numerous lawsuits has broken me financially. It is apparent that the paranormalists cannot fight me on the basis of my life work, so they strike at my reputation with lies, blackmail and misinformation. I ask you not to be a part of that system.

James Randi
Plantation, Florida

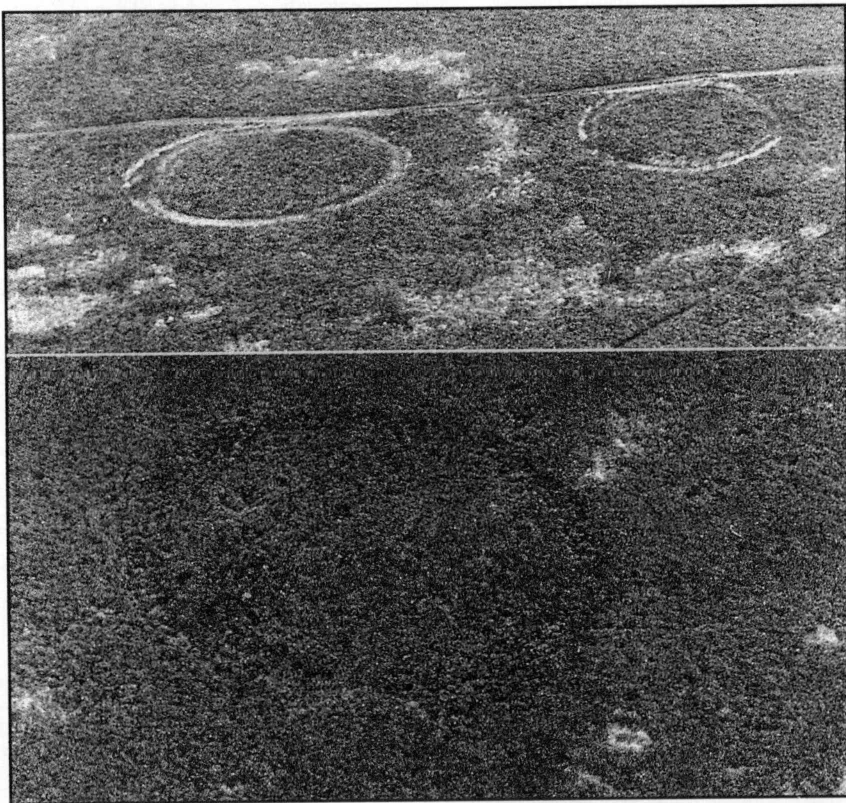

SHROUDED RETORT

■ It would be wearisome to refute Lynn Picknett's many inventions of what I am *supposed* to have said on the subject of the Turin Shroud [*FT70:54*], but one in particular takes the biscuit: "1492? Yes, the Shroud did disappear around then". Far from 'disappearing' around 1492, the Shroud had been acquired by Duke Louis of Savoy in 1453, and remained with the Savoy family, always well-documented, until ex-king Umberto of Savoy bequeathed the Shroud to the present Pope in 1983.

Despite the bigotry Ms Picknett claims, the British Society for the Turin Shroud has consistently offered a forum to serious detractors of the Shroud's authenticity, among them Dr Walter McCrone, who argues the Shroud to be a 14th century painting; Dr Michael Straiton, who argues it to be the image of a 14th century Crusader; and Professor Michael Tite, who supervised the carbon dating carried out in 1988.

As Ms Picknett's argument stood in 1991, when her followers tried to pressurise the Society into giving her a platform, her key source of information purported to come from within the mysterious 'Priory of Sion' of *Holy Blood, Holy Grail* infamy, and which could not be disclosed. Whatever the nature of the Turin Shroud, its origins will never be learned from such 'cloak-and-dagger' sources, and this is why the Society (small, and disinclined to promote itself), declined to invite her to speak.

Ian Wilson
Bristol

LEVITATION

■ Some years ago I was serving in the Royal Navy and was on leave in the Cameron Highlands, Malaya. An Indian magician and his assistant gave an impressive show of magic in the local 'village hall'. At the magician's insistence, the last trick was carried out on the padang ('village green'). There he erected a lathe and canvas 'box', similar to those sometimes seen at fairgrounds in this country. The sides could be rolled up to reveal the interior. Previously, a bamboo stick, about three feet long and six inches in diameter, had been used. The spectators were permitted to come within three or four yards of the 'box'.

Having an idea of what was to follow, I mentally recited the multiplication tables to counter any attempt at hypnotism. The magician, assistant and bamboo entered the 'box', the sides were lowered and after a brief interval raised, revealing the assistant horizontally balanced on the bamboo, which was in the middle of his back. Once again the sides were lowered. When raised, the assistant was apparently floating in mid-air. The magician passed a wooden hoop around his body from head to foot to 'prove' this. Had this trick (?) been performed on stage, I would have been prepared to accept it as a clever illusion; but in the open on an unprepared field, subject to relatively close inspection? Readers' comments are invited.

Mr R.N. Elliott
Nutley, Sussex

ODD RINGS

■ While researching for my book *Mysterious Calderdale* about oddities in West Yorkshire, David Green, a photographer from a local paper, sent me this ærial photograph, (above) which he had taken in the summer of 1989 from a helicopter above Rishworth Moors in West Yorkshire, not far from the Lancashire border, about 15 miles from Halifax. Neither he nor the pilot knew what to make of the rings, which they estimated to be around 25 to 30 feet in diameter. Jenny Randles suggested they might be grouse-shooting circles – but does that explain the circle in the foreground, which looks like a burn mark?

Andrew John Owens
Cambridge

JUNG'S DREAM

■ In the centre of Liverpool stands a small bust of the psychologist Carl Gustav Jung. It commemorates his famous (if wildly inaccurate) dream of Liverpool, in which he saw the city as "the pool of life". (Cf. *Memories, Dreams, Reflections*.)

Do any readers know of the circumstances in which this monument was erected? Or of any other instance, anywhere in the world, of a statue or public monument built to celebrate a dream?

Frank Roberts
Teddington

EDITORS' NOTE: *Ken Campbell has told us that the Liverpool monument was put there by the poet Peter O'Halligan in about 1976. We can't answer the second question, but look forward to feedback.*

noticeboard

EXCHANGE & MART

● **UFO NEWSCLIPPING SERVICE** keeps you up with the real 'close encounters'. Many fascinating UFO reports from the world's press are reproduced facsimile, along with news-wire items from the major agencies. UFONS is 20 foolscap pages monthly, with a Fortean section strong on cryptozoology. Foreign language reports are provided in translation. For information and sample pages, write today to: UFONS - Lucius Farrish, Route 1 - Box 220, Plumerville, AR 72127, USA.

● **THE SKEPTIC** takes an entertaining, rational and humourous look at pseudoscience and claims of the paranormal. Articles, reviews, columns, cartoons and much more. If you like FT you'll like The Skeptic. Sample issue £1.85; annual sub (6 issues) £12. The Skeptic, PO Box 475, Manchester M60 2TH.

● **NEW DIMENSIONS** the monthly magazine of esoteric information. The best for occult articles, qabalah, metaphysics, psychology, books and music reviews. Dynamic in origin. The best all-rounder. Magic at it`s best £1.25 UD, £175 overseas. Dept MS, 1 Austin Close, Irchester, Northants NN9 7AX.

● **WANTED** Anything relating to the visionary/occult artist AUSTIN OSMAN SPARE (AOS). In particular original artworks depicting satyrs, witches ghosts and elementals, astral and aboreal landscapes, self portraits etc. Good prices paid. Telephone 081 742 7347 FAX: 081 995 2961. Attention John Balance or write to: BM Codex London WC1N 3XX.

● **UFO NEWSCLIPPING SERVICE** keeps you up with the real 'close encounters'. Many fascinating UFO reports from the world's press are reproduced facsimile, along with news-wire items with a Fortean section strong on cryptyozoology. Foreign language reports are provided in translation. For information and sample pages, write today to: UFONS - Lucius Farrish, Route 1, Box 220, Plumerville, AR 72127, USA.

● **THE SKEPTIC** takes an entertaining, rational and humorous look at pseudoscience and claims of the paranormal. Articles, reviews, columns, cartoons and much more. Sample issue £1.95; annual sub (6 issues) £12. The Skeptic, PO Box 475, Manchester M60 2TH.

● **COMMUNE REGULARLY** into inner space? Mind machines take you places yet undreamt of. Money back if not mindblown. 2x 1st class stamps to: Highland Psionics, Scoraig Garve, Ross-shire 1V23 2RE.

● **ELECTRONIC SHAMANISM!** Mind machines and tapes to promote higher consciousness, lucid dreams, out-of-body experiences. Send two 24p stamps: to Aqualibrium, 3 East Albert Road, Liverpool L17 3BH.

● **UFO BOOKS, MAGAZINES, VIDEOS** Lists SAE to SR Stebbing, 41 Terminus Drive, Herne Bay, Kent, CT6 6PR.

● **THE ENIGMA** articles on horror, politics, psychology, the occult and religion, plus subjects enigmatic, for we are the ENIGMA. But not a puzzle. £1.50 UK, £2.00 overseas. Payment to: 1 Austin Close, Ircester Northants NN9 7AX

● **WHY IS** the public so irrational and ill-informed of this plant's properties? Mitigate with a little propaganda. Colourful designs screen-printed on top quality T-Shirts subtly convey 'Cannabis', 'Marijuana', 'Hashish'. Good buzz to wear: people study, then smile. Details: DogDooDesijn, PO Box 122 Kidderminster, Worcs DY11 6YZ.

● **CAULDRONS** Heavy black cast iron. In three sizes - 1.2 Gal capacity £37.50. 2.5 gal £45.00. 6 Gal £92.50. Credit cards accepted. Enquiries: John Ruse, 254 High Street, Canvey Island, Essex, 558 7SY Tel:0268 510608. Fax:0268 681008.

● **CANNIBALS & VAMPIRES** True cases detailed in "Everything You Wanted To Know About Cannibals and Vampires but Were Afraid to Ask". £7 from Greytown Enterprises, PO Box 3380, London, N10 3DZ.

● **STARKERS** Radical nudist magazine. New Summer issue for six first class stamps, subscription - four issues £5 cash or £6 cheque to: Islington Arts, Unit 423, 31 Clerkenwell Close, London, EC1R 0AT.

● **FREEDOM OF INFORMATION CAMPAIGN** Everything you need to know, but were never told about UFO's, aliens, cures, cover-ups, conspiracies. For free catalogue write to: Rev Anthony G. Pike, 141 Austen Rd, Sth Harrow HA2 0UU Middx. Tel: 081-426-8758.

● **GHOSTWATCH** needs YOUR experiences of the supernatural - however large or small - as they are happening NOW. Issue 1 FREE to anybody who responds to this advertisement. Please contact GHOSTWATCH, Eclipse, PO Box 54, Birkenhead, L43 7FD.

● **SPIDERWEB** limited edition T-shirt screen-printed with unusual repeating-fractal design. SAE to; 160 Stonor Road, Birmingham, B28 OQJ.

● **KHAT/QAT** The powerful coca like organic stimulant, aphrodisiac and dietary suppressant from the cradle of creation. Available fresh (approximately 3.5 oz) at £6.50 or as MIRAH tea £2.65. Both 40p P&P. Send cheque/p.o`s to KHAT at 95, Ditchling Road, Brighton, East Sussex. BN1 4SE.

● **MIDNIGHT** is a new cyclopean horror magazine that enters dimensions of psychological fear - the world of the nightmare. Strickly for the connoisseur. £2.50 cheques PO's to: New Dimensions, Dept 666, 1 Austin Close, Irchester, Northants NN9 7AX.

EVENTS

● **PUBLICISE YOUR EVENT HERE FREE** Fax us details on 081 552 5466.

● **PSYCHIC QUESTING** special conference at Conway Hall, Red Lion Sq, London WC1 - 6 Nov 1993 - tickets £9 and details from SKS, 20 Paul St, Frome, Somerset BA11 1DX - Tel: 0393 451777.

● **FOLKLORE SOCIETY EVENTS** Katherine Briggs Lecture by Dr Ruth Finnegan 'The Poetic and the Everyday', 9 Nov 1993 at University College London. For details of events, phone Steve Roud at the Folklore Society: 071 380 7095 (messages 071 387 5894).

● **DOUBLE LECTURE** ASSAP presents two lectures for the price of one (£4) on 27 Nov 1993 at Conway Hall, Red Lion Sq, London WC1, at 3pm. Jack Gale on 'Sacred Greenwich', and Ralph Noyes on the latest 'Crop Circles', more controversial than ever! Pay on door, send to ASSAP, 31 Goodhew Road, Croydon CR0 6QZ, or phone 0373 451777 for details.

● **TEMS (ASSAP)** covers S.W. London and Surrey. Meetings: 2.30pm (& tea): Sun 31 Oct, Lynn Picknett - "The Turin Shroud". Sun 21 Nov, David Percy - "The Avebury Connection". For prog ring 081-979 3148/542 3110.

● **BUFORA LONDON LECTURES:** Sat 6 Nov: Northern contact cases (Arthur Tomlinson). Sat 4 Nov: Circles video evening (John Macnish). 6.30pm Kings college London, Campden Hill Rd. W8. Tel: 081-979-3148.

BOOKMART

● **JONATHAN WOOD-LITERATURE & PRIVATE WRITINGS** Anything from Aleister Crowley to Arthur Machen and Ralph Chubb. Catalogues and No obligation booksearch. Write for latest catalogue: J.Wood, BM Spellbound, London, WC1N 3XX.

● **MIDNIGHT BOOKS** - Quality secondhand books on all aspects of the unexplained. SAE for 32 page catalogue: Steven Shipp, Midnight Books, The Mount, Aserton Road, Sidmouth, Devon, EX10 9BT. (0395) 515446

● **MILLENNIUM BOOKS** 2nd hand books on UFOs, and mysteries weird and wonderful. For free list, write, fax, phone - 9 Chesham Road, Brighton, Sussex BN2 1NB.- 0273 671967

● **EXCALIBUR BOOKS** New, secondhand and imported titles on folklore, paranormal and UFOs. Free lists - 1 Hillside Gardens, Bangor, Co Down BT19 6SJ, N.Ireland. (0247 458579)

● **MYSTERIES** old & new - we have the books! Abductions to yetis, via the New Age. Send 6x1st class stamps for 150 page catalogue. THE INNER BOOKSHOP (FT) 111 Magdalen Rd, Oxford OX4 1RQ.

● **PHENOMENAL BOOKS** catalogues of secondhand books on all kinds of anomalies! Write to: Phenomenal Books, 14 Gresham Rd, Thornton-Cleveleys, Blackpool FY5 3EE. Or tel 0253 854617 any evening.

● **SPACELINK BOOKS** Since 1967 Britain's leading stockist off UFO and Crop Circle books and magazines, plus wide range of Fortean titles. Free lists - Lionel Beer, 115 Hollybush Lane, Hampton, Middx TW12 2QY. Tel 081-979 3148.

● **FREE BOOKSEARCH** 'Wants lists' Welcome. No obligation to buy. Catalogue of current stock available on request. Write to Carcosa Books, 3 Arundel Grove, Perton, Wolverhampton, Staffs, WV6 7RF or tel 0902 758977.

● **UBIK** for Leeds' best selection of Fortean/Occult second-hand books. Catalogue available soon (SAE). 5A The Crescent, Hyde Park Corner, Leeds 6. Open 10-6 Mon-Sat. Also SF, Lit, etc.

MISC

● **INTERESTED IN A CREED OF IRON?** Read THE ODIN BROTHERHOOD (£6.95) from Mandrake Press, Ltd, Essex House, Thane, OX9 3LS.

● **WELSH HOLIDAY COTTAGE** Self-catering accomodation in historic North Wales town of Denbigh. for further details , contact Janet Bord, Melysfen, Llangwm, Corwen, Clwyd LL21 0RD. Tel: 049 082 472. Fax 049 082 321.

● **SEND ME ANYTHING** I don't care what, just send it. POB 341349 Los Angeles, CA 90034-9349 USA.

● **UNEMPLOYED MALE** 21, looking for Fortean related work in the West Yorkshire area. Write to: John Travis, 12 Lilac Ave, Thornes, Wakefield, WF2 7RY.

● **ALL ELECTRICAL REPAIRS** domestic - industrial - marine - large or small, including computer systems setup, configured & serviced - 24hr 7day service. Tel: 081 345 6789 (quote call sign F5730). No extra charge for evenings or weekends.

RESEARCH & HELP

● **WANTED** expert dowser. Must have proven track record. Target large, stone box in earth mound. As trial run. Contact M.T.B, 3 Tydraw Place, Penylan, Cardiff, CF2 5HF.

● **FORTEAN PICTURES** The Fortean Picture Library is a self-funding project for the rescue and preservation on of valuable documentary material, photographs and drawings etc. If you have anything of this nature, let FPL look after it. 50% of any revenue from the commercial use of the material (in books etc) comes to you. FPL covers all expenses from its half. Contact Janet Bord, FPL, Melysfan, Llangwm, Corwen, Clwyd, Wales LL21 0RD. Fax: 049 082 321.

● **SIMULACRA** Examples of symbolic geography (shapes on maps suggesting people, things, etc) sought by John Robert Colombo, 42 Dell Park Avenue, Toronto M6B 2T6, Canada. All correspondence acknowledged.

● **IMAGINARY FRIENDS** Accounts and references needed, especially personal experiences - write me in confidence: Andy Fish, 23 Brittany Ave, Ashby-de-la-Zouch, Leics LE65 2QY.

● **STAR IN YOUR OWN REPORT ON TV** 'THE BIG BREAKFAST' is inviting any FT reader who has an outrageous, new or theory about the paranormal; an unusual demand, beef, or need; a bizarre pet; an out-of-this-world habitat; a world-shattering discovery; etc - contact Myfanwy Moore, 'The People Report', Planet 24, Norex Court, Thames Quay, 195 Marsh Wall, London E14 9SG - or phone 071 712 9300 ext 313. This is your chance to be famous for a few minutes and help plug FT at the same time.

For credits for this issue see page 20.

HAWKWIND

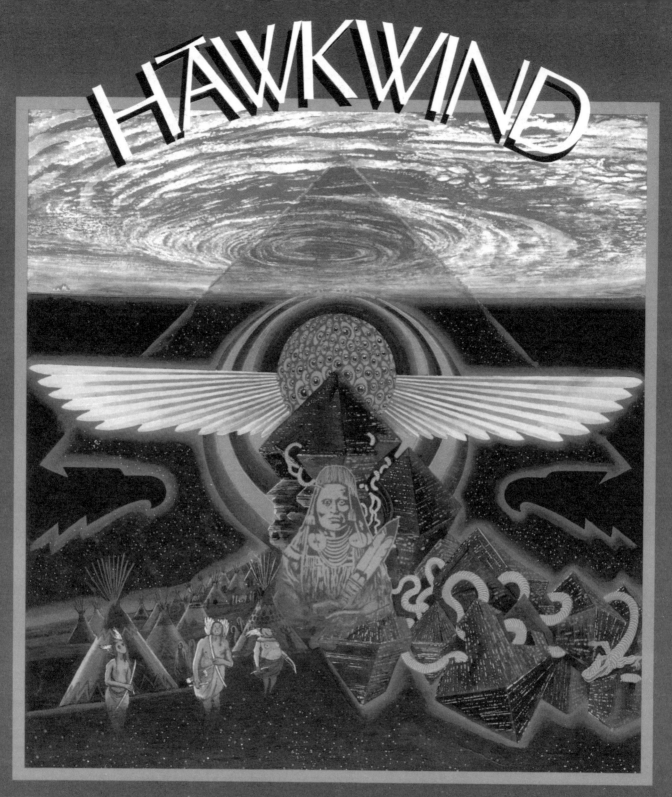

IT IS THE BUSINESS OF THE FUTURE TO BE DANGEROUS

new album out 25.10.93

CD: ESSCD 196 • cassette: ESSMC 196 • double album: ESDLP 196

CD includes 12 page booklet and special picture disc.

Double vinyl is in gatefold sleeve and a limited edition of only 3000 !!

HAWKWIND EUROPEAN TOUR STARTS 5TH NOVEMBER

SPECIAL GUESTS ON THE TOUR BEAUTIFUL PEOPLE (new album ' If 60's were 90's ' ESSCD/MC 200)

See press for details

NUMBER 72

UK £2
USA $4.95

FORTEAN TIMES

THE JOURNAL OF STRANGE PHENOMENA

THE BIG SLEEP

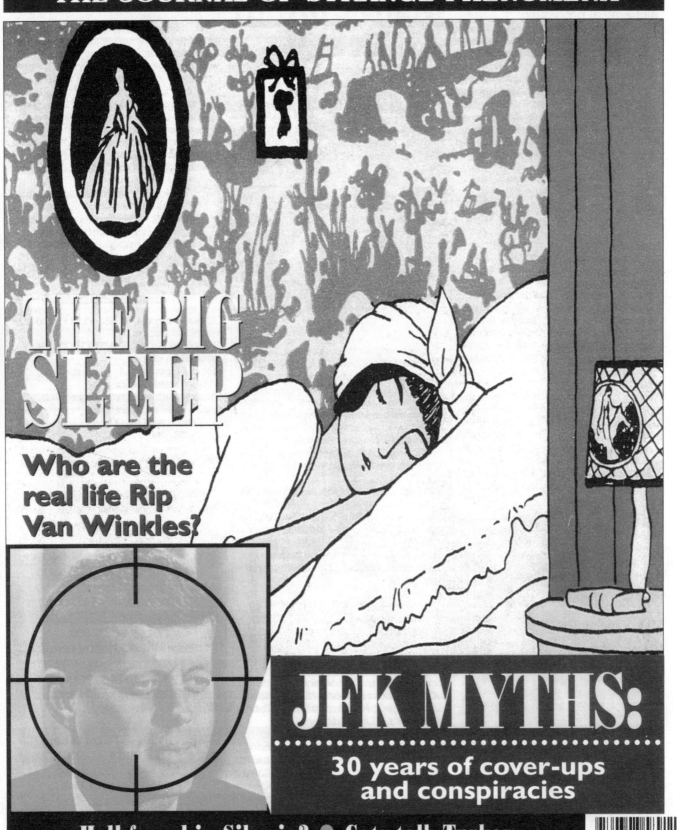

Who are the real life Rip Van Winkles?

JFK MYTHS:

30 years of cover-ups and conspiracies

Hell found in Siberia? • Cats talk Turkey
Thai nipple enigma • Satanic abuse update • Born again?

ADVERTISEMENT

WEHL Reveal Secret Recreational Drugs

Whole Earth Herbs Laboratory was established in 1982. Since then they have carefully researched over 30 different proven psycho active herb and alchemical preparations.

Up until this actual advertisement most of the WEHL range of products were only revealed when one ordered from their range of Marijuana like herbal smoking mixtures. New and exclusively for Fortean Times readers, WEHL proudly present their 100's range of Legal herbal recreational and ritual products.

Cloudswept is a combination of a stimulant and a sedative herb. Our first exclusive mixture was acclaimed by the LCC's Hookah as 'an unforgettable Buzz'. 'Highs seemed endless and controlled'. A rare psychoactive extract from Fiji is sprayed over 'Cloudswept' to create 'Rococan' .

The result is a smooth taste, an enhanced mellow high with the subtle buzz of the alchemical liquid. The mixture has up to 50% sprayed on it as opposed to a maximum of 10% sprayed on filter tip cigarettes. The final development in a line of Nicotene-free and non-addictive Herbal high alternatives to marijuana was a completely new mixture of the five very best psycho-active herbs. Formulated for a maximum 'high' with 5% mint (not menthol) for a smooth taste. The result, known as 'Yuba Gold' is an astonishing success. Why be illegal?!

Tested and proven by clients of whom 99.9% declined a refund. Testimonials of complete satisfaction regularly arrive as do multiple and repeat orders.

Exclusive to WEHL, Eclipse Cigarettes contain a similar formula to Yuba Gold with Yellow paper and marble effect filter. Available as four cellophane packets of twenty Tipped. These very rare world-wide herbs are reduced to a fine smokeable mixture. Beware of inferior imitations which will disappoint. WEHL is the only company in the world to currently produce herbal psycho-active cigarettes. Unlike THC in Cannabis, no tolerance builds up to our herbal highs. Just one cigarette required.

WEHL PSYCHOACTIVE BOTANICAL ALCHEMY RESIN POWDER LIQUID AND SEEDS

Catylist is a Stimulant/Aphrodisiac powder taken with black coffee. A mild cocaine-like effect. Costs £8 plus £2 p&p is £10 for 20g. Special offer for limited period only 40g for £15 all inclusive.

Pipe Dreams is an alternative to Opium. It is milder yet just as dreamy. Labour intensive process makes resin similar in taste, smell and texture. Pipe Dreams costs £10 plus £2 p&p. £12 for 10g. Smoke or eat.

Supana seeds are from a tropical jungle. A natural stimulant, it quickens perceptions, excellent for long drives. Costs £10 plus £2 p&p is £12 for 20g. New phiels 10 x 15ml wine, 1g Supana, 5m vitamin E - £12 inclusive.

Fijian Fantasy is a green alchemical liquid extract. Using alcohol extraction methods, no water-soluble alphapyrones are produced. These are then re-dissolved in brandy. Small amounts produce euphoria. More can create auditory and visual hallucination. An excellent aphrodisiac as warm emotions are generated. Narcotic numbing effect. Fijian Fantasy cost £12 plus £3 p&p is £15 per 100ml.

Blue Heaven seeds contain one microgram of LSA (a naturally occuring LSD-like structure) per seed. Five grammes equal approx 125 seeds. Effects are an LSD-like experience lasting 6 to 12 hours. Blue Heaven seeds are £10 plus £2 p&p is £12 for 10g.

Cloudswept is £6.45 (add £1.55 p&p) - total £8 per oz
Rococan is £8.95 (add £2.05 p&p) - total £11 per oz
Roco Cigs are £11.45 (add £2.55 p&p) - total £14 per 50
Yuba Gold is £10.85 (add £2.15 p&p) - total £13 per oz
Eclipse are £19.90 (add 4.10 p&p) - total £24 (4 x 20's)

Guaranteed psycho-active and legal. All sales are final. Sent by plain cover in 7-14 days. Write clearly please. Mail order only. Cheques/PO's payable to Whole Earth Herbs Laboratory. International: Eurocheques welcome. Sterling only. Add 20% for Air Mail (8-10 days). Exchange rate US$2 to £1. Checks add 20%. Literature and trade names copyright owned by WEHL 1993. Not sold for any medicinal purpose. For ritual use only.

WEHL (Dept FT2), 103 High Street, Sawston, Cambridge CB2 4HL England
Tel: (0223) 833343.
VAT reg no 538 5999/6

ALL PRICES INCLUSIVE OF VAT

Contents

Issue 69 June/July 1993

P30 KARMAPA CHAOS

P38 CROP STAR

HOW STRANGE ARE YOU?
Complete our pull-out questionnaire and you could win the amazing AMSTRAD PDA 600!

4 EDITORIAL

Fortean exhibition plans ● Cold Fusion cover-up ● 'Wacopalypse'

5 STRANGE DAYS

● Indian Forteana ● Japanese transfixed duck ● A new monkey ● Pig attacks ● Telecom Terror ● Electrocuted cows ● Coutts Bank haunted ● Cross dressing 'General' ● Egyptian hysteria ● Bleeding statue

21 PHENOMENOMIX

HUNT EMERSON's humorous look at the world

23 HOT STUFF

CHRIS TINSLEY reviews recent advances in Cold Fusion research, which looks set to consign conventional power generation to the dustbin.

27 THE FT INTERVIEW: DAVID JACOBS

TIM COLEMAN talks to the alien abduction researcher from America (not to be confused with the veteran British DJ).

30 GOLDEN CHILD

KARMA TENDZIN DORJE delves into the intrigue surrounding the enthronement of the new Karmapa in Tibet.

34 PHANTOM DINER

TONY CLARK recalls a remarkable meal in an Iranian restaurant which later vanished without trace.

37 PICK OF THE CROPS

The Fortean Times Field Guide to English Crop Circle Hoaxers compiled by JIM SCHNABEL

42 FROM OUR FILES

● THE CASE OF THE MISSING MOA: Recent sightings in New Zealand
● DEADLY ALCHEMY: The rumours about red mercury
● UNEARTHED: Mini mammoths and ancient footprints
● HARD TO SWALLOW: Cannibalism in China and Japan
● DIARY OF A MAD PLANET: Weather watch Feb/March'93
● THE MIA PHOTO MYSTERY: Fat Russians mistaken for US airmen
● SECRET COUNTRY : Cerne Abbas, Dorset

53 FORUM

● Mike O'Neill ● Colin Wood ● Ralph Noyes ● Loren Coleman

59 REVIEWS

● The Matter Myth ● Demons, Doctors and Aliens ● Robin Hood ● Arktos ● The Goddess Hekate ● Fire in the Sky

63 LETTERS

● Largest fish clarification ● Another face on Mars ● The age of the Earth ● The face(s) in the window ● Von Däniken

66 NOTICEBOARD

Fortean meetings, lectures, events, products and offers

Cover by Hunt Emerson

WHY 'FORTEAN'?

CHARLES FORT (1874-1932)

Fortean Times is a bi-monthly magazine of news, reviews and research on all manner of strange phenomena and experiences, curiosities, prodigies and portents, formed in 1973 to continue the work of the iconoclastic philosopher CHARLES FORT. Fort was sceptical about scientific explanations, observing how scientists argued for and against various theories and phenomena according to their own beliefs, rather than the rules of evidence. He was appalled that data not fitting the collective paradigm was ignored, suppressed, discredited or explained away (which is quite different from explaining a thing).

Fort was perhaps the first to speculate that mysterious lights seen in the sky might be craft from outer space. He coined the term 'teleportation' which has passed into general usage through science fiction. His dictum "One measures a circle beginning anywhere" expresses his philosophy of Continuity and the 'doctrine of the hyphen', in which everything is in an intermediate state between extremes. He had notions of the universe-as-organism and the transient nature of all apparent phenomena. Far from being an over-credulous man, Fort cut at the very roots of credulity: "I cannot accept that the products of minds are subject matter for beliefs ... I conceive of nothing, in religion, science, or philosophy, that is more than the proper thing to wear, for a while."

Fort was born in Albany, New York, in 1874 into a family of Dutch immigrants. Beatings by a tyrannical father helped set him against authority and dogma, and on leaving home at the age of 18 he hitch-hiked around the world to put some "capital into the bank of experience." At 22 he contracted malaria, married his nurse and settled down to 20 years of impoverished journalism in the Bronx. During this time he read extensively in the literature of science, taking notes on small squares of paper in a cramped shorthand of his own invention, which he filed in shoe boxes.

In 1916, when he was 42, Fort came into a modest inheritance, just enough to relieve him of the necessity of having to earn a living. He started writing *The Book of the Damned*, which his friend, the novelist Theodore Dreiser, bullied his own publisher into printing in 1919. Fort fell into a depression, burnt all his notes (which numbered some 40,000) as he had done a few years earlier, and in 1921 set sail for London, where he spent eight years living near the British Museum (39 Marchmont Street) and wrote *New Lands* (1923). Returning to New York, he published *Lo!* in 1931 and *Wild Talents* in 1932, shortly before he died. He left 60,000 notes, now in the New York Public Library.

THE GANG OF FORT
EDITORS:
Bob Rickard & Paul Sieveking
CONTRIBUTING EDITORS:
Steve Moore,
Mike Dash & Ian Simmons
© Fortean Times December 1993 – January 1994 ISSN 0308 5899

EDITORIAL ADDRESS
Fortean Times:
Box 2409, London NW5 4NP, UK.
Tel & Fax: 071 485 5002 or 081 552 5466.

CAVEAT
The opinions of contributors and interviewees are not necessarily those of the editors. FT itself has no corporate view except to bring the widest range of interpretations to stimulate discussion.

SUBMISSIONS
Submissions are invited of suitable articles, news, art, cartoons, letters and reviews. Preliminary discussion with the editors is advisable. Text can be submitted on floppy disks, but check with the editors first. Submissions may be edited. FT assumes no responsibility for submissions, but all reasonable care will be taken while they are in FT's possession. Requests for return of material should be accompanied by stamped addressed envelope.

CLIPPINGS
All clippings, references, etc, should be identified by source, date and clipster's name. Mail or fax them to the editorial address (above).

SUBSCRIPTIONS - UK
One year (6 issues). £12. Two years (12 issues) £20. For payment and inquiries by phone, ring FREEPHONE 0800 581409. Major credit cards accepted – or make cheques/ money orders payable to: **JOHN BROWN PUBLISHING, and send to Freepost SW6096, Frome, Somerset BA11 1YA.**

SUBSCRIPTIONS - OVERSEAS
One year (6 issues). £15 or US$30. Two years (12 issues) £26 or US$50. For payment or inquiries by phone, ring (+44) 373 451777. Major credit cards accepted – or make sterling cheques/ money orders drawn upon a London bank payable to: **JOHN BROWN PUBLISHING, and send to Fortean Times, 20 Paul Street, Frome, Somerset BA11 1DX, UK.**
US subscribers can deel direct with our American subscription agent, Fenner Reed & Jackson, PO Box 754, Manhasset, NY 1130. Tel: 516 627 3836, Fax: 516 627 1972.

US POSTMASTER
Fortean Times (ISSN 0308 5899) is published every two months for US$30.00 per year. Second Class postage pending at Manhasset NY. Please send address changes to Fenner, Reed & Jackson Inc. at PO Box 754, Manhasset, NY 11030.

ADVERTISING ENQUIRIES
DISPLAY or CLASSIFIED:
contact **Ronnie Hackston** or **Dan Squirrell** at John Brown Publishing Ltd: The Boathouse, Crabtree Lane, Fulham, London SW6 6LU, UK.
Tel: 071 381 6007 or Fax: 071 381 3930.

PUBLISHER
John Brown Publishing Ltd, The Boathouse, Crabtree Lane, Fulham, London SW6 6LU, UK.
Tel: 071 381 6007 or Fax: 071 381 3930.
Managing Editor: Fiona Jerome.
Publisher: Vic Lime.

DISTRIBUTION
UK trade distribution by UMD, Castle House, 37/45 Paul Street, London EC2A 4PB Tel:. 071-490-2020 Fax: 071-490-1239 USA newsstand distribution by Eastern News Distributors Inc, 2020 Superior St, Sandusky, OH 44870, USA.

Printed in the UK.

Bob Rickard

Paul Sieveking

Sleeping Beauties

● The main feature this issue concerns unusually prolonged sleep. Traditionally, this has been classified as an anomaly of sleep along with comas, sleeping sickness and narcolepsy, but our brief research of the sparse historical information on the subject suggests that most cases would be diagnosed differently today. They were more akin to trance and accompanied by phenomena familiar from studies of hypnoid states: cataleptic rigidity of limbs; suggestibility; multiple personalities and inspired oration; enhancement of the senses to ESP-like levels; suppression of normal body functions; immunity to pain often coexisting with hypersensitivity; and selective amnesia. Some of these 'Sleeping Beauties' might be distantly related to the self-victimisers and confabulators discussed in our previous two issues.

● Get your forward planners out! The first annual *Fortean Times Convention* will be held over the weekend 18-19 June 1994 at the Students' Union Building of London University, Malet Street, London W1. Each of the two days will be divided into two sessions ... a selection of speakers and topics in the morning and a specific theme in the afternoon: Near Death Experiences (18th) and Spontaneous Human Combustion (19th). Running concurrently will be a continuous show of rare film and TV Forteana, a special seminar each day, and a roomful of dealers in books, videos and probably alien artifacts, T-shirts etc. A special discount on admission will be offered to subscribers – more information and form next issue.

● We are pleased to announce an improvement in our service to our North American subscribers. Each issue will be specially freighted to our new US subscription agent – Fenner, Reed & Jackson, Box 754, Manhasset, NY 11030; phone: (516) 627 3836 or fax (516) 627 1972 for direct insertion into the US postal system, which should greatly improve on the present notoriously slow shipping times. As an added convenience, readers will be able to remit directly to this agent.

● We are sure that readers will join with us in wishing two of our friends and colleagues a speedy recovery: Cecilia Boggis following a stroke, and Loren Coleman after falling some 20 feet onto his back while rock climbing.

● **COMPETITION.** Beginning this issue, we plan to offer copies of our lead review (it might be a book, video, or something else appropriate) to the first three correct answers to a simple question. This issues's question is: In which country is the iron pillar, allegedly immune from rust, which Boris Yeltsin visited recently? Answers (by mail or fax to the editorial address), must reach us before February 1994. The first three correct answers, drawn at random from a suitable container, will receive *Forbidden Archeology* by Michael Cremo and Richard Thompson.

The Editors

Paul Sieveking

STRANGE DAYS

16 pages of worldwide weirdness

SANTA STUCK

The would-be burglar stuck for over an hour in this Oceanside, California, chimney, just below the Christmas stockings, is an extremely embarrassed (and sooty) Frank Morales. He was discovered by Lawrence and Margie Beavers when they came downstairs to investigate shouting and banging that woke them at 2:00am on 4 January 1993. At first the Beavers could not figure out where the anguished cries were coming from. "Where are you?" Margie called out. "Up your chimney", came the reply. Police and firemen were called and they had a good laugh as they took souvenir pictures before demolishing the brickwork to get the dangling man out of his predicament. Morales, described as a 42-year-old transient, is quite a surrealist ... not content with his poor imitation of that better-known red-clad transient and seasonal housebreaker, he told police he "dove into the chimney" to escape pursuit and then decided to steal the piano. "Ho! Ho! Ho!" chortled the police as they charged him with burglary and resisting arrest. *[AP] 5 Jan 1993.*

EXTRA! EXTRA!

Fortean headlines from newspapers around the world

5 CHINESE CAPTURED IN DUBLIN MOUNTAINS
Irish Independent, 19 July 1979.

HEAVEN IS...A WARM COW PAT
Sun, 6 May 1992.

FROG GLANDS PUT DOCTORS JUMP AHEAD OF INFECTION
D.Telegraph, 9 May 1992.

PIGEONS GET SUNSTROKE
Nottingham Evening Post, 29 May 1992.

TEACHER FIRED AS STUDENT CASTRATES PIG WITH HIS TEETH
Bangkok Post, 21 June 1992.

MASSIVE BLACK HOLE FOUND IN SKY
Cleveland Plain Dealer, 10 July 1992.

INCIDENCE OF FATAL ASIAN FISH BUG ROCKETS
China Daily, 10 Oct 1992.

POLICE 'HAMPERED BY RULES'
D.Telegraph, 17 Dec 1992.

THE FAR SIDE By GARY LARSON

"So, Professor Jenkins! . . . My old nemesis! . . . We meet again, but this time the advantage is mine! Ha! Ha! Ha!"

TERMINATION CLAWS

It was the kind of story we at FT adore - it concerned the killing of Grady Stiles, a professional sideshow freak, allegedly by his wife Mary and her son Harry Newman. His relations are accused of hiring their neighbour Chris Wyant to shoot him at his trailer-home at Gibsonton in Florida. Stiles earned a living from his deformed hands which were shaped like two massive pincers and posed as 'The Lobster Boy' in a large fake aquarium.

Unfortunately Stiles, no boy at 55, had a mean disposition and regularly beat his family. In support of their plea of self-defence, all three accused brought forward a truly bizarre line-up of character witnesses ... 'The Bearded Lady' testified that 'Lobster Boy' was a 'cruel tyrant'; the 'Fire Eater' said Stiles didn't know his own strength; and 'The Alligator Man' told of Stiles' alcoholic binges, during which he loved to 'pen cans of beer with his pincers'.

In the end a mis-trial was ruled - because a sheriff's deputy mentioned a lie-detector test which was not admissible as evidence - and a new trial was set for October 25th in Tampa. *USA Today, 22 July; D.Mirror, 23 July 1993.*

MEKONG MONSTER

Rumours have recently been flying around Vientiane, capital of Laos, that a five-headed dragon has been seen repeatedly in the Mekong River. This mottled green, brown and yellow reptile breathes no fire, measures 15 feet from head to tail, sees through five pairs of shiny black eyes and finds children most appetising. Few people acknowledge seeing the dragon themselves; most sightings are attributed to a friend of a friend. Some say that the rumours are based on a type of catfish that grows up to ten feet long and is considered a delicacy. Drought lowered the river enough in 1992 to bring these normally deep-dwelling fish to the surface. *Wall Street Journal, 21 Oct 1992.*

BALLOON WONDER

Pupils at the primary school in Nantymoel, Mid Glamorgan, Wales, released 3,000 helium-filled balloons in a fund-raising event on 23 June. Each had a card tied to its neck with the school's address and the name of the pupils who had released it. Not long after, Debbie Watkins and Stuart Jones, aged 10, received a letter on headed notepaper from the Shangri-la Hotel in Beijing, postmarked 28 June, from hotel worker Cheung Xin.

The balloon had fallen to earth in the Chinese capital, 5,053 miles away, after five days' flight. It would have had to average over 40mph. It is possible that it rose to its equilibrium height of about 30,000ft, where it might have been propelled by jet streams travelling up to 200mph. A Met Office official was sceptical. "An ordinary party balloon would almost certainly be unable to withstand heights of 30,000ft, where it would expand several times", he said. The longest reported journey by a helium-filled toy balloon is 10,000 miles, from Dobbs Ferry, New York, to Wagga Wagga, Australia, in 1982. *D.Mail, 6 July 1993.*

SIMULACRA CORNER

Like something from the *Hellraiser* films, two strange faces – like bizarre human masks set into a triangular plate of bone – were dredged up by startled fishermen trawling for sole off Newfoundland's Cape St George in October 1980. Measuring 32cm from top to bottom and 29cm across, they puzzled many, and it being just before Hallowe'en, disturbed them too. "It's not plastic, or carved, or wood," said Sgt Lorne Goode of the Mounties. "I've checked with local fishermen and they haven't seen anything like them. They say it's not a fish, and they're definitely not human." Later, the bones were positively identified by John Maunder, curator of Natural History at the museum in St Johns, as "merely the skulls of bluefin tuna, viewed from above".

We are always glad to receive pictures of spontaneous forms and figures, or any curious images or scenes. If you have one, send it to the editorial address – with SAE – and we'll pay a fiver for any we use.

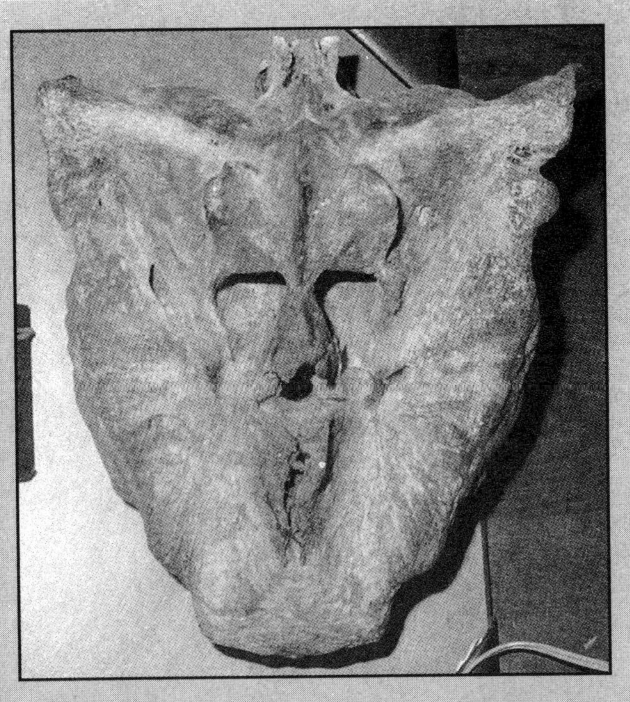

CRAPSICLE MISSES COP

Southend's top policeman narrowly escaped injury when a huge lump of green ice plummeted through the roof of his house on 12 July 1993. Chief Supt. Michael Benning, 46, was woken when the icy missile hit a metal support joist in the attic above his bedroom. "The sound was something like a loud explosion ... The ice shattered into pieces when it hit the joist. Had it been just a few inches over it could have smashed through to the rest of the house."

The immediate assumption of victim and reporter was that the ice had fallen from an aeroplane's leaky chemical toilet, so Mr Benning was said to be waiting for aviation investigators to find the flying culprit. It's our prediction that, despite his authority, he'll have a long wait. To our knowledge, no airline has ever admitted liability for any fall of ice. *Leicester Mercury, 13 July; Southend Standard Recorder, 15 July 1993.*

INDIAN TRAGEDY

A contemporary version of *Romeo and Juliet* played out in Andra Pradesh state in Southern India this year. A village astrologer told Subba Rao, 20, and his bride Nagalakshmi, 18 (or maybe 14), that although they were married they had to wait more than six months, 'until the stars were auspicious on 16 September', before they could have sex.

With a month to go, the overheated Rao feigned suicide by smearing granules of pesticide on his lips in order to make his bride's family relent and allow them to make love. He was dragged off to the nearest clinic in Sattupalli, six miles away, and was discharged in perfect health in the evening.

Believing her husband was dying, the besotted Nagalakshmi swallowed the remaining pesticide and her family rushed her to the Sattupalli clinic as her husband was returning by bus. By the time they arrived, the doctor in charge had left - to attend a wedding. The pesticide proved fatal. *Independent, 24 Aug 1993.*

NOT YOU AGAIN!

Anna Hascher, 82, had been on crutches since she was knocked down in Vienna in 1983 by minibus driver Milance Zivojinovic. On 21 May 1993, Anna was hobbling across the street about 500 yards from the site of the earlier accident when she was knocked down again by Zivojinovic, this time with a truck. He told police he didn't see the old lady until it was too late. Her left leg was crushed and had to be amputated. *National Enquirer, 14 July 1993.* Curiously, an earlier report *(D. Mirror, 25 May)* names the victim as 'Maria Schmidt'.

● A driver who lost control of his truck and crashed into a house in Salvador, Brazil, in 1966, did it again 23 years later, on 6 November 1989. Cristina Costa said outside her demolished home: "I opened the door and said 'Not you again!'". *Sandwell Express & Star, 8 Nov 1989.*

POSTBOX PERILS

The village of Chinnor in Oxfordshire has been plagued for six years by someone who rings doorbells at night and runs away. After some of his victims disconnected their doorbells, he prowled the village with tape recordings of a range of door bells and barking dogs which he blasted through letter boxes. Most of his victims were elderly women living alone.

● A late night stroller in Wrexham, Clwyd, was shocked to hear cries for help coming from a post box outside the sorting office in Regent Street. A middle-aged mailman had been collecting late deliveries 20 minutes earlier from the large post box when a gust of wind blew the door shut behind him. A GPO worker had been trapped in the same post box 25 years earlier. *D.Telegraph, 12 Nov; Wrexham Eve. Leader, 23 Nov 1992.*

Two American brains survive bullseye projectiles:

1. MOUNTAIN MAN MISSES THE MARK

Anthony Roberts, 25, an unemployed carpenter from Oregon, wished to join a rafting and outdoor group called Mountain Men Anonymous. On 1 May he was drinking at his friend Michael Kennedy's house in Grant's Pass, about 200 miles south of Portland, when he agreed to an initiation rite into the group, which involved having a gallon fuel can shot from his head with a crossbow arrow. Kennedy missed his mark, as can be seen from these photographs. He was perhaps the worse for drink - one report said that both men had downed 16 pints of beer.

Paramedics saved Roberts's life by restraining him when he tried to pull the aluminium arrow out while being taken to hospital by helicopter. "If he had succeeded", said neurosurgeon Johnny B. Delashaw, "the flanges slicing through his brain would have killed him instantly." Delashaw's surgical team at University Hospital in Portland spent 12 hours removing the arrow by drilling a larger hole around the tip at the back of his skull and pulling it slowly through. He lost his right eye and partial vision in his left eye, but suffered no brain damage. He was able to leave hospital after a few days, fitted with a glass eye. "I feel really stupid", he said.

If the arrow had been a millimetre closer to his nose, it would have fatally severed major blood vessels.

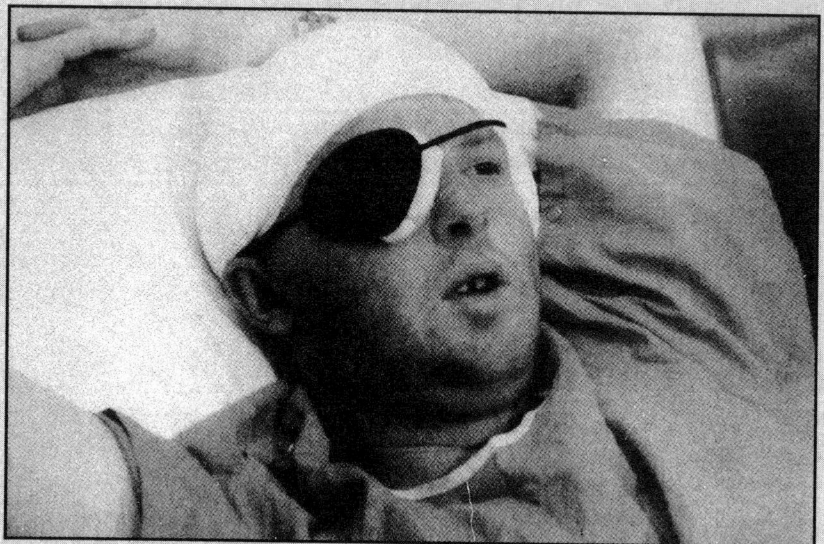

Anthony Roberts recovering in hospital after being shot through the eye.

"I've never seen anything like it", said Delashaw. "The arrow went through eight to 10 inches of brain, with the tip protruding from the rear of the skull."

We hope Roberts has earned his membership of Mountain Men Anonymous. "I don't think that's a good initiation", he said. "I think a hug would be better." Kennedy was not charged with any offence. *Oregonian, 5 May; [AP, Reuters] 6 May; Daily Record, 7 May 1993.*

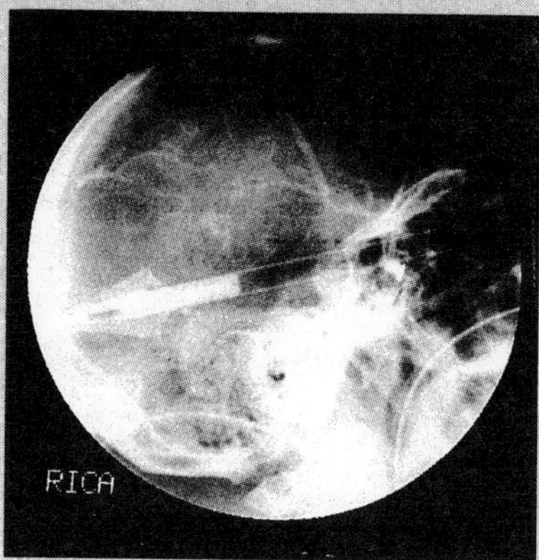

An X-ray picture showing the arrow lodged in Roberts's skull

2. NAILED

Earlier this year, a 'stuporous, inebriated man' was admitted to the Massachusetts General Hospital. Examination revealed a mild right hemiparesis (a weakness of the muscles on the right side of the body, in other words, 'a mild stroke'). Dr Michael Schwarzschild gave him a routine computed tomographic scan (shown right), which revealed a one-inch nail stuck in the man's brain near the back of his skull.

The patient later admitted that, during a depressive episode 12 years earlier, he had attempted suicide by firing a carpenter's nail gun between his eyes. Miraculously, the nail went through his brain from front to back without killing him, and the only symptoms he has now are a slight limp and a right-sided facial droop. *New England Journal of Medicine, 4 Mar; New Scientist, 25 Mar 1993.*

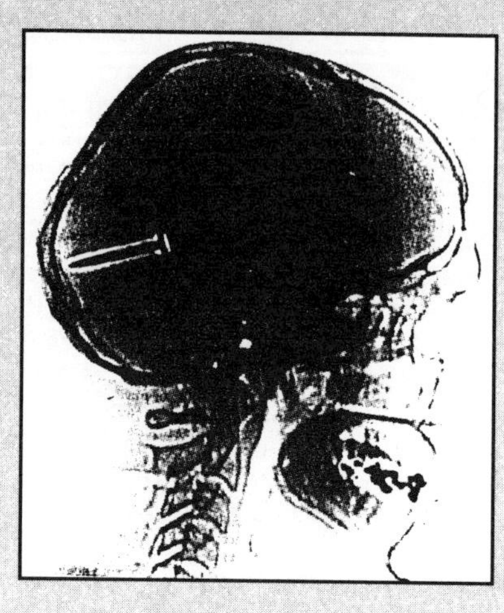

SIAMESE SUNDRIES

Our national page this issue is devoted to various odd goings-on in Thailand

● METEORITE RETURNED

Soon after a 37lb meteorite fell near Khamla Rakkorn's house in Phetchabun Province, Thailand, on 13 June, neighbours built a shrine of bamboo, incense sticks and flowers around the crater. Crowds started visiting the 10in x 6in rock, thinking it was a sacred object with special powers. One newspaper account said people bought lottery tickets with numbers they thought they saw in the meteorite. A merchant offered the equivalent of US$400,000 for the rock, but Khamla, 55, didn't want to sell it.

Four days later, the authorities seized it, saying that what falls from the sky belongs to the state. Khamla shut herself in a room and stopped eating and talking. Villagers marched in protest, demanding the meteorite's return.

Interior Ministry legal experts ruled on 22 July that the rock was an extraterrestrial object, not a natural resource or buried artifact, and therefore not state property. "It is like a cloud or the moon, which cannot be taken for commercial value", they said, according to the *Bangkok Post's* ministry source. The grey stone was handed back on a red cloth-covered platter by the deputy governor of Phetchabun on 5 August. *FT70:13; [AP] 24 June; [Reuters] 22 July; Victoria Times-Colonist, 6 Aug 1993.*

***NIPPLE SQUAD:** Thai Tourist Police race to the scene of the incident*

● BANGKOK STING

A gang of transvestites robbed tourists by enticing them to suck their tranquilliser-laced nipples and thus putting them to sleep, according to the Bangkok police. They were told the ploy was adopted because "many customers did not drink". Those tranquillisers must be damned strong!

Four transvestites and a woman were arrested after complaints from a Syrian and a Hong Kong man, who said they were robbed of a Rolex watch and nearly £2,000 in cash. *[Reuters] 29 Dec 1992.*

● SPIRIT SNATCHERS

Villagers in Long district, Phrae province, northern Thailand, became disturbed in June 1993 when over two dozen old people died in quick succession. Unease turned to alarm after stories spread that a pickup truck without a driver roared into town before the spate of deaths.

"There was a pickup truck from far away with old people and teenagers in it, and then someone walked from it into a village lane to ask if there were any elderly people in the area", one old woman told TV Channel 9. "Someone said there were many old people around, and soon thereafter they started dying." Villagers festooned their homes with banners that claim, in the local Lanna dialect as well as in Thai: "This house does not have any old people". Not every villager thought the old people died of supernatural causes. "They were elderly people who had been sick for a long time", said one sceptic.

More supposedly healthy people died in September in Thainmee in the north-east province of Surin, prompting fears that the village had been invaded by *pee paob* (living dead), who take over human bodies and kill and eat other people, including internal organs. Villagers placed human-sized straw dolls with faces like demons outside their houses and strung 'sacred string' around the village. Buddhist monks were also invited to perform exorcism rites. *Bangkok Post, 13 July; Bangkok Nation, 9 Oct 1993.*

● SPIRITS BLAMED FOR FIRE

The fire in the Kader Industrial Company plant near Bangkok on 10 May which killed 200 workers was possibly the worst factory fire in history. Thailand's mass-circulation daily *Thai Rath* claimed the fire happened because the factory had been built on the site of a cemetery without any attempt to appease the spirits.

Mr Saengchaliao Sipeung, 41, headman of a village near the factory, said four workers had been possessed by spirits since 1990. One of the four told others she wanted to take the lives of 200 workers. A medium told him the possessions and accidents occurred because the owners failed to build small ceremonial houses for the spirits. *D.Telegraph, 14 May 1993.*

● SCIENCE IN ACTION

The Thai minister for science and technology had a distinctly un-western explanation for how he escaped an assassin's bullet. Mr Phisan Moonlasartsathorn, advisor to the Buddhist Image Club of Thailand, said that the 'magnetic field' of an amulet he wears 'deflected the bullet', which missed his head by a centimetre. The amulet had 'invisible power' by virtue of 'natural science'. *Guardian, 8 April 1993.*

Sidelines

The *Birmingham News* in Alabama has published on its front page the results of a Baptist poll which shows that 46.1% of the state's population are heading straight for hell. It included a map showing which areas had the greatest concentrations of lost souls. *Independent on Sunday, 19 Sept 1993.*

•••••••••••••••

Because friends bet him £5 it couldn't be done, Pedro Guattero rolled a watermelon for 220 miles through the streets of Vera Cruz, Mexico. "It was a matter of honour", he said. *People, 25 July 1993.*

•••••••••••••••

Nearly 500 pigs were blown up or burned to death in Granada, Spain, when an electrical short circuit ignited methane gas produced by their dung. *[Reuters] 21 Aug 1993.*

•••••••••••••••

Chinese health authorities have discovered a 30-something woman in Taiyuan, Shanxi province, who likes rubber so much she has eaten more than 800 rubber nipples for baby feeding bottles since 1990. All the family like the smell of rubber, and her younger brother is fond of eating rubber bands. *[Reuters] 17 Aug. 1993.*

•••••••••••••••

Actor Gareth Gilchrist, 32, was flying home from Edinburgh to play Caithness in a production of Macbeth at the Bristol Old Vic when the X-ray scanner picked up a flick knife. He was arrested by WPC Heather McBeth, who said "Is this a dagger I see before me?" (so the press assured us). Gilchrist said it was a prop, but was fined £150. *Western Daily Press, 23 Aug 1993.*

FINAL CURTAIN: 24 NOVEMBER

Maria Devi Christos

An extreme millennial cult called Belye Bratya ('White Brothers'), led by Maria Devi Christos, self-styled Final Incarnation of God on Earth, has declared that the world will end on 24 November, about the time this *Fortean Times* goes on sale. The cult is banned in Ukraine and Belarus, but claims to have 144,000 devotees, who are forbidden money, television, computers, jobs and education. The White Brothers are violently opposed to bar codes, in which they see the Mark of the Beast. (The only constant feature in bar codes are three sets of delimiters, two thin stripes longer than the others, representing the number six, hence 666, fulfilling *Revelations 13:7:* "...no man might buy or sell, save he that had the mark, or the name of the beast, or the number of his name." It's hard to think of a more effective way for Satan to conquer than to control the world's shopping habits. (See ***FT62:13***).)

Thousands of posters of Maria Christos were plastered over the walls of St Petersburg in the summer. Texts exhorted readers to denounce the devil and his monetary system, confess and pray to Maria. Little is known about Maria, except that she studied journalism, lived in Kiev and saw the light in 1990, aged 30. Various groups have been formed to counter the influence of the cult, which lures teenagers away from families and schools. *St Petersburg Press, 24-30 Aug 1993.*

HORSE LOVER

Hanibal Cantori, a horse trainer in a Bucharest circus, went to the stable to give sugar to his stallion, Galbenus, and discovered his wife Laura copulating with the animal.

She confessed to seeking regular satisfaction in this way, whereupon Hanibal strangled her with a silk scarf before committing suicide. The report in the Romanian paper *Dracula* (1 June 1993) concludes: "Now the stallion is on tour in Holland. Desire glows in his eyes. He still waits for the beautiful Laura in his stable."

Our picture shows Laura, apparently in bridal gown, riding Galbenus. *Dracula* also published a voyeuristic photograph of the naked, strangled Laura which shows how far the Romanian press has come since the demise of Ceausescu.

A CONTENTIOUS NEW SKULL

It was an unintended coincidence that *FT70* - containing Pat Shipton's account of the village in Java specialising in faked *Homo erectus* skulls and other antiquities - was published very close to the centenary of Eugene Dubois' original discoveries of *Homo erectus* remains on Java. Inured as we are to quirky coincidences, a more splendid one was in the making.

As *FT70* was going to press, news came of a special announcement of the discovery of "the oldest fossil East Asian skull" of the *Homo erectus* type. Not only was it found on the anniversary of Dubois' discovery, according to the media, but it was found near Sangiran, a village mentioned by Shipton, that has a special market for forged antiquities.

We decided to check some of the details with Dr John de Vos, curator of the Dubois Collection at the Netherland's National Museum of Natural History in Leiden, which provided the venue for the special announcement.

Old bones

It seems that while Don Tyler, professor of anthropology at the University of Idaho, was surveying a site near Sangiran in May 1993, a farmer brought him some skull fragments which he had found recently in his field. Tyler went to the field with students from Indonesia's Bandung Institute, and recovered more bones. Under the direction of Sastrohamijoyo Sartono, a professor of anthropology at the Bandung Institute, the students studied the fossil skull – **pictured above** – and announced that they were of a woman who lived in the Sangiran area between 1.2 and 1.5 million years ago.

Tyler and Sartono were invited to Leiden to present formally what one spokesman described as "one of the most spectacular finds in palæoanthropology outside the African continent". The presentation went well until, during the press session afterwards, Sartono suddenly revised the age of the relics. His students had been wrong, he said – the skull was much younger; between 500 and 700,000 years old. His hosts and colleagues were taken aback when he added that he had not read the paper just presented and wanted to remove his name from it.

Unanswered questions

Tyler's own conclusion was that the age and morphology of the skull was strikingly similar to *erectus* skulls from Africa, and therefore its owner had arrived in Java earlier than previous estimates. Tyler also appeared to contradict this claim by accepting Prof Sartono's revised dates, at which point the meeting broke up in some confusion, leaving many questions still unanswered.

Dr de Vos, meanwhile, is in no doubt that the new Sangiran skull is genuine and sees nothing suspicious in its discovery. "Farmers are always turning up fossils there," he told us. It seems inconceivable to think that someone might have planted a genuine African *erectus* skull at Sangiran as a joke, because any such African skull would itself be famous and incredibly valuable. Dr de Vos also disabused us of the coincidence idea too: the anniversary of Dubois' discovery was chosen simply because it was an appropriate time for the announcement.

Sidelines

A dead woman was called for jury service at the trial of the man accused of her murder. Staff at Blenheim High Court in New Zealand said that the name of Ann Urquhart, whose body has never been found, was among a random selection from the electoral roll. *D.Star, 25 May 1993.*

A young mother was charged with sexual abuse and jailed in Syracuse, NY, after asking innocently if it was normal to experience arousal while nursing her child. *Washington Post, 30 Dec 1992.*

Tribesman Simphiwe Khosa was cleared by a court in Johannesburg of possessing 80lb of marijuana after he told the judge it was for burning during thunderstorms – to ward off lightning. *People, 27 June 1993.*

Last May, Randy Kraft, on death row for the sexual torture-murder of 16 men, sued Warner Books and Dennis McDougal for $60 million, arguing that their book *Angel of Darkness* was unfair in its portrayal of him as a 'sick, twisted' man. *Los Angeles Reader, 23 July 1993.*

KCAL in Los Angeles, a TV station owned by Walt Disney, the studio which boasts that it was built by a mouse, is plagued by mice which frighten reporters, gnaw through cables and invade storerooms. *D.Mail, 16 Aug 1993.*

Police in Tokyo arrested three men for selling used schoolgirl panties (price: £18 each) from vending machines in the suburbs without an official permit. *[Reuters] 22 Sept 1993.*

FORGET ME NOT

Drivers seem to have become very absent-minded recently...

According to an AP item from 12 May 1992, a couple were driving from Delaware home to Colorado, and the husband left his wife by mistake in Rostraver Township (western Pennsylvania). It took the man four hours to realise his mistake, whereupon he headed back to Pennsylvania... but hit a deer just west of Wheeling, West Virginia, and disabled the van. He walked to the nearest truck stop and told police his problem. State troopers in Pennsylvania, West Virginia and Ohio drove his wife in shifts to the truck stop, where the two were reunited.

Later that summer, a husband drove for six hours, arriving home near Milan, before realising he'd left his wife at a motorway service cafe 450 miles back. He told police that his wife normally sat in the back and talked non-stop. "I never listened to her, so I didn't notice she wasn't with me". *D.Mirror, 27 Aug 1992.*

Norwegian motorist Lars Thongruen, 35, noticed he had left his wife behind at a gas station after only 30 miles, but he couldn't remember where the gas station was. When he arrived home, she was waiting for him, having hitched a lift. "I didn't miss her because she's not a big talker" he said. *Wolverhampton Express & Star, 4 Jan 1993.*

A French tourist drove 200 miles before realising he had left his wife at a motorway service station. The 32-year-old stopped off the M6 near Carlisle for a wash, but set off again, not noticing his wife had nipped to the loo. He returned eight hours later, after a 400-mile round trip to Birmingham. He thought she was asleep in the caravanette. *Most papers, 17 April 1993.*

According to a Dutch press report on 16 August, a British tourist travelling around Austria left his wife by mistake on the Italian/ Austrian border after she went to the lavatory. He didn't realise his mistake until he reached the Austro-German border 150km away. The same mistake was made by a visitor to Bodmin, Cornwall, a few days later. He drove 20 miles before returning for the wife he left in the lavatory. *D.Mirror, 24 Aug 1993.*

In an item from the *Middlesbrough Evening Gazette* (21 Dec 1992), it's the driver's mother rather than his wife who is left in the service station. This one is set in New South Wales; mother had been asleep in the back of the car and got out for a spot of nocturnal urination. Police caught up with the son after 30 miles.

Sometimes the forgotten party is a child. On 21 June, Charles and Marjorie Miller left their daughter Kimberley (14) at a rest stop in eastern Oregon on the way to a holiday in Minnesota. They thought she was asleep in their motor home and didn't realise she was missing until pulled over by a state trooper 150 miles away in Baker City. Morrow County Sheriff Roy Drago said that in the previous year there had been four or five similar occurrences in the county. *San Jose (CA) Mercury News, 24 June 1993.*

Thomas Brown was driving to the seaside at Totnes in Devon with his wife Catherine in their Skoda on 29 August 1993. The clutch burned out on the M5 at Clevedon, near Bristol. Mr Brown, a retired rail worker of 73, parked on the hard shoulder and hobbled off on his two walking sticks to seek help. Five hours later, police found Mrs Brown, 84, sitting in the Skoda on the hard shoulder. Her husband had taken a bus to Bristol and a train home to Tewkesbury, 70 miles away. "I suppose I must have got confused", he said. "I was very surprised when the police turned up." *People, 30 Aug; D.Telegraph, D.Mirror, 31 Aug 1992.*

On the evening of 13 September, a 65-year-old Dutch tourist and his wife arrived at the municipal car park in Coppice Street, Shaftsbury, on their way to a holiday in Cornwall. In the morning he left his wife in the caravan and drove to a business meeting 50 miles away, in Swindon. He scribbled down 'Coppice Street', but failed to note the name of the town. He spent the whole day going up and down west Country roads, driving as far west as Exeter, and eventually seeking help in broken English from police in Salisbury. It took two hours' research to locate the right Coppice Street. *D.Telegraph, 17 Sept 1993.*

It seems very odd to us that all these (broadly similar) tales should come from the last 16 months, and none from earlier years. The only precedent that we know of took the form of a Max Bygraves joke about 30 years ago. Perhaps recent months have been earmarked by the cosmic joker as passenger-forgetting time. The alternative – that reality copies old Max Bygraves jokes – is too horrible to contemplate.

SLAM BAM

The odds against being dealt a perfect hand in bridge are 158,753,389,899 to 1; this has not happened in 60 years of professional tournaments, but amateurs seems to have more luck. William McNall got all the hearts in Gateshead in March 1992, as did Pat Lambert in Ludham, Norfolk, in October 1992.

Marcus Benorthan got all the spades in Elburton, near Plymouth, in May 1993. Mr Benorthan, a bridge teacher and retired newsagent, was competing at home with his wife Phyllis and another couple. The cards had been well shuffled by Phyllis, cut by her partner Ann Blades and dealt by his partner Brian Blades. The odds quoted by most papers in reporting this event – two thousand million million million million or so to one – were against *all four* players being dealt a perfect hand.

Retired GP Bernard Samuels, 70, got all the clubs in Southport, Merseyside, in August 1993. Gertrude Lutchner shuffled the cards, Bernard cut them and Joe Lutchner dealt them. Raymond Brock, general manager of the English Bridge Union, said (absurdly): "These hands seem to be coming up more often than they should". Of course, it's all in the eye of the beholder: we decide what counts as a significant pattern. Whatever hand one is dealt, the odds against it are astronomical. *FT65:6; Eastern Daily Press, 29 Oct 1992; most UK nationals, 12 May; D.Mail, 28 Aug 1993.*

IT'S A MIRACLE?

Hundreds of people testified to cures effected by the 'holy water' sold by a pedlar in Mexico City. When he was arrested, he told police that he drew the water from a local well and added a drop of home-made tequila.

Perhaps hooch wasn't the only active ingredient in Mexico's 'holy water'. It's fame spread to Argentina, where health ministry officials issued a ban on its importation on the grounds that it was untreated water from a cholera area. It's a miracle those folks in Mexico City hadn't swapped their arthritis and athletes' foot for something more fatal! *Eastern Daily Press, Sussex Eve.Argus, 18 Aug; People, 29 Aug 1993.*

WILD HUMANS SAVAGE DOG WARDEN

Early on the morning of 16 July, families living in the Withywood area of Bristol complained to the police about a terrier roaming the streets. A dog warden spotted the animal in Piggott Avenue at 8am and put it in his van, whereupon two men and two women ran up demanding that he free it.

One smashed all the van's windows and released the dog, while the others pinned the warden to the ground, assaulted him with a plank of wood and began biting him before neighbours could come to the rescue. There was blood pouring from his neck. The unnamed warden was treated in hospital for bites to neck, arms and legs. Three people in their 20s were being questioned by police. *Western Daily Press, 17 July 1993.*

OLD COBBLERS

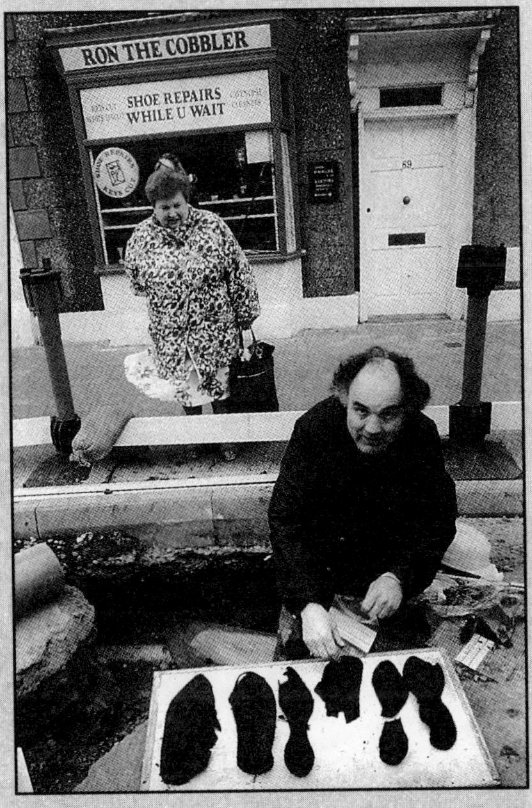

One of Wales's earliest and largest footwear hoards - hundreds of pairs of 13th century boots, lace-up shoes, moccasins and sandals - has been found buried in six feet of mud in Monnow Street, Monmouth, by drainage contractors working for Gwent County Council. Most curiously, the find was made right outside Ron the Cobbler's shop. The picture shows the appropriately named Stephen Clarke, chairman of Monmouth Archæological Society, examining some of the finds.

ENVIRONMENT-FRIENDLY JEWELLERY

When jewellery-chain chief Gerald Ratner said that some of the products sold in his stores were 'crap', he can hardly have anticipated the latest ecologically sound novelties from Sweden and Japan.

Horst Keuhne, the tourist office manager from Hede in northern Sweden who last year had a brisk trade in bottled moose droppings, is now offering varnished moose-turd earrings. "I'm really amazed at the demand", he said. In this value-added form, he is shifting the shit for £180 per kilo.

Meanwhile the Tokyo Metropolitan Sewerage Bureau has been producing a range of Sludge Jewellery including pendants, earrings and tie pins from dehydrated human waste at the Minamitama Treatment Plant. At very high temperatures, the organic matter burns off, leaving inorganic matter which solidifies. The slag is known as 'metro marble' and, when mixed with other materials, is used to make road-bed, bricks, vases and name-cards. *Sydsvenska Dagbladet, 22 July; Aftonbladet, 23 July 1993; D.Telegraph, 13 Nov 1992.*

EGG SCRAMBLE

Jamie Andrich with the Æpyornis egg

On 19 July, scientists announced that a 31.7in circumference beige fossilised egg with its 12.8 pint capacity, discovered at Cervantes on the Australian coast north of Perth *[FT70:44]*, was undoubtedly laid by the elephant bird of Madagascar *(Aepyornis maximus)* about 2,000 years ago, and not by a prehistoric giant emu. The carbon-dating was said to be accurate to within 150 years. *Aepyornis* is thought to have become extinct 800 years ago.

Many speculated that the egg floated across the 4,600 miles of ocean from Madagascar, but Dr Patricia Rich of Monash University, Melbourne, doubted this as there were no signs of barnacles or other marine organisms. "It's likely that it came off a shipwreck", she said. "The eggs were traded as curiosity items during the 19th century."

In August, a collector offered £70,000 for the egg; the Andrich family informed the Government of Western Australia, whereupon Arts Minister Peter Foss wrote to them, trying to poach the egg on behalf of the Government and accusing them of breaching the Land Act by digging it up, as the beach was state property. Foss offered a paltry 'finders' fee' of £11,000. Jamie Andrich, nine, and his cousins Kelly and Michelle Rew (not Pew), were naturally peeved; Jamie promptly reburied it somewhere in the dunes on 28 August. Within six days, the Government agreed to raise funds to match the offer and pay the finders, by charging admission to see the egg in Perth. *[Reuters] 19 July; D.Telegraph, 20 July + 2 Sept; Brisbane Courier Mail, 2 Sept 1993.*

NEW MAMMAL

DNA tests on 11 specimens from over 20 skulls, horns, hides and teeth, including three complete skins, found by Dr John MacKinnon in Vu Quang nature reserve in Vietnam in 1992 (see ***FT66:6***) have confirmed that they belonged to a mammal unlike any in the bovid family. It's the first large, new mammal to be identified since a type of wild Cambodian cow in 1937, and MacKinnon has called it *Pseudoryx nghetinhensis.* It is a cow-like creature with the glossy coat of a horse, the agility of a goat and the long horns of an antelope. The local peasants call it the 'forest goat' or the 'spindle horn'. It has a deep brown coat with black and white markings, dainty hooves and sharp, straight horns about 20in long. It weighs about 220 pounds. No-one, except perhaps local trappers, has seen a living specimen of the spindle horn. *New York Times, 8 June 1993.*

What could be the last population of one of Asia's rarest monkeys, the Tenkin snub-nosed langur, has been found living among jagged limestone cliffs and patches of forest in northern Vietnam. The two-foot-long, black-and-white monkeys were found near the village of Na Hang in Tuyen Qang province. *[AP] 29 Mar 1993.*

A GRIZZLY SIGHT

The swimming pool at the expensive Ritz Carlton Hotel in Aspen, Colorado, closes at ten in the evening and no-one is allowed to use the pool after hours. In late May, one swimmer went for a pre-dawn dip, ignoring the signs. The following morning, as staff reviewed security camera videotapes, they saw a bear enter the pool at 3:40am, swim for about 12 minutes, climb out and saunter off. It left a trail of bloody tracks, the result of a minor foot injury sustained before it entered the hotel grounds. *San Jose (CA) Mercury News, 25 June 1993.*

ALIEN STING

People eavesdropping on police radio broadcasts heard an emergency message about a flying saucer crash in a field at Appleton, Cheshire, and a warning about radioactivity from the burning spaceship. Five people raced to the scene and were promptly arrested by little blue men who charged them with telecommunication offences. Scanning devices are legally available to the public, but using them to listen to police transmissions is an offence. *Guardian, Times, 23 Mar 1993.*

HOLD TIGHT

A crewman on the Spanish yacht Galicia, training for the Whitbread round-the-world race, had his hand sliced off in an accident in The Solent off the Isle of Wight on 3 August. He was coiling a halyard when a jammer device broke and the wire whipped onto his arm. His colleagues recovered the hand from the boat, still clutching a Cadbury's Flake chocolate bar, and packed it in ice. The 27-year-old Spaniard was airlifted to Salisbury, where the hand was sewn back on. The chances that it would be functional again were thought to be good. *Today, D.Telegraph, 4 Aug 1993.*

IT'S RAINING MEN

A round-up of recent falls from the sky – from the mysterious to the lucky

Denise Buisson, 63, was on the telephone in her house in the Paris suburb of Eaubonne at about 11:30am on 8 July when she heard "a noise like two cars colliding" and the line went dead. She went upstairs and saw that tree branches were broken and telephone wires torn down. The body of a man had fallen in her garden, making a six-inch dent in the lawn. The man was lightly dressed and his swarthy complexion suggested he was Armenian. All he carried was three obsolete Russian banknotes, amounting to 55 roubles.

At first the police said he had stowed away in the undercarriage of an airliner where he had frozen to death and fallen out as the wheel doors opened in preparation for landing at nearby Roissy-Charles de Gaulle airport. (Two suspected illegal immigrants had fallen on to French airport runways in the last six months, both from flights from Africa.) Then investigator Jean-Paul Simmonot discovered that the man was certainly alive when he hit the ground. If he had hidden in the undercarriage, he must then have survived several hours at 36,000 feet where the temperature drops to minus 45 degrees Celsius, which was thought to be a medical impossibility. The average person freezes to death after ten minutes at this temperature. So, did he fall, or was he pushed?

According to our information, neither the man nor the aircraft have been identified. About a dozen possible candidates for the plane, given the time-frame, include flights from Moscow, Rome, Geneva, Milan, Dublin and several from the Middle East. One suspicion was that the outdated roubles were a plant by assassins from the Middle East to throw the investigation off course. We await developments.

Eight days after the plummeting Armenian, on 16 July, a man (believed to be Nigerian) was found frozen to death in the landing gear of an Air France Boeing 747 flying from Libreville, Gabon, to Paris. It was thought he had stowed away during a stop-over in Lagos.

On the very same day, lovestruck Mohammed Shamim, 17, fell to his death 100 feet beyond the tarmac of Fiji's main airport at Nasdi. He had stowed away in the undercarriage of an aircraft which was carrying his girlfriend Kurisha back to her family in England. The body was not found for six days. *[AFP], Guardian, D.Telegraph, 10 July; European, 15-18 July; [Reuters] 20+22 July 1993.*

Klint Freemantle, 22, of Napier, New Zealand, fell nearly 3,600 feet above Napier airport on 31 July when his main and reserve parachutes became entangled. Then, as relatives looked on in horror, he landed in a three-foot-deep pond sending ducks scattering and clambered out with only a slight cut over one eye. "I leaned back and undid my harness", said Klint. "If I was going to survive by hitting the water there was no way I was going to drown. I splashed down before I thought I would. The first thing I did was stand up and shout 'Yes!', then I reeled the chute in." He said he would be back skydiving as soon as his knees stopped trembling. *Western Morning News, D.Telegraph, 10 Aug 1993.*

Six months earlier, novice skydiver Clark Manning, 43, from Oklahoma City, survived an identical accident, falling 3,500 feet and landing in two feet of water. *People, 14 Feb 1993.*

A 45-year-old resident of Bnai Brak in Israel tried to commit suicide by leaping from a pedestrian footbridge onto a busy highway during the height of midday rush hour. He landed on a truckload of mattresses and suffered only minor bruises. *The Jewish Week, 12-18 Feb 1993.*

On 1 April, Chris Saggers, 26, plunged 220 feet from a tower block in Greater Manchester – Fitzwarren Court in Salford. His 22-floor fall, at an estimated 80mph, was captured on security video. He landed on the roof of a Nissan Micra car, which completely caved in, and after 15 seconds walked away, telling passer-by Paul Eardley he felt 'fine'. He was later treated for cuts, a neck injury and a suspected broken elbow. He said he was not trying to commit suicide, but tripped on the stairs and fell out of a window. *Most British papers, 2-4 April 1993.*

Michael Afilaka's sagging Nissan Micra car after Chris Saggers had fallen on it from 220 feet.

SNACK ATTACKS

● During the Moorish occupation, the pig became a symbol of political and religious resistance for Christian Spaniards. In a new prize-winning film, *Jamon Jamon* (Ham Ham), the pig – in the form of ham – looms large as a metaphor for Spanish society. At its violent climax, two rivals in a love triangle club each other with legs of ham until one falls dead in the sand. *Victoria (BC) Times-Colonist, 16 Jan 1993.*

● Catherine Deck killed her husband Alain after a heated row at their home in Lyon. She smacked him in the face with a giant cucumber. *Scottish Sunday Mail, 28 Mar 1993.*

● A robber staged hold-ups at a Manchester bank and three building societies, armed with two cucumbers taped together like a double-barrelled shotgun. He netted £5,000 in 20 minutes, but was arrested in a taxi after a helicopter chase. *Sun, 26 Aug 1992.*

● Thieves smashed their way into a pub at Dawlish, Devon, using a frozen rabbit as a battering ram and then left it on the bar to thaw out. *Sunday Mirror, 30 Aug; Sun, 3 Sept 1992.*

● A robber armed with a sausage raided a shop in Graz, Austria, and escaped with £1,000. Storekeeper Rudy Buckmeister was hit over the head with the ten pound wurst. "It felt like a baseball bat", he said. *Scottish Daily Record, 25 Aug 1992.*

● Mrs Carol Osbourne, 49, who was working in a mobile cafe near Lewes, Sussex, needed three stitches in her forehead after being hit by a strawberry bonbon thrown from a passing car. Police compared the impact to that of a bullet. *D.Mirror, D.Star, D.Telegraph, 4 Feb 1993.*

● A 56-year-old woman was driving from Gore to Winton in New Zealand on 9 August 1991 when, near Waimunu, a vehicle coming the other way put its lights on full beam. As it passed, a swede was hurled from it. The vegetable bounced off the bonnet, smashed the windscreen and ended up smeared across the back window. Wellington *(NZ) Evening Post, 13 Aug 1991.*

● Retired teacher Ann Mann was hit by an egg hurled from a passing car at Oldland Common near Bristol. Her leg was bruised, but there was no serious injury. Carey Turner, two, was hit in the eye by an egg thrown from a car in Doncaster, South Yorks. He needed five hours in hospital. *Bristol Evening Post, 10 June 1992; D.Star, 26 Feb 1993. [For other flying food, see **FT53:14, 57:31.**]*

NOW YOU'RE TALKING

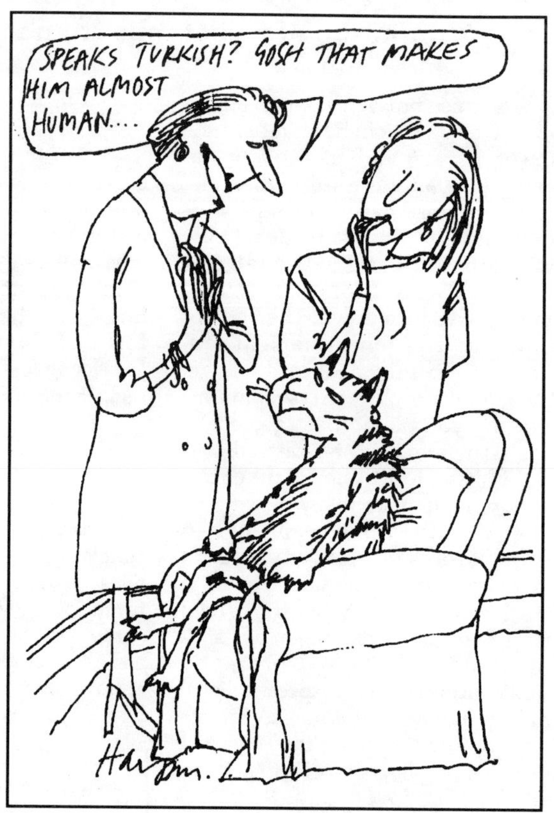

According to FT correspondent Izzet Goksu, the lead story of the Turkish television news on 20 March 1993 was a talking cat called Cingene (Gypsy) belonging to Mrs Ayfer Celik of Izmir. The two-year-old black cat had green eyes and a penchant for cheese and chicken. Cingene managed to say at least seven words on television, including *Ver* (give), *Nalan* (a girl's name), *Derya* (another girl's name), *Demem* (I don't say), *Naynay* (baby talk for music), *Nine* (colloquial word for grandmother) and *Babaanne* (formal word for grandmother). These words, Mr Goksu tells us, were clearly audible. Veterinarians examined the cat and confirmed its ability to talk.

Mrs Celik turned down an offer of 150 million Turkish Liras (about £10,000) for Cingene. She said she had first heard it talk at the age of three months when she was sitting in the waiting room of a local vet. Cingene leapt from her lap to her neck and said *'Annem-Mom'*. Everyone in the room was taken aback.

Perhaps Turkish is the most suitable language for cats. According to the *Exeter Express & Echo* of 17 December 1968, there was a cat called Pala who belonged to a businessman in a Turkish town. Pala was able to say *Anne* (mother), *Baba* (father), *Abla* (elder sister) and *Kamile* (the name of the owner's wife). The cat's gift of human language was authenticated by the chief veterinary surgeon of the (unnamed) town. It occurs to us that perhaps cats all over the world are talking Turkish, and we just don't notice. *Harriyet, Bugün, 27 Mar 1993.*

RIVER SURPRISES

Danger signs have been erected on the banks of the Rhine: 'Beware of the Piranhas'. Shoals have been spotted by people walking along the tow path in Düsseldorf. Angler Claudio Romero, 25, actually caught one. "I just dropped it and ran for my life. This is dangerous. Young children often bathe here." Police blame (without evidence, we suspect) unscrupulous pet shop owners for dumping the Amazonian predators. Shoals are surviving near power stations where the water is warm.

● A small Nile crocodile, a foot long, was found on a barge in the River Main in Frankfurt on 8 September. Where it came from was a mystery. *D.Mail, D.Record, 8 July; D.Telegraph, 9 Sept 1993.*

ASSAULT ON THE BATTERY

An interesting dispute surfaced in the pages of the London *Evening Standard* (10 Aug 1993) between the establishment of battery manufacturers and the forces of consumerism. The focus of attention was a new kind of battery charger which tops up ordinary batteries, which we have all been led to believe are non-rechargeable. Naturally, the big boys are a bit concerned that sales of the more expensive rechargeables will be affected. Behind this is the fear, regularly voiced by conspiracy buffs, that ever-sharp razor blades, eternal light bulbs, perpetual batteries, and other economical products of new technology and inventions would be available now if they didn't threaten manufacturers' profits.

In this case, the 'Battery Manager' is being imported by the Innovations mail-order company, who specialise in such essentials as nostril-hair trimmers. The *Evening Standard* tested one for four days, running standard batteries flat and recharging them up to ten times without noticeable impairment of performance. (Innovations say 20 rechargings are possible.) The only drawback was the slowness of the process.

When the *Evening Standard* asked Ever-Ready for their opinion of the charger, they first said it simply didn't work, but when faced with the *Standard's* findings, said it was dangerous and might make batteries explode. A spokesman for Duracell sniffed: "It goes without saying that our leakage guarantee would be invalid if any attempt was made to recharge normal Duracell batteries."

FISH COUNTER-ATTACK

An eight-foot barracuda hurtled almost 15 foot aboard a houseboat off Islamorada in the Florida Keys on 10 July, slicing into the arm, hip and thigh of Nasine Cloer, 46, during a family fishing trip. Relatives managed to push the fish over the side with boathooks. The school bus driver needed 200 stitches, tendons replaced and skin grafts. The razor-sharp teeth came within a thumb's width of severing an artery in her pelvis, which almost certainly would have been fatal. A day before, tourist Bobby Martin of Jemison, Alabama, needed 24 stitches after a 40-pound barracuda leapt into a boat and bit him near Bradenton. Marine biologist George Burgess of Gainesville had "never even heard of them jumping out of the water". *[AP] 13 July; USA Today, 14 July 1993.*

A MODERN CAVEMAN

When fire destroyed Ernest Dittemore's six-room farmhouse 18 years ago, neighbours in Troy, Kansas, pooled their cash to buy the 60-year-old bachelor a trailer house. Grateful, Dittemore filled the trailer with food, then spent the night in a four-by-ten-foot hole he'd dug in the ground with a shovel.

Now, shortly before his 78th birthday, he still descends into the burrow every night, using the trailer just for storage. "I'd been thinking about living underground for quite a while, even before the house burned", he said. "It's a lot easier to heat. I can keep warm and save money on fuel costs."

His nest has earth walls and floor, he sleeps on a bed of newspapers and uses a wood-burning stove for heat. A skylight built into a cement ceiling slab is darkened by soot, but still allows a little light in. There is no electricity or telephone. He's a staunch Republican who never misses an election, and he doesn't care if people think he's odd. Residents of Troy have come to accept his unorthodox lifestyle. Some affectionately call him 'The cave man of Doniphan County'.

"Ernie is the nicest guy you'll ever meet", said neighbour Jim Gilmore. "One day we'll find him dead in the hole; but he'll die happy." *[AP] 28 Feb 1993.*

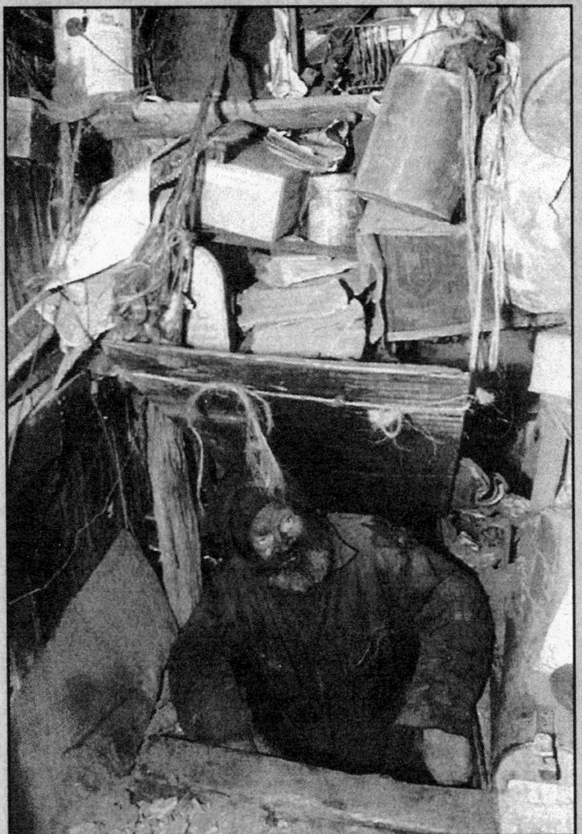

Home, sweet home. Ernest Dittemore descends into the hole that has been home for 18 years.

TALES OF DIVINE INGRATITUDE

A four-year-old boy was killed in a Maryland church in May this year, when a statue of the Virgin Mary fell on him. This kind of story seems to us typical of a category we call 'divine ingratitude'. Here are others, collected since our last assembly in FT60:13.

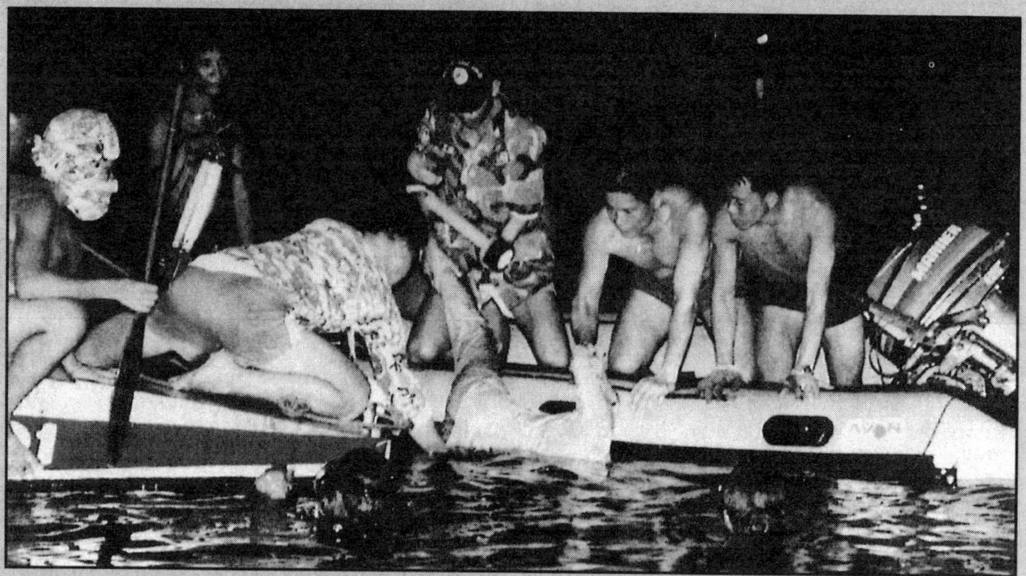

Nearly 300 devotees drowned in the Philippines when three floating shrines overturned on the Bocave River, 3 July 1993.

● **NOV 1991** - Ten people were crushed to death and many others hurt when 2,000 families crowded into the Sidi Ali Boughaleb mausoleum in Fez to watch the annual mass circumcision of thousands of young boys.

● **JAN 1992** - Thirty members of a small Mexican sect were suffocated in their temple in San Luis Potosi state; they believed breathing butane gas in a closed room made them closer to God. They were right!

● **FEB 1992** - A hostel for Hindu pilgrims collapsed during the festival of Mahamaham, held every 12 years in Kumbakonam, in India's Tamil Nadu state, killing 50 and injuring nearly 100. The disaster was triggered by several hundreds of people on balconies craning to watch the state's chief minister, Mr Jayalalitha, bathe in a holy pool at a moment designated by astrologers. (He had specialised in playing Hindu goddesses in films before turning to politics.) In China's eastern Henan province, a bus carrying Buddhist pilgrims on a visit to a holy mountain plunged off a bridge killing 28, injuring 38.

● **MARCH 1992** - Thirty people were overcome by fumes from a faulty boiler in a Catholic social club in Acton, West London. In the Gulf of Thailand, a ferry carrying mainly Chinese Buddhists pilgrims was hit by an oil tanker, drowning 87. In Peckham, London, four African immigrants died in a fire caused by 'prayer candles' as they slept.

● **MAY 1992** - A house full of mourners collapsed killing 81 in Srinagar, India. Sixteen Muslim pilgrims were killed in a bus collision in India's Uttar Pradesh state. In Ada, Oklahoma, a truck ploughed into a funeral procession, killing four.

● **SEPT 1992** - Indian crowds worshipping at a Bombay shrine dedicated to Varuna, god of rain, stampeded during a sudden downpour, trampling 11 to death. A separate but similar crush at a shrine dedicated to Shiva occurred a few days later in Bihar state killing 11 and injuring 17. In Fort Wayne, Indiana, a man was bitten by a poisonous snake during a snake-handling service at the Hi-Way Holiness Church of God.

● **JAN 1993** - A bus carrying mourners to a funeral in northern Thailand collided with another bus killing 18, injuring 20.

● **FEB 1993** - A Russian airliner, chartered to carry Iranian pilgrims from Tehran to the holy city of Mashhad, collided with a military plane, killing 134. At a gathering site for pilgrims in Dhaka, Bangladesh, a water tower collapsed killing 10, injuring 20.

● **MARCH 1993** - In a stampede to reach a holy stream near Mari, in India's northern state of Himachal Pradesh, 12 were killed and 35 injured. In Kashmir, a bus carrying people back to villages to celebrate the end of the Ramadan fast plunged into a ravine killing 38, injuring 18.

● **MAY 1993** - Eleven buses and four cars on their way to the shrine at Fatima, in Portugal, for the anniversary of the 1917 vision of the Virgin Mary, collided in fog, injuring 90.

RUSSIAN ENTERPRISE

A high-tech gang, led by an elusive Russian named 'Serge', have milked a fortune from various corporations on Madison Avenue in New York. Early in 1992, they set up two premium-rate '540' telephone numbers of the kind used by phone-sex lines. These were named 'Get Rich Fast Inc' and 'Work For Yourself Inc.' The gang dispatched fake messengers to pick up packages from reception desks. When told there was no parcel waiting, the 'messenger' asked the receptionist for permission to "call the office to see what is wrong".

He then dialled a '540' number and held a long and involved conversation (in Russian) at a cost of $225 per minute, which charge was automatically transferred by the New York Telephone Company from the business victim to the accounts of 'Get Rich Fast' or 'Work for Yourself'. It was not yet known how much the conmen made altogether, but they withdrew $240,000 in cash before the police discovered the front companies. Only one 'messenger' was arrested. *The European, 8-11 Oct 1992.*

FIJIAN SPECTRE

Security guard Pauliasi Cuanilawa and two colleagues at Fiji's Parliament House in Suva saw on a television monitor what appeared to be the apparition of a faceless Fijian warrior moving around inside a locked refreshment room for about five minutes. The shadowy figure was recorded on videotape and broadcast on Fijian TV on 2 September.

Historians said that the Parliament House was probably built on the site of a village burial ground and that ceremonies might have to be performed to exorcise the *kalouvu* (ancestral spirit). *[AFP] 3 Sept 1993.*

FORTEAN FUNNIES

His quest at an end, Neville cursed the day he decided to trace his ancestors

STRANGE DEATHS

✝ A 1920s Rolls-Royce, used for weddings, broke down in Stockport, Greater Manchester. As chauffeur Frank Jackson, 70, was working beneath the bonnet, another car rammed into the Roller and Frank's head was impaled on the Silver Lady statuette, killing him. The car was made before Rolls-Royce made the Silver Lady mascots spring-loaded, to flip backwards on impact. *D.Star, Today, 11 Aug 1993.*

✝ On 24 April, Kwarme Shariff, seven, was playing with his twin brother Kwasi outside their apartment block in North Brunswick, New Jersey. He stuck his foot in a small hole and the ground gave way, swallowing him up. People tried to pull him out, but each time he slipped from their grasp and slid deeper into soft mud. A hundred rescuers worked for over seven hours to dig him out, but he was dead on arrival at hospital. Tree stumps buried by builders, rotted by unusually heavy spring rains and the township's "traditionally high water table" probably contributed to the ground's collapse. *NY Times, 25 April; [AP] 26 April; USA Today 28 April 1993.*

✝ Also in April, Willie Murphy, 61, an employee of the Golden Peanut Company in Donalsonville, Georgia, was killed when he was crushed under an avalanche of peanuts; while in July, a 23-year-old sweet factory worker in Marseilles, France, was crushed to death when a bin filled with 5,000 pounds of marshmallows fell on him. *USA Today, 5 April; Daily Record, 15 July 1993.*

✝ North Sea oil worker Ellard Zuidema was decapitated by a helicopter's rotor blades on the diving support ship *Mayo* in April 1992. Mr Zuidema, 6ft 3in, ducked to avoid the blades, but a huge wave caused the *Mayo* to shudder and the blades dipped to 5ft 8in. *D. Telegraph, 5 Nov 1992.*

✝ Tanya Green, 22, of Dewsbury, West Yorkshire, died after having sex with her boyfriend, a week after giving birth to a healthy baby. The post mortem showed that air had been forced into her bloodstream because blood vessels had not closed again after the birth. *Sussex Evening Argus, 21 July 1993.*

✝ Stubborn Armando Pinelli, 70, won his argument with another man over who should sit in the only chair in the shade of a palm tree in Foggia, Italy - then died when it fell on him. *Sun, 18 June 1993.*

FORTEAN ALMANAC 22 November 1993 - 6 February 1994

Notable feasts and anniversaries in the coming weeks

MONDAY 22 NOVEMBER:
On this day in 1963, C.S. Lewis ascended to heaven and Aldous Huxley went out on a cloud of LSD... but the public hardly noticed, being absorbed in the JFK death drama in Dallas.

THURSDAY 25 NOVEMBER:
USA Thanksgiving and Feast Day of St Catherine, who was allegedly broken on the wheel (hence 'Catherine wheel'). She was probably derived from the Hindu Kali, who is associated with the wheel of karma.

SUNDAY 28 NOVEMBER:
Birthday of William Blake (1757).

TUESDAY 30 NOVEMBER:
St Andrew's Day. The X-shaped cross upon which he was said to have been crucified was the same as the cross of Wotan carried by Norse invaders into Scotland, where it became the national symbol.

SUNDAY 5 DECEMBER:
A day for disappearances. In 1872 the *Mary Celeste* was found with all 14 crewmen missing and in 1945 Flight 19 vanished in what was dubbed (20 years later by Vincent Gaddis) 'the Bermuda Triangle'.

WEDNESDAY 8 DECEMBER:
Bodhi Day - Enlightenment of Gautama Buddha.

TUESDAY 14 DECEMBER:
Kaspar Hauser ran from a park on this day in 1833, crying that he had been stabbed. The park, covered in new-fallen snow, bore only his footprints, but the deep fatal wound in his heart was (in the opinion of two doctors) not self-inflicted.

TUESDAY 21 DECEMBER:
Yule, or Winter Solstice; Sun enters Capricorn 20:26. The Romans called it *Sol Invictus* (the Undefeated Sun).

SATURDAY 25 DECEMBER:
Christmas Day. The birthdays of the Babylonian Queen of Heaven and of Osiris, Dionysos, Adonis, Mithras, Balder and Jesus were celebrated today, the old date of the Winter Solstice. All these deities are associated with rebirth and eternal life.

SATURDAY 1 JANUARY 1994:
The ancient British festival of Gogmagog, and *Circumcisio Domini*, the day Jesus was snipped (said to have been instituted in 487AD). It first appeared in the English liturgy in 1550.

WEDNESDAY 5 JANUARY:
The Feast Day of St Simon Stylites who spent 36 years on top of a pillar 60 feet tall and three feet in diameter. His favourite position was standing with his head touching his feet. He kissed his arse goodbye in 459AD.

FRIDAY 14 JANUARY:
St Hilary's Day, supposedly the coldest day of the year.

MONDAY 17 JANUARY:
Feat Day of St Anthony, patron saint of pigs.

THURSDAY 20 JANUARY:
St Agnes' Eve, the night when young girls can discover their future husbands by divination.

TUESDAY 25 JANUARY:
St Paul's Day (the day Saul was zapped by the Lord). It was thought the weather today determines the character of the coming year: fair weather betided a prosperous year, snow or rain, an unfruitful one; clouds, high livestock mortality; and wind meant war.

SATURDAY 29 JANUARY:
Feat Day of St Francis de Sales (1567-1622), patron saint of journalists.

TUESDAY 1 FEBRUARY:
Imbolc, the first day of Spring in the pagan calendar.

SUNDAY 6 FEBRUARY:
First day of the Regnal Year, "43 Eliz.II".

SPECIAL CORRESPONDENTS

AFRICA Cynthia Hind (Zimbabwe), Ion Alexis Will (Roving). **AUSTRALIA** Greg Axford (Vic), Paul Cropper (NSW), Arthur Chrenkoff (Qld), Rex Gilroy (NSW), Tony Healy (ACT). **BELGIUM** Henri Pr_mont. **CANADA** Brian Chapman (BC), Dwight Whalen (Ont.). **DENMARK** Lars Thomas. **ENGLAND** Claire Blamey, Bruce Chatterton, Peter Christie, Mat Coward, Hilary Evans, Peter Hope-Evans, Neil Frary, Alan Gardiner, Mick Goss, Chris Hall, Jeremy Harte, Ronnie Hoyle, Dionne Jones, Jake Kirkwood, Alexis Lykiard, Nick Maloret, Valerie Martin, Kevin McClure, John Michell, Ralph Noyes, Nigel Pennick, Andy Roberts, Tom Ruffles, Paul Screeton, Karl Shuker, Ian Simmons, Bob Skinner, Anthony Smith, Paul R. Thomas, Nigel Watson, Owen Whiteoak, Steve Wrathall. **FRANCE** Jean-Louis Brodu, Bernard Heuvelmans, Michel Meurger. **GERMANY** Walter J. Langbein, Ulrich Magin. **GREECE** S.C. Tavuchis. **HOLLAND** Robin Pascoe. **HONGKONG** Chris Williams. **ICELAND** V. Kip Hansen. **INDONESIA** Alan M. Stracy. **IRELAND** Peter Costello, Doc Shiels. **JAPAN** Masaru Mori, Shigeo Yokoyama. **NEW ZEALAND** Peter Hassall. **NORTHERN IRELAND** Caryl Sibbett. **PHILIPPINES** Keith Snell. **POLAND** Leszek Matela. **ROMANIA** Iosif Boczor. **RUSSIA** Vladimir Rubtsov. **SCOTLAND** David Burns, Stuart Herkes, Roger Musson, Roland Watson, Jake Williams. **SWEDEN** Anders Liljegren, Sven Ros_n. **USA** Larry E. Arnold (PA), Loren Coleman (ME), James E. Conlan (CT), Karma Tenzin Dorje (CA), David Fideler (MI), Mark A. Hall (MN), Myron S. Hoyt (ME), John Keel (NYC), Jim Lippard (AZ), Kurt Lothmann (TX), Barbra Millspaw (CO), Ray Nelke (MO), Jim Reicken (NY), Ron Schaffner (OH), Chuck Shepherd (FL), Dennis Stacy (TX), Joseph Swatek (NB), Joseph Trainor (MA), Jeffrey Vallance (CA), Robert Anton Wilson (CA), Joseph W. Zarzynski (NY). **TURKEY** Izzet Goksu. **WALES** Janet & Colin Bord, Richard Holland, Joe Kelly.

ILLUSTRATION COPYRIGHTS

5 POPPER **6** INTERCONTINENTAL FEATURES **7** LORNE GOODE **8 (t+m)** AP **(b)** NEW ENGLAND JOURNAL OF MEDICINE **10 (t)** ST PETERSBURG PRESS **(b)** DRACULA **11** DR JOHN TYLER/ DR JON DE VOS **12** MERRILY HARPUR **13** ROB STRATTON/WESTERN MAIL **14** REUTER/HULTON DEUTSCH **15** MANCHESTER EVE. NEWS **16** MERRILY HARPUR **17** AP **18** AP **19** COLIN TAYLOR **21** HUNT EMERSON **25-26** MARY EVANS PICTURE LIBRARY **27-28** ROLF OLSSON **29 (b)** CASSIDY & LEIGH **30** REUTERS/HULTON DEUTSCH **31** TOPHAM **32** HULTON DEUTSCH **34** TOPHAM **36** REX FEATURES **37-39** PIATKUS BOOKS **43** HINRICH SIEVEKING **44 (l)** WALT ANDRUS/MUFON **(r)** FORTEAN PICTURE LIBRARY **45 (r)** FORTEAN PICTURE LIBRARY **46** KARL SHUKER **49** PA **50 (t)** POPPER **(b)** AP **51** HULTON DEUTSCH **52** J+C BORD **56** PIERRE HOLLINS **64 (b)** NIGEL JONES **65** ELLEN LAVERY

CLIPPINGS & TRANSLATIONS FOR THIS ISSUE

Ian Abel, Jayne Amat, Bruce Baker, Jon Barraclough, K.A.Beer, Lionel Beer, Claire Blamey, Pierre Bonello, Janet & Colin Bord, Iosif Boszov, Bill Botham, Dave Bourgoin, Cuyler Warnell Brooks Jr, David J.Burns, ByRon, Cain, Rod Chambers, Brian Chapman, J.Chetwynd, Arthur Chrenkoff, Peter Christie, J.Clarke, Jim Conlan, Richard Cotton, COUD-I, Mat Coward, Joy Critchley, Paul Cropper, Karma Tenzin Dorje, Jill Doubleday, Ellen Dupont, John Eastman, Bill Ellis, Peter Hope-Evans, George Featherston, Dick Foreman, George L.Foster, Neil Frary, Rob Gandy, Alan Gardiner, Izzet Goksu, Simon Goodman, Matthew Goulding, Andrew Green, Mark Greener, Slim Haines, Robert Hale, M.K.Harris, Peter Hassall, Kevin Hayes, Steve Hexter, Cynthia Hind, Toby Howard, Myron S.Hoyt, I.K.Johnson, Dionne Jones, Joe Kelly, Graeme Kenna, David Keyworth, John J.Kohut, Naomi Lee, Chris Lonsborough, Dave Malin, Nick Maloret, Valerie Martin, David McKinnon, Barbara Millspaw, Jan Mura, R.D.Murrell, L.Naylor, Roger O'Donnell, Robin Pascoe, Matt Peach, Helen Penn, Nigel Pennick, Mark Pilkington, John Price, David Rider, Jim Riecken, Zvi Ron, Sven Ros_n, M.Rothschild, Tom Ruffles, Tom Salusbury, John Sappington, David Scoffins, Ronnie Scott, Paul Screeton, Keith Seddon, Doc Shiels, Caryl Sibbett, Adrian Sill, Ian Simmons, Andy Smith, Anthony Smith, Dennis Stacy, Peter Stallard, H.Stanton, Gary Stone, Joe Swatek, Joff Tanner, Lars Thomas, Paul R.Thomas, Pam Thornton, Fred Tomsett, Richard Turner, UFONS, Jeffrey Vallance, Dr Jon de Vos, David Wallachinsky, Sarah Walsh, Nicholas P.Warren, Christine R.Weiner, John Whiskin, Owen Whiteoak, Ion Will, Chris Williams, Jan Williams, Jason Winter, Steve Wrathall, M.J.Yates.

'HAT WE HAVE HERE IS **CHARLIE FORT**, IN "HE BOOK OF THE DAMNED", ANGING ON ABOUT HE EXCLUSION OF WKWARD DATA BY SCIENTIFIC DOGMA! E'S JUST GOT TO THE IT WHERE HE EQUATES HIS EXCLUSION WITH IMILAR PROCESSES HROUGHOUT NATURE... WHAT HE CALLS...

...UNIVERSALITY OF THE PROCESS!

A TREE! IT IS DOING ALL IT CAN TO ASSIMILATE SUBSTANCES OF THE SOIL AND SUBSTANCES OF THE AIR, AND SUNSHINE, TOO, INTO TREE-SUBSTANCE... OBVERSELY IT IS REJECTING OR EXCLUDING OR DISREGARDING THAT WHICH IT CANNOT ASSIMILATE...

YUM YUM YUM
YUM YUM YUM YUM YUM YUM YUM

PHENOMENOMIX

RIPPED WHOLESALE FROM "THE BOOK OF THE DAMNED" by CHARLES FORT, AND CARTOONED by HUNT EMERSON ... oct 93.

OW GRAZING...

EXCLUDED

GRAZE GRAZE GRAZE

PIG ROOTING...

PTOOi

EXCLUDED

TIGER STALKING...

OUT OF MY WAY, BUG!

EXCLUDED... (THIS TIME)

PLANETS TRYING TO CAPTURE COMETS...

EXCLUDED

RAG PICKERS...

EXCLUDED

..AND THE CHRISTIAN RELIGION...

EXCLUDED

BLEAT

BAA BAA BAA BAA BAA

...AND A CAT DOWN HEADFIRST IN A GARBAGE CAN...

HALLELUJAH!

EXCLUDED

NATIONS FIGHTING FOR MORE TERRITORY...

EXCLUDED

SCIENCES CORRELATING THE DATA THEY CAN...

I DON'T KNOW WHAT IT IS...IT DOESN'T FIT MY THEORIES... THEREFORE ! EXCLUDE IT!

TRUST MAGNATES ORGANIZING...

WE DON'T WANT HIM, DO WE?

NO, NO... INDEED NOT!

EXCLUDED

CHORUS GIRLS OUT FOR A LITTLE LATE SUPPER...

RITZ
Tonites Special
Pie PEAS + MASH 1/6D

ALL OF THEM STOPPED SOMEWHERE BY THE UNASSIMILABLE! CHORUS GIRL AND THE BROILED LOBSTER...

...OR SCIENCE AND SOME OF OUR CURSED HARD-SHELLED DATA...

EGAD! A HARD SHELLED DATUM! I CAN'T ASSIMILATE THIS–NOT WITHOUT A STIFF DRINK!
KEEP YOUR DISTANCE, CREEP!

THE BIG SLEEP

After centuries of research, sleep is still a mysterious phenomenon, at once a familiar part of our lives and yet forgetful, ominous, healing, surreal, magical and death-like. The archives of sleep research include many accounts of strange sleepers, and we review here some of the more extreme forms which may relate to the 'Sleeping Beauty' syndrome.

NODDING OFF

A veritable slumber party of miscellaneous notes on protracted sleepers and their ilk, compiled by BOB RICKARD

There is something profound and mysterious about unusually prolonged or deep sleep. Beliefs about magically-induced sleep have been noted in cultures all over the world. They are also very ancient, possibly even prehistoric: one European example is the story of Sleeping Beauty sent into her 100-year slumber by the prick of an enchanted needle, preceded by the story of Wotan causing Brunhilda to sleep surrounded by a magic fire through which only a brave hero can pass to waken her with a kiss.

The most famous sleepers in Christian legend were seven youths who hid themselves, allegedly in 250 AD, in a cave near Ephesus to escape persecution. They fell asleep and were discovered, still youthful, 200 years later. (Eastern churches commemorate this miraculous awakening each 27 July, a feast day commended to all who suffer from insomnia.) More ancient still is the story of Epimenides, who is said to have wandered into a nymph-haunted cave on Crete at the end of the 7th century BC and woken up between 40 and 100 years later. Another variant, called 'the king under the hill', concerns a local or national hero who is not dead, but sleeping in a secret place awaiting the call of his people in their hour of need: this is said of King Arthur, numerous central European hero-kings like Charlemagne, the Tibetan hero Gesar, and many others.

The legendary 20-year sleep of Rip Van Winkle is, in fact, a pastiche of the kind of tall story this Dutch colonist made up to cover his alcohol-induced amnesia, yet it demonstrates the relationship of prolonged sleep to the ubiquitous folklore motif known as 'the supernatural passage of time'. Typically this occurred when the story's hero was transported to fairyland or some other enchanted location and returned to find so much time had passed in the 'real' world that all the people he knew are long dead. While this is usually taken as a metaphor for sleep, it more accurately reflects the type of selective amnesia found in such strange states of consciousness as Multiple Personality Disorder (MPD), in which two or more alternating personalities have no recollection of their intervening 'sleep'. Bizarre instances include picking up in mid-speech or action at the exact point at which they were interrupted, the hiatus ranging from minutes to several years.

Prolonged sleep has to be distinguished from long-term comas resulting from neurological damage to the brain; and from African sleeping sickness (once thought to be a form of narcolepsy, but which is in fact a fever caused by protozoal parasites). Many medical commentators recognised the hysterical or neurotic nature of extraordinarily extended periods of sleep, and in reviewing many of the accounts for this summary it is clear that a significant proportion of them could be re-diagnosed today as variants of the syndromes which produce the behavioural problems discussed by Jim Schnabel in these pages.

Washington Irving's <u>Rip van Winkle</u>, drawn by Hoppin (1864)

"The legendary 20-year sleep of Rip Van Winkle is, in fact, a pastiche of the kind of tall story this Dutch colonist made up to cover his alcohol-induced amnesia."

Some people have an unusual condition in which they tend to fall asleep during incongruous activities, such as walking. This is known as narcolepsy, a rare form of which, cataplexy, can be triggered by emotional excitement. Katherine Porter, 17, from Sutton-in-Ashfield, Nottinghamshire, for example, collapses unconsciously whenever she laughs. "If I am watching something funny on television, I have to force myself not to laugh", she told the *Yorkshire Post* (5 May 1990). "If I feel one coming on, I have to pull a cushion over my face and concentrate hard. I once fell asleep during a history lesson on the Battle of Hastings when somebody said something funny. I dreamt I had been stabbed by a Viking. I woke with a start and lashed out and my books went everywhere. It was very embarrassing."

Today, conditions such as Katherine's can be controlled with drug therapy, but they are still poorly understood. Their complexity is underlined by the psychologist Ernest Hilgard, who tentatively relates narcolepsy and cataplexy to hypnotic-like states of 'double consciousness' typical of MPD. Whatever their origin and however they are triggered, he regards them as a genuine altered state of consciousness, related to the kind of 'blackout' in which someone "drives a car satisfactorily for some miles and presently finds himself registering at a hotel having forgotten how he got there or why he is there."

Gould and Pyle were firmly of the opinion that numerous related conditions, from premature burial to "the fabulous sleeping girls of the newspapers" arise from "spontaneous mesmeric sleep in hysteric patients" lasting from a few minutes to several years. As in normal sleep, there is a turning in or up of the eyeballs, lowering of body temperature, slowing of respiration, pulse and digestive tract – and even brief moments of wakefulness. Little nourishment is taken during these periods, and bowel movements often dwindle to less than one a month, and sometimes disappear altogether. In this, the similarities with animal hibernation have not been lost on some medical commentators. We have to omit discussion of voluntary suspended animation for lack of space.

Unlike normal sleep, however, there appears to be a low-level operation of consciousness resembling in almost every way a deep hypnoid state. This may include selective responses to certain sensory stimulation – being sensitive to voiced suggestions, for example, but not to pain, taste, smell or bright light. Sometimes the sleep may be accompanied by a cataleptic rigidity of the muscles, so that the sleeper's limbs hold the position into which they are moved – one hears of bizarre postures being maintained for years in this manner.

Most of the accounts we could find were of sleep lasting from most of a day up to six months, and fell into two classes – those who slept continuously, and the rest whose sleep was broken with (often regular) periods of wakefulness – the most impressive from each is given in our listing on p28. The intermittent interruptions themselves varied in length, some sleepers appearing normal and others still drowsy. They were noted with care because they were often the only opportunities for the sleeper to attend to nourishment and calls of nature, some even falling back into sleep in the act of eating or defecating.

Wilson provides brief accounts of eight sleepers (in the years 1546, 1696, 1738, 1777, 1788, 1826 and 1827) with slumber times ranging between 18 hours (daily) and three months. The earliest instance concerns William Foxley, a pot-maker for the Mint in the Tower of London, who "fell asleep" on 27 April 1546 and "could not be awaked by pricking, cramping or burning". When he awoke 14 days later he was unaware of the passage of time "as if he had only slept one night".

Many sleepers slumbered on through horrific torments – Wanley provides two detailed case histories. Samuel Chilton (see under 'Intermittent') was "bled, blistered, cupped and scarified". Doctors also pushed a pin into his arm until it hit a bone, injected him with sal amoniac, and crammed hellbore into his nostrils. Elizabeth Orrin (see under 'Intermittent') was not only burned and jabbed by over-enthusiastic medicos, but they gave her strong emetics, shouted in her ears, whipped her "till the blood ran from her shoulders", and exposed her to angry bees after smearing her with honey.

Kirby's treasure trove of Forteana yields nine additional cases (in the years 1694, 1711, 1734, 1738, 1753, 1808, 1812 and two from 1752) of between three days and four months. Nearer the present, the pioneer psychiatrist Weir Mitchell [cited in G&P] collected 18 cases from the 19th century, the longest being six months continuous sleep. A few died asleep; one recovered only to be afflicted with insomnia; the rest recovered normally.

Many other cases could be found – especially from continental and early medical literature – but, in general, they lack the detail that would aid us in making a diagnosis at this distance. Most defy easy categorisation, confusing sleep with trance, coma, possession and even melancholia with breathtaking ease.

THE BIG SLEEP

THE SLEEPING PREACHERS

Sleeping preachers and healers constitute a major subcategory of strange sleepers, but they differ significantly from the extended sleepers in that their sleep was relatively short and transient, having more in common with mediumship or channelling. It is not difficult to understand how, in archæic communities, such sleepers were thought to be in touch with the divine – it was, after all, the basis for Asclepius's sleep cures in ancient Greece. In the late 1800s, thousands of superstitious Italians brought their sick to the bedside of Bettina Pieri (see under 'Intermittent') hoping for cures.

Perhaps the most famous example is Edgar Cayce (1877-1945), the psychical healer of Virginia. Although he was known as 'The Sleeping Prophet', this epithet referred not to prolonged sleep but to the trance state in which Cayce made his diagnoses. He found it also facilitated inspired preaching.

An earlier example is Simeon Watson, aged 30, an English labourer of 'athletic habits', who, in April 1826, began spouting fluent and structured sermons in his sleep.

Edgar Cayce

During these periods, which always began with convulsions and groaning, his hands could not be unclasped and he could not be roused.

Rachel Baker, famous in her day as 'The Sleeping Prophet', is another example. Born in 1794, she grew up in a poor but devout family in Marcellus, New York, and from the age of 17 endured periods of somnambulism and morbid fears about spectres and being dragged down to Hell. These increased until she sank into daily periods of trance, during which she uttered solemn devotional sermons that impressed people sufficiently for them to be collected and published in 1815. This was 37 years before the Fox sisters began the Spiritualist movement, also in New York State, which also combined trance oration (somniloquism) with possession by spirits of the dead.

In many early observations, however, the trance state was thought to be a peculiar kind of sleep and related to possession; today, the parallels with behavioural syndromes, such as MPD, can be more clearly seen. Trance preaching had a considerable history in the Protestant tradition, even before Wesleyan revivalists became known for it in the 18th century, and can still be found in congregations today, from Quakers to Pentecostals, that invoke the Holy Spirit. Finland, in particular, has produced 'sleeping preachers' since the 1770s. [*Lazell, Shepard, Wilson*]

THE BIG SLEEP

THE BROOKLYN ENIGMA

The baffling phenomena of Mollie Fancher, a sleeping cripple with multiple personalities

Born in Brooklyn in 1848, Mollie was a tuberculous child, given to 'nervous disorders'. Shortly after her seventeenth birthday in 1866, she met with two accidents which left her blind and an incurable invalid. She spent the remaining 30 years of her life bedridden in her aunt's house in Brooklyn.

For the first nine years of her confinement, Mollie slept in a coma or trance (no one could decide which), lying on her paralysed right side, her legs twisted and atrophied beneath her. In those nine years her body functions all but ceased – she took little or no food for very long periods, and she suffered nightly convulsions. She was deathly cold – a little warmth and a faint pulse could only be detected in the region of her heart.

While Mollie slumbered, however, her crippled body manifested four quite distinct personalities who accepted and transcended their poor vehicle. Though Mollie was virtually blind and paralysed, these entities used her hands to create exquisite needlework and paper flowers. This was accomplished in a peculiar position, the work being done above and behind her head, out of normal visual range. One investigator noted that each personality had a different style of handwriting, each nonetheless 'beautiful'.

Mollie's eyes were enhanced, despite being severely damaged by years of unblinking, tearless staring. Somehow, Mollie could see perfectly in the dark and read books placed under her pillow. She 'saw' into all parts of the house (invariably being correct about the location of lost objects) and even described events in distant towns. This has been described as 'travelling clairvoyance' and recalls the statement by Rachel Baker (see under 'Sleeping Preachers'), a generation earlier. Rachel told researchers that her self-awareness was not dimmed by sleep when she trance-preached, because she was aware that she existed for that period at locations far distant from her body. Like Rachel, too, Mollie often clarified Christian doctrine for her listeners.

Mollie Fancher in 1864, aged 16

After nine years, Mollie's body relaxed, but was subject to prolonged fits of such violence that she was frequently hurled out of bed. Her original personality returned between the convulsions but had to share her body with a number of other personalities, usually at night. The five major ones were often mutually hostile and their arguments were known to go on all night exhausting their host and her carers. The conversation of each would be picked up exactly where it left off, regardless of the amount of time lapsed between those moments.

Mollie often spoke of seeing the 'angelic forms' of dead relatives and friends, and said "I am with friends in most heavenly places" during the times her other personalities evicted her from her body. She knew of the new Spiritualist movement, but refused vehemently to act as a medium for the curious and the bereaved.

As her fame spread, more and more savants and clergy came to test her. Many were turned away as she had no wish to be exhibited. Mollie would not see any but close friends, some of whom left useful records of her strange phenomena. Mollie, or rather her other personalities, passed every test – for example: Henry Parkhurst, an eminent astronomer, testified to her powers of eyeless sight when she read a torn-up letter he retrieved from a wastebasket and sealed in an envelope.

Undoubtedly, Mollie's case would be seen in a different light today. Her ailments have the ambiguity typical of hysterical phenomena, leading one to suppose her blindness and paralysis may have had a psychosomatic origin. That she also manifested unexplained psi talents while in this condition is supported by impressive evidence. *[Thurston, Shepard]*

BELOW: Mollie in 1886, aged 38, in the long second phase of her illness, with her aunt, Susan Crosby. Despite 30 years of lying on her atrophied legs, she never had a single bedsore.

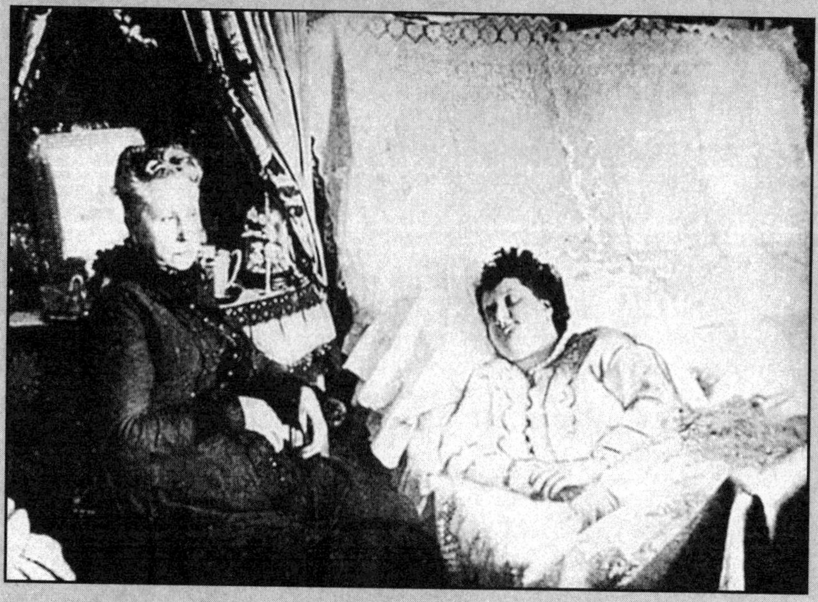

CAROLINA DREAMING

ROLF J.K. OLSSON tells the remarkable story of Carolina Olsson (no relation, apparently) whose unbroken sleep of over 32 years is the longest on record.

On 22 February 1876, a 14-year-old girl called Carolina Olsson, from Mönsteras in Småland, fell into a mysterious trance-like sleep. She did not wake up until 3 April 1908, 32 years and 42 days later. About two months after her awakening, Carolina returned to a normal life, which carried on for another 42 years. She died in April 1950, at the age of 89.

No-one else in history has slept for a longer continuous period than this girl, and the cause of her long sleep was never established. It was conjectured that she had fallen on the ice and hurt her head on her way home from school.

It is remarkable that Carolina didn't suffer any after-effects from her long sleep. Most people who, because of injury or illness, sink into a coma that lasts for years, eventually die without regaining consciousness. Those who survive and wake up are usually disabled for life. But when Carolina woke up in 1908, her life continued in much the same way from the point she had fallen asleep in 1876, and she had a normal memory of what had happened until the day her sleep began.

Carolina lived with her parents and five siblings in a crofter's cottage at Oknö, south of Mönsteras. Returning home from school one day in February 1876, she complained of a headache, saying something about having slipped on the ice. A few days later, she got so tired that she was confined to bed. In the evening of 22 February, she suddenly fell into a coma.

The days passed by, but Carolina continued to sleep. It was impossible to wake her up, and her parents didn't know what to do. Her father was a crofter and fisherman, and because he was poor he hesitated for as long as he could before sending for a doctor. The family kept the sleeping girl alive by forcing her to swallow milk or sugared water. This food was to be Carolina's only diet for more than 32 years.

As time passed by and the girl showed no signs of improvement, her parents finally called in a doctor, but he could only confirm that the girl was in a trance-like sleep. She did not react to being spoken to, nor to bodily contact. Not even needles stuck into her fingers prompted a reaction.

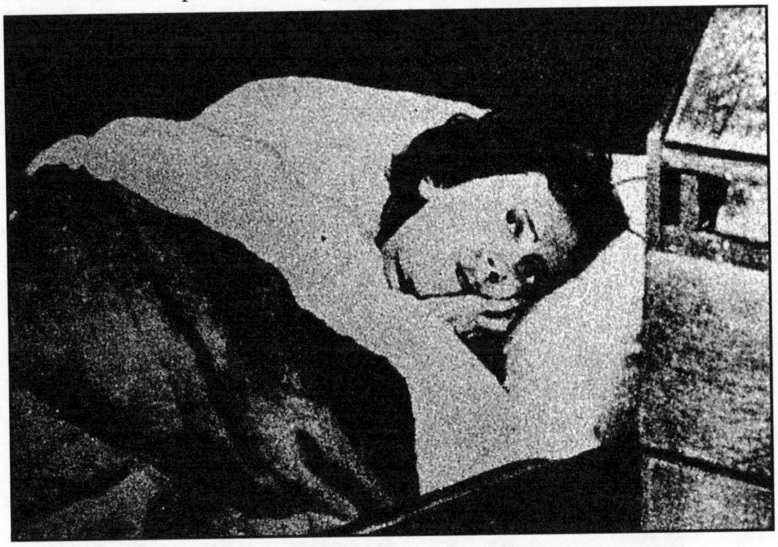

In the years to come, many physicians took an interest in the case and came up with some curious explanations. One doctor explained the girl's remarkable condition as 'hysterical paralysis', presumably caused by a sudden scare or shock. He did not, however, know how to wake her up.

Carolina's parents were now desperate, and hoping to get help from a specialist, they took her to the hospital in Oskarshamn. She was subjected to dangerous experiments, the hospital personnel demonstrating a severe lack of judgment. They even tried to rouse her with electricity, without success. She was sent home as incurable.

In their little cottage, consisting of one room and a kitchen, the Olsson family now got used to having the sleeping girl on their sofa bed. Her mother tended her carefully, and kept watch at her bedside even at night. The family got no help from the medical establishment, and it is easy to understand their despair. One county medical officer even described the girl as "a mentally backward person, pretending to be ill." Rumours flew around the village. Some thought that the girl was faking; others that her soul had been abducted by a supernatural being. Local wise women who were consulted offered no solution.

Carolina Olsson shortly after she had woken up in 1908, after 32 years asleep

As the years passed, Carolina's face became pale and thin. In 1904, when she had been asleep for 28 years, her mother died. Thereafter, a widow in the neighbourhood helped the family with the housekeeping.

At nightfall on 3 April 1908, she entered the cottage and found Carolina "jumping around the floor, like a dark shadow", exclaiming "Mother! Mother!"

"Though she was 46, she looked like a woman of 25. Her body had not grown or aged at all – it was still the body of a 14-year-old. Even more remarkable was that her hair and nails had not grown during her years asleep."

The housekeeper told her that her mother was dead, as were two of her brothers, who had drowned. Carolina looked around the room in const-ernation. Much had changed since she had fallen asleep. The door opened and an old man and two middle-aged men came in. She found it hard to grasp that these were her father and two of her brothers. "But they were small", she objected, pointing to her brothers.

Asked if she was hungry, Carolina said that she wanted cured herring. She felt faint and dizzy, but recovered surprisingly fast – "As though a miracle had taken place", one doctor said. Only a couple of months later she was fully at work in her home. Though she was 46, she looked like a woman of 25. Her body had not grown or aged at all – it was still the body of a 14-year-old. Even more remarkable was that her hair and nails had not grown during her years asleep.

The news spread rapidly that *Törnrosa* (the Sleeping Beauty) had finally woken, and newspapermen from all over the country gathered on her doorstep, followed by hordes of the curious. Carolina was looked at like a circus animal. One day, no less than 27 coaches were parked at the cottage. Finally, her family had to keep the door locked and all the curtains drawn.

About two years later, Carolina was examined by a psychiatrist from Stockholm's Hospital för Sinnessjuka (a mental hospital), Dr Harold Fröderström, who noticed that the woman looked young; her skin smooth and her teeth very well preserved. He found her "of a cheery temperament, and she gave clear and intelligent answers to all the questions she was asked". She could read and write, and remembered everything she had learned before she fell asleep.

Her father had seen Carolina get up three times during her sleep. One night he found her kneeling in bed praying to "sweet Jesus". This was the only time during the 32 years that she was heard talking. On some other occasions her family had heard her crying and sobbing in her sleep.

Carolina Olsson (centre) on her 80th birthday

The cause of Carolina's long sleep remains a medical mystery. It was not an established fact that she had fallen on the ice and hurt her head. Dr Fröderström suggested that her abnormal condition was the result of "disturbances of the internal secretions, caused by self-intoxication, generated through the influence of her sexual organs".

Carolina lived a normal life for another 42 years. Her friends described her as an industrious, humorous and talkative person, who took a natural interest in whatever happened in her neighbourhood; but whenever she was asked about the lost years, if she remembered anything about her longest night and what dreams she had had, she became silent and reluctant to answer.

*Adapted from an article published in the Swedish magazine **Vi** (September 1991). Thanks to Sven Rosén for the translation.*

THE BIG SLEEP

SLEEPYHEADS

The Fortean Times League Table of continuous, intermittent and comatose...

CONTINUOUS SLEEPERS

32 YEARS 42 DAYS – Carolina Olsson's continuous sleep is probably the longest ever recorded. See accompanying article by Rolf Olsson. Details (and probably accuracy) are wanting on the historical cases, but these notes provide a guide to other sleepers.

20 YEARS – In 1883, Frenchwoman Margaret Boyenval – later known as 'The Sleeping woman of Thenolles' – was so anxious over a visit from the village policeman that she collapsed and 'slept' for 20 years. In 1902 her doctor saw signs of returning consciousness. Opening her eyes, she remarked, "You are pinching me", and immediately went to sleep again. She died five months later, still asleep, on 28 May 1903. [Corliss (BHF33, X0); Woodall]

4 YEARS – A French woman aged 25, collapsed after a 'fright' on 30 May 1883. Her menstruation was suppressed. [G&P]

1 YEAR 3 MTHS – A Kentucky man, aged 27, fell into a 'trance' in 1874, while suffering from tuberculosis . [G&P]

1 YEAR 2 MTHS – Spanish soldier, aged 22, in Cuba, following unspecified injury and depression. Reported in 1885. [G&P]

260 DAYS – A Dutch peasant slept from 29 June 1706 to 15 March 1707, waking briefly on 11 January 1707. [G&P]

220 DAYS – Maria Cvetskens of Stevenswerth, Holland. Not much is known about this young girl, but medical investigators found no signs of deception. Sleep continued beyond the report date of 5 December 1895. [G&P]

INTERMITTENT SLEEPERS

73 YEARS – The record must go to Italian Bettina Pieri, who went to bed in 1864 when she was 15, and remained there until she died, aged 88. She was widely believed to have miraculous powers. According to the Rome newspaper *Tribuna*, when she awoke, which was once in every three or four years, people came from miles around and sent their sick to her in hundreds. Her mind was perfectly clear; her health was surprisingly good throughout her life, although her hair turned snow white. [Woodall]

26 YEARS – In 1874 a farmer named Harms, of St Charles, Minnesota, went to bed, where he remained for the rest of his life. Although he woke up for regular meals, his weight dropped from 14 stone to six before he died. [Woodall] ▷

19 YEARS – In 1884, 16-year-old Gesine Meyer, of Grambke near Bremen, fell asleep after falling from a cart. She seemed perfectly well when she awoke three months later. Two years later, she took to sleeping for long periods. In late 1886 she fell into a deep coma, from which she did not awaken until 15 November 1903, when a fire broke out in the village and the alarm bells were rung. She sat up and called for her father and brother. She asked her brother, who 17 years earlier had been a conscript, why he was not in uniform. When told what had happened, she said: "Why, I thought I had only been asleep for one night". [Woodall]

Elizabeth Perkins in 1789

18 YEARS – A New Orleans girl was aged nine when prolonged sleep began, apparently precipitated by large doses of morphine and quinine. She woke each day for 12 brief but regular moments. Reported in 1869. [G&P]

15 YEARS – John Maceachin, 75, a farm labourer from Argyle, broke his thigh in 1921 and was taken to the West Highland Rest Hospital at Oban. There, he fell asleep after a meal, and until he died 15 years later, slept 22 hours a day. He awoke for meals, but never uttered another word. [Woodall]

15 YEARS – Elizabeth Orrin, aged 36, of Hainault in Belgium, slept for four days 1738, then for 18 hours every day for 15 years. She could not be woken by the most painful tortures, and slept through the cannon-fire during the siege of nearby Mons in 1746. During sleep, her limbs would stay rigidly where they were put. [Kirby, Wanley]

5 YEARS – A New York man averaged 16 hours awake over six weeks or more. Reported in 1853. [G&P]

4 YEARS – Following a 'sudden fright', a 14yr-old German girl fell into deep lethargy, broken only by an average of four hours dreamy wakefulness every 96 hours. Menstruation ceased. Early 1800s. [G&P]

2 YEARS – In 1696, Samuel Chilton of Tinsbury near Bath, in Somerset, a smallholder of 'robust habit' aged 25, fell soundly asleep for four weeks. Then a month later he slept for 17 weeks, waking on 17 August 1698. A year later, on the very anniversary of his waking, he plunged into a five-month period of semi-consciousness from which he could not be roused (though he did wake briefly on 19 November 1697). He woke in early February 1698, returning to his usual routines. [Wilson, Wanley]

2 YEARS – In 1788, Elizabeth Perkins – **above** – of Morley in Norfolk was unconscious for 11 days 6 hours. A week after recovering she sank into a profound sleep which lasted until her death in 1790. This portrait was drawn on 26 July 1789. [Wilson]

UNKNOWN – Godofredo Souza, 49, a farm worker from Rio Branco, Brazil, cannot hold down a job because he regularly sleeps for two months at a time. Doctors are baffled. [*Sun*, 15 July 1992]

COMATOSE SLEEPERS

Because of the lack of details in the historical cases it is difficult to determine whether or not the unconscious period derived from a head wound or from some other affliction, such as toxæmia, caused by infections which nowadays can be controlled with antibiotics. Here are a few coma records for comparison.

37 YEARS 111 DAYS – Elaine Esposito of Tarpon Springs, Florida, never awoke from an appendectomy on 6 August 1941. She died in 1979. [The Guinness Book of Records]

29 YEARS – In 1963, in Florida, Anne Shapiro suffered a stoke and was in a coma-like trance until October 1992 when chest pains caused her to wake up. She wanted to watch *I Love Lucy* on the TV to take her mind off the Kennedy assassination. [Canadian Press 14 Nov 1992]

8 YEARS – Conley Holbrook of North Carolina beaten on the head in 1983. In 1991 he revived and named his assailants. [See ***FT59:34***]

A young woman from Chichester exhibited another peculiarity of sleep in 1989. "I lie in until lunchtime if I don't have to work and when I do I always come home for a nap before going out", said Tina Houghton, 18, an auxiliary nurse. She had survived a 13-month pregnancy when the fœtus went into an unexplained 'form of hibernation', before resuming normal growth. Tina weighed 7lb 7oz at birth. She had to be woken three times a day for feeding. "Her last feed was at 7pm", said her mother, "and she would sleep right through the night until nine the following morning. We were never woken by her crying in the middle of the night. It was amazing." **D.Telegraph, 23 May 1989.**

SOURCES

E. Cobham BREWER: A Dictionary of Miracles (1884). William CORLISS: Biological Anomalies: Humans 2 (1993), compiled from original sources. G&P – Gould & Pyle: Curiosities and Anomalies of Medicine (1896, p867ff), compiled from many earlier medical accounts. Ernest HILGARD: Divided Consciousness (1977). Robert KIRBY: Wonderful and Eccentric Museum, (1803-1820, 6 vols). David LAZELL: 'Sermons from Sleeping Speakers' (MS. 1993). Leslie SHEPARD: Encyclopedia of Occultism and Parapsychology (1985, 2nd ed.) Jim SCHNABEL: 'The Münch Bunch', FT70:23-29; and 'Memories of Hell', FT71:23-30. Fr. Herbert THURSTON: The Physical Phenomena of Mysticism (1952). Nathaniel WANLEY: Wonders of the Little World (1883, 2 vols.) WILSON'S Wonderful Characters (1839). Robert WOODALL: 'Peace, Perfect Peace' Lilliput magazine (December 1948).

Special thanks are due to Bob Skinner and Paul Sieveking for their contributions of source material and data.

SHOOTING DOWN THE MYTH

The assassination of President Kennedy on 22 November 1963 continues to haunt and fascinate the public, perhaps more than any other murder. Nearly everyone now agrees that Lee Harvey Oswald did not act alone – if indeed he was involved at all. The event acts as a focus for studying the nature of historical evidence and interpretation. It is a sort of Rorschach blot, prompting the world's conspiracy theorists to construct endless and labyrinthine scenarios. Glenn B. Fleming investigates.

So far, no fewer than 23 people have been 'identified' as being responsible for firing shots into Kennedy's limousine on 22 November 1963. Men in bushes, in open windows, in storm drains, in moving vans, across the Plaza, on the overpass, in the Book Depository, on the Book Depository roof, in the records Building, in the Dal-Tex building, with umbrellas. No *woman* has been named as a possible sniper, which comes as a welcome surprise, if not a relief.

These assassins, these desperados, linked so tenuously to organised crime, the CIA, the KGB, the OAS, Texan oil millionaires, US Military Intelligence, the John Birch Society, anti-Castro mavericks and a host of other faceless organisations are still, apparently, walking free.

The JFK assassination, America's darkest hour, has become a million dollar industry. Books, films and tours of the murder site are now available to everyone. The only thing that isn't available is the truth. What really did happen that day?

The history books, written by intelligent and enlightened men, tell us that a lone, crazed young man called Lee Harvey Oswald crouched in a window at his place of work waiting for the President. In his hands lay his mail order rifle, ready for murder. No motive was positively established for Oswald (himself shot dead in the custody of the Dallas police less than 48 hours later), but we are told that it may have had something to do with Oswald being jealous of Kennedy and, following a tiff with his estranged wife, deciding to get his own back on her by killing someone she admired. Oswald also admired his President and later denied shooting him.

No one actually saw Oswald commit the crime and several witnesses placed him elsewhere than the sixth floor Book Depository window (from which he allegedly shot the President) at the time of the shooting. Oswald was a poor shot, as revealed by his Marine Corps records and testimony from those he served with. The top three rifle experts in America could not equal Oswald's amazing feat of three shots, two hits, in 5.6 seconds with that rifle, in that time.

Paraffin tests taken from Oswald's hands and cheeks three hours after his arrest prove that he had not fired a rifle that day. Did he wear a mask and gloves? Neither were found. Photographs found of Oswald holding the alleged murder weapon are almost certainly fakes, as Oswald himself said during the interrogation. Over the years, the names of many of Oswald's 'acquaintances' have been linked to the CIA, the Mafia and anti-Castro movements.

A high-powered rifle was found on the sixth floor of the Book Depository that afternoon and was subsequently identified by two Dallas police officers as a German Mauser (they clearly state in their report that 'Mauser' was stamped on the barrel of the weapon). Later, after the arrest of Oswald, the rifle was re-identified as a 20-year-old Italian Mannlicher Carcano. The telescopic sight mounted on the Carcano was found to be defective. This type of rifle was notorious for jamming and was commonly known as a 'humanitarian rifle' because it would not injure the enemy. The Carcano was traced to Oswald through a post office box in Dallas. He denied ever owning a rifle.

One theory suggests that there were two plots that day and claims that several unidentified Texas businessmen were anxious to be rid of their Governor, John Connally. Connally, who died recently, always maintained that he was hit by a different bullet. (The infamous 'magic bullet', the key exhibit of the official version, supposedly hit JFK in the back, exited via his throat, hit Connally in the back, exited via his chest, went through his wrist and ended up in his right thigh. Apparently, more bullet fragments were left in the Governor's wrist than were found to be missing from the bullet. This 'magic bullet' was later found on a stretcher at Parkland Hospital, even though doctors operating on Connally told reporters that the bullet was "still in the leg".) Author and journalist Joachim Jorsten believes Connally was shot by a different hit-team, firing at the same time the President was shot.

Some people believe Lyndon Johnson, the man who inherited Kennedy's crown, was behind the assassination. Didn't Johnson have the most to gain from Kennedy's early (if not violent) demise? What about J. Edgar Hoover? He'd been at loggerheads with the Kennedy brothers, especially Bobby, for years. Then, what about Joe Kennedy's alleged links with the Mafia? According to unsubstantiated speculation, organised crime bosses like Sam Giancana bought the election for Joe only to see Jack foolishly turn his back on his benefactors. Was Jimmy Hoffa, ruthless leader of the all-powerful Teamsters' Union, involved? If anybody had a grudge against the Kennedys, it was him; Bobby Kennedy had been hounding him for years.

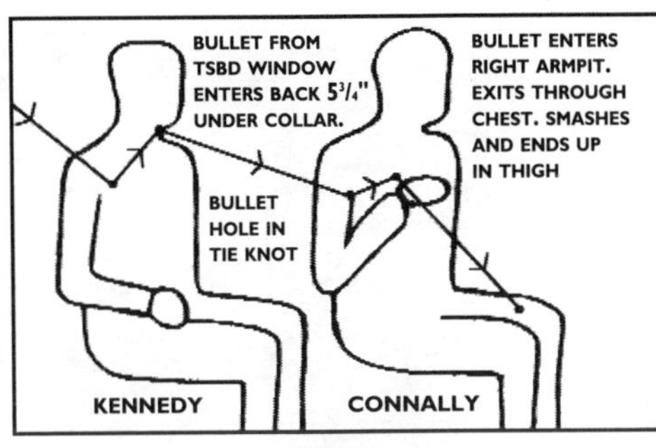

TOP LEFT: The presidential car approximately one minute before the assassination.

BELOW LEFT: A security man clambers over the back seat – or is it one of the assassins?

ABOVE: Trajectory of the 'magic bullet'

Fidel Castro became a suspect too. Could Oswald have been one of his agents? Oswald had been involved with the 'Fair Play for Cuba' movement in New Orleans that summer of 1963, when, posing as a pro-Castro sympathiser, he had been arrested by the FBI. Two days earlier, he had posed as an *anti*-Castro sympathiser.

Was Khrushchev still angry with Kennedy for humiliating him during the Cuban Missile Crisis a few months earlier? Hadn't Oswald defected to the Soviet Union in 1959, returning to the United States in the summer of 1962? Was Oswald being controlled by the KGB? Was it the *real* Oswald who came back home, or a Soviet impostor, a döppelganger trained for the assassination? British author Michael Eddowes succeeded in having the body of whoever it was in Oswald's Fort Worth grave dug up in 1981. It was found to be Oswald, though the head had somehow separated from the body…

Closer to home, Kennedy had spoken of a total withdrawal of all US personnel from Vietnam by 1965. He was going to use this stance as part of his campaign for re-election in the fall of 1964. After his death, Johnson made a complete U-turn on that policy. We all know what happened in Southeast Asia over the next decade. Kennedy declared he would "splinter the CIA into a thousand pieces". Would America's top spy agency turn against its own commander-in-chief?

Nobody today really believes Oswald acted alone, except the intelligent and enlightened, and many question whether he actually fired any shots at the motorcade. Some say he was a government agent and had infiltrated the group planning the murder; others maintain he was simply a patsy, a fall guy.

Clearly, something is not quite right concerning this crime. Through the years, the 'truth' has become tainted and, even if the 'truth' were revealed, who would believe it? Just about everybody in American officialdom was compromised that day. As American eyes turned skyward for a possible invasion from an enemy who had cut down their new hope, the powerbase in the United States shifted a little further from the reaches of the Presidency and the people.

The late Jim Garrison, District Attorney of New Orleans and the only man to bring the case to trial, called the assassination a 'coup d'état'. Witnesses to the killing and acquaintances of Oswald began mysteriously to drop dead like flies in the years after 1963. By 1973, 116 of them had died in dubious circumstances.

"The JFK assassination, America's darkest hour, has become a million dollar industry. Books, films and tours of the murder site are now available to everyone. The only thing that isn't available is the truth."

Jack Ruby, Oswald's killer, died shortly after Jim Garrison's secret probe into the assassination became public. Cancer. Rose Cheramie, a stripper at Ruby's night club, told people that the President was to be shot in Dallas two days before it happened. Killed by a hit and run driver. Dorothy Kilgannan, the only journalist to be granted a solitary interview with Ruby, declared she would blow the case right open. Barbiturate overdose.

Of the first two journalists to meet Ruby's boyfriend, one was killed by a karate chop as he left his shower, the other was shot 'by accident' by a cop in Long Beach, California. David Ferrie, a strange individual with ties to the CIA and the Mafia and a known acquaintance of Oswald, died the day before Garrison was going to arrest him. Ruptured blood vessel to the brain. And so on, and so on.

Coincidence or conspiracy?

In 1979, 16 years after the event, the House Select Committee of Assassinations recommended that the Justice Department reopen the investigation into Kennedy's death, having found evidence of a 'possible conspiracy'. So far, they appear to have done nothing.

THE LINCOLN-KENNEDY COINCIDENCES

One of the most popular documents in Xerox folklore is the Lincoln-Kennedy correspondences. The following is compiled mainly from the Wallace family's Book of Lists No.3 (1983), an item by Larry King in USA Today (21 Nov 1988) and one by E. Randall Floyd in San Antonio (TX) Express-News (16 July 1991).

Abraham Lincoln studied law, was elected a Congressman in 1846 and President on 6 November 1860. John F. Kennedy studied law, was elected a Congressman in 1946 and President on 8 November 1960. Both were civil rights campaigners.

Two of Lincoln's sons were named Edward and Robert. Edward died at age three, Robert lived on. Two of Kennedy's brothers were named Robert and Edward. Robert was assassinated, Edward lived on.

Lincoln was succeeded by Andrew Johnson, who was born in 1808. Kennedy was succeeded by Lyndon Johnson, who was born in 1908. Both Johnsons served in the US Senate.

Mary Lincoln and Jackie Kennedy both had children who died while their husbands were in the White house.

Both presidents were shot on a Friday in the back of the head with their wives present. Both men had expressed anxiety about possible assassination earlier in the day.

Lincoln's assassin, John Wilkes Booth, and Kennedy's alleged assassin, Lee Harvey Oswald, were both Southerners in their 20s. (Booth was born in 1838 and Oswald in 1939.)

Lincoln's secretary, John Kennedy, advised him not to go to the theatre. Kennedy's secretary, Evelyn Lincoln, advised him not to go to Dallas.

Booth shot Lincoln in a theatre and hid in a warehouse. Kennedy was shot from a warehouse; Oswald was found sitting in a theatre. Lincoln was killed in Ford's Theater. Kennedy was killed in a Ford Lincoln convertible. Booth and Oswald were both killed before they could be tried in court. Lincoln was shot with a pistol and his assassin with a rifle. Kennedy with a rifle and his putative assassin with a pistol.

The names Lincoln and Kennedy each contain seven letters, Andrew Johnson and Lyndon Johnson each have 13 letters, and John Wilkes Booth and Lee Harvey Oswald each total 15 letters.

TWO INTERPRETATIONS OF THE ZAPRUDER FILM

The 8mm film shot on Elm Street, Dallas, on the fateful afternoon by patriotic dressmaker Abraham Zapruder has become one of the central exhibits in the eternal investigation of the JFK mystery. Viewers have interpreted the images in many different ways. Here are two examples.

Seventeen research papers were delivered at Second Research Conference of the Third Decade of JFK Assassination Studies on 18-20 June 1993 in Providence, Rhode Island. R.B. Cutler's paper 'The Umbrella Man' suggested that the murder missile was a poison flechette fired into the President's throat from an umbrella gun. The fatal wound occurs at Zapruder frame Z-187, with the death 6.9 seconds later at frame Z-312.

The 25-30mm tracheotomy performed 10 minutes later didn't disturb the flechette, but it had to be removed, which explains the 'pre-autopsy surgery' performed on the neck at Bethesda, resulting in a gaping wound. Cutler names the Umbrella Man as George Novel, as seen on the Zapruder film. He raises his black umbrella and turns as he pumps it up and down – all on a bright, sunny day.

The collected conference papers cost $20 in USA from Prof. Jerry D. Rose, State University College, Fredonia, NY 14063. This info. comes from Paranoia, the Conspircy Reader, P.O. Box 3570, Cranston, RI 02910.

UFO researcher William Cooper, in his book *Behold A Pale Horse*, revives an hypothesis from the 1974 book *Murder from Within*, that the Zapruder film shows Kennedy's driver, Secret Service agent William Greer, turn round and fire at the President. According to a film commentary made by one Lars Hansson: "You see the .45 automatic ... in his left hand. He's firing over his right shoulder; you see it in relief. You see his head pointing backwards towards the President. The force of the shot drives him violently backward against the back of the seat". According to Cooper, all of the witnesses who were close enough to the car to see what happened were murdered within two years.

Copies of the Zapruder film cost $30 + $4 US postage & handling from William Cooper, 19744 Beach Blvd., Suite 301, Huntingdon Beach, CA 92648.

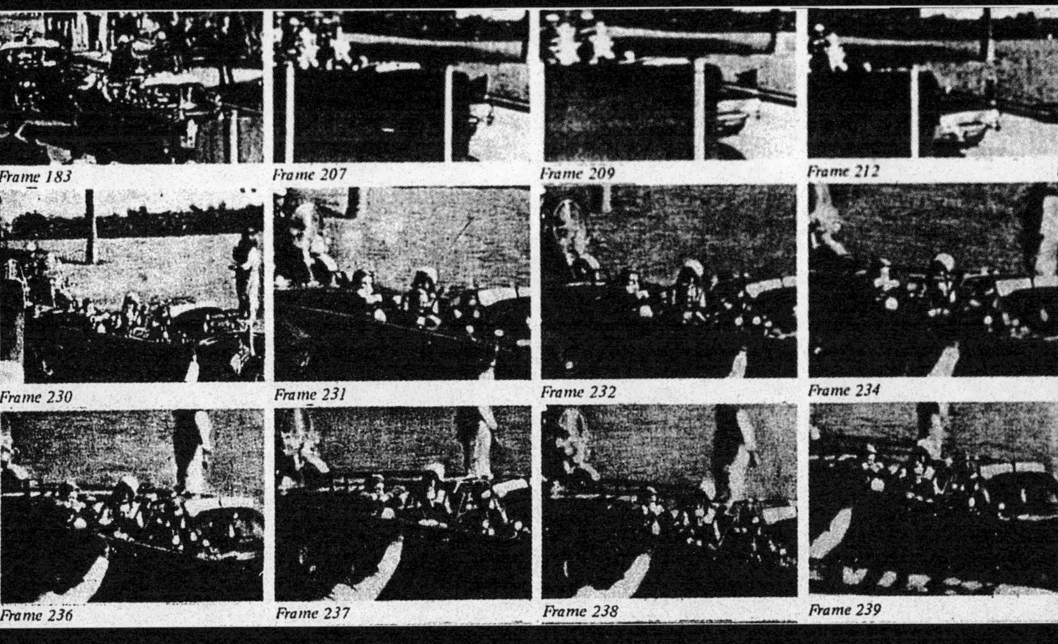

ABOVE: The Umbrella Man waits in Dealey Plaza, his umbrella at his feet.

LEFT: Frames from the Zapruder 8mm movie – a hand-drawn copy from Life's original.

THE ASSASSINATION OF LEE HARVEY OSWALD

The famous moment on 24 November 1963 when Lee Harvey Oswald (centre) was shot in the stomach by club-owner Jack Ruby (right of centre) in the basement of the Dallas Police Department building, captured by photograper Bob Jackson.

A curious aside concerns James Leavelle, the luckless cop in the light suit and hat handcuffed to Oswald at that fateful moment. In August 1992, as part of an oral history project, Leavelle was being interviewed by former newsman Bob Porter, and Wes Wise, a former mayor of Dallas. Leavelle showed the investigators a .38 Colt Cobra (as used by Ruby) and demonstrated how his colleague Det. L.C. Graves had grabbed Ruby's arm and prevented him firing a second shot (Graves can be seen reaching in on the right of the picture).

Suddenly the gun went off, and with the camera still rolling, a shocked Leavelle quickly attended to Bob Porter's wounded right arm, while Wes Wise dialled for paramedics. "I had two guns, one loaded and one not," explained the embarrassed 72-year-old lawman. "I guess I picked up the wrong one." *Washington Times, 8 Dec 1992.*

"I see life as a continuing process. I don't have any problem with the concept of energy continuing after a body wears out."

BOB RICKARD talks to JENNY COCKELL, who claims to have transcended death to reunite the children of her former life.

MARY'S CHILDREN

Mention reincarnation today and you are likely to be lumped with dotty spiritualists, dreamy New Agers or distant Indian peasants – yet there have always been people like Jenny Cockell whose claims to have lived before are based on direct personal experience. Since childhood she has relived the life of Mary Sutton, an Irish woman who died in 1932, leaving her eight children to fend for themselves.

Today Jenny, a 39-year-old chiropodist, lives happily in Northamptonshire with her husband Steve (a garden designer) and their two children. She seems to be the very model of sensibility – intelligent, articulate and thoughtful, and with no overt quirkiness or neuroses – as she tells you, with impressive calm and care, that she has somehow transcended death to find Mary's children and reunite them.

The story of Jenny's quest for details of her past life – how she recalled dream scraps of information which were later verified; how she located Malahide, north of Dublin, as the village where Mary lived; and how she found Mary's scattered children (only five are still living) – is told in *Yesterday's Children* (Piatkus, 1993), and was the subject of *Strange But True?*, a pilot for an ITV series on strange experiences.

It is a moving story that begins with Jenny's recurrent nightmare of Mary's death, alone in a room in Dublin's Rotunda Hospital, almost frantic with concern over the fate of her children. Their father was a soldier in World War I who made a precarious living as a scaffolder. He was moody, often drunk and absent, so the children were distributed among several orphanages. Once Jenny had located Malahide, and inquiries identified a Sutton family that fitted her recollections, it took several more years of patient research to discover the whereabouts of all but one child. She made her first contact in 1990, when Jeffrey, Mary's third child, answered an appeal in a Dublin newspaper. In 1991 and 1992, Jenny finally met the others in several family reunions.

FAR LEFT: Jenny with Sonny, now aged 72. He was Mary's eldest son and has confirmed many of Jenny's descriptions of his childhood home and life – including how he used to trap pheasants using brown paper sugar bags containing corn, and how he once brought home a live hare he had snared.

ABOVE LEFT: Mary's four sons – from the left, Jeffrey, Christy, Frank and Sonny – at their first reunion in 1985. Sonny stayed with his father when the other children went to several orphanages. Jenny's impressions of the number of children and their scattering was borne out by tracing baptismal and orphanage records.

FT: How did you come to feel that you had lived before?

JC: That's quite difficult because the memories had always been there, in detail, right from the beginning. I have memories of three previous lives going back into the historical past. It didn't worry me at all – I took it that I'd lived before and assumed that it was perfectly normal. I thought everybody did.

It was not until I went to Sunday school for the first time, with my older brother, that I realised otherwise. They talked about issues that I thought were important, like what happens after you die, but they didn't mention previous lives. I was a bit confused by this so I asked my mother and learned then that it was not normal to think this way.

It wasn't that I suddenly felt that I had lived before, but I did suddenly realise that other people couldn't remember.

FT: Your book describes your early past-life memories as nightmarish dream experiences. I have great difficulty remembering dreams, they tend to evaporate as the day progresses – so what made yours so memorable?

JC: There was only the one dream, really, and it was the same every time – a nightmare of dying and leaving my children behind. I had difficulty getting it out of my mind, in fact. It took tremendous effort to push it to one side because the intensity of feeling was almost unbearable.

But there were also other memories ... If you sit down now and try to remember a childhood memory of a day at the seaside, it just pops into the mind. My memories of Mary did the same. Like ordinary memories, too, they were quite fragmented – but then your childhood memories will have bits missing. I felt I was the same person, but in a different body. It was not a fleeting one-off thing. I relived it regularly, I think, because it arose from a situation which was unresolved.

FT: How did you settle on Malahide as your former home?

JC: I had always felt the memories were connected to Ireland. One day, as a child, I felt sure that if I could look at a map of Ireland, I would know where the village was located, and match it up with the maps I had been drawing ever since I could hold a pencil. Many times, when I looked at my school atlas, I was drawn to the area north of Dublin and the village of Malahide.

FT: At what point did you decide to be hypnotised?

JC: It was long after I had verified that the town of Malahide corresponded to my own drawings. That was in 1980. It was one of those things I thought I might do one day to get some extra details. I had been fairly successful in pushing the memories to one side, but after my children were born, I found new motivation, as if having them reawakened old feelings. In late 1987, while I was saving up for a trip over to Ireland, a friend said I must come and see this chap – he was not a therapist but a researcher into past lives who used hypnosis to recover memories. I went to one of his talks and later volunteered, in 1988, to be one of his case-studies.

It all came back with such intensity – not just because I was seeing scenes during the hypnosis, but because I was thinking more about my past life. Memories were continually popping up between sessions ... but this time I was an adult and able to do something about investigating them.

ABOVE: Mary Sutton in 1927, with Phyllis then aged two years. Mary died in October 1932, a month after the birth of her youngest daughter. She was alone and desperately worried about the fate of her children.

FT: What other kinds of psychic experiences have you had?

JC: Premonitions, mainly. I always knew when things happened to my younger brother. For example, the first I knew of the death of my older brother (in a gliding accident) was when my younger brother got the phonecall. I was in a motorway service station at the time and nearly fell over with the shock.

Sometimes, when my mother and I were talking, I'd go and fetch something, then we'd realise she hadn't actually named the thing she wanted me to fetch. I'm quite good at psychometry – holding an object belonging to someone and then being able to describe their feelings or other things about them. As a chiropodist holding people's feet I just have to turn off.

FT: When were you able to contact Mary's children, and how did they react to the strange story you had to tell them?

JC: I made my first visit to Malahide in 1989, and the first contact with one of the children was in 1990. It took me a long time to think about how best to approach them. I thought that explaining it gently would give me a certain amount of control, but I was caught off guard by a phone call from Mary's second son, Jeffrey. I'd placed an advert in a local newspaper – someone saw it and sent me his address.

Unfortunately, he was a little deaf, so part of our conversation went via his daughter. They re-

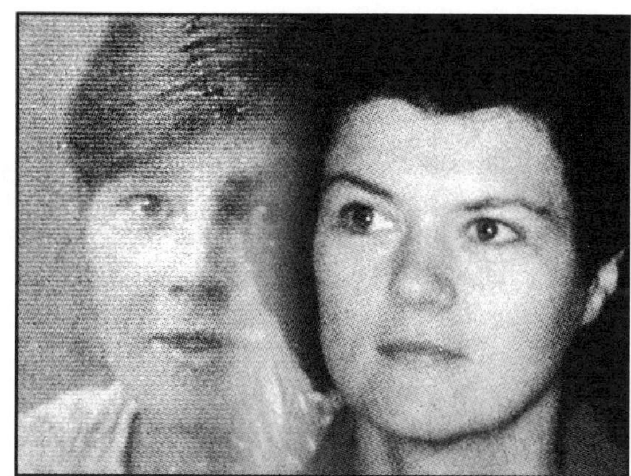

Mary and Jenny. There is a surprising physical likeness between the two women, despite the improbability of any genealogical relationship.

alised that I was not a direct member of the family but they weren't quite sure what my interest in them was. They gave me the addresses of two other sons. Then they asked me my connection, and I reeled back wondering what I could say without upsetting them. In the end I said it is very odd but I remember your family through dreams. They obviously weren't sure how to take this, but I later got back in touch with them and tried to explain again without actually saying "I *was* your mother." They didn't get in touch again.

It made me wonder whether I should have made contact another way, perhaps just finding out if they were all right. A month later, I managed to contact Sonny, the oldest son, who lived in England. I was *very* nervous when I phoned him, but he was brilliant. He was very direct as a boy, so I knew I had to be direct to him. I told him I'd had dreams about the old home in Malahide and the people who lived there. He challenged me to name one of the nearby roads, but I confessed to him that I had been there recently and seen a map so this was no real test.

We would have met, but the researcher for the TV documentary suggested we should keep apart until more work had been done on the background and statements had been taken. It was a good idea but incredibly frustrating. I didn't get to meet Sonny in person until about four months later.

FT: I believe that one of the girls, Phyllis, went to her priest after you contacted her, to get his opinion.

JC: Yes. He told her it couldn't be reincarnation, because the Church doesn't accept that. However, I've found the dogma on the subject to be very ambiguous. The priest suggested that it must have been the spirit of Mary acting through me to unite the family. There's an element of truth in that and it has been accepted by the family, though some of them now see it as reincarnation.

FT: Once you had reunited the children, did you feel any release from your nightmare, any sense of mission accomplished?

JC: Now that I had found them, and could look them in the eye and see they were happy and well-adjusted, it *was* a release. The fact that they were all together again made us all happy. I still hang on to them, keep contact, because they are important to me.

FT: When you met them in person, did you feel maternal, that they really were your children?

JC: Yes, I still feel like that but one step removed as it were. I stepped back almost too far, allowing them to get on with each other. The last time we met I had made room for them to make up their own minds how they interpreted the phenomenon. I didn't want to be in the way. It hadn't occurred to me how far I had stepped back until two of them, quite independently, asked me if I was going to keep in contact with them. In the end, they needed me to be there, which was wonderful.

FT: How has this experience affected your own beliefs?

JC: I have always had what you might call religious feelings – a sense of being – but without being attracted by any particular religion. There are bits of most religions that I find interesting, and other bits that I couldn't agree with.

I have been stopped by people who say "You are chosen, special." I certainly don't feel this has made me any better than anyone else – it just happened to me. I think it could happen to any of us. Maybe, in my case, I didn't finish very well. I had a strong maternal drive, and in my new life I couldn't forget the unfinished business.

I see life as a continuing process. I don't have any problem with the concept of energy continuing after a body wears out. I'm working on another book about my memories of other lives past and future – although that should be a premonition of a future life rather than a memory of it.

In dreams, Jenny vividly recalled Mary waiting on a jetty at dusk for someone to return. Sonny later told Jenny that he once worked as a caddy at a golf course on an island and his mother would wait on this jetty for his return in his boat.

The sense of time between lives seems to be different – linear but somehow brief. I seem to have had another life in the 21 years between Mary's death and my birth – under hypnosis I had brief glimpses, and a memory of a street that later checked out.

FT: If we can have premonitions of future lives, surely this raises the thorny philosophical problem of free will? If you have a future life, have the elements of it already happened to your future self?

JC: That's the way I would have put it. Whenever I have a premonition, it feels as though it is of something that has already happened – but you don't see it until it happens or has just happened. Other people have premonitions of things apparently as they happen or seem to be happening. I think that somewhere along the line we'll have to change our concept of time.

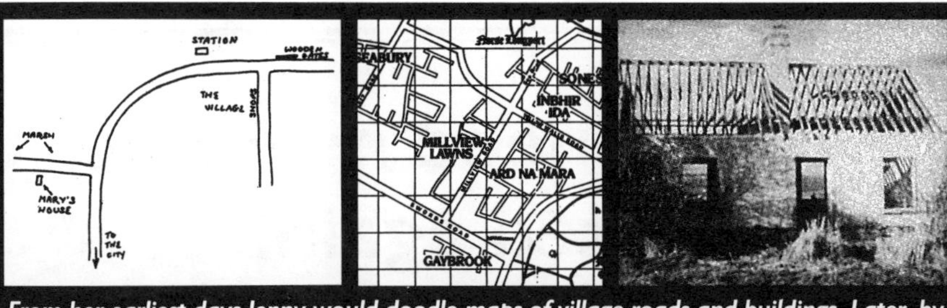

From her earliest days Jenny would doodle maps of village roads and buildings. Later, by a mysterious psychometry while looking at maps of Ireland, she recognised the layout of Malahide north of Dublin. There she saw the names she had known from dreams and memories, especially the house called 'Gaybrook' on Swords Road. When she finally met Mary's children, they confirmed Jenny's visions of such domestic details as a particular pair of oval photographs on the wall, and violent beatings by their drunken father.

LEFT – Jenny's map, and – CENTRE – the actual Malahide. Gaybrook Lodge, today, is a crumbling overgrown ruin – similar to this Malahide cottage, RIGHT – but still recognisable to Jenny as her home between 1923 and 1932, during her life as Mary.

Several times, in the course of our chat, Jenny had referred to her personality type, which she characterised as "being an introvert with an active imagination". I wondered whether she fitted the profile, emerging from current research, of the kind of person who could invent a fantasy life for herself, inhabit it, and accept it as real. It was quickly apparent that the issue is not that simple.

Certainly Jenny presents many of the noted characteristics: besides the psychic experiences she has referred to, she readily admits to having had a rich fantasy life "including imaginary friends"; she is extremely susceptible to hypnosis (at her second session, it only took a touch on the shoulder by the hypnotist to plunge her vividly into Mary's life); and she had the almost obligatory unhappy period in childhood, when her father's depressions and violence put tremendous stress on the home. A number of recent studies have focussed upon these kind of personality traits and the role they play in claims of, for example, abduction by UFOs, multiple personalities, or abuse by satanic covens, showing, in many instances, that the claimants have demonstrably *invented* a fantasy life for themselves.

When discussing fantasy-prone personalities, I have noticed that there is a tacit assumption that the fantasiser abandons objective control or any kind of critical thought. It may be argued that Jenny's early preoccupation with Mary's death amounted to an obsession; if so, it was one which Jenny tackled with precocious common sense.

When I asked Jenny how she knew her past-life memories were real and not simply imagined, she implied that they were significantly different in tone or quality. "There was never any doubt in my mind that they were real and not fantasy," she said. "I have had no problem in influencing my ordinary dreams, controlling them almost at will. Again this was something I assumed that other people could do. I remember once trying to change the ending of my dying dream and I woke up in worse tears than usual. In trying to alter the ending I was fantasising about it. It was no use because I *knew* that I died and left the children."

Another common misconception is that high fantasisers only use the talent to escape from reality. Jenny thought that was too glib in explaining her case – her experience was neither sought nor indulged in; in fact she tried to push it away because of its overwhelming feelings of anguish and helplessness. She said: "Imagination or fantasising can be used just as well to reinforce experience. Opening up a new world can inspire you spiritually as well as imaginatively, and that also is a reward." To this we might add other unresearched motivation such as self-entertainment or curiosity, both of which can be hugely rewarding.

We are just waking up to the role of the therapist in the discovery and disclosure of fantastic personal experiences – see, for example the articles by Jim Schnabel in *FT69* and *FT70*. We do not damn *all* therapists, but it is clear that, in a significant number of cases, extraordinary tales of possession, human sacrifice, bestial abuse, genetic experimentation, demonic assaults etc have been coaxed from patients by therapists who have a prior commitment to beliefs in such things, and who have then reinforced those beliefs in their unfortunate patients. It may be that the recovery of past-life memories using hypnotic regression is similarly confabulated by a therapist who already believes reincarnation is a fact, as Jenny's hypnotist did.

Where Jenny's story confounds this thesis is in the fact that the people in her life will confirm that she talked about this other life, drew maps and pictures, and began her search long before she was exposed to a hypnotist, and long before there was objective confirmation of the many tangible details she wrested from her memory and nightmare. In the end, she *did* bring together six of the eight children who had lost touch, and they are glad she did so, even if they don't quite understand *how* she came to do it. FT

F.T. MONSTER BARGAINS

Now... You need never be abducted again!

Fortean Times is proud to offer the most complete alien defence system yet devised. All the equipment you will ever need, developed by the SCHWA Corp. of Reno, Nevada.

SCHWA Corp. is constantly searching for ways to ease your comfort on this planet. With the discovery of the Xenon™ coating used in many SCHWA products, alien defence has entered a new era. This amazing coating alerts you to lost time and alien abductions you may have forgotten. (SCHWA Corp. also markets Plutonium™ coated alien repellent patches.)

EVERY PICTURE TELLS A LIE!
WRITE TO SCHWA BOX 6064 RENO NV 89513. SASE.

SCHWA STICKER & CARD PACK
Things you need! Includes alien invasion survival card, repellent patches, "Defended by SCHWA" car stickers and other cards and surprises - £4.50/£5.00 overseas.

COMPLETE SCHWA KIT
Includes stickers, cards, repellent patches, surprises and SCHWA book (T-shirt not included). Ends all doubts about the unknown now, forever! - £8.99/£9.99 overseas.

SCHWA T-SHIRT
100% cotton Hanes Beefy T will keep you safe at all times. Alien detector on front, SCHWA Corp. symbol on back. Glows in the dark on in the presence of aliens. Available in large or XL sizes - £9.99/£10.99 overseas.

SCHWA

1994 LUNAR CALENDAR

1994 8"X36" LUNAR CALENDAR
Shows phases of the moon. Printed on gloss card, may help prevent abduction - £4.50/£5.00 overseas.

SCHWA BOOK
Illustrated 76-page guide to alien defence. An ideal starting point for your survival needs. Designed to make *you* feel better - £4.50/£5.50 overseas.

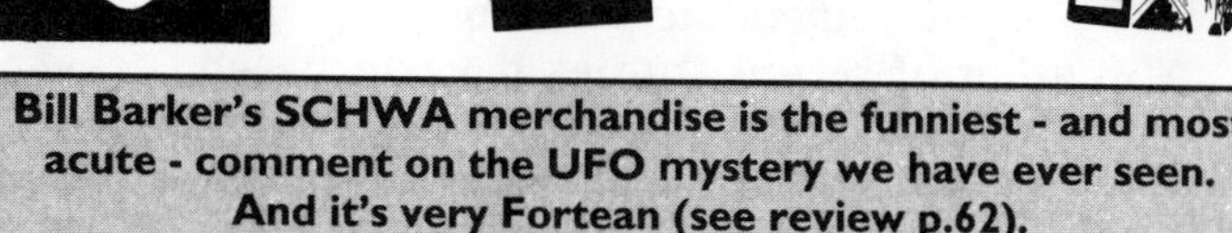
Bill Barker's SCHWA merchandise is the funniest - and most acute - comment on the UFO mystery we have ever seen. And it's very Fortean (see review p.62).

"Mind-blowing." Factsheet Five

"It's weird. I like it." PJ Stuckard

Give your home a Fortean theme with these beautiful hand-made crop circle tiles. Each tile is exquisitely detailed – you can even see the circular pattern of the flattened corn – and painted by hand.

There are five designs to choose from: **1. Silbury Hill, 2. Mandelbrot Set, 3.Three Satellites, 4. Church & Circle** and **5. Pictogram.** Each tile measures 132x90mm and comes complete with a felt underside, making it the perfect ornament for your mantlepiece or an ideal paperweight for your desk.

Makers Cropcraft of West Wickham, Kent, have been selling the tiles at £19.95 plus £2.50 postage and packing, but FT has negotiated a special price of just £10.95 inclusive for readers – a saving of £11.50.

There are even better discounts for multiple orders. Choose any three tiles and you get them at less than half price: just £30 (saving £37.35). Or take all five for £47.95 and saving a total of £64.30!

Each tile will be sent post free in secure packaging.

Hoax!

DRILLER CHILLER

Four years ago, the Christian fundamentalist press was much exercised by the story that Hell had been discovered by a drilling team in Siberia. PAUL SIEVEKING tries to excavate the roots of the rumour.

"**For a fire is kindled in mine anger, and shall burn unto the lowest hell, and shall consume the earth with her increase, and set on fire the foundations of the mountains." [Deuteronomy 32:22.]**

The earliest version of this outlandish yarn seems to be from the August 1989 edition of the Finnish monthly *Ammenusastia.* [1] Geologists in Siberia, under the direction of Dr Dimitri Azzakov (or Azzacov, Azzarov, Azzazov), found their drill spinning wildly at a depth of 14.4km (8.95 miles). "Our calculations indicate temperatures of 2,000 degrees F [almost 1,100 degrees C]", said Azzakov. "This is ten times higher than was anticipated." Micro-phones were lowered, and picked up the sound of a human voice screaming in pain. It sounded as if there were thousands (or millions) more screaming in the background. "Hopefully, what we found there will stay there" said Azzakov.

> "Microphones were lowered, and picked up the sound of a human voice screaming in pain. It sounded as if there were thousands (or millions) more screaming in the background."

The next development comes in a letter dated 7 January 1990, from Age Rendalen Jr, "Special counsellor to the Minister of Justice of Norway" [2], who said he heard of Hell's discovery in a Trinity Broadcasting Network broadcast while visiting California. On his return to Norway, he found "the newspapers full of reports about this incident". He quotes an interview with the Norwegian Bjarne Nummedal, 65, the chief seismologist of the project, in the 4 January edition of *Asker og Baerums Budstikke*, "Norway's largest and most reputable newspaper".

The crucial additions to the story are these: Nummedal described "a fountainhead of luminous gas shooting up from the drill site", out of which, he said, came "a brilliant being with bat wings". (Variations received by Christian papers across America describe fangs, evil eyes, screeching and sky writing.) Later, Nummedal saw ambulance crews circulating in the community. One driver he knew told him that they were supposed to sedate everybody with a drug known to erase short-term memory. Half the geologists involved in the drilling were Finnish and Norwegian. They were instantly dismissed and their lives threatened if they breathed a word about the discovery. The following day, a spokesman for the Ministry of Religious Affairs gave them all large [unspecified] bribes to keep quiet, and they were deported. Back home, Nummedal donated his bribe to charity and then told the whole story to the press.

So far, I have summarised successive reports in the Florida Christian paper, *The Midnight Cry* (April-July 1990). The story becomes more tangled when compared with other sources. *America's Promise Newsletter* from Arizona (March 1990) says that the televangelist Paul Crouch gave the Trinity Broadcasting Network report on Hell's discovery, and referred to an interview with R.J. Nummedal [sic]. In this version, the "brilliant being with bat's wings revealed itself with the words in Russian 'I have conquered' emblazoned against the dark Siberian sky." If this is the broadcast heard by Mr Rendalen, then he already knew of the Nummedal (R.J. or Bjarne) interview before his return to Norway. In any case, Mr Rendalen later repudiated his letter as a hoax (*Midnight Cry* Dec 1990). According to William P. Cheshire, editor of the *Arizona Republic*, the Foreign Press Service in Washington had never heard of the Norwegian paper that ran the Nummedal interview.

California talk show host Rich Buhler told the story of the chilling drilling in *Christianity Today* (July 1990). He referred to a letter-to-the-editor published in a Finnish newspaper written by an elderly man who thought he got his information from a Christian newsletter in California. His other reference was to a letter sent to a Texas evangelist from a *Finnish school teacher* who had heard the story while travelling in California and wrote the letter as a hoax just to see if the evangelist would use it. He did. This version, which seems to have turned the whole fishy story inside out, appeared in a report by Gustav Spohn for the Religious News Service, quoted in various US papers in August and September 1991.

Biblical Archaeology Review had an item about the subterranean horrors in its November/December 1990 issue, and the All Africa Press Service covered the story in its issue of 29 July 1991. They checked it out with a Finnish embassy official, who felt it was not true.

The basis for the whole yarn is probably the Kola borehole. (The Kola Peninsula is north of the White Sea in Soviet Lapland, just next to Finland.) The borehole is the world's deepest, started in 1970. It had gone down 12km (7.46 miles) by 1984. The drill was still encountering rock at that depth. The temperature increased by one degree Celsius every 100 metres to 3,000 metres, then by 2.5 degrees every 100 metres thereafter. At ten kilometres, it was a mere 180 degrees. The detail of the drill 'spinning wildly' may be based on the fact that the water content of the crust was much greater than expected. There were some small flows of gas, and large amounts of hot, mineralised water encountered. *Scientific American* Dec 1984, *New Scientist* 18 April 1985.

Our Finnish correspondent, Tuuri Heporauta, wired us on 5 December 1991: AMMENUSASTIA OBVIOUS HOAX POSTPONE PUBLISHING LETTER FOLLOWS. Alas, the letter never came. Tuuri died five days later from a cerebral hæmorrhage.

Notes:

1- *According to the June 1990 edition of The Midnight Cry (Box 3686, Tequesta, FL 33469), the article was written by Suome Jengi, ja Katulahetys r.y., Levasjoki 29880, Finland. Telephone 011 358 395 27105.*

2- *The address given for Rendalen is Stjerneblokkvn 20, Oslo, Norway.*

MISSING TIME

Peter Brookesmith, former editor of The Unexplained, reports on a UFO conference in Sheffield

Between 14 and 15 August this year, I mysteriously lost two days out of my life. Later, under hypnosis, I learned that I had gone to Sheffield, to the Independent UFO Network's conference *UFOs – Fact, Fraud or Fantasy*? An event that managed to provide as wide a sample of ufological wonders – or, depending on your point of view, horrors – as anyone could wish. [1]

For those interested, bewildered, infuriated or enormously amused at the current fashions among UFO buffs, it was a veritable feast, and one of the chief gurus of the present phase of the so-called 'alien abduction scenario', New York artist Budd Hopkins, came on stage for not one but two long lectures over the two-day event.

In his first address, Hopkins outlined his version of the now-famous, and much disputed, 'Linda Napolitano' (or 'Linda Cortile') case. According to Hopkins, at around 3:15 am on 30 November 1989, this 45-year-old mother of two was floated out of the *closed* window of a 12th-storey Manhattan apartment and into a waiting UFO. While this was happening, Mr 'Napolitano' slept the sleep of the just, but the event did not go unobserved.

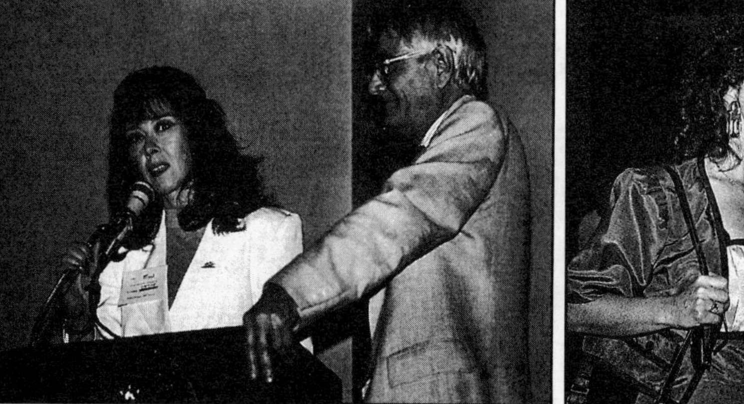

LEFT: Linda Napolitano and Budd Hopkins RIGHT: Linda Moulton Howe

On the ground nearby, two government security agents in a limo with a 'high-ranking political figure' (who has, Hopkins says, declined to *deny* the truth of his guards' account) watched all this happen through binoculars. On Brooklyn Bridge, about a quarter-mile distant, another person, a 60-ish grandmother, saw the party of aliens, the UFO and even Mrs Napolitano being floated into it. This witness's car had mysteriously failed, and the lights on the bridge blacked out. Other cars ground to a halt around and behind her. (The limo too had apparently broken down mysteriously.) Hopkins concludes that 'the aliens' deliberately stopped these vehicles to allow their occupants to witness the abduction. The event was a *demonstration*, in short, to warn us, in particular the anonymous high-powered politician, of what 'they' can do.

Cattle-mutilation chronicler and US TV documentary-maker Linda Moulton Howe also made two appearances to elaborate her belief that aliens are as avidly removing the juicier parts of animals as Hopkins thinks they are temporarily borrowing entire humans, if for different reasons. Some curious findings emerged: that, for example, cattle mutilations appear to involve a cutting instrument that generates enough heat to cook the haemoglobin in the tissues adjacent to the 'cuts'. Further, the way tissues are utterly drained even of capillary blood is quite unlike the effects of wounding by predators.

From southern Africa, Cynthia Hind – who deserves an award for being the drollest UFO investigator on any continent – came a treatment of what she called 'anomalous' alien abductions in Zimbabwe. This began for the Moslem female victim with sinister 'bedroom visitors', who felt her head, inserted something into her ears, and repeatedly raped her. No UFO as such seems to have been involved. Cynthia Hind also described the first case, to her knowledge, of a black African (an engineer) having encounters with alien entities. The core victims in another were a white mother and daughter, abducted in the early hours of the morning in Johannesburg. One of the atypical features of the case was the benign atmosphere that permeated their otherwise degrading experience at the hands of the 'aliens': indeed neither wished to leave the abductors' UFO. Cynthia Hind's suspicion is that ufonauts are not extraterrestrial, but are from other dimensions or times.

Philip Mantle gave an immaculately concise account of UFO facts, frauds and fantasies from Yorkshire in the last decade; and Andrew Collins (the well-known psychic quester) described how he and his associates had borrowed ideas and techniques from the psychologist Wilhelm Reich, combined them with infra-red photography, and come up with some very curious results that appear, despite the eccentric methods employed, to confirm the notion that some UFOs at least are natural in origin, but *may* be sentient, intelligent, or at least responsive to human activity.

Even sceptics had their spokesmen. Hilary Evans presented a devastating thesis that *everything* in the history of UFO reports since 1947 had been anticipated by science-fiction writers between the turn of the century and 1940.

Paul Devereux, meanwhile made a hugely cogent case, with admirable diplomacy, for regarding UFO phenomena – including the notorious abduction cases – as aspects of mental and physical *natural* events, little-understood though they may be. To learn that DMT, a substance secreted by the pineal gland and found in the psychoactive plants used in shamanic societies, can produce the subjective experience of entering another universe, was intriguing enough; to learn that those taking DMT see worlds replete with alien figures, whose features are common to all reports, was a revelation. Devereux made provocative links with this information and new data emerging from lucid dream research, and suggested that the abduction scenario (which he did not dismiss as a false *experience*) is a dramatisation of inner, individual psychological and spiritual alienation. Both these papers should set real ufologists off in genuinely interesting new directions of research. But will they?

In its way, this was all good stuff, whatever corner it came from. But a genuine ufology would look at every possible angle of a case as outlandish as Linda Napolitano's before ascribing it to 'aliens'. Not Budd Hopkins: he launched into his account without even a ritual nod toward the possibility that something else is at work here.

Nor did he make any attempt to address the radical criticisms and doubts about his technique and competence that others have made concerning this case and others he has pursued (for a brief review, see ***FT67:53***). And when one learns, from his own mouth, that he is – without qualification or training – hypnotically regressing children 'down to the age of two and a half' to ask them about their 'alien abduction' experiences, some instinct screams in protest.

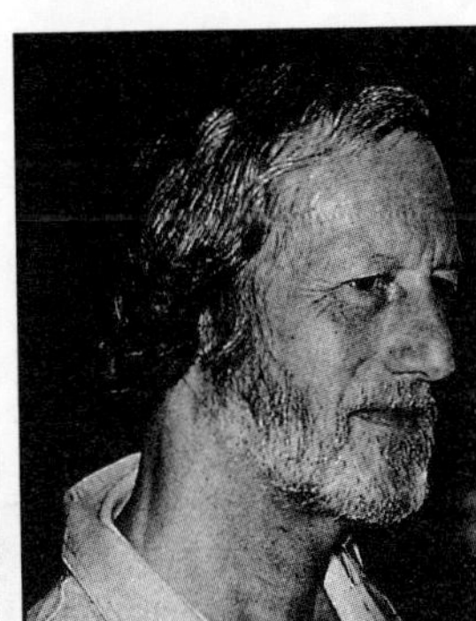

***ABOVE FROM LEFT TO RIGHT:* Jenny Randles, Paul Devereux and Hilary Evans**

The unshakability of Hopkins's belief in his scenario and his 'witnesses' became apparent in his second session, when he described a 1979 case in which, on a well-populated beach in Brisbane, Australia, a mother and her two children were abducted – beamed up into a UFO, it seems – leaving the father of the family paralysed, holding a camera, for an hour or more while they were away.

> "A similar tendency to find what you are looking for was evident in Jenny Randle's discovery of a window area, where 'something is distorting space and time' near her home on the Mersey estuary."

Amazingly, no one else on the beach noticed any of this. Budd Hopkins can tell you why: because all four *became invisible* during this period. To their conscious memory the husband and wife took four photographs of each other with their children. When developed, the pictures had a curious red cast, and showed the beach, but no figures. Hopkins thinks this case proves that 'aliens' can cloak their victims in invisibility and can themselves become selectively invisible (as they'd have to, to be able to abduct Linda Napolitano from right opposite the *New York Post's* busy night loading bay – a fact about that location that Hopkins mysteriously failed to mention at Sheffield).

'They were in a realm where they could see each other and the beach and everyone on it, but no one could see them," Hopkins suggested. ... An invisible man holding an invisible camera with invisible film takes a visible picture that shows what everyone else could see [ie an empty beach] ... This principle of cloaking can be switched on and off.'

The same kind of presumption lies behind Linda Moulton Howe's notion that aliens are up to something nasty with cattle (and even cats) in America's wide-open spaces. From the evidence she presented, something odd does seem to be afoot here. Even the famous black helicopters that used to swarm around these cases have become invisible now! But why aliens, and not the angry ghosts of American Indians, the spirit of the Great American Dragon, or worried Atlanteans?

A similar tendency to find what you are looking for was evident in Jenny Randles's discovery of a window area, where 'something is distorting space and time' just south of the Mersey estuary between Runcorn and Warrington. It struck me as not insignificant that this area is right on Ms Randles's home doorstep: that is, I suspect that in the last 50 years *any* small area of the British Isles will have seen a few scruffy old polts, a close encounter or two, some ghosts, a disembodied voice and a few earthlights, maybe even the occasional crop circle or mysteriously deceased cow, come and go.

Ms Randles also *seems* to have taken at face value the idea that some UFOs can't land in the wet – difficulty with 'electrical charges', you know. Funny how the aliens can hop the dimensions and make themselves invisible, but it hasn't dawned on them to abduct a few yards of terrestrial rubber.

Only two speakers really addressed the theme of the conference – 'fact, fraud or fantasy' – and they were the true sceptics, Evans and Devereux. The sight of a small but perfectly formed 'gray' appearing on the screen during Evans's address was made delightful by the news that this was an illustration from a French magazine published at the turn of the century. Or did Evans get this all wrong? Surely this is part of the insidious programme of 'education' (ie softening up) we've been subjected to over the years, that's to ready us for the Great Extra-Terrestrial Revelation? Is it hell.

The implication of Hilary Evans's address was supported by Paul Devereux: there is something in the human mind that creates consistent forms for alien figures.

But then isn't that what Alvin Lawson was saying more than a decade ago, if adducing his evidence from elsewhere? I called this piece 'Missing Time' because the last event like this I went to was in Chicago in 1982, where Dr Lawson first presented this thesis – and hardly anything in ufology has changed since.

In 1982 crashed saucers were making a comeback. Now abductions are the chic thing, on a curious parallel track with the more public fascination with child abuse in sundry horrible forms. When will the first *fashionable* 'transportee' case arise as a rebirth of the old 'contactee' myth? Before the next decade is out, I wager.

Note:

[1] *Anyone interested in what was said* ***verbatim*** *can write to Stu Smith at 15 Rydal Street, Burnley, Lancs BB10 1HS, UK, for audio or video tapes of the proceedings.*

LOVECATS: THE NEXT GENERATION

Dr Karl P.N. Shuker examines some possible jungle cat hybrids

Shortly after my Lovecats report ***[FT68:50]***, examining the possibility that escapee Asian jungle cats *Felis chaus* were mating with feral domestic cats in Britain to yield fertile hybrids, I contacted Gareth B. Thomas, the vet who had examined the adult male jungle cat discovered dead close to a farm at Richards Castle, Ludlow, Shropshire, on 3 February 1989.

A few days after the examination, he told me, Mrs Jeanette Powell, living nearby at the time in the Leintwardine area, brought in a male kitten, Jasper, to be castrated. Thomas was startled to discover that this kitten was more than a little reminiscent of the jungle cat he had just examined. He took various photographs before the anæsthetic wore off.

Considerably larger than other kittens of his age, Jasper had grey fur that lacked markings on his flanks; a very prominent black dorsal stripe running along his back to the end of his tail, which was heavily-ringed with a black tip; stripes on his limbs; black tufts at the ends of his noticeably broad-based ears; a white ring encircling each eye; white jaws; and notably large canine teeth. Although jungle cats are usually brown or fawn, grey specimens have been recorded, and the other features listed above for Jasper are typical of jungle cats, and were all exhibited by the Ludlow specimen.

Jasper – a jungle cat hybrid?

Thomas learned that Jasper's mother was a grey feral domestic cat who had been tamed by Mrs Dorothy Williams of Whitton Farm (also in Leintwardine) – near to which the cat had first appeared during the mid-1980s. Known as Mother, she has given birth to several litters – including the August 1988 litter that contained Jasper. Mrs Williams told me that Mother has tufted, lynx-like ears, stripes on her limbs and tail, and ginger patches on her grey fur, but unlike Jasper she has only an average-sized body.

Apparently, Mother is one of a number of unusual feral cats in the area that are similar to the jungle cat, and which the locals call 'lynxes' or 'wild cats'. As the Ludlow jungle cat is believed to have been on the loose for up to five years, could these be hybrid descendants of this non-native escapee? Thomas considers it possible that Jasper is a second-generation hybrid descendant. His father is unknown, but the *chaus* characteristics of Mother suggest she could be one such crossbreed.

I visited Mrs Powell last May and came face to face with her enigmatic pet. A sturdy, powerfully muscular cat, he was certainly very large, weighing 14lb, but with tantalising ambiguity he recalled three different types of cat. To add to the confusion, two of these, both domestic breeds, share features of the third, the jungle cat.

Jasper's face, chest and banded limbs reminded me of the Egyptian mau, supposedly derived from an undetermined species of wild cat in ancient Egypt, a region now home both to the African wildcat *Felis silvestris lybica* and to the jungle cat. The mau shares the jungle cat's white 'spectacles', its limb striping, white 'moustache' across its jaws, tufted ears with wide bases, and heavily-ringed black-tipped tail.

Conversely, Jasper's dorsal stripe and unmarked flanks, and once again his tufted ears, resembled those of the Abyssinian cat – a very distinctive domestic breed which looks remarkably like the jungle cat. Jasper's relatively short limbs and long tail, however, were not Abyssinian features, but did resemble *chaus*. Jasper had a brother, George, who shared his distinct dorsal stripe and wide-based tufted ears, but was ginger and white, more gracile in build, with longer limbs and weighing 12lb.

If Jasper had possessed George's build, he would have looked ever more like a jungle cat; yet, even without this, it was easy to see why Thomas had been so impressed by his correspondence to this species. I learnt that over successive moults Jasper was gradually acquiring brown fur; if his grey pelage is eventually replaced entirely with brown, this will enhance his resemblance to a typical jungle cat.

Could Jasper and George really be hybrid grandsons of the Ludlow jungle cat? Or are they simply unusual pure-bred domestics whose jungle cat characteristics are due to a descent from domestic breeds such as the Abyssinian and mau that themselves resemble wild species? I asked a number of mammalian geneticists in Britain and overseas whether blood samples could determine taxonomic identity – via chromosomal analyses or DNA hybridisation. The replies were not encouraging.

No features unequivocally distinguishing the karyotype (chromosomal complement) of the jungle cat from that of the domestic cat have yet been documented, and DNA hybridisation techniques are insufficiently rigorous at present for conclusive differentiation of jungle cats, domestic cats and hybrids. As for anatomic analyses, the jungle cat has not been studied sufficiently to offer much hope either. A definitive taxonomic identification of Jasper and George will have to await scientific advances.

My thanks to Mr Gareth Thomas, Mrs Jeanette Powell and Mrs Dorothy Williams for their kind assistance.

BEDEVILLED

MIKE DASH updates our 'Satanic Child Abuse' file with a major case from New Zealand and news of some continuing cases

The United States, Britain, Australia, Canada, South Africa ... allegations of Satanic ritual abuse have been made in almost every English-speaking territory. So we were less than surprised to hear from our correspondent Peter Hassall that a case being tried in the New Zealand city of Christchurch had all the familiar elements.

Peter Ellis, 35, a worker at the Christchurch Civic Childcare Centre, stood accused of abusing up to 50 toddlers left in his care between December 1986 and May 1991. Three female workers at the centre were said to have helped him conduct weird, possibly Satanic or Masonic, rituals and terrorise their charges by locking them in subterranean mazes or in cages hung from a ceiling.

So far, so typical ... after all, three prominent US cases – the seminal McMartin pre-school scare, which collapsed in a welter of ever-more-inventive accusations, New York's Wee Care Day Nursery case and North Carolina's Little Rascals saga [see below] involved allegations of ritual abuse in the pervert's paradise of a day care centre. Where the Christchurch case differed from the majority of its precursors, though, was in the guilty verdicts delivered to Ellis and the 10-year jail sentence imposed on him for 16 'proven' charges of sexual violation, indecent assault and doing an indecent act.

Peter Ellis (left) was found guilty, but his co-workers (right) were cleared of child abuse.

The story began in November 1991 when one child attending the centre told his father he did not like his teacher's "black penis". Questioned, he said that this was "just a story", but his concerned parents turned for help to a "community consultant" who had been working at the centre. A month later, Ellis was suspended from his job. The child was then formally interviewed three times without making any direct allegations of abuse.

Concern spread rapidly through the area as parents shared fears that their own offspring might also be victims. The local police conducted an investigation which was concluded without charges being brought, but three months later, in March 1992, Ellis was arrested and booked on the first of what became 45 indecency charges. On 3 September, the crèche was closed after the Ministry of Education revoked its operating licence.

The Christchurch case followed three years of growing concern at the scale of child sexual abuse in New Zealand, beginning with a 1988 telethon in aid of abuse victims and gathering pace with the heavily-publicised allegation by two female psychiatrists that as many as one in four New Zealand girls were being abused.

Social workers investigating Ellis, led by the appropriately-named Dr Karen Zelas, conducted dozens of interviews and concluded "the children had a general fear of Peter Ellis and ... he has handled them roughly." But by then, more specific allegations of abuse were beginning to emerge.

A mass of complainants (13 in all) laid more than two dozen charges concerning the abuse of 20 of the 116 children interviewed by the authorities (police said over 50 infants had made allegations), and the sheer weight of evidence meant things looked bleak for Ellis.

Many of the charges were levelled by one six-year-old, already in therapy before the case began, whose story unfolded over a series of five lengthy interviews. At first the child's allegations centred on straightforward sexual abuse in the crèche toilet, but the story gradually became more bizarre: 'Peter' had made him eat 'poos', had dressed as a witch and threatened to turn his victim into a frog if he told anyone what was going on.

During the third interview, the child told of being thrust through a trapdoor into a maze where he was accosted by two of Ellis's 'friends', called Spikehead and Boulderhead; during the fourth he said children from the crèche had been made to stand naked in a circle drawn on the floor of Ellis's house. Slit-eyed adults playing guitars stood outside the circle; they carried magic knives, wore white suits and pretended to be cowboys. After the ceremony, the adults put the children into ovens and pretended they would be eaten.

Asked why he had not mentioned these details earlier, the boy replied: "Oh, I just remembered today."

Familiar doubts were expressed at the conduct of many of the interviews. Several other children were interviewed two or three times, a process later described by Harris's prosecutors as 'peeling the onion' to get at the core of each supposed victim's experience, and by the defence as 'softening up' of confused, bored and inconsistent witnesses. Impossibilities and contradictions in the children's stories were never cleared up, and police said they were worried by parents asking their children leading questions before the formal interviews.

Much was also made, by the press at least, of the community consultant who had made the initial allegations against Ellis. She, it was revealed, was the co-founder of a private abuse therapy organisation called START and had long been interested in cases of child sexual abuse.

The case finally came to court in April 1993, and both prosecution and defence argued their cases along lines familiar to anyone who followed US and British ritual abuse cases. According to the Crown, its child witnesses (who were aged between three and five when the alleged abuse took place) gave details no toddler could have made up. The defence contended that their allegations emerged from lengthy and leading questioning conducted by desperately anxious parents, and pointed to a complete lack of generally acceptable physical evidence.

The two month court case ended when the jury found Ellis guilty on 16 of 25 charges (the acquittals concerned charges that children had been assaulted with needles and sticks) and the judge, noting that the verdicts were "obviously correct", sentenced the defendant to a decade in gaol. Ellis's female co-workers were discharged early on when the judge decided there was not enough evidence to proceed against them.

"I don't blame the children at all," said Debbie Gillespie, one of the four women. "They don't think they are actually lying. They are emotionally manipulating their parents. Every time they disclosed they would get these cuddles, they would get to stay up past their bedtime and get told, 'We love you, you're a brave boy.'"

Ellis immediately announced plans to appeal against his sentence, but we have heard nothing since.

***LEFT:* Robert Kelly**

***ABOVE:* Betsy Kelly**

SHARK SENTENCE

In Farmville, North Carolina, meanwhile, Robert Kelly has finally been found guilty of some of the 183 charges of Satanic pædophilia he was accused of committing at his Little Rascals day-care centre [***FT60:35*** and ***FT71:24***].

He received 12 consecutive life sentences for his crimes, despite the pleas of three jurors who refused to believe tales of children fed to tanks full of ravenous sharks (Jim Schnabel gives further details in his article last issue), and his wife Betsy is shortly due to stand trial as an accomplice.

The *Daily Telegraph* columnist Claudia FitzHerbert, who has joined the *Independent's* Rosie Waterhouse as a regular critic of the abuse scares, drew attention to a little-remarked, but potentially enormously important, detail of this case. "Neither the fundies nor the feminists appear to have had anything to do with the case," she observed, "but Betsy Kelly feels there is some significance in the fact that most of the accusations came from mothers who did not work, and determined to destroy the day care centre for complicated reasons of their own."

"Her tale tallies with others I have heard, of a new militancy among stay-at-home mums. 'Maternal correctness' involves the banding together of women who have forgone their careers for the sake of their children and are consumed with loathing for their less sacrificial sisters. They drive cars with 'The Mom' number plates and persecute working mothers with anonymous telephone calls detailing their children's inadequacies. That they are now banding together is very bad news indeed."

PEANUT BITTER

Further up the Atlantic seaboard, New Jersey child care centre worker Kelly Michaels was recently released from prison after serving four years of a 47-year sentence for abusing dozens of infants at the Wee Care Day Nursery in Maplewood.

Michaels, who was alleged to have raped the toddlers with cutlery, licked peanut butter off their genitals and forced them to eat 'cakes' of her fæces, was released after an appeal court ruled she had not had a fair trial. The judge questioned whether the elaborate ritual abuse Michaels was supposed to have committed over a three-year period would have been possible in a busy church.

ORKNEY SAGA

Britain's longest-running and most bitterly-disputed ritual abuse case also reached some sort of conclusion earlier this year with the suspension and eventual resignation of Paul Lee, the director of the islands' tiny social services department. He was given a bumper £57,000 kiss-off.

Lee, whose suspension on full salary was ordered at a closed meeting of the Orkney Islands council, was paying the penalty for ordering dawn raids in which nine children were taken from their homes after allegations that they had been regularly abused by a Satanic coven led by a local priest, the Reverend Morris McKenzie [see ***FT57:50***]. McKenzie (an elderly man with a heart condition) was alleged to have stripped naked in the biting Orkney winters and abused his charges during rituals in an abandoned quarry.

Sadly, McKenzie himself became a victim of the case at roughly the time his chief accuser was clearing his desk. In May he took early retirement and announced he was leaving the islands, still bitter he had been unable to formally clear his name. "As a Christian minister I ought to be able to forgive – but I can't yet," he admitted.

Also facing an uncertain future are the eight Orkney children 'uplifted' from their schools by social workers in November 1990. They belonged to a single "large and unruly" local family, the father of which had received a prison term for sexually abusing a daughter ... and it was constant questioning of these children that eventually produced the accusations that led to the seizure of the more famous nine in February 1991.

Two of the girls responsible for the original allegations have now given details of the methods social workers used to extract 'evidence'. "I was put in a room with a piece of paper and a pen and told to write down what had happened, and if I didn't write it down I wasn't coming out," one said. "I got bribed with a pair of new shoes. I was told that if I said something more I could have two pairs."

Almost three years on, seven of the original eight are still in care, their mother's access to them has been cut, and one has become involved in solvent abuse. Only when the children turn 16 are they free to leave their foster families and return home.

The consequences of the Orkney case are beginning to affect social services nationwide with the publication in late July of a White Paper entitled *Child Care Policy and Law*. It encompasses recommendations made by Lord Clyde after his enquiry into the Orkney affair, the most significant of which strictly controls an authority's option to 'uplift' children, and outlaws the notorious dawn raids.

Paul Lee, Witchfinder General of the Orkneys.
BELOW: Rev. Morris McKenzie, victim of the witch-hunt.

NORTHOLT NEWS

Yet another British ritual abuse case made headlines briefly in June, but by now the press had learned the lesson of earlier debacles. The story made its cautious appearance on the home news pages, rather than splashed on the front cover, and there was no mention of satanism – just abuse and "unpleasant practices connected with witchcraft" in a church in Northolt, Middlesex, the previous Hallowe'en.

On the stand at the Old Bailey were the father, uncle, aunt and grandfather of a 10-year-old girl who described a catalogue of abuse at the hands of the accused, including rape, buggery and indecent assault. The main defendant was her father, whom she accused of sexually abusing her from the age of three.

Several years later, she went on, she was taken to a 'devil church', where she was stripped, tied up, and abused by adults wearing black cloaks and balaclavas. "They used to have pictures of ghosts and stuff," she added.

Cross-examined on a video link, the girl said seven children were involved in the rituals, performed by around 20 adults. Two girls had tried to commit suicide to escape the group, and a boy was dangled by his ankles from an open window to force him to agree to perform sex acts on an adult. The girl denied she had fabricated the accusations after watching horror videos. If the outcome of this case has been reported, no news or clipping has reached us.

SUBTERRANEAN SUBMARINE

This summer has been a bonanza for submarines. STEVE MOORE reviews four discoveries.

It sounds like one of *those* stories: *"Turkish Miners hit German Sub"*... but it seems that very thing happened at the beginning of September, in the village of Akpinar on the Black Sea coast. In a large open-cast pit, an excavator was working through sand and lignite when it hit the U-boat, buried in a dry sand wall between the mine and the sea, 15 feet below sea level. Working back into the wall, the small submarine was uncovered, complete with loaded torpedo tubes. At this point, archæologists will probably start to weep...

Turkey's version of the SAS blew up the live torpedoes, then spent three days digging through the wreckage and piling up the contents on the sand: wooden lockers, lead basins, leather boots, human bones, a plaque in German script, a serial number tag possibly dated 1902 and a fountain pen inscribed *Der Kimmelstiel.* It seems that an explosion had twisted the metal deck and fire had charred everything inside. But how the submarine, presumably a UB or UC class boat on active service in World War I, ended up in the mine is a mystery ... and likely to stay that way. There being no sign of treasure to be found, what remained of the submarine was scooped out of the sand by an excavator and, presumably, dumped.

This, however, is only the latest in a rash of U-boat discoveries. In June, the *U1226* was found by divers four miles off Cape Cod, Massachusetts, with the remains of 50 sailors and spies aboard. She had been sunk by an allied bomber in October 1944, on its way to drop the spies on the coast.

In July, the *UB30* was found in 160 feet of water, three miles off Whitby, N. Yorkshire. She was sunk on 13 Aug 1918 after being rammed by an armed trawler, the *John Gilman,* and hit by shore batteries and depth charges. The remains of up to 20 sailors are said to be on board, and the 121-foot-long, 257-ton vessel is reported to be in 'perfect condition'.

On 23 August, salvagers raised the 230-foot-long *U534* from the seabed near the Danish island of Anholt, where she had lain since being sunk by a British Liberator bomber on 5 May 1945. Being part of the long-range 33rd Flotilla which specialised in runs to Japan, expectations were high of finding treasure, documents and possibly the remains of high-ranking Nazis, fleeing in the last days of the war. After six tons of torpedoes and ammunition were removed, examination began. No treasure or Nazis so far, but 100 bottles of vintage wine have been found, almost 2,000 condoms ... and a safe which is apparently stuffed with documents, diaries and film canisters. It seems that although the rest of the sub was flooded, the diaries and documents were stuffed into the safe so tightly they remained sealed and are mostly legible. Whether they'll contain any surprises remains to be seen.

Independent, 27 July, 24&25 Aug, 8 Sept; D.Telegraph, 12 June, 27 July; Times & Sunday Times, 24 Aug; NY Post, 23 Sept 1993.

ABOVE: Turkish workers uncover the German U-Boat found on 4 September 1993 in a mine at Kemerburgaz, on the edge of the Black Sea, 40km from Istanbul. LEFT: Another German submarine, 'U534', being raised in the Kattegat Sea off Denmark on 23 August 1993.

DIARY OF A MAD PLANET

August - September 1993

This diary aims to record, in two-month segments, the geophysical highlights of our planet: the tempests and tantrums, the oddities and extremities.

LANDSLIDES ***7 August JAPAN: Vehicles stranded after torrential rain triggered landslides in Kogoshima on the southern island of Kyushu. Some 80 people were killed in southern Japan during July and August as the country experienced the coldest and wettest summer since the war.***

FLOODS 30 July MISSOURI: The Midwest flooding [see *FT71:47*] lifted and carried downstream over 50 coffins from the cemetery in Hardin, western Missouri, some ending up 10 miles away, snagged in trees and bushes, some of them open.

A survey found that 18% of Americans believed the floods were "God's punishment on the people of the US for their sinful ways". *Plus ça change...*

EARTHQUAKE 8 August MARIANA ISLANDS: (12.97N 144.74E) 8.0R, 61km down. The world's strongest quake since an 8.2R event in the South Pacific in May 1989. Extensive damage on Guam, 48 injuries and a general power outage. Moderate tsunami and heavy damage of port facilities. (Japan's 12 July earthquake [see *FT71:47*] moved Okushiri island about two yards westward.)

HAIL 9 August FRANCE: At least 100 vehicles were damaged by tennis-ball-sized hailstones in a freak 10-minute storm outside Lyon. Steve Edington and his family, returning to Lincolnshire, had their Ford Sierra badly battered and all the windows smashed. Equally large hailstones fell in the Dordogne region on 15 August.

FLOODS 12 August UKRAINE & BELARUS: Heavy flooding from weeks of rain increased background radiation levels in areas stricken by the 1986 Chernobyl nuclear disaster – between 19 and 24 curies per week in the Dniper River, for instance.

SWARM 13 August POLAND: An unprecedented mosquito plague hit the northwestern coast, clearing the beaches and endangering drivers. The insects fell like rain in Szczecin province, near the German border.

Meanwhile, Pakistan faced its most serious locust attack in 30 years.

DROUGHT 20 August AUSTRALIA: Thousands of hungry emus moved south from drought areas in New South Wales and Queensland. Mobs of up to 300 of the four-foot, flightless birds damaged crops and jeopardised road traffic.

FLOOD 27 August CHINA: A dam burst at the Gouhou reservoir in the remote western Qinghai province, wiping out several villages and killing more than 240 people. Another 150 were missing. The reservoir, in the Hainan Tibet prefecture, was holding about 92 million cubic feet of water.

SWARM 21 September CHINA: A Chinese oil tanker was attacked by a swarm of millions of dragonflies in the Yellow Sea. A frightened crewman jumped overboard. Lookouts had sighted an 'obstruction' five miles long by two miles wide skimming quickly towards the tanker.

EARTHQUAKE 29 September INDIA: (18.05N 76.42E) 6.3R, 6km down. Deathtoll: 10,000 (official), 30,000 (media). Extreme devastation in Latur-Osmanabad area of Maharashtra. Khilari (pop. 18,000) destroyed. Felt in Bombay, Hyderabad and Madras.

Special thanks to the Global Seismology Group of the British Geological Survey for the earthquake data.

Secret Country

Mysterious places to visit in Great Britain compiled by Janet & Colin Bord

11: Silbury Hill and West Kennet long barrow

These two sites form part of a tight nexus of major enigmatic monuments including Avebury Henge, Kennet Avenue (standing stones), the Sanctuary (once the site of a circular wooden building), and Windmill Hill (the largest British causeway enclosure yet found).

Silbury Hill is the largest prehistoric man-made mound in Europe, 130 feet high and covering over five acres. It has been estimated that it took 18 million man-hours to construct. The hill's significance is still hotly debated; archæologists have failed to prove that it was built as a tomb for a high-ranking chieftain. Other suggestions include a gigantic sundial, with a large pole erected on the top – though why go to all the trouble of building a huge mound for this purpose? Michael Dames in his book *Silbury Treasure* (now available again in paperback from Thames & Hudson) saw Silbury as a representation of the winter goddess.

In 1776, the Duke of Northumberland got Cornish tin miners to dig a shaft down from the summit and in 1849 a tunnel was dug into the centre from the base, and this was re-excavated by Professor Richard Atkinson in 1968-70, but no trace of a burial was found (though it may still await discovery). Something was learned of Silbury's construction, however. The first phase dates from 2500BC, when a 16ft mound was built. It was soon enlarged; then the plan was changed and a much larger mound was constructed in steps. Finally, the steps were filled in to give a smooth slope.

Inside West Kennet long barrow

According to legend, Silbury is the burial place of King Sil, who is somewhere inside, upright and on horseback, wearing golden armour, or in a golden coffin; or it was a load of soil dumped by the Devil, who abandoned his plan to bury Avebury (or Devizes) when he met a man (who was in fact a cobbler carrying his work with him) who said he had worn out a sackful of shoes while coming from there; or the Devil made the hill when he wiped his spade while building the Wansdyke.

At one time it was the custom for local people to gather on top of the hill on Palm Sunday, and there to consume fig cakes and sugared water. In recent years, it has been a centre of crop circle activity, which has led to a body of modern folklore: the Devil has been supplanted by extraterrestrials.

On a crest of a hill overlooking Silbury lies West Kennet long barrow, one of Britain's finest chambered tombs. It is Neolithic, more than 320ft long and 8ft high, made largely of earth. A stone passage runs 33ft into the mound at its eastern end. There are two small chambers either side of the passage and one at the end, all of which contained burials. Forty-six burials have been found and there is evidence that many more remains were removed in the 17th century, some by Dr Toope of Marlborough who used the bones to make medicines. Also found were flints, beads, animal bones and pottery, the dating of which indicates that the tomb was in use for about 1,000 years. The only recorded belief connected with this once-important place is that the ghost of a priest enters the barrow at sunrise on Midsummer Day, followed by a ghostly white dog with red ears. **FT**

Silbury Hill

LOCATION
Beside the A4, 5 miles west of Marlborough, and just south of Avebury. Silbury Hill: SU 100685.
West Kennet long barrow: SU 104677

Janet and Colin Bord are authors of Mysterious Britain, The Secret Country, Alien Animals, The Atlas of Magical Britain, and modern Mysteries of Britain among many others

GENETICS
Anthony McLuskey is a genetic scientist from Glasgow

PHENOMENOLOGY
Robert Anton Wilson is a prolific American trickster and author best known for his sf trilogy with Robert Shea, *Illuminatus!*

SCIENCE WATCH
Dennis Stacy, a freelance journalist living in Texas, edits the monthly *Journal* of MUFON, the largest UFO organisation in the US.

FOLKLORE
Michael Goss writes about folklore and mysteries. He has compiled a bibliography on poltergeists and a book on phantom hitch-hikers

GENETICS

Cloning Recipes

Anthony McLuskey explains why he won't be producing living dinosaurs

I'm a genetic scientist, and everyone seems to think that I want to take over the planet with my specially-engineered, super-powered *Jurassic Park* T-rex clones. No, I'm not paranoid: people actually think that I spend my time making two-headed babies, nasty die-bastard viruses and the like.

People assume that we geneticists have god-like powers. The reasoning goes like this: "They're always saying that DNA is the blueprint for making a human-being. It's very easy to follow a blueprint, so it must be easy to change it into something else, if you want, right?" Wrong. The blueprint thing is a misleading analogy. It's more useful to think of the genome as a *recipe* for a human.

Think of it like this: you've got a book that has the recipes for a five-course meal, comprising a starter, soup, main dish, sweet and after-dinner thingy. Now come the complications. First of all, the recipes are all in a foreign language. You can follow the instructions, step by step, but you have no idea what it is you are making, and won't know until you eat it. This would be OK if the recipes were in sequence, but they aren't. They're all mixed up. There's worse. The recipes aren't set out nicely on separate pages, but are joined together by gibberish sentences which can't be separated from the recipes. There's gibberish *inside* the recipes as well. Like this:

"A large onion, a pound of chicken pieces, a half pint of – cludgy coloured sproggets for the large nippled onions of Bingo land! Aha cries Rodney, it's time for my – chicken stock."

Except, of course, that there's no punctuation, all the words are run together and it's all in a foreign language which you don't understand. What's more, you get bits of one recipe stuck in the middle of another.

The individual recipes are the genes, made up of DNA. The words are made up of the letters A,T,C and G, which correspond to molecules called *nucleotides*, which are attached to the DNA and spell out three-letter words called *codons*. It is the order of these codons which make up the so-called sequence of the gene. The bits of the sequence that make up the message are called the *exons* and the gibberish bits are called the *introns*.

> **"The idea that *anyone* can alter the DNA sequence in order to make superhumans is just a load of nonsense."**

The above describes the composition of a genome encoding five genes, whereas the human genome has approximately 50,000 genes, of which scientists understand about one per cent – if we're lucky. A big problem is there can be lots of genes which are pretty much alike, but are found in different cell types. Genes also switch themselves on and off as the organism ages, as if by magic.

The development of the fœtus is still largely a mystery. Oh, you'll hear scientists on *Equinox* talking about 'developmental switches', 'differential expression patterns', 'gastrulation', 'neuralation' and the like, but don't be fooled. They really don't know what the hell is going on, any more than you do. The idea that *anyone* can alter the DNA sequence in order to make superhumans, or take a sample of Hitler's blood and use it to make lots of little cloned Hitlers in a jar, or even (I'm afraid, Mr Spielberg) get some T-rex DNA, put it into a frog and make a new little dinosaur, is just a load of nonsense.

What we want to do is help people: finding cures for cancer and AIDS, and genetic diseases like cystic fibrosis and muscular dystrophy. We want to help feed the world by making crops that can survive under conditions of extreme heat and/or cold; by improving yield and making our plant friends less susceptible to destructive viruses and insects.

Science fiction is just that: fiction. We can't bring back the dinosaurs. Scientists are not the demi-gods that you see at the movies, but ordinary people – some nice guys and gals, some bastards and some absolutely *barking mad*.

Preposterous Perception

Robert Anton Wilson plays cat-and-mouse with hypno-hype

The doctrine of Preposterous Perception holds that almost all of us see crazy and 'unbelievable' things most of the time – almost *all* the time – even when we're not on acid. Why don't we remember this? Because we repress the memory in order to fit into a repressive society. Many experts vehemently deny that PP exists at all. Other experts claim that denying PP marks one as akin to those who deny the Greenhouse Effect or the Second Law of Thermodynamics.

In fact, the whole PP feud has opened a 'can of worms' that begins to look more like a can of cobras. We face here the almost unthinkable question: Who has the objectivity to distinguish scepticism (in the scientific sense) from denial (in the neurotic sense)? Or even from denial (in the legal sense)?

Perhaps the problem began with Whitley Streiber. As Prof. H.H. Sheissenhosen (University of Heidelberg) has written, "Maybe somewhere out in space, in a galaxy far away, some especially perverted little aliens do exist. Maybe these vicious little buggers (I speak precisely) occasionally get their hands or tentacles on some especially nefarious drug.

"*Maybe* after these aliens have all become totally 'wasted', one of them cries, 'Hey, fellas, let's hop in the flying saucer and buzz over to Earth and have another go at some of that sweet Whitley Streiber ass.' And *maybe* they all whizz across billions of light-years just to ram the poor man's rectum with weird instruments one more time.

"*Maybe.* Nonetheless, some doubts arise in any dispassionate contemplation of this scenario."

Dr David Jacobs, on the other hand, insists that, after careful study of extraterrestrial sexual abuse, he believes these people have indeed literally suffered alien rape, an experience so much more traumatic than ordinary rape that most victims block out the memory entirely – until Dr Jacobs skillfully helps them recall it.

Do these hypnotic visions belong in the category of the real or the hallucinatory? Don't expect me to answer such questions. Maybe "the Shadow knows", but I'm as uncertain as Hamlet after he encountered what seemed to him a possible appearance of his father's ghost.

Perhaps the *real* Memory Mystery began not with these Alien Abductors but with the McMartin Pre-School follies in Southern California in 1983 which kicked off the Satanic child-abuse business. Sociologist Jeffrey Victor has written that at least 33 'rumor panics' similar to the McMartin case have occurred in 24 states in the last decade.

The False Memory Syndrome Association, funded by sceptical psychotherapists and families who have been on the receiving end of bizarre accusations, attempts to educate the public about the simple fact that many 'memories' – even (or some would say especially) those activated under hypnosis – do not always correspond with real events in real space-time.

> **"Do these hypnotic visions belong in the category of the real or the hallucinatory? Maybe 'the Shadow knows'".**

Dr Jean Piaget, generally considered the world's leading authority on developmental psychology, has recounted how he 'remembered' an alleged (non-violent and non-sexual) event in his childhood all his life – until he learned that he had only *heard* about it from his parents, who *heard* it from a maid, who had invented it to avoid admitting a minor malfeasance.

At this point Preposterous Perception appeared in the literature, thanks to Prof. Timothy F.X. Finnegan of Trinity College, Dublin. I should mention at once that Prof. Finnegan serves as President of CSICON – the Committee of Surrealist Investigation of Claims of the Normal – and has developed, in several books, the system known as Patapsychology (not Parapsychology, although that error seems ubiquitous). Scholars trace Patapsychology to Alfred Jarry's Pataphysics and Jacques Derrida's Deconstructionism, but Prof. Finnegan has always insisted he got his basic inspiration from one Sean Murphy of Dalkey. Murphy's First Fundamental Finding states succinctly: "I have never met a normal man or woman; I have never experienced an average day."

The Patapsychological 'school' holds that Preposterous Memories do not have any less 'validity' than other memories, since (in de Selby's words) "All that we know derives from our own perceptions, which a thousand well-known experiments have proved fallible and uncertain, and from the instinct to gossip, sometimes called Public Opinion, which sociologists now consider equally unreliable."

In Finnegan's own words (*Archæology of Cognition*, p.23), "A world where most men prefer sex with little children to sex with grown women, mostly allegedly Christian parents secretly engage in bloody Satanic rituals and every third person has suffered anal, genital and other harassments by demonic dwarves from Outer Space makes just as much sense – and just as little sense – as a world where the universe is run by the ghost of a crucified Jew and George Bush had rational reasons (which nobody can now remember) for bombing Iraq again two days before leaving the White House."

FORUM is a column for anyone with something to say about a particular field, theory or incident. If you'd like to join in with an opinion on any area of Forteana, send it to the editorial address. Ideal length: 500-1000 words. Please enclose an SAE, a three-line biography and a head-and-shoulders photo of yourself, preferably in black and white.

Roswell the Terrible

Denis Stacy looks into the most famous'Crashed Saucer' case

Among the most interesting type of UFO reports are the so-called crash/retrievals, in which witnesses, usually with a military background or connections, report seeing a crashed saucer on the ground which is subsequently spirited away by the 'authorities', also commonly military in nature.

The most famous of crashes is the one said to have happened near Roswell, New Mexico, in the first week of July 1947, within a couple of weeks of what is considered the beginning of the modern UFO era. Although the case didn't receive widespread attention until 30 years later, it was initially announced in an official US Army Air Force press statement released within days of its discovery. "The many rumors regarding the flying discs", read the opening sentence, "became a reality yesterday when the intelligence office of the 509th Bomb Group [the world's only then extant atomic bomb wing] of the Eighth Air Force, Roswell Army Air Field, was fortunate enough to gain possession of a disc through the cooperation of one of the local ranchers and the Sheriff's office of Chaves County."

The press release went round the world, but before the media could pursue the story of the century, a press conference was called in Fort Worth, Texas (several hundred convenient miles from Roswell) where the military authorities admitted – "Whoops!" – it had all been a magnificent mistake. The flying disc was a weather balloon, pieces of which were spread over the office floor of Brigadier General Roger Ramey, Eighth Air Force commander, for reporters to inspect and photograph. In pictures, the UFO 'wreckage' looked like an aluminium foil kite that might have been caught up and spat out by a tornado.

What gives Roswell its legs is the now more than 200 first- and second-hand sources interviewed over the last decade who support the contention that the weather balloon story was just that: a clever cover-up aimed at getting the press off the Army's back. According to many of these sources, which include local townsfolk, retired pilots, intelligence agents and even one general, the real wreckage – assumed to be extraterrestrial in nature – was flown to Wright Field in Dayton, Ohio, now Wright-Patterson, home of the Air Technical Intelligence Center (ATIC). The uncertainty about what really happened at Roswell has fuelled a cottage industry of articles, monographs, books, videos and movies.

Roswell is merely the most notorious of such cases. In the July/August issue of the *International UFO Reporter*, editor Jerome Clark lists a total of 38 early crash claims, beginning with an 'event' in September 1862 in the Indian Ocean, which Clark considers spurious. In fact, Clark concludes that none of the 12 cases that date from 'The Airship Era' (c.1862-97) are credible. The most famous of these – the crash of a large airship near Aurora, Texas, on 17 April 1897, along with the body of a pilot said to be 'not of this earth' – Clark calls "One of the great UFO hoaxes".

> **"How many 'UFO crashes' have there been? UFO alarmists like John Lear suggests that there may have been 80 or more."**

The Aurora airship allegedly collided with the windmill of Judge J.S. Proctor before exploding and killing the pilot (thought to be from Mars), who was then buried in the town cemetery. Attempts to locate the grave were in vain, although there *was* a Judge Proctor in Aurora at the time... but he didn't have a windmill.

Fortean lexilinkers will be interested to learn that four more Proctors were pivotal witnesses at Roswell. Floyd and Loretta Proctor were nearest neighbours of Mac Brazel, the anonymous rancher mentioned in the initial press release. It was Brazel who first found the debris in a field (not an intact disc as implied), while in the company of Timothy Proctor, seven, younger brother of Norris. Brazel reportedly showed the other Proctors a few pieces of the unusual debris he picked up, but they declined at least two offers to accompany him back to the site. (See *UFO Crash at Roswell* by Kevin Randle and Donald Schmitt.)

How many 'UFO crashes' have there been? Discounting the 12 Airship Era cases, Clark came up with 26 separate possibilities. UFO alarmists like John Lear (son of William, developer of the Lear jet) bruit that there may have been 80 or more. A slightly more conservative ufologist, Leonard Stringfield, has identified at least 49 candidates, 16 outside the US, 27 inside, the others unknown. 1952 seems to have been the most 'popular' year for UFO crashes so far, with eight on record. In fact, all but 13 of Stringfield's extraterrestrial catastrophes occurred before 1970.

The Roswell event took place over 45 years ago; many witnesses have died and those that remain are relying on very old memories. The potential for error is enormous. By way of comparison, we could look at a roughly contemporary case causing a current sensation of its own: that of Ivan the Terrible, the sadistic camp guard who terrorised Jewish prisoners at Treblinka.

Eighteen Treblinka survivors, working from photographs, positively identified retired Cleveland autoworker John Demjanjuk as Ivan the Terrible, and five of those witnesses, aged 61 to 86, actually confronted Demjanjuk in court in Israel and pointed him out as their tormentor. He was sentenced to death by hanging, but the conviction was overturned this year by the Israeli Supreme Court after new evidence had surfaced from KGB files. Whoever else Demjanjuk may have been (his name was originally Ivan and he apparently worked as a guard at the smaller Sobibor camp in Poland), he was almost certainly not Ivan the Terrible.

Factors leading to the misidentification probably included the eyewitnesses' age and the fallibility of their memories, as well as the desire to nail *someone* for the atrocities perpetrated at Treblinka. Hanging the wrong man, however, would hardly make for satisfactory revenge.

Could Roswell the Terrible be in similar straits, a complicated case of mistaken identity? Convicted as a balloon, was it really a space ship from another planet, or merely a curious artifact from that much larger (and greyer) area in between the two extremes? Memory would tell if it could.

Down In The Jungle

Michael Goss looks at the folklore of the Candyman

"To be buried while alive is, beyond question, the most terrific of those extremes which has ever fallen to the lot of mere mortality", declares the narrator of *The Premature Burial.* Far be it from me to argue with one who has evidently Been There and Bought the Tee Shirt, much less with he who made it possible for him to narrate of being prematurely buried, namely Edgar Allan Poe. But... "beyond question...?"

Is being inhumed alive really worse than getting trapped in a broken-down lift with someone who's just discovered Chaos Theory? Or, worse yet, with someone who thinks that the British National Party winning a seat at Millwall is a good thing?

From the creation of an early 19th century literary master to that of a late 20th century one, from Millwall to New York: in chapter one of Tom Wolfe's *The Bonfire of the Vanities,* Sherman McCoy experiences "that deep worry that lives in the base of the skull of every resident of Park Avenue south of 96th Street": alone on the benighted street, he is accosted by a young, rangy black man. It's not merely the terrific extreme of mugging by a stereotypical mugger; as Wolfe has written elsewhere, the average American white male fears the average American black male because of the latter's suspected supernatural powers, his "Tarzan mumbo jungle voodoo". Could it be the same in darkest Millwall?

Our fears take the form of legends, sometimes. That's neither Poe nor Wolfe. It's a precis of something uttered by a contemporary folklore professor in *Candyman,* recently released on video and fairly essential if you want to see more in urban legends than amusing schlock-horror themes revisited.

That *Candyman* is schlock-horror (or, if you prefer something more academic-sounding, New Gothick) is an unavoidable conclusion. It nods knowingly to the Dracula-Vampire mythos by having the statuesque and saturnine anti-hero strike impressive middle-distance poses reminiscent of Christopher Lee at his most dominant. The irresistible revenant forces a paranormal intimacy and soul-union upon the heroine with lines like "You will come to me ... The pain will be exquisite ... Come with me and be immortal ... You are mine now" – delivered in a wonderful, liquid, sexually charged depth of tone. There are vampire kisses, a sharp stick shoved in the region of the heart, a female victim carried in Candyman's muscular arms (again, Lee-fashion) and deposited upon an alter-like table. Etcetera etcetera.

> **"Is being inhumed alive really worse than getting trapped in a broken-down lift with someone who thinks that the British National Party winning a seat at Millwall is a good thing?"**

But Candyman, urban maniac killer-ghost who can be invoked if you recite his name five times while looking in a mirror, is primarily a *black* urban legend. One in whom white academics can show suitable detached intellectual interest, but in whom the blacks of the grim, criminally-ruled Housing Projects believe actually and instinctively. You can only understand him if, like Helen the research-student heroine, you run the gauntlet of this Caucasian no-go zone. More – Candyman is a legend of black revenge. He slaughters those of his own colour, but what propels him through after-life is the ghoulish mutilation-murder perpetrated against him in 1890 when he was punished for loving and impregnating a white girl with social pretensions.

Urban legends not infrequently exploit white fears of blacks which it is uncool to confront openly: with deflating humour in the tale of the ostensible elevator-mugger who turns out to be Eddie Murphy, or more crudely in the case of the Castrated Boy who suffers terrible things in the washroom (a legend recalled in *Candyman,* incidentally). The central character here has that Wolfian mumbo jungle voodoo with a vengeance. It is a racist nightmare because it exceeds the material.

Two optimistic things remain to be said of *Candyman.* The first is that the end of the film brings the two communities together when the Project blacks attend Helen's funeral. Secondly, it reveals fictively the aforementioned mumbo jungle voodoo terrors which shape some of our legends – including those which inform the political policies of some recently-prominent right-wing groups... **FT**

REVIEWS

FORBIDDEN ARCHEOLOGY

THE HIDDEN HISTORY OF THE HUMAN RACE
by MICHAEL A. CREMO AND RICHARD L. THOMPSON

Once upon a time there was a new idea called 'evolution' and all the brave scientists and academics set off to find the evidence with which they could trace the origins of the human race. It was the 19th century and the evidence soon mounted up, got reported and interpreted; some of it was explained and some of it explained away. These days, of course, we have a nice cosy picture of the way it all happened and if we can just find a few more pieces of the jigsaw, then we can all live happily ever after ...

It isn't often that one can say that a book is truly imbued with the Fortean spirit, but *Forbidden Archeology* undoubtedly is, in spite of the fact that Fort's name is not mentioned once. Cremo and Thompson have launched a startling attack on our whole picture of human origins and the way that we've arrived at that picture: not only is the evidence impugned, but also the scientific method of handling it.

A Pre-Cambrian cricket-ball? This metallic sphere was found in strata said to be 2.8million years old, in South Africa.

The book falls into two main sections, the first dealing with anomalous evidence (finds which seem to contradict the dominant view of human evolution), the second with defects in the accepted evidence on which that view is based. But just as important as the evidence itself are the preconceptions of the interpreters, and C & T manage to demonstrate how, as the prevailing dominant built up, those preconceptions became more important than the quality of the evidence, thus consigning the anomalous to oblivion.

C & T have taken on an enormous task. Much of the anomalous evidence dates from the 19th century and exists now only as reports; the extensive quotation from those reports accounts in large part for the vast size of the book. Beyond that, the controversy over each piece of evidence is fully covered, and we're allowed to see the process of exclusion at work, with its accusations of misinterpretation, its hints of cheating and its simple "I'm a more famous scholar than you ..." And yet, of course, many of the adherents of the anomalous were among the most famous scholars of their day, and such technical matters as the stratification of deposits were as well understood then as now. Indeed, more than a century later, there still remain serious questions about our modern dating methods, as is pointed out in a lengthy appendix.

There are occasions where the book strays into the more familiar (and possibly sensational) Fortean territory by dealing with the notion that the yeti / sasquatch / wildmen reports suggest co-existence of species rather than linear evolution, and with more outrageous anomalies (though handled with suitable reserve) such as apparent shoe-prints in ancient strata and puzzling artefacts found in solid coal. For the most part, however, it deals scrupulously with matters of palæoanthropological record. It might be thought that 900 pages of detailed material on anomalously dated flint tools, broken bones and fragmentary skeletons might not make the most absorbing reading, but by providing the human controversies as well, the authors tell a gripping story. Thus, with a clear conscience, one is able to say "I couldn't put the book down", rather than simply "I couldn't pick it up"!

C & T avowedly believe that modern man has been upon this earth longer than currently believed and that our picture of human origins is seriously flawed. Be that as it may, they appear to have given a commendably even-handed treatment of the material and have certainly made a compelling case for its re-examination, both accepted and anomalous. Their own ideas on human origins are deferred to a promised second volume. If you have any interest in fossil humanity or, perhaps more importantly, the way scientists put together our picture of the universe, then you ought to read this vast and surprisingly cheap book ...

Govardhan Hill Publishing, 1380 Garnet Ave, Suite E-5, San Diego, CA 92109, USA - or in UK, Bhaktivedanta Books, Box 324, Borehamwood, Herts WD6 1NB. 1993, hb $39.95 or £28.95 (inc. post), pp952, index, bib, illus, tables.

Steve Moore

THE PARANORMAL YEAR: 1993

By Jenny Randles

This annual record of the previous year's odd doings is a nice idea as far as it goes ... however, this is not far enough to be the record for posterity one presumes is intended. Jenny charges rather breathlessly through 10 major categories of phenomena, from a few general science oddities to ghosts, psychic questing and cryptozoology, but she is at her most interesting in those areas – like UFOs, crop circles, ETs and NDEs – which she has actively researched.

This is an idiosyncratic progress report of which a number of features could be usefully developed in any further yearbooks – the 'top 10' listing of favourite cases should be extended to include selections by other researchers *and some references;* the review chapters on books and the media should be more complete; and so could the reference section of useful contacts.

Robert Hale, London. 1993. hb £15.99, pp192, refs, index.

Bob Rickard

PRIME CHAOS

By Phil Hine

With his first full-length book on Chaos Magic, Phil Hine shows himself to be one of the leading thinkers in the field ... and, perhaps, one of the least dogmatic. Rather than laying down specific guidelines, Hine is more interested in exploring the *mechanics* of magic practices ... how rituals are constructed, how magical groups work together (or otherwise), how 'reality' can be transformed.

It's this last aspect that should be of particular interest to Forteans, for in so many of our cases (e.g. UFO abductions) a transformation in the perception of reality occurs with apparent spontaneity. If it's possible to make such an alteration with conscious intent, as a magician would claim, then whether reality is actually changed or only perceived to be changed (if there's any difference between the two anyway), obviously this is something worthy of study. How much more so if 'reality' is such a flexible concept that it's possible to work with, and get results from, a purely fictional system such as Lovecraft's Cthulhu mythos. Excellent and intriguing stuff.

Chaos International, London. 1993, pb £10.00, pp144, bib. (Mail order: £11.00 from Chaos International, BM Sorcery, London, WC1N 3XX)

Steve Moore

Dreamtime, Dreamspace

SHAMANISM AND THE MYSTERY LINES

By Paul Devereux

Quantum, London, 1992, pb £7.99, pp238, index, refs, illus.

SYMBOLIC LANDSCAPES

By Paul Devereux

Gothic Image, Glastonbury, 1992, pb £14.95, pp192, index, refs, bib, illus, b/w + colour photos.

Fashions come and go in all things, and this is as obvious to Paul Devereux as anyone else: thus he spends the first half of *Shamanism and the Mystery Lines* providing us with a potted history of the whole ley-line/earth mystery field that runs through the theories from Watkins' *Old Straight Track* to the present. It's an eminently sensible and laudably humane review of an area where theories abound, keeping the useful and gently disposing of the useless, and it clears the decks before Devereux moves on to present a new interpretation which forces us to put aside our preconceptions and view the landscape with new eyes: the eyes of the shaman.

A 'dreamstone' in Lithuania, with engraved footprint.

Shamanic landscapes turn up in both books in fact, and it has to be said that there is a certain amount of overlap between the two. The emphasis is different however: *Shamanism* ... concentrates on interpreting the land's linear markings in terms of shamanic magical flight and the out-of-the-body experience, while Symbolic Landscapes is more concerned with shamanic modelling of the entire landscape, and takes the Avebury complex as its exemplar. Even so, reading the two together one does get the impression that we're dealing with material that would have been better handled as one large book, rather than two medium ones.

This quibble aside, I have to say that I found both books very worthwhile reading, with a lot of careful research and many thought-provoking ideas. Quite apart from the earth mystery aspects, Devereux's investigations throw interesting light on various ways that we encounter 'reality', from dreams and trances to 'waking' UFO encounters, mythology, and much else besides. And I, for one, am pleased to see him bold enough to weave the tale of his own personal investigations into the more academic material at his command.

And yet ... and yet ... at the back of my mind is that slight niggling worry that, after all those other fashions, shamanism may be just another whose turn has now come. But that, of course, only time will tell ...

Steve Moore

THE ONLY PLANET OF CHOICE

Compiled by Phyllis V. Schlemma and Palden Jenkins

Unwritten history is a safe refuge – you can say what you like about the ancient past with little fear of contradiction. Similarly, you can claim that any intelligent beings live anywhere in the universe – save, perhaps, in our Solar system – and nobody can prove you wrong.

Add together these elements, and mix in a claim by one individual that she receives copious mental messages from a non-human intelligence and you have the premise of *The Only Planet of Choice*, an impressively produced, substantial and literate book subtitled 'Essential Briefings from Deep Space'. The non-human entity is Tom, emanuensis and general messenger for the all-knowing, cosmic 'Council of Nine' who, apparently, live "beyond the Universe".

To afford the book respectability, much is made of the support and interest of some slightly famous people, like David Hemery and the late Gene Roddenberry ... but it is a book of ancient history, cosmology, philosophy and moral instruction, *not* a book about hurdling or making SF programmes for TV.

The 'history' is unprovable and untestable. For example: "The civilisation Hoova, in charge of your planet Earth elevation at this time, seeded your planet Earth three times. Your myth of Adam and Eve came in after the first installation by the Hoovoids." The cosmology is unlikely: "Those that have been seeded on this planet Earth have also been seeded in other systems in your galaxy. The Pleiades are in your Earth galaxy."

The philosophy and moral instruction is rather uncaring and unimaginative. The Nine offer no way to cure cancer, no way to control the weather, the sea, earthquakes or epidemics and no miracle food to alleviate world hunger. The wisdom of the Nine is restricted to very specific, much less significant areas.

The best test of the origin of any communication alleged to be from any non-human source is simply this ... is there any content that could not have been available to those who are passing the message on to us? For all this book's extravagant suppositions, there is nothing here that passes that test.

Gateway Books, Bath. 1993, hb £14.95, pb £9.95, pp398, notes, index.

Kevin McClure

A THEORY OF ALMOST EVERYTHING

By Robert Barry

Notable for the modesty of its title, this layman's index of the current state of human thought and knowledge is readable, stimulating and surprisingly unsensational. Barry, a statistician and doctor of psychology, conducts a whirlwind tour of psychology, physics and evolution theory which is useful to anyone without a scientific background, but he is most lucid in his own sphere.

We are told that research for the book took ten years and converted the author from an agnostic who believed that an omnipotent science had all the answers ... but what is Dr Barry now? The non-scientific aspects of the book have a distinctly Christian tone – this religion, for example, receives more than double the space and enthusiasm given to other world religions in his survey. His view of spiritual phenomena is entrenched in the *Encyclopedia Britannica* and *National Geographic* school in which astrology is only for the gullible, philosophy only began in Graeco-Roman times (no discussion of 'Wisdom of the Ancients' here), and the 'mystical state' is only a passive one that cannot be induced. The history and influence of Magickal arts and sciences is completely ignored, even when the author acknowledges they might contain the very answers he commendably seeks.

The book emphasises the interconnectedness of all things, and that the 'illusion of separateness' is at the root of many modern problems. This leads Dr Barry to propose a theory of a universe divided into seven 'dimensions' which he claims is original. He explains it neatly and clearly and it is surely a welcome contribution to the emerging 'subjective sciences' and all the more refreshing coming from a scientist.

The New Age can only go forward if it discards as well as creates, and only if it leads beyond comfortable territory will it become revolutionary and inevitably dangerous. This *Theory of Almost Everything* is neither revolutionary nor dangerous – though its urging towards mysticism and promotion of the Baha'i faith as an ideal interface between all religions will seem progressive to some. The New Age must be more than new bricks on old foundations, but, for now, a little extra height is always welcome.

Oneworld, Oxford. 1993, hb £9.95, $18.95; pp200, notes, bib, index.

Alex Brattell

THE DAMNED UNIVERSE OF CHARLES FORT

By Louis Kaplan

In principle, of course, any book that helps bring Fort's work to the attention of a wider audience should be welcomed, and as a sampler of his prose (some 20-odd pages from each of the four books), this works very well. Beyond that, though, it's deeply flawed, mainly because Kaplan has decided to write the remaining half of the book himself: and Kaplan has learned nothing of the lucidity, wit or intelligence of the man whose work he reproduces and professes to admire.

Perhaps the greatest mystery here is how anyone involved with the book, from author to publisher, can expect the reader to get through the 20-page introduction without having had every vestige of interest in Charles Fort totally eradicated. Kaplan is obviously more concerned with writing something "intellectual" than telling us anything about Fort, and the result is a morass of painfully laboured puns, desperate cleverness and vapid posturing which is perhaps the most pretentious and unintelligible drivel it has ever been my misfortune to read.

His concluding chapter, 'Telepathic Technologies', is marginally better, purporting to be a proposal for the establishment of an Institute of Telepathy to investigate the (mainly commercial) potential of certain concepts, such as teleportation, originated by Fort. Yet Kaplan seems incapable of doing more than quoting a passage from Fort and saying, in effect, "wouldn't it be great if we could learn how to do this". There is no constructive thought here as to *how* the investigation might be carried out, or even (with regard to military applications) *why*; and one is left once again with the conclusion that this is no more than a literary piece, an empty display of "Kaplanism" rather than Forteanism. For masochists and completists only.

Autonomedia, New York, 1993, pb, pp156, illus. Available in UK (£8.70 incl. p+p) from Counter Productions, PO Box 556, London SE5 0RL.

Norma Mysta Nosegay

MagWatch

Two Fortean-related magazines have changed hands recently. **THE CEREALOGIST**, after three years in the hands of its founders John Michell, designer Richard Adams and his son Sam, Christine Rhone, and Patrick Harpur (novelist brother of our cartoonist Merrily) is conducting business as usual under a new team led by George Wingfield and John, Lord Haddington. Issue 10 (Autumn 1993) proves the field is still active (so to speak), and includes much anger at the exploits of Jim Schnabel.

In the USA, an ideological split has riven the International Fortean Organisation forcing the withdrawal of former president Ray Manners and his supporters. We understand that the remnant will continue to produce its excellent **INFO JOURNAL**, and that Manners himself wants to publish a Fortean magazine. The last *Journal* (June 1993) had research into the discovery of a prehistoric crocodile skeleton In New Jersey in the mid-1800s, beneath which was found a Roman coin – a fascinating antiquarian conundrum.

The other prominent independent Fortean mag in the States is **STRANGE**, edited by our colleague Mark Chorvinsky, who tells us he plans to publish three times a year from 1994. Its long, dense articles and experimental graphic style might daunt the less dedicated Fortean, but it is always worth the effort. Each issue carries a themed clutch of articles – the current issue (#10, Summer 1993) revaluates Lovecraft in a Fortean context.

Two smaller – but no-less dedicated – mags of Fortean-related interest deserve a mention ... **ALIEN SCRIPTURE** is a new venture from Kevin McClure, and devoted to an erudite analysis of channelled material – motto: "If we are not alone, then who is speaking to us and what are they saying?" **THE JOURNAL OF METEOROLOGY**, edited and published by Dr Terence Meaden, is a good example of high standards in an independent science publication and often includes phenomena of the kind that interests us (ball lightning, unseasonal or extreme weather, odd vortices, etc).

Bob Rickard

■ ***Alien Scripture:*** *42 Victoria Road, Mount Charles, St Austell, Cornwall, UK.* ■ ***The Cerealogist:*** *20 Paul St, Frome, Somerset BA11 1DX, UK.* ■ ***INFO:*** *Box 367, Arlington, VA 22210-0367, USA.* ■ ***Journal of Meteorology:*** *54 Frome Rd, Bradford-on-Avon, Wiltshire BA15 1LD, UK.* ■ ***Strange Magazine:*** *Box 2246, Rockville, MD20847, USA.*

ALSO RECEIVED

● **OTHER MERIDIANS: ANOTHER GREENWICH** by Jack Gale. A look at the geomantic and sacred significance of Greenwich, its alternative history, alignments, tunnels and psychic phenomena, etc. We need more of this sort of in-depth research. *Adelphi Press, London, 1993, pb £4.95, pp102, bib, illus, photos.*

● **FANDEMONIUM!** by Judy and Fred Vermorel, is a clipper's guide to showbiz consumerism from the fan's viewpoint. There are three chapters – a twirl through dance crazes from Tango to Disco; a 'Strange Days' style sampling of allegedly true stories about the extremes of fandom and cults; and a mainly pictorial essay on showbiz, hysteria and fetishism. It's a good idea, but too many pictures are printed too large to allow for depth or width of reaction. *Omnibus Press, Book Sales Ltd, 8/9 Frith St, London W1V 5TZ. 1992, pb £9.95, pp128, illus.*

● **GMICALZOMA** An Enochian Dictionary by Leo Vinci. In the 16th century Dr. John Dee and Edward Kelly used skrying techniques to take down a number of messages from the Angelic world, in the 'Enochian' language. Vinci provides both Enochian-English and English-Enochian lexicons, with biographical and explanatory material. *Neptune Press, London, 1992, pb £9.50, pp136, illus.*

● **THE BEAST WITHIN** by Adam Douglas. Yet another look at the history and lore of the werewolf, from ancient myth to modern cinema. A reasonable introductory volume which rounds up all the usual explanatory suspects: shamans, hallucinogens, porphyria, 'wild children', psychopathology, etc. The dust-jacket illustration is a dreadful piece of junk. *Chapmans, London, 1992, hb £15.99, pp294, index, refs, illus.*

● **SELL YOURSELF TO SCIENCE** by Jim Hogshire. The complete guide to selling your organs and body fluids. The cover blurb says it best: "Learn how to harvest your body while you're alive and how to sell the leftovers once you're gone." Tap your human potential! A drug developed from one man's spleen earned him millions. Weirdly entertaining. *Loompanics, Port Townsend, Washington, pp160, 1992, £12.45 (incl.p+p) from Counter Productions, PO Box 556, London SE5 0RL.*

● **SCHWA** by Bill Barker. *Schwa*, represented by an upside-down e in pronunciation tables, stands for "the indeterminate vowel sound of most syllables not stressed in English". For Barker, it is the symbol for indeterminate menace or wordless dread. This picture book of stick people and spare ovals presents a surreal narrative involving aliens. As SubGenius guru Ivan Stang says: "It isn't really about UFO abductions. It's about religion, belief, self-subjugation and all control systems ... Somehow Barker manages to sum up the mystery and terror of the UFO experience in a non-verbal way." On one page, Barker gives some deathless instructions - "In case of abduction: 1. Remain where you are. 2. Give or do whatever they ask. 3. Forget everything that happens." *Schwa Press, Box 6064, Reno NV 89513-6064, 1993, pp76, £4.50 (incl.p+p) from Mark Pawson, PO Box 664, London E3 4QR. Mark also sells SubGenius stuff.*

● **THE AVALONIANS** by Patrick Benham. Essential reading for those interested in the lure of Glastonbury and the motley of colourful characters associated with the place since the 1906 discovery of a blue glass bowl, rumoured to be the Holy Grail, in St Bride's Well. The cast includes Basil Wilberforce, Fiona MacLeod, Bernard Shaw, A.E. Waite, Annie Besant and Frederick Bligh Bond. The in-depth, never-before-told story of the Glastonbury Revival long before New Age Yoof arrived. *Gothic Image, 7 High St, Glastonbury, Somerset BA6 9DP. 1993, pb £12.95, pp286, photos, index.*

● **GHOSTS AND LEGENDS OF YORKSHIRE** by Andy Roberts. Mainly concentrating on ghosts, but broadening out into mystery animals, UFOs and more straightforward folklore and legend, with a chapter for each geographical region of the county. Occasionally one could wish for a little more detail, but Andy Roberts has certainly packed in the material here, and the sheer quantity of cases is fairly astonishing. Recommended. *Jarrold, Norwich, 1992, pb, pp128, photos, bib. £5.50 (inc p+p) from Andy Roberts, 84 Elland Rd, Brighouse, W.Yorkshire HD6 2QR.*

● **THE BEST OF BRITISH MEN** and **THE BEST OF BRITISH WOMEN.** These two heavily-illustrated books are organised by occupation, so that pawn brokers jostle with party organisers, astronomers with head porters, TV personalities with chiropractors. The lookalikes sections are particularly amusing, but we were sorry not to find any swindlers or serial killers. Under 'Paranormal' we find Janet Bord, Caroline Wise, Jenny Randles, Mary Caine, Susan Blackmore, Serena Roney-Dougal, Paul Devereux, Hilary Evans, Arthur Ellison, Andrew Collins, Maurice Gosse, Brian Inglis – and FT editors Bob Rickard and Paul Sieveking. These books seem too quaintly arbitrary to be much use for reference; but they're fun for browsing. *Reed Illustrated Books, 1993. hb £14.99 each, pp346 each, photos, indexes.*

● **THE COLDRUM LINE** by F. Russell Clampitt and Leslie J. Peters. This modest booklet brings together a series of articles that ran in *IGNews* in 1979 and 1980, and details the authors' discoveries of a strong ley running roughtly northwards through Kent and East Anglia to the mysterious 'Witch Ground' in the North Sea, as evidenced by ancient stones, landscape features and associated folkore. Interesting. *Akhelarre Publications, Box 3, Llandeilo, Dyfed SA19 6JY. 1993, pb, price unknown, pp36.*

● **EXTRA SENSORY PERCEPTION** by Alastair W. MacLellan. A curiously intriguing booklet which sets out the author's ideas linking brain physiology with psychical phenomena, spiritualism, and Theosophical ideas about 'etheric bodies', leading to a theory of clairaudience and clairvoyance based on a kind of radiation from the brain. To date, this radiation is only inferred from several odd experiments (described herein), and the author pleads for their replication. A "hither-to closely-guarded secret of witchcraft" is said to be revealed in the text, but this uninitiated reviewer failed to recognised it. *Excalibur Press of London, 13 Knightsbridge Green, London SW1X 7QL. 1992, price unknown, pp40, bib.*

● **THE LITTLE DUTCH BOY** by Ronald Hearn. Mr Hearn is a medium with a considerable reputation, and this is his solid account of 15 taped communications allegedly with a young boy who had died of leukæmia and which impressed the boy's parents as being authentic. It provides an excellent glimpse into a medium's life, beliefs and methods, but whether it will convince you of the existence of an afterlife depends on the level of evidence you require. *The Book Guild, Lewes, Sussex. 1993, hb £14.95, pp298.*

Steve Moore, Bob Rickard, Paul Sieveking.

DEAR FT...

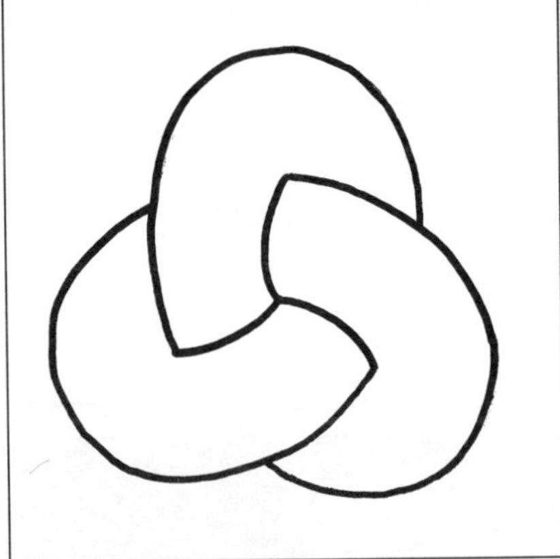

AN 'IMPOSSIBLE' SOLID?

■ Years ago, I discovered a topographical conundrum which orthodox mathematicians have told me shouldn't or couldn't exist and which seems to have escaped Euclid's attention.

It is a three-sided solid which is a close relative of the sphere, being two-thirds the area and nine-sixteenths the volume. My *Trinoid* (see drawing), as I call it, exists in left- and right-handed forms and provides an answer to the question of how much an overhand knot shortens a rope – eight times the diameter.

I'd welcome any correspondence on the subject.

Anthony Bruce
59 Gorse Way, Jaywick, Clacton, Essex

FRACTAL CHALLENGE

■ I must admire the gallantry of Dr D. Fisher [letter, ***FT70:64***] in rushing to the defence of a book he admits to not having read (*Fractals* by John Briggs). What an honour, therefore, he bestows upon me in even glancing at my review [***FT69:60***]. I just wish he'd paid more attention to what I actually said. I criticised a caption in that book describing a portion of the (graphically represented) Mandelbrot set as having been 'explored by' Newton's method.

Yes, Dr Fisher, I know that the Mandelbrot set has fractal properties (furthermore, Dr M. Shishikura of the Tokyo Institute of Technology has shown that its perimeter has a fractal dimension of precisely 2.) I also agree that Newton's method may be used to generate a fractal. I did not say there was no connection, I merely scoffed at the notion that Newton's method could be used to generate the Mandelbrot set. If anyone can demonstrate how this may be accomplished I would be delighted to hear of it. I suggest they send the algorithm to me c/o *Fortean Times* with a copy to the Nobel Prize Committee.

K. Tendzin Dorje
San Jose, California

EDITORS' NOTE: *Our correspondent K. Tendzin Dorje is a former Software consultant and author of several fractal programs. We would like to mention here some errata for his article* ***Golden Child [FT69:30]****. P.31, col.3, l.17: bracelet should be amulet. P.33, caption: delete 17th. P.33, col.2, l.42: protestations should be prostrations.*

WHO'S IN CHARGE HERE?

■ With regards to crop circle faking - who's to say 'who' put the original ideas in the hoaxers' minds to get them to carry out their plans? It's like the 'Philip' table-turning experiments in Canada some years back - isn't it possible that 'he' programmed and controlled the experimenters and events himself, and not the other way round as they assumed?

Tony Sandy
Inverness, Scotland

ELUSIVE PIG

■ The *Buxton Advertiser* (Derbyshire) carried the following item on 22 September 1993: "Workmen carrying out tests for the proposed new bypass at New Mills have reported seeing a wild boar in the woods. The men were drilling in Gnat [should be Knat] Hole Wood, close to the Swizzels factory, when they apparently spotted the animal. New Mills police are investigating and the owners of the wood have been informed."

I discussed the sighting with a local farmer, who has had the bypass survey team on her land, and had spoken to them about it. She said the men had seen one of a group of ordinary pigs living wild in the wood, having escaped from captivity some years ago. She told me the description given was of a normal pig, although a dark-coloured one. On the surface, it appeared to be another case of misidentifying familiar animals glimpsed briefly out of context.

However, the explanation, as is often the case, itself needs explaining. I spent a great deal of time in the Knat Hole Wood area while living in New Mills, searching for tracks and dung from the badger population. I never found any tracks or dung indicating the presence of pigs, and as far as I am aware, nobody has ever reported seeing pigs, or any animals larger than dogs and badgers.

Indeed (shades of *A Private Function*), I imagine that the presence of free-ranging pigs in the area would have served as a magnet for many of the local residents in search of free pork. There are a fair few dubious types in the neighbourhood with very large hunting dogs and guns, and I don't believe piggy would have lasted very long.

Jake Kirkood
Taddington, Stockport

RIP-OFF

■ Am I the first to say that the 'cheap cannabis' ad. [***FT70:58***] is a rip-off? Intrigued, I sent off and received some vile-smelling, very unpsychotropic herbal mixture. I sent it back for the promised refund, but never heard anything. I suppose these picaroons don't reckon many people will bother complaining to their local Fair Trading about not getting stoned!

Name and address on file

EDITORS' NOTE: *We will not be carrying ads from these people in future.*

MARKETING BLUNDER

■ In the last issue of *Hi-Fi World*, I read a test report on a new shelf loudspeaker called 'Minette Mk.II'. Then I read your 'Naff's the Word' item [***FT70:6***]. I suggest you add Minette to the list. A salesman might well have trouble selling one of these speakers in a French-speaking country: in French slang, 'minette' means cunnilingus!

Robert Dehon
Elewijt, Belgium

MEETING PAN

In the spring of 1964, when I was 16, I was staying in a village in South Wales, at the home of Peter, a friend I had made the previous year. One evening, Peter suggested we try a 'Wine Glass Seance'. I was uneasy about this, having heard of potentially harmful side-effects, but was not confident enough to say so.

I would telephone my parents periodically when I was away from home, and I decided to make one of the calls that evening. While Peter was setting the table for the seance, I walked the quarter mile alone to the telephone box in the village centre, as there was no phone in the house.

It was quite dark and the street lighting barely adequate, but I set off happily enough, rehearsing what I would say. After about 100 yards, I got that 'some-one is behind you' feeling. I was slightly annoyed with myself for succumbing, but I couldn't resist turning round and looking. As expected, there was no one there and the feeling disappeared. I continued on my way. The sensation, when it almost immediately returned, was stronger, and it felt as though the mysterious entity was walking with its toes actually touching my heels and never losing contact as we walked. Again I turned, again the sensation disappeared, again it returned, almost immediately, as I continued.

This time, the impression had taken on another dimension. I felt it was head-and-shoulders taller than myself and was walking on tip-toe! What on earth was going on? Was this the Devil? Had all this talk of seances conjured some entity? I looked again, turning full circle this time. Nothing! I felt decidedly uncomfortable as I continued walking. I was getting near the village centre by this time; surely if this was a creature of darkness it would be disturbed by the brighter light of the shopping area, and would leave me alone.

As I neared the friendly neon of the shops, my perception of the entity increased as it seemed to manifest ever more strongly. It was towering over me, even though I was already near my adult height of over six feet. It was, as before, walking on tip-toe and literally on my heels and I became aware that it was laughing at me – not a malicious laugh, but a teasing, playful, mischievous laugh. I knew then that whatever or whoever it was meant me no harm.

I tried something I had read about in book on the paranormal. I turned around and, while concentrating on trying to project caring, loving thoughts, said quietly and carefully: "Are you a troubled spirit, can I help you?" I hadn't the faintest idea what I would do if it said "Yes", but the problem didn't rise. As I finished speaking, I got the impression of absolute amazement, followed by the sensation of the entity moving away from me at enormous speed somewhere to my right front. The feeling was exactly like that cartoon image of Wile E. Coyote falling into a canyon and becoming, within a second or so, a vanishing pinpoint. When I continued on my way, the sensation had gone, and never returned.

I made my telephone call and returned to tell my tale, but nobody was particularly interested. During the seance, we apparently contacted a Roman centurion. Peter asked him how he had died and the glass moved rapidly and apparently randomly, whereupon I broke contact by removing my finger. I felt we had gone far enough.

Many years later, during the 1970s, I came upon a book about the Findhorn Foundation containing a lucid account of a meeting with Pan on Edinburgh's Princes Street. The description of Pan, whom I'd always thought to be quite small, was intriguing. Half man, half goat, some seven and a half feet tall, and walking with apparent ease on the tips of his hooves, he has a wonderfully warm, jovial, bubbling personality that constantly bursts out in shouts of laughter. No-one but the narrator saw him, and they walked up and down Princes Street with Pan's arm round the shoulders of his human companion. For myself, I was left wondering about that night in Wales.

After seeing Michael Bentine's one-man show, 'From the Ridiculous to the Paranormal' in September 1992, I wrote him an account of my strange experience, and he phoned me to talk about it. He said I had encountered a Pan archetype. Such meetings, he said, are a rare event and not always pleasant. People who had been cruel to animals, in particular, meet a fearsome and vengeful entity. He then, unprompted, endorsed my own belief that I would have another visit. I await that meeting with interest!

John D. Ritchie
Doncaster, South Yorkshire

SOLAR PHENOMENON

This photo of an 'upside-down rainbow' **below** was taken by a gamekeeper on a North Wales estate, and witnessed by others. The rainbow appeared above the trees and below the clouds, and the sun was behind the photographer. I was assured that it wasn't part of a 'solar halo'.

Nigel Jones
Chester, Cheshire

EDITORS' REPLY: *Despite those assurances, Nigel, it is highly likely that this inverted arc is indeed part of a parhelion (or sun-dog), most of which was probably too faint to be seen. The diagram* ***right*** *shows the major elements of the phenomenon – caused by the refraction of sunlight through ice crystals in the atmosphere – only parts of which are usually seen at any time, the whole quite rarely. Your photo seems to show the top-centre one of three inverted bows which form tangentially to the main circle of about 22 degrees diameter.*

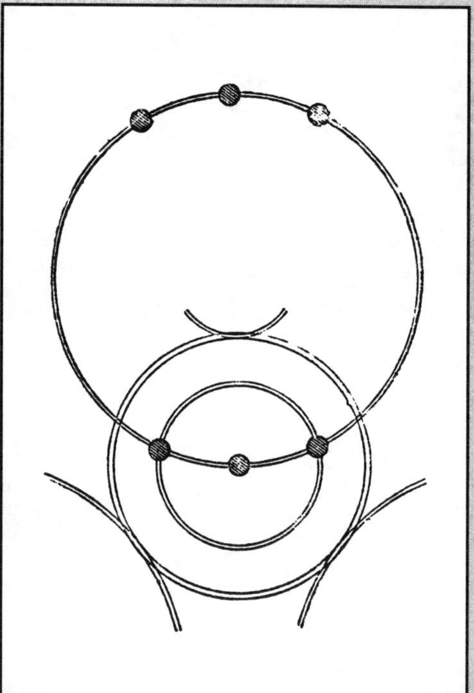

MUNCHAUSEN'S SYNDROME

■ I loved FT70, especially the very interesting and provocative section on Münchausenianism. In fact, I haven't seen a model that seems to fit so much Fortean data since Persinger argued his case for geomagnetic fluctuations that can cause real energy anomalies together with altered brain waves and hallucinations. A blend of Münchausen syndrome and Persinger magnetic wobbles may account for a good deal of the madness of the planet...? Maybe?

Tim Leary in Los Angeles a few weeks ago: "I have found a new way to get high and spacey for hours and it's legal. It's called senility. It improves long-term memory – in walking to the kitchen I remember fighting another kid when we were four and all my grade school teachers and my first date. It destroys short-term memory – when I get to the kitchen, I don't know why I went there. And I forget the third effect." Leary is 13 years older than me, but I see more and more of these memory lapses in all my contemporaries, including myself.

Do you know what Alan Watts said to the hot-dog salesperson? "Make me one with everything".

Robert Anton Wilson
Santa Cruz, California

QUAKE MIRACLE

■ On 12 December 1992, an earthquake (Richter scale 7) on the Indonesian island of Flores killed 2,700 people and destroyed many buildings, including three quarters of the town of Maumere where my daughter Sharon lives while she teaches English as part of Voluntary Service Overseas.

In one destroyed church, a statue of the Virgin Mary (illustrated here) looks as if her throat is cut and bleeding. This happened at the time of the quake and the local people are in awe of it. My husband and I visited the island earlier this year and made a video of the statue.

Eileen Lavery
Torquay, Devon

FLASHES IN THE DARK

■ With regard to the 'Blue Flash' [*FT70:8*]: I've seen this phenomenon and similar ones myself many times. I first noticed it on a meteor watch in 1983 when I needed to change the batteries on my red-covered torch while still out in the field. The red cover (to prevent ruining my dark adaptation) was provided by several layers of red cellophane attached to the torch cover with masking tape. As I pulled the tape away from the torch body to allow access to the battery cover, I noticed a line of yellow light where the tape was pulling away. Investigation quickly revealed that this was the adhesive, not the tape or the torch body.

Subsequent experiments indicated that all types of self-adhesive tape produce this effect, including self-sealing envelopes, some producing a blue or purple light (particularly envelopes), others a yellow or white glow. The best type, for which the effect is most pronounced in my experience, is Sellotape's masking tape. It seems to have just the right mix of adhesion and ease of pulling to generate the effect for a long period (a great way to use up large amounts of it rather wastefully!) The light is not bright enough to do anything useful with, but it is fascinating to watch.

There is another phenomenon which I'm certain I must have seen for many years, but which only in the last year have I came to recognise. This is called the Blue Arcs of the Retina. It was first described by Purkyne (now usually written Purkinje) in 1825, spotted while kindling a fire. To see the effect (and anyone with normal colour vision should be able to do so), you need a dark room with a small red or orange light in it – the small lights on a central heating clock, or the LEDs of a clock or TV will do very nicely. As you look slightly to one side of the red light, a short blue arc should flash across your vision.

The effect is best seen before the eyes are fully dark-adapted (this usually takes up to 20-30 minutes for normal eyes). The nature of the arcs is still unknown, as far as I can ascertain, but the shape is virtually identical to some of the nerve fibres in the retina. Experiments have shown that this is not due to bioluminescence of the fibres, however, and it remains something of a mystery. Anyone wanting to find out more should refer to "On demonstrating the blue arcs phenomenon" by J.D. Moreland in *Vision Research* (1968) (vol.8, pp.99-107.)

Alastair McBeath
Morpeth, Northumberland

EDITORS' NOTE: *Thanks to all those who wrote to us about odd flashes in the dark – from packs of photographic developing paper and polyester clothing (Gary Buckham); from a partially-collapsed plastic bottle (Ian Clifford); from self-seal envelopes (D. Willis); from a beach of wet sand (Andy Inman); and from peppermints (Ian Liston-Smith).*

LOCALISED COMBUSTIONS

■ There is one aspect of the phenomenon of spontaneous human combustion (SHC) which has not received much attention, but which should be carefully considered by those who believe that SHC exists as a well-documented occurrence. The geographical and demographical spread of SHC is all wrong or, at the very least, makes little sense. Of 120 apparent cases listed in the Appendix to Jenny Randles' and Peter Hough's *Spontaneous Human Combustion* (1992), 53 (44%) took place in Britain, 35 (29%) in the USA, 9(8%) in Ireland and the remaining 23 cases everywhere else on earth. Of the 41 cases between 1970 and 1990, 20 took place in Britain, 11 in the USA and one each in Canada, Singapore and Hungary.

Such a geographical distribution of what is presumably a random phenomenon is, I would suggest, statistically impossible; indeed, if this account of the frequency of SHC is accurate, its geographical occurrence is more extraordinary than the phenomenon itself. Great Britain, with just over one per cent of the world's population, has been the locale of nearly 50% of all cases during the past 20 years.

Three explanations might be offered for this distribution. Most obviously, the vast majority of SHC cases in other countries remain unknown to researchers in Britain and America, being reported – if at all – only in provincial foreign language newspapers inaccessible to them. The problem here is that not a single case has been reported in this century in France, Germany, Japan, or Scandinavia, while it is simply impossible to believe that not a single case is known to our researchers from China, India or Latin America – where there must be dozens every year. The last known case in Ireland occurred in 1889, although eight others had been reported between 1800 and 1889: again, a virtual impossibility.

Secondly, assuming that the reported geographical distribution of SHC is indeed accurate, one must look to some geographical, meteorological, demographic, dietary, or life-style factor or factors to explain it. This might be a fruitful approach, although the obvious question here is – what?

Thirdly, one might bear in mind that far more ghosts have been reported in England than in any other country, just as more UFOs have been 'sighted' in the USA. A sceptic might offer the most obvious explanation of all of these strange distributional patterns – that Britain and America contain far more credulous people than any other country.

Professor Bill Rubinstein
Deakin University, Geelong, Victoria, Australia

noticeboard

EXCHANGE & MART

● **UFO NEWSCLIPPING SERVICE** keeps you up with the real 'close encounters'. Many fascinating UFO reports from the world's press are reproduced facsimile, along with news-wire items from the major agencies. UFONS is 20 foolscap pages monthly, with a Fortean section strong on cryptozoology. Foreign language reports are provided in translation. For information and sample pages, write today to: UFONS - Lucius Farrish, Route 1 - Box 220, Plumerville, AR 72127, USA.

● **THE SKEPTIC** takes an entertaining, rational and humorous look at pseudoscience and claims of the paranormal. Articles, reviews, columns, cartoons and much more. Sample issue £1.85; annual sub (6 issues) £12. The Skeptic, PO Box 475, Manchester M60 2TH.

● **NEW DIMENSIONS** the monthly magazine of esoteric information. The best for occult articles, qabalah, metaphysics, psychology, books and music reviews. Dynamic in origin. The best all-rounder. Magic at its best £1.25 UD, £1.75 overseas. Dept MS, 1 Austin Close, Irchester, Northants NN9 7AX.

● **THE ENIGMA** articles on horror, politics, psychology, the occult and religion, plus subjects enigmatic, for we are the ENIGMA. But not a puzzle. £1.50 UK, £2.00 overseas. Payment to: 1 Austin Close, Ircester Northants NN9 7AX.

● **MIDNIGHT** is a new cyclopean horror magazine that enters dimensions of psychological fear - the world of the nightmare. Strictly for the connoisseur. £2.50 cheques PO's to: New Dimensions, Dept 666, 1 Austin Close, Irchester, Northants NN9 7AX.

● **READ WYNN WESLEY'S** "A Course in Male Sexual Potency and Permanent Penis Enlargement". Only £14.50. Available now from Solutions (World-wide) Ltd, PO Box 95, Southsea, Hants, PO5 3EF, UK. Tel (0850) 232007.

● **WEIRD NEWS AFICIONADOS:** The wildest, funniest, most bizarre news items are found in "Strange, But True News" newsletter. Sample copy $2 (US dollars please). Write to: "SBTN", 7522 Campbell Rd. Suite 113, Room 162. Dallas, Texas 75248 USA.

● **UFO REPORT...** They are here! They are real! And people are disappearing! Previously classified information from USA ... UFO REPORT is a "must read". 3 volumes available @ £13.50 each, or all three volumes for just £29.95. Order now. BVM, 79 Lee Lane, Horwich, Bolton BL6 7AU.

● **TIBETAN DHARMA SCARVES**, hand woodblock printed, blessed individually in Himalayan Monasteries for protection against Snakes, Tigers, Water, Fire, Wind, Demons, Unseen Gods and Goddesses, price £6.99 post £1.00. Sacred Tibetan Tanka Paintings, each different, Three Grades, £10, £15, £30, post £3.00. Palette, 7 Airlie Street, Glasgow G12 9RJ, Scotland.

● **ALEISTER CROWLEY – THE GREAT BEAST SPEAKS.** Official spoken word CD. Mastered from 1920 cylinders, surface noise evident. Excellent packaging, great item. Available now from 'Mysteries' and all good record shops, or £13.50 payable to 'Humbug'. PO Box 2903, London, N1 3NE. Wholesale enquiries welcome. Volume two available next year.

● **TERENCE MCKENNA** describes with vibrant, lucid details the effects of the most powerful hallucinogens on 'DREAM MATRIX TELEMENTRY' with music by wizards of tribal ambience Zuvuya. Also available 'Liberation Through Hearing' – Prayers and Rituals from The Tibetan Book Of The Dead. Many other titles available including voodoo drumming, Tibetan ritual music, shamanic chanting, Buddhist drums and bells and much more music from the indigenous peoples and traditions of the world. Details from Labyrinth Distribution, Unit G, 44 St Pauls Crescent, London, NW1 9TN. Telephone - 071 267 6015.

● **THE SMOKY GOD –** Anthony Chamberlaine-Brothers recounts Willis George Emerson's amazing 'ghosted' tale of Hollow Earth travel, on cassette. Send £5 (UK & EEC) £7 (elsewhere) to: 48 Hill Road, Old Town, Eastbourne BN20 8SL, UK, Tel 0323 727907.

● **FREEDOM OF INFORMATION CAMPAIGN** Everything you need to know, but were never told about UFO's, aliens, cures, cover-ups, conspiracies. For free catalouge write to: Rev Anthony G. Pike, 141 Austen Rd, Sth Harrow HA2 0UU Middx. Tel: 081-426-8758.

● **LEGAL HIGHS** - We supply over 18 herbs at 30p to £2.50 per ouncce – a fraction of the price of rivals! Also: full background information on these and many others in a £7.50 book. SAE: Sirius (F) PO Box 524, Reading, Berks, RG1 3YZ.

● **KHAT/QAT** The powerful coca-like organic stimulant, aphrodisiac and dietary suppressant from the cradle of creation. Perfect party preparation. Available fresh (approximately 3.5 oz) at £6.50 or as MIRAH tea £2.65. Both 40p P&P. Send cheque/p.o`s to KHAT at 95, Ditchling Road, Brighton, East Sussex. BN1 4SE.

MISC

● **INTERESTED IN A CREED OF IRON?** Read THE ODIN BROTHERHOOD (£6.95) from Mandrake Press, Ltd, Essex House, Thane, OX9 3LS.

● **SURREALIST GAMES, RESEARCH, CREATIVE WORK** -sound, video, cut-ups, photomontage – dreams, trips, visions, provocations – enthusiasts wanted to form new surrealist group. Write to – SRG, c/o 16 Triangle Place, London, SW4 7HS.

● **WELSH HOLIDAY COTTAGE** Self-catering accomodation in historic North Wales town of Denbigh. for further details, contact Janet Bord, Melysfen, Llangwm, Corwen, Clwyd LL21 0RD. Tel: 0490 420472. Fax: 0490 420321.

● **UNEMPLOYED MALE** 21, looking for Fortean related work in the West Yorkshire area. Write to: John Travis, 12 Lilac Ave, Thornes, Wakefield, WF2 7RY.

● **ALL ELECTRICAL REPAIRS** domestic - industrial - marine - large or small, including computer systems setup, configured & serviced - 24hr 7day service. Tel: 081 345 6789 (quote call sign F5730). No extra charge for evenings or weekends.

RESEARCH & HELP

● **FORTEAN PICTURES** The Fortean Picture Library is a self-funding project for the rescue and preservation of valuable documentary material, photographs and drawings etc. If you have anything of this nature, let FPL look after it. 50% of any revenue from the commercial use of the material (in books etc) comes to you. FPL covers all expenses from its half. Contact Janet Bord, FPL, Melysfan, Llangwm, Corwen, Clwyd, Wales LL21 0RD. Tel: 0490 420472 Fax: 0490 420321

● **REPEATED ENCOUNTERS?** If you believe you might have had repeated alien encounters in England write to: Roland Rashleigh-Berry, Appt 33, 25 Rue de la Baignerie, 59800 Lille, France.

● **WANTED** expert dowser. Must have proven track record. Target large, stone box in earth mound. As trial run. Contact M.T.B, 3 Tydraw Place, Penylan, Cardiff CF2 5HF

● **SIMULACRA** Examples of symbolic geography (shapes on maps suggesting people, things, etc) sought by John Robert Colombo, 42 Dell Park Avenue, Toronto M6B 2T6, Canada. All correspondence acknowledged.

● **IMAGINARY FRIENDS** Accounts and references needed, especially personal experiences - write me in confidence: Andy Fish, 23 Brittany Ave, Ashby-de-la-Zouch, Leics LE65 2QY.

● **STAR IN YOUR OWN REPORT ON TV** 'THE BIG BREAKFAST' is inviting any FT reader who has an outrageous, new or theory about the paranormal; an unusual demand, beef, or need; a bizarre pet; an out-of-this-world habitat; a world-shattering discovery; etc - to contact Myfanwy Moore, 'The People Report', Planet 24, Norex Court, Thames Quay, 195 Marsh Wall, London E14 9SG - or phone 071 712 9300 ext 313. This is your chance to be famous for a few minutes and help plug FT at the same time.

EVENTS

● **PUBLICISE YOUR EVENT HERE FREE** Fax us details on 081 552 5466.

● **SOCIETY FOR PSYCHICAL RESEARCH.** Lecture 9 December – 'Squatters in the Mind' (Prof. Archie Roy) followed by Christmas party. Venue: the Lecture Hall of Kensington Central Library, Campden Hill Road, London W8, at 6.30pm. Non-members £3, student cards £1. Further info from SPR at 49 Marloes Road, Kensington, London W8 6LA. Tel 071 937 8984.

● **GLASGOW FORTEAN SOCIETY.** Next meeting 26 January 1994 at 7.30pm. Society of Musicians, 73, Berkeley Street, Glasgow. New members very welcome. Further details: Desi Atkinson tel 041 339 5725.

BOOKMART

● **DISCOVER ORBITAL SPACE PROPULSION.** Advanced Spaceship Propulsion (UFO Technology?) Governments Supressed book titled *Spaceship Conspiracy* ISBN 0-9695767-0-6 UK £7.00, US $10.00. Postage Included. Knapublishing – 936 Peace Portal Drive, Blaine, Washington, U.S.A. 98230.

● **MIDNIGHT BOOKS** - Quality secondhand books on all aspects of the unexplained. SAE for 32 page catalogue: Steven Shipp, Midnight Books, The Mount, Aserton Road, Sidmouth, Devon, EX10 9BT. (0395) 515446

● **MILLENNIUM BOOKS** 2nd hand books on UFOs, and mysteries weird and wonderful. For free list, write, fax, phone - 9 Chesham Road, Brighton, Sussex BN2 1NB. 0273 671967

● **EXCALIBUR BOOKS** New, secondhand and imported titles on folklore, paranormal and UFOs. Free lists - 1 Hillside Gardens, Bangor, Co Down BT19 6SJ, N.Ireland. (0247 458579)

● **MYSTERIES** old & new - we have the books! Abductions to yetis, via the New Age. Send 6x1st class stamps for 150 page catalogue. THE INNER BOOKSHOP (FT) 111 Magdalen Rd, Oxford OX4 1RQ.

● **PHENOMENAL BOOKS** catalogues of secondhand books on all kinds of anomalies! Write to: Phenomenal Books, 14 Gresham Rd, Thornton-Cleveleys, Blackpool FY5 3EE. Or tel 0253 854617 any evening.

● **SPACELINK BOOKS** Since 1967 Britain's leading stockist off UFO and Crop Circle books and magazines, plus wide range of Fortean titles. Free lists - Lionel Beer, 115 Hollybush Lane, Hampton, Middx TW12 2QY. Tel 081-979 3148.

● **FREE BOOKSEARCH** 'Wants lists' Welcome. No obligation to buy. Catalogue of current stock available on request. Write to Carcosa Books, 3 Arundel Grove, Perton, Wolverhampton, Staffs, WV6 7RF or tel 0902 758977.

● **UBIK** for Leeds' best selection of Fortean/ Occult secondhand books. Catalogue available soon (SAE). 5A The Crescent, Hyde Park Corner, Leeds 6. Open 10-6 Mon-Sat. Also SF, Lit, etc.

● **UFO BOOKS, MAGAZINES, VIDEOS** Lists SAE to SR Stebbing, 41 Terminus Drive, Herne Bay, Kent, CT6 6PR.

TO ADVERTISE ON THE NOTICEBOARD OR BOOKMART

simply fill in the form below and send it, together with a cheque made payable to JOHN BROWN PUBLISHING LTD, to: FT Classifieds, John Brown Publishing Ltd.The Boathouse, Crabtree Lane, Fulham SW6 8LU.

Classifieds cost £15 for the first 30 words, 50p for each additional word.

I enclose my message of __________ words plus payment of £__________ No of insertions ________

Message reads: ____

Preferred section: ❑ **Exchange & Mart** ❑ **Events** ❑ **Bookmart** ❑ **Research** ❑ **Miscellaneous**

Classified adverts should reach us by 14 January 1994.

For credits for this issue see page 20.